ELISSA WYATT

Elissa Wyatt

A *Novella*

in

Three Acts

by

Stuart Shotwell

δὲ τυπικῶς συνέβαινεν ἐκείνοις, ἐγράφη δὲ πρὸς νουθεσίαν ἡμῶν, εἰς οὓς τὰ τέλη τῶν αἰώνων κατήντηκεν.

Now all these things happened unto them for ensamples: and they are written for our admonition, upon whom the ends of the world are come.

—1 Corinthians 10:11

Mermaid Press of Maine

The method for ascertaining cube roots described in chapter 4 is explained more fully in *Figuring: The Joy of Numbers,* by Shakuntala Devi (Penguin 1990, 79–84).

Publication Data
    Shotwell, Stuart (1953–).
    Elissa Wyatt; or, Aeons' End/Stuart Shotwell
    p. cm.
    ISBN 978-1-941864-06-7 (Paperback)
    1. England—19th century—Fiction. I. Shotwell, Stuart (1953–).
    II. Title.

Conceived, written, edited, designed, typeset, and produced by Stuart Shotwell.

This book is distributed directly by the publisher at stuartshotwell.com.

Mermaid Press of Maine regrets that it is not able to respond to queries, comments, reviews, or marketing suggestions concerning this or any other publication, and that it is not able to acknowledge, consider, or return manuscripts submitted in any form.

For the Onely One

And for my part if onely one allow
    The care my labouring spirits take in this,
    He is to me a Theater large ynow,
    And his applause only sufficient is:
    All my respect is bent but to his brow,
    That is my all, and all I am is his.
And if some worthy spirits be pleased too,
    It shall more comfort breed, but not more will.
    But what if none? It cannot yet vndo
    The loue I beare vnto this holy skill:
    This is the thing that I was borne to do,
    This is my Scene, this part must I fulfill.

—Samuel Daniel

The Warp
of the Words Within

The Usual Polemical
Preface

by the Author

When I was sick and lay a-bed,
I had two pillows at my head,
And all my toys beside me lay,
To keep me happy all the day.

And sometimes for an hour or so
I watched my leaden soldiers go,
With different uniforms and drills,
Among the bed-clothes, through the hills;

And sometimes sent my ships in fleets
All up and down among the sheets;
Or brought my trees and houses out,
And planted cities all about.

I was the giant great and still
That sits upon the pillow-hill,
And sees before him, dale and plain,
The pleasant land of counterpane.

—Stevenson

This book was written during a prolonged illness, and like the marching of Stevenson's toy soldiers up and down the counterpane, it served as a physic to me. I have said the same about other books, but in this case I mean it in a more literal sense. I undertook it to keep the inner life alive. Everyone needs something that can keep that life alive when the body itself has committed treason and turned against one. To my mind (perhaps because my illness included that indescribable distortion of reality called subjective fever) the story has a febrile quality that readers of my other books may find unusual. But of that I have said more than enough in mentioning it at all; I shall leave the pronouncement vague and mysterious. Suffice it to say that the writing of this book has been a strange detour.

On another point: My readers may assume that in this book I merely amused myself by ringing the changes on certain narrative themes and devices that will be familiar to any person acquainted with English literature. And it may be read that way. To those who read it thus, and who thereupon complain that it all seems too much the same . . . well, I can only quote some lyrics from a song printed as early as 1605, by someone whose name has been long forgotten by the world:

> Fain would I change that note
> To which fond love hath charmed me
> Long, long to sing by roate,
> Fancying that that harmde me;
>   Yet when this thought doth come,
>   Love seems the perfect summe
>   Of all delight—
>   I have no other choice
>   Either for pen or voyse,
>   To sing or write.

Others may detect in the book a more serious theme. For them the above excuse will not be necessary; or rather, it will be read in a very different sense. For them I may quote a different epigraph, from Campian:

> Old Stories onely, goodnesse now containe,
> And the true wisedome that is just, and plaine.

Confession

by the Same

The anonymous old songs quoted here come from many sources. Those familiar with them will observe that I have sometimes felt free to change the lyrics to suit my purposes. After all, such has been their constant fate since they came into being; and I view them now as the common possession of humankind. I have taken similar liberties with the spelling of the old manuscripts, sometimes preserving it for the sake of its quaintness, and sometimes burnishing it a bit for modern readers.

Having pled common ownership as granting me the right to alter anonymous lyrics, I must by contrast throw myself on the mercy of the reader when I admit that I have extended the same license to at least one of the very old poems cited here whose author we actually know. But again, I have done nothing more than editors have been accustomed to do for centuries. Editing, if practiced long enough—and I have practiced it for decades now—promotes a *changing* cast of mind, one necessary to the trade; and where some see me as a ferocious and unrelenting critic of writing, I see myself as merely engaged in my calling. More negatively, I might say that editing is a kind of mental disease, a compulsion; once it grips you, you can never refrain from it, and nothing you read is ever really good enough to pass without some improvement; including, and even especially, your own writing. So I suppose I can plead that I have not done unto any writer that which I have not done unto myself.

Dramatis Personae & Loca

The Wyatts and Their Kin

Elissa Wyatt	*The Soul of the Book*
Merry Wyatt	Younger sister of Elissa
George Wyatt	Deceased, brother of Elissa
John Wyatt	Father of Elissa, Merry, and George, husband of Jane
Jane Wyatt	Deceased, mother of Elissa, Merry, and George, wife of John
Obed Wyatt	Deceased, father of John Wyatt

❧

Frances Crustall	(Née Wyatt) sister of Obed, wife of Xenophon Crustall and mother of Nicholas Crustall
Xenophon Crustall	Father of Nicholas Crustall
Nicholas Crustall	Son of Frances Crustall and Xenophon Crustall, and heir of Aeons' End

The Newsomes and Their Kin

Charles Newsome	Son of James Newsome and Agnes Newsome
James Newsome	Father of Charles Newsome
Agnes Newsome	Wife of James, mother of Charles Newsome, daughter of Alexander and Ellen Rowcliffe
Daniel Newsome	Cousin of Charles Newsome (son of James Newsome's brother)

❧

Alexander Rowcliffe	Father of Agnes Newsome
Ellen Rowcliffe	Mother of Agnes Newsome

Michael Rowcliffe   Son of Alexander and Ellen Row-
                       cliffe, younger brother of Agnes
                       Newsome
Anne Rowcliffe   Michael Rowcliffe's wife

The Brights and Their Kin

Louisa Bright   Friend of Elissa Wyatt, daughter of
                       Samuel Bright
Samuel Bright   Father of Louisa Bright
Eugenia Bright   Mother of Louisa Bright
Sam Bright   Brother of Louisa Bright

David Boulder   Louisa Bright's cousin, son of Josiah
                       and Kitty Boulder, friend of George
                       Wyatt
Josiah Boulder   Father of David Boulder, husband
                       of Catherine Boulder, brother-in-law
                       of Samuel Bright, uncle of Louisa
                       Bright
Catherine Boulder   "Kitty," sister of Eugenia Bright, wife
                       of Josiah Boulder

Servants of Aeons' End

Mrs. Northaker   Housekeeper
Mr. Jens   Head manservant
Mrs. Tottle   Cook
Mabel Dean   Kitchen maid
Lucy Brown   Housemaid
Laney Brown   Upstairs maid
Dick Broad   "Dickon," coachman
Jim Riggins   "The boy"
Mr. McBean   Gardener
Joe Wiley   Assistant to Mr. McBean
Mr. Tempest   Estate manager

Other Servants

Mr. Blaickie	Daniel Newsome's manservant
Mr. Dover	Charles Newsome's manservant
Mr. Curtis	Manager at Lakeholm

Others in the Story

Alfred Herbert	Rector of Deepclough
Susan Bruit	Daughter of manager at Landseye
John Gunne	Magistrate in Deepclough

Places

Aeons' End	Home of the Wyatt family
Deepclough	Valley and village near Aeons' End
Landseye	Home of the James Newsome family
Lakeholm Hall	Home of Daniel Newsome
Rowantree	Home of the Rowcliffe family
Ryderly Hall	Home of the Bright family
Casa Solitária	Estate of Daniel Newsome in Madeira

Act I

In the Garden

In June there grows the red rose vine,
As red as your own hart's blood;
And round and round you it does twine
Till you long to pluck its bud.

'Twas in a gloryous summer hour
And the angels all asleep,
I helped a man to pluck the flower
And I was piercèd deep.

The rose he took, but left the thorn
That pierct me to the hart;
And in that hour my pain was born,
My sufferings, sighs, and smart.

I've lockèd up the garden gate
And vowed to keep the key,
But all my care is come too late
For my rose is stoln from me.

My garden it is past its prime
With the roses red it grew;
And all the beds once deep in thyme
Are now o'errun with rue.

So now a knot of rue I'll wear,
That no man e'er shall touch,
A knot of rue in my jet black hair
For I loved that man too much.

—Old Song

Sketching

And this was on the sixte morwe of may,
Which may hadde peynted with his softe shoures
This gardyn ful of leves and of floures;
And craft of mannes hand so curiously
Arrayed hadde this gardyn, trewely,
That nevere was ther gardyn of swich prys,
But if it were the verray paradys.
The odour of floures and the fresshe sighte
Wolde han maked any herte lighte
That evere was born, but if to greet siknesse,
Or to greet sorwe, helde it in distresse;
So ful it was of beautee with plesaunce.

—Chaucer

*A*gain I come bearing the old tale: *All we are is our stories.* *To say: No matter how the outline may read, we can make our story either beautiful or wretched. Within the outline our story can become not trivial but profound; can become (beyond all expectation) not individual but universal.*

So we must not fault the outline and neglect the story. That would be as if the weaver condemned the warp and so never came to weave the cloth. The story must be woven, and the warp, however it may have been laid on, must serve for it.

And if we weave well, then when our story comes to its whispered end, when all our work unravels and blows away in the careless breeze of time, we will have served the human purpose; and, if you will believe it, a higher purpose as well.

3

The story of Elissa Wyatt is one such tale, a human tale with a definite purpose. We could begin her story anywhere—with her birth, her childhood, her coming into womanhood; but let it begin where its images begin to crowd most thickly in the mind, on that summer day when she sat looking down on Aeons' End from a few hundred yards distant, sketching the house in which she had lived all her life; and let us, while she sketches, take a sketch of her.

A human is a house unto herself. Consider for what innumerable things on this earth a woman or a man serves as home and habitation over a lifetime: for dreams, plans, thoughts both merry and serious, moods that pass like the clouds over the Cotswolds, casting shadow, and between them leaving broad swaths of sunlight; and for ideas, images, that draw in and include everything eyed by eye, felt by flesh, scented by nostril, heard by ear, tasted by tongue.

Thus Elissa, seated in the grass, sketching Aeons' End: a human house sketching a house of humans.

On most humans, the flicker of longings plays on the face endlessly; not on hers. If her calm expression fooled you, you would have said she was serene and had no longings to show. If you were not fooled, you would have realized that she was only waiting to show those longings until she had someone to show them to.

The drawing hand moved with certainty; it caught what the mind wanted it to in the scene before it; and at moments, alone there on the hill, she smiled faintly as she smudged and softened the line of the pencil with her finger and changed its hardness into heartfulness. This was her home, after all, and she loved it.

The year was 1811; the place, England, the Cotswold hills; she, a woman; and so she wore the clothing of that time and place and sex, a morning dress borrowing much from the Empire Style, but more modest than an evening gown. It was blue, blue as if some blue had fallen from the sky and in falling had grown pale and splashed upon her. She had arranged it somewhat carefully around her after she had seated herself, so that it would not be too much wrinkled; but then her concern for that had melted away as she grew absorbed in her sketching.

So still did she sit, except for fingers chasing down the image of the house, and eyes constantly checking image against reality, that a wren, a bird of the coverts, thinking this human was a natural object affording shelter, flew down and began to hop through the long grass around her. And so it always was: whether Elissa Wyatt sat or moved, she was strangely silent. In moving, it was as if she weighed nothing; she came and went without sound, with a grace so complete as to effect silence in itself. Even if not perfectly silent, quieter than one expected. She came into a room and if one was not looking where she came, it seemed she had suddenly appeared there, the way Homer's Aphrodite appears before Odysseus, an inner reality suddenly manifest in space and time, and one found oneself looking her directly in the eyes though she had not been there a moment before. It was not an unpleasant phenomenon at all, though it was often surprising; it was like the sense of happy discovery one has when one wakes up, and turns over in bed, and remembers only then that something particularly wonderful is going to happen that day. The other inhabitants of the house, from the master to the lowest servant, felt that as long as she was present somewhere, there was always hope that the difficulties of life could be resolved; because of her, they felt a sense of well-being pervading every room of the place; and without knowing it, they hoped they would find her present whenever they happened to move from one room to another. On those moments when she suddenly appeared beside one, whether in the house or outside it, or was found to be already present, waiting for one in a chair by the fire, or at the beginning of a path or at some point along its length or at the end of it, one had the feeling that there was after all something steady and calm in this world, something that made existence not just a state to be endured but a state to be desired. Perhaps this sense people had of her could be summed up by saying that they felt she was *present in life,* or that she *had presence.* A rare gift. We are so often absent from the lives of others, even when physically in the same place.

Her younger sister Merry said that Elissa was capable of being anywhere at any time, and one had only to snap one's fingers to make her visible; and she had come to depend on that constancy of presence as a child depends on her mother. ¶ In many ways, in fact, Elissa had been a mother to Merry. She had been five years old when their mother had died in giving birth to her sister. Their father, John Wyatt, had been shattered by this loss. Usually at times of difficulty he retreated to his gardens, for he loved them as much as he loved his house, and worked in them with his own hands like a common laborer; but after that terrible event, not even the gardens offered consolation enough, and he became simply absent—rode out in the mornings no one knew where, came back late, and never spoke of where he had been. The women of the house had had to take matters in hand. ¶ Not that there were many women in question, for Aeons' End was not a large establishment; and it was mainly Mrs. Northaker, the housekeeper, who had seen to it that the infant had a nurse. And thereafter it was little Elissa, so brave and solemn, who took it upon herself to make sure that sorrow should not become the exclusive spiritual diet of this new little baby, by befriending her and loving her; and as she grew, teaching her and becoming inseparable from her. She had often secretly pretended that the little red-haired moppet was her own baby; and though this fantasy had fallen away as she grew older, she still watched over the feelings and fortunes of her younger sister almost to the exclusion of proper care for herself.

And at this moment, Merry comes out of the house; and by a kind of instinct, she looks across the garden and field separating her from her sister, up to the side of the ridge that stands protectively over Aeons' End to the east, and she puts up one arm and waves her hand energetically, merely to say, "I see you, Elissa! I love you!" And her whole body becomes, in that motion, an expression of laughter, and it is almost as though the waving hand is jerking her body about with its merriness. ¶ Merry's name had come upon her irrelevantly: her mother, Jane Wyatt, who had always disliked her own given name as too plain, had during her pregnancy expressed the wish that if she had another girl, the child might be called Merry. And though bestowed in ignorance of Merry's future character, the name was a prophecy and became, as names sometimes will, a kind of destiny; and the daughter Jane Wyatt never saw, except for a moment as she passed from the world, had become indeed a merry girl, and was now a merry young woman.

To sketch Elissa is, in a way, to make a sketch in negative of Merry, an apophatic exercise. ¶ Elissa had hair so black that it gleamed. It is curious how blackness has accumulated so many trite descriptors: black as night, black as a crow, black as a raven's wing, black as coal, black as jet, black as soot, black as pitch. For the color of Elissa's hair, none of these was correct. It had not the iridescence of a clucking starling or the flatness of a exhausted cinder. It was purely and merely black, but beautifully so, wondrously so, and people often found themselves staring at it as if trying, in vain, to detect some other shade in it. Merry's hair was, or had now become, an auburn color, very pretty, but somehow by contrast with the color of Elissa's, *not quite serious.* ¶ And Elissa's complexion was also pure and, though white, healthily so, with health-wealthy pink highlights that spoke of the time she spent outdoors, walking the ridge, or ascending and descending the hills, on visits to neighbors and to the nearby village and church; highlights that stood out especially when she was pleased, or on those occasions when she was angry at some wrong done to others; while Merry's face had been splashed with a pale but dense crowd of freckles that thronged her cheeks from the corners of her laughing lips right up to the corners of her laughing eyes. In that era, freckles were thought to render beauty impossible; but Merry paid no attention to this prejudice, in the same way that those from foreign parts have no fear of a local god unknown to them; and her laughter would have made her pretty no matter how far out of the canon of beauty her features might be. ¶ As for Elissa's features, you would not have thought them beautiful unless you were of a mind to think the soul that showed through that face was beautiful; and many of that day were not so minded; and perhaps even fewer of ours would be. If you were looking for lightness and self-seeking rebellion against all the rules great and small, for someone who would leap with you headlong from the Cliff of Trespass onto the Stones of Consequence beneath, all for the sake of the few free-falling seconds in between—then you would be repulsed, and think you had found a great prudish waste of womanhood. But if you were looking for intelligence, sincerity, a warm authenticity, and a heart and intellect always probing the moral dimensions of her own and others' actions and thoughts—then your heart would give a half-guilty and half-joyful thump when that face turned to you and those large dark eyes opened upon you as if they were drinking up the aura that radiated from your opposite being. ¶ Elissa's figure was womanly: she possessed, in shoulders, breasts, hips, and thighs, a handsome bigness, and in waist and neck and wrists and hands an inviting slenderness. To put it another way: though she was tall for her time, her shape was well proportioned to her height. She was what in her day was called "stout," which was a compliment meaning "well-built," the opposite of scrawny or thin; had she lived in our day she might have been the captain of three college varsities at once. But as is often the case with such women, she was all the more a woman for her lack of slightness. Men encountering her for the first time, seeing her ahead of them along a path or a road, often muttered "Goodness!" to themselves, as if suddenly realizing that they had never actually seen a woman until that moment (or perhaps had not understood goodness until that moment); and their minds would go, in a tumble of speculation, to all kinds of things they oughtn't to be thinking or had never thought before; and even bachelors of solid brass would find themselves thinking of being the father of tender babies. They would exert themselves to catch up to her to see the face that went with the figure; and they might be pleased, or they might be disappointed, depending on their own preference and their perception of her disposition. The female fashion of that time, with its high waistline, was apt to negate the advantage a woman like Elissa possessed in the flatness of her stomach and the narrowness of her flanks, which produced an abruptly incurving outline of her back as it descended to her hips; but so much the more surprising and pleasing it was then, when her figure showed despite that concealment, when her dress was pulled tight against her in sitting or in walking. And if the high waist was a disadvantage, the low bustline of the gowns typically worn in the evening made up for it. Merry's figure, by contrast, was indeed slight. The styles of the times did nothing for her, either by exposure above or concealment below. ¶ But it hardly mattered: Merry was like a flame, snapping and leaping; she was like energy without a body at all. You could not miss Merry if you were anywhere near her, and people were drawn to her because of her humor, her disposition, the flashing color of her spirit. Furthermore, Merry would talk, so much and so fluently and so continually that it could be difficult for others to add their own part to the conversation. Her speech was the figurative little brook, and you might close a figurative sluice gate to block it for a moment, but it would soon rise to top that height and flow on again. If you entered a room full of people, it was Merry that took your attention; and you only gradually became aware of that maiden Juno, her sister, and only by small increments became aware that she was, spiritually and intellectually and morally and in physical beauty as well, much the superior of the sprite that had initially caught your attention. Perhaps, in fact, this was why neither had ever attracted a suitor: that any man looking on both of them would see in Merry the lack of the qualities so visible in Elissa: steadiness, thoughtfulness, loyalty, a graceful personal integrity; and would see in Elissa an apparent lack (for they were only hidden) of the qualities so evident in the younger sister: humor, liveliness, vivacity, charm. And any such man was indeed likely to compare them, because Elissa was not likely to be far from Merry at any gathering. To say it again: She still watched over Merry, if not like a mother, then like a big sister; and sometimes big sisters are more assertive of their care even than mothers.

Perhaps this role was what had given Elissa her serious turn throughout life. ¶ When their teacher had assigned them the memorizing of the major rivers of Europe, or the English counties, or the kings and queens from Alfred and Ealhswith to George III and Charlotte, the black-tressed head would bow over its task with powerful absorption, as if in her success lay the saving of the world; while the red-tressed head would bob up and down and turn to this side and that side, as its owner saw silliness in everything before her. For the silly people of the world see everything serious as silly, and the serious see everything silly as silly, and take the fault of that silliness very seriously. ¶ In church that black-tressed head would be held upright, looking upwards with earnest attention at the rector when he spoke, or bent forward in prayer when called upon to do so; while the red-tressed head would look anywhere but upward or inward, finding interest in human character and dress and incident among the pews around them rather than in reflection on things divine. ¶ When they were taught to dance, Elissa astonished their dancing master with the rapidity of her learning and with the natural and effortless grace of her movements; and though in some respects Merry seized upon knowledge of the dance quickly, she never acquired what their master would have called elegance of motion— "Miss Merry," he would scold her, "you dance like a sailor!" And yet the result was that more men danced with Merry than with Elissa. Their father would often say that it took a better sort of man to stand up with Elissa, one sure of himself, morally and corporeally. "A lesser man will shy from exposing his failings beside a lady like Elissa," he used to tell Merry, "but anyone may dance with a wild young filly like you." And then Merry would grin, and he would smile broadly and shake his head.

People often said to Elissa: "You should smile more" or "You are so beautiful if only you smile" or "You should be happy" or other such foolish things, judging the content of that tall stack of deep tomes in which her thought and emotion was writ by the solid black on the cover of the first alone. She knew that the people who made these cheap remarks were frightened by the seriousness of life and needed to hide it under a thin buckram of artificial happiness—and not only did they do this themselves, but they insisted that others around them do so too, for a serious person disturbed and beriddled them. And yet she herself thought that it was the more serious-appearing people in life who were the most beautiful. A sunny appearance was to be treasured, certainly; but was it ultimately to be trusted? Was it not more likely to be a fair house built on sand? And wash away with time and tide. ¶ The universe was a joyful place, true; and yet it was a serious place as well, and there were hard facts in it, like sickness and death and struggle and sorrow. One had to find a way, she thought, to contain that suffering within joy, to see how the joy was greater and held everything else; or one would founder without foundation. It was as Scripture said: one ought to live *sorrowful, yet alway rejoicing;* and elsewhere: *Sorrow is better than laughter: for by the sadness of the countenance the heart is made better.*

And yet Elissa's seriousness was not dour; it did not make her frown at or openly reproach her cheerful sister or anyone else. If we can make a Daphne of her, this seriousness was instead like the roots of a tree, a fully formed but supple and graceful tree, that could bow in the wind and bear up ice and snow and yet never topple; such a tree as you see from a distance standing alone on a hill, and it is yet young, but has already put out strong and handsome limbs and raised a fine shape upwards toward God, as if grateful for its own wild planting in that spot, and for every drop of rain, every beam of sun, every atom of nourishment it has drawn up out of the fostering soil. ¶ Yes, graceful and grateful: Elissa's seriousness was a kind of gratitude: it said *Thank you* and *This is what we are given here and it is more than enough if we only pay attention to it.* ¶ It was indeed a kind of *attention* to life and living, in all their difficulties and blessings, while Merry's laughter was a way of glossing over the hard parts of life, as if life were something to be shied away from instead of confronted and welcomed. And were Elissa to be grappled to the rack of mistaken love and of ill chance and of all the unforeseeable changements that time and life and death bring with them, and on that rack tormented, she would not be twisted and broken, because she possessed always the spring-steel spine of her seriousness, whereas Merry had only a spine of reed—that is, an ability to dodge from trouble into jollity, which would not avail once she was bound fast to trouble. ¶ Spring steel, yes: but Elissa's seriousness was a metal even more noble than steel, true and hard and unriven. Though she could doubt, though she could falter, though she could be misled by misappearance and fate, the metal of her morals was true and would not be bound, but would rebound, would redound to her happiness.

This was the graceful steadiness and seriousness that made Elissa the rock of the household. It was no surprise that Merry doted on Elissa and brought every decision to her, whether a weighty matter or as trivial as what gown or even what ribbon to wear each day; more striking was that John Wyatt wanted her opinion frequently himself, in matters of all kinds—from the plantings of his beloved gardens to his dealings in the business of his little manor; from the question of which book he ought to take up next, to whether a particular horse would serve to pull the carriage. And this was to say nothing of entire provinces of decision and knowledge to which John and Merry simply abrogated all claim, leaving them entirely in the hands and head of Elissa, trusting her to take requisite action in the realm of the house, to rule over the housekeeper and the other servants, and to act in their interest even in larger, more important realms, even the realms of spiritual things. For John and Merry somehow felt that if Elissa believed in God and prayed to the Lord on their behalf, that was enough, and in fact that was better than if they had prayed themselves; for they knew their own defects of character, and they knew none of Elissa's. Elissa was a kind of interceding saint in their eyes.

The granting of these many responsibilities to Elissa, beginning in childhood and increasing into adulthood, had convinced even her that she was indispensable to her sister and father. Some people thought her devotion to her family had caused the delay in her marrying; for she was now twenty-seven years of age, and never a man had proposed to her, for all her beauty and her good character and her five thousand pounds. The society in the neighborhood shook their heads over this puzzle: Elissa seemed to be determined not to marry until Merry was safely embarked in matrimony; but how was such a girl as Merry to be married off when her more handsome and virtuous and wise sister was always present by her side? It was a *circulus vitiosus*, a vicious circle caused by virtue.¶ She had in fact been courted, wooed, suitored, but she would have denied it if she had been asked if that were so, because what men became in the act of wooing her did not seem to her sufficiently serious to be accorded that designation. To woo was, to her way of thinking, to become serious about the most serious decision in human life, the choice of a mate, a spouse; and yet, when men wooed her, it was as if they became antic apes, unsuitable by their very suit, anything but serious. ¶ Not that a wooing need be a dull affair, a dour and humorless business; indeed, it should be the very opposite, lightsome: but it should be, as well, deliberate and aware. For the best wooing is both joyful and intelligent, driven as it is by an impulse of the intentional heart. ¶ Such a wooing she had never found; only a lurid, lewd, ludicrous gauntlet of genteel grinning that thought itself gallantry; or what was worse, a mocking abuse that was intended to incite her desire, by what perverted mechanism she knew not. ¶ So, suitorless, truly without serious suitor, she had remained to this day.

But Elissa knew, and it caused her a secret grief, that she must leave her father and sister and cleave to another and live elsewhere with him. When she saw those words in the Bible, whether in Genesis or in the speech of the Son of Man, they filled her with a pain and awe, and she saw her destiny written in them. She was certain that she would find a man to marry and would leave home; and it seemed irrelevant to her that such an expectation has failed of fulfillment in this world many and many the time. Many a woman of twenty-seven, rich in goodness and vitality and intelligence, has gone on to live alone, to her own bitter astonishment; but this was not what Elissa feared. Instead she feared and dreaded the day that she must part with her sister and her father and leave them to whatever support they could find in this life without her. Thus the marrying of her sister to a good and steady man was of keen interest to her; and if she could have found a suitable wife for her father, she would have worked in every way to promote that marriage as well.

And it ought to be said, more explicitly, that she had within her, utterly unknown to her family, a vast and secret life. How could they have known of it? It was only rarely known to Elissa herself. She glimpsed it from time to time in church, or on her walks over the hills, at dawnings and at dusk: what she could be if she had the love of a good spouse and the raising of a brood of children about her and the management of her own home. If she had been compelled to describe it, she would have said that she could have lived in greater awareness of God, because she would have had a field of good and loving action in which to excel. Often, of course, we picture such fields of action lying elsewhere but in our current lives, and it is our real task to see that field as lying before us, around us; it is our task to take up the circumstances that we have been given and live in *them* to the ultimate and maximum of our love. Perhaps that would be what would happen to her: that she would spend her love on her own family of John and Merry. But she did not believe it. The potential for her greater loving was so enormous within her that it persuaded her that her future held more than caring for the family of her birth. She was, fortunately, not prey to ambition; she knew already—arrival at her death bed after a wasted life did not have to teach her—that no glory won in the world held any value whatsoever. What had value was utterly different, infinitely more glorious: those everyday mornings waking up beside another, those evenings falling asleep beside him; the drawing up of children from the deep well of her body in childbirth; the raising of those children into good men and women; the growing old, rising to meet suffering and loss through a certainty of the Good. And also of value would be the moments of solitude in the midst of this activity, when God shone in upon her and told her that her journey and path were true. People err in trying to make themselves exceptional. Joy is found in the ordinary. This she knew; in part by listening to God, and in part by listening to that gift God had given her, her own body; for it promised much; indeed, it promised miracles of pleasure and labor on behalf of her spirit.

When you came right down to it, was it any surprise that such a serious young woman had never married? Find one man in ten thousand who could match her. And how espe-cially rare such a man was among those of her years.

And yet, serious though she was, and serious though her sister and father and friends understood her to be, the role she took, of *the serious one of the family,* was largely in reaction to Merry and John Wyatt. She felt someone must be seri-ous; and since no one else agreed, she was the serious one by default. With a peer whom she respected, she could be, if nowhere near as merry as Merry, still lightsome as light. Then indeed was the rather wanton cheer that ran like a touch of wine in the Wyatt blood moderated into a truly winning blend of thoughtfulness and good humor.

For she was right: this is the theme of all wisdom, and it must be said again and again: The most beautiful part of life is its sadness; and yet at its beauty we must feel joy. Elissa, and those like her who can see this, found herself thus locked into a cycle of grief and transcendent joy; or not a cycle, but an upward spiral, always lifting her upward.

And there was a very palpable grief that lay over them all, of which nothing has yet been said, a grief now greater than the loss of Jane Wyatt some twenty-two years before, because fresher, and boding trouble for the future: the death some three years before of the heir of the family, brother to Elissa and Merry, George Wyatt.

George had been sent to school quite young, and then to university; and then, since Europe had been in the turmoil, he had gone on his grand tour belatedly, and elsewhere—to India. It was a mad idea, and much against the wishes of his father; whose reluctance to see his son go so far away had achieved ghastly vindication when George died of a fever aboard ship returning around the Cape.

The loss of George as son and brother had been brutally painful to the little family at Aeons' End. The father had looked to him as the very continuation of himself; the sis-ters had idolized him. Though they saw him seldom—only on holidays, when he came home like a conquering hero, showering smiles and jests and gifts, chucking Elissa under the chin until he made her laugh, and carrying Merry about on his broad back—to them he was everything good. He had inherited the Wyatt cheerfulness that ran underground in Elissa. He was like his father, affable, cordially courteous; but on his own he possessed a bright laugh and a quick eye and a lively but loving wittiness.

This brother, Elissa had once believed, was everything that a young man ought to be. But as she had grown older, she had seen faults in George—lovable faults, true, but faults all the same. In her eyes, the chief root of all these faults was that he was never serious. Though free of many of the more vicious traits that young men of those times fell into so readily, namely gambling and drinking to excess and frequenting loose women (there once was such a concept), he did not wisely use the many advantages that position and wealth had bestowed on him. If he was given money, he soon had none. Time was a matter of indifference to him—he was always behind it, never on it. Knowledge, too, was of little weight for George: though he was intelligent, and picked up much information almost without trying, he had almost been sent down from university. And the height of what Elissa understood as his lack of seriousness—his whimsical plan to tour India—had actually killed him.

And so, as is so often the case, her love for her older brother both taught her to like and trust men, and encouraged her to hold out for a spouse that met a higher standard than her own brother had attained. And sometimes it is that extra, that increment, that makes a woman's waiting fruitless; for no mortal man can reach it.

Beyond inflicting a deep emotional blow on all the Wyatts, the death of George Wyatt destroyed the future they had all planned, for reasons that will be shown more in their place. But to put it simply for now: with the death of John Wyatt's heir, his estate must descend to someone else, and his daughters must be left homeless and penniless.

Remaining single was thus not a practical choice; it meant dependence on others, perhaps even that final degradation to the workhouse. They might stave off that fate for a time by taking employment as governesses or companions of wealthy ladies or seamstresses or the like; but Merry was in particular ill-suited to such occupations, and in any case, age and its eventual sickness or at least feebleness would pull them down into misery at the end.

And George's death meant that his sisters were at risk to lose not only a better future, but a beloved if minor past as well. The history of the Wyatts at Aeons' End was not storied in any book, not enhanced by any tale of heroism or romance. It was sometimes said that they shared in the stock of that sturdy courtier whose varied accomplishments include being the High Sheriff of Kent, an ambassador for Henry VIII, an alleged lover of Anne Boleyn, the man who premiered the sonnet in English, the writer of disputed and rather difficult poetry, and the subject of a sketch by Holbein the Younger—that is, Sir Thomas Wyatt. But this connection, if indeed it existed at all, was very faint, and had nothing to do with Aeons' End. These Wyatts had lived in the place for eight generations, over three hundred years; a dynasty not especially long by the standards of British history, but one remarkable for its prosperity and for the goodness and kindness of the family. They had been thoroughly ordinary members of the lower part of the upper class: gentlefolk, moderately well educated, civilized, church-going people, successful in managing their estate. Today we would probably call them and their values middle class. But it is in the lower and middle classes that virtue lives, if it remains anywhere at this day; and so it was in those times as well. If today virtue seems a luxury to many of the invisible poor, and if the middle class muddles along only on faint reminders of truth and beauty, it is worse among the celebrated and conspicuous rich, to whom morals are a laughingstock. It is the nondescript who can best value virtue for what it is worth—namely, everything.

Indeed, the line of Wyatts in the house of Aeons' End might be said to be humanity itself, the better part of it, in microcosm: humanity moving onward to its eyeblink end.

But the moralizer digresses from his topic, which is the death of the son of the family and the inevitable loss of Aeons' End. So deep did sorrow at this catastrophe run through the lives of the Wyatts that they felt it every day, and sometimes every minute of every day. It was this lurking grief that had brought Elissa out on this fair noon and set her to drawing the place; and she had actually thought, as she had settled down to her sketching, that what she drew now would someday be all that remained to her of the house she loved.

And having sketched the lady herself, we can show what her drawing showed. Aeons' End was originally a Tudor construction, though it had none of the half-timbers often associated with smaller and poorer buildings of that era; instead, it was constructed throughout of a Cotswold stone the color of strong tea and scant milk, with abundant tall though somewhat narrow windows of leaded diamond panes. The architect had slightly jettied the second story, though in this open country there was no call for such an expansion; and he had added other Tudor elements as well that had no other justification except as an expression of the taste of that time: chimneys, of which there were many, topped with elaborately carved stone pots; a kind of crenellated parapet at the roof edge, stepping up in curved segments over the gables; arches, varying from the broad curve over the entryway in the four-centered style, to round-headed arches over the side doors, to high and almost fantastical arches over the windows and in the gable ends; and other and numerous such features. (And speaking of round heads, the house had scars, which it bore with silent pride, of the bullets of Cromwell's musketeers, who had stormed it one day in the to-and-fro of battle in the Cotswolds during the Civil War.)

In such blunt description, it might seem that Aeons' End was overwrought and overdecorated, but in fact it appeared rather simple. This was perhaps partly the effect of its size, which was smaller than that of most other English country houses built in the same intensity of style. There were, in fact, only five bedrooms in the place, not counting some rooms for servants on the upper floors of the two stubby wings that projected from the back. ¶ To digress for a moment on this head, these servants were: Mrs. Northaker, the housekeeper, now quite elderly; Mr. Jens, who was a sort of butler and footman and valet combined; Mrs. Tottle, the cook; Mabel Dean, the kitchen maid; Lucy Brown, the housemaid, a sturdy engine of toil who kept the place immaculate; Laney Brown, cousin to Lucy, and physically her opposite, a diminutive, even delicate creature who acted as a maid to the two sisters and as an upstairs chambermaid; Dick Broad, the coachman and stablehand; and Jim Riggins, usually called just "the boy," or "bwoy" in Cotswold dialect, a lad who might be put to almost any work. Two servants lived in their own dwellings elsewhere: the gardener, Mr. McBean, and Joe Wiley, who maintained the outside of the place (for like all houses, Aeons' End was constantly wanting to disintegrate). In the English country house of the time, this was somewhat of a skeleton crew. The land itself was worked by tenants, all of very old families as well, strongly rooted in the earth of the place. ¶ To resume on the point of the simple appearance of the house: Another feature that contributed to this effect was that the construction was low to the ground. It did not sit on a high foundation with openings for windows of a "downstairs" containing the kitchen and pantries and other offices; instead these facilities were in the wings. ¶ Nor were the ceilings within, and nor thus the ground floor and the first story, at all lofty; its dwelling spaces had been built for people of an earlier time who tended to be somewhat shorter than the average today or even in the early 1800s. ¶ But the main reason that the house was not overwhelming was its contrast with the wide gardens in which it was set (of which more shall be said later), which formed a kind of vegetative moat around it, virtually lapping against it like a virid and vividly bespangled lake. Upward the garden swept as well, like an ascending torrent, but by way of terraces and inclined walks, to the high ground behind it, merging its greenness with the grove that grew on that height, all of dark yew trees fifty feet or more in height, planted in time out of mind. Aeons' End was thus on a sort of shelf in the greater ridge; and as Elissa sketched, she tried to catch that sense one had, even when within the house, of being cradled, held, even immersed in garden; and of being backed, protected from the winds of the north by hill and sky-high tree. The house appeared to have grown out of the landscape—this was what she tried to capture. English soil had given birth to English men and women; and they, as part of that organic process, had given rise to this home. ¶ So it was not an overly large house, Aeons' End, nor indeed particularly elegant or imposing or even regular in appearance, though it was certainly pretty, especially in the sun that fell on it now, summer-bright but still mellow and northern as light in England is, even in the summer; mellow as the limestone of which it was built.

And when one was in the house, the view over the land below and before the house drew one's attention away from the interior. One saw, near and far, the cicatrices of ancient valleys, and the shoulders and long hips of the high wolds; the roll and dip of pasture and field, and the hedge or stone wall or stream or lane or ribbons of wild border-growth following and framing them; the occasional dwelling, diminutive in the distance, with its outbuildings; white spots on the green land that betrayed their identity as sheep only over long intervals by their random, drifting movement; and the sky, a vast stage on which played out by day the drama of cloud and sun, and by night gave forth the visual lullaby of star wheeling and moon inching above the shadowscape below. Indeed, on the stage of that sky the angels could have waged the battle of Armageddon, so wide it was, so deep, so pregnant with presence. ¶ In this view Nature was both awe-inspiring and benign; it was charitable in what it had allowed humanity to accomplish; it blessed rather than damned; it nurtured rather than blasted; it was lulled into harmony with humankind for a time, a wink of time, a few thousand years, before its inevitable changes would come.

All this must go some faint part of the way toward explaining why the Wyatts felt toward Aeons' End as they did. The rest, the greater part, lay in the human history of the place. Here for generations men and women had met in marriage and the toil of love; new generations had come forth from between the legs of the old; children had played and learned and grown; from here they had moved forth into the world, remaining always attached to the place by blood and memory; or here they had stayed, here they had worked to make a living for themselves and their kin, however ephemeral that prosperity was in the gaze of the ages; here they had died and been mourned; from here they had been carried forth to sleep in the churchyard; here new masters had come into their own, with new wives, new Wyatts beside them. The Wyatts had formed and become, in that house, a flight on the Ladder of Jacob stretching from earth to heaven.

In short, Aeons' End was not just a house; it was a heart, both loved and beating with love. And this was what Elissa strove to draw; but only the eyes of the heart could see what Aeons' End really was; and so the more she drew, the further she felt herself from achieving what she wished, because she could not make that heartedness leap forth from the lines on the flat paper.

Two horsemen now appeared, ascending the drive that wound along the hillside. One was John Wyatt. The other was a stranger, a much younger man than John, beside whom he appeared a boy, barely Merry's age. And yet they were speaking together very eagerly and animatedly—John's arm was up, his finger was pointing out the features of the place: his gardens first, then the house, then the dark grove beyond. Elissa watched them stilly and silently, making no motion or sound to attract their attention, wondering a little, and waiting to know more. As they rode up to the front, Dick Broad appeared from the stables, calling rather roughly for Jim; whom, it seemed, he rousted from a nap in the kitchen garden, where he had been set to weeding; for the boy came forth from that quarter, rubbing his eyes with dirty fingers. Dick took the bridle of the master's horse, and Jim that of the stranger's horse; words were exchanged that Elissa could not hear; and then, while the servants led the horses in the other direction, the gentlemen strolled along the front of the house, as if they could not bear quite yet to go inside and forfeit this fine day—or no, of course it was so that Mr. Wyatt could show the newcomer the garden, the part of Aeons' End he loved before any other. At that moment, Merry came almost running around the side of the house, with a bunch of culled flowers in one hand, and met the men near one of the gates of the garden.

Elissa, from that distance, saw it all with great interest: how Merry stopped short; how her father introduced the newcomer; how the young man bowed, and Merry curtsied (or made as good a semblance of a curtsy as she ever did); and how, even while John Wyatt went on speaking and gesturing, the young man and Merry continued to look at one another without seeming to notice John at all.

A hint of a hopeful smile played over Elissa's face for a moment, only to fade into more sober protectiveness; and she very carefully set her drawing materials into their case, and rose from her place in the grass, putting the drawing board under one arm; and she descended to the house.

By the time she came down from the hill, the others still had not moved an inch, for Mr. Wyatt had already begun lecturing his visitor on botanical matters. "And here we have a new little pink rose," he was saying eagerly, fondling the blossom on a spray of a volunteer that had escaped its enclosure. "It is the smallest bloom on any rose you have ever seen, is it not?"

"Indeed it *is*, sir," affirmed the newcomer happily. "A very wonderful and precious thing—almost like a pearl of a rose." From the visitor's mere tone Elissa could tell that he had rarely if ever looked closely at the bloom of a rose before, or compared the size of one to the size of another; but he had looked now, and had been able to meet the pleasure of his host with genuine pleasure of his own.

"Yes, yes," said John Wyatt, gratified at the thought. "Perhaps I should call it that—my pearl rose. I am glad, sir, to learn that in showing it to you, I do not cast it before swine."

And he laughed at this contrivance of his humor, and the newcomer, after taking a moment to think over the joke in some surprise, and evidently realizing that it was not harshly meant, laughed as well.

At this point Elissa set down her drawing materials on a bench; and the little scraping sound they made drew the attention of the others.

"Ah, here is Elissa!" said John Wyatt then. "Mr. Newsome, I should like to introduce my elder daughter, Elissa; Elissa, this is Mr. Charles Newsome."

Charles Newsome had turned toward Elissa when his attention was directed to her; he now smiled in a somewhat startled way that was familiar to her from her introductions to other men, but which she had never quite understood or believed when she encountered it. Such a surprised smile is in fact quite usual when a man meets the better-looking sister after the merely pleasing one; it is a kind of "Oh!" of recalibration. And yet Charles Newsome seemed not immediately comfortable with Elissa: he was daunted by her, she could see; and perhaps somehow he sensed that she was inspecting him in her role as protectress of her sister.

He bowed, she curtsied, and John rattled on. "Mr. Newsome is the grandson of Mr. and Mrs. Rowcliffe, dear; I happened to stop by Rowantree on my ride this morning and met him there; and I was so taken with him as an affable young man that I proposed he visit us here and make our acquaintance." And see the garden—that was probably much more John's purpose than he would have admitted.

"Ah," Elissa said to Mr. Newsome, "*you* are the grandson of whom we have heard so much over the years. You will find yourself famous in these parts.—You have never been here before, have you?"

"Never, in fact."

"But you live only just over in Oxfordshire, do you not?"

"Yes, I do."

"Your home there has an interesting name—Landseye, I believe it is."

"Your information and recollection are excellent," said Charles Newsome; "that is the very place." He looked both pleased at her recalling the name and yet strangely pained by the mention of it.

"As my daughter says, we have known of your family for years, for many years," said John then. "And if you will allow me the freedom to say it, sir, the praise we have heard of your person and character eminently matches the man himself." Even in making this effusive speech, John seemed to be holding himself back; he seemed inordinately pleased, even deeply excited at making this acquaintance; but his compliments only made Charles Newsome look a bit less comfortable still. Clearly he could not return them by saying that he had ever heard of the Wyatts from his grandparents; or if he had, he certainly had never paid attention to the reference.

To show him she did not hold this against him, Elissa continued, "And how long do you stay in our county, sir?"

He appreciated her perseverance in friendliness. "Why, I do not know," he said, as if suddenly realizing that he might remain some time in their neighborhood, and might enjoy doing so. "I do not know how long I shall stay with my grandparents. I should like to be . . . out on my own, so to speak; though unfortunately, I do not have the means for it."

"Of course," said John. "Every man must have his own home, his own castle—and his own garden, if he is like me. But we are sorry to hear of your not having means, sir; it is a grief. We are not unacquainted with grief here, and we can sympathize."

"I am sorry that you can sympathize so readily, then," said Charles Newsome. "But I hope you will understand that when I say I do not have the means for it, I do not suggest any slight on my father. He is very good to me—a most good and kind father." As he said this, he looked puzzled somehow, as if he were secretly thinking of something about his father that was not as good and kind as the man must necessarily be represented to new acquaintances. Some trouble lay between this man and his father—Elissa could only guess that it was the cause of his present pennilessness, or perhaps the effect of it. And for her the most important point was that no penniless and homeless man, however affable and attractive, could ever make a good husband for her sister. She wrote him out of that role at once; but she glanced at Merry and found her smiling on Charles Newsome and looking on him with that certain look she reserved for young men who intrigued her. Often and often had Elissa seen that look before; for the truth was that Merry was inclined to fall in love all too easily. All she seemed to want in a man was that he match her zeal for laughter and fun; and most men were captivated enough by her essential merriness to summon up a deceptive semblance of it in themselves, at least for a day or an evening.

"Indeed," Elissa said then, by way of probing Charles Newsome's circumstances, "our patrimonial system, though revered and ancient in origin, can be a cruel one."

Merry added, somewhat improperly: "I hope you are not utterly without the prospect of a living, sir; for that is something every gentleman ought to have."

Charles Newsome again looked puzzled and distressed. "Indeed," he said, "that is my difficulty precisely. My father wishes me to find myself a profession."

"But you are the only son, are you not?" asked Merry.

"Yes," answered Mr. Newsome. "I know you must think it strange, and so do I myself. The truth is that my father has said he will not leave Landseye to me, or any part of its income. He does not want to, for reasons unknown to me; and he is not obligated to do so. After he came of age, his father tried to make him settle; but my father then had other funds to live on, and waited his father out, and so when the estate came down to him at his father's death, it was not under a settlement, and so he turned it into a fee simple. And under those terms, he can do as he wishes. I have a right to it *in custom*, you see, but not in *law*."

This was so very shocking that the three Wyatts did not at first know what to say. Elissa's primary thought was that it was remarkable she had never heard of this before, for she visited Mr. Newsome's grandparents at Rowcliffe very often. She was instantly certain, in fact, that Mr. and Mrs. Rowcliffe knew nothing of this blow to their expectations for their grandson, and she made a mental note to instruct Merry to say nothing of it to them.

"You see," Charles Newsome went on, in that mixture of bashfulness and excessive openness that seemed to be his normal mode of engaging with everyone, "I have thought a great deal about it; I have decided that I do not really deserve my father's wealth. I mean, if you stop to think about it, not many people do. I knew fellows at school who were to inherit vast estates and had absolutely nothing to recommend them. Once they came into their own they did nothing but sink their patrimony in debt, and what is the good of that? I certainly am not a person who ought to be given wealth. I am no better than the next man. I have not the first idea how to keep my father's estate from simply being eaten up by bad tenants or tradesmen or servants, let alone how to improve it and use it to the benefit of others.

I should *like* to, and that is good; but I am ashamed to say that there is always a large gap between my intentions and my performance."

It was Merry, with her quick sympathy, who now managed to speak. "I am sure you do not give yourself enough credit, sir," she said. "But this is all very strange. To whom else would your father leave Landseye, if not to his own son?"

"He intends to leave it to the son of his brother, my cousin, Mr. Daniel Newsome."

"Why," said Merry in instant dislike, "is this Mr. Newsome not ashamed to have the estate on those terms? What kind of a fellow is he?"

"Oh, no, you do not understand!" exclaimed Mr. Newsome. "Daniel is not only my cousin, he is my best friend. He is like a brother to me. He is a guardian angel to me. He has watched over me and guided me and protected me through every step of my life."

"Then how can he take the estate from you?"

"If he refuses it, it will only go to someone else. If he accepts it, he will be able to use it to assist me in some way. That is his intention."

"Oh, but people's intentions often change when they come into their own," said Elissa. "All of a sudden they find their previous commitments and promises not at all as compelling as they previously believed them to be."

Mr. Newsome laughed and said, "Ah, Miss Wyatt, you do not know Daniel! If you ever know him, you will find it is impossible to doubt him. He is wiser and kinder and better than anyone else I have ever known. He will assist me as he can—indeed, he has already assisted me out of his own purse many a time, for my father gives me no allowance."

"No allowance!" said Merry.

"That is so. It is very awkward, but so matters stand. I must find a way to earn a living, that is all. And I am having a very difficult time of it. Daniel tried to convince me to pursue theology; but I have no head or heart for the church. Though he is right in saying that there is many a clergyman in England today who is less studied in that field than I am, still we cannot pretend that I would fill the role as I ought."

"Your scruples do you great honor, sir," said Elissa, "however unfortunate your lack of interest may be in this case."

"I have hoped that I may catch fire in the law," Mr. Newsome went on; but his choice of words was grimly comical, for his tone was despondent, even gloomy. "I have spent some time in reading it, and I mean to use my time here in the country continuing to do so. But, of course, 'reading the law' means apprenticing in it, and you see that I have cast off that bond and fled here to the country. Indeed, I fear I could never be more than a middling lawyer at best. And as for politics—" Here he made a face. "Why, I agree with Daniel. He says the great puzzle of society, of governance, is how to get the right things, wealth and power, into the right hands so that good may be done with them. He says that humankind has never sorted that out and never shall. He says we can indeed do better than we have done, but we shall never perfect ourselves. You see, chaps like me, or worse than me, keep coming into power, and so the whole world stumbles along and never improves."

Elissa was beginning to find this relentlessly frank self-assessment almost unnerving.

"And you have no interest in the army?" asked Merry.

Mr. Newsome now made a face that expressed both disgust and terror. "I could never follow that calling," he said. "It requires . . . crossing the ocean. That I could never do."

"But is it not exciting—more exciting than the law?" asked Merry.

"It has moments of excitement, certainly; but for the most part it seems to consist of waiting and idleness. As you may imagine, I am sick of waiting."

"Yes," John put in now. "I remember feeling the same at your age."

"I have always been waiting for the next stage of my life to come into view and begin," said Mr. Newsome.

"Precisely," said John.

"And it is a particular difficulty in my case," said Mr. Newsome, "because I have always been uncertain as to what was to come after my schooling."

"I understand you absolutely, sir," said Merry. "I loathe waiting. I must be *doing* something all the time."

"Indeed, that is so," said John.

Mr. Newsome smiled at John and Merry, pleased at their sympathy. All in an instant, Elissa saw the man's great failing: he was unable to go forth into the world and, of his own accord, engage himself with it; instead he could only wait until it offered him something he could endure to do. For all his own perception that he detested idleness, he was in fact cut out to be an idle gentleman, and could endure nothing else.

"Well," said Mr. Wyatt, "you may be sure that my daughters and I wish you the best success in life; and for our part we are sure that such an amiable gentleman as yourself cannot be far from a place and profession that will suit him. There is ever a need for good company in this world, and you will be sought after for that quality alone, if for none else."

This last compliment seemed rather backhanded to Elissa, but neither did Mr. Wyatt intend it so nor did Mr. Newsome receive it in such a sense.

"But let us not speak of sorrowful and puzzling things," said Mr. Wyatt. "Not on such a glorious, young-summer's day as this. I have the garden to show you.—Elissa, you will accompany us?"

"With pleasure, Father."

"'With pleasure,' she says! Did you hear that, Mr. Newsome? What good girls I have! They have heard my ecstasies concerning my flowers and trees and plantings ten thousand thousand times since they were little, and yet they are so gracious as to be willing to hear them again."

"You are blessed indeed, sir," said Mr. Newsome; and now his uncertainties seemed to fall away, or he seemed to transcend them; he seemed to forget the troubles of his own life; he looked on Elissa and Merry and saw them through the eyes of their father, and he pronounced his benediction warmly and genuinely. Elissa could easily see why her father had liked this man so readily, despite the difference in their ages: he was nothing if not winning; his way of entering into the passions and interests of others was very endearing. Perhaps he was a little too winning for his own good, she thought; he might in his winningness be won over himself to run in a course for which he had not the stamina.

"Well, do come in," said Mr. Wyatt, turning toward the gate. "I shall go first, to explain everything, and to make sure you do not miss a thing—that would be too bad, too bad!"

"Indeed it would, sir," said Mr. Newsome, as if he genuinely believed that by such an oversight he would be deprived of his only opportunity to view some of the greatest beauties on earth.

To enter the garden at Aeons' End was to plunge seemingly into another world. The gate was set in a fragrant boxwood hedge; and the vegetation grew so dense around its fissured, weathered wood that the tiny, fragrant leaves of the hedge threatened to engulf the gate entirely from time to time, and had to be clipped back sharply, only to swarm over the gate again. The boxwood leaves in fact reminded Elissa of a stationary swarm of little green and yellow bees, saturated with some odor culled from a thousand different flowers, both pungent and sweet, both oily and dry. The gate opened on a path, and the path led on through the boxwood, which was as wide as the foundation of a fortress, ten or even twenty feet thick in some spots, and seven or eight feet in height, and all of it clipped to form a kind of formless topiary that, seen from the windows of the house above, resembled nothing if not the swells of a green ocean. The path, as old as the house itself, was laid of Cotswold stone set deep and flat in the earth, and zigged first five feet this way and then zagged five feet that, and so on, so that one could not see straight through it from beginning to end; and here in the path, as at the gate, the boxwood crowded on the visitor, forming nearly a tunnel—shadowy, secret, initiative, testing—through which those passing must walk in single file.

Then the stones underfoot, emerging from the hedge into the light, were almost lost in the extraordinary profusion of John Wyatt's garden.

John loved every flowering plant with a passion bordering on the absurd, the obsessive; he loved flowers, their shapes and hues and deeps and scents, almost as a voluptuary loves flesh and its curves and tints and fragrances. And yet there was nothing obscene in his love: it was romantic in the extreme, idealizing; one might equally have said that he loved flowers as a geometer loves the five Platonic solids, it was that elevated a love, a love of elegance and abundance and the mysterious affinities among the various blossoms of the world, in all their colors and forms. When, on this occasion, he stepped out of the hedge into the sunlight of that flower-world, it was as if a drug had run through his blood; for an instant he stopped, in pleasure and satisfaction, heedless of those behind him, until Elissa touched him on the back of his shoulder, to remind him of their presence.

She herself never entered the garden without feeling a fresh sense of amazement at the enormous diversity to be encountered there. The pantheist—so she had read—argues that there is a soul even in matter such as stones and earth and air and water. Aristotle, she knew, was less generous and more specific. He said that there are three souls:

the nutritive, the animal, and the rational. Plants, the Philosopher averred, were vivified by the first, animals by the first and second, and humankind by all three. But all four types thrived in John Wyatt's garden.

For even the stones here—and there were many, set in the earth as paving and as uprights, as walls and as banks—seemed ensouled and living, because wrought to a higher purpose. They formed benches, either worked by tool and labor to that function, or naturally suited to it where they happened to rise from the soil; they reared and jutted here and there, defining niche and allee and bower, and served as the spine and ribs and legbones of the labyrinthine innards of the garden's plan; they rose in ramps and descended in steps; they marked the borders of gleaming pools and glowing flowerbeds, of rows of shady overhanging trees and a sunny-grassy amphitheater; they gave forth a speaking clatter underfoot in herringbone block or patchwork flag, or voiced a sibilant friction if brushed in passing, or a bright patter if rained upon; they curved, they crouched, they leaned, they loomed; they soothed the eye with their weather-worn surfaces, or teased and intrigued it with carvings ancient and allusive and arcane. Just as we are dead matter ensouled by something higher, but mysterious and vasty, so the stones of John Wyatt's garden were not dead, but living, because they had been set there, or exposed where they lay, or carved into shape and ornament, by a greater power—in their case, the hands of men. When speaking mutely among themselves, the foolish stones perhaps doubted John's existence; but they partook of him, and so they lived of him, whether they knew it or not. ¶ The water of the garden, by contrast, was a thing that spoke aloud; however it went, whether in channels or jets, it chuckled mirthily in the hearing ear. It ran down from a little gurgling spring on the hill, through pools in basins worked in monoliths of natural rock, shallow pools a cubit in depth and *pav'd beneath with jaspar shining bright,* as Spenser tells it. In the limpid water over this gleaming and lapidary pebblery there flew fulvous fainéant fish, flashing and fluttering and feinting, flirting and fanning and flicking their trailing tails. Nowhere did John let plants grow in these clear and pristine basins, except in one side pool where water lilies—those called brandy bottle and swan-among-the-flowers—gave protection to frogs and minnows.

Then there were, of course, the vegetative souls, the plants; but these were legion, beyond counting, beyond full description, beyond any ordering. It was true that in some patches Mr. Wyatt had imposed order for some particular purpose, with stake and string and trellis and wattle and pergola; so that, for example, a type of cucumber whose flowers he liked might have the room to grow (it was a peculiarity of his that he liked the blossoming of the cucurbits as though that were all the reason for their existence), or so that roses might run their peaceful riot along the walls, or ivy scale stone to provide handhold and backdrop for hydrangea. But for the most part the plants grew thickly, one upon the other, so that one felt almost that one would be borne up on their masses if one lay down upon them.

All the plants had this in common: like John and his daughters, they were an English breed. A more shallow enthusiast might have faulted John Wyatt's garden for its lack of exotics, but he preferred to work with plants native to England and those that had been acclimated to England's air and soil for centuries, though he did relax his horticultural xenophobia in the case of roses; for the roses of France in that era were exquisite. This passion for the native plant was not so much a conscious inclination as an instinctive tendency. When he was offered plants from Europe or the Americas or the Far East, as regularly happened in his winter correspondence with seed and bulb and stock agents, or with other gardeners in England, he would pause to listen to his heart on the matter, as another person might listen inwardly in an affair of friendship or love; and the absence of his customary zeal to acquire some new specimen made him promptly decline.

But there was no lack of variety in his garden for all that. The colors—it was as if God's palette had tumbled over and left its smears upon the place, for they either intermingled daringly or jostled together as discrete patches that were sometimes wide and sometimes brief, in swathes that merged and shifted with the passing of the seasons, washing and clashing and combining. Over spring and summer and fall, over the acreage in which they throve and strove, the hues erupted and faded from here to there: yellow ranged from the most sodden, succulent apricot to the most faint and pale yellow lily; purple from the Tyrian and purpureous lavender-bush and claret-colored hyacinth to the fading tones of the bellflower; red from the shouting scarlet of the opium poppies and Jerusalem cross, from the double red of the peonies, to the faintest pinky blush of the nigella and eupatorium; and then there was the dun and tan and brown and buff as well, such as in the muted teasel and fennel; and silver in the dusty miller; and there was white and cream, as in the umbels of Queen Anne's lace.

The diversity of roses alone was endless. To name a few: apothecary rose, rosa mundi, damask rose, rosa alba, double velvet rose, the lilac-pink early cinnamon rose, briar rose and double-blush briar rose, maiden blush rose and royal virgin rose and thornless virgin rose, the hundred-leaved rose, the burgundy rose, the wide-hipped apple rose, York rose, marbled rose, and that rose of lowly name but splendiferous flower, the cabbage rose; roses rambling and roses climbing and roses in dense bushes, and even roses that were not roses at all—*exempli gratia*, the rock rose. ¶ The garden had also its flowering trees and shrubs of full fruit and bright berry: cherry, apple, pear, rowan, apricot, peach, quince, elderberry, bilberry, lingonberry, blackberry, currant; these were often espaliered, or trimmed into clever conceits. ¶ Beneath the leafage of these plants, in damp and cool times, the garden had the volunteer color, sometimes subtle and sometimes strident, of its fairy growth: the delectable button mushrooms, blewitts, beefsteaks, parasols, chanterelles, and puff-balls; the ravishing fly-agaric, poison pie, and death cap.

And this is to leave aside entirely that corollary, the extensive kitchen garden of Aeons' End, so productive that it fed many a pauper in both summer and winter.

The names of the flowers in John Wyatt's garden were in themselves an incantation on his lips as he ran through them for curious visitors over the seasons. A mere fragment of the song ran *delphinium and nasturtium, auricula and clary and columbine, anemone and peony, lupin and loosestrife, convolvus and clove pink and copper pink and pinks of every color, sweet William and sweet Alice and sweet pea, lady's mantle and mourning widow, masterwort and mignionette and marigold, houseleek and hollyhock and bleeding heart, doronica and dahlia, gillyflower and bellflower and moondaisy, thistle and tulip, jonquil and lily of the valley and valerian, feverfew and forget-me-not and love-in-a-mist, pansy and primrose, saxifrage and syringa and snapdragon and Solomon's seal, violet and rocket.* He knew the Latin names of all his plants as well, though he could not have parsed *odi et amo;* but these he did not inflict upon his visitors, unless he was asked for them. For each shade of color he had a term of his own determining—celestial blue, indigo, blue madder, peacock blue, steel blue, azure; blood red, cherry red, carmine, iron red, magenta, maroon; ocher, peach, carrot; butter, saffron, gold; jade and aquamarine and bottle green; and very private names that seemed to stem from objects and incidents in his childhood, such as dogbark blue and teapot yellow and ladder brown, which he gave out as if everyone should know them.

With respect to the color green it should be said that in this place the variety of the leaves alone of that color would have made a garden in itself—yellowish box and privet, the sallow sedge, the mahogany-tinged foliage of the bush rose, the feathery faint verdigrisy fans of the fern, the bicolor of the broad imbricate pantiles that roofed the grape arbor, the waxen holly, the wan chlorine of the fluted pillars of arbor vitae and cedar, the glaucous fir, the mysterious sea-green depths of the hemlock, the dark and stark emerald of the yew. Some of this leafage was that of creepers and climbers like ivy and clematis and scarlet runner and briony and jessamine and bindweed; some of it was shrubbery, no few specimens of which were carved and trained in tunnels and mazes and knots and arches and spirals and topiaries, such as the boxen horse rearing at the staunch yew turret— vaguely evoking the knight and rook of chess, or perhaps the rescuer's mount and prisoning keep of fairy tale.

But forget color and shape. A blind man might have wandered those paths and been overcome by the fragrance alone, of herbs such as thyme and oregano and marjoram and rosemary and lavender, and also of the summer jasmine, woodbine, musk rose, and eglantine, to say nothing of all those roses, those roses. Here one might, in the poet's phrase, *die of a rose in aromatic pain,* so very intense was the scent of John's garden. For odor alone, it was such a place as made old men weep remembering, and stirred old women with long-forgotten desire.

As for the second of Aristotle's souls, the animal, John Wyatt's garden held a menagerie of creatures both domestic and wild: narcissist peacocks like vibrant living bouquets, meek rabbits and bold squirrels, silent butterflies and droning bees, dozens upon dozens of nesting songbirds, and wild duck that sometimes set down to rest an hour in the pools before winging onwards.

And to fill the third Aristotelian category, here was humankind as well. Looking upon the garden's profusion, one might have thought that it was simply let to grow by itself. But like all art, its simplicities disguised a labor more ceaseless and assiduous than did its complexities. Day after day, Mr. Wyatt; and the gardener, Mr. McBean; and the boy, Jim Riggins; and sometimes that jack-of-all-trades Joe Wiley would guide and nourish the garden by weeding, by watering, by plucking spent blossoms, by pruning dead

                                      Elissa Wyatt

growth, by tearing out annuals that had had their flower-time and by replacing them with later-blooming plants, by gathering seed to be saved for next year, by setting bulbs or dividing root stock, or any of the thousand other chores that gardeners even of less populous plots repeat according to the season. So much work there was to be done here that often John Wyatt brought in laborers by the day or by the week, though he seldom found any worker that suited his own passion for perfection.

This labor, considered in his day so coarse and ungentlemanly, affected John Wyatt physically and spiritually. He was wiry and sunburnt, and outside his own grounds he kept his hands gloved, so roughened they were. But his spirit was well fed and rosy and smooth; he was at peace, though it was an active form of peace, as long as he was in his garden. It was to him his church, his *ecclesia* of varied souls, his choir, his monastery cell, his desert cave. He knew essentially nothing of the doctrine of his nominal church, which ran through his mind like fine loam through a gappy screen; he could not have recited the Ten Commandments in ten centuries of attempts; his knowledge of the Bible was limited to scraps here and there, and it might be said that he knew it more by hearsay than by true acquaintance, as a citydweller has heard of the stars but never truly seen them, much less navigated by their constellations. But he had his garden, he loved his garden; that garden was the liturgy of John Wyatt's worship; it was a mass not in the vulgate, but in a secret language whose meaning could not be understood by the profane, and all were profane but he within those walls and hedges. And though the living image of that garden was transient, temporary, passing, and doomed, it was, in its annual revival, an allegory and promise of resurrection; it was yet permanent in its beauty and its loss. This last, the most precious arcanum of the universe, he understood and relied upon, without knowing he knew it—because he worked in his garden.

Or, to put this truth more simply, gardens are where everything begins for us, as we toddle about in the dirt; and where, if we are fortunate, everything ends for us, as we sit warm in the sun.

This was the wondrous place into which Charles Newsome unknowingly stumbled. Stumbled, at least in the figurative sense; for in fact he strode in behind Merry with all the confidence and curiosity of a young man following a young woman whose shape distracts him. The garden hit him like a stone hammer. He stood staring around himself, his eyes wide, his mouth open in flehmen like a cat let outdoors for the first time, sensing a world hitherto unimagined. The Wyatts took their places around him in a little group, looking at him; and on viewing his reaction, John was gratified, Merry pleased, and Elissa amused.

When he could finally speak, he said, "What an extraordinary . . . ! I say, what a remarkable . . . ! I say, sir, what a . . . !"

It was almost as if he could not say the word *garden,* because this was so far from any garden he had ever known. What were those vacant and paltry places to this?

"But there is more, sir," said Mr. Wyatt. "You have not even begun to see the place."

"Mr. Newsome," said Elissa, "this is only one *court,* so to speak, in a great palace of delights."

And Mr. Newsome allowed himself to be led on, alternately open-mouthed and grinning, alternately staring and shaking his head.

They went through arches and tunnels, down aisles and allees, past beds and pools, over little bridges, up stairways and along the winding trickle of the stream. Elissa could guess at the wonder Mr. Newsome was experiencing, though she herself was long past familiar with all of this. John narrated it all, the passion of his speech a fitting audible accompaniment to the richness of the spectacle.

At last they came to a long wooden bench set into a niche in the hill behind the house, and here Mr. Wyatt, having talked himself out for the moment, proposed they sit. So they did; and somehow Merry and Mr. Newsome wound up in the middle, and Elissa and Mr. Wyatt at the ends. Such a position was not likely to improve Merry's self-restraint, for if she did not have her chaperones in her visual field, she tended to forget they existed; and so she sat looking more at Mr. Newsome than at the view before them.

Which included not only the garden but the valley of Deepclough beyond it. One could see in the distance the roofs of the village and even the mirror of the millpond lying in the course of the threadlike river. "We could see Rowantree from here, sir," John told Mr. Newsome, "except that it lies behind that little knoll you see at the end of the wold—the little rise, with the orchard on it. But you can just make out parts of the road that winds up to your grandparents' house along the side of the valley, though not the house itself or the grounds proper. It is about two miles from here, but as you have discovered, it is a very brief and pleasant ride."

"Indeed it is, sir," said Mr. Newsome. "And if I may make so bold, I should like to make that little journey in this direction on many a day during my visit here."

"You would be most welcome," said Mr. Wyatt.

Elissa noticed what Mr. Wyatt did not: that this particular topic caused Mr. Newsome and Merry to exchange a shy glance and then look away.

After a moment, Mr. Newsome said, "But I must say, sir, that seeing your garden makes me wish I had such a place myself. And since I am not likely to have that good fortune for quite some time, I wonder if you might . . . take me in as a sort of apprentice, and teach me a little of what you know. About . . . making gardens, you know. Planting them, I suppose I mean; but it would seem as well that you have . . . *designed* this wonderful place."

He could not have pleased Mr. Wyatt more. "Well, of course I have," said Mr. Wyatt. "That is the work of the cold winter nights, you know, when one cannot be outside digging and pruning."

"Papa takes to his desk in the sitting room," said Merry, "and draws maps and pictures of what he wants; and we sit there by the fire with him, with our sewing, or Elissa reads to us. It is very cozy, I assure you."

"So it sounds," said Mr. Newsome approvingly. "I do have a bit of skill at drawing, if I dare say so—if that would be of any service to you, sir, I would most humbly undertake anything for you. An elevation, say, or a cross-section."

"Ah, elevations! That is exactly where my skill is wanting, I am afraid," said Mr. Wyatt. "Perspective on paper is simply not my strong suit."

"I am rather good at perspective," said Mr. Newsome, with a commendable sort of eager humility.

"Well, that is excellent," said Mr. Wyatt.

"And how are you with a spade, Mr. Newsome?" asked Elissa.

He shook off this dose of reality quickly. "I should very much like to find out," he said. "I think I could be quite useful in that respect as well.—But do you do much of your own work, sir? I imagine you have gardeners for that."

Mr. Wyatt frowned, and Mr. Newsome looked stricken. "I *do* have some men who work for me," said Mr. Wyatt, "but they only follow my lead. I am a put-my-hand-to-it sort of man, Mr. Newsome, a put-my-hand-to-it sort of gardener; I am not afraid to get my hands dirty, and I think no true gardener is. Indeed, that is what we live for—getting our hands into the dirt."

Mr. Newsome gazed at him as if he were a veritable Nelson speaking of commanding the fleet. "I should *very* much like to give that a try, sir," he said. "My mother loves her garden, and she spends much time in it; and when I was a boy, she would try to bring me along with her when she went to give the gardeners their directions. But my father did not believe in her soiling her hands."

Mr. Wyatt's contempt for this attitude was palpable. "Oh, did he not?" he said. "Well, you shall find no such belief here. Miss Merry often helps me with little tasks that are not too taxing. I insist that she wear gloves, of course, to preserve her hands." He had shed his own gloves when he entered the garden, and he now looked down at his roughened palms with some satisfaction. "I myself am not the least bit concerned about such matters."

"So, Miss Merry, you help Mr. Wyatt?" said Mr. Newsome.

"Oh, with little things. Binding up, and plucking the faded flowers, and watering sometimes, and sometimes pulling up weeds. It is very pleasant on a fair day, you know—to be out of doors, and to be useful to Papa."

"And a very pretty picture she makes, too," said Mr. Wyatt, "with her wide-brimmed hat over her locks, and her smock tied around her little waist, and her long leather gloves, kneeling on the rug we have for her—a particular one we save for her."

"I should like to see that," enthused Mr. Newsome.

I wonder that Mr. Newsome does not notice how artful Papa is being, thought Elissa to herself. *Or perhaps he takes it as a compliment to himself and enjoys it.*

Almost as if Mr. Newsome could tell that she was thinking of him, he turned to her now in one of the rare moments on that first day of their acquaintance with him in which he took particular notice of her—or indeed, in one of those moments rare on nearly any day that summer. "And you, Miss Wyatt?" he asked. "Do you too work in the garden with your father and sister?"

Merry answered for her. "Oh, no," she said, in a tone of assertiveness that greatly amused Elissa. "We do not allow it. She works so hard for us in the house, you see. She takes care of everything—consults with the housekeeper, and keeps the household accounts, and—well, simply *manages* everything. I do not even know *what* she does! But it is a great deal, and she never would dream of complaining, and everything runs like the great clock in the hallway—"

"Which, as a matter of fact, she winds up and keeps well oiled," Mr. Wyatt pointed out.

"Precisely," said Merry. "She frees us from thinking of any of it. She holds all the keys of the household! So we have all the pleasure of the garden. And so when she visits us in it, we do not allow her to work. We have even had a special chair made for her, a kind of wicker sofa chair, so she can put her feet up."

"She must sit in the shade, or in the sun if it is cool," said Mr. Wyatt. "We are happiest of all when we see her dozing peacefully, though that does not happen often."

"She sometimes tries to help us," said Merry, "but we are quite firm with her. It is the only time we are ever firm with her! Usually she is the one who must be firm with us."

Mr. Wyatt laughed in agreement with this statement.

"Sometimes," Merry went on, "we let her read to us if we are doing something quiet enough to hear her."

"How fortunate you are to have such a sister," said Mr. Newsome. "I myself have absolutely no head for such things. If I ran a household, it would be all topsy-turvy. Why, when I lived alone in the City, my lodgings were a chaos. My cousin had to engage a woman to come in once a week to clean, and she would require the greater part of a day to set it to rights—though I thought she worked rather slowly, I must admit. Daniel would like to engage a manservant for me, but I drew the line at that. It is too expensive, and besides, I might well drive such a fellow mad."

"Your cousin is indeed very solicitous of you," said Merry.

"Oh, he is! He is! I could not possibly want a kinder friend. The man is an angel who was sent to earth to make sure I do not stumble. He carries me over every rough patch. I do not know what I would do without him. I have not a doubt that he would die for me if it came to that, and I would rather die than see him do so."

Elissa, guessing that this line of conversation would soon provoke something inappropriate from Merry, interposed to say, "Your love for your cousin is admirable, Mr. Newsome."

"Not nearly so admirable as his love for me, I assure you! He would never let me starve, or be in the least uncomfortable."

"Then he is noble in character, would you say?" asked Merry.

"He is indeed. Why—"

Merry had a bad habit, when agitated, of asking questions and not listening to responses; she often hurried ahead into asking new questions or making related statements before her own questions were answered.

"Then he is like my sister," said Merry. "And that puts you and me, Mr. Newsome, in exactly the same position of having excellent models to emulate."

Mr. Newsome was pleased at the comparison. "Yes, I suppose it does," he said happily. "But I could never model myself on my cousin. I could never be like him."

"But why not?"

"Because he is ever so far above me. His intelligence, his wide reading, his wide *thinking*, his moral sense, his . . . his quiet sort of dignity—I do not know how else to put it, but you would know what I mean at once if you ever met him— he quite puts me in the shadow, though without meaning to. And in fact sometimes I think he holds back and says nothing when we are in company, out of fear of exposing my foolishness."

"What foolishness is that, Mr. Newsome?" asked Merry in a skeptical tone.

Mr. Newsome was again pleased. Elissa saw how these little complimentary strokes buoyed the man up socially; she guessed he was forever being grateful and pleased by being noticed and approved of. This was the very sort of attention that Merry had a natural and inexhaustible ability to provide.

"If you only knew me, Miss Merry—" said Mr. Newsome, beginning what probably would have been a long demurral.

"As I hope we all shall," Merry cut in.

Mr. Newsome must of course here reiterate his own hopes on this matter, which Merry again soon interrupted, and with a typical non sequitur.

"And where *is* your friend and cousin at present, sir?"

"Why," said Mr. Newsome, with some slight evidence of uneasiness, "I do not perfectly know. But then again, I often do not know where he is. He travels about so rapidly. I never know when he will drop in on me in my lodgings—just to see how I am faring, you know, and to help me in some way. He is like a thief in the night, but a thief who leaves you gold rather than steals it from you."

"He sounds like a very noble fellow indeed," said Mr. Wyatt. "I like the man already, and would like to meet him."

"And I myself would like to see him. But he may be preparing to go to Madeira."

"Really!" exclaimed Merry. "How interesting! Madeira?"

"Yes; you see, his father was the younger brother of the Newsome family, and he was forced to make his own way in the world, as I am. He did not scruple to . . . form extensive connections with Madeira."

Elissa saw at once that Mr. Newsome did not like to mention that his uncle's family was involved in trade, most likely the wine trade; and this guess was at once confirmed when Mr. Newsome continued, "They did not *need* to be connected with the place, I suppose; my uncle could have found a profession. But it has brought a source of wealth that is most useful; and wealth in an old family creates its own dignity, even for a younger son."

"Any such increase is agreeable," agreed Mr. Wyatt, "even for the best of good families. It is our obligation to improve our estates, sir; and mine is carefully husbanded by a manager of the most excellent skill and probity, Mr. Tempest."

The young people could not be drawn off by this sober topic. "So you believe your cousin is in Madeira?" asked Merry, trying to track Mr. Newsome's point, though she would likely not let him make it if he tried.

"Oh, no," said Mr. Newsome. "He has not left yet. He would tell me if he were going there. But he might have gone to Falmouth—he often goes to Falmouth, where . . . ships put in."

Yes, thought Elissa with a little sharp humor she would never have expressed aloud, *ships do indeed put in at Falmouth. You mean your cousin's family's ships put in there, Mr. Newsome, the ships that bring the wine in which his family trades so extensively and successfully; you need not be ashamed of saying so.*

"I think you will find, Mr. Newsome," she said then, "that the Wyatts have not that prejudice against men like your cousin that you may meet elsewhere. He is a gentleman, and we honor him for that. We do not let the necessity under which he operates—that of his being in trade, I mean—detract from the more important fact that he is of good family. Indeed, if he discharges his duties in trade as a gentleman ought, we shall esteem him more than we would if he were the idlest of squires on the most fabulous of country estates."

Mr. Newsome looked at her gratefully; she had precisely eased the fears he was feeling on his cousin's behalf. He seemed too full of emotion to reply aloud; instead he made a little seated bow in her direction.

He probably could not have spoken in any case, for Merry was quick with another non sequitur: "Have *you* ever been abroad, Mr. Newsome?"

At the mere suggestion implied in this query, Mr. Newsome showed an almost violent reaction: he physically recoiled, shuddered, turned pale, and looked deeply unsettled. It was a more complete version of the revulsion he had displayed when he had been asked about going into the army.

"Oh, no!" he exclaimed. "I shall *never* go abroad! I shall *never* leave England! But it is not from zealous patriotism, though I hope I have that, and in as good supply as any Briton. It is because . . . *I could never board a ship*, Miss Merry. I am as terrified of the water as . . . as I do not know what. Nothing terrifies me more than . . . the idea of a ship, or even a boat, a little boat, on the water, even on a very little water—a cowpond a yard deep, Miss Merry, I could not do it. It is not rational, I know, but . . . it is the way I am."

He paused a moment. They were all embarrassed by the passion and discomfort of this confession, and remained silent out of compassion for him; but he seemed to take their silence as expressive of disbelief, and he plunged on: "It is because I almost drowned when I was a boy—indeed, I would be dead, if my cousin had not saved my life. Daniel himself almost drowned saving me; but you will never hear him admit that, because as I have already said, he would gladly lose his life to save mine—unworthy though I am of any such devotion!"

Then, as if casting about to bring this outburst to a conclusion, he said: "Water! No! Why, I hate even going over a bridge in a carriage.—So I shall never go to Madeira! My cousin has been to Madeira, and talks of going to Madeira again soon, but I shall never go. Never!"

Even Merry must continue silent in the face of this emotion. It was John who was able to reply and bring Mr. Newsome back to some semblance of calm and good cheer. "Then gardening is the thing for you, my good fellow!" he said. "Indeed, I think gardening is the thing for everyone. I remember my Horace from my school days, and how he talked of the impiety of going to sea in ships, and even at the time I heartily concurred with him. We are an island nation, and by rights have a mighty navy to defend ourselves, and to trade with the world and bring us its wealth; but someone must also work the garden that England is, sir! That is no less noble a calling. And when you have your two hands deep in the soil—when you have those twin anchors down, as it were—you shall know a contentment you have never felt before, I assure you."

"I do believe I shall," said Mr. Newsome, seizing on this hope as if it were all that was saving him from the pressgang and a watery doom.

Merry was now able to help distract him from his anxiety with another detour. "Your cousin must be familiar with Bath," she said.

"Bath? Why, yes, he is. He travels through Bath of a purpose, whenever he goes from Landseye to Falmouth. He has friends in the environs with whom he stays."

"We have a friend in Bath," said Merry. "That is why I mention it."

"I would not be surprised if my cousin knows your friend; I think he is much liked in society there, though he makes only flying visits through the place."

"Her name is Miss Louisa Bright. Her family has a seat not far from here—how far is Ryderly, Elissa?"

"About eight miles."

"Yes, eight miles. It is Ryderly Hall, Mr. Newsome. I do not suppose you have heard of it? But at present our friend is living with her uncle and aunt at Bath, where there is more society. They are quite in need of her—her uncle and aunt, I mean—for she takes care of everything for them. She is to them what our Elissa is to us."

"Ah," said Mr. Newsome, with a generous affectation of interest, though he was clearly and understandably not sure why he was being supplied with this information. He was able to tie up the topic by resorting to a stock sentiment from the general book of manners: "I shall ask my cousin about your friend when I see him again."

"She is really more Elissa's friend than mine," added Merry. Elissa, who knew the reason for this odd correction, wondered if Mr. Newsome might guess at it.

Perhaps sensing Mr. Newsome's continued perplexity, Mr. Wyatt added, "The Bright family is often in our thoughts, you see, because Miss Bright's cousin, Mr. David Boulder, went out to India with my son, George. Mr. Boulder, however, is still overseas. He is trying to make his fortune there. His father was not able to manage his expenditures well, and in retrenching has had to let his own estate. I believe his parents live comfortably enough in Bath, however—if it is possible to live comfortably without the possession of a garden."

"Well, I wish Mr. Boulder the best of success," said Mr. Newsome, who was evidently able to shower genuine goodwill on anyone, even on those who had no idea they were receiving it from him. "That is something I should like to do—make my fortune! But as I have said, India, or even Madeira, is out of the question in that respect. My cousin recently had a . . . a kind of scheme for me in Madeira, a way to maintain myself. But I could never overcome my reluctance to go there."

"I do not believe Mr. David Boulder likes to be away from home either," said Merry; and then she blushed.

Elissa was amused by her sister's confusion: obviously Merry did not know whether to defend Mr. Boulder—one of the many gentlemen with whom she had been infatuated in the past—against an imaginary slight, or to forget her passion of yesterday and continue to compliment the man who might be her suitor tomorrow.

Mr. Newsome was, fortunately, incapable of misunderstanding Merry's remark as a reproach to him. "I am sure he does not," he agreed affably. "Especially as he was acquainted with all of you before he left, and must certainly regret his absence from you."

Merry, disconcerted by this near hit, turned away; and noticing Elissa's amusement, she rolled her eyes as if to say, "I am fairly caught!" But Mr. Newsome, looking out again over the valley, did not notice, and the awkwardness passed with no harm done. Merry was glad to drop the topic; and her temporary silence gave Mr. Newsome a chance to seize the initiative in the conversation.

"And you, Miss Merry?" he asked. "Have you traveled much?"

Elissa could not but feel that his singling Merry out was somewhat rude to her father, and perhaps to her; but she was as ready to forgive people's petty failings as she was quick to observe them.

"I have but seldom traveled anywhere," said Merry. "My sister and I attended school at Mrs. Wright's in Gloucester, and I have been to London twice, but I have never been even to Bath, and that is a very easy distance from here."

"I have never been to Bath either," said Mr. Newsome. "But if you have not traveled far, you have not much to lament; for this is surely the prettiest little valley in all of England."

"Do you truly think so?" asked Merry happily.

"I do," enthused Mr. Newsome. "It is not only fair to the eye, it is fair to the ear. It is so wonderfully quiet here! All one may hear is the sound of nature at work, and that is in no way an annoyance, not after the rumbling of carriages on city streets, and the cries of the sellers, and the hubbub of the mobs passing to and fro. The birds, and the sheep, and the breeze in the trees and the hills and the wold—the river running along the lowermost reaches—it is all wonderfully picturesque and pastoral. Lovely, truly; truly lovely." And he looked into Merry's face as he said this in a manner that made Elissa think he was forgetting one theme of beauty for another; though he did somewhat spoil the effect by adding, "And I am sure there is wonderful shooting here!"

"You are a hunter and shooter, then, Mr. Newsome?" asked Elissa. Her own opinion of such sports was not high, and it amused her to find that this idle man professed enthusiasm for what she considered to be so idle and unprofitable a pastime.

"Indeed I am," he said warmly. "You have found out one of my great enjoyments."

"Well, I am afraid we must disappoint you in that respect," she said. "The shooting is rather poor on our hill."

"It is not something I have kept up," explained Mr. Wyatt.

"Well, it hardly matters," said Mr. Newsome generously, "when you have all this beauty around you."

"My dear sir," said Mr. Wyatt, with his own brand of enthusiasm, "you have not even begun to see the beauties of our valley. Why, from this spot, if you sat here only for one hour a day, you would soon think you had seen ten thousand valleys. The way the clouds move over the land, and the shadow of the clouds beneath, and the way the colors of everything change as the sun comes and goes with those shadows! It is far better than human life, I shall tell you that, with its loves and its dislikes, its disappointments and balkings, its pains and its perilous pleasures. Here you may see only changements of beauty, not changements of suffering. Stick to nature, my good sir, and you will not go wrong! And the garden, the garden is the best place to do that."

Mr. Newsome responded in the same key, and it was clear that his warmth and goodwill had plenty of scope to take in all nature. And the conversation continued in this pleasant vein for quite some time, warmed by the enthusiasms of Mr. Newsome, of the pretty young woman beside him, who looked so merrily into his face, and of the father of the family, who skillfully coaxed him to adopt a new mania. Elissa herself made no attempt to cool any of them. Certainly her wry observations would have chilled their companionship, but she reserved them for her private enjoyment.

Eventually they wound their way back through the garden again and concluded the tour at the back of the house, where they walked through to the parlor. As they entered there, Elissa interrupted the conversation long enough to ascertain one critical point. "Is Mr. Newsome to stay to dinner, Papa?" she asked. In that era, the invitation would be nearly understood; it needed only to be formalized.

"I am sorry, but he shall not do so on this day," said Mr. Wyatt. "He has told me that he must dine with the

Rowcliffes at Rowantree. But we shall have them all to dine as soon as possible.—Still, perhaps we should have something to tide us over. Would you take some tea, sir?"

"I should like that very much," said Mr. Newsome.

None of the servants were about, so Elissa undertook to go to the kitchen to give directions. When she returned, Mr. Wyatt and Merry were chatting with Mr. Newsome about the name of Aeons' End.

"Here," said Mr. Wyatt, "Elissa will tell us. What Bible verse is it, my dear, that has the name of our house in it?—Elissa is quite clever about all these things, Mr. Newsome, as you shall see for yourself soon enough."

"Elissa *knows everything*," said Merry with the reverent certainty of those who have no idea how very little they know themselves, and to whom any knowledge seems prodigious.

"Papa," said Elissa mildly, "you know I would know nothing about this matter if Mr. Herbert had not taken the pains to point it out to me."

"Well, do show it to Mr. Newsome.—Sir, you imagine how it tickles my pride to see the name of my family's house written in the Bible, as it were."

Elissa went to a side table and turned the pages of the large family Bible that lay open there. Either Mr. Wyatt or Merry could easily have found the passage themselves, since it was marked by a slip of paper that the rector, Mr. Herbert, had written up for Elissa on the occasion they had discussed the passage together; but neither Mr. Wyatt nor Merry would ever have thought of seeking the page out, regarding the actual printed Bible as they did as a kind of Holy of Holies they were not permitted to enter; or rather, as something which, despite its venerability, was a source of overwhelming boredom that would have suffocated them had they attempted an interview with it.

"It is in Hebrews 9:26," Elissa told Mr. Newsome.

"Ah," said Mr. Newsome uncertainly. She could see that he had never read that book of the Bible, and perhaps not any of them. Despite the training he must have received at university, the sole reference of the word "Hebrews" in his mind was those people from whom certain of his classmates had borrowed money.

"*In the end of the world he hath appeared, to put away sin by the sacrifice of himself,*" she read. She looked at the note Mr. Herbert had written for her. "Apparently," she added, "the words 'in the end of the world' in the original language include the word *aeon*. Mr. Herbert says the phrase may more properly mean 'in the conclusion of the ages' or something of that sort. So 'Aeons' End' is . . . the end of everything, like Judgment Day."

Mr. Newsome almost seemed a little frightened. "Is that not a portentous name for a dwelling, though?" he asked.

She laughed in a manner that relieved him. "I do not think you need to take it quite so seriously, sir," she said. "I think our ancestors may have been learned in Greek, and seen this as a play on words, a gentle joke of sorts."

"But what exactly does it all mean?" asked Mr. Newsome, still puzzled.

"They meant this house to be the abode of the Wyatts until the end of time."

Instantly she wished to recall this last remark, as she knew it would send her father's thoughts in a gloomy direction. "And," she added quickly, "the verse as a whole is a reflection on how we put away our own sin by sacrificing ourselves, through the grace and in the pattern of the self-sacrifice of Jesus Christ."

This theological reflection was far above the heads of her listeners, who saw it as irrelevant in any case; and in her purpose of deflecting the topic away from gloom—which was, in effect, to overwhelm her father with what was to him only abstruse church-language—she was thoroughly unsuccessful.

"And we have failed them!" exclaimed Mr. Wyatt, thinking of his ancestors. "*Aeons' End* indeed! We have come to the end of the aeons! We have come to the end of time, of the Wyatts' time in this house! Judgment Day it is, indeed—judgment on us for . . . what we have done."

"But what have we ever done, Papa," asked Merry, "that would make us deserve to lose the home we love?"

Mr. Wyatt did not immediately answer, and to Elissa his hesitation seemed curious. "Indeed, I know not," he said then. "I have certainly made mistakes in my life, but I hardly know that they are worse than most men make at some point, sooner or later."

"You have never erred, Papa," said Merry simply.

"Well," said Mr. Wyatt, with the air of one shifting the subject, "I can tell you where I erred in one point, and that was in letting George go to India."

"But you did *not* let him, Father," said Elissa. "You cannot blame yourself for that. He went without your blessing."

"So he did, so he did," said Mr. Wyatt. "And I wish he had proven me no more than a foolish and worried father. I wish he had not proven me right!"

"Mr. Newsome must be surprised at this reference to our family troubles, Father," said Elissa. "Let us choose some more sociable topic."

Mr. Wyatt took half the hint: though he did not change the topic, he did realize that Charles Newsome was ignorant of the difficulties he alluded to; and this latter oversight he sought to correct. "Mr. Newsome," he began, "of course you may know nothing of this; but I had a son, and my daughters had a brother—I mentioned him in passing before—a fine young man, a fine, fine young man; who was to inherit this house after me. He would have been the means of preserving his sisters after my death, as well as the means of perpetuating this estate of ours into centuries to come—until the very end of time, truly. But he perished at the Cape, in that passage from India that is so often perilous to men hale as well as weak. And since then, we have lived like the condemned, waiting for the worst to befall."

"But this is terrible," said Mr. Newsome, genuinely sympathetic.

"Indeed, sir, it is; terrible, terrible, terrible. And that I, John Wyatt, who have loved this house and property as much as any of my ancestors, or more—it is just possible that I have loved it more, I say, as the care I have lavished on my garden may testify—that I, sir, should be the means of its passing to a man of another name, a man decidedly inferior to the Wyatts in blood and bearing! This is, for me, not to be borne. I think sometimes that as I die I shall set the place afire, rather than pass from this world knowing it shall go into *that* man's hands!"

"Is he so very bad, then, this fellow?" asked Mr. Newsome, evidently a little shocked at Mr. Wyatt's passion on the subject.

"He is, sir," said Mr. Wyatt. "I have met him several times in my life, particularly at the assizes. He is a brute, no better than a brute. I would sooner bequeath Aeons' End to a foul dog or a pig, to make a kennel or a sty of it."

"Truly!" said Mr. Newsome, impressed by this emphasis. "But must you leave it to him? I gather it is entailed upon the oldest male in the line—and thus the sympathy with me that Miss Wyatt expressed earlier on our patrimonial establishment—I see it now. But entails can be broken; I understand that much from my reading of the law."

"The entail of Aeon's End cannot be broken now," said Mr. Wyatt. "When I came of age, my father and I signed a strict settlement that ensured the property would be mine as life tenant after my father's death, just as my father was in his. In the event of my having no heir, the property was stipulated to pass to the son of his sister, a man who does not even bear the Wyatt name, this most degenerate and disgusting Mr. Crustall."

Mr. Newsome looked at Elissa and then asked Mr. Wyatt, "And it is a tail male, and not a tail general? I believe that has something to do with it."

"I am far more well acquainted with the settlement than I wish to be," said John, "but I regret to say that I do not know the meaning of those terms, sir."

Here Mr. Newsome's authority in the matter apparently collapsed. He looked unhappy at being called upon to be specific, though Mr. Wyatt had not intended to force him to disclose his ignorance. "I believe," he said hesitantly, "that a tail general can descend to the females of the line, while a tail male cannot. At least, that is what I recall."

"Oh, no, there is no hope of my dear daughters coming into the estate. Believe me, I have questioned the lawyers on that, I have had the best advice. The thing is unbreakable."

"But . . ." began Mr. Newsome, and then hesitated.

"If you have a thought, sir, speak it," said Mr. Wyatt. "Though again I assure you, I have looked into every possibility without success."

"Well, if the ladies will forgive me for raising this somewhat indelicate point, and if you yourself will forgive my presumption . . . why not marry again, sir, and beget an heir?"

Mr. Wyatt visibly shuddered in repulsion. "I am past that," he said.

"But older men than you have done the same."

"It is not that I doubt the possibility of it. I am sure I am capable; it is only that the idea of marrying again offends me. I loved once, I married, and I lost my wife. You would not understand it, being the age you are; but as a widower of my age, I am both too far from returning to the passion for the opposite sex that once I felt, as a natural part of my youth, and too set in my ways as a man who lives without a wife. I could not endure to take a wife again. It would seem a farce. And she must needs be young, to breed, sir; and like as not she would seek to quarrel with my daughters, and to set me against them; and *that* I could not endure, truly. And it seems likely that any woman willing to marry a man so much older than herself would be desperate and poor and without standing in society; and forcing my daughters to keep company with her, and indeed, to give her precedence, would be wrong of me."

"But for the *sake* of your daughters . . ."

"However concerned I might be for their sakes, *she,* this new wife, would not naturally be so. She might well conspire with my son, if I had one by her, to turn them out of the house after I am dead. And she might just as likely compound the problem by giving me more daughters—who would add their sufferings to that of the beloved pair I have already."

"This *is* a grief," said Mr. Newsome. "I am sorry to learn, my new friends, that you have your share in the troubles born out of our laws of inheritance that are . . . what did you call them, Miss Elissa? Both ancient and cruel."

Then the tea was brought in; an event which, as it so often does, resulted in a change of subject, which suited them all.

<h1 style="text-align:center">❋ 2 ❋</h1>

Sister, Awake!

Sister, awake! close not your eyes,
The day her light discloses;
And the bright morning doth arise
Out of her bed of roses.

See the clear sun, the world's bright eye,
In at our window peeping;
Lo, how he blusheth to espy
Us idle wenches sleeping!

Therefore awake, make haste I say,
And let us without staying
All in our gowns of green so gay
Into the park a maying.

—Bateson's Madrigals

The breakfast room at Aeons' End had been added shortly after John Wyatt had wed Jane Abel. It projected from the east side of the house, so that it caught the sun at once; and it was surrounded on three sides by—what else but the garden: a small, *U*-shaped sward of emerald lawn backed by heavy banks of roses. In each of the three walls was set a pair of French doors (that is, doors made of smaller panes of glass extending from floor to ceiling). These doors could be and often were opened in fair weather, and thus the garden and its scent of vanishing dew and warming air and freshly clipped grass and billowing, blowing roses poured into the room as does vapor into a perfumer's alembic, there to be distilled after the doors were closed and the day proceeded.

And the morning after the day on which Charles Newsome entered the lives of the dwellers at Aeons' End was just such a fair, early-summer's day; so when Elissa entered the room, she was met with the facts of the day: beauty, warmth, fragrance.

She found to her surprise that both John and Merry had risen before her. Merry, in fact, had finished her breakfast and already walked forth outside; and though the impulse to walk outdoors early on such a day would not have been extraordinary in anyone else, in Merry it was rare.

"Our sleepyhead is up and has breakfasted and gone outside, then?" said Elissa when she had seen the evidence on the table.

"Yes," said John Wyatt. "She was waiting for me when I came down; she was impatient to make a request of me."

"And what was that, Papa?"

"She wants me to go to Rowantree today."

"Ah," said Elissa.

"I think we can guess why," said John.

"To take her there, or to bring our new acquaintance back."

"Precisely," said John.

He had expressed his approval of Mr. Charles Newsome in general terms to his daughters after that gentleman had left, but now Elissa pressed him further.

"Papa," she said, "do you not think it may be a mistake to encourage Merry in this new infatuation? For I see that is exactly what it is."

John seemed oddly reluctant to agree. "Well," he said, "I suppose you mean that he has no means of support."

"That is just what I mean—no means of support, nor the sort of ambition to acquire them. He is dependent on others to help him."

"Perhaps those others shall," said John. "The Rowcliffes are very fond of him; I saw that yesterday. And his cousin seems a very noble and generous man, from his description."

"The Rowcliffes are obsessed with patrimony, as I said yesterday, so any fondness they may have for their daughter's son is both consistent with their character, insofar as Mr. Newsome is male, and liable to bear no fruit, insofar as he is not their own son. They do have a son of their own, after all; and Mr. Michael Rowcliffe is likely to give them an heir soon enough. They may offer Mr. Newsome a room at Rowantree as long as they live, just as his cousin may offer him a room at Landseye, but so far as we know, they cannot give him a house of his own, or the funds to keep it up. Surely that is too much for him to ask of anyone, or for him to count on anyone supplying."

"But he is such a good boy," said John.

She was now surprised the more at his reluctance to concede her point, which seemed almost too obvious to need expression. "He seems to be a very sweet-tempered gentleman, that is true," said Elissa. "But I doubt if his good nature would survive long under the strains of poverty or ill-use by the world."

John shifted his ground. "I do not think we ought to interfere between them," he said. "Who knows? They may tire of each other in another meeting. Merry falls out of love as quickly as she falls into it."

"Papa, that is not true! It may seem that way, but believe me, each of these attachments takes away another shred of her innocence and happiness when it is torn from her."

John made the face he reserved for those occasions when he thought Elissa was being too prudent or too prudish. It always especially alarmed her, because it had often been the first indication that in addition to being very wrong, he was about to be very stubborn.

"But Papa," she said, "Mr. Newsome has no plan for his future. The future, the future, Papa! We must think of it.

If we do not, we will condemn Merry to a life of poverty. Certainly Merry never thinks of it; it remains for us to do so. You could interfere at this moment, and speak firmly to her about not forming an attachment to Mr. Newsome, and you might have some effect."

"I will not do it," he said.

She found his persistence extremely puzzling.

"I understand why you like the man, Papa," she said. "But really—"

"It will all come right, my dear," said John. "I do not know how, but I am sure it will."

"Papa," she said, "it will not come right unless we use the powers that God has given us to make it come right—prudence and rational thought."

He rose from the table now. She saw she had lost the battle, or at least that he was making his escape.

"Dear girl," he said fondly, "do not fret yourself. I know you feel yourself a mother to her, but she must be allowed to find her own way in this."

"But you will not go to Rowantree today," she said, hoping for at least this concession.

"I am busy today, and I told her so. I am quite happy to have the Rowcliffes and their grandson over to dinner at any time; but I leave the arranging of that in your capable hands."

"Thank you, Papa."

He took her hand in his own rough hand and kissed it—it had been a quirk of his since she was a child—and then he went out into the garden. She knew she would not see him until dinner unless she went to find him.

She served herself some breakfast and had nearly finished it when Merry came into the room through one of the garden doors. She approached Elissa directly and kissed her good morning.

"You are risen early today, dear," observed Elissa.

"I had to speak to Papa," said Merry.

"So I heard."

"Did he tell you? But he must go to Rowantree today, and he refuses."

"Do not be too alarmed at his refusal," said Elissa, with a little irony in her tone. "It is not for any prudent reason; it is only that he prefers to work in the garden."

"But we must see Mr. Newsome again," said Merry.

Elissa smiled. "*You* must see him today, perhaps," she said. "Pleasant and amiable though I find that gentleman to be, I believe I can live without him for a day—or even a week, if need be."

"Well, Papa seems to be of your opinion," said Merry. "He talks vaguely of our having the Rowcliffes to dinner some-day this week, and of course Mr. Newsome with them, but he leaves it all to you to arrange. And that is all very well; but I want to see Mr. Newsome *today.*"

"Perhaps Mr. Newsome will come here."

"But perhaps not."

"Well, we can hardly go to him at Rowantree. You cannot *chase* him, dear."

"No," said Merry, with uncharacteristic primness. "I would not do that. But you are going to the village today, are you not?"

This had been Elissa's previously announced intention; now she sought for some manner in which to retract it. But none immediately came to her, and she had to admit that she had planned so to do.

"Well, then, I shall walk with you. Mr. Newsome will likely pass through there if he goes anywhere beyond Rowantree."

Elissa opened her mouth to say more, but the kitchen maid, Mabel Dean, happened to enter the room at that moment and began cleaning up the breakfast things; and Merry turned the topic elsewhere, seemingly with an effort, though she continued to speak in that ready, easy way of hers—about everything except the subject that Elissa guessed was on her mind. She spoke of gowns, and of household matters, and of books to take back to the little library club at the shop in the village—which chore she would doubtless forget when it came to the actual performance—but no further of Mr. Newsome. This studied attempt to dissimulate was impressive to Elissa; she had never seen Merry infatuated enough with any gentleman to even think of concealing her interest in him. It was to prove only a brief intermission in her enthusiasms on the subject, however.

Since Elissa could think of no way to prevent Merry from coming with her, she was determined to set off shortly after breakfast. She guessed that Mr. Charles Newsome might be a late sleeper, and the earlier her visit to the village, the more likely it was to miss any sally he might make from Rowantree.

The village was in the long valley below Aeons' End; the descent to it was easy, and Merry found plenty of breath to continue speaking; and on this walk, whether it was because she was not overheard, or because she could not help reverting to the subject, she spoke almost uninterruptedly of Charles Newsome. She rehearsed the previous day's meeting with him in detail, showing an unusual degree of perspicacity with respect to those traits of his character that his conversation had revealed. Inevitably she happened on the more practical topic of his means, or his lack of them; but that, too, was seen by her in a positive light.

"Do you not think it noble of him to tell us at once that he is not rich?" she said.

"I would not use the word 'noble,'" said Elissa. "But I would indeed say that it was candid and kind and proper of him not to misrepresent himself."

"How well can one live, do you think," said Merry, "on a settlement of five thousand pounds?" This was the amount the sisters understood they were each to have when they married. It was not inconsiderable, but—

"One may live well for about a decade, if one spends the principal," said Elissa, her tone making it clear that she dismissed that option. "Otherwise, I am afraid, one's life must be more limited. It will produce in interest only two hundred and fifty pounds per year—enough to keep a spinster well enough, but not enough to support a genteel family."

"But such an amount might considerably *assist* someone to support his wife and family, if he also has a profession."

"Indeed; though I must say, my dear, that I do not think Mr. Charles Newsome is such a man. Even he does not think he will make much of himself as an attorney."

"But he underestimates his powers," said Merry. "I feel that he is not sure enough of himself. He wants encouragement. He sounded quite lawyerly when he made his foray into the topic of fee tails, or whatever it was."

"And his little foray came to a quite sudden halt and retreat, as I recall," said Elissa.

Merry could not deny this.

They were silent for a moment or two, both thinking uneasily of this obstacle.

"His cousin may be able to give him something after all," said Merry then.

"We do not know his cousin and cannot well judge his intentions. Despite Mr. Newsome's handsome opinion of his cousin, it is as I said yesterday: people in Mr. Daniel Newsome's situation soon find that, much though they love their relations, they have enough expenses of their own with wife and family and an estate to keep up. Mr. Daniel Newsome may come to think Mr. Charles Newsome ought to provide for himself. And he will have the world's opinion with him in that respect, I do believe.—And while we are on this topic, dear, I hope you will not forget that Mr. Charles Newsome gave us this information about his inheritance in confidence. I do not believe the Rowcliffes have heard a word of it."

"Of course not," Merry said, "I shall be scrupulously silent on the matter, I assure you." Then her mind jumped back to the topic that most interested her. "But do not forget," she went on, "that when we marry, we shall have also have as much as a hundred pounds per year while Papa is alive."

"Yes, while Papa is alive. But when he has passed on, and Aeons' End has gone to Mr. Crustall, that annual hundred pounds will vanish."

This caused a slight diversion in the topic.

"I think," said Merry with a sudden increase in emotion, "that Mr. Newsome was right to put the matter to Father so directly. Papa ought to marry again. It would be the salvation of us all."

"Salvation is a strong word, dear. I hope that no matter what happens to us, we shall not lose our salvation."

Merry did not like to yield points constantly to her elder sister, and she now shifted the grounds of her argument. "But whether it is *our* salvation or not, it would be the defeat of Mr. Crustall," she said. "And given what we have heard of Mr. Crustall, that is a goal to be worked toward at any cost," she added. "So Papa truly *ought* to marry again."

"But Papa's objections to another marriage were quite well taken," said Elissa.

"But is it not silly that he objects to loving another wife so strongly? I think it is. He has not loved a woman since Mother died, and that was when I was born. It is high time for him to love again."

"Not everyone loves as readily as you, dear," said Elissa.

Merry laughed at this rebuke. "I suppose not," she allowed. "But he has been without a spouse fully as long as I have! And you must admit that twenty-two years is a decent interval of mourning for anyone."

"Yes, so it would seem. But I think that sometimes the death of a spouse changes one in such a way that there is no going back to what one was before. The power to love freely is broken in one, I believe. Of course, I am only guessing at things I know little of; but so it seems to have been in Papa's case."

"Broken! It is hard to imagine. If I were a widow, I should marry again as quickly as I decently could—and perhaps even quicker. Why, it is like old Mr. Philbrick and his dogs, you know; he has terrible luck with his dogs, but no sooner does one of them die of some horrible or mysterious disease or accident, than he goes out and finds another to love. It is almost as though he is not in love with any particular dog, but with the idea of dogs, and he cares not which particular dog he has to coddle and spoil, so long as he has one on which to lavish his love and attention."

"I know what you mean with respect to Mr. Philbrick; but affection for another human is, or ought to be, deeper than love for a dog; and so an injury to such an affection wounds us the more deeply."

Merry, as she often did when brought up short by what she called Elissa's scruples, held her tongue obligingly but rolled her eyes humorously at her sister's scrupulousness.

Then Elissa said, "Besides . . ." But she did not complete her thought.

"Besides what, dear?" asked Merry, instantly curious.

"Oh . . . nothing."

Merry would not be content with this, and pressed Elissa's arm tightly against her side (they were walking arm in arm) to show she would not.

"It is just . . ." began Elissa again, and again paused.

"You must tell me now; you know you must," said Merry.

Elissa smiled a little ruefully in acknowledgement that Merry would never leave her in peace if she did not complete her sentence, and said, "It is just that once I thought from something Papa said that he had loved someone else before Mother."

Merry was very surprised. "Indeed!" she exclaimed. "You have never mentioned this before, ever. How is it that you never mentioned this to me? What did he say?"

"I cannot remember, really; it was so long ago. You were too little for me to say anything to you at the time. And now I cannot tell you what his exact words were; they just left me with the feeling that it is not only Mother whom he mourns."

"Really!" said Merry excitedly. "How romantic! Do you not realize how romantic this is, Elissa? A lost love before Mother! I shall ask him about it directly we are come home again."

"No," said Elissa forcefully. "You must not do that, whatever you do. It would be too painful; you know it would. We must not stir up painful memories to satisfy our idle curiosity."

"Very well," said Merry. "But I shall from now on be alert to any references of this sort."

"You shall never hear any," said Elissa. "All I ever heard was a faint one, and that was, as I said, very long ago. It was so faint that I do not know if it was even real."

"Well," said Merry, "in any case, I shall forgive Papa the more readily if he has lost more than one love in this life.— 'The third time's lucky,' though. Has he never thought of that?"

"It is just a silly proverb, dear. 'Once bitten is twice shy' is just as much to the purpose."

"But he was not 'bitten' by Mother. He loved her."

"No, but he was bitten by losing her."

Merry could fence with her sister no longer. "Oh, I cannot understand it!" she protested.

"That is because you live in a continual present, dear," said Elissa in the gentle, elder-sister tone she often used with Merry. "To you, mourning someone you have lost would be living in the past." Though she did not mention their brother, it was during her own period of mourning for him that she had discovered her difference from her sister in this respect.

"Well, yes, it *would* be like living in the past," said Merry. "How could anyone think differently?"

"Because," said Elissa, "for some people the past and the present and the future are all one. I believe that is true for most people, though they do not realize it."

"How could the past and the present and the future be one? Elissa, that is nonsense."

"Not so much nonsense as you think. I believe that is the way things seem to God."

This enigmatic statement was very baffling to Merry; it silenced her for a moment.

"We are, after all," said Elissa in a thoughtful, distant tone, "not only what we do in this moment, but what we have done in the past; as well as what we hope to do in the future. Indeed, I believe that we are, more than anything else, what we hope to do in the future. And to lose someone we love is to lose the possibility of their presence with us in times to come. That is what makes the loss so difficult."

Merry still said nothing; but she looked at her older sister with a respect that verged on uncomprehending adoration.

"Losing the future," Elissa went on a little mournfully, "that is what slays us. It makes us give up on life. We can live without having what we once had, as long as we think we shall have something like it again, or something even better; and we can live in an absolutely wretched present, as long as we think it will someday end in happiness. It is the future that we absolutely must have. That is what makes people so afraid of death, you know: they cannot see a future in it! That is why the preachers speak so much of the life to come, to cheer us. And that is why the very old, who can no longer delude themselves that their life on earth will return to easiness, so often sink into mourning."

Merry shook her head. "My dear," she said, "you think about all these things, and I do not."

"I know," said Elissa, with a fond smile.

Merry smiled too. "Then I shall leave it to you to think all weighty and sad things for me. Will you do that?"

"It will be good for you to think a few of them yourself," said Elissa.

"I shall have all the good of them from hearing you say them, my love," said Merry.

Elissa shook her head in disagreement, but smiled at Merry's expression of fondness; and the sisters were content to walk arm in arm in silence for a time.

They soon descended the side of the valley and reached the river that ran through it—the river that had run through it since time out of mind and indeed had formed it, made it the deep clough, or cleft, that gave the village of Deepclough its name. The lane from Aeons' End intersected the road that followed the river not far from the point where its waters flowed over a steep and even an abrupt dam about ten feet in height. Here in seasons of flood the river broke with great vehemence on a jumble of jagged rocks that had been heaped there to shore up the base of the dam and prevent erosion and undercutting. Above this dam was a narrow impoundment, which was at least nominally a millpond, but in actuality was more of a long chute about thirty feet wide that penned in the water so that its excess could be drawn off by the fulling mill. It was here, as the sisters were walking beside the mill pond, that Merry's pursuit of Charles Newsome had an outcome satisfactory to her, if not to Elissa: for now they saw him approaching them on foot from the opposite direction.

His entire demeanor and posture when he realized who was advancing to meet him revealed even better than words that he had set out deliberately to visit them, walking rather than riding perhaps in order to disguise to some extent the purposefulness of his journey. His pleasure at the sight of them fairly glowed from him, and his stride gained a certain bounce. His gait in fact reminded Elissa of the distinctive, floating, prancing, lightfooted trot of a fox, though a less foxlike human could scarcely be imagined: his delight was almost painfully patent and ingenuous.

He had eyes only for Merry as the two parties drew close together, though when they actually met he recollected his manners enough to bow to Elissa and murmur, "Good morning, Miss Wyatt!" before turning again to Merry and saying, in a louder and obviously more interested tone, and with a lower bow, "Good morning, Miss Merry!"

"How pleasant to meet you, sir!" said Merry.

"I was . . . just strolling about," said Charles, uttering a fib the more forgivable for being so transparent.

"And we were on our way into the village for some little errands of my sister's," said Merry. She blushed a little as she said this—Elissa could not remember having seen her blush for many years—and Charles seemed not the least deceived by this answering fib, as his cheeks seem to redden a little too.

What a pair of original innocents! thought Elissa to herself. *Either they will have declared themselves by day's end or they will go on in a state of unthinking mutual hope for years!*

"May I walk back toward the village with you, then?" asked Charles.

"We would be most pleased if you would," Elissa put in quickly, in the hope of deterring Merry from disclosing her infatuation still more openly; but Charles hardly seemed to hear her or to think that consent was truly required; for without a further word he turned about to fall in with them as they continued walking.

"Your father is well today, I hope?" said Charles.

"Indeed, sir, quite well," said Merry. "He is in his garden, where he loves most to be, as you have seen.—And Mr. and Mrs. Rowcliffe?"

"In excellent health, I thank you," said Charles.

After this successful exchange of felicities, Merry and Charles looked at each other with such a transported expression that Elissa doubted they could have recalled the words they had just uttered.

"I believe you have never told us," said Merry, "exactly how long you expect to be among us in Gloucestershire." Elissa had asked this very question yesterday, but Merry must not have been satisfied by the indefinite nature of the answer they had received then.

"My plans," began Charles, and then he smiled in a kind of happy confusion. "My plans," he went on, "are not yet settled. But I see no reason to run away elsewhere at any time soon. Mr. and Mrs. Rowcliffe are happy to have me as a guest as long as I wish to stay; there is really better opportunity here to study, as I must, and there are far fewer distractions; and then there is the dirt and noise of London, which I am not the least sorry to do without."

"And might I hope the company is better here?" asked Merry.

Charles was very glad to affirm that it was so; in fact that it was very much better, excellently better, better than any place he had yet visited in his life. He probably would have gone on insisting upon this point for ten minutes, but Merry seized on the topic to elicit even more effusiveness from him.

"But do you not find country company dull, sir?" she asked.

Charles looked almost horrified. Elissa understood now, seeing his response in the light of some of his behavior the previous day, that he made the habitual mistake of taking ordinary conversational gambits much too seriously. "Not in the least!" he protested. "You forget, Miss Merry, I was raised in the country, I adore the country. When I went up to school I thought I should die for lack of the country; and in London I feel I am in constant danger, that I have not the wits to protect myself from sharpers."

"It was wise of you to come down to stay with the Rowcliffes, then," said Elissa.

"Very wise," echoed Merry.

"Indeed, I do believe it *was* wise," said Charles. "I have at last realized that in order to be safe, I must go either to them or to my dear cousin. But I believe he is at his wits' end for some way to take care of me, and I wish to do anything but become a burden to him."

They were now passing the little wood on the outskirts of the village and entering more upon the village proper. In the land on the left of the road the valley climbed steeply up to the wold, and the village houses were perched in occasional hollows or natural terraces in the flank of the ridge; on the other side of the road the land fell away equally steeply, with only an occasional house built into it, and that of the poorer kind, as the land there was prone to flood in storms. As the road wound into the village proper, however, the valley grew more wide; here was room for larger and better houses, as well as for a goodly church on ground that was level with the road on the side nearest the river. Out of the rectory associated with this church the village rector, Mr. Herbert, now happened to emerge, evidently with the purpose of exchanging greetings with the Wyatts.

Mr. Herbert was a gentleman of about fifty-five years of age. But that statistic tells so little, for the fifties are an age in which one may be in the prime of life or already declining. In Mr. Herbert's case, age had not assisted him in maintaining his looks: his fair hair, once full and golden, was now a very pale blond and rather thin; his skin, particularly on his high brow, had acquired a certain craquelure consisting of parallel lines; and his waistcoats had had to be let out and finally replaced as the beef and port wine had insisted on exacting their charges from him. He had, or so he liked to say, been quite the athlete at Oxford in his days there, with the oar and the bat; but what had been muscle on his chest and back was decidedly slacker these days, and might be doubted to be true thews at all. His eyes, as well, had grown dim over his books, and both white and lid were red, and the orbs were a little sunken, and he squinted when he removed his spectacles, which (people noticed) he was apt to do when approaching the company of Miss Wyatt. His shoulders were rounded, and his head hung forward, and he was in danger of developing prematurely that hump at the back of the neck so common among the elderly. ¶ Merry had once remarked that his looks were not entirely repulsive; and Elissa had replied a little archly that her sister must mean that Mr. Herbert was just a human being like others, possessing an ordinary appearance, and having nothing remarkable about him superficially to make him particularly noticed or remarked upon; to which interpretation Merry, after a moment of reflection, had agreed, without realizing how much her agreement had amused Elissa. "In other words," Elissa had added, to make the point, "unless God has blessed a person with particular beauty, in your estimation he or she is to be classed as 'not entirely repulsive.'" But Merry saw nothing reprehensible in this, and agreed further, and missed the lesson. But still Elissa, more generous than her sister in this and indeed in most respects, would have said that Mr. Herbert was a man whom his wife might well have thought adequately handsome, ordinary though he might be to others.

Wife he had none at this time, his spouse having perished about five years ago; and he was also childless. The village thought that he, like Mr. Wyatt, ought to marry again; but then again, villages always think along these lines, pairing off the unmarried in theory, as a housemaid instinctively pairs off china figurines while dusting a mantelpiece. This particular pairing, however, did not arise simply from the fact that Elissa and Mr. Herbert happened to be marriageable and resident within two miles of one another on that narrow ridge that formed half the valley of Deepclough; rather, they shared a certain characteristic, or seemed to do so. In the eyes of the villagers, Mr. Herbert's primary quality was extreme seriousness, perhaps even humorlessness; and Miss Wyatt had always been renowned among them as a serious girl, and then young woman, though she was in no way without good humor or a good sense of humor (for these two are as different possessions as are long-suffering and bravery). In the uncritical estimate of those who knew Mr. Herbert and Miss Wyatt only as figures striding about on the far-off stage—or the mantelpiece, if you will—of a higher social level, as actors rarely heard and even more rarely understood, this appearance was similarity enough. But those who knew them better thought that no two people could ever have existed who were more unlike. It seemed to them that Mr. Herbert was seriousness in its superficial and, it must be said, unpleasant incarnation. He seemed the very type of a "studying rector," more interested in thumbing antique tomes with fingerless gloves than in dirtying his digits tending his flock. He had a book underway, which he even alluded to from the pulpit upon occasion, and which he expected would set the theological world by its ears from the conventicles of the British nonconformists to the halls of Halle. None of his parishioners but Elissa knew what the exact subject was, but they did have a fear and awe of Mr. Herbert's erudition, and they had always believed his knowledge of church history, the creeds, the Bible, theology, and all related matters to be an inexhaustible ocean, though they themselves never sampled it at a rate greater than a spoonful at a time, on Sundays, and much as one takes cod liver oil.

The great error into which an observer ought not to fall, however, was to think of Mr. Herbert as a mere caricature, because he was all too real a figure to all in the valley to deserve that characterization. For there he was, in his house at Deepclough; and anyone who has ever lived in a small village knows how inescapable the presence of any of its residents is. He was an authority to be reckoned with: for the poor, in the dispensation of whose succor he had great say; for the girl who got pregnant by mistake, on impulse, of a summer evening, as well as for the farmhand who so mistook her, and could be brought to the rector in manacles to marry her; for the villagers who loved church only for the choir, over whose hymnody he had final say; and for the better sort, who felt compelled to include him in their society as one of their own, though they also felt him to be an eternal outsider. Elissa's neighbors at Rowantree, Mr. and Mrs. Rowcliffe, quite idolized Mr. Herbert as a being above them. If he was dry and unintelligible in his sermons and conversation, why, it must be their own fault; and in fact they would have respected him far less if they had actually understood him. Even John Wyatt had a kind of quiet admiration for the rector, born ungrudgingly of John's generosity toward all humankind, but based in his recognition that the rector simply knew a great deal more than he himself on bookish topics. To Merry, Mr. Herbert was a subject for her cheerful version of sarcasm. In fact, like the folk of the village, she was a little afraid of him. He was so dour! And inscrutable. And she listened too much to the wife of Mr. Jens, the Wyatts' own butler, who was housekeeper and cook to Mr. Herbert; and so Merry was forever hearing through that lady of various acts of oppression the rector had committed against her—sending back a dish, for example, to be cooked more, or remade entirely; or faulting her for attempting to clean the mounting mess of his study, with its heaps of books and papers, its spilled ink and rusty pen knives and dead candle stubs and moldy quills; or calling for more coal just as she was about to go away home; and so forth.

As for Elissa, there were various things that saved Mr. Herbert from becoming a living caricature. She had known him most of her life, and he could not be anything but a distinct and particular human being to her. He emitted Latin and English tags that every British schoolboy knew, but very few British girls had the privilege of hearing; and these she pursued as best she could in the sources she had. Words he spoke on the occasions when she saw him, whether at church or in society, entered into her mental life, either because their polysyllables were novel to her, or because they offered (inadvertently on Mr. Herbert's part) some insight into higher intellectual and spiritual realms—into things that other human beings had thought about God and the universe and humankind. He flung her scraps of literature as the morsels rejected at the high table are thrown to the dogs; and often she felt, on deep study of what he gave her to read, that he himself must not have fully understood what he recommended to her. They were not just intellectual and religious—Watts's *Logic*, those old stalwarts *The Whole Duty of Man* and *The Ladies' Calling*, for example. No; it was from Mr. Herbert that she first heard of Pope's *Essay on Man*; which led her to read and to memorize those lines of almost Shakespearean power:

> Know then thyself, presume not God to scan:
> The proper study of mankind is man.
> Plac'd on this isthmus of a middle state,
> A being darkly wise, and rudely great:
> With too much knowledge for the sceptic side,
> With too much weakness for the Stoic's pride,
> He hangs between; in doubt to act, or rest;
> In doubt to deem himself a god or beast;
> In doubt his mind or body to prefer;
> Born but to die, and reas'ning but to err;
> Alike in ignorance, his reason such,
> Whether he thinks too little, or too much:
> Chaos of thought and passion, all confus'd;
> Still by himself abus'd, or disabus'd;
> Created half to rise, and half to fall;
> Great lord of all things, yet a prey to all;
> Sole judge of truth, in endless error hurl'd:
> The glory, jest, and riddle of the world!

And for her these verses became (until circumstances arose, yet to be told, in which she discovered their most mordant application to herself) a sketch of Mr. Herbert. He *was* "a being darkly wise," for he knew much of value, but could not apply it to himself or his life; he was, in this little hamlet, "rudely great"; his reasoning often ran aground on petty prejudice; often he overthought crucial matters, and at other times failed to think of them at all; in the midst of a most reasonable discourse, empty passion would intrude and spoil his argument; he was the lord of souls in Deepclough, and yet an endless prey to ridicule and disdain, secret and otherwise, from no few of his own parishioners. He was, indeed, the glory, jest, and riddle of the valley.

Still, Mr. Herbert occupied Elissa's thoughts more than he could have known. How could he not, given the narrowness of their lives there? He had always treated her with a striking reverence—but no, not reverence, rather a favoritism bordering on what that age called *particularity.* He had often spoken to Mr. Wyatt in a congratulatory and possibly even self-congratulatory manner about her excellent mind and morals; in particular, he had once told her father that she was "seriousness *in eminentia,*" that is, in its highest, transcendent form. This had pleased Elissa more than any compliment on her looks could ever have done; for to her, seriousness was not a height from which to look down at the people of the valley; it was not a dry, dull stare that proclaimed one's intellectual superiority, but a loving and embracing and understanding gaze signifying that the person whom she viewed had her full spiritual attention. This quality in her had perhaps impressed Mr. Herbert so much because it was something of which he felt himself incapable. Perhaps he so frequently sought her out, even at stray moments and wayside meetings like that which was to take place on this very day before the rectory, because he felt she could supply a sympathy with his neighbors that he knew he ought to have and that he knew he lacked.

When he spoke to her, especially when they chanced to meet alone together on their different walks about the village, he spoke almost as an equal. An example of this has already been mentioned: he had trusted her, and her alone, with the secret of the subject of his great dissertation. It was to be a definitive denunciation of the regulative principle of worship. He had defined this principle for her as an insistence that church worship must be founded on the directives in Scripture—as one old confession put it, "so that God may not be worshiped according to the imagination and devices of men, nor the suggestions of Satan." In other words, this principle could be used to declare that such ornaments of the divine service as musical instruments and hymns were to be forbidden. Fortunately, Mr. Herbert was, as Elissa thought, on the right side of this question, and quite forthright in his condemnation of the principle. ¶ He often discoursed to her of his thesis, and described his progress, and she did her best to enter into his interest; and perhaps in doing so she made the common error of conveying more warmth of intellectual sympathy than she actually felt, if only because she regretted her intellectual failure in this respect. She need not have; she was no trained theologian. Her world and her times had not allowed her to partake in any rigorous education; and though she had done her best to make up for that lack of opportunity by determined reading, still that reading had left her quite inadequate to fully comprehend the niceties of the debate over such matters as whether or not one ought to sing something other than a psalm in church. She loved hymns, and felt one ought to be able to sing them in church, and it horrified her that anyone might be restricted from this wholesome practice, and she was vaguely pleased, in principle, that Mr. Herbert was readying a blow for this right. But at the same time she was not the least foolish, and she could see through the rector's delusions of importance all too readily. The world would wag on—would sing its hymns—with or without his treatise; she had no doubt of that.

Add to these proofs and effects of Mr. Herbert's powerful presence in Elissa's life this one more: that the thought had often crept through her mind (egged on by Merry's jokes on the subject) that Mr. Herbert would willingly have had her to wife. This is a potentiality that must, once it has intruded there, inevitably cling to the mind of a woman of twenty-seven who has never had a sweetheart, or even a flirtation, let alone an active suitor. The idea was thoroughly moot, true; he was so unlike anyone Elissa had ever pictured as her spouse that her imagination balked at the notion with a sort of metaphysical perplexity. It was like trying to imagine division by null or a square circle or *being that transcends being* or any of those other logical impossibilities with which philosophers tease themselves to the point of madness and beyond.

In addition to the metaphysical oxymoron posed by this possibility, there was the very physical impossibility of the thing. And this, strange to say—for Pope forgot to mention this particular quirk of our kind, which we share with the animals—this physical revulsion was far more deadly a blow to any hopes of her that Mr. Herbert might have had than any philosophical consideration. It rested, simply put, on the *smell* of the man. Yes, his odor put him out of all consideration as a husband. And that odor was all too often in her nostrils as it was, that murky stink compounded of the roast that had cooked in his kitchen, of the wine that had spattered his collar on its way to his mouth, of the port that had reached said port unspilt, of tea oily with clotted milk, of the cloyingly sweet hecatomb and holocaust of Latakia offered in his postprandial pipe, of his black wool suit, of the lingering staleness of the rectory privy, of mildewy books, of lamp soot and candle smoke and coal dust and beechen charcoal, and especially, oh especially, of his body (for people did not bathe so very much in those days). And it is not *appearance* that most often deters younger women from allying themselves with older men—not the wrinkles of those men, their clawlike and arthritic hands, their potbellies or their baldness—but the smell of age upon their bodies and their breath, which rises like a miasma when their clothes open for a moment at neck or waist. That smell is like a whiff of

approaching death, when the body becomes the mere excre-
ment of the soul. How could youth, with its own fragrance
of ripe juice and fertility, endure *that?*

He had once discoursed to her of a Scholastic axiom:
*Quantum distat potentia ab actu, tantum potentior debet esse
agens.* Which was to say, *The further a potency is from act, the
more powerful an agent must be to actuate it.* He was as fond of
these logical and metaphysical taglines as the most recondite
and convinced Jesuit, and he often drew them out of the
folio of his brain and spattered them on her like scholar's
dust. And in this case, as was often so, his erudition blew up
upon him. For to her, the potency of any marriage with Mr.
Herbert was far, far from becoming act—so far that she was
quite certain he had not the power to achieve it.

To this point in time, Mr. Herbert had said nothing to
Elissa on the subject of marriage—fortunately for the continued ease of their encounters at church, and in the village,
and in company. Instead he had confined himself to long,
speculative, visual inspections of her face and person, all
carefully contrived so as not to be noticed by her or to offend
her; but which of course were quite obvious to her, and
which were, after all, not so very offensive because they were
simply a fact of her life, being like those she had for many
years now received from other men. All she really could
think was that if the gentleman intended to propose marriage, he seemed to be endlessly postponing his declaration.

The rector was thus real to all the valley, to each in a different way, to all in the little village to which he supposedly
provided spiritual guidance. What he really provided was
something quite different, for he was really no more spiritual
than the least of them; what he provided was a presence with
which they must learn to live—and, if the Master whom
Mr. Herbert nominally espoused was to be believed—a
presence that they must somehow learn to love.

On this occasion, he made directly for Elissa, doffing his
hat and bowing, surveying her very keenly, and taking little

if any visual notice of Merry and Charles. After mutual greetings between the rector and the sisters, it became clear that Mr. Herbert did not yet know Charles, so he was introduced; and once this ceremony was complete, Charles received more, if constrained, attention from the rector as the grandson of the Rowcliffes.

Mr. Herbert began, as he often did in meeting new acquaintances, by divulging everything he knew about Charles: "If you are Mr. and Mrs. Rowcliffe's grandson, sir, that would make you the son of their daughter, Mrs. Agnes Newsome, of Landseye, in Oxfordshire, and thus the son of Mr. James Newsome."

"Do you know my father, sir?" said Charles in surprise.

"No, but I know my own parishioners, Mr. Newsome. Your grandparents have spoken well of you, in a manner surpassing mere progenitorial pride.—You are reading law at Lincoln's Inn, I believe?"

Charles looked embarrassed. "I hope to read a little while visiting my grandparents," he said. This lame little tale was doubly pathetic to Elissa on a second hearing.

"Well, sir," said Mr. Herbert, "*reading* of anything can take place anywhere; but *reading the law* is a somewhat more serious procedure, and often requires *listening* as well as *attending;* and they will not like you much at Lincoln's Inn if you do not put in an appearance there. But you could do much useful *learning* of the law here, I allow that, if you discipline yourself properly."

There was then an awkward pause while Mr. Herbert regarded Charles speculatively, seeming not to think the man's open and honest face promised well for that profession. "I thought of the law myself once," he said then. "But I find the church much more congenial to my tastes. It possesses ampler room to undertake a greatness that will have a truly worldwide effect, an effect to aeviternity."

"As rector of a village church?" asked Charles quite innocently, doubting he had heard Mr. Herbert rightly.

"As an *author*," Mr. Herbert said in correction.

"Ah, splendid!" said Charles. "I never got on much in writing, myself. I am remarkably slow at it."

"The law does often require a great deal of writing," Mr. Herbert pointed out drily. He was beginning to get Charles's measure, or at least so he thought; for the good qualities of people like Charles were invisible to him.

"That is the great perplexity of the law, I find—the writing," said Charles. "After the reading, of course; for I had far rather be doing almost anything other than reading." Then, seeing Mr. Herbert's stare, he added, as if in explanation: "I am not much of a reader."

"Neither a writer nor a reader," said Mr. Herbert. "Well, are you an orator, sir? Are you inspired before audiences? For if you can neither write nor read with ease, I hope you can at least talk."

"I *am* a tolerable talker," admitted Charles, obviously glad to have at least one good report of himself.

"But on technical subjects?"

"What sort, sir?"

"Legal subjects, sir—subjects having to do with the *techne* of your profession. Can you speak on them? For forensic oratory is not small talk."

"Well, perhaps I *am* better at small talk," allowed Charles, with another smile. It was a smile that would have disarmed any critic but Mr. Herbert, and Elissa was all the more won over by it. Self-doubt and humility made Charles regal in the company of self-assurance.

"I say, sir," said Mr. Herbert, "if you are at Lincoln's Inn, perhaps you know my friend, Mr. Robert Standish. He is an attorney in the City. I do not mean just an ordinary attorney—he comes of the best sort of family, you may be sure, if he forms part of my circle."

"I am afraid I have very little acquaintance there as yet," said Charles.

"And you are like to continue to have none, if you do not frequent the place," observed Mr. Herbert. "But who could endure the City out of season, eh? Still, you ought to cultivate acquaintance. It will advance you more than all the reading in the world—that is the way the law works, and perhaps I should say, the way the world works: knowing the right people.—I suppose that as yet you have no family to support?"

"None, sir."

"That is just as well! A man must be well settled for that."

Here Elissa had an inkling that Charles was receiving this odd dressing-down because she herself was present. She cast about mentally for a way to put a stop to it, but the conversation continued, Charles exposing his own gentle and pleasant nature, and Mr. Herbert dismissing and doubting and mocking it, quite undetected by Charles. Elissa did not like it at all; she had seldom seen Mr. Herbert in this particular sort of a disagreeable light.

It happened that while they were standing thus in the road, the mail coach to Gloucester came along from the east. Its approach forced Elissa and her companions to leave the metalled way and step onto the rough bit of lawn between the road and the rectory fence; and with the curiosity that country folk often feel toward strangers traveling through their land, both Elissa and Merry looked up at the coach with interest and scrutinized its passengers.

The coaches of the Royal Mail carried four paying customers inside, and three on the outside—one on the box (the seat on which the coach driver sat) and two behind him, all well segregated from the guard at the rear with his red coat and his blunderbuss. In those days the coach was an institution, and the location of the village of Deepclough on the mail route between London and Gloucester was its cultural salvation. Without the passage of the mails, it would have been a backwater indeed. The village did not, however, rank as a place in which the horses were changed; instead the mails were often virtually thrown into the arms of the innkeeper, who was alike the postmaster of the place, while the coach rumbled on, clinging to its iron schedule.

And iron it was: one old writer tells the tale of the regular meeting of two mail coaches, one northbound and the other southbound, at the same bridge in the middle of their six-hundred-mile journeys. And rumble the passing coach did; though kept always in perfect condition, it was a great, noisy machine, drawn by four horses, which added the thunder of their hooves to the creak of harness, the banging of the harness pole, the rattle of metal fittings, the grinding of the great wheels of iron-shod oak in the ruts of the road, and the overall groaning of the joinery of the thing as it bounced and lurched and swayed through pools of mud and over hillocks of dust. An added noise on this day was a shouted conversation between the driver and the passenger beside him, which became audible as the machine drew alongside the little group at the side of the road, though no individual word was intelligible; and the passenger called out as he noticed the pretty women there, directing towards Elissa and Merry the attention of the other men on the outside.

Of the two sitting behind the driver, one was much younger and better dressed than the other. He was about Elissa's age; and it seemed likely that he had resorted to one of the cheap seats on the top of the coach only when he found the better seats within were taken; that is, he looked very much a gentleman, and well-to-do. She had no more than a glimpse of him, but he caught her attention immediately, because of the way his own attention was arrested by the sight of the group by the road. She at first guessed, in that instantaneous egocentric response that is naturally human, that his gaze was attracted to her; but as he turned about suddenly on the bench (he was sitting at the near end of it) and stared down at them, and back at them as the coach rolled on, she realized that it was not her or Merry or

Mr. Herbert that held his attention, but Charles. Surprise registered at once on his face, but this emotion was at once succeeded by pleasure and by another feeling she could understand only as considerable affection. Clearly he had recognized Charles, and Charles was someone he greatly liked.

The coach proceeded; and though she would have followed it with her eyes, she was too polite to neglect the conversation by doing so. She thought she would wait until she and Merry and Charles had walked on before she mentioned what she had observed. However, this day was one of those rare occasions when the coach must actually stop for a few seconds to discharge passengers at the inn. The groan of its brake was distinctive, but if that had not been noticeable, the mere cessation of the noise of its passage would have been striking enough to call the attention of the little group by the roadway from a hundred yards' distance; and even Merry, who had resumed listening to the conversation between Charles and Mr. Herbert, looked for a moment at the coach, before forgetting it again and focusing on Charles. Elissa, however, continued to watch it; and the position in which she happened to be standing allowed her to do so without the others noticing that her attention was elsewhere.

Two men descended from the top of the coach—the gentleman who had recognized Charles, and another who seemed, since he took charge of some luggage from the coach, to be the first man's servant. The master threw a coin each to driver and guard, and the coach stirred into motion again, gradually, like a great beast stiff in the joints, resuming its passage, with all the accompanying groan and rattle and thunder, which grew into an indistinguishable tumult and at length faded away.

Meanwhile the gentleman, leaving his servant behind with the baggage, walked back towards the group by the rectory. For a moment Elissa considered interrupting the

conversation and pointing out the newcomer to Charles—
for she now had no doubt that the man was a friend of his,
and it is, after all, gratifying to one's self-importance to
deliver information of this kind. But then she decided that
she would simply wait and watch the encounter develop
without giving any warning of it.

She thus had an opportunity to study the stranger, if
somewhat surreptitiously. But he would not have noticed her
interest in him even if she had not tried to conceal it, for he
was not looking at anyone but Charles. His appearance was
not displeasing, but not specifically pleasing either: he was
in some respects striking to look upon, being somewhat tall
and well but not stoutly built. His face was made distinctive
by the shape of his cheekbones and his high, smooth brow;
his hair, though covered by the inevitable hat and showing
some dust from his journey, was dark and thick and perhaps
a little unruly—it was hard to say what it would look like
when it had the advantage of being freshly groomed. These
were all good or at least interesting qualities in his appearance, but—as in the case of Mr. Herbert—she would not
have said he looked handsome. And yet if she compared him
with the rector, she found there was a profound difference
between them.

Mr. Herbert was . . . *ordinary,* and somehow this stranger
was not. What *was* it about him? She could not isolate and
identify the feature of his appearance that made him so
striking.

Now he had come up to them. Charles was speaking,
having finally asserted the natural advantage in oral activity
that he had described to Mr. Herbert previously; and the
newcomer laid his hand gently on Charles's shoulder.

"Charles," said the man softly.

Charles ceased speaking and turned about in surprise.

"Daniel!" he cried. His voice resonated with the same
pleasure and affection with which he had been addressed.

Both men laughed; then they seized each other in an
embrace—an impetuous, boyish, bear-hug of a grip, as

if they were instantly struggling each to knock the other down; and then they each pushed the other away, and Charles struck this Daniel on the chest with a strength that would have knocked Elissa flat on her back, but which its object seemed not even to register; he only laughed.

"Found you," he said.

"So you did!" exclaimed Charles. "And however did you?"

"By means no more mysterious than these: I was looking for you, and I thought you might have come to Rowantree."

"But I was not hiding from you."

"You might as well have been."

"You were in the mail coach?"

"On the outside seats, yes."

"No wonder you look so dirty! I have never seen you look so disreputable!" Charles looked the newcomer up and down with the happiness of one who has latched on to a good reason to tease a favorite friend.

His friend only grinned, as if pleased to appear out of character.

Mr. Herbert then said, "If you will excuse me, gentlemen and ladies—I must return to my studies." Elissa suspected that the rector, for all the pleasure he had apparently taken in skewering Charles, had been looking for an excuse to escape once Charles began to out-talk him.

"Of course," said Charles. "So good to speak with you, Mr. Herbert—we shall see you again."

"I hope so, sir," said Mr. Herbert, with an excellent pretense of affability. He bowed to them all, murmuring Elissa and Merry's names, and made a quick retreat before he could be drawn into the additional complication of meeting the newcomer. And he smiled as he went, as if congratulating himself for having shown up Mr. Charles Newsome for what he was; but in point of fact, his departure was to prove only one more mistake in a badly mismanaged campaign. But that was to come to light only later.

When Mr. Herbert had left them, Charles seemed to realize that he had missed the opportunity of introducing this stranger to the rector; but he immediately made sure he did not commit the same error with his female companions.

"Daniel," he said, "I must introduce you to these new and excellent friends I have made but yesterday.—Miss Wyatt, Miss Merry, do allow me to present my cousin, Mr. Daniel Newsome, who has hunted me down in my hiding place.— Daniel, please: This is Miss Elissa Wyatt, the daughter of Mr. John Wyatt of Aeons' End, and her sister, Miss Merry Wyatt."

Now Mr. Daniel Newsome looked at Elissa, and at Merry in her turn; he bowed to them, smiling, and they curtsied, both of them pleased with him.

"Of course I know of Mr. Wyatt," he told the young women. "I have heard his name mentioned by my aunt, Mrs. James Newsome, on several occasions over the years; but I have never had the opportunity to meet him." Elissa was here struck by the fact that Mr. Daniel Newsome recalled hearing of her family, though Charles had not.

But Charles made up for any previous neglect with present enthusiasm. "We have been missing a fine acquaintance, Daniel," he said. "I cannot tell you how much I like Mr. John Wyatt. We took to one another at once, despite the difference in our ages. You will like him greatly—we must see to it that you two are introduced as soon as may be. But you will first see the quality of the man reflected in his daughters."

Although Mr. Daniel Newsome had taken appropriate notice of Merry, he did not look at her more than that; like Mr. Herbert before him, his eyes, and indeed his face and his entire frame, turned back toward Elissa. He smiled at her, in a polite and friendly manner, not offensively; but then his brow seemed to contract somewhat; he seemed to be studying her, as if he had discerned some quality in her that required confirmation.

And by this attention Elissa felt inordinately pleased. She could not have explained the feeling to herself; she did not even attempt to do so; but she felt secretly thrilled that such a patently superior man was interested in her and seemed to approve of her. She certainly did not require his approval, or that of anyone outside her family and friends; and yet guessing that she had it was still a very pleasing matter.

"Will you walk up to Rowantree with us, Cousin?" asked Charles.

"Of course," said Mr. Daniel Newsome. "And with pleasure. I shall stay with you there till tomorrow, if you think your uncle and aunt will not mind."

"Oh, never! They will be delighted to see you."

"The Rowcliffes adore company," Merry told Mr. Daniel Newsome. "And it seems your cousin must have you stay, Mr. Newsome—so you must."

"And my grandparents have complained they do not see enough of you," added Charles.

"But we have met often enough at Landseye over the years," said Mr. Daniel Newsome.

"Well, they will be in raptures now. They have great plans for you, you know. Why, they told me last night that you ought to be Prime Minister!"

"They have great plans for everyone, as I recall," said Mr. Daniel Newsome in an even tone. To Elissa it seemed that he spoke in the manner of one firmly shutting a conversational door that might lead toward criticism of family members. Charles seemed to take the hint, since he changed the subject.

"And Blaickie?" he asked. "You have not left him behind—dear old efficient Blaickie?"

"He is up ahead with the baggage, at what I take to be the inn."

"Oh, it *is* the inn, Daniel, and the oddest little place you have ever set foot in."

"Do tell us what is odd about it, sir," said Elissa, "since we have long regarded it as the paradigm for all inns everywhere." She spoke in a droll and somewhat teasing tone.

"I do not believe we have ever set foot in it, have we?" added Merry, for the first time in her life unwilling to let new acquaintances receive a false impression.

"I should hope not!" said Charles humorously. "It is but three rude tables in a room barely big enough for them—a lady could not find a seat there, I assure you. There is sand on the floor—river sand, I take it—to lap up the spills, of which I believe there must be many, in all the jostle of the place when the farm labor comes down off the hills. But what a wonderful place! Perfect of its kind! It makes me wish I could dress as one of those laborers myself, and sit there on a Friday night unrecognized!"

"*That* could never happen," said Mr. Daniel Newsome, and Elissa found herself smiling rather broadly at his tone. It was both matter-of-fact and humorous; it was the same sort of tone she often used with Merry, when she was saying something loving and teasing that she knew Merry could not quite understand or appreciate. Mr. Newsome noted her smile with a little surprise; he must have realized she knew exactly what he had intended by his remark. But he could not help teasing his cousin a little more: "Imagine *you* sitting in silence for five minutes!" he said to him.

Charles laughed happily. "Oh, yes, that is impossible, is it not?" he said.

"And if once you opened your mouth, it would all be over," said Mr. Daniel Newsome.

"Yes, do you know, the local accent is quite thick—quite pleasant, but quite thick; I find I can hardly understand the local folk."

This topic enlarged naturally into a description of all the singularities of Deepclough Valley, for which Charles expressed his usual enthusiasm. He continued, it seemed, to love every thing and every one, or to think he did; and they listened to his flowing and glowing praise of the place while they walked on. They did not need to pause at the inn; it appeared that Mr. Daniel Newsome's servant, the aforesaid

Mr. Blaickie, was an enterprising individual—he had hired one of the multitudinous local boys to push a wheelbarrow with the gentleman's luggage, which, though modest in quantity by contemporary standards, was heaped in it almost higher than the boy himself; and the two of them, servant and boy, were already well ahead on the road. And so instead of coming to a natural halt, Elissa and Merry and their new gentlemen friends walked on.

Elissa did, however, have a moment of uncertainty. The sisters had not been planning to walk as far as Rowantree. It did not seem quite proper to Elissa that they should do so now, though they had walked there without a second thought on many a day in their lives when they were not in the company of eligible men. But somehow she could not quite bring herself to call a halt, when she saw how happy Merry was; and the day had acquired a certain momentum that outweighed and overbore the faint misgivings of her discretion. And there was something about Charles Newsome's cousin that intrigued her; perhaps it was her curiosity on that point that overcame her faint scruples.

In any case, on they went.

After they had passed the inn, a gig came rapidly toward the group of four, and they were compelled to move to the side of the road. As it happened, they divided into two pairs, one pair going to one side and the other to the other. In those days people of their class instinctively did such things by order of precedence; and though the ladies should have gone first and the gentlemen last, somehow after the gig had passed, Elissa and Mr. Daniel Newsome wound up walking ahead of Merry and Charles. Elissa was not exactly pleased that it had come about so, as it revealed the increasing predilection the younger pair had for one another's company. She tried to engineer a return to their four-abreast configuration, but Merry and Charles, carrying on their laughing conversation about the peculiarities of the village, seemed to lose all awareness of the presence of their respective elder sister and cousin, and dropped back even farther. Her attempt was thus thwarted, and rather than draw even more attention to Merry and Charles by forcing them to regroup, she desisted; and so she and Mr. Daniel Newsome preceded Merry and Charles down the road. This struck her as improperly intimate. What was worse, Merry and Charles were so engrossed in one another that they continued to dawdle on their way, opening the gap between the two couples minute by minute. And what was still worse, none of this—Elissa's attempt to rejoin the two couples, Merry and Charles's obliviousness to her purposes, and their intensifying preoccupation with one another—eluded Mr. Daniel Newsome's notice.

Elissa was not exactly sure how she knew this. Perhaps it was that Mr. Daniel Newsome seemed too studiously neutral. She would have thought that he must be surprised that his cousin's warm welcome could so quickly vaporize into inattentiveness toward him, but if so, he gave no sign of it—aside from giving no sign of it. Or perhaps he was not surprised; perhaps he knew his cousin's distractibility very well by now.

The silence between Mr. Daniel Newsome and herself had now extended too long; it was becoming embarrassing in itself. Mr. Newsome seemed to think so too; he turned to Elissa rather suddenly and said, "How strange it is for me to see this place at last! I have heard of it so often from my aunt over the years—she has described the valley, the river, and of course her own home, and mentioned your family and other neighbors in the society here. I feel as if I am walking in a dream in which I remember another dream much like the one I am in, but not exactly so." Then he seemed to think he might be speaking in terms too odd for a new acquaintance. "Do you know what I mean?" he asked.

She was glad to be able to say reassuringly, "I have had such dreams, yes." Then she went on: "Do you know Mr. and Mrs. Rowcliffe well?"

"I do not know if 'well' is the word, but my family always joined Charles's family at Landseye for the holidays, and occasionally the Rowcliffes came too. Thus I am acquainted with them, though we are not directly related. That is, my Aunt Agnes—my father's brother's wife—is their daughter."

"Still, how is it that you never came here? Your cousin has told us that you are often in Bath. Do you not go home from there this way?"

"Never on this specific route, no," said Mr. Daniel Newsome.

"But do you like what you see, now that you have come to this little land of dreams at last?"

He smiled at her. No other answer was really necessary.

How very, very pleasant his smile is! she thought then. *So warm, so friendly, and yet so sweetly* . . . serious *as well.*

About halfway through the village, the road forked; on their left, through some unmarked pillars roughly built of stone blocks, a lane led up the side of the valley to Rowantree. They now reached this turning, and it was with a little embarrassment that Elissa found that she was the one who must indicate to Mr. Daniel Newsome that their path veered from the main road—the servant and the boy were already out of sight ahead of them, and Charles was too preoccupied to so much as call ahead to his cousin to give him directions.

This hint she gave Mr. Daniel Newsome with a little inclination of her head, to which he responded with a slight bow and the words, "This is the way up to Rowantree, then?"

"It is, sir."

"The lane is wonderfully unostentatious," he said with another smile.

"Indeed, you would not guess what a fine house stands ahead of you, judging from the humble beginnings of this avenue."

"But I did not mean to suggest that I thought the Rowcliffes to be presuming people," said Daniel.

"Absolutely not," she agreed; though her emphasis was addressed more to the fact that he would not have presumed to suggest such a thing rather than to the fact that any such suggestion would have been incorrect.

He seemed to perceive this distinction; for he felt it necessary to say, "I must confess I like them. They have somewhat odd manners, I am not afraid to say; and yet one loves them all the same."

"One does," agreed Elissa. Then, in a moment she added: "Is it not strange, how you and I, though strangers to one another, have both long known and mutually loved the same two people?"

He smiled, and that was all the response she required.

They walked on. The road, angled as it was across the side of the valley, was not steep, but after a few hundred yards they had ascended higher than the roofs of the village; and as there were sheep pastures on either side here, they had a clear view of the little vale where the village lay.

"How pretty it is," said Daniel. "These houses—the stone walls—all the green pastureland—and your little river, soaked in sunlight where it appears through the trees. And so quiet! How free of harm and, from this distance, how free of pain it seems."

"Ah, I wish it were that last," said Elissa. "But I will agree with you about the rest. It is all very pretty—to my eye, beautiful to the highest degree."

"Yes, I am sure there is pain enough. Wherever humanity is, there is pain; though it is a relative suffering, either great or small, depending on the people and the place. Still, I would guess that the suffering here is less, on a relative scale."

"Perhaps it is," she agreed. "Much less than what I read about as the lot of those in the great cities of the world. But you must know that even the best workers here, in the valley and on the wolds, live a very hard and difficult life."

"Yes," said Daniel. "And it is the duty of people more privileged, such as we are, to make that life less difficult."

"A very laudable sentiment, sir."

She paused, uncertain as to whether she ought to ask a further question; and after considering it, decided to do so.

"Forgive my raising this matter," she said, "but Mr. Charles Newsome has told us that your uncle means to leave you in possession of Landseye."

He was surprised; but recovering from that emotion instantly, he said, a little ruefully, "Sometimes my cousin's candid nature outruns even my expectations of it! Or perhaps I should say, my fears of it. And I am afraid that is exactly what my uncle threatens to do, much to my distress and chagrin. I thank God it has not lessened my cousin's love for me by one jot. I might even say it has increased it as he has seen how much this injustice pains me. I still cannot believe my uncle will do such a wrong thing. It is utterly out of his character."

"I did not mean to cause you distress, sir," said Elissa. "I had understood it to be a settled matter; and the only reason I mentioned it was in regard to our discussion: Would you consider yourself bound to make the lives of your tenants less difficult, should you become the possessor of Landseye?"

"Oh, Miss Wyatt, believe me, I would! That is the only pleasure I take out of the prospect. I *would* do good, I assure you. My recent visits to Landseye suggest that the houses and farms of the tenantry need much improvement; my uncle seems to have let them go in his later years."

His fervor on this point was extremely pleasing to Elissa.

"And I," she said, not as one boasting, but as one speaking to another who might understand, "I have made it my work to help the folk in the valley in whatever ways I can, and encouraged my father to think of his tenants more."

He smiled approvingly at her. "Indeed," he said, "it is the true work of Christians."

"Yes," she replied, almost eagerly. "We know that that is what Christ wishes us to do most of all after loving God—I mean, to help one another. That is his entire theology in a nutshell, and He said as much."

Again that smile, which she returned.

They were silent then for a few minutes, but it was a pleasant silence. She felt they had progressed with unique rapidity to a topic very important to both of them, and understood one another perfectly.

Then he said, "Is it bad here, in your valley? The troubles of the millworkers and weavers, I mean."

"It is, fortunately, not so bad here as in some of the other valleys round about. At this point in its course, the flow of the river from day to day varies so greatly that it is not as dependable as might be wished for a mill. We do have one, but it is used only for fulling wool, most of it brought in from the surrounding valleys. When the river is in spate, you can hear the mill pounding away like artillery; but when the river becomes lazy, the hammers fall silent. The greater part of the workers here are shepherds and farm laborers. We have some weavers and glovemakers who do piecework out of their homes, but fewer all the time."

He had listened to this summary with evident distress, and now he shook his head. "The lot of farm laborers can be so hard that sometimes I wonder why they continue in life," he said.

"I have sometimes wondered about that myself," she said. "And the answer I have come to is that they do so by holding on to a strong zest for living. They taste and feel every act, every moment, both the difficult times and the pleasant. They are not cut off from the meaningfulness of action and bodily labor as gentlefolk too often are."

He gazed at her quietly and seriously, a look that invited her to continue. She made an effort to enlarge upon what she had said.

"I do not know quite how to say it," she went on. "They taste the *implicit flavor* of life, of being alive. It is like having an appetite for food. It keeps them going as they wade through the suffering of every day. As long as they have that, the hold life has upon them is greater than any longing they may have to escape from toil and suffering merely by dying. If they lose it, that zest, they are apt to give up, not to care if they die. I believe one can see that quite clearly in those who commit self-murder, though thank God that does not happen often here—I have known of only one such case."

She was conscious that this was a somewhat morbid topic to pursue with a stranger, but she was reassured by Daniel's air of quiet attention, and by what he said to her next.

"Yes, I know what you mean by that zest for living. I have often marveled how my uncle's tenants, whether men or women or children, have that zest unconquerably, even when they are in pain from some injury, or weary with the endless repetition of labor. If they are knocked down, they get on their feet again and seize upon that zest once more. It is their balance, it steadies them, it keeps them upright. And we gentlefolk think that the only way to get through life is to have the leisure for conversation, for calling on others, for reading, thinking, writing; deprive us of that and we are forlorn and see no reason to go on. It is as you said: the zest for life is like appetite. Your laborer enjoys it all, whether what he gets of life is coarse food or fine; whereas we gentlefolk too often know how to enjoy nothing but what is fine."

"Quite so," she said.

He was silent for a moment, and then he said: "And would you attempt to amend this difference between the gentlefolk and those who do the labor?"

She did not understand what he meant, and she must have looked at him blankly.

He tried again. "We have agreed that it is our duty to lessen the sufferings of the poor. But what if *we*, the wealthy, are by our very existence the cause of those sufferings? Do you believe we ought to mend that inequity?"

She was still only vaguely aware of what he meant; and by way of making some sort of response, she said, "In Christ we are all the same. I know that; I believe that."

"Indeed," he said. "I honor you for that answer. It is the right answer, the deep answer. And yet it does not put food in the mouths of the poor."

"No," she said, thinking that she caught his drift. "That is what we must do ourselves, from our position of privilege."

"But some," he said, "would change our entire system. Look at the Americans, for instance. They have declared that all men are equal."

She was still a little confused by this line of questioning, and he had invoked a counterexample she did not feel knowledgeable enough to address. "But we cannot change our system," she said. "We must have order in the world, from top to bottom; to change it would be like trying to think with our feet. It is not natural. Without order, we would have no farming, no manufacture, no buying and selling of food or goods. We would have famine, chaos, despair."

"The Americans seem to be muddling along well enough," said Daniel. "Their trade is increasing by the year, and they are not starving."

"But I believe, sir, that they still have gentlefolk and laborers. The distinction is still preserved in practice, if not in theory. They give lip service to leveling, as I believe it is called, but they do not *do* it—if my understanding of their society is correct, at least."

"To some extent I must agree," he said. "But I wonder. It is an interesting experiment. If these distinctions in rank truly do dwindle away among them, can their nation survive? We shall know soon enough."

"Oh," she said, somewhat impulsively, "surely you cannot think well of the Americans! They are ingrates and troublemakers, all of them, from what I can tell."

He smiled. "Perhaps that is so," he admitted. "But I do not think they are entirely fools."

She was upset with herself for not knowing enough about the subject to meet him on his own ground; and she was filled suddenly by a hunger to know more, to know as much as this man did, so that she would be able to converse with him as an equal. His smile was not condescending, but she guessed from it that he was reserving his full opinion in order not to offend her by any intimation that she was ignorant on the topic at hand; and that annoyed her.

At this point, however, their attention was diverted by a burst of bright laughter from the pair that was walking behind them.

Daniel said: "I think my cousin and, if I may be so bold, your sister have found some of the zest of life for themselves."

"They *do* seem to be enjoying one another's company," said Elissa. She meant her remark to be cheerful, but she could not keep a little worry out of it, as she saw further signs that Merry's partiality was gaining upon her too quickly.

Daniel cast a glance back at them and then said to her, evidently in response to the concern he heard in her tone: "I think we need not be alarmed. My cousin is of a very lively disposition when he is pleased, and it would seem your sister is as well. To you and me, their liveliness may seem to be too much; to them, it is simply in accordance with their natures."

Another look of what she would at the time have termed perfect understanding passed between them.

Despite this act of mutual reassurance that all was well, they did pause to wait for the other two to catch up; which took a surprising length of time; for Charles and Merry, seeing that Elissa and Daniel were not proceeding, took that as a license to dawdle, rather than as a request to them to hasten their steps. During this interval, Daniel looked out over the valley and the river and the village below. His demeanor, even the stance he took, breathing deeply and turning from side to side, sweeping the landscape with his gaze, all showed her that he took a great deal of pleasure in what he saw. It was only after a considerable silence that they spoke again.

"To revert to our previous topic," said Daniel, "I am reminded, on surveying your pretty little vale here, that nature itself gives us the most powerful implicit reason to live. I know that when I am despondent, a walk in the fields or the woods will set me up again. Those who live constantly in those fields and woods have that medicine constantly applied to their spirits."

"That is so," she agreed. "But there is a medicine in human company as well. We band together on our journey through life, we humans, as naturally as wild birds gather in passing from north to south."

At that moment, a little flock of blackbirds flew overhead, clucking lustily.

"And like the birds," Elissa added, "we chatter together and sing to express our love of company. Our farmhands and weavers here—how they love singing! It gives them a kind of human companionship even when they are alone. And when they are together, they sing at every task. And if it were not for the choir and the singing in church, I think most of those who do attend would not."

"Yes, singing!" he said with an enthusiasm that was surprising to her.

"Are you musical?" she asked.

"Indeed, I love music. My mother taught me to sing and play the pianoforte when I was a boy—I insisted upon it, or at least I may say I begged her to do so."

"Do you mean you neglected the hunt to practice your scales?"

It was a somewhat sharp little squib, given her unfamiliarity with him; but he smiled again, and she saw that he understood her teasing.

"As a matter of fact," he said, "I was always wild for the hunt, whether by horse or on foot, whether following the hounds or following the birds. I am a better shooter than I am a singer; but I do love to sing.—And you?"

"I love to sing as well, though I am not a wonder when it comes to performance before others."

"And what do you most enjoy?"

"I have some books of very old airs. I cannot tell you how much I love them."

He was surprised. "I, too," he said. "One of my great treasures is a book of old songs by Dowland and others."

"Perhaps you would be interested in looking at my books, then; I have several. They are for the lute, but I manage to play them on the pianoforte. They include songs composed to words by Thomas Campian and Samuel Daniel and Fulke Greville and writers unknown. I would be glad to copy out some pieces for you."

"It is too gracious of you to offer your time in this way."

Elissa was hardly sure why, but she was seized by a sudden passion to do this service for Mr. Newsome, and she said nothing further about it in order not to provoke his absolute prohibition.

"And you prefer the pianoforte to other instruments?" he asked then.

"I do. I had only an old spinet here until my sister and I went to Gloucester, where we attended school for two years. That was where I discovered the pianoforte; and when we returned home, I pined for it—I am quite ashamed when I look back on how much its loss affected me. My father bought me an instrument as soon as he understood what I lacked. God bless him, he feared at first that I had formed a connection with some gentleman in Gloucester, and I believe he was glad to learn from my sister that my grief could be so easily mended."

Mr. Newsome smiled at this.

Again Elissa thought: *He has a wonderful smile. It is so cordial, and it makes one feel so perfectly understood.*

"Yes, we need music," said Daniel then. "We need music daily, or at least so I find. I did not say it before, but on those solitary walks I take to cheer me in a fit of melancholy, I often add singing to my cure. And as you say, the laborers in our fields know instinctively that we all need music; they know it better than we do, with all our airs of superior education.—Perhaps you and I can find time during my visit to sing together. Apart from the judging ears of others, I mean."

"I should enjoy that."

He made a little bow in promise of his accompanying her, and resumed looking over the valley.

For some reason for which she could not account, she found herself then inquiring of him, quite suddenly: "Where do you live, sir, if I may ask?"

He looked back at her with that pleasant suggestion of a smile. "You must come and see," he said.

She laughed to cover her embarrassment at having asked so pointed a question.

He then went on: "I live at Lakeholm Hall, in Oxfordshire, not far from my uncle's home at Landseye. It is an old family place that came down to my mother, and then to me after my parents' death."

"You are an orphan, then. I am sorry to hear that."

"And you are bereft of your mother, if I remember correctly?"

"Yes, sir."

He looked at her with an expression that somehow both understood and eased her pain.

"Well," he said, "it is fortunate for us both that we have another Parent who watches over us."

"Indeed; indeed it is; and that is a great comfort, a wonderful comfort—indeed, it is all we should need of comfort."

He smiled again and looked back at the valley.

And in that last minute before Merry and Charles came straggling up to join them, Elissa stood to one side watching

Daniel, and a flock of strange thoughts flew through her mind, thoughts she had never thought before or ever had to think; but the first, which came there not birdwise but bursting like a skyrocket from nowhere, was the strangest and most shocking of all.

This is the man I shall marry, she thought.

At once she was frightened that this idea had ever occurred to her. *It is dangerous*, she thought, *it is wrong, even to say such a thing to myself! I know nothing about him, nothing. If I were to set my heart on him—to say nothing about doing something so foolish as to set my cap at him—he might break my peace of mind in pieces. Why, for all I know, he is already promised to another. Indeed, it is likely that he is so, considering how gracious and generous he is. But he might even be married, for all I know, despite my having heard nothing to the contrary. No, I shall not be so stupid, so foolish, so hasty, as to even speak that thought privately to myself: "This is the man whom I shall marry." That is exactly the sort of thing that Merry might say— in fact, has said, and not privately, on more than one occasion. I am not so foolish.*

Despite this self-scolding, she studied Daniel more attentively now. *What is it that has made him so attractive to me?* she asked herself. Again she found herself thinking that he was not particularly good-looking; that no one would ever call him handsome. *But still*, she thought, as she had thought before, when she first laid eyes on him, *there is* something *about his looks. Or maybe it is not really his looks at all, but something above and beyond his looks; or deep within his looks.*

And she remembered some lines from Chaucer she had read in school, in a sort of primer of English literature—in the prologue of the Canterbury tales:

> And though that he were worthy, he was wys,
> And of his port as meke as is a mayde.
> He never yet no vileinye ne sayde

In all his lyf, un-to no maner wight.
He was a verray parfit gentil knight.

She had thought, reading them a decade ago, that these were the words that would describe the man she would want to marry. And this man was the first whom she had met in all the time since who seemed to her to fit those lines.

Then she thought to herself that the aspect of this man that had so instantly and powerfully affected her was some kind of moral authority. One felt the difference between that morality, however marred it might prove to be in the actual practicalities of life, and one's own halting attempts to be good. The contrast with Mr. Herbert immediately came to her mind: the rector was a man who understood the goodness of being good only in an abstract way; he had sought it out on intellectual grounds. But this Mr. Daniel Newsome truly was good; and if not absolutely good—for no one but the Lord was that—then one certainly felt that he was better than oneself, and one ought to be more like him, one ought to try to be better than one was for the very reason that this man was good. One felt that he had repented already; that he knew that he was full of mortality, humanity, shortcoming, and he never lost sight of that. One felt that he was humble. One felt that his heart, however knocked about it must be by the tumults of life, was still pure. *Look at him!* she thought to herself. *How he stands there, so tall, so upright, so square in the shoulders—why, it is he that is the innocent, not Merry and Mr. Charles Newsome. No, they are Adam and Eve all over again, more foolish than pure; while Mr. Daniel Newsome is like the new Adam who has had sin flung upon him but has shrugged it off—has cast it off. It could not stick to him!* She had a sudden sensation of lightheadedness and heat. It astonished her; and the images that flashed through her mind, as she looked at this stranger and imagined him as her husband, they astonished her too; until she turned away in distress at herself.

Good gracious, Elissa Wyatt! she thought. *Whence this wild and instant infatuation? This is exactly what Merry must go through with her sudden passion for a particular man. Be* Elissa, *be yourself, do not be other than what you are!*

And yet she felt, somehow, and very disturbingly, that she had never been so much what she truly was than at this moment.

Nor was it her mind alone that was roiled; her body, too, was perturbed, in a manner she had never experienced before, in all of her twenty-seven years. Her fingers spread and flexed, almost itching to run through his hair, and her knees trembled.

She looked back at him; and she had time for just one more fleeting, intrusive, overmastering thought: *I know what it is I love about him. He is* serious, *as no one else I have ever known has been serious—only that stranger who looks out of the mirror at me. And he is* present. *When he looks at you and speaks to you, you feel that he is engaging with you, wholly and earnestly. His eyes* look into *you, not askance, just as his thoughts freely meet your own, and do not run off sideways in evasion.*

"And what are you thinking, sweet Sister?" said Merry teasingly as she and Charles closed up the gap between them at last.

"Yes, Miss Wyatt," said Charles a little naughtily. "You are looking at my cousin very seriously and thinking something very serious."

Daniel turned to look at Elissa. She would have thought he would be surprised that she had been watching him, or annoyed on her behalf by his cousin's imputation, but as before he seemed calm, neutral, patient, tolerant of everyone, and especially of his cousin.

Meanwhile, there was no point in denying what Charles had said; that would just make it worse. "Yes," she said, returning Daniel's gaze quite frankly, but speaking to Charles. "I am indeed thinking something serious. I am thinking that your cousin Mr. Daniel Newsome is a serious person, in the best sense of that word."

"Serious!" exclaimed Charles. "That he *is*, indeed! Far, far too serious, and I make it my business to try to lighten his mood at every opportunity."

"Do not attempt it," said Elissa. "You will only annoy him—if he *can* be annoyed, which I take the liberty to doubt—and you will not succeed. And if you did succeed, you would find that he was your cousin no more, but someone else entirely; and you would miss him, miss what he was, I assure you."

"But no one should be wholly serious all the time," said Merry with a smile; this was a sort of conversation she had had with Elissa before, though never about anyone other than her sister.

"On the contrary," said Elissa. "We should all be serious—serious in our woes and our joys. You will never find a man who enjoys the world so much, who takes as much joy in the world God has made, as a man who is serious in his heart. The rest, I am inclined to think, are triflers; they see the surface and are amused by it; but the serious man sees deep into things, sees them with the eyes of his soul, and whether it is joy or sorrow he discovers in them, they are all beautiful to him."

"I declare!" said Charles. "Miss Merry, till this minute I thought your sister quite sober-minded; now I think she has a passion for the fantastical."

"You would not understand it, Charles," said Daniel. Again, his tone toward his cousin was not condescending in the least; it was in fact affectionate. "Miss Wyatt overestimates my perspicacity, but she understands me—she understands something about me that you have not understood in twenty-one years."

"Really!" exclaimed Charles. He and Merry exchanged a glance.

There was a silence; a longish silence.

"Let us walk on, shall we?" said Elissa then.

They went onwards together, in a foursome now, and spoke of other things.

Whereas Aeon's End virtually hid in the landscape, the house known as Rowantree seemed to want to make itself a foil to its environs. If a significant mansion in the heart of the finest district in London had been disassembled, block by block, transported to the Cotswolds, and reassembled on the height over a deep valley, it could not have looked more alien. In fact, if a Bavarian palace had, by the same scrupulous means, been imported from its own setting, it might have seemed more at home where Rowantree stood than the current dwelling. Though built in the time of George the First, it kept still an air of something that had been purchased sight unseen and unpacked from a box. Not a tree or ornamental shrub softened its sharp lines; it was surrounded by a wide and open lawn. Here, in this pleasant but stringently artificial hilltop meadow—clipped rigorously short once a week by gardeners crawling about with shears, occasionally assisted by a flock of sheep—Rowantree-house reared up out of the soil, gray, polished, staunchly Georgian, and aspiring to be perfectly symmetrical in every respect, no matter from what angle it might be viewed. It seemed almost like that lonely house that has somehow survived the terrible shelling of an entire city district; and the rubble has been cleared away, the ground leveled to an absolute flatness, and grass has been planted, and yet the house remains so clearly requisite of company that one thinks, on encountering it, *Where is the rest of the city?* In a more country metaphor, it was a duckling or a pup, orphaned and without siblings, with no warm body nearby to which to attach itself. This was the scandal or the glory of Rowantree, depending on whose view one took. Elissa always thought the place sterile, though admittedly grand; but Mr. and Mrs. Rowcliffe would be the first to tell you that Mr. Rowcliffe's ancestor, then a London-dwelling merchant of some sort, had "gone to the best architect" and required the best sort of country house that could be had; the strong implication of the story being that this was the explanation of the perfect success that had been achieved.

Or rather, Mr. Rowcliffe would tell you this, not Mrs. Rowcliffe. But if you thought back on who had told you, you might not be able to remember which of them it was. They had each absorbed the anecdotes of the other, the very biographies of the other; they used a common pattern of speech; they each told the other's stories as often as they urged the other to do so, and if the other told a tale at that urging, the urger in any case promptly retold it in virtually the same words, though sometimes with surprising variations that negated the point of the first narration. They had even begun to look like one another somehow, though Mr. Rowcliffe was rather tall for his times, and Mrs. Rowcliffe rather short, and though he remained the very figure of the masculine Briton, and she that of the feminine. It was as if their long life together had melted them into essences that had then been mingled and perfectly homogenized before being reinstilled into their physical husks. This likeness was assisted by the fact that their bodies were elderly, and age imposes on human corporality a generic sameness, an indistinguishability: their backs were hunched, their faces and hands were crazed with wrinkles and stained with spots, their voices quavered, and either one might be seen to tremor at any time—it was almost as if they took turns. This sympathy extended through much of their physicality: Elissa had in fact seen Mr. Rowcliffe flinch once when Mrs. Rowcliffe had stubbed her toe in hastening out of the parlor; and one was never ill but both were ill. They had become twins over time; for, since death is a birth, life itself is a womb, and their life as a married couple had knit them together at the hip, in bone and flesh and soul. They could not abide to be long apart from one another, and "long" in their case meant no more than a few minutes; they were even known to begin to fret if the other was *in absentia* for an unaccountably long period in responding to nature's call.

Aside from that one obligation, they performed and did everything together. They each simultaneously and spontaneously rose from their seats to walk outside; they sat beside one another at the spinet, which is not a spacious instrument; they read the same book aloud, by turns; they had played two-handed games of cards in contests that spanned decades, each win and each loss carefully recorded and summed in a series of dated notebooks. When they heard a knock on the door, they would each jump to their feet and rush, with age's shambling, tottering stride, to make the footman who had answered the summons superfluous, crowding past him in the hallway to view their visitor with eyes that were strikingly bright under lined and drooping eyelids. Their method of greeting a newcomer was idiosyncratic in the extreme: often only one of them would do the greeting, and the other, judging social obligation had been observed by his or her better half, would turn away in silence before the greeting was even complete. But once their guest had entered the parlor, they would both talk at once—and God save the visitor who came alone, for they would combine against her or him, and chatter unmercifully, usually on the same topic, but sometimes on diametrically opposed theses, until one felt like a confessor caught between two sinners intent on unburdening themselves of sins too slight to require contrition.

People who met them for the first time thought that they were becoming dotty. But this was nothing new: Elissa could attest they had been "that way" as long as she had known them, and Mr. Wyatt could extend that testimony even further back in the past. It was not that they were forgetful, so much as that they were unreliable with respect to others—thoughtless, though in a trivial rather than in a cruel way. For example, if they took salt at table, they would put the saltcellar as far as possible from the nearest guest, almost as if they intended to force her or him to ask for it. If Mr. Rowcliffe handed over the newspaper to Elissa when she was visiting, he never returned it to its original condition beforehand, but left it folded to the particular article he happened to have been reading last, as if he expected her to be interested in the same item of news. They often never said farewell at all after a visit, but simply turned in silence to other pursuits once their guests had said goodnight, as if by doing so their visitors had ceased to exist or vanished like ghosts. They, or one or the other of them, would suddenly rise to their feet and declare the room too hot, and open the window to winter's deadly breath behind one, and then go off and stand by the fire. And yet, it must be repeated, all these thousand little acts of forgetfulness were performed without any malice whatsoever. They simply did not think of others in a helpful way. Mrs. Rowcliffe was perhaps the less likely to commit these little social oversights, and her son relied upon her to treat his new and rather grand wife with more tact than Mr. Rowcliffe; but this reliance was often defeated, and he must spend many hours of each visit he made to his home explaining away his parents' little failings of consideration; which were quite baffling to the new Mrs. Rowcliffe, well brought up as she was.

This son was one of two offspring of the Rowcliffes. He had been achieved, by an almost Abrahamic (or perhaps Aphrodisic) miracle, very late in their lives. Schooled elsewhere, he now lived in London, but visited upon occasion. Their daughter, Charles Newsome's mother, Agnes, had preceded him by such an interval that she was nearly of the previous generation. She had spent her early childhood at Rowcliffe, but was schooled in Bristol and then married into Oxfordshire, and never visited. Perhaps this was for a reason Daniel did not perfectly appreciate or had felt he ought not in good taste to mention: namely, that the Rowcliffe parents shared a very patriarchal prejudice: they doted on their son, and on Charles, their grandson. Agnes must have grown tired of being treated as a nonentity; and though it must be insisted that they did love her, they tended to speak of her only as a staircase that had allowed their grandson to arrive by birth at what they believed would be a very fortunate position, the proprietorship of Landseye. Yet one felt again, upon encountering this bias, that it was not cruel or heartless, for the Rowcliffes were not cruel; it was only that they looked ahead to the future so eagerly that they forgot the rewards and duties of the present. They would live on in their son and his children, who would own Rowantree; they would live on in Charles and his children, who would own Landseye—as they apparently still believed. This, too, was Abrahamic: they longed for an uncountable posterity.

And indeed, why else would they be remembered, how else would they *matter* beyond this generation, if not for their offspring and their offspring's offspring? It would not be for their thousands and thousands of card games, or for their idiosyncrasies, however endearing or irking to their neighbors. This was the assumption and indeed the fear that lurked behind their bias toward their male descendants. They had never observed that each one of us—childless or not—constitutes a particular stellar mass in the great galaxy of galaxies that is humanity, for each of us exerts a gravity that pulls upon the others and holds us all together, and especially in the gravity of good deeds. This thought was beyond them; they had no way to think it.

Patriarchal myopia determined much that the Rowcliffes did and did not do. For example, it explained the gardens at Rowantree. The house did have a garden, for every English house must, but that ground was separated from the house by some two hundred feet and walled in like a beast that might escape. And despite this strict imprisonment, it was only a very tame garden, consisting of a prettyish grass court where some boxwood was kept at strict attention along the perimeter of a gravel path, and of a second enclosure for kitchen purposes. Elissa, in those few times when she had entered it for one reason or another, thought that it was not really a garden at all, but an excuse for one; and Mr. Wyatt had been known to look solemn and even shake his head sadly whenever the garden at Rowantree was mentioned, as people react when a demented person claims to have seen something that never existed.

This garden was explained by the Rowcliffes' misunderstanding of the future and their place in it, in this way: A garden is a participation in an eternal cycle. It is a willingness to be a part of a far larger entity than oneself, an entity that has been in progress for an untold number of years—in one sense, since the universe began. John Wyatt knew this, without knowing he knew it. The thought of his garden, and his work in it, sustained him because it connected him to eternity. In the cycles of the seasons, the growing and blooming and then the fading and dying of his plantings, he had grappled a great truth to himself with bands of steel: life, greater life, of which he was a part, if a vanishingly small part, does not die.

Of this, again, the Rowcliffes knew nothing. They had turned away from everything that might teach them this, except for their hopes for their son and their grandson; and that was a feeble crutch, as any parent knows. Indeed, their own case proved it, unbeknownst to them as yet, since Charles was to be disinherited of the future they had expected for him. And their son had once confided to Elissa, on one of his visits, that he could not stand Rowantree, did not know how his parents endured to live in the country, and would sell the place as soon as it came to him.

Their hopes for their son did, however, have this good effect: it made them very zealous in preserving the estate on his behalf. Though nearly a century old, the house seemed absolutely new. Its floors were swept, mopped, waxed, and thus immaculate; its woodwork too, waxed, polished, and thus gleaming; its carpets were beaten free of all dust and dirt; its window glazing was so clean as to be invisible. Its lawn, as has been mentioned, was kept shorn and even, and its garden never varied, as though it were a place out of time, a place that did not participate in time, which in many ways it was. And the orchard at Rowantree—of course the Rowcliffes maintained it as an asset for their posterity.

But by contrast with the house and the garden, that orchard was something quite remarkable. Mention of *that* made Mr. Wyatt turn from his spading and listen. Not even the assiduous tendance of the orchard by the Rowcliffe gardeners could deprive it of its essential mystery.

It had first been planted by the Kestons, the family that had held the land for centuries previous to the Rowcliffes. Its origins were thus lost and dim. It lay at a great distance from Rowantree-house, nearer where the Keston house had stood, between Rowantree and Aeon's End, at the end of the long ridge that ran between the latter and the former. Elissa sometimes made the orchard a destination of her walks. It had—Mr. Wyatt was not shy of saying—the finest rowantrees in all of England. He claimed they were of the true *sorbus domestica* variety, the service-tree, and he had taught the Rowcliffes how the brilliant red fruits would, if bletted, make a wonderful wine. One of these rowantrees, the great-grandfather of them all, was five feet thick; and though it was no more than thirty feet high, its boughs extended twice that far over the ground below. The rings of another that had fallen in a storm had been counted at some three hundred, and it was believed that the great rowantree was many centuries older than that. Mr. Herbert had once said it ought to be cut down, as it had likely been worshiped by the Druids; but Mr. Wyatt had on this point felt the confidence to contradict the rector, saying that the tree could not possibly be that old. Still, it looked like a tree that *ought* to have been worshiped by the Druids. In any case, no matter what Mr. Herbert might say, there are far worse things for heathens in this world to worship than trees. Perhaps it was with some vague sense of propitiating a tree-spirit that the Rowcliffe family, on purchasing the property and beginning to build on it in the early 1700s, had named the place after the great rowantree; and in some local histories the place was in fact called not just Rowantree but Great Rowantree.

The rest of the orchard consisted of trees either excellent or extremely curious—for example, cherries as bitter as cyanide, far too tart for even the most heavily sugared pie; transparent apples from Astrakhan; golden crabapples; and giant medlars whose open *et caetera* would make any young maid curl her lip in disgust. Elissa thought that the place was a kind of curio cabinet of fruits. Mr. Wyatt had taken many grafts of the better specimens; and as for the odd ones, he liked to maintain that they were ancient sports, one of a kind, experiments the Great Gardener had launched long ago and then forgotten.

The orchard, however, in its position at some distance from the house, was not on the route of march on this day. The four walkers ascended the long lane directly to the house, where, the news of their arrival having preceded them, they found Mr. and Mrs. Rowcliffe actually straying across the lawn in anticipation of them, hatless, and so pleased at the young people's coming they barely spoke at all upon being approached, but instead tremored together. In their excitement, Mr. Rowcliffe shook Charles's hand again, as if he too were just arrived in the county, as well as that of Daniel; and Mrs. Rowcliffe kissed the Wyatt daughters on the cheek as if they were some distant spur of the Rowcliffe family come on a visit for the first time.

When these overtures had been made, and the young people had said good morning, the Rowcliffes looked over this promising foursome and began to speak; and then the torrent was loosed.

"You have never been here," said Mrs. Rowcliffe to Daniel.

"No," he agreed. "I have not had that good fortune. But here I am; and if you will have me, I shall stay a day or two."

"But Charles has never been here either," pointed out Mr. Rowcliffe.

"You shall stay the summer," said Mrs. Rowcliffe.

Daniel laughed at her insistence; and when he laughed, everyone smiled.

What a wonderful laugh! thought Elissa. *It is so loving, and yet it does not surrender one jot of his personal dignity—indeed, of his personal sovereignty.*

"I feel blessed to have even a few days," said Daniel.

"Charles shall stay the summer," said Mr. Rowcliffe, "and perhaps more."

"I am delighted to hear it," said Daniel. "It is an excellent place for him to do his reading, though perhaps he is far afield from his mentor."

"He has not cracked a book yet," said Mr. Rowcliffe.

"But he has found the finest young ladies in the valley," said Mrs. Rowcliffe. "And that is far more important.— And what need has he of the law, anyway? He is to have Landseye."

The smile faded from Daniel's face, and he looked at his cousin, who, unobserved by the Rowcliffes, gave a helpless little shrug. Elissa saw that it was not in Charles's character to willingly bear bad tidings.

"But knowledge of the law will stand him in good stead should he become magistrate," Mr. Rowcliffe was saying.

"Yes, he is likely to become magistrate someday," said Mrs. Rowcliffe. "But he will do no reading here! He will take his ease, as he ought, and visit our many fine families.— Why, on his first day here, he toured Mr. Wyatt's garden, and that is something many a visitor aspires to do in vain."

"Not all our visitors are as amiable as Charles," said Mr. Rowcliffe.

"None of them!" said Mrs. Rowcliffe.

"And you too have met our lovely neighbors," Mr. Rowcliffe said to Daniel.

"Yes, I have just been granted that privilege, sir," said Daniel.

"Well, we must have your father to dinner," said Mrs. Rowcliffe to Elissa. "And you all must stay."

"I regret we cannot, Mrs. Rowcliffe," said Elissa.

"But—" began Merry.

"We cannot," said Elissa firmly but kindly, silencing her sister with a look. "My father expressly said he would not go out today, that he had things at home he wished to do; and we would not be so disrespectful as to discommode him, simply because we have had the pleasure of falling in with your visitors while in the village. Indeed, we have some errands there that still must be done."

"But you will come in and refresh yourself with a cool beverage, certainly," said Mrs. Rowcliffe.

"That would be most welcome," said Elissa.

"And we shall send you home with an invitation to dine here with your father tomorrow," said Mr. Rowcliffe.

"That, too, would be most welcome," said Elissa, "though I cannot speak for my father's time."

"Well, if not tomorrow, then soon, soon!" said Mr. Rowcliffe.

"Indeed, I know he would wish it," said Elissa "for he spoke to me of inviting you all to Aeons' End this week."

"There, there you have it!" said Mr. Rowcliffe happily.

The Rowcliffes were already turning away toward the house as this final comment was uttered; the assent to take refreshment was all they needed to hasten into the house, calling on the housekeeper for a table of beverages to be set out. The young people again divided into couples as they followed the Rowcliffes; and so Elissa was able to observe Daniel's reactions as he entered the house.

Not that the house called for any particular response: it was well-appointed but somewhat conventional. It was rather that Daniel evinced none. He was studiously neutral, conducting himself with that perfect tact that is invisible and only discoverable when it is absent. He neither pretended to be impressed, nor pretended to be unimpressed, nor really was impressed, nor really was blasé. He seemed detached somehow, as if he thought it would have been bad manners to judge as either good or bad the manner in which someone else lived. And yet Elissa knew he had an opinion; it was just that he did not judge his own judgment worthy of imposing on anyone else.

And these good manners were an earnest of those which he maintained, and maintained effortlessly, throughout the remainder of Elissa and Merry's short visit there. He was not just amiable; he had something of the same sort of charm as his cousin, but his was founded on a more solid basis of intelligence and of respect for others. The Rowcliffes had foibles enough to elicit an ironic jest from anyone less circumspect, but Daniel forbore at every opportunity to raise an eyebrow or exchange an ironic glance with his cousin or the Wyatts. Some of the Rowcliffe's oddities of manner must have been surprising and challenging to him—he could not possibly know the couple as well as did Elissa; and yet he bore it all with authentic equanimity. Elissa was impressed.

The content of the conversation itself, by contrast, was not particularly enlightening as to his character. The Rowcliffes commandeered all the talk, and the Wyatt ladies and the Newsome gentlemen were left to keep up as best they could; which meant that they might manage to insert a statement of agreement here and there, or address a question to one of their hosts; but the discourse was all on topics of interest to the Rowcliffes—their son; his wife, who was expecting a child within months; the status of their card-playing series (Mrs. Rowcliffe was currently several games ahead); the death of a shepherd who pastured his sheep on one of their fields; the departure of a chambermaid from their service; the effect of the war on the wine trade (they would not listen to the only person who could have perhaps enlightened them on this matter, Daniel); and some trouble they were having with their private carriage.

After an hour of this, Elissa saw that even Merry would be glad to escape. She rose, Merry followed her signal, and they made their farewells to the Rowcliffes and the Newsomes. There was another discussion on both sides as to when they would meet again, and Charles suggested the very next day, since Daniel planned to leave so soon. "And he cannot be trusted not to go," he added, with a laugh. "I never know when he is coming or going."

"Tomorrow is Saturday," said Daniel. "If I do not leave then, I must stay until at least Monday, for I do not travel on the Sabbath."

"Then since I believe my father has given me *carte blanche* to arrange matters, may we ask you all to dine on Sunday?" asked Elissa. "You do not mind such a gathering then, sir?"

"I should prefer Monday," he said.

"If we can be sure you will stay until then, let it be Monday."

"Since my hosts seem amenable to my staying even longer, I shall give you my word to stay at least until Tuesday morning."

"Then we shall see you all at Aeons' End to dine on Monday," concluded Elissa.

The Rowcliffes now, in accordance with their usual quirk, ceased to pay any attention to their visitors, but Charles and Daniel went with them to the door of the house. There was an interesting moment there: the couples paired off again, and Charles said something to Merry that made her laugh, while Daniel said something to Elissa that pleased her just as much, since it was serious. It grew naturally out of the mention he had made of the Sabbath.

"Do you regularly attend the church here, Miss Wyatt?" he asked.

"Every Sunday, sir."

"And the rector—that was he whom I saw when I met you and your sister and Charles in the road, was it not?—how do you find his care for his parish?"

"Yes, that was Mr. Herbert with whom we were speaking. He is as good a pastor, I suppose, as the usual minister in the church these days. His knowledge of theology in general and of the doctrines of our church in particular are probably superior to those of most, I should think. Some fault his sermons as too long, too technical, I will even say too *dull*. But he has helped me at times, and he assists me in my efforts to care for the villagers who need the charity of those more fortunate; so I rather like him and appreciate his labors than not."

"Ah," said Daniel. There was no need to say more, but he added something she thought rather wise.

"I have heard it said, and truly, I think, that one ought to attend a church for its doctrine and not for its sermons. The giver of sermons may be anyone, fit or unfit for the task, whom God has appointed there for His own purposes; but as long as the teachings are true, we ought not to mind the dullness of the rector."

"Yes," she responded, "but how little people know or care of the teachings of their own church!"

"Indeed," he said, "how little, how very little."

"You have no idea how much this deficiency has been a concern to me," she said.

"Have you read Wilberforce on this point?" he asked.

She knew the name: William Wilberforce was a member of Parliament and had written a well-known book on the state of the Anglican religion—it had been what today would be called a bestseller—but she had to confess to Daniel, with some chagrin, that she had not read it.

Then Merry came to her, and the encounter was over. Daniel bowed to her, with a look that seemed to say, "We must speak more of this"; and in a few moments more, the sisters were on their way back down the lane.

Throughout that entire walk to the village and again home, neither Elissa nor Merry spoke of what was most on her mind. The Newsome cousins were not mentioned, not so much as alluded to. At first Elissa was amused by Merry's deliberate avoidance of the topic, then disturbed by it; and then, gradually, she realized that she, too, had no inclination to introduce the subject until she had thought more on it. Thus they were rather more silent on their way home than on their way to the village.

But that night Merry came to Elissa's room after they had prepared for bed. They both spoke of being particularly weary; and then Merry, almost cutting Elissa off, precipitately asked: "What do you think of him now?"

"Of Mr. Charles Newsome, I presume you mean?"

"Yes, of Charles."

"You refer to him by his Christian name?"

"Oh, Elissa, are you teasing me, or are you being prudish?"

Elissa thought back on some of the feelings she had had in the course of the day and shook her head slightly at the idea that she was prudish; but she said nothing of that.

"Of course I call him by his Christian name," Merry went on. "But I only distinguish him from his cousin by doing so." When Elissa made a face expressive of amused disbelief, Merry gave up this pretence and said: "Well, how could I not call him so? We are . . ." She hesitated tellingly, and then concluded her sentence by saying, "We are so much alike."

"That is true," said Elissa. "But that is not necessarily a good thing."

"Not a good thing in a man and wife, do you mean," said Merry, "that they should be alike?"

"Oh, are we talking about marriage?" said Elissa a little coolly. "I had not realized that Mr. Charles Newsome had made any offer to you."

"Now you *are* being a prude," said Merry, but in the tone of one stating a matter of fact rather than of one expressing irritation.

"No, dear Merry," said Elissa, seeing that the conversation they both now earnestly desired was going off in the wrong direction. "I am not being a prude. I am only saying, rather badly and obscurely, I admit, that you must not go too fast. I see that you like . . . Charles. He is very amiable, very fun; and we saw yesterday that he is already winning Father's affection, which cannot help but endear him to us. But I think he is not . . . not a *steady* sort of man. He would like to be one, I admit. He would like nothing better. One sees that he would give anything to be like Mr. Daniel Newsome in that respect, if only he could, even though he teases his cousin for being serious—that he would give anything, that is, except what is required, which is, among other things, an effort to control his impulses and discipline himself to the unpleasant task of acquiring a means of living."

"Oh, I knew you would reproach him with that!"

"How can I not, dear? I love you. I do not want to see you dragged down into poverty; and he has no prospects at all, so far as I can see, except to live off the alms and the leavings of others, which may or may not materialize."

"Oh, dearest," said Merry, smiling, "if that is the only objection you have to him, then I do not fear anything."

This caught Elissa up short. "Why?" she asked. "Do you have any information about his prospects that I do not?"

"No," said Merry. "It is just that I have every confidence that all *that* will be sorted out in no time as soon as he does pay his addresses to me. I shall have my settlement, and his father will give him something after all. You saw that the Rowcliffes have not an inkling that anything is awry there. Even if his father does cut him off, the Rowcliffes will give him something, and Papa will find a little extra somewhere, I am sure. It will not be a great deal, but it will be more than enough to allow us to live as well as we Wyatts have lived here at Aeons' End. I want nothing more, and I dare say that Charles needs nothing more, either. He has no use for a great house and estate like Landseye; he told me so. He said that it is a blessing his father does not wish to burden him with it, for it would have pulled him down into matters of business that he simply cannot care for. No, it is much better if Landseye goes to Mr. Daniel Newsome. From what I hear from Charles, his cousin is certain to carry off the whole supervision of the estate superbly, and without any particular effort."

"*That* I can readily believe," said Elissa. "His cousin is most impressive."

"Which brings me to another topic," said Merry, with a smile and a twinkle in her eye.

"No, no," said Elissa, "we shall not so easily drop the present one. Do you not see that we can have no clearer proof of Charles Newsome's inability to manage money matters than we see in what his father has done, or is planning to do? When a father refuses to pass his estate *to his own son*—that is so unnatural, so monstrous an act that we can only understand it as a deep, a profound disbelief in his son's ability to manage his own affairs."

Merry cast about for a rebuttal, but was at a loss.

Elissa pressed the advantage she had won. "You *must* go more slowly, dear. You are rushing into this affection for Charles Newsome at all too headlong a pace."

"But that is the way of love, dear Elissa," said Merry, smiling.

"Love! You talk of loving him already? You have not known him for two whole days!"

"What are two days when you have found the one you know you were made to love?" said Merry. "Two days are like two whole years of being acquainted. When I look in his eyes, when we laugh together, when we talk together on any subject, it is as if I have known him for a thousand years.

It is not just that I *know* him; I *recognize* him as the man I have always wanted to marry."

Elissa shook her head. "But this is an illusion," she said. "Talk sensibly, *think* sensibly. You do *not* know him, you *cannot* know him. Two days cannot make a deep acquaintance; you have supplied the sense of being acquainted with him out of your own imagination.—And how many times have you said something similar to me about some gentleman you have met in passing at some ball or party? How many times have I heard similar speeches about the value of instant acquaintance? And then we found out that your proposed beloved had some insuperable defect—that he was a drunkard, like Mr. Keynes, or a gambler, like Mr. Clare? Do you not see that the same lesson applies in this case?"

At this reproach, Merry looked away in considerable embarrassment, for she was justly convicted of having made such a mistake before; but after a long moment of distress she shook off the charge and, turning to Elissa brightly, said: "But this is different, dear."

"It is exactly the same, I say."

"No, it is different, because Charles is different. You know as well as I do that he is *not* vicious. He is not a drunkard—indeed, he would have nothing to do with any beverage on the table that had spirits in it; you may be sure I was watching that. And he has told me that wine and spirits make him ill. And he is no gambler; he has expressed a very healthy fear of such people. And besides, if he were vicious, how could his cousin, who is clearly a good and honest man, love him with such unreserved affection?"

"We do not know what reservations Mr. Daniel Newsome may have in this respect. Compare my reservation about *you:* I think you not practical enough. But I would be slow to tell the world about that flaw in your character. Mr. Daniel Newsome is the very soul of discretion, and we are not likely to see any comment from him about his cousin's flaws."

No sooner had Elissa said this much, however, than she remembered that moment of understanding she had had with Daniel; it was nothing if not a tacit acknowledgement of the imperfections of their respective relatives. But she clung to the main point.

"And that is what most concerns me," she said. "Neither of you is practical. And at least one party in a marriage ought to be; and since it cannot be you, in your case it must be your husband. And Charles Newsome is not that man."

This caution had caught Merry up short a moment ago; but now she only laughed happily. "And this is your great objection to him?" she said.

"It is," said Elissa stoutly.

"Then I ought to marry his cousin, do you think?" asked Merry teasingly.

"His cousin would make you a much better husband."

"Except that I would be miserable with him. I should feel oppressed by his seriousness."

"Do you feel oppressed by mine?"

"No; but I would if you were not my sister—if I did not know how much you loved me, and that your prudishness is all lovingly intended."

"But so would be the prudishness, as you call it, of a husband who loved you. I would call it loving prudence rather than prudishness. He would take care of you because he loved you."

"No, Sister," said Merry, "I shall take Charles to be my lawful wedded husband, if you please; and do you then, take Mr. Daniel Newsome to be yours."

"Do not marry me off so quickly, please," said Elissa. "I prefer to make far better acquaintance with the gentleman you have so readily destined for me."

"Take all the time you need, dear," said Merry, in the same teasing tone. "Charles and I shall afford you plenty of opportunities when you visit us at our house."

Elissa had come to the point where she thought it best not to encourage this kind of talk, so she was silent.

"But seriously, Sister," said Merry, "do you not like this Daniel Newsome? I dare say he likes you. Charles thought he would—he very nearly said as much when we were walking up to Rowantree."

"I *do* like him," said Elissa, since there was little point in denying the fact. "He does seem, as I said myself, to be serious in a most excellent way."

"He is not handsome," said Merry, as if testing her.

"I dare say I would care nothing for that, so long as he is a truly good man. Or perhaps I should say that in his goodness, he would be not just handsome, but beautiful."

"I am glad that one of us can be so spiritual in outlook," said Merry. "But Charles, I think, truly *is* handsome, and any woman would agree with me."

"Well, I cannot say that I for one perfectly agree, but I can see why you say so about him."

Merry grinned happily. "You are only teasing me," she said. "Do you not see what I am getting at? You are only pretending that you do not. How convenient that sisters should marry cousins! You shall rule over Landseye, and Charles and I shall live on at Aeons' End."

"You know *that* cannot be so," said Elissa, referring in specific to the disposition of Aeons' End.

"It cannot be that Mr. Crustall will inherit," insisted Merry.

"It can be and it shall be, whether we like it or not," said Elissa.

"No," said Merry. "That simply cannot happen."

Elissa was quite familiar with this quirk of Merry's, this maintaining stubbornly and without reason that an unpleasant event could not come about—as if God himself would forbid it; there was no argument effective against this insistence, so she refrained from attempting any. Instead she fell back on the most important point in their conversation, which she wished to carry if she possibly could.

"Be careful, dear," she said. "That is all I urge. I understand—the play, the flirtation, the smiles and the laughter, are all so intoxicating that they become a reason in themselves. But the intoxication and the fun of it have serious consequences."

"Oh, yes," said Merry in a droll tone, "I agree. Happiness for the rest of one's life is a very serious thing."

"It is, dear," said Elissa. "It is as I said earlier this very day, and I suppose on many other days as well: every beautiful and good thing is serious beneath the surface, no matter how much laughter it comes clothed in."

Merry was silent then. Perhaps the lesson had penetrated. In any event, she seemed for once a little more serious as she rose from the bed where she had been sitting beside Elissa, and kissed her, and said goodnight, and took her candle, and went away to her own bed.

❦ 3 ❦

Saturday and Sabbath

The mouth of a righteous man is a well of life: but violence covereth the mouth of the wicked.

—Proverbs 10:11

At the breakfast table on Saturday morning, Merry told Elissa that she expected the day to be tedious. Elissa encouraged her not to miss the rewards of daily life in regret for the absence of her new love interest—although she did not phrase it so bluntly. But in the aftermath of the Saturday that unfolded, both sisters would have preferred it to have been utterly dull.

At about noon Elissa was at her writing desk in her bedroom. She heard footsteps in the gravel drive below, proceeding directly to the front door; and if she was not mistaken, she heard as well a somewhat labored breathing, as of someone not particularly fit. People who ascended on foot from the village road were often breathless by the time they reached the door; but such foot travelers were usually of the lower class and presented themselves at the back of the house.

She went to the window, but by then the visitor had approached so near the house as to be almost out of her view; she caught a glimpse only of broad shoulders and of the flat surface of a top hat, by which she confirmed her guess that the arrival was male. Almost simultaneously she heard, both through the window and through the intervening rooms and halls of the house, the sound of the front door opening.

Such was the informality of the Wyatt household, and such was the Wyatts' relative lack of paid servants, that it was not unusual for a member of the family to open the door to visitors, if none of the household help was nearby. Thus Elissa now dimly heard Merry's voice greeting the visitor, and a deep and grating voice resounded in response. Though Elissa could make out only a muffled exchange of words, she did not like what she heard. She knew, even with those very faint clues, that her sister was somehow uncomfortable or even alarmed.

She went at once out of the room and down the stairs. The stranger's voice was now coming from the parlor on the left of the hall, and she proceeded there; and this was what she found.

Even in the very short time that had elapsed since the newcomer had gained entrance to the house, he had driven Merry to the far side of the room, where she stood now with her back against the wall, as if she had been compelled there against her will and penned in. Between her and Elissa, with his back to the doorway, stood the visitor, a man of about forty years of age. Though Merry wore a look of fear and revulsion, the visitor by contrast was looking about himself with a proprietary coolness. His clothes had once been rather fine, but were now shabby and astonishingly dusty and dirty—he must have come into the village on the top of the mail coach this very morning. He had taken off his hat, and his thinning hair was long, greasy, and disheveled. He was large in frame and, though not by any measure tall, appeared powerful, with that sort of slouching strength that nature randomly gives sometimes to those who have never earned it by any exercise or labor, and which they augment with flabbiness until it forms a prepossessing bulk. His size combined with an intangible, inexpressible air of heedless-ness to project unpleasantness, willfulness, even danger to others. For this menacing appearance Elissa would have immediately disliked him, even if he had not alarmed Merry; but there was, too, the strong odor of the man to put her off. The instant she stepped through the doorway, she could smell it trailing like a vapor in the air behind him: a dark but invisible aura, a stench like the burning of a rancid steak.

She spoke at once. "May I ask your business here, sir?"

The man turned around to face her, almost the way a bear will turn that has reared onto its hind paws—in a stiff, lumbering manner, but certain of its strength. When he saw Elissa, he leered at her with open lust. She could not help thinking that the very openness of his lasciviousness was meant to unsettle his potential victims.

"Ah," he said, "an even prettier one! Much prettier, much more to my liking! One with more meat to her bones! And very fine meat it is!"

"I do not like your manner of speaking," said Elissa coolly. "State your business."

"You are the elder sister, ain't you?" he said. "*Elissa,* that is your name.—Oh, I know all about you, all about your little family. Well, where is John today, Missy 'Lissy?"

"Mr. Wyatt is expected back at any moment," said Elissa, though in fact John was likely to be away for most of the day.

"Well, then, I shall just wait for him," said the man, look-ing about for a chair.

"That will not be possible," said Elissa.

"Not possible? How is that?"

"Because I shall not allow it," said Elissa. "You may leave your card and return at a suitable time on Monday morning."

"My card?" said the man with a leer. It was clear that he had carried no visiting card for many a year. "No, I shall stay here and wait." And with that he sat down in the best chair in the room. His affectation of ease was false, however; he leaned forward in his seat, with a crouching, slovenly air, as if he knew perfectly well that he ought not to be there; and he continued to look Elissa up and down in the rudest possible way.

Elissa said to Merry, "Please go ask Mr. Jens to step in for a moment."

"Mr. Jens is not here," said Merry foolishly.

"Dickon, then," said Elissa curtly, expressing by her tone that she did not want to reveal how vulnerable they happened to be at this particular juncture. Though calling the coachman to the parlor was quite unheard of, Merry obeyed without further comment, slipping quickly around their visitor, who watched her with a continuation of his leer, evidently enjoying her discomfiture.

When Elissa was left alone with the stranger, she suddenly wondered if sending Merry out of the room had been wise. He sat up on the edge of the chair, and his look of lust hardened in a frightening way, as if he interpreted her dismissal of her sister as an invitation to him.

And at that moment she realized who he was.

"Mr. Crustall, I believe," she said.

If a grin could be called dangerous, such was the grin that his face presented now. "The very same," he said. "You have heard of me, I see. Just as I have heard of you—of you and your fine bosom and your fine, wide hips. Those hips shall breed some lucky gent a fair troupe of brats someday. And why should that man not be me?"

"You are not wanted in this house, Mr. Crustall," she said, "and I cannot imagine why you have come. If you do not leave of your own accord, you shall be ejected."

"Why, I came to see what must be mine soon enough," he said. "My house—and my girls. My two little girls; though I must say, you are far the finer of the two, and the one I shall sooner take to my bed."

"We shall never be *yours,* Mr. Crustall, and again I cannot imagine how you could imagine that."

"Why, where will you have to go, when your Papa is dead? You must bide on with me. Fear not, Miss 'Lissy; old Nick Crustall will take care of you both—*good* care of you." And he grinned with sickening effect, showing his teeth. Some of them were long and some were broken short or missing; some were stained brown with tobacco and some were stained yellow with neglect.

"I do believe you *are* Old Nick," she said. "Nay, I believe you are Hell itself."

He laughed. "Some say so," he said. "And those that don't say it, think it."

"In any case, Mr. Crustall, I assure you that you will not advance your cause by insulting me or my family."

"It is not a matter of advancing my cause," he said. "No one can stop me from getting my own. No, Missy 'Lissy, I take what I want; and I take what I want when I want it."

"I pity your illusion on that score," she said. "If you have any wisdom at all, you will go from this house before you are thrown out."

"Nay, why should I go? Is Papa John here to throw me out? And indeed, he could not if he wanted to. I am far the stronger of the two of us. I have met Papa John before, you know, at the assizes.—No, it will not be easy work to throw me out, Missy. I doubt if *you* have the strength for it, doughty little dame though you be."

He laughed at his little joke, and then stopped very abruptly and listened. The house was utterly silent. The servants were likely outside or in the back wings. He must have realized this; for now he stood and looked at her with that leering, menacing air.

"I take what I want when I want it," he said again.

She hardly dared think what he intended now, but she was very frightened, and the only thing she could conjure to do was to speak to him, in the hope of distracting and delaying him. So she said: "One must pay a heavy price when one takes things that one wants but ought not have, no matter how much one wants them."

"I find that when Misses are the things that are taken, they do not report such things," he said. "It spoils them so for further use, you see, if others find out. They prefer to hush it up."

And he advanced toward her several steps, each step quicker than the previous.

As it happened, she was standing by a table that held various items common to drawing rooms of the times, and among them was a silver paper knife, an implement used to cut open the pages of books. The edges of its long blade were dull, like a modern letter opener, but—unlike most paper knives of the day—it was as sharp at the tip as a dagger. Though she would have preferred not to given such clear evidence that she was frightened, she seized the book knife and held it at her side, hoping to suggest that any assault upon her would indeed bear a price so heavy as to ensure it would not be worthwhile.

But the knife only provoked him the more. With a sneer he closed the space remaining between them and took hold of the blade, which, being dull, did not hurt him in the least. He twisted it out of her grip easily and flung it aside.

And then he seized her and swung her against the table, where he forced her down on her back; and he sprawled at full length over her, pinning her down with one arm as he clamped a dirty hand over her mouth. With his other hand, he grasped at the skirts of her dress, trying to pull them to her waist.

All this took only one long moment; she hardly had time to feel her own terror and revulsion. But this was as far as he got; for suddenly he gave a high-pitched scream and lurched backward away from her.

Dick Broad had him by the hair; and Dick, twice as strong as Crustall and thoroughly loyal to the Wyatts, had no mercy

on the man. He twisted him and swung him about and literally tore a piece of scalp from his head; and when that gave
way, he bent one of Crustall's arms up behind his back and
used that as a kind of rudder to steer the man out of the
room. All this time Crustall did not stop screaming in that
odd, bitterly aggrieved voice, so high in pitch that, in a bizarre
reversal of the roles of this fracas, it seemed almost the cry of
a outraged woman. There was a loud crack when they passed
through the outer door of the house—Elissa could not see
what happened, but she was certain that Dick had knocked
Crustall's skull on the doorframe as they went through it.

Merry, who had followed Dick back into the room, now
ran to Elissa, uttering choked cries that would have been
screams of her own if she had not been too out of breath to
make them such. She helped Elissa up off the table, groaning in anguish for her, and unable to form any articulate
speech.

"I am quite all right," said Elissa firmly, seeing that firmness was required, and hoping that her own trembling did
not give the lie to her insistence. "Thank God you brought
Dickon in time!"

"Oh, Elissa, are you—? Did he—?" cried Merry now,
once more able to express herself, if brokenly.

"I am quite all right," said Elissa again. "He injured nothing but my dignity, and no one need know about *that*.—Do
you hear? No one need know of this. Dickon and you and
I alone shall know; we shall not tell Papa or anyone else."

"No one?" said Merry; and now finding her power of
speech again, she protested: "But ought we not? He must
be charged, he must be tried, he must be punished for this!"

"No," said Elissa. "It is as he himself told me: no lady
wants to become notorious for having been attacked by a
man. Who will believe he did not carry out his intention? It
is better if no one knows. I shall tell Dickon not to tell anyone—I do believe I may trust him; if only Jim is not here—"

And with this thought she judged it better to leave
Merry and go outdoors at once, straightening her dress and

smoothing her hair as she went. Merry followed her help-lessly, and would have actually clung to her if Elissa had not been too quick for that.

As she strode through the front door she found that Dick had not finished teaching their visitor about the type of hospitality he might expect at Aeons' End in future. He had let go of Crustall now, and the man was on the ground, crawling sideways like a crab in order to keep one eye on Dick, which posture made him the perfect target for the tremendous kicks Dick periodically delivered to his mid-section. His scalp and face were bloody, and his nose and mouth in particular seemed to have received bone-crushing blows. Elissa could not be sure that his arm was not in fact broken, for it dangled oddly beside him as he groveled along, and he did not put his weight on it.

She ran to Dick and seized his arm just as he was about to strike Crustall again. "That is enough, Dickon!" she said.

"God bless you, Miss Elissa," said Dick, "that could *never* be enough! This snake could *never* take enough of a beat-ing!" But he desisted nonetheless.

They stood together as Crustall crept away, moving faster the more he opened the gap between him and Dick; and when he was well out of his tormentor's range, he rose to his feet and, turning about, ran, or rather stumbled, bent over with pain and in evident terror for his life.

"I could kill him!" said Dick then.

"Thank God you did not," said Elissa. "He is not worth the sin of it!" Then she turned to him and took his hand. "Good Dickon," she said, "thank God for you!"

"Did he hurt you, Miss?"

"No, no, not at all! You came just in time."

"He has torn your dress, Miss!"

She looked down at herself and said, "Yes, he has torn my dress—and I shall not feel clean again until I have scrubbed myself for a hour; but he did me no other harm."

"Thank God indeed for that, Miss! There is no doubt he would have if he had not been stopped!"

"Indeed, there is no doubt of that."

"Who *is* the fellow?" said Dick.

"Did you not guess? This is Mr. Crustall, who shall turn us all out when my father dies."

Dick was speechless for a moment with disgust and dismay; then he said, "*This! This* is the man! Hellspawn! Forgive me, Miss, for using strong language—nay, I am sorry to add that to what you have been through.—But *this* is the viper!"

"The very man."

"Hellspawn!" he said again.

"That is what I called him; though I believe I omitted the second syllable.—But Dickon, you must tell no one of this."

"What?" said Dick. "Not tell the master?"

"Especially not Mr. Wyatt."

"But why not, Miss? The man must hang for this!"

"Because I would not have anyone know he ever attempted it. Do you see?"

This thought outraged Dick even more. "Are you saying that someone could—!"

But he broke off as he realized she was right.

"Yes," she said. "The world will see me as dirtied, even though Crustall never had his way."

Dick did not reply immediately to this; his eyes searched hers, and he shook his head in anger at the ways of that world, even as he knew she was right. "I wish I *had* killed him," he said finally.

"No, Dickon; then you would only be caught up and dirtied by him yourself. That is another reason you must tell no one. Do you understand? But if he ever comes after you, claiming you beat him for no cause, then you must tell the full truth, at once, and do not concern yourself for me. I shall tell the truth myself, immediately, if there is ever any trouble to you for what you have done, so you might as well be forthright—if that time ever comes, which I hope it shall not."

"Nay, I doubt it shall," said Dick. "He will not like to admit that he was beaten by a common coachman."

"There is nothing common about *you*, Dickon," she said. "I am sure he has been beaten before, but never by a better man." Then, resuming the matter uppermost in her mind, she went on: "No one else knows, I believe. Jim is not here?"

"Jim left early for his half-day," said Dick. "The others are in the back office and the kitchen garden. I am sure none of them knows, or they would all be here a-gawking at us."

"Yes, that is true."

Elissa now turned to Merry and said, "There, do you see, Merry? Dickon will not tell, and neither shall we. We must be quiet about this as much to protect Dickon as to protect me."

"Of course," said Merry.

"There," said Elissa again with finality. "Come with me into the garden, then.—Dickon, do please go rest." She looked at his hands; there was blood on them. "I hope you have not hurt yourself?" she asked.

"No, Miss," he said almost scornfully. "Why, the man was too soft to hurt me, no matter how hard I might hit him."

"Well, thank God for that, too.—Come, Merry, before we are all seen."

With a final grateful nod of her head to Dick, she turned for the nearest entrance to the garden, and Merry tagged along with her.

"But why the garden?" asked Merry.

"I must find some mud there to dirty myself with," said Elissa. "How else am I to justify calling for a hot bath in the middle of the day?"

"You think of everything!" exclaimed Merry.

"Let us hope that I have," said Elissa.

Then she thought of an additional way to impress her sister with the need for silence. "We would not want our new friends to know of this, would we?" she said.

Merry looked truly disturbed at this thought. "No!" she said.

Elissa was now satisfied that enough had been said on that score; but she was sorry that someone as innocent as her sister should be burdened by such a secret.

When Elissa went to wake Merry on Sunday morning, her sister protested that she did not wish to go to church at all. Elissa could not help sympathizing with her; both sisters were deeply disturbed by what had happened the day before, as people with little knowledge of the world are when the brute reality of violence intrudes upon the security they have taken for granted. But she insisted.

"You are always seeking an excuse to lie a little longer in bed on a Sunday morning," she said. "And this time, more than ever, I shall not listen to you. A little attention to religion will go far to putting yesterday in perspective, and it will remind us both to be grateful for the providence that saved us."

Merry groaned and turned over to hide her face in the pillow.

"Besides," said Elissa in a softer voice, "it is most likely that Mr. Charles Newsome will be there."

This reminder provided a more readily accessible change in perspective, and put an end to all reluctance.

In fact, the Sabbath tradition itself promoted healing. On these days the entire household rose with the constrained buzz of a common purpose—to be at the church on time. Although Miss Merry might try to evade that duty, not a single servant would ever have thought of missing the morning service; it would have been felt by the master, though he was no tyrant in this or in any other respect, as an affront to him personally. That was not the only compulsion they were under: some of the servants, waking up at five o'clock on a cold winter morning, might have flirted with the idea of staying home and risking the astonished but silent displeasure of their master; but at the thought of the slight to Miss Wyatt's piety that their absence would imply, they threw back the covers and flinched forth into the day.

The servants walked to the village, and therefore left earlier than the master's family; but so perfectly was everything coordinated by Elissa and Mrs. Northaker and Mr. Jens that, no matter what the season or the weather, the master's carriage caught up to the flock of servants on the near approach to the church. The manager, Mr. Tempest, as well as the Scottish gardener, Mr. McBean, and his second-in-command, Joe Wiley, nearly always arrived at the same moment with their families from their separate houses.

On this particular day, Elissa found even the journey to the church salutary. For the past year Mr. Wyatt had yielded his place in the carriage to Mrs. Northaker, who was really too elderly to walk that distance, and there was something reassuring to both of his daughters in the presence of this woman who had been a virtual mother to them. And there was Father, too, riding along beside; and up on the box was Dick Broad.

The carriage descended trippingly from Aeons' End, and the views of the little journey, familiar as they were, offered reassurance that all was right in their little world—the fields, the river, the mill dam and its long pond, and the straggling but pretty village of Deepclough itself. The sky was overcast, but not darkly so; Elissa thought of it as a kind of fairy daylight, without oppression by bright sun or heavy cloud.

Thus even the thought of Mr. Crustall was soon rendered powerless.

Prompt though they were on this occasion, the Wyatts found the Newsome cousins already in church. Elissa had had no doubt that Daniel would attend; but she had wondered if Charles might share Merry's customary reluctance to rise early merely to hear a sermon. Evidently he did not, or else his cousin had herded him out of bed as effectively as

Elissa had performed that duty for Merry; or perhaps he had discovered the same interest in attendance that had finally spurred Merry to rise.

On that Sunday the Wyatt sisters suffered the same disappointment as young women have for centuries in such circumstances: the holy service proved a poor time to extend their acquaintance with intriguing young men. Here they were, in their own pew, and there were the Newsomes in the Rowcliffes', and the Rowcliffes and Mr. Wyatt and even the whole aisle were between them; which could have been the English Channel, for all it helped communication between the parties on opposite sides of it. How much more pleasant it would have been, to stand beside the Newsomes, and sing with them, and engage in all those gentle flirtations afforded by the sharing of a hymnbook, such as leaning close together over it, seeking out the proper hymn together, and sending forth a mingled song. Merry missed these opportunities much more than Elissa; but even the latter did at first think of them with some regret.

But it must be admitted that for Elissa there were other things to think of. Incredible though it may seem, those gentlemen in the opposite pew did fade from her mind for that hour, as she set her thoughts on matters beyond the earth, beyond space and time, on a Love that moved both beyond her ken and within her heart. She sang; she prayed; she listened earnestly to the discourse and tried to learn from it. If Merry's eyes and thoughts strayed to that opposite shore where the Newsomes were in exile, hers did not.

But when the service was over, then with a little rush of pleasure, much like the one that awakening daily on this earth can bring, the thought of the Newsomes recurred. Those delicious moments arrived when neighbors emerged into the open air and exchanged greetings, some brief and some more lengthy, before the return to house and home and dinner. In this interval, resourceful young women have never found it difficult to linger strategically and to thus be available to the approach of young men; and this both Elissa and Merry contrived, though separately, while Dick Broad was seeing to the harness of the horses. Charles Newsome found his way to Merry, and Daniel Newsome to Elissa.

Out of the corner of her eye, she saw the man turn and seek her out the moment he was clear of the door. He made a beeline toward her; and that was especially flattering.

And as he came across the lawn, his manservant Mr. Blaickie, whom she recognized though she had seen him only briefly and distantly on Friday, came forward from the roadside on a diagonal, intersecting course, and handed him a book as they passed one another. Indeed, the deliberate nature of their meeting and the exchange of the book had the hallmarks of what today we might call "a pass" in sports. It was clear that Mr. Blaickie had been instructed to bring the book to his master immediately after church; and Elissa was extremely curious to know why.

"Good morning, Miss Wyatt," Daniel began.

"And to you, sir—a pleasant enough morning for those who can appreciate it."

"Indeed it is," he said. "There is a kind of cool glow over everything; it reminds me of certain mornings closer to the coast, in Falmouth and even in Bath.—Do you recall, Miss Wyatt, that as we were parting the other day, I mentioned Mr. William Wilberforce's book to you?"

"Ah," she said. "I do recall, yes."

"Well, as it happens, when I first read the book, I was so impressed by it that I gave my cousin my own copy, with many urgings to read it. It was foolish of me, indeed; he is not so dedicated a reader as I could wish, and though he loves me and would try any book for my sake, he could not make much progress in this one. When he mentioned having brought all his books to Rowantree, I remembered the Wilberforce book, and asked him if he still had it. He admitted he did, and was only too glad to give it back; and so I can offer it to you now, if you think you might find it of interest."

And he held out the volume in his hand. She took it with a warm feeling of pleasure at his thoughtfulness.

"How kind of you!" she said. "I shall indeed read it, and read it through, I promise you."

"Oh, make no promises. Keep it and look into it when you have the opportunity, until I leave Rowantree; and if it does not appeal to you, say so freely, and I shall take away with me both the book and any obligation to read it that might inadvertently be implied."

"It is not an obligation, I assure you. I have long heard of the book and wished to read it. It is kind of you to offer me the opportunity."

He was pleased by her response and stood watching her gladly while she looked into the book as far as the title page, which read:

A

PRACTICAL VIEW

OF THE

PREVAILING RELIGIOUS SYSTEM

OF

PROFESSED CHRISTIANS

IN THE

HIGHER AND MIDDLE CLASSES IN THIS COUNTRY,

CONTRASTED WITH

REAL CHRISTIANITY

"I have always admired the epigraph chosen by the author," said Daniel. It was a passage from Milton; she read it aloud:

How charming is Divine Philosophy!
Not hard and crabbed, as dull Fools suppose,
But musical as is Apollo's lute

> And a perpetual feast of nectar'd sweets,
> Where no crude surfeit reigns.

She looked up at him sharply, unable to suppress a little smile; she sensed a subtle reflection on Mr. Herbert's sesquipedalian sermon. But Daniel was awaiting her reaction with no hint of wry humor about him.

"How true," she said. "Solemn things need not be dull."

Now he smiled, a smile that was so subtle it was all in his eyes and not in his lips; but she saw it, and the little flash of understanding passed between them again: he perfectly agreed with her.

In the next moment they were joined by John Wyatt and Mr. and Mrs. Rowcliffe, and in a minute more by Charles and Merry; and the plan to dine at Aeons' End the next day was confirmed. Elissa had to be content with that; her father was missing his garden and eager to go home.

Another incident occurred, however, when the two families had parted ways to return to their separate carriages—one of those little presages of later events that is not recognized as such at the time. Mr. Herbert intercepted Elissa just a few steps short of the carriage, and catching sight of, or affecting to have just caught sight of, the book she was carrying, he inquired after it.

"It is Wilberforce's *Practical View*," she said.

"Ah," he responded, raising his eyebrows in a show of distaste. "The work of a *lay* theologian."

"But an earnest believer, if what I hear of it is true," said Elissa. "I shall soon find out if that report is correct."

"I can supply you with better reading, Miss Wyatt," said Mr. Herbert. "Butler's *Analogy*, for example."

"And I am sure I would be interested in all such books that you think are not above my training," she replied. "But for now, I shall content myself with this one."

He bowed stiffly; and turning away rather brusquely, he left her.

She found that Mr. Herbert's disdain for the book had exactly the opposite effect from that which he had intended; for as the product of a passionate amateur, Mr. Wilberforce's efforts actually acquired luster in her eyes.

She carried the book home with a pleasure that seemed to her to arise from an eagerness to be reading it and improving herself as soon as possible; but her zeal might have had more to do with her dawning hopes concerning its giver.

The afternoon service on that day was, as was often the case, much more agreeable to Elissa than the morning service. Very few attended, as a general rule; and the greater space thus afforded her thoughts and prayers always seemed to help them rise and expand. Neither John nor Merry could ever be persuaded to come with her, and the servants, too, seemed to melt away into their respective nooks and busy themselves at their respective tasks, in order to avoid seeing the implicit reproach of Miss Wyatt's departure for vespers. And it would only have been implicit, for in truth Elissa regarded it as a minor miracle that the servants attended even the morning service, and she never attempted to compel them to evensong.

Daniel was present, as she had expected he would be, though the Rowcliffes stayed at home, and Charles with them. This time his pew across the aisle seemed much closer to hers; if she let her mind stray into fantasy, she could almost imagine that they stood and sat together. Afterwards she had the pleasure of a smile, a nod, a bow from him, a cheerful mention of seeing her again tomorrow, and all these she took home again very happily, as she had the book.

By reading in every spare minute on Sunday, and in the midst of directing the preparations for the dinner on the following day, Elissa finished a good part of that book before the guests arrived. Something more, therefore, must now be said of it.

William Wilberforce is perhaps best known today (if he is known at all) as the member of Parliament instrumental to the abolition of the slave trade in the colonies of Great Britain. He was also a devout Christian; and since that title has become a synonym among the heathen for evil and close-mindedness, it may surprise some that as a Christian he managed to do anything useful at all. He was, however, a man highly useful to British society, and even to the course of progress (if there is such a thing) in the world at large.

As has been mentioned, the particular book by Wilberforce that Elissa began to read that afternoon was a great bestseller in its day; but like virtually all bestsellers, it soon and inevitably passed from the common mind. It can be purchased still in a weakened form, true, a kind of bowdlerized thing. Its original prose is intense, vivid, and immediate, more like the spoken preachment of an Isaiah than the inky scribbling of an English M.P. But readers in those days actually preferred complex and intelligent prose, and Elissa had been raised on it; so she ate up the writing of Mr. Wilberforce at a furious pace, with nothing short of delight in the challenge it offered to her mind.

The basic purpose of the book was to set out to Christians the unfortunate fact that their beliefs had grown so lukewarm and dilute that they themselves did not in fact deserve the name of Christians at all. Every dodge and excuse that such people make to avoid living by the difficult injunctions of their Master was laid out in devastating review; and Elissa felt the sting. It was, she felt, a book very good for her soul, and very good for anyone who had any pretense of being a Christian at all. After reading it, one must either redouble one's efforts, or else implicitly acknowledge that though one claimed that title, one was not at all what the title proclaimed one to be.

She could see, however, why Charles had not been able to read much of it. (She found a note in the margin on page twelve that said READ TO HERE, and she assumed it was his.) He was only instinctively avoiding correction that he knew would serve no purpose.

She came across a passage that in fact struck her as very instructive with respect to Charles's character. At that point in the text, Wilberforce was demonstrating the error of, as he put it, "exaggerating the merit of certain amiable and useful qualities, and of considering them as of themselves sufficient to compensate for the want of the supreme love and fear of God." On this head he said:

> It would not be difficult to show that the moral worth of these sweet and benevolent tempers, and of these useful lives, is apt to be greatly overrated. The former involuntarily gain upon our affections, and disarm our severer judgments, by their kindly, complying, and apparently disinterested nature; by their prompting men to flatter instead of mortifying our pride, to sympathize either with our joys or our sorrows, to abound in obliging attentions and offices of courtesy; by their obvious tendency to produce and maintain harmony and comfort in social and domestic life. . . .
>
> But where the benevolent qualities are genuine, they often deserve the name rather of amiable instincts, than of moral virtues. In many cases, they imply no mental conflict, no previous discipline: they are apt to evaporate in barren sensibilities, and transitory sympathies and indolent wishes, and unproductive declarations; they possess not that strength and energy of character, which, in contempt of difficulties and dangers, produce alacrity in service, and vigor and perseverance in action. . . . And here it may be observed, that persons thus defective can ill establish the claim which is often preferred on their behalf, that they are free from selfishness; for if we trace such deficiencies to their true source, they will be found to arise chiefly from indisposition to submit to a painful effort, though real goodwill commands that sacrifice,

or from the fear of lessening the regard in which we are held, and the good opinion which is entertained of us.

Yes, here were the cousins in miniature: Charles all sweetness and compliance, but in all likelihood lacking "that strength and energy of character" that resulted in "vigor and perseverance in action"; which by contrast Daniel seemed to possess. The one had been raised as the only son of an eldest son of landed gentry, the other as the son of a son dispossessed by the patrimonial system; the former had grown up soft and almost helpless, the latter active in mind and in all his course of life. No wonder Charles's father had chosen to disinherit the son in favor of the cousin; faced with that choice, it would have been taking parental love to an unjustified extreme if he had not. In the care of the estate there were too many lives at stake to trust it to Charles, amiable though he was (and it struck her now how often, in her very brief acquaintance with that man, the regretful phrase "amiable though he is" had recurred to her mind). The Newsome estate, with its tenants and the great company of servants it doubtless supported, needed and deserved more than "transitory sympathies, indolent wishes, and unproductive declarations" in its support. And there was a danger as well that in his weakness, Charles might be the victim of others who saw a way to drain and exploit his wealth—a common outcome to which Wilberforce, too, seemed to allude when he went on to say that such people are "often drawn in to participate in what is wrong, as well as to connive at it." Indeed, Charles himself had seemed to sense this danger around him in London; and perhaps he had fled from the city in order to escape a particular companion or set of companions who wished to take advantage of him.

Yes, as for Charles's ever being an adherent of the "real Christianity" of the sort Wilberforce commended, Elissa saw no hope of that. Charles could no more have been a truly good Christian than he could have been a priest in the days of old Israel. He could only be loved as he was, and held by those who loved him to as straight a course as they could manage; and left for God to judge, in the hope that a life that was at worst harmless constituted a plea for some kind of leniency. Wilberforce, of course, did his best to dispel this hope; but what else was there?

So much for a sketch of the book. Now to describe that odd meeting of personalities at Monday's dinner.

John Wyatt had of course worked in his garden all day, and his mind was full of that, and his body slightly wearied with it. He would speak of nothing at all if he could not speak of his garden; so he spent most of the dinner listening to the others, as a man who has only slight acquaintance with a foreign language tries as best he can to catch the drift of the conversation of native speakers. But he did contribute immensely in one way: he sat at the head of the table and exuded the quiet and steadying presence of a good host. Perhaps his steadiness was a result of his having had his hands in the earth so much.

Mr. and Mrs. Rowcliffe were the most voluble. Having them to dinner was much like having two excited birds perched on chairbacks opposite one another, chattering and nattering at one and all. They would give all the latest news of their son—of the anticipated happy event—of the likelihood of a visit to him afterward in London, to see the new heir. No one spoiled this prospect by mentioning the possibility that the baby, when it arrived, might be discovered to have been appointed to be a girl; a fact that might have presented itself to their minds when they openly extended their regrets and condolences to Mr. Wyatt (it was a compulsion of theirs) on having lost a son. They cast some aspersions on their daughter-in-law as haughty and reserved, but they allowed she was handsomely formed and a fit rooting pot for a scion. They would speak at great length of the virtues of Charles and, to a far lesser extent, of Daniel; indeed, Elissa thought the ratio of praise in that respect was probably in inverse proportion to what was just. They interrupted each other, and if anyone else attempted to talk, that person as well; Mr. Rowcliffe told stories he had told at every dinner for twenty years and more, and then Mrs. Rowcliffe retold them. They begged Daniel to send them a case of his best wine, and then did not let him speak long enough to agree to do so; they asked Mr. Wyatt his opinion on a dying apricot tree in their orchard, but evinced no understanding when he suggested what they might do to save it; they requested that the Wyatt's cook should send their own cook the receipt for an excellent meat pie, and did not notice when Elissa gently explained that she had arranged for this several years ago. And so forth.

The hubbub generated by the Rowcliffes did not daunt Charles. He at times seemed not to know that his grand-parents were speaking, and often turned to Merry, who sat beside him, and kept up a steady flow of enthusiastic con-versation with her, only occasionally interrupted by demands from Mrs. Rowcliffe to let them know the reasons for the merriment between the young people; which that good lady did not subsequently pause long enough to hear.

This side conversation tended to isolate Charles and Merry from the rest of the table. Elissa saw this as some-what rude, but she could think of no way in which to com-municate her disapproval to Merry, and no reason to hope Charles would suddenly realize his little social fault. She did what any wise hostess would: once she saw that no one else was concerned about the irregularity, she ceased to worry about it herself.

Daniel dealt very graciously with all of this, though to do so must have been tiresome. He responded to the Rowcliffes when they allowed him to; he deftly eased the conversation through its awkward moments; and he avoided the tempta-tion to create a third conversation with Elissa, though he sat near her end of the table. Rather than being miffed by his reticence in that respect, Elissa was relieved at it; for however much she would have enjoyed the conversation for itself, she would have disliked it as being disrespectful of the general table.

The ladies withdrew, but they had not been in the drawing room for more than a few minutes when the gentlemen followed them. This was usually the case on such occasions: Mr. Rowcliffe so soon grew uncomfortable without his twin.

Cards were called for. A table was promptly made up by the Rowcliffes, Merry, and Charles. John Wyatt said he would read, but Elissa knew that meant he would soon be nodding over his book. And this left her virtually alone with Daniel; and more alone because they went at once to the far end of the room, through a double door, and into the adjoining music room, where the pianoforte stood. There, if they spoke in low voices—which they did instinctively—they could not be heard over the avid discussions of trumps and tricks and rules and revokes that went on throughout the card play.

Their conversation began, however, before they even reached the destination toward which they were drifting. And, in its mutual engagement, its earnestness, its seriousness as well as its quiet humor, it was an extraordinary conversation, utterly outside anything Elissa had experienced in her life.

It begin very simply.

"Have you by any chance looked into Wilberforce's book, Miss Wyatt?" asked Daniel.

She said, "I have read nearly the whole of it, sir, with great interest, and I hope with great benefit."

He was deeply pleased by this response, and said so; then asked: "And were there any passages that come to mind, as you look back on it, that you particularly enjoyed?"

"Yes, indeed. I put markers in at several places. But it would be easier to refresh your memory of them by quoting them than by summarizing."

The book was at hand in the music room (not by coincidence, since she had eagerly anticipated this discussion), and she picked it up. She made a gesture toward a seat, but he would not sit down until she had done so herself, in the chair opposite. She then read one of the passages aloud.

> It is another capital excellence of Christianity, that she values moral attainments at a far higher rate than intellectual acquisitions, and proposes to conduct her followers to the heights of virtue rather than of knowledge. On the contrary, most of the false religious systems which have prevailed in the world have proposed to reward the labor of their votary by drawing aside the veil which concealed from the vulgar eye their hidden mysteries, and by introducing him to the knowledge of their deeper and more sacred doctrines. . . . It is part of true wisdom to endeavor to excel there, where we may really attain to excellence. This consideration might be alone sufficient to direct our efforts to the acquisition of virtue rather than of knowledge.

"Yes," he said emphatically when she was finished. "And that is the crux of the whole matter: that we must *acquire* good characters; we are not born with them. I hope you do not mind if I speak frankly, Miss Wyatt, and use my own dear cousin as an example. He has a kind of natural goodness. Indeed, Wilberforce speaks of this kind of thing elsewhere."

She was struck by the fact that his thoughts had gone exactly where hers had already been; but then again, they had probably preceded hers in going there long since. But she only said, "Yes, I recall the passage."

"What I fear for Charles," he went on, "is that natural goodness is like natural beauty; it is not a lasting thing. It has no foundation in the facts of how our lives proceed. The girl who is a beauty today, or the handsome young athlete, will be an ordinary-looking middle-aged lady or gentleman tomorrow; the same is true of those who are naturally good when they are young. I fear that as Charles grows older, his natural goodness will lead him to feel a hollowness in himself, an emptiness at the core of his life. I believe that a moral life, which is the only *good* life, the only possible *happy* life, must be built on a solid ground of understanding and belief; we cannot just drift along half-asleep without knowing *why* we ought to be good. As Wilberforce says, many other religions in the world mumble about secret wisdom that is to be gained when we practice their precepts; but when we pursue that wisdom, it turns out to be mere mumbo-jumbo, delusion, smoke-and-mirrors. Christianity, by contrast, *has* no secret wisdom. It is not about arcane practices. It is about becoming good, about becoming constantly more good. When Proverbs talks about the importance of wisdom, we quickly discover it is not some convoluted nonsense from the Kabbalah that is intended; we see that the only use of wisdom is to show us *how to be good*. Just as the only true freedom is the freedom to do what is right, the only true wisdom is the knowledge of how to be good. No more and no less! Every other kind of wisdom is a sham and a seduction. Those who describe God as Love and Wisdom can mean no other thing—that loving others teaches us that we *must* be good, and wisdom teaches us how to go about it. All we have in this world is our love for God and our kindness toward one another. That is really all we have left when the fog of worldly fortune and success blows away in the morning sun. It is wonderfully simple to understand, and yet, given our propensities, prodigiously difficult to do. Charles, God bless him, understands none of this. With respect to goodness, he is like a beauty of seventeen before her mirror, thinking her looks will never fade. How will his goodness last when it is challenged?"

No one had ever spoken to her like this before, so seriously, at such length, and with such intimate emphasis. She felt she could sit and listen to this kind of talk all day, every day, for the rest of her life; she felt bathed in the earnest sweetness of it. It was only the desire to provoke more from him that led her to speak herself.

"Yes," she said. "I have often feared the same thing for Merry, though I dare say I have never understood the problem as clearly as you have stated it. Heaven knows, I have tried to teach her how to run a household, and have had little enough success in that; she will need an excellent and honest housekeeper to make up for what she lacks. But what I have feared far more for her is that she will not have the resources to deal with vicissitude in general. She will marry—someone; that seems certain, for she is such a lively, fluttering thing that she attracts suitors as a butterfly draws a flock of hungry swallows. Then, certainly, once she is married, she will find that her husband will have his moods, for every man does. How will she understand them, cope with them? She will have babies, for every woman does; and those children will have their illnesses and setbacks, for every child does. What strength has she to mother them?

"Perhaps I underestimate her. Perhaps she will rise to the challenge of being spouse and parent as she has risen to the challenge of being cheerful—I do not know. But I confess myself concerned. Happiness in life is not just a matter of being jolly—of being *merry*. My sister faults me for smiling more seldom than she does; and though I do not see this as a matter for competition with anyone else on earth, yet I dare say that in some deeper way, I am happier than she is."

"I believe you are," said Daniel. "And I share your concern about how our respective relations will meet adversity."

"It seems to me," said Elissa, slowly voicing the thought as it slowly came to her, "that they will only be gradually weakened by hard times. They will not grow in strength because of adversity, as people often do in trials. They will never really meet the difficulties of life; they will have to avoid them, have to pretend those difficulties simply do not exist."

Evidently his projections on this point had not gone so far. "Do you think so?" he said.

She made a gesture of uncertainty for answer.

They sat for a moment in a somewhat somber silence. Then she said, "And you, sir? Do you not believe you have a natural goodness? For it seems to me you do, though you have an acquired goodness as well."

He laughed softly, shaking his head. "Oh, no," he said. "I was never the lamb that Charles is. I was as naughty a boy as most, though I do think I was not an unkind lad, or a bully, or anything of that sort. But I did my fair share of stealing apples, and fishing where I ought not, and getting into the leftover wine, and even breaking a window or two for the sheer wanton pleasure of watching it shatter. These were things that horrified Charles as a boy, or at the least made him very uncomfortable. No, I had to commit my petty wrongs in order to begin to learn what right was."

It was her turn to laugh, and laughing she said: "I can scarcely believe you ever did such a naughty thing as to break a window on purpose."

"It is true," he said.

"But you had good impulses as well, as a boy—I am sure it is so."

"Yes, I admit I did. I looked around me at the injustices of the world, and I thought about them, and I resolved to mend them."

"And have you?"

He smiled. "I confess there are a few injustices that still beg for my attention," he said. Then he grew more serious and went on: "But that is another point I should like to pick up from Wilberforce. He says, in that passage you have just read, that it is part of true wisdom to endeavor to excel where we may achieve excellence. And that means not just in the *nature* of our sphere, but in the *scope* of it."

"What do you mean?"

"I think we start out—or perhaps I should say that I started out—hoping to mend the ills of the world in some significant way, on some large scale. But I have come to see that very few are really blessed with that opportunity. I have read books written by simple and quiet men that would change the world, if only everyone in the world would read them. But that is not to happen. At most those books are read by a small circle, perhaps five people, perhaps a hundred, or a few hundred over time. And those readers are indeed deeply affected, and their lives are changed. But that is an end of the little ripple that that one kindly thinker has sent forth into the world; that is the limit, the periphery of his sphere, or his aura; and I should say *her* sphere or *her* aura as well, for women work for good and succeed in reaching as wide a sphere as men. The difficulty lies in being content with what you *can* do, do you see? That is what God gave you to do, and no more. If you are tied to the shore by a rope of circumstance, you cannot blame yourself for not swimming across the sea. That does not mean you ought not to try; but I do believe real wisdom lies in becoming what we are and doing what we can within our sphere, however large or small that sphere may turn out to be. I have seen men grow bitter because the larger world had no time to take interest in their works; but it is as the writer of Hebrews says: *Be not forgetful to entertain strangers: for thereby some have entertained angels unawares.* We must *entertain* our lives, our possibilities; we must welcome them and live fully within them, because at the end of them we shall look back and see that in that process we were entertaining goodness, angelic goodness, a goodness of achievement, an achievement of goodness. And however large or small it may seem in the eyes of others, we will see it then for what it is: large enough to please God. It is truly a sin to want more than that! It is a sin for us to complain and be bitter because we have not accomplished more. God knows how little we are and how little we can truly do—how spoiled that little is by our self-love and our weakness. And yet, *because* God loves us, that little shall be enough. *Well done, thou good and faithful servant; thou hast been faithful over few and small things—* that is enough. We must know what we have been given to use, and recognize that it has been given us for a purpose; otherwise there is no purpose anywhere in the universe. It as if you, Miss Wyatt, were to fret your life away wishing you had been born with your sister's auburn hair, or if she were to fret hers away wishing for your jet. You have understood that you are beautiful with what God gave you, and you are happy within that.

"Let me tell you a little parable, as it were. I remember when I was a very little boy, perhaps three or so—I should say first that my father always wished and expected me to take up the family trade, and would tell me that someday I should excel him in the business; and once, after he had sat me on his knee and given me such a talk, he asked me, 'Now, my boy, what is it that you want to be when you grow up?'—expecting me to answer, "I shall be the first importer of wines in all Britain.' But I was too young to perceive what response he was expecting; and I answered, with great earnestness, 'I should like to be a pony on Exmoor!' For I had encountered some ponies of that sort on a trip we made to Falmouth; they were wandering in the mist on the moor, and their life seemed the most wonderful that could be had. My father had the goodness to laugh out loud, realizing that he was beforehand in expecting me to follow in his footsteps. And I recall the moment, perhaps a few months later, when I was old enough to realize that I would never *become* a pony, since I was a human being, and was to become a man. I dare say I was silly enough to be disappointed!

"I might take another example in you, Miss Wyatt. Clearly you have not repined—I hope!—because you were not born a pony, or six feet tall, or green-eyed, or a princess of England. You have accepted your particular place in the universe and are doing the most and the best you can with it. We are each and all of us particular, specific beings—for some reason we are never content in being so, and so we never truly realize ourselves. Talk about mysteries! We are mysteries to ourselves. And to grasp that mystery is wisdom; and it is wisdom, simple wisdom of that sort, that makes us happy, in the end."

"I do indeed know what you mean," she said. "But I have to add how very ungrateful I would have to be if I *were* unhappy, for I have had everything I could possibly want—except, I suppose, a mother."

"Well," he said, smiling ruefully, "do not underestimate the power of human ingratitude and blindness. There is many a young woman such as yourself in England, fortunate in ways too many to count, who frets under the weight of her particular circumstances. And as for the young men of that sort, I know all too many examples. I am convinced, you see, that God owes us nothing—He has given us everything already: he has given us our being in this universe. How much more can we demand of him? The universe is a difficult place, true, and being alive in it is not necessarily all pleasant. But that is as it must be. What we have cannot be any other way and still be physical existence. But I do believe you understand that."

"Yes, oh, yes, absolutely. I know exactly what you mean. Of course . . . I would not be fully honest if I did not admit that sometimes I wish certain matters in this world were proceeding differently."

"Of course," he said. "That is very natural. Just as I mourned my not being a pony! And I am not saying that we should merely rest easy in the character with which we were born; as I have said, we should *acquire* a better self, through the grace of God, for the sake of others even if not for ourselves. That is the labor we are given on earth—to strive, ever to strive, to accept no seductive whisperings telling us to rest easy with the character we have. No person but one was ever perfect. We must strive to be kinder every day. *In caritate perfectio mundi:* 'In kindness lies the perfection of the world.'—But tell me, what are these matters that you wish were proceeding differently?"

"Oh," she said, wondering at once whether she could really tell him what she meant; and being immediately surprised to find that she could, she went on: "If I were to give you examples, I would mention my father's loneliness, or Merry's sweet silliness, or my own . . . well, I do sometimes wonder *when* I shall marry and begin to achieve what I wish for in my life."

"And these things darken your world," he said, in a tone of deep sympathy.

"Yes. The darkness comes in seasons: it never goes away, it only returns in its cycle. But pray, do not give my worries too much weight, Mr. Newsome. Even in the most difficult of those times, it always happened that a kind of light breaks into my darkness, or perhaps I should say that it breaks *out* from the center of things, the heart of things, where I imagine God lives. God is love, as you would say, and I do believe it, because I have felt it; but I also believe that God is joy. *Joy* is at the heart of everything—do you know what I mean? Do you not feel it too?"

"Indeed I do," he said, in that quiet, grave way he had, which she was already beginning to know and love; and he looked at her with that expression she could never have described. It was not a smile, but the deeper foundation of a smile.

And now when she saw that expression on his face, she stirred restlessly in her chair: her body moved, without her conscious will, as if calling to his. Though it was a vague movement, so vague that no one else could have understood it, it seemed he understood it subconsciously when he saw it, and it awoke some deep response in him, so that he must turn his face away; and a little color came into his cheeks as a betrayer of his subconscious confusion. And a matching confusion came to her, and she too looked away.

He spoke again now. It seemed to be with the purpose of easing them out of their mutual consternation, and she was grateful to him for that.

"I understand you well about how difficult it is to wait," he said. "I know you will say that my own waiting cannot compare to yours—what with the busyness of my years at university, and then at work in the family concern. And it is true that I keep active, but . . . I am haunted by a sense that what I do is only prologue for something greater."

"And what is that something greater?" she asked. "Do you aspire to Parliament or some office in the government?"

"Oh, no. What I think of as a greater thing is something much more domestic than that; as I said, something more within my personal sphere."

"Ah," she said, realizing suddenly that he was talking about having a family—that in fact he was talking about the very goal she herself had had in mind. She could not think of any time before now that a man had spoken in these terms to her.

"Does that surprise you?" he asked.

"Well, it is unusual to hear a man speak in such a way."

"Of family, do you mean?"

"Yes. Usually a man speaks of marriage as . . . forgive me if I put it this way, but as if his purpose in marriage was only to licitly acquire the company of a woman. He does not speak about the rest—which, as I have said, inevitably follows: I mean a family."

"That is very true," he said. "Generally a man's thinking on the subject goes no further than that purpose you mention, or at least at first. But I think that is the way God planned it; otherwise men would shy away from marriage and live like wild animals."

"So that is why God has given beauty to women, is it?" she said in a teasing tone. "To trap the men into the propagation of humankind?"

"If that is so, it was certainly wise of Him," said Daniel wryly.

"But you claim you do not share this general fault of your sex?" she asked.

"I do so claim," he said.

"And so you are, like me, waiting with interest till your family shall . . . come about?"

"I am."

Her teasing had gone as far as she dared take it. It was, again, tremendously exciting to her to speak in this way with him. Since she said nothing now, he took his turn.

"I think," he said, "that we do not realize how important, how vital our times of waiting are. *Let patience have her perfect work, that ye may be patient and entire, wanting nothing.* It is in the waiting that we become equipped for what we must do—and because of our waiting we appreciate what we do when we are at last able to do it. Otherwise we might unwisely cast the opportunity aside when it finally comes.

"And every act of waiting is a little model of life as a whole. We wait for, we look forward to, eternity. We do not necessarily have what we want here. Far from it, indeed. It is curious fact, which most people do not observe, that Jesus really cared nothing for our lives here. Of course, he wished us to feed the hungry, tend the sick, visit those in prison, and the like; but he made it clear that he would not lift a finger to change the injustices we see about us. When his followers asked him to rid them of the Roman oppressors and of the puppet king the Romans had set over them, he said he had not come for that, that his kingdom was not of this world. He was concerned only that the individual should look into himself or herself, see the errors there, and seek to mend them—to repent. And of course, we never perfectly can; instead we have to rely on grace and forgiveness."

"But you spoke just a moment ago of wanting to end certain injustices in this world."

"Yes, those within my sphere; they are my way of feeding the hungry, and so forth. But the point I mean to make is that my first obligation is to God, and to living rightly in His eyes. Without that, nothing else I do has any meaning."

"Yes, I see what you are saying."

"All this talk of eternal life is, of course, repugnant to our age," he went on. "We are all determined that this life is the only one, and we mean to make the most of it, and not be put off by promises of the next. And it *is* good to make the most of this life; but not in the way most people intend. Often the best we can do here is to be patient."

"'They also serve who only stand and wait,'" she said.

"Yes, precisely. As Milton says in that same sonnet, 'Who best bear His mild yoke, They serve Him best'—by whom he means those who love God and, looking within, work to make themselves more like His image."

"Well," she said, "I do honor your wise words; but how difficult it is, all the same, when we are waiting to begin what we hope is to be our appointed task."

He smiled. "Then there is that other promise," he said.

"What is that?"

"*They that wait upon the Lord shall renew their strength; they shall mount up with wings as eagles; they shall run, and not be weary; and they shall walk, and not faint.*"

"Yes, that is a lovely thought," she agreed.

At that point the card playing came to an intermission; and the card players, noticing Elissa and Daniel deep in conversation, called to them with the instinctive jealousy that superficial people have of the earnest, and asked for music, asked for a song, though none of them was particularly ready for or interested in one. John, too, stirring out of his doze, called fondly for a song. And Elissa and Daniel, jolted out of their quiet rapport into a consciousness of their intimacy, rose and went somewhat hurriedly to the piano and began looking through the music. They settled very quickly, almost at random, on a song from one of her books, which she played and they both sang.

His voice was well-trained—indeed, she thought, better trained than hers, though there was nothing amiss with her natural tone—and it was very pleasing. She could not help glancing at him as he sang; and she found that in that act he revealed a boyish artlessness that was not all that different from his cousin's. Singing, after all, is a very revealing act, if you know how to listen to it: you may hear all the uncertainty about herself that a young singer intends to cover with bravado, or hear all the conceit of himself that an older singer thinks is rendered invisible by his affectation of modesty. It is like watching a poet read his own verse. Performance, like wine, strips us bare.

What Elissa heard on that first occasion, and on every occasion thereafter when they sang together, was that Daniel Newsome was a good man, neither uncertain nor conceited nor a fool; that he was honest, candid, and true. And the way their voices joined was very pleasing to her; and it occurred to her that the sweetness of that mutual sound had as its cause that she, too, valued honesty, candor, truth.

But this was not all she heard in his voice. Anyone, any thoughtful bystander, might have heard those things and understood them. She heard something no one else could have heard.

She heard the future. She heard her life. She heard his voice beside her as her head lay on the pillows beside his; his voice in her ear, in the dim and in the dark; and also in the bright day, rallying her to live always in the light. She heard his voice in the wind of all her future days; and indeed, she was never to hear the actual wind again without hearing his voice hidden in it, distant and haunting.

These things she heard moving through her heart as all mysteries move through the mind, untouched, ungraspable, but leaving a resonance there, the ringing ricochet of deep longing and desire.

And as luck (was it luck?) would have it, they had hastily seized upon this ancient song:

> Dear, if you change, I'll never choose again.
> Sweet, if you shrink, I'll never think of love.
> Fair, if you fail, I'll judge all beauty vain.
> Wise, if too weak, mo'e wits I'll never prove.
>> Dear, sweet, fair, wise—change, shrink, nor be not weak:
>> And, on my faith, my faith shall never break.

> Earth with her flowers shall sooner heaven adorn,
> Heaven her bright stars through earth's dim globe shall move,
> Fire heat shall lose, and frosts of flame be born,
> Air made to shine as black as hell shall prove:
>> Earth, heaven, fire, air—the world transform'd shall
>>   view,
>> Ere I prove false to faith, or strange to you.

The meaning of these words—*Before I prove false to my faith, or be estranged from you, the world shall turn inside out and upside down*—made the heat rise in her face as she sang them. They seemed a kind of declaration the two of them were making to one another.

Indeed, she was never to forget those words, or that first evening when she and Daniel sang them together, she at the keyboard, and he beside her, turning the page; and at times the taste of those words in her memory would be bitter.

Bitter indeed; bitter when in fact, in the time to come, they two were estranged.

✢ 4 ✣

A Mutual Opening of Minds

[Amor vere conjugialis] ascendit a primo suo calore progressive sursum versus animas nisu ad conjunctiones ibi . . . per aperitiones mentium jugi interiores.

From its first passion, love that is truly worthy of marriage soars progressively higher in lovers, straining to be united in their souls. And this it accomplishes by opening their minds ever more intimately to one another.

—Swedenborg

Mr. Daniel Newsome did not leave Deepclough the next day, though it had been vaguely projected that he would. Elissa did not know—or told herself she did not know—whether this was a surprise to her or not. The day after the dinner party, in fact, he and Charles arrived at Aeons' End at precisely eleven in the morning, which custom held as the appropriate time for visiting to begin. It was as if they were determined not to waste a minute.

Elissa and Merry met them at the door, and by common consent they all went forth into the garden. Daniel had not seen it yet, and Charles was eager to begin to work in it. Elissa led the way, utterly conscious of Daniel as he walked behind her, and secretly very proud of showing him the beauty of the place, knowing that he would associate it with her as the brainchild of her father. She took the liberty of turning from time to time to view his reactions, and they were extremely satisfying: he walked along in a kind of spell of wonder and enjoyment, smiling at the beauty around him; and smiling, when he saw he was observed, at her . . .

But to describe that day would be to describe many days of that summer, and to describe the summer would be to include that day. So let the summary stand for the summer; and let the summary be cast in the various themes of the companionship that Elissa Wyatt and Daniel Newsome formed together.

*I*dyll—to use the familiar term, such that summer was. Elissa often thought it so, and she once said something to that effect to Daniel; and he told her how the word originally meant a little picture, and came to be applied to a short poetic sketch of some incident between lovers or friends, often in that *faux*-rustic setting of the pastoral; and from there came to mean a time of peace and contentment.

During those months, Daniel came and went at irregular intervals; but he was present for at least a few days of every week. He had matters to see to on his own estate, and sometimes business to attend to in London or Falmouth. He never promised to come back, and no such promise was ever demanded of him; but he always returned; and after Elissa had missed his company for several days, the morning would come when he would reappear with Charles as the latter returned to Aeons' End.

For Charles did not leave the valley so much as once. His nights were given over to the company of his grandparents at Rowantree, but all his days were spent—or gained, depending on one's point of view—at Aeons' End. After all, our days are gold; we win them, second by second, and bank them; and if it proves in the end that the vault has a hole at the back and some thief has stolen them all away, suddenly we find the possession of them makes no difference, since it was the winning of them that matters.

Charles helped John Wyatt in the garden. And he truly did help. He worked with spade and trowel and rake and hoe; he carried water, he shifted rock, he weeded, he pruned, he trimmed; his hands took on that same ungentlemanly roughness as the hands of his host, since no more than John did he have the patience to wear gloves for long. He put himself totally under the direction of his teacher, and by being naturally docile and biddable he increased more and more in John's estimation and love. The gardening men, too, Mr. McBean and Joe Wiley, though they at first thought him an annoying dilettante, were won over by his unquenchable enthusiasm for hard work and his newly discovered passion for plants and soil; and if they thought him a little touched in the head, for wanting to work hard when he did not have to, at the same time they respected him for the earnestness of his labor.

The cause of Charles's enthusiasm was, of course, liable to some suspicion in the beginning; for if he was in the garden, then so was Merry. Certainly the gentleman must be coming for that company, rather than for the opportunity to dirty his hands and strain his sinews and cover himself with sweat. But it soon became clear that even if Merry had not been there, Charles would still have come, to become a gardener.

In fact, without the gardening, the attachment between Charles and Merry might have moved along faster than it did and come to a point that required open commitment. But as it was, they could enjoy one another's company without the pressure of any further purpose than garden work. She did not labor as hard as he did, being more lightly built; but she was as eager and active as ever. They both, over the course of that summer, took on more of the beauty of figure that fitness lends to its possessors, the narrower waist, deeper chest, and wider shoulders. On Charles's form, this hardness was conspicuous; on Merry's, it was more subtle, as when a master draftsman darkens the lines of a shape he has previously sketched in only roughly.

During these days, if Daniel was not there, Elissa was very busy, either running the household or managing the informal charitable operations of the parish, which was the duty of women in the upper class in those times. The latter activity in particular required a great deal of traveling about, sometimes in a small gig driven by Jim Riggins, but often on foot, for some of the poorest homes were on slopes of the valley so steep no cart could climb them; so she was often away, and was often weary when she returned.

For this reason Merry and John, and indeed the household servants as well, combined against her on those days when she was at home and begged her to go into the garden and rest. She knew not where this instinct of theirs came from, but it was an old tradition with them, and it was her custom to meet it sometimes with a laughing refusal and sometimes with gracious acquiescence. In a previous summer John Wyatt had had a chair made for her, of light canework; it was kept in a shed with the tools and brought out by Joe Wiley, who tried to spoil her by finding exquisite locations for it, either in sun or shade depending on which she preferred on any given day, and not far from where the gardening work was ongoing, and giving out on a view of the valley and its far side. This chair was a kind of divan with a backrest, and she could put her feet up and lean back in it; and truly then she did relax, and enjoy the comfort and beauty of her surroundings.

On those days when Daniel was in Deepclough, another chair was brought out for him as well, and placed near hers. It was of a more common variety than her divan, but he did not seem to mind that. Typically his chair faced the side of hers, so that she sat or actually lay at right angles to his line of vision; and this arrangement gave her a sense of being under his care and attention that, though strange at first and unfamiliar to her, became deeply enjoyable.

And what did they do? They talked. They talked nearly without ceasing. They spoke in that earnest and intimate fashion they had discovered in their first conversations together, on deep topics, beautiful topics; and their conversation together became greater than the thoughts of either of them individually. In their talk they built a lofty castle—more than a fortress, rather an entire world—of thoughts, ideas, values shared. When they conversed he never interrupted her; and this was new to her, because she had known only the lectures of her teachers, and the butterfly conversation of Merry or of the Rowcliffes, and her father's somewhat distracted musings, and Mr. Herbert's attempts to guide her thoughts where he believed they ought to go. She felt respected; she felt her opinion was genuinely wanted and seriously considered when she voiced it. And yet often, too, they were wonderfully playful in their conversation, teasing one another and laughing together and heaping up jokes as a bulwark against the outer world. Merry commented more than once that she had never known Elissa to be such a merry creature; but at these remarks Elissa only smiled and thought how little the serious are known to the superficially cheerful, who cannot believe a reserved person can harbor even a spark of liveliness. Merry would quiz her to discover the cause of that delicious mutual murmur of laughter that came drifting through the intervening shrubbery of the garden while the others were at work, and she seemed not to believe Elissa when the latter only shook her head and opened her eyes wide and confessed not to remember particulars.

And in truth Elissa did not; for the seriousness and the playfulness she shared with Daniel Newsome were woven together without seam, without beginning or ending. Indeed, where they two had left off their conversation one day, they resumed on the next as though the twelve-hour lapse between was nothing; as if—somehow—they themselves did not exist unless in one another's company.

At times he read to her. He might bring a journal or newspaper from London, or a book of new or old poetry. He read from Milton often, and sometimes from the Bible; they read a play together, taking different parts; and sometimes—and these were the intervals she loved best—he would simply put down the reading and continue in the same vein himself, giving her his own thoughts on the subjects that the book or poem had evoked in his mind, and soliciting hers.

They often sang as well. They would stand side by side and lean their heads together over the pages as he held them, and sing the old poetry that had come down from Good Queen Bess's time; and their voices would drift up over the garden, until those delving would pause and listen, as if to a fairy music. On days of rain they sat at the pianoforte and sang together until they almost began to be hoarse.

In midsummer, after one of his brief absences, he returned to the house with a lute in hand—he had never before made mention of being able to play one, and his suddenly appearing with it made her wonder how many other abilities he possessed still unknown to her. And if this one ability was typical, those other hidden abilities must also be remarkable; for to her ears, he was a virtuoso. She loved to lie back in her chair and listen as he played and sang, or sometimes simply spoke softly over the music. And it was sweet to be coaxed into singing while he played, there, under the sky, in the deep privacy of the garden—with her father and Merry still within earshot, so all was proper.

And sometimes, though not often, they made neither speech nor song nor music. They were silent. How could Elissa ever have explained *that* to Merry? For in those interludes in their conversations, she felt a deep intellectual and spiritual intimacy and oneness with Daniel that required no words, one that in fact would have been lessened by words.

The only way she could describe the feeling was to compare it to the sense of wonder one has in the presence of nature, of awe at a mist-shot dawn or of solemnity on viewing a sunset of blood and fire.

She had, too, a sense of *recognizing* him, as a sheep is said to recognize its shepherd, in some way unknown to human knowing. It was as if she had been with this man, who in some real sense was so new and unknown to her, somewhere before, but not on earth or in heaven, not in this age or in the past or in the future, but in some timeless otherwhere. She liked to tell herself that she and he had long been companions together as ideas in the mind of God (though Mr. Herbert would have been horrified at that idea for any number of reasons).

All this, this unspoken acknowledgement of their spiritual bond, led to something else that she could not describe or articulate even to herself. She only called it *the bliss*. It would come over her suddenly, without warning: a mood of blessed and even transcendent well-being. In these moments, she knew with vivid clarity that the universe had a purpose, and she a purpose within it. As it was the work of the stars to shine in the darkness, in their immense distances and countless numbers, so it was her work to shine here in her little circumstances, in this little school called England, in this little time on earth. And of Daniel Newsome, this man so new and yet so familiar to her, she knew it was his work to shine beside her, so that the rays of their shining would join together, intimately, so that their individual warmth and love and light could not be discerned separately, so that they would be one common if little and finite shining in the infinite shining of God.

And strangely, in comparison to these moments of bliss, she scorned anything that others called *happiness*. That construction was a pathetic thing, a desperate idea patched together from bits of transient gladness and moments of good cheer; her *bliss* was all-powerful, and even if it was felt only for short times before it was interrupted, it was anchored deep down in the twin realities of this world, love and suffering. The only thing she thought might be like her bliss—though infinitely greater than her own understanding—was the infinite suffering that the Human God had taken on Himself on the Cross, in a love for all humankind that surpassed anything humans could themselves experience. In that moment on the Tree, all human suffering had been extinguished in love and had been transmuted into joy; and some crumb, some mote or mite of that surpassing *bliss* had slipped through time and fallen upon her, as she lay on the divan, had fallen on her womb and heart and mind, till she was become one whole and entire embodied perfection of being.

Yes, it was there that the seeming-unlikely bedrock of her bliss lay, in love and suffering.

She felt her love coming upon her all that summer, as waves advance over the horizon from the unseeable center of the sea, buffeting shore and strand inexorably, growing in size from small to great.

As for the suffering, it was still distant and unfelt; but it was hiding where it always does: in the heart of love.

Ideality. Did she know him? Or did she only think she knew him? At first the question worried her the more she felt that she did know him. It was like a religious question; and one day she asked him, "Do you think that we can really know anyone?" It was as if she were saying, *I believe; help thou mine unbelief.*

He did not think the question odd; he never thought anything she said or asked was odd.

"I do," he said. "I believe we can know people better than they know themselves."

"Truly?" she asked in surprise.

"Yes, truly."

"But how can that be? Everyone has thoughts and feelings, and a history of actions, that can never be known to us."

"And is that what makes someone known to us, truly known to us, do you think? Knowing all their thoughts and feelings and acts?"

"Well, what else is knowing someone, but that?"

He thought for a moment, and then he said, "That is *part* of knowing someone, certainly. But of course we can never know all the things that a person will think and feel and do in the future; they may be very different things than he or she does now; and yet we say we know the individual despite our ignorance on that point."

She said: "And if their actions do become so very different, and do deviate from what we expect of them, ought we not then conclude that we do not know them after all? If they violate our expectations, I mean, the expectations that are built on what we think we do know about them."

He replied, "That is what I mean about how we know them better than they know themselves. It may be—I am not saying it is necessarily so or always so—that when some man, for example, violates our expectations in that way, he is losing his way and betraying his own better self."

"Sometimes, yes," she agreed. "But more often, I think, it is rather that we have imposed our ideal of him over his real self, so as to conceal who he truly is. And when he apparently violates that ideal, he is finally showing his true self."

"Ah, I think not. That is exactly the point I am trying to make. Some will tell you that we construct an image of another in our minds and cling to it, and it always disappoints, because it is a false image. But I think often—and especially when we love someone deeply—what we really are doing, in our love, is to see that person as God sees him or her. You could call it an ideal, but in fact it is the *reality* of that person's being; it is what he or she could aspire to, and be, if some weakness of material life did not block the way."

"But what about all the complaining of our poets when they are thwarted by those they love? Does it not seem to you, when you read them, that they have done exactly that—fallen in love with a false image? They have foolishly chosen to love someone who cannot return their love."

"I would say that they do love something real in that person. But I admit that because of the brokenness of our material world, often the beloved cannot live up to the reality. It is the broken beloved who is false to the ideal, to the true image held by the lover, rather than the other way round—the lover having a false idea of the beloved, I mean. Of course, this is not universally true. People do delude themselves and pursue a spouse who genuinely wants nothing to do with them; and certainly there is a great deal of that behind the complaining of the poets. But if . . ."

He hesitated a moment, and she encouraged him by saying, "Yes?"

He plunged on.

"If a person like you," he said, "able in mind and judgment, and a good observer of your fellow humans, were to conceive an image of another, and that person should fail to live up to that image, or ideal, or reality, or whatever we call it, then I think we could be certain that it was you who were in possession of the reality of what that person was, just as God knows it, though of course not as completely as God knows each of us."

"But if," she said, "this person who disappoints me is the one to blame for not living up to his own ideal self, what consolation would that be to me?"

He looked surprised at the question. "A great consolation," he said emphatically. "A great consolation indeed. It means that the goodness and truth you see in him is real; it means that if circumstances were different, if he were in some way stronger, and not broken and bent by this world, he could indeed be what you know him to be ideally. And that is a great consolation. Knowing that you have seen the truth is far better than believing you have been deceived."

She was silent a moment, thinking of this; and then, on an impulse she could not control, she said, "And do you think you know me?"

"I do believe so," he said.

"Me, I mean, with all my sins?"

He smiled. "Your many sins," he said.

"Because I do have them."

"Of course you do. We all do. But that need not leave us paralyzed in guilt. Our awareness of our sins should only urge us to grow in spirit, to move closer to goodness and perfection. People today would just as soon not even *use* the word 'sin.' It offends them. They would rather speak of peccadilloes or failings or faults or flaws or errors or defects of character, or anything that removes the problem from the realm of our relationship with God. But our failings with respect to one another *are* necessarily problems we have in our relationship with God. It is important to realize that, because that is the best reason we can ever have to outgrow them."

She said, "The wonderful thing about our faith, I think, is that it teaches one to look inward. And there—what a spectacle of pettiness and error and selfishness! When I stop to take that view—how absurd I am! All my little pride in myself is exposed as the delusion of a mote of dust that believes itself a world entire. But from that crushing sense of absurdity I take refuge in the knowledge that God allowed me to *be,* to come into being; that God sees my absurdity, better by far than I see the absurdity of others, and loves me despite it, loves me as I stumble onward in my life. And this mind, this body, these hands, these legs and feet, all of me—absurd as they are, they are what I am. And then I rise above my sense of foolishness and absurdity, because *this,* this, is what God created and what God loves. I know of no other philosophy that can so raise one above the absurdity of being a lone and temporary being in the universe."

"*Brava,*" he said then. "Amen, Miss Wyatt."

For a moment he smiled again; and then he said, "And do you think you know me?"

"I do," she said softly.

"I think you do too," he said.

It was peerless moment in which they were perfect spiritual peers; and the *bliss* fell over her again, and she was silent.

Spirit. They spoke often of things beyond the material world. If anyone else had discoursed to her of such matters—Mr. Herbert, for example—she would have said the topic was religion. But this, the subject they addressed in those summer days, was not religion in its rigid form—dead, mere words and phrases without meaning. Often they spoke together of life itself, and it was only belatedly, looking back on what they had said, that she realized they had been talking of the spirit and the transcendent.

He had a way of speaking of Christian practice as the ancient philosophers spoke of the Good, and yet he also spoke of Christian belief as those ancients spoke of how to live. The two aspects of Christianity, belief and practice, were united in him. Most of his acquaintance, she suspected, never thought of him as a Christian; instead they thought of him as a genuinely good man who helped them when no others would and who understood them when no others could. Even Charles seemed to be only dimly aware that his cousin was driven by a living faith as much as by a personal love. If Elissa had confronted Charles and asked him if Daniel was a Christian, he would have said, after a pause for reflection, that of course he *was,* but not like one of those . . . those *Christians.*

There was only one occasion when Daniel spoke of Christianity per se. They had been speaking of their times—full of war and unrest and political farce, as all times are—when she said something about how she wished the national religion might mitigate the madness of the day. "The only truly national religion," he had replied, "the only real religion most people have, is a longing to prove themselves right and to follow their own will. The notion that something is greater than they are and more right than they can possibly be is repugnant and baffling to them; the idea that they can obey that greater thing rather than wallowing along helplessly through life, driven by the demon of their own will, is one they have never seriously considered. They are a law unto themselves, and they live in misery in consequence, never realizing why."

"But there are a few who do not," she said, thinking specifically of Daniel himself, and of people like Wilberforce. "And if they could only be allowed to lead us, they might do much good. Why cannot the sheep elect the shepherds instead of the wolves?"

"That is the way the world must be," he said simply. "Otherwise it would not be the world, it would be heaven. Besides, the opposition Christians face in this world is the very thing that makes their struggle to love Christ noble and beautiful—that makes their lives in fact Christlike. Even their own blundering attempts to accept and love Christ are beautiful in their way. To draw on the ancient metaphor used by Christ himself, theirs is like the action of a beloved bride who, through some mistake, spurns her future husband, and must make her way back to him through pain and sorrow. Who would not pity such a bride, and rejoice all the more when she succeeds, despite her suffering?"

"Indeed," she said, with a little smile. And to herself she added: *But I dearly hope we are speaking in metaphor only.*

This metaphor was typical of the creative way Daniel drew upon that deep and often puzzling book, the Bible. But when she learned how he read it, she was not surprised; for he had borrowed a Catholic practice and followed the *lectio divina,* the method of reading, meditating, praying, and contemplating on individual and almost isolated passages of the Bible, assimilating and weaving them into his own life and thought. This method he taught to her, or at least in its rudiments, and by so doing he forever changed her encounter with the chief source of her religion.

Still, and most unexpectedly and oddly, he refused to make overmuch of Bible reading. Jesus, he said, did not ask his disciples to write a book; instead he sent them out in the world to be an example. "Christians," said Daniel, "could learn more about *being* Christians by *acting like* Christians than they usually do by reading Scripture. Indeed, I think Christians rely too much on the reading of Scripture. They think that if they read it, that is enough. But it is not enough to read it; you must *do* it. You will learn more about God by doing as Jesus commands, and helping someone, than you will ever learn from reading the Bible. He himself said, *Search the scriptures; for in them ye think ye have eternal life,* and went on to point out that for all that perusing of Scripture, people do not do what is truly needful: *Ye will not come to me, that ye might have life.*"

And next she said: "But do you not think that the Christian religion is very difficult, or at least our living of it in the face of the world? Jesus calls it a light burden, but how can it be so?"

"It is the world that is a heavy burden," he said. "Our existence does not feel light until we have given up the world—until we have fully come to prefer God's love to our love for the world, and to prefer it to that love we so crave but can never gain, the world's love for us. As long as we have failed to sever the chain that binds us to that one last millstone we long to carry with us to heaven, there is nothing heavier than the life we live. But when that bond is broken at last—we soar."

"But who knows that in these latter days? Who believes it?"

"In our hearts, we all know it and believe it, even the godless."

"My dear sir, how can that be so? Atheists, too, believe this? Do you really think so?"

"The true atheists have proven themselves such by committing suicide; the living who boast that name are only hypocrites. They are only in vain flight from something beautiful and good. They have set up for themselves, or adopted from the scanty understanding of others, a picture of God as a brute; and no wonder they flee. But they are like a man fleeing from a monster that exists only in his own mind.

"Indeed, I have sometimes thought that an atheist is like a man who has caught his arm in a trap and attempts to cut it off in order to escape. But when he has finished this grisly operation, he discovers that he has somehow cut off the wrong arm! And then he finds himself without options—for the limb that is caught fast cannot free itself. Likewise the man who has shunned the love of God cannot understand the purpose, either of his own life, or of the universe entire. He has cut off and discarded, in the most painful possible manner, his own freedom to know and love God. And yet he still goes on living as if he did believe in the purpose he claims does not exist. That is why I say that in their hearts, all humankind believe that there is a reason to live; and that reason is that there is a purpose to the universe, and a place for us in it; a purpose and a place that only God could have given."

She did not want to mar this sweet rhetoric with a single further question or rejoinder. Instead she was silent and thought: *If this is all heresy, and he a heretic, may I burn beside him!*

*K*nowledge. One of the ways in which she bloomed that summer was in the great reawakening in her of her desire to know new things.

And not simply to know them; but to *think* new thoughts every day, not to be stuck in the stale round of things thought before, but to encounter and strive to understand new ideas, to see matters from a constantly fresh perspective. Daniel told her once, in one of their conversations, that he believed the angels in heaven lived that way: that the Beatific Vision was not some continuous, static display of the glory of God, but a constant, ever-fresh and ever-deepening *thinking about* that glory, a deep seeing of it from constantly new perspectives, of being drawn deeper and deeper into the beauty and complexity of both the Creation and the Uncreate, of enjoying the ultimate joy of wonder.

And she caught a glimpse of this very sort of wonder that summer, though in things sometimes seemingly very small and trivial. But Daniel said that the more you looked at anything, no matter how small, the more you saw; and he quoted to her that poem now so familiar and even trite, but then still virtually unknown:

> To see a World in a Grain of Sand,
> And a Heaven in a Wild Flower,
> Hold Infinity in the palm of your hand,
> And Eternity in an hour.

One of these grains of sand whirled into her ken from a conversation that her father and Charles had one hot, bright mid-day. Mr. Jens and Mabel Dean had carried a luncheon into the garden, and John Wyatt and Merry and Charles had ceased work, along with Mr. McBean and Joe Wiley; and the little party of garden workers had come together at the spot where the two garden enjoyers were sitting in the shade, so that all could eat together. It was, by the standards of polite society of that time, an odd meal. Mr. McBean and Joe Wiley sat within earshot, though at a slight distance and perched on some stones, and ate food they had brought, which consisted of a coarse bread, cheese, cold meat, and an early apple or two, doubtless quite tart. The gentlefolk sat in chairs, ate off china plates, and drank from cut glass; but their meal consisted of cheese, meat, and only slightly less coarse bread than that which Mr. McBean and Joe were eating, and some fruit dried in the past season and plumped up on this day. The servants drank ale provided by Mr. Wyatt; the gentles all drank water from the spring on the hill, though wine was on offer. But this was the sort of relatively simple meal Mr. Wyatt had come to prefer for his gardening days, and no one would have thought to complain about it. In fact, the few guests who tasted those garden lunches thought them delicious, and much better than more complicated fare.

The conversation Elissa had been having with Daniel of course lapsed; and instead Charles and Mr. Wyatt continued their own, with occasional requests to Mr. McBean for his corroboration of this fact or that. At one point Charles began talking about planting more hydrangeas in a large bed dedicated exclusively to that plant. "I should like to see a thousand hydrangeas there!" he enthused. "What a lovely sight that would be! A sea of ivory blossoms!"

Mr. McBean could not refrain from a low chuckle when he heard this. Though he had come to like Charles—and who would not?—he looked upon him as a kind of genial madman.

"You see Mr. McBean does not approve of your plan for a thousand new plants," said John Wyatt.

"Well, of course, a thousand is too many—I admit there is not enough room. But can we not put more plants in the bed?"

Mr. Wyatt nodded at Mr. McBean to invite him to tell Charles why this was not a good idea.

"The more plants, Mr. Charles," said Mr. McBean, "the fewer blooms ye'll have."

"How can that be so?"

"For every plant ye add to that bed, ye'll rob each of the rest of some of the earth and food that produce the blooms. So by adding more plants, ye shall have fewer flowers."

"Oh! I suppose so," said Charles. "I never thought of that. But surely there must be a way to put a few more into the bed—there must be a way of knowing how many we can put in before it becomes *too* many. Surely we can add *some*."

"Aye, but how many? Can ye puzzle that out? How many before we start having fewer blooms?"

Charles opened his eyes wide in bafflement and shook his head, and Mr. McBean, too, shook his head. "There is no way to predict that," said the gardener. "We could only try it and see."

Daniel laughed softly, but said nothing.

"What is it?" Elissa asked him.

"Oh, nothing. I was just thinking that it sounds like a kind of problem they used to put to us in mathematics. So-and-so many plants, so-and-so many blossoms, and so forth; and find the maximum."

"Well?" she said teasingly. "Can you solve it?"

He smiled at her and thought for a moment. The others were silent, curious, waiting to see what he would say.

"Can you take a guess, Mr. McBean," he asked then, "how many fewer blooms a plant will have if we add one plant to the bed?"

Mr. McBean scratched his chin. "Oh, I don't know," he said.

"I should think . . . perhaps five," said Mr. Wyatt.

"Aye," said Mr. McBean. "That's as good a guess as any."

"And how many blooms do you think each plant has?"

"Oh," said Mr. McBean expansively, "I should say about four hundred. Them's muckle big 'drangeas."

This seemed wildly improbable to Elissa—Mr. McBean was known to be somewhat of a stretcher of the truth—but as her father did not contradict him, she thought that certainly she should not take it upon herself to do so.

"And how many plants are in the bed now?" asked Daniel.

Mr. McBean and Mr. Wyatt consulted and agreed the number was about fifty.

Daniel gestured toward Elissa's drawing pad and pencil, looking at her for permission, and she made a gesture that said, "Of course, take it."

He put the pencil to a blank sheet of paper, and as he went on speaking he made a few notes on it. "Now," he said, "let us say that the number of new plants is designated by x. If we have fifty plants already, then the number of total plants after we have done our gardening will be fifty *and* x. If there are now four hundred blooms per plant—that is what you said, is it not, Mr. McBean?—and there will be five fewer blooms for every plant we add to the bed, the total number of blooms per bush when we are through will be four hundred less five times x. So the total number of blooms for the new bed will be those two quantities multiplied together: fifty and x, multiplied by four hundred less five times x."

Elissa leaned over the side of her chair to look at what Daniel had written, and saw this:

$$(50 + x)\,(400 - 5x)$$

"But *that*," he went on, is nothing other than—"

And he wrote the following:

$$= 20000 - 250x + 400x - 5x^2$$
$$= 20000 + 150x - 5x^2$$

And then, without explanation, he wrote:

$$f' = 150 - 10x$$
$$0 = 150 - 10x$$
$$x = 15$$

"It would seem, Mr. Wyatt," he said, "that you could safely add fifteen hydrangea plants. You would then have—let me see—" and here he scratched the pencil on the pad for a moment— "21,125 blooms instead of twenty thousand." He did a couple of further calculations and then said: "You could add any number of plants up to thirty and still have an increase of some sort; but after that, you would actually start having fewer blooms in the bed. And fifteen plants remains your maximum."

Charles and Merry looked confused, Mr. Wyatt looked doubtful, and Mr. McBean looked positively scornful. "Beggin' yer pardon, sir," Mr. McBean said, "but I dinna think ye can garden with a pencil."

Daniel grinned and glanced at Elissa.

"A prophet goes without honor in his own house," she said. "Never mind the unbelievers, Mr. Newsome. Will you show me how you did that?"

"Of course," he said.

And then he began to show her, in very brief form, how he had found his answer. He started with the idea of finding a derivative, and that led him into graphing the problem. They completely forgot the others; they forgot to finish their meal; the servants cleared away, the gardening party went back to work and left them alone; the sun moved onward in the sky, clouds came and went, a breeze rattled from time to time in the privet near them, and they neither saw nor heard anything but what they two were doing. It was almost as if they were making love.

She had of course heard of Newton, and heard the word *calculus,* but she had never heard of a derivative. When Daniel drew the problem of the hydrangea bushes as a parabola on a Cartesian graph and showed her how the high point of the curve was at fifteen on the ordinate, she was appalled that she had never been taught any such glorious thing. She stared in wonder at the paper as he proceeded, and listened to him as though he were an oracle. It was as if there were a light shining from his mind, reflecting off the drawing paper, and shining into hers; as if truth itself in the abstract were resonating in his chest and overflowing through his voice into her hearing.

She knew not how long they sat thus, only that her limbs seemed stiff when they had finished; but her mind was entranced, astonished, pleased, enchanted. She sat back and looked at him with an admiration she could not possibly have disguised.

"I hope I have not bored you," he said with a little concern in his tone.

"Bored me! Nothing of the kind! You have fascinated me, sir. If this is a token of the wonders with which your head is stored—why, it must be ready to burst!"

He laughed. "Nothing of the kind," he said.

"How I wish I knew all you know!"

"How I wish I could give it to you in the twinkling of an eye—in the twinkling of one of your own eyes, Miss Wyatt; for they are sparkling with interest at this moment as I daresay I have never seen them sparkle before. But how much better still, if we did not take that moment to exchange what little I know, but this entire day, if this day could stretch on for a year and a day, and each day of that year could be a day and year in itself; or better still, for eternity. What could be sweeter than this, this glorious summer day; and two minds alike, in company with one another, enjoying and rejoicing in the wonders of knowledge that God has created and humankind has discovered?"

"Amen, Mr. Newsome," she said fervently, "Amen."

The *bliss* came over her again, and they were silent for a minute.

"Well, you know," she said then, with a smile, "I can perform a few parlor tricks with numbers—not up to your calculus or your Cartesian pictures, but enough to impress the ignorant."

"Well, by all means," he said, "do impress me!"

"For example," she said, "I can find the cubic root of a number up to nine digits in length, as long as the root is exact and does not drift off into fractions."

"Ah, but that is just a good exercise of trial and error on paper," he said.

"In my head, I mean—I do not need to resort to your *paper.*"

He laughed at her mock scorn; but then he said, "That is no mere trick; I should imagine it is rather difficult."

"Try me," she said. "Pick a number."

"Oh, but I believe you if you say so."

"No, no, sir, you will not be sweet and polite and *not* put me to the test for fear I shall make a fool of myself. I insist upon proving my claim. Pick a number, Mr. Newsome."

Still he seemed to evade actually testing her. "But who taught you this?" he said.

"When I was at school in Gloucester, the headmistress had a nephew who came down from Cambridge to visit her. He used to sit with us at tea—"

Daniel smiled. "I am sure he did," he said. "And I am sure that his visits were very frequent in the time Miss Wyatt was at school, and that he was very thirsty every afternoon as well."

She laughed off the implication. "He was quite a good mathematician. Indeed, I think he knew nothing else but mathematics. And so he taught me a few tricks."

"To retain your interest in him, I suppose," said Daniel.

She laughed, delighted at the humorous pretense of jealousy in his tone.

"Very well," he said. "Let me give you such a number." He calculated a cube from an integer, covering his work with one hand, as if he thought she would cheat—which made her laugh again; and then he said, "Your number is 638,277,381." Though she did not ask him to, he tore off a scrap of paper with the number on it and handed it to her.

She sat back in the seat and stared at the scrap. "The root is a number of three digits," she said. "The first of the three digits—the *hundreds* digit—is eight, because 638 is between the cubes of eight and nine."

"And you have memorized the cubic numbers up to—?"

"Up to nine, sir."

"Oh; I thought perhaps you had memorized them all."

She giggled.

"The last digit, the *ones* digit," she went on, "is one, because your number itself ends in one."

"And that is a rule?"

"It is, sir."

He laughed as if appalled; it was a wonderful, playful laugh; it made her grin. "And I suppose you make up all these rules as you go along?" he said.

"No, not at all. They are part of the mysteries of mathematics."

"So you have eight for the first digit and one for the last. But what is in between them?"

"That is trickier," she said. "For that, I must add up all the digits in the odd positions in your number. Let's see, that would be . . . *twenty-five*. Then I must subtract from that the sum of the digits in the even places, which is . . . *twenty*. That leaves five. Now, by the secret knowledge that was given me, I know that if the remainder is five, I must subtract three from the sum of the other digits in the root, eight and one. That gives me nine less three, or six. So the cube root of your number is 861."

He threw back his head and laughed aloud, delighted and pleased and astonished all at once. Then he said, "Wonderful!"

"That is correct, is it not?"

"Indeed it is! Indeed it is! Wonderful!"

She was enormously pleased that she had entertained him, though she still felt that her little trick paled in comparison with what he had shown her. They sat in silence for a minute looking at one another, smiling, smiling; and again the *bliss* came over her.

He suddenly said, "Do you know—" Then he grew silent, looking at her.

"What is it?" she asked.

"Oh, it is only that when I talk with you, I have a little dream."

A shiver of pleasure ran through her.

"And what is your dream, Mr. Newsome?"

"I dream that someday every woman will be offered the chance to be educated."

"Do you really? I must say I have never really thought of that. Do you think it could ever happen?"

"Well, why not?"

"Well, it has never happened before in the history of the world, has it?"

"Ah, but that means nothing. I think God wanted women to know everything that men know. And when that day comes—what a change we shall have in the world!"

"Indeed, it is difficult to imagine."

"I know; it is difficult. But not impossible. Think! Twice the number of brains at work on our problems! What shall we not accomplish!"

"But women have so much to do as it is. Would you not be placing an extra burden on them?"

"What, to have a mind alive with knowledge? Would that make them any less excellent as mothers or wives or whatever it is they do? I do not think so. And it would give them something to do if they did not want to be wives or mothers, or could not be. I think it would make them better at whatever they do—certainly happier. My mother, you know, was a highly intelligent woman, very well read, in addition to being an excellent musician."

"I can believe that she was so, since I know her son."

"Everything she learned only made her happier. There must be some way to give women all the learning they want, without detracting from their other excellences in the process."

"You are a visionary, Mr. Newsome."

"Indeed, you make me one, Miss Wyatt. I have never had this thought until this very day."

"What, because of my little trick?"

"No, because of your delight at learning, always learning more."

"Perhaps that is something *you* give me, Mr. Newsome."

"Would that I could take credit for it! But no, Miss Wyatt; I think it is something God gave you. And who knows how many other women there are in the world to whom he also gave it?"

"Yes," she said. "Who knows? Maybe all of them."

And he smiled.

But she said to herself inwardly, with a little inward laugh, *Oh, but do not talk about* other *women, Mr. Newsome. Talk only of* me, *and tell me only how wonderful* I *am!*

*W*orld; meaning the world not in the profane sense, but in its best sense, Creation.

Daniel showed her the wideness of the planet and the cosmos. She felt her mind open and expand as he spoke; she told him that in his descriptions of things he had seen, he put her on his back and flew to faraway places with her, like the roc of Arab legend. He freely gave her his own eyes to see; and because they were the eyes of his mind and memory, her vision through them was clear and bright.

One place he showed her was Madeira.

"It is a very small island," he said. "I doubt it is a third the size of Gloucestershire. It is very steep and rugged. There is not even a proper harbor, just a roadstead at Funchal, though for most of the year that is well sheltered, because the winds blow predominantly from the northeast, and the town is on the southwestern side. Perhaps 'town' is too big a word for it; it is almost like a scattering of houses at the foot of a mountain; that is what you see first when your ship casts anchor. But that would not do Funchal justice: it *is* charming. It has whitewashed houses and walls, tile roofs, church towers, winding streets.

"The ancients called Madeira one of the Islands of the Blest, and for good reason. The climate is like heaven—it is always cool, never too hot, as are the West Indies. You are always comfortable there with no more than a light coat at most, though in the winter you sometimes see snow, distantly, on the heights of the mountains. The soil is wonderfully fertile; I have been told that the place used to be covered in forests, but now it is planted in tropical fruits and sugar cane and of course grapes. But the vineyards are not what you might picture—not like those of France, rolling endlessly over hillsides and plains. Madeira is like some Alpine mountain that was snatched up by a sorcerer from its true home and cast down in the ocean; the highest top of it stands up above the waters by quite a mile in height. It is all jagged, and full of ravines and of valleys not unlike your Deepclough, though rockier for the most part. But the industry of the people over the centuries has terraced much of it, and so the vineyards are little ribbons of land clinging to the sides of the steeps. In the center is a plateau that I loved the moment I saw it; it is like Dartmoor, bare and deserted. On the northern coast there are great cliffs fronting the sea, and they make the island a fortress on that side.

"The Newsome land came into my family on my mother's side as part of what the Portuguese call a *morgada,* an entail. It is a strip of fertile soil at the base of cliffs on the southern shore; it can only be reached from the sea. It is a magical place—lonely, full of sky. At your back is the cliff, with a waterfall falling in stages down twelve hundred feet of vertical stone; before you is the endless plain of the deeps, constantly moving and heaving. There is danger in its isolation, of course; it was once, long ago, sacked by pirates. The house had no name for a long time, but the people called it *a bela casa solitária,* 'the beautiful, lonely house,' and now the English too call it *Casa Solitária.*"

"*Casa Solitária,*" she repeated, captured by the image of it. "Lonely House. How sad and strange, and yet beautiful too."

"Indeed, it is," he said. "And I think the most beautiful places in the world have that lonely, sorrowful grandeur about them that strikes us through and through. It haunts us so because the grandeur is larger than we are, whether as individuals or as humankind in total. In being humbled by that grandeur, we become closer to God. It is our arrogance and self-centered assurance that throws up the barrier between us and the Divine, and such places shatter the barrier."

"I know what you mean; I have felt that humbling."

"I am sure you have," he said.

"And you feel it often there, in Madeira?"

"I do. Not, of course, when I am in the toils of business with other men, managing or bargaining with them, or in society there. But when I climb those steep, rocky heights, and look out over the sea, I would have to be numb not to feel it. I know you would understand and feel the same awe I do if you could look out from those heights."

He ceased speaking for a moment; and then he added, in a low coda that seemed as if it had been spoken aloud only by mistake: "I would love to take you there."

There was a longer silence between them then as she thought of this, of their seeing that place together; and the *bliss* came over her.

Then he went on. "And we, the Newsomes," he said, "grow the finest crop of the finest grapes on the island, what the Portuguese call *malvasia,* but the English call Malmsey. Such a wine it makes! Sweet, but endlessly rich and deep; truly a wine as sweet as a kiss. I will freely tell you that most of the wine that Madeira makes today is debased and coarse.

It is mixed together from lesser grapes, then overheated in hothouses they call *estufas,* and it is no better than cheap wine you might find anywhere; but the Malmsey is not so, and it is known to be such not only in England but in all the world."

"But has not the war cut into your trade?" she asked.

"You would not believe it, but the war has doubled our profits, merely by doubling the price of wine. The wines of France are now out of reach of the English, and Madeira is producing more than ever—fifteen thousand pipes a year, twice as much as in my father's time."

"And a pipe is how much?"

"It is just over a hundred gallons. So the Madeira wine trade has reached over a million and a half gallons *per annum.*"

This seemed a staggering quantity to her, especially given the small size of the place.

"And is the entire Madeiran trade in the hands of the English?" she asked.

"Society there is an oddity. There are perhaps sixty or seventy thousand Portuguese, and a few hundred of the English; and yet we are of vast importance to the trade of the place, so that the Portuguese must contend with us, though in truth they might more happily be rid of us. My family has a little house in Funchal in addition to the *Casa Solitária,* and that is where we stay in the winter months especially, when the wind blows up from the south and it is difficult and even dangerous to land at our own property. We English visit amongst ourselves for the most part, as you may imagine; but we do have good friends among the inhabitants of the island—there are many admirable people there. At the moment, the King's troops have occupied the place, to keep the French from taking it, and there is considerable friction between the governor and our generals; which makes us all uneasy, I am sorry to say."

He smiled then. "So we shall have to postpone our visit until the war is over," he said.

And until we are married, she thought.

"Very well," she said aloud. "But I shall consider that a promise and look forward to it."

They were silent again, thinking of it.

*B*ody. Now and for the first time in her life, Elissa came fully into the knowledge that her body was a divine gift. And what a wonderful thing it was, in its warmth and livingness and beauty and moodiness and breath, even in its hunger, thirst, its need for sleep, its appetite for exercise as well as comfort.

It was not despised by God nor to be despised by her. God had made it for her to enjoy, so long as she did so in the knowledge of the One to whom it ultimately belonged, the Giver, and so long as in that knowledge she kept it holy.

She felt its holy power when she saw the power it had over Daniel. God had meant it to have that power, and she rejoiced when she saw its effect.

One day he returned unexpectedly in mid-afternoon after an absence of some five days. She had been out for a walk to a particularly distant and lonely cottage and came back to the house to hear that he was already in the garden. She went directly to him, and found him with the others.

In the evening of that day, Merry cornered her before they went to bed and tried to tease her about that moment. "You looked so windblown and fresh with the air of the wold," she said. "And the pinkness in your cheeks, and your breathlessness—I could not tell if they were because of your walk or your excitement at seeing him again; and if *I* could not tell, I am sure he was asking himself the same question. Dear, I have *never* seen you so beautiful! And you had a little certain knowing *something* in your walk, I dare say, Elissa: you *knew* the effect you were having on him."

"Not at all!" protested Elissa, but with a laugh that gave the lie to her denial.

"You looked . . . I do not know how to describe it," Merry went on. "So . . . *wifely*, dear, as if you . . . *knew* everything, as if you were certain of him."

"Well, I am *not*," said Elissa.

"Well, you soon *shall be*, if you continue like *that*," said Merry.

And Elissa chased her out of the room.

But it was true: she did know her effect on him. Even when she sat in her wicker chair, she had to be careful to keep her legs covered right down to the tops of her shoes; but even that was a token effort, and made little difference, because she could clearly see that he was distracted by her body, from her feet to the hair bound up on her head. His interest in her body thrilled her. And she thought, with a wisdom beyond her years, that to be desirable is another of God's great gifts and a great joy to obtain from Him. (If you are old, you will remember how, when you were young, you thought that gift would never be withdrawn; if you are young, you will only smile and not believe it.)

There were times that she became someone she had never been; or rather, times when she became an Elissa who had been waiting to steal forth from her hiding, but had never done so. She blossomed in his company, feeling like a woman and a grown woman as never before. She flirted with him, in a feminine way, as she had never flirted before, giggling and laughing in a soft voice, and she could see that he was ravished by her mere femininity as much as he was enthralled by her mere humanity.

And she—as if her body had become a great shout of reply and response to his—she felt the same way about him. She doted on his masculinity. All other men seemed paltry and (though she would not have used this word) sexless beside him. She lay awake in bed at night and thought of him—his shoulders, arms, torso, hands; his height, the *cut* of his figure; the way he moved as he walked toward her, the way he leaned forward in his chair, speaking to her, watching her; his smile, so often wonderfully subtle, but all the more forceful for that; the resonance of his laughter and of his voice, in speaking or singing, especially when it became soft, when it became *only for her.* When she thought of him in this way later, as she lay in bed in twilight or in the dark of night, she had the most delicious sensations, such as she had never had before; for she was still quite innocent about her body's potential for pleasure, and sensed it only as one feels a carving in deep relief through a thick woolen cloth, not sure what it depicts, but certain that it must be beautiful. She would drift along in a warm, delectable half-dream, until sleep took her away; and sometimes her dreams continued as had her vague fantasies, and she could not tell the difference.

Indeed, there was a day when in his presence an even more wonderful thing happened to her, a merging not of fantasies and dreams but of reality and dreams. She was weary, but in a most pleasant way, and he seemed to see that she was, and he did not speak to her or press her to speak. Instead she lay back in her chair, her eyes half-closed, as a sweet, warm sun played over her through the leaves of a little poplar, the light shifting as the tree branches were moved by the occasional swelling of the breeze. He played his lute; and as she drifted into dreams and out again, the music followed her, like a kind of warm breeze in itself. She was aware of him constantly, and aware that he was aware of her; that from time to time he looked at her and took pleasure from that looking; and she felt very safe beneath his gaze, and willingly gave herself to be looked at, because there was a gentleness in his looking, as there was gentleness in everything he did in her presence. She could feel almost palpably how her womanhood made him gentle. Without her, he would have been always rough and ragged, whatever his outward manner; but she woke in him a protectiveness that prevented him from ever harming her or even conceiving of harm to her.

And at the very point when she might have fallen completely into sleep and missed this moment, he began to sing. It was one of the songs from the books of old Elizabethan airs that they had sung together several times; and thus it ran:

> Rest, sweet nymph, let golden sleep
> Charm thy star-bright eyes,
> Whiles my lute the watch doth keep
> With pleasing sympathies.
>   Lulla lullaby, lulla lullaby,
> Sleep sweetly, sleep sweetly,
> Let nothing affright thee,
>   In calm contentment lie.

It was magical—was she truly awake, or did she dream as well, dream while awake? And if so, did that not mean that one could have all those wonders of which one dreamt, if one could continually find, as it seemed she had at this moment, the open gate between sleeping and waking, through which the angel-dreams came and went from heaven on slippered feet, bringing that calm contentment of which Daniel sang, and yet bringing also the excitement that thrummed in her veins, piquant as the plucking of the lute, echoing sibilantly with the murmur of Daniel's voice?

The *bliss* rushed through her body.

And she thought to herself, *If only this moment could go on and on forever . . .*

And so where did this summer tend? Where—for so she had to wonder from time to time—where would it take them, leave them?

As for Elissa: Somewhere in those first days of knowing Daniel, the belief that he was to be her husband had overpowered every reservation and caution. She barely felt her earlier checks upon her feelings as they loosened, barely knew that they fell away forever. She felt only how *right* it was to be with him. God *intended* her to love Daniel, and him to love her in return; and against the decree of providence nothing could avail in any case, so she cast herself into its flow. It was a right thing in the same sense of rightness as the apostle used when he spoke of a person becoming right in the eyes of God, becoming justified. Her love for this man justified her—made *her* right and righteous, confirmed the purpose of her existence in her obedience to divine order and divine law. Indeed, their love for one another was a further proof (though she needed none) of the working of God's providence. It could not possibly fail.

It was significant that she and Merry, who had shared everything in their lives to that time, spoke less and less of the Newsome cousins as possible husbands as the summer went on. Partly this was, perhaps, because each secretly feared that by discussing their odd situation, they would prevent the outcome for which they both hoped. And partly it was because the summer rushed by them; they were very busy. Surely tomorrow would bring on the resolution that was in the offing. The cousins must speak with one another, they must share their plans; and so when a proposal came for one sister, a proposal would come for the other.

Or the other sister would know for a certainty then that no proposal was to come; and that would be dreadful for both of them.

As for Daniel: On him she made no demand to clarify or make verbally explicit what he felt for her. But why did she not? She would ask herself that question later. Part of the answer, perhaps, was that she could feel her power over him. She never doubted her power, on those summer days when they spoke, sang, read, or simply sat together, close to one another, in the heart of the green labyrinth that was her father's garden. Her power over him was the mirror of his power over her; and when a man and a woman each have that power of evoking and receiving love in the other, the danger is that their love may become self-caused and lose its connection with its deeper Cause.

Though there was no proposal between them, their conversation was so wide-ranging as to make the subject of marriage impossible to forever avoid. And yet even at those times when they spoke of marriage, they did not speak of it as occurring with one another. They spoke only of marriage in the abstract, or if of a particular marriage, only that which might possibly occur between Charles and Merry, though that topic they touched upon only skirtingly and fleetingly, as if they were under the same spell that made the subject taboo between Merry and Elissa, as if invoking it directly would jeopardize not only all connection between her sister and his cousin, but their own connection with one another.

The last such generalizing conversation occurred in late July. The setting was the same: they sat by a little rill of water, now dried almost to temporary extinction. By now the heat of the summer Cotswolds lay heavy on the land, and on them, so that they barely moved against it, like fugitives in shadow who cease to move in order to avoid being seen; it was as if by not moving they could evade the weight of the heat. Only their voices moved, as well as their eyes, as they looked into one another's faces, as if they drank relief there from the atmosphere that oppressed them.

They had been talking about miracles, and why in the estimate of the world they did not appear in this latter day. "They would be, I think, a form of compulsion," said Daniel.

"How so?" she asked.

"If Jesus were to appear to unbelievers, would they not be compelled to believe?"

"I dare say not," she said. "Most people today would find reasons to doubt still, as people did in Jesus' own time; and indeed, the world seems to be determined on the constant creation of more and more reasons that would allow them to doubt their own eyes in that case."

"True," he said. "But it is too bad for the rest of us that we do not have signs and miracles."

"Why would we need them? What purpose would they serve?"

"There are many things that we do in life on the basis of our best hopes that we would probably do with more of a will if we had absolute certainty about them."

"Do you mean in our daily lives, or our business arrangements?"

"No, nothing so petty. In more important matters. Say, for example, Christ were to appear to me and direct me to my proper spouse. Would not the certainty of such a vision give my wooing of her that much more zest?"

She was amused by his example. "Against that," she said, "I would argue that in fact we *can* know to a certainty which person ought to be our spouse. It occurs by an everyday kind of miracle, very much the product of grace; and that is that by doing what is right, we see what it is right to do."

She saw that he did not quite understand her.

"I mean, sir," she explained, "you are a Christian; you ought to marry a spouse who espouses the doing of good."

"Of course," he said, catching on.

"And so *that* should give you certainty. Your proper spouse may, on that ground, be obvious to you when she appears."

"Indeed," he said.

"And as a practical matter," she added wryly, "how many ladies do you know who, merely by their goodness, tempt you to marry them? Is it so very many, then, that you are in doubt about which to choose?"

He laughed. "No," he said.

"If you find even one," she said, "it is a miracle."

"Indeed," he said again, "God would not spare Sodom for less than ten good men, and in the end they could not be found. I do not expect to find more than one good woman, or at least one who is marriageable and approves me; but then again, one is all I need." In the last part of this comment, his tone was more serious, and their eyes met, and then she had to look away, as a little wave of the *bliss* ran through her from head to toe.

Then, to cover her own distraction, she went on: "Finding the right spouse is an *ordinary* miracle, or at least an *everyday* miracle, but I suppose it feels much like those miracles that occurred so long ago."

"I do believe it is a similar thing," he agreed. "But the wise of the world tell us, you know, that it is a mistake to look for some great epiphany in the presence of a potential spouse, or to wait until we have fallen madly in love with someone before we marry."

"Many of the *worldly* wise were bachelors, I believe," said Elissa, with that playful archness that always made Daniel laugh.

Which he now did; but then went on to protest: "Ah, but there is wisdom in what they say. Steele, you know, says something like, 'Do not first love, then consider. First consider, then love.' And there are other old writers who say similar things. One named Gataker, as I recall; he said, "It is not evil to marry, but good to be wary." And a old preacher named Henry Smith said, 'First he must choose his love, and then he must love his choice.'"

"I see you are primed with quotations. Does that mean you hold to this point of view?"

"Well, I do, I suppose. Or at least I would say that one should be careful not to marry someone whom, in the long run, one cannot love. One should indeed marry someone whom one can love more and more as time passes, even if one feels only liking and respect at first."

"And so if you fell in love, you would distrust that feeling?"

"I suppose I would, somewhat. I would school myself to look for good and durable qualities in the lady, and hope my affection did not blind me to faults that would make our life together difficult."

"It all sounds very cold-blooded.—And suppose we reverse the question: Do you think that you really could separate yourself from a woman you loved, merely on the basis of a few faults?"

"I would hope that whether I loved her at once or not, I would not fail to consider her as a wife merely because of a few petty faults, since we all have those. But I hope I would discount her and avoid her if she evinced faults that would ultimately be fatal to our happiness; or perhaps I should say, to our godliness."

She forced a smile, but said nothing.

"But you do understand this, do you not?" he asked earnestly. "You do approve this sort of caution?"

She considered for a moment before she spoke. "Yes," she said, "I suppose I must, if I consider the matter rationally. But there is something in me that says that you are putting the cart before the horse—that the passion of one's early love and marriage will serve as a kind of account of mutual joy and pleasure that one may draw upon to tide one over in any estrangements and difficulties that may arise in love's later stages. A marriage coolly entered will proceed coolly—that is what I fear. And what if passion finally does awaken in old age? Will it not be silly fondness then, and . . . past performance, if I may say so? Past fruition? It is the way of all humankind to love passionately in youth; and to set yourself up against that, and think you can avoid it and love as your reasoning mind directs—why, it is expecting too much for the mind alone to perform. To say nothing of the fact that if you wait for the spouse whom your mind deems perfect, you may well never marry; for the mind is infinitely scrupulous and nice. The heart, on the other hand, is much more realistic about love. It knows that rational perfection is not attainable, so it draws up its own terms of perfection. It makes excuses for the loved one's faults, and loves despite them. And if it were not for that—if we were all the perfectly reasoning beings you would have us be—why, the species would die out, sir. God gave us hearts to form bonds with others, so that we could go through what must be endured for love's sake."

"No one should love and marry, then, on the basis of reason alone? Is that what you are saying, Miss Wyatt?"

"Perhaps it is, sir; perhaps it is."

They were silent; and for the first time in their acquaintance there was a little unhappiness and tension in the silence, because they did not agree.

He seemed to want to remedy this. "Do not mistake me," he said. "I am a creature of flesh and blood like anyone. When I speak of first considering with the mind, I am speaking in ideal terms."

"I am glad to hear you say that, though in truth it is only what I suspected must be so."

"Yes, you know me. You know I am not some cold-hearted, calculating person, concerned only to work out the future of his marriage like some problem in calculus before he proceeds with it."

"Yes, sir, I do know that."

"But still . . . one must be concerned. One must look ahead. One must consider."

"I would not have one rush into marriage without consulting one's reason and confirming that it approves one's choice, certainly; it is only that I think the mind alone should not dictate that choice. That would be a cold way to go about marrying, and indeed I think it would fail far more often than it would succeed."

"I understand what you say," he said. "I think the disagreement in our views is slight; and in effect it is of no importance."

She was surprised at this last statement, and wondered what he meant. Did he perhaps mean that the argument he made was moot because he already loved her? Or did he mean that he was not considering marriage to her in any case? Or was he still speaking only in general terms?

She puzzled on these questions for a few minutes without speaking. The longer this silence continued between them, the more agitated he seemed to become; until finally he said, with a smile, and as if shaking off his worries, "But I feel, Miss Wyatt, that as to the purpose and the manner of marriage, we agree perfectly."

She did not know how to reply to this; and her uncertain look brought more explanation from him.

"I mean," he said, "that you believe, as I do, that marriage is the best state of humankind. Not everyone can achieve marriage, I know, and I do not fault those who do not find their way to it, for whatever reason. But for such as you and I, it is the perfecting of our lives. It is the ground where we mean to practice and to better learn the virtues that are enjoined on us by God—kindness, thoughtfulness, patience, steadfastness, love, hope, and all the rest. And more than that, marriage is a great act of creation, an act of art, carried on by husband and wife under the direction of grace and providence. It is a beautiful thing, a duet, if you will. We might say that life itself is a song made a thousand times more beautiful by being sung by two voices. Is it not?"

She had turned to him fully now and raised her face to his. "Indeed," she said, "it is this exactly. We could not agree more."

Still he seemed concerned that some difference of opinion stood between them. "Perhaps I can better explain if I recite you one of my favorite poems—or at least a passage from it."

"But all means," she said. "You know I am always delighted to hear the poets that you favor."

"It is Ben Jonson's 'Epode.' Do you know it?"

"No, I am not familiar with it."

"I was compelled to learn it in school, but it has stood me well since. He begins by describing the common conception of love. That part runs like this:

> The thing they here call Love is blind Desire,
>> Armed with bow, shafts, and fire;

> Inconstant, like the sea, of whence 't is born,
>   Rough, swelling, like a storm;
> With whom who sails, rides on the surge of fear,
>   And boils as if he were
> In a continual tempest.

"He then sketches true love in contrast:

> Now, true Love
>   No such effects doth prove;
> That is an essence far more gentle, fine,
>   Pure, perfect, nay, divine;
> It is a golden chain let down from heaven,
>   Whose links are bright and even,
> That falls like sleep on lovers, and combines
>   The soft and sweetest minds
> In equal knots: this bears no brands nor darts,
>   To murther different hearts,
> But in a calm and godlike unity
>   Preserves community.
> O, who is he that in this peace enjoys
>   Th' elixir of all joys?
> A form more fresh than are the Eden bowers,
>   And lasting as her flowers:
> Richer than Time, and as Time's virtue rare:
>   Sober, as saddest care;
> A fixèd thought, an eye untaught to glance:
>   Who, blest with such high chance,
> Would, at suggestion of a steep desire,
>   Cast himself from the spire
> Of all his happiness?

"Do you see what I am saying, Miss Wyatt?" he went on
then. "The love I seek, and the love I believe you seek, too,
is 'richer than time' and 'rare'; it is as serious and sober as

sadness itself; and yet we know it is joy, the deepest joy of all, the highest joy of all, 'the spire of all our happiness.'

"So all I am saying is that we ought not be deluded and deceived by the rough, boiling passion, the 'steep desire' that deceives us into thinking it is love. True love is as powerful in its way, for the very reason that it *is* serious in its purposes and preparations. It does not deceive us, because its varying seriousness precludes that necessity."

She was caught up in the topic and failed to couch her next question in terms of generalities. "And do you think you are deceived, Mr. Newsome?" she asked.

And he—apparently as caught up as she, and eager and even anxious to reassure her—also forgot the screen of generality they had been operating behind, and replied definitively: "Not at all, not in the least."

And in that moment they were interrupted by the others.

❊ 5 ❊

A Heart in Hold

Your looks so often cast,
Your eyes so friendly roll'd,
Your sight so fixèd fast,
Always *one* to behold:
Though hide it fain ye would,
It plainly doth declare
Who hath your heart in hold,
And where good-will ye bear.

—Wyatt

But they were so often interrupted. Each visit was circumscribed; business, either at his home or in London or in Falmouth, always took Daniel away after a few days. It was the many interruptions, Elissa now began to think and hope, that explained why their conversations never came to the point to which they so obviously tended: the proposal of marriage.

And yet still, as August came on, she felt a curious lack of pressure with respect to that outcome. The *bliss* persuaded her that the fulfillment would come—the fulfillment of that prediction made so abruptly by her intuition on the day she first met Daniel Newsome. She no longer attempted to silence those certainties when they welled into her consciousness; she only said, *Of course; of course it must be.*

Indeed, she no longer had cause for doubt. She was deeply in love with the man. She loved everything about him, body and mind. There was in all the world no one more pleasing to look upon, more deeply stirring and stimulating to converse with. Her brain was pregnant with countless spiritual offspring after they spoke. When he so much as entered the room or whatever part of the garden she might be in, the rhythm of her heart burst into a rapid patter of applause, her breath blew away, her soul seemed to crush her chest from within as it stood up on high the better to see his. When he was not present, his absence was both a stone that pulled her down into a blue sea and yet, even in its suffocation, a glorious martyrdom; for she loved him, she loved him, and that was a blessing and bliss so far beyond anything she had known or dreamed of knowing that she almost did not care about the pain bound up in it.

Often she thought to herself: *Such a man!* For her this brief phrase, which would have puzzled anyone who heard it, bore a mighty freight of meaning. As in: *It shall be my blessing to marry such a man,* or *What a miracle that such a man walks the earth, and I have found him, and he favors me,* or *Such a man he is as cannot be compared to any man in times ancient, times present, times to come.*

And this was no vain idolatry; it was a love properly subordinated to her other love, for God and all His gifts, for the ordinances of her religion, the commandments she had been bidden to hear and to do. But curiously (for so much was new and strange to her in those days), her love for Daniel reinforced her and supported her in her love of God, merely in being consonant with it. To go to church, that simple church by the river in the valley of Deepclough, with its self-important and pomp-speaking priest, was now not just a mild refreshment but a burgeoning of her *bliss.* It was like going to stand in a chapel on the verge of heaven. She felt God near her as if He were flowing into the church through the windows with the sunlight; and that sense of His nearness would linger deeply in her throughout the following week. To compose our thoughts to suit divine order has that effect; and thoughts not in that alignment read to us as woe, misery, blank and intractable depression, causeless anxiety, and lead to desperate and misguided attempts to set everything right, which plunge us only into more agony. During that summer she rose above that turmoil, which is so constant and typical with the benighted human race; she drifted forward immune to it, as a nymph of story rides upon the wave, her shining, tapered feet resting lightly and easily on its foam.

If she had in the beginning needed to make an effort to work out Daniel's character, she need do so no longer. He was perfectly, if soberly, affable and kind and open-hearted. He loved all humankind, he made no distinctions, he accepted people as he found them, though he was no fool, no pampered stripling unaware of evil. It was as if he had a secret reason to love each person whom he encountered; as if he looked into their souls and said, "See—there! There is the goodness in you, given you by God, though you always doubted its existence. Well, I see it, and I love you for it, whether you perceive it or not."

In all this he remained utterly without pride or pretension. Rather, it was his study to defer to everyone else in the social interactions of the two families he visited in Deepclough. He made no attempt to openly school or reprove anyone, even his cousin; instead he set himself to be a living example—finding that difficult enough to keep him occupied, as mortals must.

This humility he had learned stood him well in his encounters with Mr. Herbert, for the rector was the one person who became acquainted with him that summer who did not come to love or at the very least respect him. Perhaps it was in part because Daniel was what Mr. Herbert ought to have been; but the larger reason was not so far to seek: it lay in the growing connection between this interloper and Miss Elissa Wyatt. Sometimes when the three of them stood together after a service, Elissa saw Mr. Herbert glaring at Daniel and could practically hear him growling: *She's mine—marked out for* me! *Be off with you!* In these brief confrontations, the lesser man treated the greater with condescension, but to the confounding of his own purposes: Mr. Herbert never stopped to think how Elissa's opinion of him sank with each stare of dislike he shot toward the man she preferred. The more Mr. Herbert tarted up his speech with obscure terms—*quiddity, haecceity, essentia, singulars* and *particulars, generals* and *universals, distributivity* and *univocality,* and all the rest of the cant of an Anglified and hyperrationalistic and utterly outdated Scholasticism, exhumed solely for the purpose of outshining Daniel—the more Daniel took on the pellucid glow of humility by contrast. On one occasion, Mr. Herbert deliberately engaged Daniel in some theological question and then wagged his finger at him and scolded, *"Ne ultra crepidam judicaret."* It was, as Daniel later explained to Elissa, the Latin version of "Shoemaker, stick to your last." She could hardly refrain from laughing; but Daniel showed no intention of scoring any points against an adversary who, in his silliness, had virtually delivered himself into his rival's hands; instead he endured the rector's superciliousness without even the faintest indication that he felt in himself the contempt these efforts deserved. And Elissa likewise: the rector's rudeness toward Daniel would have annoyed her, if there had been at that time any room in her spirit for annoyance. Rather, it was as if she were in love with everyone living and everything existing in the subsolar realm; and she would sooner have blessed Mr. Herbert for his silliness than marred her love for Daniel by despising it. So what, if the Christian minister flew in the face of his own doctrine and proved himself petty; well, who would not come off the worse, she asked herself, who *could not,* when matched against Daniel?

In these encounters and many other little incidents that summer she came to understand Daniel well. She sometimes thought that he was both the boy who had broken windows and the man who now knew better, for the unthinking boy was continually father to the thoughtful man. That summed up his progress from being driven by the impulses of boyhood to give himself over to the work of Good, driven from the child's willfulness to the mature man's surrender. To the question, *Who has ultimacy?* he had in his youth made this answer: *I do, this person I am; I in the pride of my knowledge and reason may judge God Himself and all His laws;* and now he answered, *God, not I, is ultimate in all things.* One felt this about him at once, that in his humility he had allied himself to God.

That was perhaps why he became a kind of surrogate for God for many people who knew him. Elissa's was not the only heart and soul that grew lighter when he entered the room; all grew more cheerful and secure, simply in knowing that he was with them. His cousin virtually worshiped him and would defer to him in any matter. Merry treated him with a deference and awe that caused Daniel to tease her, in his mild way, until she would smile or laugh with him and by doing so admit that he, too, was merely human. Even the Rowcliffes eventually came to the point where they would fall silent when he spoke, and listen to him, and consider what he said, and discuss it between them in his very presence at the dinner table, as though it were an oracle delivered from Delphi. As for John Wyatt: Elissa always watched closely on those occasions when Daniel spoke with her father. Any daughter, any good daughter of a good father, must feel some trepidation about whether the man she has come to love is accepted by the man who once was previously the central masculine influence in her life. And see how John responded to Daniel, looking up at him—for Daniel was much the taller man—with a kind of awe, even a love of his own. And afterward he would look at Elissa with a deep, almost tearful pleasure, as if he might be thinking, *At last, my dear! A man who is good enough for you!*

And seeing this, she would say inside herself: *This man, my Daniel, is an angel come down to earth. Everyone knows it. He is everything I ever wanted in a husband, and nay, better still than that, for I had not the goodness to know such a man in thought, I had not the wit nor the imagination to conceive of him. If there were arts I could practice that would ensure he became mine, I would undertake them; but such arts do not exist, and the only power I have of making him my husband is to be as good as I can be, broken mortal as I am. Sincerity, sincerity alone is what he respects. He would scorn me if I attempted any feigned or artificial route to his heart; the only way he will love me is if I be most perfectly who I am, the one whom the perfect God intended me to be—if I find the source of love and goodness within me that is inexhaustible, because it comes from a power higher than any place I have ever stood.*

Dear God, she would pray, *Make me worthy of this good man. That is all I ask, though it is much, I know; but it is all I can ask, and it is all that will be required if he is to love me. For if I become as good as he is, then he must love me as I love him.*

If Daniel had any flaw—and of course he had many, but she would admit only this one so far—it was that he was reluctant to divulge concrete information that might prejudice one person against another. This prohibition was configured in a manner she could not fathom. He was willing to talk quite freely with Elissa, though with no one else, about his concerns about Charles and his future, but he would never have divulged the nature and extent of Charles's financial assets, if he had any. He spoke candidly to Elissa about Charles's parents, their strengths and foibles, but he never further mentioned Mr. James Newsome's radical plan to bequeath his estate to Daniel himself rather than to Charles. If Charles ever alluded to it, the subject seemed to distress Daniel, as a wrong he still hoped to make right; but he never expatiated on those plans privately to Elissa. There was, as well, an entire cast of characters in the unseen part of his life, of which he spoke with apparent openness . . . but only up to a point. Their characters might be colorfully sketched for her information and even amusement, but their circumstances remained vague, as if he thought it improper or even a violation of right conduct to discuss the particulars of their way of living upon the earth; or deemed doing so a form of gossip and thus beneath him.

Sometimes she thought this inhibition was not a flaw but actually a strength of character in him. Perhaps he believed that the specific material circumstances of someone's life were irrelevant; they would be shed forever someday, but the person personally, and the self itself, would live on; and so he paid little attention to them. Or perhaps he was thus secretive merely because he thought that divulging his knowledge about others might somehow lead to their hurt.

But at other times she was less certain about the beneficial nature of this characteristic. It resulted in curious blanks in her knowledge of his life, and she wanted to know everything about him. She felt like a child given cake. She would not be content until she had eaten every fact pertaining to him. Like that child, perhaps—and this was the risk she took—she would not be content until she felt surfeited and sick of the eating.

Meanwhile she played, and with the zest of one discovering them for the first time, all those games in which lovers indulge in their imaginations. She often went about the house chanting *Mrs. Daniel Newsome* over and over in her thoughts. She pictured herself out in company with him; how all would look on them with wonder and approval; how perhaps his acquaintances would say of her, "Where did he *ever* find her? How much she loves him! How perfect a spouse she makes for him!—And one can readily see that our sober-minded friend *dotes* on her to distraction." Indeed, when she thought of the dignity and honor of being the wife of *such a man,* the *bliss* would well up in her and make her for a moment useless for ordinary tasks.

And what did he think of her?

She was certain that he loved her. So certain.

It was in the very way he looked at her, unmistakable. The delight he took in her was beyond all denial: delight in her thoughts as she spoke them, in her physical presence, in the way she walked and the way she sat, in her coming in to where he was, in the way she turned to him, in the liveliness of her countenance as she beheld him, in their serious conversation, in their light and flirting repartee. He showed it in the sweetness of those dialogues they shared on topics dear to them both; in his little courtesies; he showed it in the joy he found in being with her, time after time; in his returning to her, again and again that summer, as a treasure seeker returns to a shore where gold is known to be hidden.

Yes, she was very certain that he loved her. Perhaps that was why she felt no urgency about their coming to the point, to the purpose, of this courtship.

And she did feel, although they had never made it explicit between them, that it was indeed a courtship.

Then one day towards the end of August, Merry said to Elissa, blurting it out, as a nonsequitur, when they had bade goodnight to Charles and Daniel at the door and had watched their carriage descend the drive: "Everyone says, you know, how perfect a couple you and Daniel make."

Elissa paused on the steps—they had left John dozing in the drawing room, and they were alone together.

"Everyone?" she asked.

"Everyone," affirmed Merry.

"Merry, dear . . . does *everyone* talk of us, of Mr. Daniel Newsome and me, in . . . that manner?"

"Of course they do, darling! Did you really think they did not?"

"I suppose I do not know what I thought about it. I suppose I expected that since Mr. Newsome and I have never spoken in that way—I mean, on that topic—that the tongues of others would not speak on it either. That was foolish of me, I suppose."

"I suppose it was!" laughed Merry. "But you cannot mean that you have not been encouraged to think he will pay his addresses to you soon?"

"I think he will," said Elissa. "It is just that I do not know when."

Merry was suddenly silent, and Elissa, wheeling her thoughts about from her own situation to train them on Merry's, said to her: "And what of you and Charles, dear? Has he spoken to you?"

"No," admitted Merry. "But I know he will. I know he will speak soon. And you know they *must* speak to us on the same day. It would be horribly awkward if they did not. They know that perfectly well."

"Yes," said Elissa vaguely. The oddness of the situation forced itself on her attention for the first time. The four of them were now long past the point when these matters should have been settled. But it was uncomfortable to think of this.

"And others speak of us in this way?" she asked again.

"Of course," said Merry again.

"But I think you exaggerate, dear."

Merry laughed. "Think so if you will, my love," she said, "but you fool only yourself."

To end the conversation, Elissa went on into the house. John was coming out of the drawing room; goodnights were said, and goodnight kisses given; and Elissa would have gone to bed at once if she had not thought of another task, that of asking Mabel Dean to make up a basket to be ready first thing in the morning for a family in the village.

At this late hour the offices were deserted. Mr. Jens, the butler, and his wife were, however, in the servants' hall, drinking tea and eating some pudding left over from the master's table. This was not unusual; Mrs. Jens generally stopped by as she walked home from her job as house-keeper to Mr. Herbert in the village; and if she was weary, sometimes Mr. Jens offered her a little refreshment before they both continued on to their little house, which was more than a mile farther along the ridge.

They both now rose and greeted Elissa when she entered the room and inquired for Mabel; but the girl had gone to bed. When Mr. Jens heard what she needed, he offered to put the basket together for her, but she would not let him; instead she urged him to continue at ease with Mrs. Jens, and she herself went away to the pantry.

As she gathered the items she needed, she could not help overhearing Mrs. Jens as she resumed the conversation. The distance between the pantry and the servants' hall was so short, and the house so quiet otherwise, that the woman's voice carried to her quite distinctly. The substance of what she said, ironed smooth of the wrinkles of its thick Gloucestershire dialect, was this: ". . . the dearest, finest lady in all Deepclough, and I dare say in all the county, and why she has not been snapped up a hundred times over, I do not know, except that no one knows what a gem we have here, hidden in our little valley—and her and her sister to have five thousand pound a piece! It is as if you was to bribe a man to welcome an angel into his house—into his bed!"

At this point Mr. Jens murmured something Elissa could barely catch; but she thought it was: "Quite so, my dear, quite so."

"We can only hope this Newsome gent has got his wits about him and can see her for what she is," Mrs. Jens went on. "He's her best chance for many a long time, or ever, unless she gets away and goes to London or Bath and gets herself *seen*. Sure, there is no one *here* good enough for her." Then she laughed, in the bold, sarcastic manner she used when speaking of her employer; and at this point her voice became louder, and Elissa began to wonder if she actually intended to be overheard. "And guess what Mr. H's latest plan is in that line," she said.

Another murmur from Mr. Jens.

"Why, he is so desperate with jealousy that he came to *me*—to me, of all people! The rector, a man of the cloth, edyecated at Oxford, a gentleman of old stock—comes to his own housekeeper for advice about what he ought to do. And you can tell he's at his wits' end. 'Mrs. Jens,' he says to me, 'do you have *any* idea what sort of thing it is that young ladies like to do, that will get them away from the house and whatever company they might happen to be keeping there?'

"And of course I knew right away what he was about, and I says to him, all the while laughing up my sleeve, 'Why, with all this rain we've had lately, Mr. Herbert, the river is running well all the way up to the sward. I should think any young ladies who might happen to live about here might like to be taken in a boat upriver, sir; and I could pack you a lunch of some of that cold mutton you liked so much. If you made up a little party of, say, three or more, it would all be quite proper.'

"Then he guessed that I knew whom he was talking about, and he grew quite angry with me for that, the poor silly man, as if I could help it, or was such a fool as to miss knowing, and he denied having anyone particular in mind, and said he was only asking in *hypothetic* terms, as he put it; but finally, when he was done huffing and puffing about that, he owned as it was a topping idea, and he would see to it; and he went on for a good quarter hour about what a fine rower he was at Oxford, and all the races he won, and he kept me from turning the roast, and was angry all over again later for *that*. Aye, let him take Miss up the stream all he likes! We all know who she has an eye for. But that older Mr. N. is a deep one, and no one ever quite knows what he thinks, or so I've heard tell."

Here Mr. Jens murmured something.

"Well, I do hope so," said Mrs. Jens. "I do hope so indeed!—Though I should be sorry to see the lady go, and I shall weep all through that wedding with a will, I shall! But

I shall be as glad for her as I am sorry for the rest of us. She is that sweet and good, she is, and one smile from her is as good as an hour of laughter from *anyone else.*"

At this point, Elissa was so overcome by various emotions that she abandoned her chore—in fact, she had been standing motionless throughout and had hardly begun it—and, leaving the basket until morning, went hurriedly back to her room. As she fled away, she thought she heard Mrs. Jens say, "Ah, I have upset her now! I did not mean to do *that!*"

Of Mr. Herbert's foolish attempt to distract Elissa from Daniel—of this Elissa thought not in the least. Instead she thought about the very person whom Mr. Herbert did not wish her to fixate upon. *Everyone knows!* was the general thrust of her thoughts, and they did indeed thrust themselves rudely on her peace of mind. She knew the way news went through the village—faster than the first rays of light over the rim of the valley at dawn; that is, with an almost impossible quickness; and if a thing was known by one, it was known by all.

All the servants know, she thought, *and if the servants know, the village knows, and if the village knows, Mr. Blaickie knows, and as he is Daniel's man, Daniel knows! And yet he does not avoid me, as he would if he did not have intentions of his own— good intentions. If he heard that Miss Wyatt at Aeons' End was head over heels for him, and if he did not reciprocate her affection, he would promptly go away, so as not to injure my feelings or mislead me about his own feelings any further—I know he would. He is an honorable man if any man ever was! To this point, he could easily have been misled by the pleasant life in our society here at Deepclough to spend more time at Aeons' End than he ought to have, if he does not really intend to marry me; but if he hears through the servants that he is at risk of injuring me, he will go away promptly—he will seize some opportunity, magnify some trivial matter of business in order to spare appearances as he departs. If he should suddenly announce that he is on his way home, then I will know!*

With these thoughts she both comforted herself and tortured herself: He had not said anything about departing—and yet he might at any moment. He had often gone away, so how could she be sure in any future case that his departure would be significant? And yet still her thoughts tumbled on: *We shall see him tomorrow. He promised to come. If he means to leave, it will be the first thing he says. If he does not, then I shall know . . . well, I shall* know *nothing for a certainty, but I may have a strong intimation that he . . .* does *love me and* does *intend to ask me to marry him; and given that intention . . . he will likely make his feelings clear sooner rather than later.*

It was some time, perhaps an hour, that she sat on the edge of her bed in her room, completely immersed in these ruminations; and then she came to, with a start, and grew conscious of the hour, and of all the hours that lay between that moment and the next time she would see Daniel; which was the hour she would be able to guess, with more reliability than ever, what his feelings were.

Such are the illogical devisings of those in love, and such is the precision of the pacts they make with the future.

The next morning the Wyatts received the following invitation:

Dear Mr. Wyatt,

Please be so kind as to do me the honor of accepting the herewith extended invitation to your esteemed self and daughters to accompany me on a rowing trip on the river tomorrow morning. The reasons for my making this invitation are as follows:

1. *The recent rains have made the river navigable as far as the fine sward at Toomey's Farm.* It would be a shame to miss this opportunity, which comes so seldom at

this time of year. Furthermore, at other seasons the river current is generally too strong, whereas it is now sufficiently moderated by the absence of spring or fall flowage.

2. *Mrs. Jens has a good leg of mutton, a part of which we may take cold with us in a hamper, along with all the other accoutrements of a picnic, which I shall be honored to provide.* Mrs. Jens is known to you and all in our society as a highly adequate cook, and I am sure you will be pleased with her fare.

3. *The weather promises to be clear and warm, both by the glass, and by the prognostications of Mr. Willis, whom many in these parts turn to as deeply knowledgeable of future meteorological conditions.* Mr. Willis's knowledge, while not scientific, seems to stem from some God-given sympathy with Nature, and is highly dependable and reliable. I myself have conferred with the glass this very morning, and it indicates that the column has been steadily if incrementally rising.

4. *I have secured Mr. Wiggot's boat for this purpose, which is the finest to be had in the valley.* It has ample room to carry us all in safety and comfort to our destination and back. It has been newly painted and is quite clean. Furthermore, I will provide rugs and pillows so that the ladies may not fear soiling or dampening their raiment.

5. *In all modesty I must add that I was a very able rower in my days at university.* You will not suffer the least inconvenience or encounter the least risk. Such an adventure on the water was in my student days so common an occurrence that you might almost reproach me for neglecting my studies if you knew how often I resorted to it (and if you could overlook the implausibility of the charge).

Please to do me the honor of sending a reply by this afternoon at earliest, so that the proper preparations may be made. I shall meet you at ten o'clock sharp at the riverside above the weir.

I await your reply in hopeful anticipation of a memorable event.

I remain always your servant in Christ Jesus,

ALFRED HERBERT, M.A. OXON.

Merry rolled her eyes repeatedly at Elissa as Mr. Wyatt read out this curious letter, with all its propositions and explanations; but Elissa herself, having overheard Mrs. Jens's story the night before, was prepared for it and kept a tolerably straight face.

It was the very sort of plan in which Mr. Wyatt was well known to have little interest, and Elissa was sure Mr. Herbert had counted on her father's declining the offer. "A day on the river!" he exclaimed when he had read the invitation aloud to them. "As if such a thing could tempt me from my garden! What a waste of a perfectly good day! Whatever is Mr. Herbert thinking?"

"I myself have no interest in going, Papa," said Elissa.

But Merry, after a momentary hesitation, brightened a little, and said, "I see no reason why we may not ask Mr. Newsome and Charles to go along with us."

"You are forgetting that Mr. Charles Newsome cannot endure to be in a boat," said Elissa.

"Oh, I am! You are right," she said. She then turned to Elissa with a teasing expression and added: "It does not seem kind to leave him; perhaps you and Mr. Daniel Newsome should go with Mr. Herbert, and I shall stay behind with Papa and Charles."

"I am sure that would be very pleasant for all concerned," said Elissa ironically. "But I think I would decline."

"In any case, you must go without me, dear girls, if you wish to go at all," said Mr. Wyatt. "Mr. Herbert is a steady, good sort of fellow, and from what I saw of it the other day, the river is full but hardly in spate; and as Mr. Herbert says, the glass promises a fair day tomorrow. So by all means, go if you wish."

"I think we are agreed, Papa," said Elissa, "that Mr. Herbert must make his voyage by himself."

"His voyage in life," added Merry mischievously. "Alone! So alone!"

Elissa ignored this squib. "So, then, shall I answer for you, Papa?"

"Oh, would you please, dear? It is you he will be expecting an answer from, I am sure."

But Elissa did not immediately undertake the reply, since the household accounts intervened; and the letter from Mr. Herbert lay still on her writing desk unanswered when the Newsome cousins arrived, much in advance of their customary hour; so much, in fact, that John had not yet gone out into the garden for the day. He was going over the accounts with Elissa in the parlor, or rather, undergoing her interrogation concerning them, while Merry sat somewhat fretfully by, attempting to read, but in actuality waiting impatiently for Charles to appear.

When the Newsomes were announced, Elissa immediately noticed something unusual in their manner, though neither Merry nor John seem to observe it: both young men were rather somber.

"We have had bad news, I'm afraid," said Daniel, when greetings had been exchanged. "We must leave you and return to Landseye."

Elissa was stricken with the memory of the little predictive arrangement she had made with fate.

"Is something wrong?" she asked.

Both men looked somewhat evasive—Charles more than Daniel, who did, after a moment's hesitation, meet her eyes and say: "No, nothing is truly *wrong*. My uncle has reported having a minor cold—nothing at all dangerous, an ailment common to him; I am sure it will pass off in a few days. But between that and some . . . business there, we have determined to go as soon as we may."

This was exactly the scenario that Elissa had imagined as a test of his intentions. He had heard the talk of the village and meant to curtail his visits to Aeons' End; he was seizing upon this excuse—this illness of his uncle's, which he himself admitted was trivial—to absent himself. And equally shattering was Charles's intention to go as well. Perhaps Daniel had explained to him the misimpression their attentions to the Wyatt sisters were creating—surely Charles himself would not *want* to go of his own accord.

"But must you *really* go?" asked Merry in sudden distress. Elissa could not attempt speech; she had too much difficulty as it was merely in appearing appropriately calm.

Merry had directed her question to Charles; and now his uncertainty vanished in irrepressible affection. "It is only for a short while," he said with a smile. "I could not possibly live without you . . . I mean, your family, for long."

This was a satisfactory answer from one suitor, but the other made no similar attempt at reassurance. His determination not to do so seemed to cause even him some pain.

"This is too bad, too bad!" exclaimed John to Charles. "We shall miss you, my dear sir, in the garden—we shall not accomplish half so much, or enjoy it a thousandth as much." And turning to Daniel he added: "And you, too, Mr. Newsome! You will be much missed."

Here was the perfect point at which Daniel could have expressed a wish to return quickly, but he did nothing of the kind. True, he seemed to want to speak; but it was as if that mysterious inhibition of his held him back.

"And how shall you travel?" asked Elissa abruptly, to cover the deficit in the conversation.

"The Rowcliffes have offered us their carriage," said Daniel, "and it seems best to take it, if it can be repaired in time."

"Oh, they are endlessly repairing their carriage," said Merry. "You would be better to go by the mail coach, or even by postchaise."

"I understand it is difficult to hire a postchaise from Deepclough," said Daniel.

"That is so," said John.

"Impossible, in fact," said Elissa, as if that obstacle should deter them from attempting to leave at all.

"And the mail coach goes to Oxford. That would put us some miles out of our way; so we have decided on taking the carriage and going directly."

"Well, can you not stay with us here this morning until the repairs are made?" asked Merry.

"We would like nothing more," said Daniel, "except that from what we understand, the carriage may be made usable within the hour. So we must return to Rowantree as quickly as we have come here to you, and we must apologize for the false drama and suddenness of our departure."

He is not leaving any room for further awkwardness, thought Elissa: *He is making the break as cleanly as he can.*

No pleading could deter him. He heard none from Elissa—she was reduced to silence again; but John and Merry held out to keep the company of their friends for at least that hour until the carriage should be ready. Daniel was courteous as always, and firm as always: they would not stay. Furthermore, when Charles showed signs that he was willing to be worked upon, Daniel strengthened his resolve with a penetrating glance.

The Wyatts followed them to the door. Their horses were still being held in saddle for them; the gentlemen said their goodbyes—the same sort of goodbyes they always said in leaving, nothing particular, nothing that marked the finality of that parting—and they mounted up and started away.

But Merry ran out into the drive and called to Charles. He looked back and stopped; she went up to the side of the horse and he leaned down close to her.

They spoke softly to one another; Elissa could not hear what they said; no one but the two of them could hear. Daniel, too, had stopped, but at a sufficient distance that he, too, must have been out of earshot.

Then, with mutual smiles of satisfaction, Charles and Merry broke off. He rode on, and she stood in the drive and watched him for a few minutes before returning, with a dawdling step and many a backward glance, to the house.

"Well," said John then, "I shall miss them both, I truly will. I have come to depend upon Charles in particular. But he shall be back, soon enough, I am sure." He studied Merry carefully for a moment to see how she was taking this; and being reassured by her air of cheerfulness, he bid them good morning, and evaded further study of the accounts by going at once to his garden.

When the sisters were alone, they went—with unspoken purpose and in perfect unison—in the opposite direction from John, to sit on a bench in a niche of the garden wall, where they could not be overheard from the house. Elissa was aching to ask Merry what she and Charles had said to one another, but she would not let herself; and Merry was the first to speak. "What do you think?" she asked.

"I think we shall never see Mr. Daniel Newsome again," said Elissa.

"What?" said Merry. "You cannot mean it!"

"It is all too clear—do you not see? He has heard his name and mine connected—his man has doubtless told him the rumors circulating in the village. He realizes that he is in danger of misleading me, and he is doing the honorable thing by taking this trivial excuse to go away."

"The honorable thing!" exclaimed Merry. "Why, Elissa, you err utterly! You know perfectly well that at this point the honorable thing would be to declare himself to you, not to steal away from you on some pretext!"

Elissa made no answer to this; instead she said: "I do believe that you yourself have nothing to fear, dearest.

Charles's affection for you was written all over his face. He is merely being taken away as a cover for his cousin's sudden departure. He will be back with us in a day or two, as soon as he has paid his respects to his parents and seen his father returned to good health."

"Oh, Elissa!" said Merry. "How perfectly wrong you are! I have never heard such a foolish thing come out of your sensible mouth! Do you not see what is happening? Daniel is taking Charles away to Landseye so that he, Daniel, can plead for him. He wants Charles to have some assurance from his father that he will not be utterly cut off. Do you not see? And once he has it, they will be back from Oxfordshire as soon as may be, and we shall both be married before the year is out.—Why, it is as I told you the other day: neither of them can speak unless the other does. That is why Daniel has said nothing; he wants to make sure that Charles can offer me a home before we all go ahead. Why, Charles practically said as much, just now when I spoke to him in the drive. I teased him about how the garden would go to ruin without him if he were gone long, and he said to me, 'Look for me soon; and, I hope, in changed circumstances.' That is what he said."

This theory was wonderfully seductive. It could explain everything just as easily as her own negative hypothesis and yet offer her hope, where her own did not; and so in an instant she seized upon it.

"Do you think so?" she said.

"Of course I do, silly!—Oh, now, who is the silly one? I thought I would never see my serious sister have her wits turned by her passions; but here you are, unable to see an explanation that is as plain as the freckles on my face."

Elissa, still thinking this possibility over, and beginning to hope again, said nothing; and Merry laughed at her. "Look at you!" she said. "There is nothing you want more than that I should be right."

"That is the truth," admitted Elissa.

"Then trust me," said Merry. "I have no doubt that Charles loves me. He did not say anything definite; but the other day he said something about wanting to discuss something with his cousin. Now we can guess what that something was, and what the outcome was—this sudden trip to Landseye. Charles will be back, and Daniel will be back. I admit I do not like the waiting, and I wish they had done it the other way around—made their declarations, and then gone to Landseye; and that probably is the way Charles would have done it, if he had been left to his own way of thinking; but Daniel does not think that is the honorable course. If Charles is going to be penniless, then he must say so when he makes his offer.—At least, that is the way Daniel would have it. I myself do not think there will be the least difficulty. Charles and I will have plenty to live on. I have worked it all out in my head."

"You are right about this much," said Elissa. "That would be the way Daniel would want to see it done.—But Merry, can we be sure? I told myself that if he left like this, suddenly, without a word of warning, it would be because he meant not to put me in a compromised position."

"Yes, you told yourself that," said Merry, "but you were wrong. Do you not always tell me that one ought not fear the worst until one has reason to do so? That is exactly what you yourself are doing. I can only repeat your own wisdom back to you."

"Yes . . . I suppose."

"We have only to endure the next few days of waiting," said Merry. "That will indeed be difficult, I grant you."

They sat in silence for a moment; and then Merry said, "Well, I see no reason now why we should not go up the river with Mr. Herbert tomorrow."

"Are you serious, dear? There is nothing I would not rather do. It would seem strange to me, to be hoping that one man will propose marriage to me, and to go on an outing with another."

"If Daniel ever came to know of it, I should think it might do him some good to be jealous of Mr. Herbert," said Merry.

"Daniel, jealous of Mr. Herbert!" Elissa actually laughed aloud. "That would be impossible."

"Well, then, why shall we not go?"

And Merry said more on this head; so much that finally Elissa began to think it might be just as well to take up Mr. Herbert's offer. Though Merry was cheerful enough at this moment, the absence of Charles, after the daily visits of the past months, would soon enough begin to wear upon her—Elissa knew her lack of resilience well, having seen her pine after the departure of other beaux. None of them had raised half the hopes in her that Charles had, so her depression, when it arrived, was likely to be more than twice as deep.

Much against her own inclination, then, she went back to the house and wrote an acceptance to Mr. Herbert's offer.

The moment she had sent the boy off with this message, it went directly out of her mind. She thought over Merry's theory instead; and though at first it had seemed more plausible as well as more attractive than her own, her anxiety and uncertainty soon began to find flaws in it.

These she had to counteract with the brute force of reason; and it did gradually dawn on her that she might be victim of her own fearfulness. In retrospect she saw that the Newsomes' departure had assumed its importance because of her own dread of it and her presumption about its cause, not because of any objective evidence. In particular, she saw that it was foolish of her to determine in advance that Daniel's departure must be motivated by his sudden awareness of any talk about the two of them in the little society of the valley. He had been coming and going from Deepclough all summer. This departure was different only in that he took Charles with him.

But she found it slow going, to work against her fear and overcome it. At length she felt spiritually exhausted by the effort. This dejection brought on a consciousness that she had not made use of the best resources available to her; and she prayed—prayed that Daniel loved her as she believed he did, that he would return, and that her hopes would come true.

And then she consigned the outcome to God and felt some peace.

At supper that night, they heard from the servants that the Newsomes had not been able to depart as they wished; the carriage had required an entirely new wheel and axle. The wheelwright was to work through the night if necessary; the cousins would likely not get away until sometime the next morning.

This news affected both sisters a great deal. They had not minded so much the losing of their companions at once, when they had thought a sudden departure would bring the gentlemen back all that much sooner; but to miss their company for a day when they might have had it, and to see that return postponed by the same additional interval, was a double loss. Merry began to lose her good cheer, and now declared that she did not want to go on the outing in the morning after all; and Elissa felt the irony keenly when she had to remind her sister that it was too late to change her mind, now that all the plans were in motion—though she herself would gladly have given them up.

✳ 6 ✳

Swept Away
and Gone Away

I'll kiss thee through, I'll kiss thy very soul.

—Cowley

The valley where Further Deepclough lay was indeed deep at its lowest point: it was as if a broad indent had been made in the land with the edge of a great hand, and then within that valley a knife had been used to cut a narrow line, winding within the wider one. This narrow course was sufficient to hold the river except in periods of exceptional rain, at which times it flooded abruptly and even surged into the lower floors of the houses beside it, as has been mentioned before. During summers, however, it was generally tame, and followed its limpid way from its sources in the higher part of the valley, through pasture and past farm field, through a weir made of wattle where fish might in season be caught in plenty, through the little village, between some bosky banks, into a slightly wider and deeper stretch above the mill, over a small dam there, and then away through the windings of the land to Nether Deepclough. The river had no name of its own, or at least so far as the natives were concerned, though distant cartographers had assigned it one; to the people of the valley, it was called only "the river" or at most "the Clough," the latter quite illogically; and outsiders were sometimes confused when they heard a river called by a word that means "a valley."

Given the geography of the river, the place to begin rowing upon it was upstream of the weir, which was in turn upstream of the village. From there it was quite safe to go against the current; the only danger one might encounter would be the inconvenience of water that was too shallow for travel. But as Mr. Herbert had promised, conditions after the rain were such that running aground was not likely to be a difficulty on this particular day.

It was at this point, just above the weir, that the Wyatt sisters met Mr. Herbert at about ten the next morning. He had just launched the boat into the water, with the assistance of a few of that ever-present population of boys who were always willing to earn a penny for assisting the gentlefolk in their pleasures. The Wyatts' carriage arrived just as the boat was drawn alongside the short wharflike stone that, with a few accompanying pilings, served as the village dock. Mr. Herbert was at once drawn away to the business of welcoming the ladies, handing them down from the carriage, and leading them to the boat. "We shall put you aboard," he said to them, "before we stow the picnic things; that way you can be sure to be comfortable, and we shall let the freight shift for itself." The personification of the picnic things was a little joke, Elissa saw; in fact, for Mr. Herbert, it was a soaring joke, and she could have no doubt that he was putting himself out for her.

The English have always had a knack, or really it should be called a genius, for making watercraft, whether small or large, that are so beautiful one almost doubts their very floatability. The boat in question was a swift, pretty little thing: so narrow in the beam that only one passenger could sit on any bench, and possessing a long, curving, jutting bow and an hourglass stern. Towards this stern Mr. Herbert gestured as he murmured, "Miss Wyatt, if you please." Elissa understood that he wished to look at her while he rowed, and briefly contemplated foiling his plan and taking her seat in the bow; but she told herself this would be merely perverse. She let him steady her by holding her hand as she boarded at the stern; and as the narrow boat seemed a trifle unstable, she immediately sat on the bench there. Merry, standing behind Mr. Herbert where she could not be seen by the rector, gave her sister another of her merry looks; the maneuver to put Elissa within view had not eluded her notice.

The reason for what happened next was never perfectly known. One of the boys had been holding the gunwale of the boat against the dock by the bow, and he let go of it and moved away as Mr. Herbert approached Merry and prepared to help her step down to her seat. The stern was not fastened at all; and as for the bow, it was conjectured later that one of the boys had been assigned, or had taken upon himself, the task of tying off the boat there, perhaps at the exact moment when Mr. Herbert had been distracted by the arrival of the ladies. But the boy was a farm lad, not the son of a sailor, and though he knew many useful knots, it had not occurred to him how critical that one knot might be, and how he ought to use the best bend in his repertoire; instead he deliberately and thoughtfully tied a very simple slip knot.

Which, it appeared, simply slipped.

Suddenly Mr. Herbert and Merry, startled and uncomprehending, were looking at Elissa and she, likewise startled and not understanding, was looking back at them, and at the gap that had suddenly opened up between the land and the boat. The boys who were standing about likewise looked on with surprise, at the young lady drifting slowly away, in parallel to the shore; clearly they thought that this was something none of the ladies of Aeons' End ought to do, and like Merry and Mr. Herbert, they could not comprehend why Miss Wyatt was doing it. The oars, after all, still lay on the dock, along with the rudder; the lady had no way to control where she was going.

There was a long moment of silence. And in the silence, Elissa turned her head and looked toward the weir.

The water was running over it briskly; it might upset the boat or it might not.

She did a rapid calculation in her head that went roughly like this: *I cannot swim. If the boat capsizes at the weir, I shall likely be thrown out, and if I do not cling to the overturned boat, I shall drown before anyone can reach me. If I do cling to the boat, still the river shall bear me away; and the river shall bear me away in any case if I do somehow pass over the weir. If I do not happen to run close enough to the shore to seize upon something, I shall be borne down through the village, past the woody banks, down to the mill. The river is running over the dam quite strongly there—we saw it on the way here—and I shall be thrown over it onto the rocks; and even if my body is not shattered at once, I shall drown there below the falls.*

The calculation was dreadful and yet ineluctable. She sat in the boat and looked still upon Merry and Mr. Herbert as the boat glided away from them—it had only been a few seconds, but already it seemed like hours; and she had a strange double sense, as if she were two different people, one who was frightened and saw her life rushing away from her at impossible speed with the departing shore, and one who was eminently calm and collected and steady of mind, to whom all this seemed to be happening with the unreal slowness of an unfolding dream.

A moment ago death had been distant; no one had thought of it. The sisters had been planning to row upstream under Mr. Herbert's careful guardianship, and make landfall somewhere by a pasture, and eat the country delicacies his housekeeper had prepared, and then return home, and never think of death at all. But now there was nothing else to think of; it loomed so large that it blocked out the very sun of life.

Then Merry shrieked. And shrieked and shrieked again. The boys sprang into motion and began running along the shore, following the progress of the boat with a kind of instinct, not knowing what they were going to do, but wishing to save Miss Wyatt if they could, just as they would have wished to save a sheep or a piglet that had fallen into the river, merely out of that compassion that is, for all its infamous absence at times, still the deepest thing and the truest thing that makes a human a human. Mr. Herbert, too, gave a cry (Elissa was not sure it was not an oath) and ran away from Merry, passing the boys in a few swift, long-legged steps, but like them, running to no purpose in an attempt to stay alongside Elissa as she drifted closer to the center of the stream.

No, she told herself: neither Mr. Herbert nor this impromptu *posse comitatus* of rural urchins could save her. If anyone would save her, it must be herself.

She looked around at the weir again. It had been built of raw willow saplings and branches, woven into a loose hurdle at a time when the river was dry, but now it was submerged almost completely. If the boat should merely catch on the tops of the willow wood, the weir might hold the craft there until some sort of rescue could be effected—another boat brought, for example, and rowed out to her. Or, as she had already imagined, between the thrust of the current and the resistance of the barely exposed weir the boat might be capsized. Which was her best chance, then? To try to get the boat over the weir and hope she might be driven near the shore further down, or to try to be caught by the weir and halted here?

She knew nothing of boats, but she realized that that particular vessel was more likely to be caught if it drifted upon the weir while traveling sideways. It occurred to her that she might be able to control it somewhat if she paddled with her hand; and in a trice she scrambled to the bow, where it would be easier to reach the water on whichever side might become necessary; and she knelt on the bench there, and dipped her arm and cupped hand in the river, and took a powerful stroke at it, and then another, and another. The water seemed icy cold to her, and smothering even to her hand.

Her efforts had no effect whatsoever. The boat was now turning on the surface, lazily defying her to direct it. It was gathering speed, in fact, as it entered the central part of the current. In a moment more it would run up against the weir; she gave up her useless attempt to control it—indeed, in paddling as she had, she had alternated between trying to make the boat run parallel to the weir and perpendicular to it, to make it catch there or make it slip over the willow barricade—and she sat on the bench in the bow, gripping the gunwales, as she might have gripped the sides of a bathing tub in preparing to exit it; only in this vessel, the water was beyond the sides she gripped, not within them.

She was dimly aware of the shouting of Mr. Herbert, who seemed to be calling some directions to her, though of what use they could have been, she did not know; and the boys were still shouting too, shouts that were half excitement and half horror and consternation; and Merry was still shrieking. Merry had run up to the road to follow the river's course, in her insensate terror rather sensibly or at least instinctively choosing to go where the going was easier, since she had no idea what she might do to help Elissa anyway.

As the boat swept up to the weir, Elissa looked up at her sister and thought, inchoately, something to this effect: *Merry, dear, farewell! If this is to be the end, then may God go with you the rest of your life, and protect you—though I really do think He meant for me to be your special angel here on earth and look after you myself.*

Then her sister became a blur in her vision and she thought: *And Daniel too—I had begun to have such hopes—no, I really already have had such hopes; but that is all moot now. May God grant you happiness and a good wife!*

And finally she thought: *And poor Papa! To lose another child! Dear God, look after Papa—do not let him break!*

At the last instant the boat spun slightly on the current and went over the weir bow first, as neatly as if it had been steered from the stern.

Another shout went up from those on the shore, but a different kind of shout. The tone of it (it was inarticulate, as far as she could tell) struck a chill into her. Mr. Herbert and the boys and Merry had by now all done the same calculation she had so instantly made; they knew she was bound for the mill dam.

On she went. The boat turned about again, very slowly, as if the current were taunting her. She looked to the shore in the hope that the river would carry her close enough to leap out or at least to grip something there; but the boat seemed to be held away from the shore by a kind of buffeting or buffering effect; it continued to travel where the channel was deepest and the current was swiftest.

In a moment more, she was riding alongside the first house in the village, where Mrs. Brough was hanging her washing. Mrs. Brough stared at her, and then threw up her hands like an actress in a theater and called, quite clearly, "Miss Wyatt! Miss Wyatt! Whatever be ye a-doin'?" But onwards Elissa went, before she could answer, if there were any answer to be made to such a question—such as, perhaps: *I am on my way to the dam, Mrs. Brough, where I shall surely die.*

As she was carried on through the village, it burst into activity in her wake. Cries could be heard; those of the women and children who were at home on this fine workday came running forth from their houses and looked down at her. She could see Mr. Herbert running frantically, although with rapidly flagging strength and energy, along the edge of the road, and Merry not far behind him, and the boys interspersed between them, now jogging along with a kind of holiday air, as if glad that something interesting was finally happening in their little village. And was not a pretty woman of fine figure, or—as Elissa, in some incongruous flash of her imagination, pictured herself—a woman in a

handsome and new dove-gray morning dress and matching
dove-gray hat with white fillets, an object of interest enough,
even without the piquancy added by her sitting so calmly
and quietly in a runaway boat, or by the fact that she was
about to die?

There was no doubt, though, that she was—at least in
spatial terms, if not in others—gradually leaving all these
mortal companions behind. They could not run as swiftly as
the current was carrying her, and so they would not be able
to help her when she went over the dam.

As the boat turned, she kept turning about within it, the
steady part of her mind telling her: *Stay calm, Elissa! You
must be aware of the banks and not miss the chance to grab for
something or to jump out near the shore—yes, you must jump,
jump into the water, if that is your only chance to be saved!* And
yet the frightened part of her was sure she could not do any
such thing.

Halfway through the village, she passed the lane that
descended from Rowantree. It was deserted; and she
thought to herself, *Daniel and Charles must have started by
now—the carriage must have been ready to go long since.*

But then, as she was carried farther on, *she saw the
Rowcliffe's carriage,* making along the road for Oxfordshire.
They had not left long since; they had just started out.

The carriage was traveling at good speed, and so as she
drew abreast of it she stayed more or less alongside it for a
minute, and she watched it, suddenly deeply grateful for this
last glimpse, if not of Daniel, then at least of the carriage in
which she knew he must be riding. Perhaps she even smiled,
looking up at him, though she could not see him.

Then the door of the carriage banged open with a report
that she could hear even from where she sat. Daniel was in
the doorway, and Charles behind him, and they were staring at her as she sat quietly in the boat, as the boat turned
relentlessly and silently, as the current carried her onward.

She heard Daniel shouting at the coachman, and the words came faintly to her over the tumult of the water: "Go, man! Go as fast as you can! You must get to the mill before the lady does!"

The driver understood instantly. He swung his whip—the horses gave a sharp lunge forward—they had probably never before felt the lash in all their lives. Still Daniel clung to the doorway, watching her, never taking his eyes off her.

Now, here nature had given Elissa one hope: the river wound sharply to the left, as if the knife that had cut its course had wobbled in the hand that held it. It described a long loop through a parklike covert, and the road went by a shorter route toward the dam. This meant that the carriage might reach the mill before the boat did, if that was worth anything with respect to the saving of her.

But of course it also meant that she was swept out of sight of the carriage, even out of sight of any human habitation. She traveled now under great trees that towered over the river, leaning their branches over it as if to enclose it, forming a green and watery tunnel; she could see up onto the banks—banks where she would be safe, if she could only reach them—and into the shady ground of the woods, uncluttered by any understory, where the pillars of the trees were ranged in wide and random colonnades.

This was the longest terror she had yet endured, and yet also the swiftest and shortest. She traveled in this solitary way to the outermost part of the loop, hoping all the while that the boat might slip into an eddy at that point and drift up against the banks; but the current at the turn was swift and bore her around the corner without giving her a chance to seize any brush along the bank or even to glimpse a shallow place where she might leap out and crawl ashore.

Now she was on the last reach of the river before the place where it widened slightly above the mill. She had no hope the water would slow down there before the dam and

so permit her rescue; having seen this place, so mislead-
ingly called the mill pond, only a quarter hour previously,
she knew the water in it was churning at haste toward and
over the dam. To make matters worse, the river was now
augmented by the addition of another small tributary just
before the mill pond.

It was at that very point—where the new stream of water
that had been gathered off the wolds and the steep sides of
the valley entered the river—that she saw Daniel again. She
was traveling still among the dark and incongruously pleasant woods, and he came running through them headlong. In
the slow, excruciating extension of her perception, she saw
and noted that he had lost his hat, if he had been wearing
one when he leapt from the carriage, and that his coat was
ripped and that there was dirt on the legs of his trousers.

He reached the bank opposite the incoming tributary just
before she did. Here the torrents of years had carved out a
hollow of sorts in the bank and left a litter of stones on the
bottom—in short, here of all places the River Clough was
somewhat shallow at one side, Daniel's side; and when he
came to the edge of the bank, he ran into the water without
an instant's hesitation. She had no doubt that he had known
of this spot, had seen it before, perhaps, on some solitary
walk along the river, and had come here deliberately in the
hope of catching her as she passed by.

And in fact, as she came up to him, the entering stream
forced the boat sharply and suddenly sideways in Daniel's
direction. She gazed at him, and even as she saw that the
course of the boat was not going to take her within his
reach, she felt not terror but only love, love for him for having tried so vigorously to save her.

Then he held up his arm—she saw that there was something in his hand—he drew his arm back and brought it
down again, though with a carefully measured force.

It all happened in an instant. The object in his hand was
the coachman's whip, which he must have taken from the

man when he left the carriage behind. Instinctively she reached out for it, opening her hand to catch the long lash before it could fall across the gunwale and slip away. It stung harshly, and she cried out in surprise and pain.

"Hold to it!" he cried.

And despite the shock of her pain, she did hold to it, with all her strength.

As the boat came up against the resistance of this impromptu mooring, it swung about so that it was pointed upstream. She would have thought that the force of the current would jerk at her arm and shoulder and pain her, but in fact the boat was of very shallow draught. It further obeyed its new instruction; it swung closer to the shore, though a perilous gap still stretched between her and the bank. She had been priming herself to leap at the first chance, and now the thought came to her again that she must do so, and she rose to her feet.

But Daniel guessed what was in her mind from this change of her position and from the way she looked at the shore, now so tantalizing close to her, and he shouted, "No! No! Do not leap out! Stay as you are! Hold fast to the whip! It is the whip that shall save you, not the leap!"

She trusted him. She renewed her grip on the leather, using both hands, though the boat was trying to continue its course, tugging at her as if trying to terrify her.

Daniel was up to his waist in the water; he waded back toward the shore—no easy work, for the stones on which he stood were slippery; and Elissa, watching him fearfully, thought to herself: *If I think for a moment you require it to save your life, dear man, I shall let go this whip and take the consequences.* But he soon was out of the water, treading along the narrow margin of sand at the river's edge, keeping tension on the whip the entire time, like nothing so much as a fisherman carefully drawing in a prize fish. He made his way to the boat; he seized the bow with one hand and held it powerfully so that it did not so much as quiver or waver in the current; he drew it close to the shore, so that it bumped up against the rocks there; and then he said, "Now—climb out onto the bank. But do not let go of the whip!"

She did as he said.

As she stepped onto the sand, she was suddenly overcome with the weakness of deferred terror. She swayed; he let go of the boat, rushed to her side, and put his arm around her; and the boat, with nothing to hold it now, drifted free, was caught by the increased current, and shot away even faster than before.

He flung the whip aside and helped her up onto the bank, his arm still tightly around her waist. To her it seemed that she was lifted effortlessly by his strength. They went a little way into the wood, she tottering, he still supporting her.

Then, when they were quite clear of the river, he turned and faced her.

"Are you all right?" he asked urgently, desperately. "Are you hurt? Are you well? What about where the whip struck you? I did not mean to hit your hand, only the edge of the boat—"

She held up her hand and looked at it. There was a red weal across both the palm and the back of it, and he groaned in distress as he saw it.

"It is nothing," she reassured him. "I barely feel it. And besides, it is what saved me."

"But are you hurt in any other way?"

"No, I am perfectly all right," she said. She looked down at herself. "Look," she added, "my shoes are barely wet."

He looked too and saw that this was true. "But your arm," he said. "Your arm is wet."

"Oh . . . I was trying to paddle the boat. But it did no good."

"How did this ever happen? What idiot . . . but never mind that.—Merry, little Merry, is she all right?"

"I do believe she is so—she was never in the boat. She must be half out of her mind for fear of what has become of me, but she will recover from that when she sees that I am safe and sound."

Then he was silent, and she was silent.

He looked at her. He passed his hands over his face once, as if pushing away the thought of having come so close to losing her.

And she, looking at him, knew again, but this time with a kind of final terror and absolute, consummated exaltation, that she loved him and would never love anyone else—never like this. She felt she would die for him quite readily—it would mean nothing to her to die for him, or perhaps it would mean everything.

She opened her mouth and made a sound. Perhaps she meant to say, "I love you," but caught herself. The sound was perhaps the beginning of that first word, "I." But it faded into silence. She could not say that to him, not yet.

He looked at her as if he knew what she had been going to say better than she did. That look made her feel dizzy, and she swayed a little again, and he caught her again; he put a hand on each side of her waist, and the pressure of his hands made her feel her narrowness there and made her think of her own womanliness.

Suddenly he drew her closely, tightly, even crushingly against himself. Because her arms were outside his hands, she raised them and gripped him in return around his shoulders, and she raised her face to look in his.

"If I had lost you!" he whispered, in a kind of terror.

And then somehow—she did not know how it happened—they were kissing one another. It was not just that he was kissing her; she was also kissing him. Neither had initiated that kiss; it was instantaneously mutual.

It was only one kiss, one long kiss; but it was such a kiss as she had never experienced before. This was no sisterly kiss, girlish kiss, paternal kiss, brother's kiss. This kiss set up a current, vaster and faster by far than the river's current, between her lips and her woman's parts, a warm, dark, melting current that ran back and forth inside her and churned every atom of her until it danced and sang in joy.

Dearest! Daniel! she thought. *Am I me, or am I you?*

She heard, from quite close by, voices calling in the wood.

He loosed his arms and stood back, still looking into her eyes. She read there the same ineffable joy that she felt herself; and she thought to herself, as she had many times since she had met him, but now with absolute certainty and satisfaction, *I shall marry you, Daniel Newsome.*

Some boys came running through the wood. "She's here!" they shouted to themselves, to no one. "They're here! She's safe!" and some of them went running away, and some stayed, orbiting around the lady and the gentleman like miniature planets, talking among themselves in wonder and excitement.

"Come," said Daniel, offering her his arm. "Your sister must be frantic—we must find her. And we must get to your father before he has word of this.—Do you feel able to walk?"

"Of course," she said, though she wondered if her feet were even on the ground.

She took his arm and he led the way up out of the woods. It was bliss to press against his side; it was bliss to know her future now, indubitably. If she had suffered terror, it was all for this, and this made everything she had suffered into nothing, a single twinge of pain that prefaced an eternity of love.

They came to the road at the point where the woods ceased and the river and road ran on toward the mill side by side; the carriage had been drawn up here, and the footman was holding the horses, but looking onwards, toward the dam at the foot of the mill pond. Following his gaze, there they saw Charles, and the coachman, and Mr. Blaickie, all gazing in horror over the side of the dam, evidently aghast at the remains of the boat.

Daniel called to Charles at once; he turned; and even at that distance, his overmastering relief was evident; even at that distance, she could guess that he was actually weeping for joy at seeing her safe and well.

Though Charles, stumbling in his emotion, came toward them more slowly, the coachman and Mr. Blaickie ran to them in a mere minute. "We saw the boat come down all alone, Master," shouted the coachman as they drew near. "We thought the lady might ha' fainted and be lyin' down in't. The boat be all smacked and broken on the rocks!"

Daniel waited until they had reached him and said, "As you can see, my good fellow, the lady is quite well. All is well, except for the boat; and I am afraid I may owe you a new whip.—You, boy, go back into the woods where you found us, and search along the banks for the whip I left there. Nay, all of you go, and I shall give a penny to each of you if one of you finds it."

The scene was thus rapidly emptied of otherwise useless boys. The villagers, however, continued to appear on the road and to crowd around the carriage and gawk at Miss Wyatt and the gentleman; and in a minute more, Mr. Herbert arrived, and not long after him, Merry.

What Mr. Herbert felt, finding Miss Wyatt under the protection of his rival, Elissa neither knew nor cared; but she went at once to meet Merry, who was severely distraught, gasping for breath, and barely able to stand, let alone walk another step. The sisters gripped each other, each with a cry, Merry's sharp with grief, and Elissa's soft with reassurance.

Daniel managed to bundle the Wyatt sisters into the carriage eventually, and they drove at once for Aeons' End. As they passed the dam, Merry could not be restrained from looking at what her sister had escaped; and there they saw, shattered on the rocks and still being pounded by the water of the falls, the remains of Mr. Herbert's borrowed boat. "And so might you be!" cried Merry, and made herself further inconsolable.

Perhaps the worst effect of her irrationality was to promote a similar emotion of terror in Charles. The incident fed upon his preexisting fear of bodies of water; and though he did not weep and sob and carry on and cling to anyone, he turned his head this way and that in a panicky manner, he rolled his eyes, and at times he looked appealingly at Daniel as if for assurance that the carriage was not going to fall into the river and vanish with them all.

Fortunately, the journey to the house was a matter of a few minutes; and when the carriage was approaching its destination, pure exhaustion made a lull in Merry's hysteria, and that cessation seemed to allow Charles to take a grip on his emotions. After a moment of relative silence, he suddenly spoke up and said to Elissa, "I declare, Miss Wyatt—you are a most remarkable lady! If I am not mistaken, you were sitting in that boat *smiling.* I do say, *smiling!* You looked up at us in the carriage, and *you smiled.* I am sure I cannot be wrong, though at the time I did not believe it.—Did you not see Miss Wyatt smile, Daniel?"

"I did," said Daniel. "And I hope to see the same on many another occasion, under more auspicious circumstances."

And then—did she not smile then? And blush, too, if the heat in her cheeks meant anything.

"Miss Wyatt is a very brave lady," Daniel told Charles—as Elissa thought, as much to distract Charles from her obvious confusion as to distract the man from his own fear. "She is a very steady lady. She is a lady who will stand true no matter what terrors life brings. You have seen it yourself—she smiles in the face of terror." Then he added vaguely: "You mark my words, Charles; you mark my words." Charles seemed a bit puzzled by this remark, and looked at his cousin as if for enlightenment; but when he received none, he did not press for it.

There was much to be gone through when they arrived home. Mr. Wyatt unfortunately met the carriage and saw the worst effect of the event—Merry's state of terror and grief—before he knew that in fact his daughters had suffered no physical harm, and Elissa therefore required more time than she otherwise would have to explain and to reassure him that all was well. She then took Merry away to her bedroom, to force her to calm down and rest. Daniel changed into dry apparel from the supply in his luggage; and then he and Charles lingered until Elissa felt it was safe to leave Merry under the watch of the maid.

Now Elissa and Daniel must say their farewells again—though even more hastily than they had yesterday, and just as publicly. She apologized for detaining the Newsomes by her misadventure, adding, "You have a long road to travel, and your starting out was already later than you might have wished."

"Indeed," said Mr. Wyatt, seconding her, "so it was; and though I would keep you gentlemen here for another year to thank you, I understand that you must go, and without further ceremony."

Daniel looked at Elissa and then at Mr. Wyatt, as though there were something more he wished to say to the latter; but perhaps in his best judgment he deemed this not to be the time to do so. Instead he stepped up to Elissa, took her hand, bowed over it, and kissed it.

"Stay well, dear lady," he said. "I shall return to . . . to Deepclough, as soon as I can. *As soon as I can*, do you understand?"

"I do, sir," she answered, "and I could neither wish nor expect anything more of you in these circumstances. With that promise I shall be satisfied—for the time being."

He looked into her eyes; and his gaze was so full of love, of joy, of hope, and of shared understanding, that she had no doubt of his intentions. She knew that he knew he was accepted by her, and that for the moment he would be content with that. He would return, he would ask her father for her hand, they would be wed. No gentleman, no man worthy of the name of man, would do anything less after having shown his love for her so openly.

In a minute more, the Newsomes were gone again. But this time their going hardly mattered, because Daniel had left her that promise that he would come back to her soon.

Yes, now her doubts about what he intended were all banished. It was only a matter of waiting; of waiting for his return.

Act II

As Strange as Strange Might Be

When thy joyes were thus at height
My love should turn from thee;
Old acquaintance then should grow
As strange as strange might be.

—Campian

{ 7 }

With Firmest Faith

Where waters smoothest run, deep are the foords,
The diall stirres, yet none perceives it move:
The firmest faith is in the fewest words.
The Turtles cannot sing, and yet they love.
True hearts have eyes and eares, no tongues to speake:
They heare, and see, and sigh, and then they breake.

—Attributed to Sir Edward Dyer

But Daniel did not return.

It was as if some great recurring natural event had ceased; as if the solstice never happened, and the sun just kept receding farther and farther below the Tropic of Cancer until night became permanent.

At first the two sisters sailed along, pursuing that fading sun, on the failing wind of expectation. The first week of the absence of the Newsome cousins was not so very difficult; they had few expectations of a return. When the second week ended, they concluded that something was wrong; and staging a visit to Rowantree, they learned of an event that was enough to assuage their uneasiness for the time being.

"Mr. James Newsome has died," Mrs. Rowcliffe told them bluntly when they came through the front door behind the footman.

"Come in, come in," said Mr. Rowcliffe from the door of the parlor behind her. "You must hear everything."

What little that everything was came out in a rush, told by one Rowcliffe and then the other, and then both of them together simultaneously; and when that was done, they began again.

"We had the news from Mr. Daniel Newsome," said Mrs. Rowcliffe. "The little cold that Mr. James Newsome had when the two gentlemen left Rowantree for Landseye grew upon him—upon Mr. James Newsome—very suddenly, and he died Tuesday week."

"Tuesday it was," agreed Mr. Rowcliffe. "'Twas indeed that cold he had, which was the very reason the young gentlemen went off to visit him like that. It grew on him, you see; it worsened. It seems so very sudden! But he must have been weak in the lungs to begin with, that is what I say."

"That is what Mr. Rowcliffe suspects," said Mrs. Rowcliffe. "And I think it all too probable. Some existing weakness in the lungs—the cold probably led rapidly on to pneumonia and pleurisy and then that was an end of it. These summer colds! They are the worst of all, you know."

"Far the worst," said Mr. Rowcliffe.

"And, if I may ask, how did you hear of this?" asked Merry.

"We had a note several days ago from Mr. Daniel Newsome telling us all about it," said Mrs. Rowcliffe.

From this fact, which the Rowcliffes had not mentioned on their first telling, Elissa understood at once that Daniel had written to the Rowcliffes in the expectation that they would pass the news along to her. He had not written directly to her because until she and he were engaged, it would not be proper; though she did think, for a moment, that he ought to have written to her father. But then even that little pique vaporized, as she thought that, in all likelihood, he did not understand how unreliable communication via the Rowcliffes must be; and she praised him inwardly for his scrupulous protection of her reputation.

"He told us very little," continued Mr. Rowcliffe. "It was a very hasty note. It would seem that our own daughter Agnes, Charles's mother, is also ill."

"I hope not dangerously!" said Elissa.

"Apparently not; but given that the illness has laid one parent low, of course Charles will not leave her side."

"Of course not!" said Merry.

"And Daniel will not leave Charles," said Mrs. Rowcliffe.

"Indeed, he will not," said Elissa.

"He quite dotes on Charles, you know," said Mrs. Rowcliffe. Elissa would have thought that the doting, strictly speaking, flowed in the opposite direction, but she only nodded in affirmation. "And who would not?" Mrs. Rowcliffe continued. "He is such a good, sweet, boy! And now, to have all that wealth and state thrust upon him!"

The Wyatt sisters were silent at this, but the Rowcliffes did not notice.

"And so it has all fallen out to the good," said Mr. Rowcliffe. "That they went to Charles's father just when they did, I mean. It is Providence, as Mr. Herbert would say. Indeed, that is precisely what he called it when I told him of it yesterday."

Elissa had seen Mr. Herbert that very day, but the rector had said nothing of this news; which Elissa thought was rather spiteful of him, unless it had slipped his mind in all innocence. But she did not see how it could have.

"And now Charles may be married," said Mrs. Rowcliffe.

Merry reacted physically to this remark, turning suddenly in her chair, and sitting up straighter; and she darted a look at Elissa, and could not help smiling.

"Yes," said Mr. Rowcliffe with great satisfaction. "Though it is too soon to think much of that, of course; there are things to be done—the arrangements, the lawyers, and caring for his mother. His cousin will be a great assistance to him in these things. And we have even thought, Mrs.

Rowcliffe and I, that perhaps now Charles may take his cousin on as the manager of his estate, and Daniel may get out of trade; which, for all he is a gentleman, still sullies him, you know, and in a way that is now unnecessary. Why, he may be Charles's private secretary—that is a gentleman's title and office; many a nobleman has been secretary to a man of greater wealth and precedence; and *secretary* is a more acceptable title than *manager.*"

Elissa felt mixed emotions at hearing this delusion expressed—irritation at the slight to Daniel it implied, and both compassion and embarrassment for the Rowcliffes. Furthermore, she feared they would not welcome Daniel to their house again when they found out the truth about the legacy Mr. James Newsome had left.

"Besides," Mrs. Rowcliffe said now, "we do not think dear Charles has set his sights on any particular young lady as yet. Perhaps our Michael will be of assistance to Charles next season in London. Why, as the master of Landseye, he will have his pick of the belles!"

"Indeed he will," said Mr. Rowcliffe with still increased satisfaction.

He and Mrs. Rowcliffe looked at one another fondly, and she murmured happily, "More babies!"

"Yes," he said. "More babies in the Rowcliffe line!"
Merry had grown very pale.

Though the conversation wandered for a time among other topics, from that moment it was devoid of interest to the two sisters. After a decent interval, they took their leave.

I am sorry you had to hear that, darling," said Elissa when they were in the carriage going home.

"It is no matter," said Merry. "You and I know he loves me, even if Mr. and Mrs. Rowcliffe do not—or pretend they do not. Did they not notice that he came to our house every single day last summer? Did they think that meant nothing?"

"Yes, but still, it was ugly."

"And as if I were not good enough for him!"

"We shall forgive them," said Elissa. "We have always known they can be obtuse, and it has never stopped us from loving them before."

"Well, the important thing is that now we know why Charles and Daniel have not come back," said Merry.

"Yes, thank goodness! Now we know! And there is no doubt in my mind that Daniel expected the Rowcliffes would tell us immediately."

"I am sure," agreed Merry. "I should have liked Charles to have written to me; but as you would probably tell me, and as Daniel probably told him, it would not yet be proper. And besides, how can I ask him to think of me in that way, when his father has died, and his mother is ill? I only wish I could go to him and be with him. I am sure I could keep his spirits up."

"Yes," said Elissa. "This has been a difficult time for us, but all our uneasiness vanishes in a flash when we find out the troubles with which Charles and Daniel have been dealing! I only hope that Daniel prevailed upon Mr. James Newsome to leave a better legacy for his son; and I would expect that on his deathbed, and with Daniel urging him strenuously, the man might well have relented."

"Oh, I am sure that he did," said Merry. "But in any case, I am sure there will never be any trouble about the money, not for Charles and me; and of course, not for Daniel and you."

Elissa made no response to this, and instead said an inward prayer that Merry's expectations would not be foiled.

The next chapter in their waiting opened a few days later, when the Rowcliffes came storming to Aeons' End, full of bitterness, and craving some outlet for it. They found the sisters in the drawing room. When Elissa heard their news, she was glad that her father was in his garden, because he would have been distressed at the vehemence of their fury against Daniel. She herself weathered it with a mixture of compassion and contempt, her patience buoyed by the sympathetic support she received from Merry.

"You will not believe it!" exclaimed Mrs. Rowcliffe as she came through the door, speaking before Mr. Jens could even announce her.

"That is what we have been saying all the way over," said Mr. Rowcliffe. "They will not believe it at Aeons' End! They will not guess what a viper they harbored in their bosom all this summer!"

One iteration of a cliché was never enough for the Rowcliffes. "And we, too! We harbored him in our bosom as well!" said Mrs. Rowcliffe.

At this Elissa guessed what was coming, and exchanged a glance with Merry, as if to say, "Fortify yourself!" Aloud she said, "Do please be seated, dear friends."

Mrs. Rowcliffe took a seat, but Mr. Rowcliffe did not; he could not contain himself enough to do so, but flung himself, so to speak, by jerks about the room, sometimes stopping to grip objects at random in a dangerous way, as though he might, without being aware of it, throw them through a window.

"It is that cousin of our Charles!" said Mrs. Rowcliffe. "Mr. Daniel Newsome!"

"We shall *not* utter his name again!" said Mr. Rowcliffe.

"Mr. Daniel Newsome will be a name never spoken amongst us again!" said Mrs. Rowcliffe.

With such a beginning, Elissa would have preferred that they kept to their vow; but of course they did nothing of the kind. At this point both the Rowcliffes looked rather fiercely at Elissa, expecting her to ask them to explain themselves; and when she did not, they seemed suddenly to feel some pity for her. Perhaps her distress showed; or perhaps the strict command she attempted to keep over her features succeeded, and they guessed at why she kept it.

"But it is terrible how he has used you, my dear!" said Mrs. Rowcliffe.

"Yes!" said Mr. Rowcliffe. "Coming here all summer! So observant, so *particular* in his attention! Why, it has been the talk of the whole county!"

"And now he will cast you off," said Mrs. Rowcliffe.

"Yes!" said Mr. Rowcliffe. "Who will want our dear, sweet Miss Wyatt, with her five thousand pounds, when he may have any lady he wants, with tens of thousands, or millions of pounds, for that matter?"

Merry made a movement, suppressed as quickly as it arose, as if she would come and sit closer to her sister. Now Elissa was receiving the smart that Merry herself had felt at their last meeting with the Rowcliffes.

There was a peculiar silence. The Rowcliffes, recalling their grounds for anger, now forgot their momentary pity for Elissa and began to glare at her; they needed to glare, and they were looking at her already, so it was at her they glared. Perhaps they still expected her to ask them to explain themselves. When she did not, they plunged on with their vituperation. Mrs. Rowcliffe led off this second attack.

"He has stolen Landseye from Charles," she said. "Do you believe it? Stolen it right out from under him! The *Judas!*"

"He worked on Charles's father," said Mr. Rowcliffe.

"Yes, we are sure of *that*," said Mrs. Rowcliffe. "While Mr. James Newsome was ill, he did it; that Mr. Daniel Newsome crept into the sick chamber like a serpent and whispered in the dying man's ear, whispered and whispered until somehow he turned the father's heart against his own son!"

"There must have been lawyers involved in it as well," Mr. Rowcliffe told his wife, as if just thinking of this. "Corrupted by a promise of a reward if a new will was written."

"Of course," said Mrs. Rowcliffe with a nod, as if she had long since thought of this fact.

"Charles," said Mr. Rowcliffe to the sisters with particularly dramatic emphasis, "is to have *nothing!* Nothing! He is to be left penniless! He is to make his own way in the world!"

"But it may serve *you* well," said Mrs. Rowcliffe to Merry, and in a rather unpleasant tone.

The sisters would have exchanged a glance, but they did not need to. They were both thinking how the Rowcliffes had previously pretended that there was no connection between Charles and Merry; that pretense was now being abandoned, apparently.

"Now, my dear," Mrs. Rowcliffe went on, "your five thousand pounds may look quite useful to Charles; and indeed they will be, unfortunately they *will* be, because Charles has not a penny! But—think of it! To be reduced from a fortune to . . . *only five thousand pounds*, and at the stroke of a pen! To go from marrying the pick of the land to marrying the daughter of a country gentleman! Why, it cannot stand! It *shall* not stand, not while there is a lawyer in England to resort to. That is what we are going to counsel Charles to do—to take up arms and fight for his right to his own estate!"

"My sister," said Elissa briskly, "is good enough to be the wife of any man in this island, Mrs. Rowcliffe, no matter where her father may reside."

"Oh, of course, my dear!" said Mr. Rowcliffe. "Mrs. Rowcliffe did not mean to cast a slight on dear Miss Merry, whom we all love. But just think of our Charles and what a comedown this is for him! To have expected to be a man of means, of ample means, and now to be—though as Mrs. Rowcliffe says, it shall not stand—to be a *nothing*, a *nobody*."

"Charles will *never* be a nobody," said Merry rather fiercely.

"Of course he shall not," said Mrs. Rowcliffe, agreeing with this assertion for reasons quite different from those for which Merry had made it. "He shall not, because the law of this land shall not allow it!"

"I believe," said Merry, refusing to look at Elissa, whom she knew would not approve of her foray, "that Mr. Charles Newsome knew all along that his father had this intention."

If she had cast a firebrand at the Rowcliffes she could not have astonished them more. They stared at her.

"Impossible!" cried Mr. Rowcliffe.

"Indeed," said Merry, "I heard of this same intention on the very first day I met Charles; and so did my father, and so did my sister. He bore his cousin no ill will for it. In fact, he more than once said to me that he was relieved not to be faced with the necessity of carrying on the business of Landseye; for he said he had no head for it, no heart for it, and no stomach for it. He said that all would be much better served if his cousin were master there."

"Impossible!" cried Mrs. Rowcliffe.

"And what is more," Merry went on, "he told us that Mr. Daniel Newsome was deeply distressed by all of this, and meant to prevent it if he could."

"Ah!" cried Mr. Rowcliffe. "That is just it! He, Mr. Daniel Newsome, whose name I shall never permit to cross my lips again, practiced upon Charles, upon poor innocent Charles! Do you not see? If what you say is true, dear Miss Merry, why, it only goes to show that Mr. Daniel Newsome has been planning this and working toward this for years, out of hate and spite and jealousy and greed! And poor dear Charles was taken in! Taken in, all this time!"

"Yes," agreed Mrs. Rowcliffe suddenly. "Yes, this only makes everything worse—that it has been going on for years! And of course Daniel Newsome would deceive his cousin with false promises of setting everything right—how better to allay Charles's suspicions and disarm any attempt he might make to appeal for his rights on his own? I can just imagine it—how Daniel Newsome told him, 'Leave it up to me, dear Cousin, and I shall speak to your father and tell him that I shall refuse to take the estate, and that he *must* give it to you.' And Charles, being the innocent he is, would not see through this wicked ploy, and would go along patiently for years and years, until—suddenly it was too late!"

"Oh, it is all too *wicked!*" said Mr. Rowcliffe.

"Yes, yes, wicked!" said his wife. "And this testimony you give, Miss Merry, only makes the depravity of this vicious man all the more vile!"

"And how does Mrs. Newsome do?" asked Elissa suddenly, in the faint hope that she might change the subject.

"She grows worse by the day," said Mr. Rowcliffe. "That is what we hear from Landseye. The death of her husband was, of course, a terrible shock to her; and then certainly this new catastrophe."

"I am grieved to hear that," said Elissa quite sincerely. "But do you not wish to go attend her?"

"Go near Daniel Newsome?" said Mrs. Rowcliffe. "Hardly, my dear! For he is still with Charles at Landseye, or so we hear. No doubt he is administering the same poison to *her*, to our Agnes, that he gave to her husband, and for a similar purpose—to get sole possession of Landseye and make a mockery of dear Charles's hopes."

The Rowcliffes' lack of affection for their daughter was a scandal with which the Wyatts were well acquainted by now, and there was no point in upbraiding them with it.

"For Charles's sake, then?" said Elissa. "I am sure if you went to Landseye, all this would be explained to your satisfaction."

"No," said Mr. Rowcliffe in a tone of absolute finality. "We shall never go near *that* place until it is firmly in the hands of its rightful owner. But of course Charles may come to us, and we will assist him in his battle to reclaim it—assist him morally, I mean. We cannot divert resources from our own son and grandson to . . . our other grandson for this purpose."

"No, God bless him," said Mrs. Rowcliffe. "He is not a Rowcliffe, after all; he is a Newsome, though Rowcliffe blood flows in his veins."

"You would never know it," said Mr. Rowcliffe. "Not if he stands for this."

"In any case," said Elissa, "I dearly hope that your daughter will soon be out of danger."

"To what purpose?" demanded Mrs. Rowcliffe bitterly. "So that she may live on at Landseye as the dependent of that villain? Better for her to die with her husband!"

"Now, now," said Mr. Rowcliffe, for once thinking his wife had gone too far.

"It is true," insisted Mrs. Rowcliffe, and Mr. Rowcliffe withheld further reproach.

"She may live here with us, if it comes to that," said Mr. Rowcliffe.

"She will not like it if she does," said Mrs. Rowcliffe.

Elissa thought this an odd remark, though she could see how it was likely to be a true one. What mother would wish to move home to her parents and hear how she had been a failure to the family?

"But certainly," said Elissa, "none of this is Mrs. Newsome's fault."

The Rowcliffes were suddenly silent. They glared at Elissa as before, and the silence continued for what seemed a very long time.

"Well," said Mr. Rowcliffe, "we wanted to let you know what had happened. And why you will not be seeing Charles again for quite some time. And Mr. Daniel Newsome—never."

"Do not say his name!" said Mrs. Rowcliffe.

"And we would thank you, my dear Misses Wyatt, never to mention Mr. Daniel Newsome's name to us again," said Mr. Rowcliffe.

"Mr. Daniel Newsome's name?" said Merry wickedly. "It is Mr. Daniel Newsome's name you do not wish mentioned again? But how will it be truly possible to avoid mentioning Mr. Daniel Newsome's name ever again, considering what has happened? For we are sure to discuss these events again, and their consequences, and Mr. Daniel Newsome is intimately involved in them."

"That is certainly true," said Mrs. Rowcliffe. "But his name need not be expressly stated."

"Mr. Daniel Newsome's name, do you mean?" said Merry, with a defiant look at Elissa, who did not need to signal her disapproval of this taunting in order for Merry to guess at it.

"*That man,*" said Mrs. Rowcliffe. "That is what we shall call him from now on: *that man.*"

"And that will do, indeed," said Mrs. Rowcliffe.

"Well," said Merry, "if you hear anything further about *that man* and Mr. Charles Newsome, do please let us know your news. They have been good friends to us over the summer, and of course we are concerned about them."

The Rowcliffes stared, but said nothing further. Mrs. Rowcliffe rose from her seat, and it was understood that they would now leave. As Elissa followed them to the door, she tried to paper over this unprecedented breach in the neighborly relationship between the Wyatts and the Rowcliffes with some talk on other topics; but she could barely find the heart for it. She had never seen the Rowcliffes in such a bad light, and was especially sorry that they had been the ones to cast it on themselves.

When they had gone, she returned to the drawing room.

"Do not reproach me," said Merry. "I am not the saint you are, dearest. I could not sit here and listen to your Daniel slighted—nay, maligned—in that way without protesting."

"Dearest Merry," said Elissa, "you must school yourself not to mind people who are foolish."

"Yes, I know; so you always tell me. 'Only a foolish mind minds fools.' But honestly, are we to have no emotions, no passions that need expression?"

"Express them to someone who can hear them, that is all; to me, or to Charles when the time comes."

Merry started to contradict her, but then submitted to her reproof. "Of course you are right, dear," she said.

"After all," said Elissa, "We have been expecting this upset all along. The Rowcliffes had to find out about Charles's disinheritance sooner or later. It was just awkward that the Newsome cousins kept it from the Rowcliffes. I suppose they did so because they hoped everything might be set right, long before the catastrophe ever happened, and so the Rowcliffes would never need to know."

"Yes," said Merry. "Well, I for one am glad it has happened. Charles will come back free to pay his addresses."

She now looked at Elissa with a particularly impish grin. "And *that man*, as well," she added. "*He* will come back free to do the same."

And she took such mischievous zest in turning the Rowcliffes' spite to this happy purpose that Elissa could not help but laugh.

Another two weeks or so dragged on without any word from the Newsomes. It seemed the sisters had lost an irreplaceable source of information when Merry's wit had driven the Rowcliffes away.

It was Mr. Herbert who was the next to provide news of events at Landseye. The Wyatts noticed that the Rowcliffes were not in church, and fearing some illness might be the cause, inquired after them of the rector after the service. He reassured them that both Mr. and Mrs. Rowcliffe were well; they were only away in Oxfordshire.

"In Oxfordshire!" exclaimed Elissa.

"Yes, that is the place," said Mr. Herbert evasively.

"At Landseye, do you mean?"

"Yes," Mr. Herbert confessed. "That is the place."

"I hope their daughter has recovered," said Elissa in alarm.

"She has recovered from this world, as we say."

Elissa and Merry were speechless, and John seemed devastated.

"Agnes Newsome gone?" he said, after a long moment of silence. "Can it be true?"

"I believe the two of you were of an age," said Mr. Herbert. "Did you know her in her childhood?"

"I did," said John.

"Ah, the loss of our childhood acquaintances—how difficult it can be," Mr. Herbert said. "Even if we do not know them well, just hearing that they have preceded us past that great bourn and gone on into the world to come—"

"How dreadful for Charles!" exclaimed Merry, breaking into this pious soliloquy. "Both his parents within a month! Why, he ought to return here as soon as he may—Papa, you must write him and propose it. There is no finer place to recover from a loss of that sort than in a garden."

"Poor Charles!" said Elissa, in the same distressed tone. "But he has Daniel with him. At least he has Daniel with him!"

Mr. Herbert was astonished; and for a moment Elissa could not think why, until she realized that she and Merry had spoken of the Newsomes by their first names, against ordinary custom.

"Well, we may hope that Mr. Charles Newsome has *spiritual* comfort from some quarter," said Mr. Herbert then. "That would be more to the purpose, Miss Wyatt."

"And so the Rowcliffes *had* to go to Landseye at last," said Elissa. "But how will they treat Mr. Daniel Newsome?— Well, I suppose we ought not concern ourselves with that. The important thing is how he will treat *them;* and we know he will behave like the excellent Christian he is, and not fault them for their feelings against him. He may even succeed in overcoming their prejudices against him."

"It is all very awkward," said Mr. Herbert. "Mr. Daniel Newsome's coming into that estate, I mean." He looked sharply at Elissa, as if to warn her that Daniel's accession to this wealth could only be proof of his wickedness.

"If Mr. Charles Newsome does not mind it, as we believe he does not, then it is only awkward for those who are such as to willfully take it amiss," said Elissa. "Have you not always told me that, Mr. Herbert? You said it was an old principle of the Schoolmen: 'Whatever is received is received in the mode of the receiver.'"

"Ah!" said Mr. Herbert unhappily, at a loss as he found his own teachings used against him. "We shall just have to abide the outcome, Miss Wyatt. We shall just have to see what the Newsomes do in this change of their condition—how they themselves receive what has been sent them by Providence. That is the test of people, you know: what happens to them in ill fortune, as has been the lot of Mr. Charles Newsome, who is now a penniless orphan; and what happens to them in great good fortune, as has been the lot of his cousin. Will they return to Gloucestershire, or not? That is what we must see. Perhaps neither of them will think to return here ever again, for their own different reasons."

He had turned the tables on her, or so he believed, and looked upon her gloatingly. Elissa felt sickened by his cynicism.

The worst blow did not come until some two months after the Newsomes had left. By then the Wyatt sisters were living in a state of profound uneasiness. The Rowcliffes had returned from Oxfordshire, but on those occasions when the Wyatts and their neighbors had encountered one another, the Rowcliffes would only speak at length about how they would *not* speak of "the Charles affair," as they called it. "It is a scandal, and the less said the better": those were the very words they seemed to be intending to repeat *ad infinitum.* They could or would give no news as to the whereabouts of either Charles or Daniel; and as to the state of mind of either, they had only their own conjectures to offer, which were as bad as naked lies. And thus Elissa discovered how quickly neighbors who have lived on good terms for decades may fall out when they can no longer gloss over their deep differences in temperament and interest.

Finally, however, a letter arrived.

It was for Mr. Wyatt. Mr. Jens, having read the return address—which read only "Lakeholm Hall, Oxfordshire," the property of Mr. Daniel Newsome—and realizing the importance of the thing, brought it to Elissa at once; and she at once called on Merry and went with her to find their father in the garden.

His hands being quite dirty, he asked Elissa to open the letter and read it aloud. Her own hands, though perfectly clean, were perhaps even less serviceable than his for this purpose; for they trembled as she read it; as did even her voice.

It had apparently been written in considerable haste. It bore the heading "Off Gravesend." "My dear Sir," it began,

> It is with the deepest regret that I must write to tell you and your family of my departure for Madeira at this very moment, on business both urgent and delicate. I shall return to Gloucestershire and Deepclough and Aeons' End as soon as I possibly can. More I cannot say at this time—they are holding the last boat for this letter.

> With the deepest respect for you and your daughters,
> Your servant ever,
> Daniel Newsome

"Madeira!" said Merry. Her voice was a whispered cry of incomprehension.

Then she turned to Elissa and caught her arm as though she feared some extreme physical reaction from her.

"I am quite all right," said Elissa. But her voice was faint, and she was not all right in any sense.

"It *is* a shock—certainly a surprise," said Merry. "What can possibly be so urgent as to take Daniel away like this?"

"The trade," suggested John. "It is his living, God bless him. He must see to his living."

"Yes," said Merry, catching hold of this. "I am sure he wants to preserve Landseye for Charles somehow; and to do that, he must retain his own living. In any case, perhaps he must complete some arrangements in Madeira before he returns to . . . complete arrangements here."

"So it would seem," said John.

"But where is Charles?" said Elissa suddenly. The question rang in the air like an accusation.

Merry found a reply to it. "Doubtless he has seen Daniel off and will return here any day—perhaps even today," she said, "or tomorrow. I am sure he will explain everything then, and make Daniel's apologies in better form."

"At least we know *he* has not gone to Madeira," said John.

"Yes; thank God for giving him his fear of the sea," said Merry. "It will preserve him. It will preserve . . . *us.*"

Elissa said, "I shall just go inside for a while."

"Of course, dear," said Merry. "The sun *is* rather dazzling all of a sudden."

Elissa turned away and then remembered that she was still holding the letter. She paused and looked back at her father. "May I keep this?" she asked him, indicating what she meant.

"Of course, dear," he said. He himself never kept letters.

She went away to her room, kicked off her shoes, and crawled onto her bed. Then she perused the letter again, not once but a half-dozen times.

It is curious that he does not send us his affection, she thought. *It would not be improper in any way; people far less well known to me have used that term to me in many letters. And could he not think of some little remark for me that he could add to the letter, to let me know that he is thinking of me in particular? He does say he* regrets *having to write us this news. That I can believe, merely because he says it. No, it is not what he* does say *here that is troubling, as much as it is what he does* not *say.*

She remembered the doubts she had had at the end of the summer, when she had feared he would look for an opportunity to leave Deepclough and go away forever. Had those fears come true?

But she lapsed then into a memory—it was more like a vision or a dream—of that moment after he had rescued her; and for some time she lay on her bed, seeing nothing, hearing nothing; and though few people would have realized it, Elissa Wyatt was smiling, ever so slightly.

For her love ached so strongly in her, remembering the way he had looked at her, the things he had said, how he had kissed her—how joyous he had been, how *proud* of winning her love.

No, there was no question that Daniel Newsome loved Elissa Wyatt. Whatever this difficulty was, it would be nothing in her recollection when he came back. And he could be back very soon—though not soon enough for her wishes and preferences, still soon enough by any ordinary standard, no more than a few months.

No doubt Merry was right, and Charles would soon rejoin them and explain everything. Elissa would not lose faith in the truest, finest, most faithful man on earth merely because he had been overset with troubles and was taking some time to work his way back to her. It was hard; but harder for him, surely, than it was for her.

She rose from the bed, and all unconscious of her actions, drifted to the window and looked out on the drive. Then she realized what she was doing: she was already looking for Charles to come, bringing with him Daniel's explanations.

She forced herself to go elsewhere and do something useful; but her thoughts were all in anticipation of Charles.

But even though winter came, Charles did not. Neither did they hear a word from Daniel.

As the time passed, Merry drooped. The change day by day was almost imperceptible, but when Elissa looked back, week by week, and compared the present with even as short a time as seven days before, the slow withering of Merry's spirits was unmistakable. It was as if the sap dried out of her merriment with the fading of the season.

Here the contrast between their characters became evident. Merry had no resources with which to withstand the increasing chill of that absence, while Elissa, even if continually uneasy and even alarmed at times by the absence and silence of her own lover, stood fast in her faith in him.

The fertility of Merry's invention carried her through for some of this time. Charles had gone back to reading law, she said; he did not want to appear in Deepclough again and propose marriage to her until he had a way of earning his living. This was certainly noble, but even as she advanced this theory, she protested against his actions as an unnecessary compunction. To Elissa, it seemed unlikely that Charles could have so easily overcome his own impulsiveness and affection, to say nothing of his aversion to hard study, for this or any purpose. ¶ Then Merry said he must be ill—that he had caught whatever his parents had perished of; and this worried her for some time. To Elissa, it seemed implausible that Daniel had left Charles behind if he were ill, no matter what crisis threatened in Madeira. ¶ Then Merry's imagination had Charles in debtors' prison, the Rowcliffes refusing to help him, and Daniel knowing nothing of his plight. Elissa could only point out how unlikely it was that Charles, in so short a time, could have incurred debts of such a magnitude to have put him in such a predicament.

John Wyatt's mood did not lift his daughter's. The business with the Newsomes affected him deeply; he was, in those months after the cousins left, often absent mentally, and in querying him on some household matter, Elissa often had to speak to him several times to call him back to the present. He was never unkind, but he was certainly depressed. In some ways, Elissa thought, he seemed to miss the company of Charles more than Merry did; as if, despite any demurral he might make, Charles had supplied the place of the son he had lost; as if Charles had taken the burden of that grief from John and borne it for months, and John now found that he could not take it back, could no longer carry it himself. Furthermore, his gardening soul always found the transition to winter a difficult one; the cold days and lengthening nights left him too much time to brood in inactivity.

They made a sad pair, father and daughter, as the winter came on. Elissa strove to cheer them: she argued away Merry's fears and distracted her father from his gloom. But in those hours when she was by herself, despite her certainty that all would come right, she worried, and sometimes she wept, and she wished for just one sign, one word by post or person, from either of the Newsomes.

The holidays passed, and the London Season began. In general the Wyatts had no interest in the Season—had never had any interest in it, though if they had done so, the Misses Wyatt might well have attracted the attention of serious suitors long before the Newsomes happened into their part of the world. To the Wyatt sisters, the Season might as well have been taking place in St. Petersburg. Certainly John would never have taken them to London for any reason, since he had no use for the city himself; and they had no close relatives residing in town who might have invited his daughters without him. But now Elissa received a letter from a former teacher of hers, a Mrs. Harmony, now married and resident in London, at the desirable address of 15 Marmaduke Place. She pressed Elissa to come and visit, for a month or for as long as she liked.

Elissa's initial thought was to kindly refuse this offer; but when she mentioned it to her father and Merry, she met a surprisingly strenuous resistance to her decision.

"You *must* go, dear," said Merry. "Why should you not? It will provide you with diversion during Daniel's absence. And you may learn something of Charles—of what has happened, of what *did* happen when old Mr. Newsome died. That will tell us something."

"Yes," said John. "I am lonely at the mere thought of being without you, dear; but you *must* go. You will never have an opportunity like this again, I dare say."

"An opportunity for what, Papa?" asked Elissa. "To see London? Should that place interest me more than my own home?"

"Well," said John, and came to a pause.

"Yes, Papa? What is it you would say? That I might have an opportunity to meet other men besides Daniel Newsome?"

"I did not *say* that," said John.

"But I do believe you were thinking it. Not that I blame you—I know that you wish only the best for me; only that if you *were* thinking it, I need to tell you that you need not do so. I have every confidence in Daniel's returning to us when he can."

"Yes," said John vaguely. "But still . . ."

Merry took up his words and applied them to her own argument. "But still you must find out what you can," she told Elissa. "We are starved for information, dear; and you may learn more about the Newsomes in a London drawing room in five minutes than we will learn here in five years. For *my* sake, dearest, if not for your own, do please go. You may come home as soon as you have learned anything, if you find you really do dislike London."

As Merry well knew, this argument that Elissa might assist her was compelling; and after dodging it for a few more minutes, Elissa had to agree that London was their best resource.

So she wrote a positive reply to Mrs. Harmony, candidly telling her that her visit might be brief; and her friend wrote back at once with perfect satisfaction, openly expressing the thought that if she once had Elissa with her in London, she could persuade her to stay until April at least.

And so the matter was arranged. Elissa went up by the mail coach, with Dick Broad escorting her as an inside passenger; and from the end of the coaching line, they proceeded to the house of Mr. and Mrs. Harmony in a hired cab.

❁ 8 ❁

The Cause Is Strange

I love, lovèd, and so doth she,
And yet in love we suffer still;
The cause is strange, as seemeth me,
To love so well and want our will.

—Wyatt

It took two weeks of going about in society before Elissa achieved those five minutes in a London drawing room (actually, it was a parlor) that Merry had been so sure awaited her sister here. Her friend's social calendar was quite full; there were continual visits, teas, and dinners to attend, and even one sumptuous ball. Mrs. Harmony's country friend was welcome everywhere, though she found she had to redo certain aspects of her wardrobe that proved to be not stylish enough. The novelty of these London adventures—of dirty London itself, which did not present an attractive face in the colder months—quickly wore off; but Elissa persevered; and the long-sought intelligence was found at last.

She and Mrs. Harmony were on a morning visit to a certain lady, wife of a knight. The parlor was astonishingly busy; there were more people coming and going and sitting and talking than Elissa would ordinarily have seen in all the winter at Deepclough. The footman had announced name after name she had never heard before, and indeed she never expected to hear a name she knew in such circumstances; and now she was surprised to hear one she did: that of Mr. and Mrs. Michael Rowcliffe.

She turned suddenly in the diminutive sofa on which she was sitting and looked toward the newcomers. The movement caught the eye of Mr. Michael Rowcliffe, and he recognized her at once. When he had paid his respects to their hostess, he led his wife straight to where Elissa sat.

"Miss Elissa Wyatt!" he exclaimed. "What a pleasure to find you here!"

She had risen, and now curtsied to his bow, replying, "I may say the same, sir—you know how fond I am of my home, and you shall be the little gleam of it that shines into my London exile today."

He laughed and said, "And you know how little fond I am of Rowantree, so if I may afford you any pleasure by my connection to it, you have done better by it than I am wont to do.—Miss Wyatt, I think you have not met my wife, Anne."

The ladies greeted one another, the one with the warmth of curiosity at a new acquaintance, and the other with the warmth of patent surprise that the country could yield so fine a specimen. For Anne Rowcliffe was, as was soon apparent from their conversation, a creature of the town, and baffled and repulsed by all things rural. Her experience was much limited by her age; for though her husband was himself not too much more than thirty, having been born considerably later than his sister Agnes Newsome, Mrs. Michael Rowcliffe was considerably younger. Indeed, Elissa guessed her to be twenty, or one-and-twenty at the most.

After five minutes spent in the expression of pleasantries—when had Elissa arrived in town, where was she staying and with whom, in what health the Rowcliffes had been when she last saw them, how Mrs. Michael Rowcliffe was now for some months happily delivered of a son (she still had a blowsy, postpartum look)—Elissa took the conversation into a more somber subject by condoling Michael on the loss of his sister.

"Yes," he said easily. "I thank you for your kindness, Miss Wyatt, but of course I knew her so little. She was married away before I was born, and never came home to Rowantree after I was eight or ten. I did sometimes visit her at Landseye when I was at university. It is a splendid place, and not so very far from town—" and in parenthesis to his wife he added: "You would not mind it, dear," and then continued: "But we had so little in common, and my parents favored me so—it was always for us a little uncomfortable to be together.—And her son, Charles, was not such as I would have struck up an acquaintance with."

"Oh, no?" prompted Elissa.

"He is quite a bit younger than I am, you know," said Mr. Rowcliffe. Then he seemed to remember his own wife's youth and, seeking to add an explanation, went on: "I am sorry to say that I always thought him a bit of a simpleton."

"But you cannot fault his disposition, surely?"

"Oh, absolutely not. He is very sweet-tempered. He is like a pianoforte that absolutely cannot go out of tune."

Elissa acknowledged the justice of this description by laughing at its whimsy. And Mr. Rowcliffe, encouraged by that, continued: "But I suppose he is not set in a good light by the contrast with his cousin. Mr. Daniel Newsome, now—there is a man to be admired—solid as a rock; a man of parts, of capability, of principle, of true gentility; one could not help liking *him*. I believe even if one hated him, one would still be forced to like him, to admire him."

"I am especially pleased to hear you express such admiration for Mr. Daniel Newsome," said Elissa, "not only because I believe it is just, but because I find that your parents have, despite your assurance of its impossibility, taken a strong disliking to him."

"Ah, this business about the disposition of Landseye, yes. Well, it *is* odd, on the face of it, but really, if you know Charles at all, it is not hard to understand. One would as soon leave an estate to a baby. Much better to have a sound intellect in charge of things there. I have heard that Charles's father actually forbade any payment of an annuity to him out of the estate—quite cast him on his own in that respect."

"Did he go so far as that, then?"

"That is what I hear, and on good authority."

"It is quite mysterious, is it not?" said Elissa. "Did Charles and his father ever have a quarrel or a falling out?"

"I once put that very question to Charles. He said it was nothing of that sort; and indeed, considering his character, I have to believe him. It is impossible to imagine him quarreling with anybody. The way he described it to me was that on the day he was going away to school, Mr. James Newsome called him into his study and told him, in what Charles described as a perfectly kindly way, that he would not make him his heir. And Charles said that periodically his father would repeat those remarks—I suppose because he thought Charles might not believe him, or might even forget what he had said."

"I do not think Mr. Charles Newsome to be the simpleton you do, Mr. Rowcliffe. I rather admire his freedom from resentment, and think him wise for preferring it to a life of spite and recrimination and regret."

"Oh, it will all come right. Charles will be the better for it in the long run—his cousin will take care of him, have no fear of that. I think Charles has perfect confidence in that eventuality, as well he should. But as you can imagine, Mr. James Newsome's last will and testament quite scandalized my poor parents. No one in the family had ever dared warn them of it, though all the rest of us knew. It even caused a burst of tattle here in town."

"And where is Mr. Charles Newsome these days?" asked Elissa. "We saw quite a bit of him last summer, but since his parents died, he has blown away like smoke."

"Why, he is in London.—You said you were in Marmaduke Place? He is not far from you. You might walk to see him."

"Well, so I shall, if I have a free hour some morning.—Do you know exactly where he resides?"

"I do indeed. I visited him there when he first arrived in London some months ago. You may remember the number easily, because it is the same as your own, fifteen. The street is Courtwalk. His cousin has set him up in a very pleasant place there."

This fact secured, she moved on to a topic even nearer to her heart.

"Do you hear anything of Mr. Daniel Newsome?" she asked.

"He has gone off to Madeira. That is all I really know."

"Yes, we have heard that much ourselves."

"And when he shall return, who can say? The seas are so uncertain in time of war."

This disquieting truism was not what she wanted to hear from anyone.

Though she made a few further deft incisions with her conversational scalpel, she could discover nothing further about Daniel's doings, since Michael Rowcliffe knew no more. The talk lapsed back into pleasantries—she found an opportunity to introduce Mrs. Harmony; and soon she and her friend took their leave, going on to another engagement.

O n the surface of it, it was not utterly unrespectable that she should go visit Charles by herself; after all, she had come to know him in a proper manner, through the introduction of her father, who had approved the acquaintance.

It was, however, a little odd; and she did not tell Mr. and Mrs. Harmony what she was doing. She chose a morning when they were going out to a far part of town; she begged off accompanying them, and they naturally assumed she must be weary of constant visiting; and then when they had left, she set out by herself to purchase some embroidery floss in a shop she and Mrs. Harmony had visited before. It lay on the far side of Courtwalk Street, and so made a convenient destination to mention to the housekeeper; who could only be dissuaded from sending a footman with her by the shortness of the proposed walk.

She arrived in Courtwalk Street at the beginning of the usual visiting hours, eleven o'clock in the morning. The neighborhood was good, even fashionable. She had the distinct impression that Charles had come up in the world since the death of his mother. The door of No. 15 was answered by a manservant, whom she guessed to be, if not a dedicated personal valet, at least a man capable of playing the valet as needed; and this, too, suggested an improvement in Charles's circumstances, for he had not had his own servant before. Perhaps, then, Daniel had seen his way to paying him some kind of annuity, despite the testamentary obstacles raised by Mr. James Newsome.

The man opened his eyes wide along with the door, and after she had inquired for Mr. Charles Newsome, he stood there for a long moment in surprise. Evidently ladies walking alone did not visit here often. Then he recovered himself, bowed politely, murmured that he would convey her message, and showed her into a pleasant parlor to wait. Before he turned to go, he cautioned her that it might be several minutes before his master appeared.

She need not have feared being left long, as it proved. No more than a minute after the message had been taken to him, Charles came bounding down the stairs, and rather burst into the parlor than entered it; but as evidence that he had been called before he was really ready to receive visitors, he was wearing a dressing robe of the sort that was then still called a powdering gown, though men no longer wore powder. She was somewhat shocked by this, but relieved to see that he had on shirt and trousers beneath it.

His greeting could not have been more satisfactory. He was unrestrained in his pleasure at seeing her. "Miss Wyatt!" he exclaimed. "Miss Wyatt! Miss Wyatt! Why, I could hardly think of anyone I would rather see! God bless you for coming to visit!" He seized her hand and bowed over it and kissed it; he held it in his own a little too long; he kept looking her face over in delight as he rattled on. "You are well, I see," he said. "Glowingly well! But you always were so! You bring all the health of the country with you! As I see you again, I can only think what a handsome lady you are! If you will permit such a one as I to offer that compliment, that heartfelt compliment—I see it all anew now, meeting you again after this interval—it is a pleasure to rediscover it!— But how am I so fortunate as to have this visit from you?"

"Why, sir, I must offer you my condolences on the losses you have suffered since last we met."

For a moment grief could be read in his face. "That is so kind of you," he said. "I cannot tell you how the thought of . . . of your family has buoyed me up through all the grief and turmoil I have experienced. It was a gift of Providence, as I think you would say—having that summer with your family before the loss of my own."

"It would be sweet to think that we had in any way helped you in your difficulties, even unknowingly and in advance. We all so wanted to help you when we heard what you were suffering."

"But how do you come to be in London?"

"I am staying with a friend, a former schoolteacher of mine, Mrs. Harmony, in Marmeduke Street."

"Why, that is a short distance from here! Is that not extraordinary?"

"I happened to run into your cousin, Mr. Michael Rowcliffe, at Lady Huston's, and he told me that you were not very far from me."

"Excellent! How fortunate for me!—Now, do tell me: Is your family well?"

"My father and Merry are quite well," said Elissa. "Indeed, we can only be said to be unwell in missing our friends of last summer."

Though he had not flinched in the least at the previous allusion to their history, this one was framed in such a way as to be painful, it seemed. He suddenly became very unhappy and awkward. He stammered through an invitation to her to be seated, and when she had done so, he sat down himself, not quite opposite to her, and looking almost miserable. His rattle had died out; he seemed to know not what to say. She, too, was nonplused; she must wonder if this pain he displayed was a definitive statement that there was no hope for Merry.

After a silence uncomfortable on both sides, she decided to leap in where she had already stepped and said, "We had hoped you would be returning to Rowantree soon."

He blinked once, unhappily, and managed a thin smile. "Rowantree!" he said. "How I do love Rowantree! But I must say, I love it so much only because it is near to Aeons' End."

She kept silent for a minute again, hoping he would draw his own conclusion from this; but he seemed not to. She tried a new tack.

"You seem happily situated here," she noted. "It is a pleasant street, and this seems a very comfortable and pretty house."

"Oh, it is," he assured her. "Daniel found it for me. I am sure I would have slouched back to my old dwellings at Lincoln's Inn, but he . . . he does everything in a trice that I struggle to do in a year."

"That was very kind of him, of course," said Elissa.

This was a topic that elicited a return to warmth. "Kind is hardly the word!" said Charles. "Daniel looks out for my every need. If it were not for him, I do not know where I would be. Why, at this very moment he is in Madeira, with the express intention of—"

He came to an abrupt halt, had no idea how to cover for it, and seemed deeply embarrassed.

She did not know what had caught his tongue, but she had a hunch that finding it out would resolve much of the mystery of the absence of the Newsome cousins.

"With the express intention of . . . ?" she repeated.

"Yes," he said. She was not mistaken: he was turning red.

If she had said anything further to provoke him to complete his sentence, she would probably have failed. But she had an inner monition to remain silent, and she obeyed it.

And it was the silence he could not stand. The unfinished sentence buzzed like a gadfly in the air between them, and he was not conversationally agile enough to swat it out of the way by starting another topic.

"Well," he said at last, "the truth is, he is looking out a wife for me."

She was absolutely shocked. There was a long silence between them until finally she said, in a faint voice: "A wife? Daniel? Daniel is looking out a wife . . . for *you?*"

His own voice in reply was low and faint, and he could not look her in the eye.

"Yes," he said.

"But . . ." she began. She meant to say: *Why should he do that? Why should he do that when Merry, who loves you, and whom you love, is waiting for you in Deepclough? Would Daniel, my own beloved Daniel, do such a thing to you, and to Merry? And to me?*

But she caught herself in time. She only said: "Daniel is doing this?"

"Yes," he said. Then he seemed to fear that what he was saying was being misunderstood in some unknown way, and he added: "He is doing this on my behalf, of course—you understand that he does not act *for himself.*" And he smiled at her. It was clear that he meant to reassure her that Daniel's feelings for her had not changed.

"I believe I understand you correctly," she said, "that your cousin is acting for you, not himself; but the mystery is—why?"

He cast about for some way to navigate these difficult shoals; and the best he could do was to say: "There is a lady we know in Madeira . . . it is a connection my family has with the place."

"A lady?"

"Yes, yes . . . I think she could be called a lady. She is a widow; and is very amiable; and we knew each other some years ago; and Daniel says she will be . . ."

This aposiopesis was less abrupt than his previous one, but equally suggestive.

"Will be?" prompted Elissa.

"Will be good for me," said Charles.

"In what way good for you?" she pressed him.

"Well," he said, a little defensively, "she is a little older than I am. Not so very much older—perhaps about your age, Miss Wyatt. Not that she is so well favored as you; but she is, or at least she was, very pretty; and she cannot have changed so much."

She thought that perhaps some gentle humor might help him. "So," she said, "let me see: She will be good for you by being my age and not unattractive? As to the matter of age, I see that you flatter my sense of the value of my maturity; and as to the matter of looks, I always think that a man ought to have a pretty wife, if he can get one. It makes everything so much easier for them both, if he admires her, and she knows he does."

He was confused; he could only dimly sense that she was teasing him. "No," he said, "it is not *that*. The thing is that she will be . . . steady, and wise, and keep me from doing . . . I do not know . . . foolish things. Particularly with respect to money. Daniel has ever so good an opinion of her in that regard."

"Ah! I see! And perhaps she *has* money as well—I would guess that she does?"

"Yes," said Charles uncomfortably. "She is a widow, as I said; a widow now. Daniel says that she possesses . . . what were his words? 'A substantial estate,' yes, I believe that is what he said."

She did not torment him further by pretending she did not understand how all these qualities were to benefit him. "Well, then, in respect of money, she will indeed be good for you, I should think," said Elissa.

"Yes," he said miserably.

"But are you pleased with this . . . arrangement?" she asked. "Do you think you can love the lady? And that she will love you? Love is not something biddable, in my experience; though I do believe people do sometimes bid money for it."

"Well," said Charles, suddenly relaxing in capitulation, "I would have to agree about that. I should much rather have a wife I can love than a wife who is . . . good for me."

He actually grinned at her, he was so relieved not to have to pretend he agreed with his cousin's plan.

"As I said," he went on, with the air of a man making a clean breast of things, "I have met the lady before."

She was not entirely sure what he meant by this.

"Yes, you said that," she replied. "But where and when?"

"She was my . . . she was the daughter of my father's steward. And she is her father's daughter, you see; a good steward in herself. So Daniel says."

"I see. You know her, and she knows you. And you know her perhaps . . . somewhat well?"

"Indeed, we have known each other from a young age."

"Yet I sense that you remain dubious about your cousin's . . . mission on your behalf," she said.

"I suppose I do," he said. "Though of course, I know it is well-intentioned."

"No one could doubt that," she agreed; though inwardly she was shouting, *Daniel! Daniel! What* are *you up to?*

Meanwhile, her instinct again told her to hold her tongue at this juncture and say nothing further until prompted; and Charles could not endure too much of the resulting silence before he obligingly said, "But you *do* have some doubts?"

She paused for a moment; and then she said, "I shall not trifle with you, Mr. Newsome. No one could help observing how happy you were last summer."

"How happy we *all* were," he corrected her, with a smile. He was certainly alluding to the feelings she and his cousin had for one another.

"Yes," she said, though she could not keep the note of strain out of her voice as she thought of this strange behavior of Daniel's.

Fortunately, he did not notice this discomfort. "That garden!" he said. "What a paradise it was! How I loved every minute I spent there, with your father, and with Mer—I mean, with your sister, with Miss Merry Wyatt."

"Yes," she said again, managing to sound more cheerful this time. "It was heaven, as close to heaven as we shall get on this earth."

"But you said you would not trifle with me," he said. "And how could recalling that summer have anything to do with trifling with me?"

She was impressed that he had been able to track the theme of the conversation so closely.

"You do not understand me, sir," she said. "I meant that to speak of it would be the very opposite of trifling. To speak of it is to be serious, quite serious."

"You mean, I suppose, that anything we might do to continue, to prolong, to repeat that summer would be . . . the best and wisest thing we could do?"

"Something like that, yes."

He sat smiling at her for a long moment in that truly affable manner that he had; and then he said, "I cannot tell you how that very same idea—the idea of continuing that summer—is in my thoughts every day. You see me comfortably situated here, thanks to my cousin; but I would cheerfully move from here, and never see this pleasant house again, if only I could work in the garden beside Mr. Wyatt and . . . and Miss Merry."

"Well, then, why do you not do so, sir? What holds you back?"

He looked puzzled for a moment, as if there were some reason, but he could not remember it; and then, with an effort, he dredged it from his memory.

"How could I live?" he asked. "The money, you know. How am I to live? My cousin constantly tells me that I do not think of that enough, and he is right. I cannot be an attorney, that I now know. I have not the head nor the heart for it. Indeed, I think the only things for which I have found the head and the heart are gardening and . . ."

And he stopped there; and instead of looking happy, or affable, or in any respect as he usually looked, he looked sick, sick at heart.

She again said nothing.

"You see," he said finally, in a thin, strained voice, "the deuce of it is that . . . I really love your sister, Miss Wyatt. But I cannot marry her, as I have not the means."

She chose her words carefully. "I am no one to counsel anyone to absolute poverty, Mr. Newsome," she said. "But I do believe it is better to be happy on a little living than to be unhappy on a great one. If your cousin means to give you something, and Merry brings her settlement, modest though it is, and if the Rowcliffes can in the end see their way to providing something . . . I do believe there would be enough for a small house and a big garden, and . . . for a great deal of love, of laughter, of happiness. That is what I think, at any rate. I am just a woman, with little knowledge of the business of the world, but I think I do know something about running a household; and I think it could be done—if you were careful."

He did not reply immediately. In fact, he did not reply at all. She could see that he was thinking hard, trying to puzzle it all out. After a few minutes, he rose to his feet, went to the window, and looked out on the street. She felt the need to prod him from his reverie, which did not seem to be a positive one.

"I am, of course," she said, "only a sister, looking out for the best interests of my sister."

"Yes," he said, turning eagerly at this. "And you would counsel me to this, would you? Knowing that your sister would be entwined with my fortunes?"

"I confess to you that I have given a great deal of thought to it, Mr. Newsome," she said. "And that is my counsel.—Of course, Mr. Daniel Newsome is only looking out for the best interests of his cousin. And he thinks those interests are best served by an arranged marriage with an heiress from Madeira, who possesses a good head for money matters. I cannot say that he is wrong; indeed, even as I deplore that plan, I see that it has at least the specious appearance of wisdom. But can it be wise, Mr. Newsome, to *marry*—to *take to wife*—a woman you do not love, in preference to one whom you do?"

He looked at her and shook his head. "No," he said. "It cannot be wise. I should hate it. I should regret all my life that I gave up Merry for money."

"I understand you do not love this lady in Madeira. Perhaps that is presumptuous of me."

"No," he said. "I do not love her at all."

"You know her, and you do not love her?"

"No, not at all. I dare say she was . . . fond of me once, and that is why my cousin thought of her. Perhaps I was a little fond of her, I admit; but she was older than I was—her liking was in that respect a bit unaccountable, as young women do not often fall in love with very much younger men. But in any case, when her father discovered how she felt about me, he married her off to a rich factor in Madeira, whom he knew through my uncle's connections there."

"I am puzzled, then. Aside from the practicality of an arranged marriage—the wealth, in particular—which I would be the last to deny, still . . . why would your cousin seek her out now, if you are not likely to love her?"

He made a gesture with his arms, a little shrug. "As you say," he said, "she does have wealth."

"And good looks," she added. "And she takes after her father in being a good manager of her wealth. We have established all this. But you do not love her, and do not believe you ever can."

"No," he said then, rather quietly. "I do not believe I ever can."

He was suddenly very happy; she would have said he overflowed with happiness. He came from the window and sat down in his chair again; he looked at her fondly; he smiled in that charming way of his, a little bashful, hoping to please; and throughout the rest of this interview, though that happiness ebbed and flooded, he leaned toward her, as if he wished not to miss a word she said. It occurred to her that his eager attitude would have been enough to win any woman, and that it was a shame that it should be wasted on her; she felt as if she should tell him to save it for Merry. But then the thought occurred to her that in the case of this gentleman, there would always be more affability where this came from. He was constitutionally incapable of being unpleasant.

"Miss Wyatt," he said, "shall I tell you a secret? I have . . . often lost sleep at night, thinking of Miss Merry and how I was forbidden to have her."

She could not refrain from teasing him a little, as she might have teased Merry. "I am sorry you should miss your sleep, Mr. Newsome," she said. "It is seldom beneficial to miss one's sleep for thinking on matters that cannot be resolved in one's nightclothes. I dare say bed is the worst place to solve any of life's puzzles, and four o'clock in the morning the worst time to do so."

"But I do not mind missing my sleep, you see," he said.

"Truly?" she said, a little archly.

"I should rather lose sleep over Merry than not think of her at all."

"If I may say so, I think you are expending too much effort *worrying* over the problem, and too little in solving it."

"Do you think so?"

"I do," she asserted, with a relenting smile. "I must say, in fact, that I really do not see the difficulty."

The statement seemed to shake him a little. "Well," he said tentatively, "It is just that Daniel . . . that my cousin does not think that . . ."

He came again to one of his tantalizing little halts.

"But you must think for yourself, sir," she said. "You may honor your cousin for his opinion, and yet have a quite opposite one on your own account."

"Indeed! And yet Daniel was so positive in thinking that Miss Merry *does not* love me; and you . . . I am sure, Miss Wyatt, that you would not have . . . said the things you have just said if you do not believe she *does*."

This was a very strange thing to hear. How could Daniel possibly think Merry did not love Charles? She did not believe it; there must be a misunderstanding somewhere.

But again she said nothing of this puzzle about Daniel now; rather she said: "Whom my sister loves and what she shall do with regard to you or anyone are locked away in her heart at present. I cannot make you any guarantee, Mr. Newsome. I must emphatically repeat that—I cannot make you any guarantee of her feelings. There is only one way to find out what they are, and that is to unlock the information with a query. I *can* guarantee that she will answer you frankly, no matter what her feelings may be."

"Oh, yes, I am sure she will tell me frankly whatever she thinks."

"But whatever gave your cousin the impression that Merry is . . . averse to you?"

He looked a little pained, but still he did not lose his smile or cease leaning forward in his chair. "It is not that he thinks she is *averse* to me, specifically," he said. "It is more that . . . well . . . that my cousin believes Miss Merry is—I think this is the way he put it—such a *merry* lady that her affections would seem just as much engaged by anyone else as they have seemed to be engaged by me."

To herself, Elissa had to concede that this was an understandable objection; but to Charles she said, "She is affable to everyone, that is true. But that does not mean that she can never dedicate her deepest affections to a particular person. Do not confuse an open, candid, and loving nature with a reckless and undiscriminating one. And we must remember that your cousin never saw my sister in any other company but yours; so how is he to judge of her behavior in other situations?"

"That is so," said Charles. He seemed happy to be convinced and grateful to her for her arguments. "So you do not think that she would as easily . . . fall in love with someone else?—Not that I presume, you understand, that she is in love with me."

"No, we cannot presume that."

"Indeed, we cannot. That would be an offense against the lady. But we can hope she is so, and we can ask, as I think my cousin himself asked, whether this is a love that is likely to last."

"Sir," said Elissa, with a seriousness that obviously impressed Charles, "I assure you that when my sister has once given her heart to a husband, nothing will shake it loose. Before she marries she may, as young women do— and I believe as young men do as well—have an eye on the entire field, to put it in coarse terms; but once she has found the man she likes best, she will stick to him with absolute loyalty. I know it from the way she has always behaved to me and my father and our friends; which, though that is a different kind of love, still proves something of the true mettle of which she is made."

He smiled so happily at this little speech that she could not help smiling back at him almost as happily. Whatever their financial prospects, Merry and Charles certainly seemed perfectly suited to one another in temperament, and he demonstrated his part of that potential mutuality with every moment of this conversation.

"Well, then," he said, "do advise me, Miss Wyatt, on this point: How am I to tell my cousin of all this? He has counseled so strongly against the marriage—how am I to go against him?"

Her voice had a somewhat cold edge to it now: "That is not for me to say, Mr. Newsome. It is up to you whether you will let your cousin decide how you are to be happiest in life."

This response was patently painful to him. "It is not *that*," he said, "not *that* at all. It is not that I am in doubt *whether* to go against his recommendation, but only *how* to do it."

"Why, that is simple. When and if you and my sister have come to an understanding, you merely write to your cousin, informing him of your plans."

"Yes; write to him. In Madeira."

"In Madeira or wherever he happens to be at the time."

"But the mail to Madeira takes some weeks under the most favorable circumstances. The mail packets, I understand, have to take special precautions in this time of war. And then there is sailing home."

"Sailing home?"

"Yes; my cousin must come home.—Surely you do not think I could marry without my cousin present?"

"I believe the only person besides yourself who absolutely must be present, if we exclude the clergyman, would be my sister. But I do understand your wish to have your cousin present. Indeed, I would myself wish him to be present." Inwardly she added: *There is nothing more in the world that I could hope for, than that my own Daniel should come home again; if for no other reason than to explain his strange actions in this matter!* She then went on: "The thing to do, Mr. Newsome, is to set the day of your marriage in consultation with my sister, and then to announce that date to your cousin. Give him ample time, of course; but do not wait for him, do not delay, if he does not then appear at the proper hour. It is best not to give anyone, even a relation we dearly love, the power of causing a delay in our own happiness. What if he were to put you off, in the hope that his own plans for you might be carried through in the end?"

He had to think about this for a minute.

"But how would I put such a thing into words?" he asked.

"Again, sir, it is simple enough. If my sister accepts you, you write and say, 'My Dear Cousin, I have determined to marry Miss Merry Wyatt, and she has accepted me. We shall be wed on such-and-such a date, and I have every hope that you shall be with me in the little church in Deepclough on that day.'"

"But what of his plans for me? How can I merely brush them aside like that?"

"You merely add to your letter some words to this effect: 'I thank you for all your efforts on my behalf, especially as I recognize the long and difficult voyage you have made in support of my future prosperity; but I have determined that it is, after all, a union with Miss Merry that constitutes my best hope of happiness.' Mr. Daniel Newsome is a man of superior intelligence, and he will doubtless see how the ground lies; he will return from Madeira posthaste and attend you at the marriage ceremony. And knowing his loving and forgiving nature, I have no doubt that he will wish you joy, and in all sincerity."

He now brightened a bit. "Miss Newsome," he said, "you make it seem so . . . doable, so possible! I see that it *can* be done; though I must say that I wish I had your words written down for me, so that I could consult them when the time comes."

If this was a hint, she found it pathetic, if not actually repugnant. "You must speak for yourself then and throughout all this business, Mr. Newsome."

"Of course," he said hastily. "It is just that my cousin . . ." His voice trailed off again.

"I understand, truly I do," she said. "It is just that your cousin is very dear to you, and that you value and respect his advice. And Mr. Daniel Newsome is a man of such integrity, of such deep love for others, of such goodness, that he is redoubtable, and one properly dreads to offend him. I could never bring myself to do so, I know; the very idea makes me shrink. I understand all this, Mr. Newsome. I offer you only my own thoughts on the matter, and only at your own invitation; I would never presume otherwise. And as I have said, I speak as a sister of a most beloved sister, and perhaps

in that role I do not take your best interests into account—
though I truly believe I do. But we are all blinded by our
love; and perhaps I am blinded by my love for Merry, and
do not counsel you wisely."

"Oh, no, no," he murmured, "I can hardly believe that."

She suddenly felt that she could not bear to play this role
any longer. If Charles was truly worthy of Merry, he must pay
his addresses to her without being thrust into it by anyone's
cleverness, and especially not by that of Merry's own sister.

And so, without any warning, she now rose to her feet.

"You are not going?" he said.

"I am, sir. I fear I have stayed too long and said too
much. And perhaps I have elicited too much from you. Mr.
Newsome, rest assured: I shall say nothing of this to my
sister. Do you think on it at your leisure. Weigh the words
of your cousin and the words of your heart, and see how the
scales of wisdom incline. But I do not wish to influence you
further. You have heard what I have had to say, and that is
enough from me on this head."

He was at first distressed at the thought of her departure;
but after he had followed her in a miserable and anxious
silence to the front door, he suddenly said, "Miss Wyatt!" in
a tone that was happy again.

She turned to face him.

He took her hand in his. "God bless you!" he said. "You
have done a great good deed on this day, for which we shall
all thank you for the rest of our lives."

"Think well what you do, sir," she said; but she could not
help smiling at him. "Good day, Mr. Newsome."

"Good Day, Miss Wyatt! And God bless you!"

She curtsied; he bowed; and he opened the door and held
it for her as she passed through.

When she had descended to the street, she had to
school herself to give no indication of her exulta-
tion—Charles might well be watching her from
a window.

And she felt like exulting; she had no doubt he meant to return to Deepclough and to Merry. Only the direct, personal intervention of his cousin could stop him.

And as she realized this, she found she was troubled still. *Daniel,* she said to herself, *what are you doing? Surely this story Charles tells of you cannot be true!*

Was this why Daniel had stayed away from her—because he wanted to prevent Charles from marrying her Merry? Did he honestly believe that Merry would not make Charles happy, after all the proof of it they had had last summer? Did some specious standard of monied contentment count so much with him, that he would cut Charles off from Merry's overflowing affection, for the sake of some heiress in Madeira?

What was it Charles had said of that person—"She is steady . . . particularly with respect to money." So *she* would hold the purse strings. Was this what Daniel wished on his cousin, this kind of life, to be always beholden to his wife for his living, made to beg for a few shillings to buy tobacco?

She recalled with a sudden chill the conversation she and Daniel had had once last summer, when Daniel had spoken of the need to "first consider, then love." Was this that philosophy in practice—or at least in practice on behalf of another? It was mad; it was cruel; it was unworthy of Daniel and of his lovingkindness. "First find the way to love, and then love will find the way"—that is what she should have retorted to him then.

Michael Rowcliffe had said something about an obstacle in the Newsome will to any support for Charles; but surely Daniel could have found some means around that. He could have supported Charles from his trade in wine; surely there could be nothing in the will to prevent such a thing. And he seemed, in fact, to have provided well for him already, if she could judge from the house where Charles was now established.

How, then, could Daniel have made such a serious, such a terrible, error in judgment? As she walked back to her friend's house, forgetting altogether the putative errand on which she had left it, she confronted that possibility in her mind again and again; and ultimately, she found she could not believe it. Daniel was not such a man as to err in such a way. There was more to this story than Charles had told her—perhaps more than he knew or could rightly understand if he did know it.

And with this decision, her thoughts reverted more directly to her own affairs; and she now thought she had one answer at least—she had caught upon it at last, the reason that Daniel had not come back. He meant to marry Charles off, and then, after his cousin's affairs were settled, return to her—return to explain and apologize as best he could and at last pay his addresses.

And how should she feel about that? Could she forgive him for making Merry miserable? Could she go on and marry him and love him when he had done her sister that wrong?

This question was deeply perplexing to her. She felt she could not, should not, ever like or trust Daniel again, if the facts bore out this appearance that he was trying to drive his cousin away from Merry; and yet to dislike the least thing about him was impossible. *Of course I shall love him,* she told herself, *even if I hate myself for it; indeed, I shall love him even if I hate what he has done. It is too late now—I have come to love him, and I cannot change that. I could never marry* anyone *else, I know that—*

And she shuddered at this thought, this thought of marrying someone other than Daniel.

But perhaps all shall be right somehow, she thought. *Perhaps he shall come to the wedding, and he shall see Merry and Charles again, how happy they are; and the money matters will sort themselves out, and they will have a cottage not too far from Deepclough, with a good bit of garden ground, and some honest servants, and perhaps a steward to help them with their accounts. And they will have children and dote on them, I know they will.*

And when Daniel sees all this happiness, and even long before, he will own himself wrong, and he will come to me and he will say, 'Miss Wyatt'—no, I hope he will say, 'Elissa, I did a wrong thing when I tried to interfere between Charles and Merry.' He is that kind of man, he would at once admit that he had made a mistake, the moment he realized it, and he would make up for it, and in the sweetest words and the sweetest manner possible; and all my hard feelings against him for what he tried to do will melt away like the last snow in the coomb come a warm day in February; and then—

And then she slid into a delicious fantasy of what would happen when he had made this confession, of how she would convey her forgiveness to him: how they would kiss as they had in the wood on that summer day when she had last seen him.

❧ 9 ❧

Two True to Love

I was more true to love than love to me.

—Anonymous (from John Dowlands's *First Book of Songs,* 1597)

Elissa expected to hear something from Charles the next day. She rather thought he would ferret out the number at Marmaduke Street and visit her; but though she stayed behind again when Mr. and Mrs. Harmony went visiting, he did not appear. Then she expected a note from him; she expected him to tell her his plans. But nothing came.

These Newsomes! she thought at last, when it was clear that she would not hear from him at all. *They are not at all as communicative as a lady would like.*

But what had happened? Had he perhaps, without her encouraging presence, lapsed back into his awe of his cousin despite her certainty he was clear of it? Or had he rashly run off to Aeons' End as soon as he could secure a team, a carriage, a postilion? Was he at this very moment proposing to Merry?

This last thought was overwhelming; and once she had had it, she wanted nothing more than to go home. And yet she knew that doing so might be a mistake. What if he required another visit from her, another push from behind, to take the step he most wanted to take?

With this consideration came another reversal of feeling: If he required another push from her, she was done with him, and she would do her best to persuade Merry to have done with him as well.

In either case, her work in London was finished.

Her friend Mrs. Harmony was more amused than offended when Elissa told her she was going home. "The country mouse has had all she can stand of the town," she said with a laugh. "There is a cat in every room, and she longs to go home where she can nibble her hay in peace."

As it happened, the Harmony household had a stout old servant who needed to return to Bristol on some family matter; and Mrs. Harmony now dispatched her to accompany Elissa on her way. She arrived thus in Deepclough unexpected by anyone. The mail coach put her down in the village; and leaving her trunk at the inn to be fetched later, she walked up the hill to Aeons' End. When she opened the door and called out that she was home, Merry came running forth from the parlor, laughing aloud, her countenance lit up as Elissa had not seen it since the previous summer. She flung herself on Elissa and hugged her, hung on her, nearly pulling her over; and her laughter changed abruptly to tears.

It did not take long, however, to ascertain that these were tears of joy.

"You have done it, dearest!" said Merry.

"Done what, dear?"

"He has been here! He has proposed marriage, and I have accepted him, and Papa has given his blessing."

Elissa hugged her in return for a minute, as they stood by the door; and then, drawing Merry along with her, and tugging off her bonnet as she went, she led the way into the parlor.

"I want to hear everything," she said, when they were seated there.

"And I want to hear everything from you," returned Merry. "Charles said that he had seen you in London, and that you persuaded him that his cousin was wrong about me—that I truly do love Charles and Charles only, and shall love him forever."

"That is not quite how I put it!" laughed Elissa.

"But why does Daniel think so poorly of me?" said Merry.

"Oh, I am sure it is all some misunderstanding," said Elissa.

"But Charles said the whole reason Daniel went to Madeira was to arrange a marriage for him! That is how determinedly Daniel dislikes me. It is not enough to voice his disapproval; he must actively seek out a rival to displace me."

Elissa could see that Merry was much hurt by this.

"Dearest," she said, "we know Daniel cannot do anything *morally* wrong. But he is mortal, he is human; he can make a mistake in perception and understanding. And you know he loves his cousin; he is only trying to do his best by Charles. If *I* were not absolutely confident that Charles would love you as you ought to be loved, I would be counseling you not to marry him—I would be encouraging you to look at other suitors. It is the same with Daniel."

"But how could Daniel ever think such a thing of me?" said Merry again.

"He does not *know* you, dear, as I do, as we all do—as Charles does."

"Well," said Merry, pushing aside this shadow and smiling again, "he shall soon see that Charles is the one for me—the only one for me; the only one I have ever *truly* loved or ever truly will love."

"Of course he shall see that. And then it will be his duty to apologize to you for ever doubting you; and you may rest assured that he shall fulfill that duty, sincerely, and with a glad heart. For he is the kind of man who relishes the opportunity to declare he has been wrong if he has underestimated another. There is no evil pride in him that would make him wish to pass over an error of that sort; rather, he would be properly proud to make all right again by confessing that he has been mistaken. The only pride he could ever have is in doing right."

This defense of Daniel tumbled out of her before she even knew what she was saying; and yet as she said it, she felt the truth of it deeply.

Merry smiled the more—beamed at her. "I am sure you are right," she said. "I *know* you are right. And in the same spirit, after having complained of him, I must confess that he is not without his reasons for doubting me. In the past I *have* been rather flighty, though I was never untrue to any particular prospect whom I had fixed upon. But that shall be no more, because Charles is to be my husband until the day I die. And nothing could make me happier!"

"I much approve of your view of the matter," said Elissa with a smile. "Now, tell me, dear, how it all came about."

"He arrived here early in the morning yesterday. He had come down from London in the night and stayed at Rowantree."

"He came here yesterday morning! Why, he must have left London by the first coach after I spoke with him."

"I believe he did."

"A very approvable impetuosity in a lover, after such a long delay."

"Well, even then he was put off for a long time by Papa, who was delighted to see him, and kept talking about what had been done in the garden in his absence, and wanted to take him away into the garden at once, and no doubt wanted to keep him there, all to himself. I kept wishing you were here, so that you would find a way to distract Papa and give Charles an opportunity to speak. But eventually Papa talked *himself* into going into the garden, and Charles said he would sit with me for a few minutes more and then follow after him. And then I think Papa suddenly realized what was afoot, and made all haste to leave us alone—it was almost embarrassing."

Elissa laughed at this sketch of events.

"And *then*," continued Merry, her tone becoming dreamy and ripe with her happiness, "Charles paid his addresses to me in the most *satisfactory* manner—full of regret for having lost his way all these months, but the same Charles he always was, cheerful and sweet, and expressing his love over and over in terms *anyone* could not help being happy with. And of course I said yes as soon as he would let me speak; and we sat together on this very sofa, and held hands for I know not how long, and it was *delicious*, and he told me all about how Daniel had tried to dissuade him, and how you had come to him and removed all his doubts in a twinkling. He said you are the patron saint of our marriage! And of course we want you to come on our wedding tour, though we have not decided where it will be—perhaps Wales, or Scotland, anywhere pretty and far away, as long as we do not have to cross water to go there."

"And where is this most satisfactory lover now?" asked Elissa with a smile.

"He has gone into Gloucester to buy rings."

"Rings? Not just your wedding ring?"

"No, I am to have a ring for the engagement too."

"Ah, he continues most approvably impetuous! But I hope he does not bankrupt himself. We do not know how his finances stand."

"He and Papa had a talk about that. You must ask Papa for the details; but I understand that Daniel has left a large sum with his banker while he is away, with instructions to his attorney to pay it out to Charles as a monthly allowance. And he has a house in London, on which the lease is paid up for another eight months, I believe. And of course Papa says that he would be quite happy if Charles and I lived here."

"But Charles has no other income except what Daniel chooses to give him?"

"None. That is what I understand. But how can Daniel not give him something?"

"Indeed, it would be impossible," said Elissa. But she had a lurking misgiving about the correctness of relying on the future generosity of the very person whose hopes and intentions they were all so deliberately thwarting.

"One thing I *do* know," she went on. "And that is that we must see your settlement is continued to be invested soundly. It must not be spent down in the excitement of setting up a new household."

"But there are all kinds of things we shall need," said Merry. "I should think we shall need a carriage, for one thing."

"A carriage is the last thing you need or ought to have, dear," said Elissa. "They are nothing but an absolute vortex to drain away all your wealth, what with upkeep on the vehicle itself and care for the horses; and the wages of a coachman, if you were so foolish as to hire one. You must live in a place where you do not need a carriage—either in London or here in Deepclough, for example.—Tell me, is there any chance of your living at Landseye? Did Charles say anything about that?"

"He is forbidden to live there by the terms of his father's will."

"Really? How very strange all that is."

"Yes. Charles said that the will was written with extreme care to prevent him from having any benefit whatsoever from the estate."

"Really, it is scandalous that people think more of how their money may live on after them than of how their own children are to do the same. How does Charles feel about this? Is he not greatly hurt?"

"Oh, you know Charles. All he says is that he loves his father, and he is confident that his father loved him, and he thinks that it is all for the best for Daniel to have the estate."

"Well, he is the true saint here, then—a true natural saint. To cherish his love for his father in spite of this very unnatural behavior in the man!"

"I am glad that Charles is not resentful. I should be sorry to see that spoil his good temper."

"Indeed, you speak wisely, Merry. As long as it must be so, it is best for Charles's peace of mind and for yours if he does not hold it against his father. And you and I ought to follow his good example and not hold the man to blame."

"Yes, though it *is* difficult," agreed Merry.

They were both suddenly silent; and that the same thought had occurred to them both was proved when Merry suddenly voiced Elissa's own doubts: "Do you not think, though," she said, "that this strange behavior on the father's part is much like the strange behavior we have seen in Daniel?"

"Yes, but only because the way each has behaved is surprising to us."

"No, I mean more than just that. Each man claimed and evidently believed he was acting for the best, though his actions were quite clearly harmful to Charles."

"Yes, I admit that there is a superficial similarity in that respect. But I do believe that Daniel is acting under a misunderstanding and will set all to rights—and somehow will make right even the actions of Charles's father."

"I, too, am sure of that," said Merry.

And then she smiled again.

"Meanwhile," said Elissa in a more upbeat tone, "have you set a date?"

"We are agreed our engagement shall not exceed three months, but we have not set the exact day of the wedding. We are to consult with Mr. Herbert when Charles comes back from Gloucester."

"Three months, you say?"

"Yes. Does that seem too long or too short to you?"

"I only wonder if Daniel can be expected to return in so short a time. He must be told what is taking place, and then make his way back."

"Charles is for going ahead, with him or without him," said Merry.

And it occurred to Elissa suddenly that perhaps Charles was *hoping* that Daniel would not return until the marriage was a *fait accompli;* that even now he did not trust himself to withstand his cousin's will.

She had an opportunity to question Charles about the date of the wedding later that day. He returned from Gloucester long before he was expected and at once came up to Aeons' End to give Merry the one ring and to show her the other.

She hesitated to bring up the topic for quite some time, in part because the extremity of Charles's happiness was reassuring to her. He had found his bride, his companion in life, his spouse; she had accepted him; in a matter of months they were to be wed, and were thereafter to live together. Life in that moment was complete for him; one felt it, one saw it in him. He greeted Elissa with deep affection and gratitude; he took both her hands, he kissed her with a truly touching awe and respect on both cheeks, he praised her for helping him to achieve the greatest happiness of his life, which, he said, meant all the more to him inasmuch as it followed so closely on the sadness of losing his father and mother.

Indeed, seeing him with Merry, it was clear that the hollow of his former sadness, whether deep or not, had been filled up by the gladness of his engagement. There was now no room left in him for mourning. It was a contest between him and Merry as to who could rattle away the faster, who could laugh and smile the more; and more than once they talked at the same time, laughing at themselves as they did so.

At length, however, Elissa raised the issue that was on her mind.

"Merry tells me you are to be wed in three months," she said to Charles.

"That is what we thought best," said Charles, "though I would just as soon be wed today."

"Have you written to your cousin, then?"

Charles looked more serious. "No," he admitted, "but I shall do so tomorrow. First thing tomorrow; and I shall post the letter before I come up to see Merry."

"That would be a very good idea; there is not much time for Mr. Daniel Newsome to receive the letter and make his way home."

"Well, it is as you said," replied Charles. "I dearly hope he attends the wedding; but it is Merry that I absolutely must have there."

This cheerful evasion seemed to evidence the weakness of willpower that she had feared to find in him.

"But ought you not make every effort to include him?" she asked.

"Do you not think three months sufficient?"

"Just barely, I would say. And for the sake of your future friendship with your cousin . . . it seems rather important to wait until he returns; unless, of course, he declines to return at all. Which I do not believe possible! But perhaps six months would be safer."

Charles now looked unhappy and uncertain, and apparently could not think of anything to say.

"Perhaps," said Elissa, softening somewhat, "you could say you wish to wed in three months, but offer to give him more time if you hear from him that he needs it."

Charles still did not look happy at this. There was now no doubt in Elissa's mind that he was hoping Daniel would not return in time; she could draw no other conclusion from his reaction.

She was disappointed in him, but she did not force the point any further.

Thus began a time of great happiness at Aeons' End. Sometimes Elissa even wondered which of them was the happiest: Charles and Merry in their delight in one another and their anticipation of marriage, or John

Wyatt in his delight in Charles as a new son and fellow gardener, or Elissa herself, in the deep joy she took in Merry's joy. And it would not be wrong to say that Elissa felt her joy at Merry's joy even more deeply than Merry was capable of feeling her own.

Very few have ever experienced how happiness can transform a household. I have known a man who lived for years and years with a bitter wife; and on one weekend, for reasons he never knew, her sadness and her loathing of him fell away, and she sang to herself as she went about. He had never heard her sing before; he had not known she *could* sing. And for those two days, the hope lived in him that she might at last have transcended her chronic sorrow and let go of the mysterious resentments she had so long held against him. For those two days, their marriage was a bliss. And then it all stopped, as inexplicably and instantly as it had begun. She was miserable again; she hated her life, she hated him, she hated herself; and so the whole household was dragged down into despair with her.

The love of Charles and Merry was like that singing, but it did not stop. The very servants caught the infection of their happiness. And its effect did not stop there: it spread to Rowantree, where Charles was ostensibly staying, and Mr. and Mrs. Rowcliffe soon came to be reconciled to the marriage. Social visits between the two houses resumed after a long lapse. The village, too, felt the effect of the good cheer radiating forth from Aeons' End. Elissa could not walk down the main street of the place without being saluted in the most benevolent terms by everyone who saw her, or asked after the health of Miss Merry and Mr. Newsome; and she must repeat the date of the wedding a dozen times a day, and hear the promises of all persons she met that they would be present for the ceremony, that they would not miss it for anything.

Indeed, the forthcoming wedding of Merry and Charles became a symbol of something—Elissa could not have said exactly what. Perhaps everyone hoped that, in a broken and disappointing world, the union between these two young people would be the one thing that was perfect. Bride and groom were ideally suited to one another and patently happy in one another. Their characters were so fixed that it was impossible for most people to imagine vicissitude ever corrupting them; and this vicarious perfection fulfilled the incomplete lives of many who knew them.

For Elissa, furthermore, the marriage of Merry and Charles meant a link would be formed between her family and the Newsomes. She did, it was true, feel troubled when she reflected on Daniel's expectations and his active efforts in the opposite cause; but so much confidence did she have in him that it was easy to discount those doubts. If Merry and Charles were right for one another, then how much more so were she and Daniel? She could not help looking at the situation in this way.

So she took part, with ever-increasing gladness, in the preparations for the wedding—the assembling of the trousseau, the planning of the wedding tour, and (insofar as she could) the legal business attendant upon Merry's settlement. She supplied a little ballast when Merry and Charles grew absolutely giddy, but she never squelched their high spirits completely.

As the months passed, she became and remained busier than she had ever been. The large obligations, like the care of the parish, she clung to successfully; but other, smaller obligations fell away from her—her usual correspondence with Louisa, for instance—and later she looked back and wondered at how that had happened, how she could have forgotten such things, and whether in fact it was because in her heart she knew a secret that she could never have consciously admitted to herself.

The only concern that marred Elissa's happiness was that they had no reply from Daniel. As the day of the wedding drew near, Elissa waited with increasing anxiety for some word from him to reach Charles, even if it was a letter strenuously attempting to dissuade his cousin, or no more than a terse note to the effect that he was making his return. Anything would have been preferable to the silence that instead obtained. But it was quite possible that he was sailing with the mails, and that the first notice they would have of his coming would be his arrival itself.

She had somehow expected Charles to partake of this anxiety of hers; but if anything, his nervousness tended in the other direction. Whenever she spoke of Daniel, Charles became uneasy and even a little confused. At such times he at once began talking of how Daniel was certain to approve of his marriage when he finally returned, and he even ran on at length about it, until he had talked himself back into his customary state of certainty and excitement. She did once wonder if he had actually sent the letter to Daniel of which they had spoken, but when she asked him about this, in the most discreet and kind manner she could devise, he assured her that the letter had gone out on the very day after her return to Aeons' End, exactly as he had promised. And she found she did believe him. However much he might shy from harsh truths, he was not a liar.

And so with mounting excitement on the one hand, and with increasing uneasiness on the other, she assisted Merry through the final days of preparation for the wedding.

The ceremony would take care of itself: all Merry need do for that was to arrive at the church as punctually as possible in her new gown and shoes, with her hair dressed; but at home there was to be an extensive wedding breakfast after the service, for which much needed to be done. By the evening before the day, the house was full of flowers in every turn and corner, despite the fact that in that era it was not common to decorate weddings lavishly with flowers. But this was the wedding of John Wyatt's daughter, and every level surface that was not set aside for food and drink bore the blooms of his garden—in bowls, lilies of the valley, ribwort and stitchwort, cowslip and milkmaid, bluebells and buttercups, purple bugle and more; in taller vases, tulips and daffodils, branches of blooming shadblow, cherry, and some late blackthorn. Indeed, Elissa felt almost as if the garden had come inside. Mrs. Tottle and Mabel Dean had taken on a temporary crew of helpers, and kitchen and pantry shelves were full of every good thing that could be baked or assembled ahead. Neighbors and friends throughout the valley sent foodstuffs for the celebration, which were constantly arriving by messenger and cart. In the yard outside, the carriage stood gleaming in the fitful sun of a cloudy day, having been scrupulously polished by Dick Broad and Jim Riggins. Merry's trunk, and Elissa's as well, were packed in readiness for departure on the bridal tour.

From this scene at Aeons' End, Charles was banished on that last day, though he sent frequent notes to Merry by his personal servant, notes that made her laugh outright, and one or two that made her blush and giggle. John Wyatt strode about in a state that could only be described as exaltation, and made somewhat of a nuisance of himself to Elissa by attempting to find still more places for flowers. Merry dashed upstairs and down, forgetting what she had come for when she entered a room, and only remembering it when she returned to the place from which she had set out, only to forget it again when she again went in search of it. Elissa went about with a fistful of lists and a lead pencil, checking off detail after detail, and marveling that their plans for the breakfast, which had grown up gradually over the months, becoming throughout that time more and more complicated, now seemed actually on the verge of accomplishment.

The great day dawned on a heavy rain; but that could not impede the joy that all the household felt. The bride and her sister and father were in the carriage in good time and descending the hill to the village. It seemed, from the rows of carriages and carts and wagons drawn up along the edge of the road near the church, that all the country round had come to see Miss Merry wed.

❈ 10 ❈

Sorrow Awaking

First Voice:
>   What sound is that, so soft, so clear,
>   Harmonious as a bubbled tear
>   Bursting, we hear?

Second Voice:
>   It is young Sorrow, slumber breaking,
>   Suddenly awaking.

—Beddoes

Mr. Herbert began the service. The preamble of the Anglican Solemnization of Matrimony is a stern lecture on the purposes of marriage, and for many a couple it has been the first glimpse they have ever had of the difficulties and disappointments awaiting them; but Charles and Merry, like most young people at the altar, stood smiling through it all, thinking its gloomy strictures could not possibly apply to them, and they remained irrepressibly joyful and certain in their choice. Of course, only Mr. Herbert could see them smiling; but to the congregation, their very stance even from behind spoke their assurance in the matter, and, one might even have said, told their *glee* at being wed to one another.

The call for anyone who could show just cause why the couple should not be married was made and the customary moment of silence was observed. During this interval, Mr. Herbert looked dutifully and sternly about the church, as if to warn anyone who dared to interrupt the service that he or she must have certain proofs of any impediment that might be declared. Then he said to the couple: "I require and charge you both, as ye will answer at the dread day of judgment, when the secrets of all hearts shall be disclosed, that if either of you know any impediment why ye may not be lawfully joined together in matrimony, ye do now confess it." And following the prayer book, he added more solemn language to the same effect; and still Merry and Charles stood in a dream, and the congregation sat behind them in a dream, and all smiled at the formality.

And then the door of the church—built by a carpenter two hundred years before, of oak planks three inches thick, bound with bands of wrought iron, ever before slow to turn on its hinges—burst open with a bang like a cannonshot. All turned in amazement to see who had so rudely disturbed the ceremony.

And into the church strode Daniel Newsome.

Elissa's first reaction was an instant delirium of joy. Merely to see him again woke all her passion for him; she twisted about in her seat, turning toward him, and almost said his name aloud in her delight at seeing him.

But then she felt a pang of fear. She saw at once that something was wrong.

He came immediately to the foot of the aisle. He was reeling slightly—for a moment she thought he was drunk, but then she saw that he was exhausted, barely able to walk or even to stand up straight. Indeed he looked ill, as if he were suffering from a fever. His clothing was filthy. He wore a riding coat with several capes, and high boots, and these were covered with mud, mud so thick that as he came to a halt, chunks of the coating it had formed on his boots and trousers sagged away and fell on the stones of the church floor.

But more striking and alarming than these irregularities was his expression, when he stopped at the end of the aisle and looked on his cousin. It was one of ineffable pain, deep, inner pain. And the marks of that psychic pain and the features of his physical state were strangely blended, as if he had an arrow in his heart, a poisonous dart that was bleeding some toxin into his blood, a hidden wound that would never be healed, which stained all his external appearance with its misery.

There was absolute silence in the church; no one gasped, no one so much as whispered.

Then Mr. Herbert had the presence of mind to say: "Mr. Newsome! What is the meaning of this, sir? Will you be seated? Your cousin is about to be wed."

Daniel spoke; but his first effort was inarticulate. His voice was choked and hoarse.

"Sir?" said Mr. Herbert, still puzzled. "Please either come forward and stand by your brother or be seated."

Daniel cleared his throat, as if with painful difficulty, and spoke again. "No one," he said, "shall be married here this day."

And Elissa, before she knew what she was doing, rose from her seat and cried out: "No, Daniel! You cannot stop them! They are *happy*—they *must* be married."

At the sound of her voice, Daniel stood as if struck; indeed, he seemed almost to shrink for a moment, as a man does when a blow that he has anticipated falls at last. He closed his eyes in agony, and then looked upward, into the high spaces of the church, but he did not look at Elissa.

"What is this?" asked Mr. Herbert, in wonder and frank disbelief. "Do you declare an impediment, sir?"

"I do," said Daniel.

"No!" cried Elissa.

"Well, then, sir," said Mr. Herbert, his voice now betraying contemptuous skepticism, "what is it? Speak up that all men shall hear; speak now, or forever hold your peace."

Daniel did not reply; instead he shifted his gaze to Charles and walked up to his cousin, with that same lurching, weary step.

"Daniel!" said Charles. "What is the meaning of this?"

Still Daniel did not reply; but when he had come within a yard of his cousin, he looked down, away from Charles; and stood there for a moment as if overcome by a weariness so intense that it nearly put him to sleep on his feet.

"Mr. Newsome," said Mr. Herbert with bitter irritation, "do be so kind as to declare yourself so that all men may hear."

"No," said Daniel. "We shall go into the vestry, and you shall shut the doors." Then he added, "Charles, and Miss Merry Wyatt and . . . Mr. Wyatt. We shall go into the vestry; and no one else."

"Nothing of the kind," said Mr. Herbert adamantly. "If you have something to say, let it be said openly, in the hearing of all, so all may know. I shall not skulk in secret and hear calumnies. Speak out, sir!"

"In the vestry," said Daniel again.

"We shall hear you here or not at all!" responded Mr. Herbert.

"No," said Daniel, "you *shall* hear me, and hear me in private. Charles, and Miss Merry Wyatt, and Mr. John Wyatt, and you, Mr. Herbert."

And with that he took Charles by the elbow and led him away into the vestry; and Charles went with him like a sleepwalker.

Mr. Herbert was in a quandary, and stood for a moment shaking his head in irritation and confusion.

"You cannot do as he says!" said Elissa. But her protest, instead of steeling Mr. Herbert, seemed to decide him to the very course she meant to discourage.

"It is irregular," said Mr. Herbert, "but I must. I cannot let the ceremony proceed without hearing his objection.—My good people, please be so kind as to remain where you are. This is some misunderstanding that will soon be got over.— Mr. Wyatt, would you be so kind? And Miss Merry.—We shall soon sort this out. Come with me."

John Wyatt, in a state of some shock, rose from the pew and went to Merry; who stood, frightened and confused, until he had taken her by the arm; and then they, with Mr. Herbert following behind, went into the vestry.

For a moment Elissa was frozen in her dismay at these proceedings; but before Mr. Herbert could close the door of the room, she ran to it and entered there.

Daniel was now standing on the far side of the vestry, paying no attention to the confused little group that had gathered near him, but looking out the small window that lit the place. He turned slowly about now to face Elissa as she paused in the doorway.

For one long moment he looked her piercingly in the eyes. Again she had the overwhelming expression that he was in profound pain, a pain that was worse than anything physical, a sickness of the very soul; and more than anything, she wanted to go to him and take him in her arms and hold him and try to soothe away that pain, whatever the cause.

Then he turned his eyes to Mr. Herbert. "I said Mr. Wyatt and Miss Merry Wyatt and my cousin should attend. No one else. What I have to tell—what I must tell—belongs to the people to whom I tell it; and if they wish to tell it to others, let them. But it is not *mine* to tell, except insofar as I tell it to you and to these few today; and would to God I did not have it to tell! Would to God it were not so!"

They were awed by the fervor with which he spoke, and for another moment they could neither move nor speak in reply. Then Mr. Herbert said, "Miss Wyatt, I am afraid I must ask you to go back to your seat and await the outcome of this strange interruption."

She would not go. But he carefully, and with all the courtesy he could muster, thrust her back through the doorway of the vestry and closed the door, though when it was shut the panels were almost in her face.

For a moment it occurred to her to remain where she might overhear what was said within; but then she scorned to do any such thing, and turned and walked quietly back to her family pew.

As she sat down, an outraged murmur arose behind her.

And then, for the first time, Elissa heard the speculation that arose spontaneously, as rumors will, seemingly from nowhere: "He *has* a wife already!" someone said.

"In Madeira!" said someone else.

No! Elissa thought. *He is not married to anyone else—it is only that Daniel wishes him to be!*

But the rumor grew. The speculation that Mr. Charles Newsome was already wed went through the congregation as an aural contagion, and the folk were soon abuzz with it, and then openly discussing it, until it seemed that their voices must drown out the conversation taking place in the vestry, even for those engaged in it.

At last Elissa stepped out of the pew again and faced them, and a hush fell over them.

"If you would be so kind," she said, "as to keep silence, all my family would be most grateful to you. If we have ever done you a kindness, as your neighbors, please respect us in this, and say nothing until the facts are known. This happenstance is strange enough—I hope we shall soon clear up the matter—but let us at least preserve what decorum we can here in the church."

After that, no one said anything.

How long they waited in total, she could not have guessed. It seemed an hour, an age, an aeon; in reality it might have been ten minutes or fifteen or twenty.

He cannot stop them, she told herself. *What can he have to say? That he has arranged a marriage for Charles already? That he has contracts, documents, that all is agreed and signed and sealed? But they mean nothing without Charles's consent— unless somehow Charles gave his consent in advance . . . if that is possible. No, no, all Charles must do is be firm for once in his life. And how can he not be so, when his own bride stands before him? When it is a choice between wealth and happiness, surely he cannot choose mere money! And when it is a choice between Daniel and Merry, surely he must choose Merry!*

But the longer the delay, the more all strength and certainty flowed from her, until she felt weak and unstrung with anxiety.

At last the door of the vestry opened. Mr. Herbert walked out—rather briskly, in fact, as if he had steeled himself to exercise his authority as rector in a proper manner. As he came forth, he shut the door behind him, which Elissa took to be no good sign. For all his attempt at propriety, his face was pale, and for a moment after he had turned to face the congregation, he looked almost ill.

"There will be no marriage today," he said. "Go back to your homes."

Elissa sprang to her feet, but then she could not move.

"Is it postponed?" asked some daring person.

Mr. Herbert seemed to struggle to find exactly the words he wanted. "This couple shall not be wed," he said. It seemed a kind of prevarication; it was impossible to be sure what he meant by it.

"He is already married!" said someone; and a half-dozen others echoed him.

But Elissa was no longer frozen. She ran to the vestry; and once inside, she closed the door before she did anything else. Otherwise all the village would have crowded in behind her.

She turned at once to find Merry. Her sister was stretched out on a bench, as white as the bridal garment she wore; she was looking into the rafters of the room with unseeing eyes; and indeed, if her eyes had not been open, Elissa might have wondered if she was even conscious. John Wyatt was on his knees at a little distance from her, holding his head with both hands, nearly as pale as his daughter, and saying something that sounded like: "We did not know! How could we know!" in several variations, over and over.

Through the little window of the room, in that fraction of a second before Elissa ran to Merry's side, she saw

Daniel and Charles walking away through the churchyard.
Charles was reeling, and Daniel was helping him and trying
to steady him, though he himself seemed to have to make
a superhuman effort against his own weariness. When she
thought back later on that glimpse she had of them at that
moment, they seemed to her like two soldiers who had been
caught near the explosion of a mine. It was as if they were
helping one another off a battlefield, shocked and witless
and dizzy, unable to hear or see.

But at that instant, she saw only that they were leaving.

And is that it? she said to Daniel silently in that brief
slice of time. *Is that all? You destroy my sister, and then you
run away? You and your cousin, you run away without another
word? Daniel, Daniel, how is this possible?*

She now rushed to Merry, and throwing herself down on
her knees beside her sister, she gathered her in her arms and
held her limp and unresisting body as if she could infuse
it with the fire and strength of her own anger against the
Newsomes.

"Merry, darling, darling, what is it?" she cried. "Whatever
has happened?"

Merry rolled her eyes to look at Elissa, but said nothing;
instead a shudder went through her.

"Will you not tell me?" begged Elissa. "How am I to
comfort you?"

"Never," said Merry then in a faint voice. "Never! Let
us never speak of him again! Of the Newsomes—none of
them!"

"So be it!" said Elissa fervently. "If he has cheated you of
your hopes, then let us never mention his name in our house
again!"

And then she broke into furious tears; and she added,
though it tore her to say the words: "And his cousin! They
are both cheats, liars, breakers of promises!"

And Merry cried out and began to weep too, as if at
Elissa's example.

As awful as her sobs were, this was a good sign, much better than the dry shock in which Elissa had found her. But she continued to shudder periodically, as if attempting to shrug off some filth that had fallen on her; and this Elissa found most pathetic and disturbing.

"Darling," she said, "you are not to blame! You could never have known what sort of people they really are!"

"No," said Merry, between wrenching sobs, "who could . . . ever have known? . . . Only . . . his cousin!"

"His cousin?" said Mr. Wyatt suddenly. "Where is there blame in all of this for his cousin? Only that he did not tell us as soon as he knew. Yes, yes, for *that* I blame him; for *that* I must blame him. But who am I to blame anyone? The man—Charles—came to *me* and asked *me* for the hand of *my daughter* in marriage, and I said . . . I said yes! But how was I to know? How was I to know? Only if his cousin had told me could I have known! But Mr. Daniel Newsome . . . said nothing! Nothing until now!"

"Papa!" cried Elissa then in anguish. "You should not have believed him! What did he tell you? What lie did he tell you?"

"Oh," said John, "it was all true, all true. It was no lie. He had the documents. He showed us the documents! Signed by her hand! And witnessed! All legal, all legal."

"What documents, Papa?" asked Elissa. "What did he show you?"

But John only cringed strangely and would not speak; and at her request, the violence of Merry's sobbing increased so greatly that Elissa suddenly feared that she would hurt herself.

So Elissa now said to John, "Papa, let us not dwell on it—not here, not now. Are you well? Can I ask you to call for the carriage, or should I go myself?"

"The carriage?" said John Wyatt in a stupefied manner. "Yes, yes, the carriage! Let us go home, let us get away from here! Let us go back . . . to the garden! *All will be well in the garden,* do you not see? I shall fetch the carriage. We shall go out the side door here and across the churchyard."

He rose to his feet with a clear resolution of carrying out this errand; but once upright, it seemed that the blood drained from his brain, for he turned very pale and swayed and almost fell. "Are you all right?" she asked him. "Do you stay here by Merry, and I shall go for the carriage."

"No," he said. "I am all right. I shall go."

And he went out by the side door.

No sooner had he left than Mr. Herbert came back into the vestry. He stood slightly apart from the women; Elissa, when she reflected on it later, thought it odd that he had kept his distance.

"This is a terrible thing," he said. His comment had the effect of making Merry sob harder.

"Your commiseration does not help us, I am afraid," said Elissa bluntly.

"I am sorry," said Mr. Herbert; but then he plunged on with the same line of commentary. "How dreadful that it all got so far!" he said. "But I understood from what Mr. Daniel Newsome said that he has come direct from Madeira, direct from Falmouth to this very church, riding through the night, to put a stop to it. For that we must always be grateful to him."

It was a strange thing for him to say; Elissa knew that he had never approved of Daniel. In any case, there was hardly anything he could have said that would have pained her more, and she turned on him, saying, "For the love of God, Mr. Herbert, can you not see that you only increase our suffering? Is this your role here, sir? If you cannot assist and support us—I beg you be gone!"

Mr. Herbert showed both shock and shame at this reproof. "I shall pray for you," he said. "I shall pray for you all."

Yes, thought Elissa, though she refrained from addressing him aloud, *if among your books you find an appropriate prayer, you will mouth it on our behalf! Bookish priest! What use are you?*

Mr. Herbert went away; he had the decency to close the door of the vestry behind him.

A Homeless Heart

Send home my harmless heart again,
Which no unworthy thought could stain ;
Which if it be taught by thine
   To make jestings
   Of protestings,
   And break both
   Word and oath,
Keep it, for then 'tis none of mine.

—Donne

None of them spoke on the way back to the house.

On their return, Elissa ordered the entire wedding breakfast distributed to any of the poor who might benefit from it. The floral decorations were to be taken far from the house and cast into the woods in a spot where neither John nor Merry would see them. She gave direction, too, that the long table be dismantled and put away, and all the furniture rearranged into its old places.

As the servants undertook these tasks, John went into his garden, and Elissa took Merry up to her room and sat with her. These were the respective hiding places in which father and daughter stayed, with only the interruptions of dreary and silent mealtimes, for several weeks. Elissa came and went between them like a nurse.

The most terrible part of those times for Elissa, as she watched over these two people she loved, was that she did not know exactly what had wounded them. She several times begged Merry to tell her what Daniel had said; but her sister's reaction was so extreme that the topic could not be pursued. After one of Elissa's attempts to question her, Merry passed out; after another she vomited violently; after another she seemed almost to lose her mind or to go into a state of shock, and lay pale and speechless and shuddering. John was similarly unapproachable. When Elissa questioned him, he sank into something like an unseeing trance, and only hours in the garden by himself would set him right again.

She soon saw that they might never be able to discuss what had happened. Talking out the pain they had suffered was not their way; they wanted only to forget it. And so she ceased trying to find anything out from them.

The two of them, as the principal parties, were unique in refusing to talk of it. The servants, by contrast, could be brought to maintain a silence about the event only by the most rigorous and earnest and constant lecturing from Elissa; for of course they all wished to comfort the young mistress after her failed attempt at matrimony. The folk from the village were equally impossible to silence. It was confirmed from all quarters that Mr. Charles Newsome had secretly wed a young woman from Madeira a few years ago, but had refused to follow her when she returned to that island, because of his fear of the sea; and though it was allowed that he had thought her to be deceased, he received no sympathy for that mistake. Mr. Daniel Newsome was better spoken of, since his agonizing ride to stop the wedding (that story got into circulation somehow) was almost something out of a song or a story; but still folk wondered why, if he had known of Mr. Charles Newsome's previous marriage, he had not at least mentioned it to the Wyatts, even if he too had been acting under the error that the lady was dead.

In confirmation of this theory, it was said that Charles had at once—on the very day of the abortive wedding—followed his cousin back to Madeira. Whether the source of this story was the Rowcliffe household or not, it was assumed to be.

Thus the mill of rumor sped round and disgorged its unappetizing grist; which folk ate till their hearts choked on it.

Of course, Elissa knew all this to be nonsense. These theories simply did not fit any of the known facts. Charles had told her and the rest of the Wyatts of the widow in Madeira, and never once intimated that he thought her to be deceased, much less described her as his former wife. Furthermore, it was impossible that Charles should be going to Madeira now; the sheer terror of the voyage would have killed him.

What had in fact happened, what *must* have happened, was clear to Elissa, even if her sister and father would not corroborate it: Daniel had accomplished his objective. He had come home with the Madeira widow's agreement to marry, drawn up in legal form and signed by the lady; he had convinced Charles, and Elissa and John and Mr. Herbert as well, that this document was binding upon him. As she thought about this, it seemed to her that it might in fact be legally possible that it was so: that Daniel had had Charles give him a power of attorney that enabled him to contract an indissoluble marriage on his behalf. It might not be possible in England, where the Church had a say in marriages; but who knew what customs and laws obtained in Portugal, or in some international setting?

Charles had wished to present Daniel with a *fait accompli;* but Daniel, the more adroit, had turned the tables on him by presenting another marriage instead as accomplished fact.

After Elissa had spent much time in reflecting on this scenario, however, it began to seem farfetched to her. It was much more likely that Daniel had simply, by the force of his own superior personality, compelled his cousin to desist from a marriage of which he did not approve. The signed documents, whatever they were, had only been part of a misleading presentation by Daniel intended to confuse the officiating rector.

Exactly how Daniel had persuaded Charles to abandon Merry—how he had torn Charles virtually from the embrace of his bride—Elissa could not imagine; but she knew that Daniel had enormous influence over Charles. If she, Elissa, had been allowed into the vestry, she might have been able to support Charles against his cousin's disapproval and against the monstrous act of rejection his cousin proposed—but that was exactly why Daniel had excluded her.

There was, in the final sum of things, much in these events that remained mysterious to her. But one fact was inescapable, and that was that Daniel had done wrong, truly violent wrong to the feelings and even the mental health of Elissa's family, to say nothing of their reputation.

And that it was *Daniel*, Daniel of all people who had done this—that fact was crushing to her.

He was, of all the people in the world, the one she had considered to stand above the capability of such moral wrong. She had built her love for him on the rock of his moral good, and through this one terrible deed, he had wrenched that foundation away.

Daniel—the man she had once believed was destined by God to be her husband; the man she had loved, even adored, from the moment she first met him; the man who had once kissed her and promised to return for her.

Well, he had returned! And how ironic was that return! He had returned to destroy not only her final hopes, but those of her sister.

Like many people who believe they have seen through the workings of divine providence, only to suffer the overturning of their expectations when they are crossed in their own will, Elissa's understanding of the world was utterly shaken. *God knows the falling of every sparrow,* she told herself. *Why, then, did He let me so deceive myself in this man? Why did He let me so love this man—love him so much that surely I can never love another so? Was it to make me bitter, to make me old before my time? To cancel in contempt the spring season of my love, and cast me directly into the winter of my despair? Yes, God knows the falling of every sparrow—and lets each of them fall unaided!*

Thus it was not just her heart that had been broken, in the romantic phrase; it was her cosmos, it was her understanding of God Himself and His workings. For much of our supposed understanding of God's operation is only the fevered imaginings of minds too arrogant to perceive their own puerility. Vast libraries of theology testify to this conjoined poverty and hubris of conception; but it has been well said that the God who can be known is not a god worth knowing. Such a god is only a scarecrow clothed in the paltry dress-up of our human thinking.

Merely to ask why, though there is a good God, we must suffer all the same, is to fail to understand what God is; or rather, to fail to understand how little of God we can know.

This challenge to Elissa's faith, however, did not mean that she stopped believing in God. She still went to church the next Sunday morning, and every Sunday after that, and to the evening services too. She often called to mind those lines from Pope's *Essay:*

> Nor God alone in the still calm we find,
> He mounts the storm, and walks upon the wind.

Even in this storm of emotion, she found God walking beside her. It was one thing to revile Daniel in her thoughts, another thing to revile God. She still loved God, she had no doubt of that; she simply no longer could assume she understood Him. And at times it occurred to her that it was perhaps a good thing that she had lost the illusion of comprehending the Divine. Such false comprehension in fact cheapens our love for God and makes it vulnerable to the very sort of shock Elissa had received.

For quite some time the Wyatts saw nothing of the Rowcliffes. They did not come to church; at times Elissa doubted they were even at Rowantree, though everyone said they were. But in such a small village, in such a small valley, the two families must meet sooner or later; and it was at a dinner party on neutral ground that this acquaintance of many years standing was—again—revived.

If *revived* was the word. The Wyatts went away from the meeting feeling rather poisoned than rejuvenated.

The first striking occurrence of this event was that in the parlor where the guests had gathered to await the announcement that dinner was ready, Mr. and Mrs. Rowcliffe looked with evident compassion upon the Wyatts, and bowed and curtsied, respectively, from their place across the room; and in a most friendly way.

The Wyatts returned this greeting without stinting in kindness, ready to forgive anyone who allowed them to do so. But the Rowcliffes did not cross the carpet to speak to the Wyatts, and Elissa, having a foreboding, did not suggest that her family should do so.

"I see we are admitted to favor again," said Merry in an undertone to Elissa.

"It seems so," said Elissa. "But I doubt that can be good."

The dinner party was large, and allowed of no real private discussion at table; so it was not until afterward, when the ladies withdrew, that the Wyatt sisters were seized upon by Mrs. Rowcliffe. There was no escaping her. In fact, their attempt to do so by retreating to a corner of the room only made it easier for Mrs. Rowcliffe to isolate them. She came and sat down opposite their sofa, and leaned close, and said in tone of thunder: "Well!"

"And how have you been, Mrs. Rowcliffe?" asked Elissa. "We have not met in ever so long."

"My dear, there is no need to gloss over it all. Not with us! We understand your heartache all too well. We, too, have been *grievously* injured by the machinations of that . . . that *villain.* It was not enough that he swept in like a harpy and snatched away the patrimony of our dear grandson—but he had to sweep in and snatch away *the very man himself* on the brink of his wedding!"

Elissa thought "brink" an unfortunately negative choice of words, but said nothing about that; instead she began casting about for some plausible way of distracting Mrs. Rowcliffe and changing the subject.

"Yes," said Elissa, "it was a most unfortunate and mysterious business.—But do tell, Mrs. Rowcliffe: For quite some time I have wondered after the health of Mr. Michael Rowcliffe and his wife and son—hoping they are well. We see them so seldom in this part of the world."

But any avenue out was again denied her by Mrs. Rowcliffe's specific prohibition.

"No, my dear," she said, "I will not have it. You will not turn the subject. I must insist upon saying it: that Daniel Newsome is a *wicked, wicked* man." Then she addressed herself directly to Merry: "And you, Miss Merry! Poor Miss Merry! The very light and soul of *merri*ment indeed, in our little village! To have been *used* so! I shall never cease to think of it with anger in my heart, every morning and noon and evening of my life, until I cease to breathe! It was not Charles's fault—you know that, I hope?"

Merry remained silent; she had turned very pale.

"It is better not to talk of such things," said Elissa firmly.

"Not to talk of them!" said Mrs. Rowcliffe. "Why, you might as well ask us not to speak of a murder committed on our very doorstep! For that is what it was—a *murder,* the murder of a young girl's innocent hopes. It is absolutely the scandal of the county!"

"I do not think, Mrs. Rowcliffe," said Elissa, "that the county at large concerns itself too much with our doings in little Deepclough."

"But how is she to be married now?" asked Mrs. Rowcliffe. "How are *you* to be married, Miss Wyatt? For you must come into this as well. There is no escaping it. Any man who meets you must be told by his friends how your dear sister was *jilted at the altar* by her fiancé. And what will he think then?"

"I would hope, Mrs. Rowcliffe, that he will be sensible enough to know that the incident in question does not and cannot affect the value of my sister in the eyes of God or of good people wherever she may go."

"Well, of course it does not. But they will still think about it, and still talk about it."

"Then pray let us not join them, Mrs. Rowcliffe."

Elissa never knew whether she had made any headway with this remark; if she had, it was immediately reversed by the arrival of Mr. Rowcliffe. In accordance with his usual custom, he had left the dining room before the other gentlemen and sought out his wife; and now he appeared in their corner before Elissa had even noticed his entry into the room.

"You must be speaking of this heinous Daniel Newsome," he said, taking a seat beside Mrs. Rowcliffe.

"We are indeed," said Mrs. Rowcliffe.

"Everyone else in the village—" began Mr. Rowcliffe.

"What do *they* know?" said Mrs. Rowcliffe.

"—believes that Charles was in error and Mr. Daniel Newsome was an innocent guardian angel trying to protect him."

"Which is absurd!" said Mrs. Rowcliffe.

"It is both wrong *and* absurd," said Mr. Rowcliffe.

"No matter what the right or wrong of it," said Elissa, "this is hardly the place to discuss this painful subject."

"Absolutely not," said Mr. Rowcliffe. "You are absolutely correct, Miss Wyatt. And that is why we must say, once and for all, that this fellow Daniel Newsome is—despicable! His sins ought to be published to the world so that he may be banned from all good society; and so that everyone will understand that Charles, our Charles, is not in the least to be blamed."

"Not in the least," said Mrs. Rowcliffe.

"We are seriously considering an action at law to bring these facts out into the open," said Mr. Rowcliffe. "But the expense! And all for—what? Why, the bruit of this sad affair might reach as far as our boy in London. And *that,* we absolutely cannot have."

"Well, sir, you have expressed yourself very finely on this point," said Elissa. "Now let us speak on other, less disagreeable subjects."

"It would be best," put in Mrs. Rowcliffe, "never to speak of this matter again."

"Indeed it would," said Mr. Rowcliffe.

"Sometimes it is just best to *let the stain lie and be done with the jacket,*" said Mrs. Rowcliffe.

"Exactly what I say," agreed her husband.

"Think of him!" said Mrs. Rowcliffe. "Why, now he may divide his time between Lakeholm and Landseye, while Charles wanders homeless through the capital! And alone as well—very lonely. What lady will have him now, now that he has lost his patrimony and left a bride standing at the altar? What father would allow his daughter to risk herself on any such man?"

It now seemed to Elissa that she had to engage with them on this topic at least partially in order to persuade them to abandon it. Otherwise it would recur at every meeting for years to come.

"But what possible motive could Mr. Daniel Newsome have had?" she asked them.

They looked startled at her ignorance. "Why, to prevent Charles from bringing a country family such as the Wyatts into the Newsome line," said Mr. Rowcliffe, in a tone that made it clear that he felt he was stating the most obvious of facts.

"Oh, come, sir," said Elissa. "Are we country families so looked down upon? Why, every day you may read in the paper of some London family whose son has fixed upon one of our rural daughters."

"Ah, but you forget—that Daniel is a climber! He longs, he *lusts* to ascend the social ladder. Do not forget, he was the son of a second son, a man forced into trade to support himself."

This explanation seemed to chime in with Elissa's own suppositions; and yet, hearing it from the Rowcliffes, she could not help thinking somehow that it was preposterous.

"Ah," she said, "they are serving tea. Let us get some, Merry." And she rose from the sofa; and Merry, a little unsteadily, rose beside her.

"You cannot run from it, Miss Wyatt," said Mrs. Rowcliffe dourly.

"At the moment, all we should like is some tea," said Elissa.

They stared at her, dissatisfied; but she calmly led Merry away to fortify her with tea and then to seek another part of the room—anywhere the Rowcliffes were not.

There were many such difficult encounters in those days; but when that first epoch had passed, strangely enough it was not Merry and not John but Elissa who suffered still and could not forget what had happened. Merry's spirits began to rise again, irrepressibly; and when John saw that, his spirits too began to lift. At first Elissa found it disturbing and shocking that Merry could give up her love for Charles so easily; but then she was only glad for her sister's healing, and thought it a blessing of God.

She realized, as further time passed, that even though Daniel's crime had not been committed against her, she herself was wounded far more deeply than Merry had been, because her love for Daniel had been far deeper than Merry's love for Charles.

The more cheerful Merry became, the less need there was for Elissa to feign cheerfulness to buoy her sister up, and thus the more she began to feel her own sense of loss. It was almost as if she took on the grief of her sister and father, curing them of it, but continuing to bear its poison inside her.

And she saw this clearly and finally on a day when Merry and John were doing conspicuously better. It was the first day that Merry had gone back into the garden. She did no work there, but she chatted with John, much as she had been accustomed to talk to him in the days before; and Elissa, coming and going from time to time, as was her custom, to see how they were doing, could hear Merry's voice drifting through the hedges and down the walks, rendered a sweet whisper by distance. Elissa felt like the thirsty traveler who hears, for the first time, the far-off rushing of a brook in a rocky desert; and she realized how much she had thirsted for this evidence of Merry's good cheer. And for the first time she was fully certain that Merry would be well again.

She made the last of these visits into the garden to look for her father and sister at mid-afternoon. This time they were not readily located, and finally she heard from the gardener that they had both returned to the house. Given the size of the garden and its many exits, this sort of mischance was not unusual. She went towards the house now too, and came out of the garden at the gate near the front door.

Here she was surprised by the sight of an unfamiliar carriage on the sweep. Beside it stood her father, holding an opened letter in his hand; and before him was the man who had evidently brought it: Mr. Blaickie, Daniel's servant.

She was so overcome with emotion at this unexpected appearance that for a moment as she stood there, she could hardly see or stand; mist seem to come over her vision and a weakness into her joints.

When her father saw her, he called to her at once; he sounded oppressed and confused. She went to him; but for a minute he did not say anything; he only looked at the letter in evident uncertainty about what to do with it.

She glanced at Mr. Blaickie. He had doffed his hat already and held it in his hand, but now he bowed to her.

She had seen this man only occasionally during that great summer; she truly knew nothing of him, except that he had been attached to the Newsome family for many years. He was in his late forties, perhaps, somewhat weather-beaten—as she supposed, from his time in Madeira; but however tarnished his skin might be by the action of sun and time, his eyes were bright and keen with intelligence. He typically bore himself with the particular sense of assurance that she had seen in Scots who made their living among Southrons—as if wishing to give notice that all but true Scots were dimwits; but now, as he stood before her, his attitude seemed unusually respectful, almost as if he had compassion for what she and her family had undergone at the hands of his master.

Then her father seemed to come to a decision. He held out the letter to her. "Elissa," he said, "Mr. Blaickie is waiting for a reply; and I think you yourself must give it, or else tell me what to say to his master."

She stared at the thing in her father's hand.

Obviously it was from Daniel. Should she read it? Would it not be better to make an answer without even deigning to hear what Daniel said? *Better to cut off all communication between us immediately,* she thought. And then, with rising irritation: *How* dare *he write to us—send us a message in this common manner? What could he possibly have to say to us? Does he attempt to excuse or explain or apologize for what he has done? Impossible! And yet what other purpose could he have?*

Despite her inner refusal to take the note, her arm, as if against her will, extended toward it and her hand opened to receive it. The motion was like an act she watched someone else perform; her body seemed not to be operating at her own command.

Her hand stopped, however, some inches short of taking hold of the note. Her father had to move it the rest of the way, pressing it against her palm.

Thus, in this state of reluctance and confusion, she took the thing. For a long moment she stared down at it, sickened by her own curiosity, raging inwardly to know what it said, and bitterly, determinedly uninterested in it. She noticed that her hand was trembling slightly—she looked up suddenly at Mr. Blaickie to see if he had seen that tell-tale quivering of the note, and she saw that he had, though he was trying his best to preserve a completely neutral expression.

This is what she now read:

Mr. John Wyatt
Aeons' End

My Dear Sir:

I beg that you and your daughter Miss Elissa Wyatt will do me the honor of permitting me to speak with her. I shall come to you for that purpose, if you both will permit it; or I beg you to come to me if you deem that more appropriate.

I hope that you will accompany Miss Wyatt; or, if you do not wish to meet with me, that another suitable companion may be chosen instead.

I have engaged the cottage I believe you know as the old Deane place, on the Oxford road, for the next few days. If you have any uncertainty as to the house, my man Mr. Blaickie can escort you there. The carriage in which he comes to you is at your convenience should it facilitate your visit.

I apologize for sending Mr. Blaickie as a proxy at this juncture, but I am sure you will understand that I did not wish to further irritate any wounded feelings by appearing in person, unexpected and unannounced.

I am at the cottage now, hoping that you and Miss Wyatt will either come at once or, through Mr. Blaickie, vouchsafe an answer and an indication of the time I may visit, or of a later time that you will visit me here.

Your servant,
Daniel Newsome

What is this! was her first thought. Then: *Does he dare to assume I am amenable to his explanations?*

She looked up at Mr. Blaickie. As he saw the look of outrage on her face, he could not hide his surprise. This was not the reaction to his master's letter that he had expected.

Then she turned to her father. "This letter is mine to reply to as I wish, Father?"

"Of course," he said. He sounded relieved that she was taking the responsibility out of his hands, and yet at the same time he seemed alarmed at the tone of her voice.

His alarm, if such it was, as well as the surprise of Mr. Blaickie, increased to a state of utter astonishment, as she now tore the note in half, and in half again, and so on until the thickness of the sheets defied her fingers; and as, that point being reached, she took each separate fragment and rent it again individually, until she had reduced the entire letter to shreds no bigger than the nail of her little finger. These scraps she let fall from her hand as they were produced, and the air took them, and the slight breeze that was wafting over the hill carried them away into the grass by the side of the drive and dropped them there like a shower of unnatural snow.

Mr. Blaickie seemed unable to speak; his Scots jaw was set, and he looked positively grim.

She said to John, "Let us go back to the house, Father."

John turned about slowly, as if he felt in physical effect the psychic pain that Daniel's letter had awoken in him. She took his arm and they made one slow, deliberate step together toward the house; and another; and another. She felt as if she were pushing each leg forward against a resisting object.

"Miss Wyatt—Ma'am!" Mr. Blaickie called to her suddenly.

She stopped and looked back over her shoulder at him. "Mr. Blaickie?" she said.

"Will there be any answer now, Miss?" he said urgently. In his state of continued surprise, his voice took on more burr than he customarily allowed in it.

She let him wait for a moment, and then she said, "I have made my answer, Mr. Blaickie. You have seen it; you may report it. But if you are asking if there will be any further answer, then I shall make it clear: There will be no such answer now—*no such answer ever.*"

He made a noise expressive of his amazement, a Gaelic-sounding syllable with which she was not familiar. She had pierced even the heart of this cool Scot. He shook his head in wonder; and then slowly—as if, like John, he felt the pain in his own limbs that his master would feel in his heart on hearing of this repulse—he turned and ascended into the carriage.

She faced forward again and, accompanied by her father, resumed her approach to the house. She did not turn around as she heard Mr. Blaickie speak to the driver and as the carriage started away, though there was part of her that wanted to shout, to stop him, to insist upon seeing Daniel at once. But the impulse was borne down by her outrage.

When the carriage had gone away down the hill, her father stopped and turned to her again. His face was contorted with anguish.

"Do you really need to send Mr. Daniel Newsome away?" he asked.

No question could have astonished her more, and she stood unmoving and unspeaking, staring at him for so long that he gathered his wits and went on, in a pleading tone: "Must you suffer in all this as well? I know you love him, and I know he loves you."

At this painful acknowledgment of the situation, she found her voice again. "Papa!" she cried, "Do not even speak of it! Under the circumstances, I could not even begin to consider marrying Mr. Newsome—you must know that, you must feel the same way!"

He did not answer immediately; but then he said, "I am very sorry for it, my love. Very sorry for it."

Then, instead of going into the house, he turned away to go into the garden alone.

"We must not mention this to Merry," she said to him.

"No!" he agreed in a wretched tone. "No, we shall not put this, too, on her frail shoulders! She already carries a crushing burden, and one that is not of her own devising or deserving."

He made for the garden gate, staggering with visible exhaustion, as if he were the victim of a wreck ascending out of the surf after swimming to shore.

Though Elissa at first made a show of going to the house after the carriage had left, she did not enter there. Instead she skirted the building, going through the kitchen garden, and taking a path that led up into the woods behind Aeons' End. Her progress was slow: she was trembling so violently that she could hardly walk.

When she had cleared the gardens and made her way under the cover of the woods, she sat on a great moss-covered stone there, trying to think, trying to gain some clarity about what she was feeling.

What she seemed to think at first was that she was angry, and perhaps she was; perhaps that really was why she was trembling. But as the moments passed, speeding away like sparks flying upwards from a bonfire, the anger, if anger it was, was vaporized in them; and into the vacuum that her departing anger left behind, her love for Daniel came roaring back from wherever it had been hiding these past weeks.

She cried out, loudly and inarticulately, in her anguish; the sound was something between a wail and a shriek.

Daniel, Daniel! she thought then. *I loved you! I loved you! How could you do this to me?*

And then aloud she said, in a voice that rang through the little wood: "Oh, Daniel, Daniel! I *wish* I could say 'I *loved* you'—I *wish* it were over! But I love you, I love you still!"

And so for the first time she realized that her love for Daniel shared one characteristic with the love she felt for God. Hurt by him though she was, she had not stopped loving him, and she never would.

❊ 12 ❊

A Scholastic Proposition

Observe that two propositions properly contradict each other only when what is affirmed by the one is denied by the other, (a) in the same degree, (b) in the same respect, (c) at the same time.

—Shallo, *Lessons in Scholastic Philosophy*

Now began Elissa's passage through what today would be called depression, and even then would have been accorded that name, though not in a clinical sense. And yet it was not that grimmest form of depression that occurs when one is without any spiritual rock on which to stand. Elissa felt firm footing under her; it was just that a flood of unease rose around her and buffeted her.

And she was a serious person to begin with; and such people tend to fare better when life becomes difficult. For Elissa, this time of grief was only a portion of the fabric of her existence where the threads of life's sorrow came to the surface of the weave: she remained aware of the strands of joy that were woven beneath and beside it.

She never felt that she would lose her mental and emotional footing and be swept away, but she did believe that she ought to do something positive and deliberate in order to move out of her grief. This was not a selfish goal; this was a duty she owed to God and her family. Her family was, unfortunately, likely to misread her seriousness as depression in the normal course of things; and when there was real sorrow active in her, they became far more alarmed than the case actually warranted; so she felt it would be best to counteract their anxiety by taking clear steps to raise her spirits.

The crux of the problem, as she had discovered after receiving the note from Daniel, was that she still loved a man whom she could no longer respect. For it is one of the great paradoxes of the human heart, whose very beating is a miracle and a mystery, that one can continue to love, and even passionately love, someone who has proven unworthy of one's affection.

To her, and especially because of her particular age (her time in life as well as the time in which she lived), it seemed that the only way out of the puzzle that her existence had thus become was to find a legitimate object for her affections. Among her acquaintances, she was widely acknowledged to be a valuable commodity in the marriage market: their primary considerations were her settlement, which was middling good, and her appearance, which was acknowledged by all to be pleasing. For potential suitors whose requirements went beyond these superficial qualities, she had many attractive characteristics—she was of good disposition, intelligent, well-read, well-mannered, and skilled in the usual female accomplishments of running a household, playing and singing, sewing, and the like. Her friends and family had always urged her to seek a wider field in which to be seen and known, and now they redoubled their exhortations. Merry actually went so far as to write secretly to Louisa Bright and Mrs. Harmony and ask them to invite Elissa to visit, though the Season was over; and though Mrs. Harmony never answered, Louisa wrote Elissa promptly, scolding her for her long silence, and requiring her immediate presence in Bath.

It would have been quite sensible to take up this invitation at once, but Elissa could not. It was not the housekeeping she was concerned about; Mrs. Northaker, aged though she was, could hold the household together for a few weeks or a month or even more. Elissa told herself she was still concerned about Merry, though she could not deny the fact that Merry's greatest source of worry was now Elissa herself. In those moments when she considered her reluctance most clearly, she saw that the mere idea of another husband was still spiritually nauseating to her. It was as if she had lost the appetite for love—for any other love than the love she still had.

She told herself that if she was to marry, then her husband must come to her—must find her out, hidden as she was in her obscure dwelling in her obscure valley in the countryside. God would provide for her if He wished to—so she told herself; thus extending the same error of anticipating, even dictating to, Providence that she had made in her response to Daniel heretofore.

But there was, also, a good and positive reason why she did not go to Bath. There was something in her that was awaiting a maturity of understanding she had not yet achieved. Often on her mind in those days was the conversation she had had with Daniel about waiting. She remembered quite clearly what he had said: "We do not realize how important, how vital our times of waiting are. *Let patience have her perfect work, that ye may be patient and entire, wanting nothing.* It is in the waiting that we become equipped for what we must do—and because of our waiting we appreciate what we do when we are at last able to do it. Otherwise we might unwisely cast it aside when our opportunity finally comes." She felt the truth of these words deeply now; and so she stayed where she was for some time longer, hoping that she would feel compelled at last to move forward with her life.

But it was not the achievement of any new insight that released her from her home. In that respect, she left prematurely, thrust out of her retirement in Deep-clough by an unexpected agent: Mr. Herbert.

Since she had found that the biblical verse Daniel had quoted to her offered her much comfort, it occurred to her that there was likely to be more of the same in the same source. But she had no concordance and no easy way to search the Bible; so one day she visited Mr. Herbert to ask him for Bible verses on the topic of patience.

Mrs. Jens showed her into the rector's study, announced her to Mr. Herbert, and left her there; and the next several minutes consisted of a little lesson in patience in themselves. For Mr. Herbert noticed her only so far as to raise the index finger of his left hand for a few seconds to signal that he was otherwise occupied and would be with her in a moment; then he continued to read in a folio that was closely printed in several columns—tracing the lines with the index finger of his right hand, squinting closely at the text, and mouthing the words to himself as he went.

She actually wondered if this was a show to demonstrate that his occupation was superior to any business she might have; but when he stopped reading and looked up at her, he seemed a little chagrined to discover whom he had kept waiting.

"Miss Wyatt!" he said. "Why did Mrs. Jens not say it was you?"

"In all fairness to her, sir," said Elissa, "I believe she did."

"Well, well—my apologies. I am reading a most absorbing dissertation by a German fellow on Psalm-singing in the early church—something I must address in detail in my own treatise. As you know, the Scottish church is quite bent on this practice. It is salubrious, but I believe it must not be taken too far, not too far. And likewise I find that my discussion of all such matters must unfortunately be limited. My theme of the regulative principle of worship indeed touches upon, and I might even say embraces all of our life not only in the church, but all of our dealings in the world in one way or another; it is a model of the cosmos, and might have readily taught the great Newton what he won only by great difficulty with his petty human researches and calculations. But I must prune back the many shoots and branches of my vineyard so that it may bear the sweeter fruit. And as the Schoolmen used to say, *Qui nimis probat nihil probat*— that is to say, Miss Wyatt, 'He who proves too much proves nothing.'"

"All things in moderation, of course, Mr. Herbert."

"Exactly, Miss Wyatt. 'Tis a pagan motto, that—it can be traced back to Hesiod—curious how little the Bible actually speaks in terms of moderation *per se;* though of course Proverbs says, *It is not good to eat much honey,* and *He that hath no rule over his own spirit is like a city that is broken down, and without walls.* And we are always taught to be sober-minded in the Epistles. Now, if we consider—"

She saw that he was about to start off on an unasked-for private discourse, so she made so bold as to interrupt him.

"That is the very thing I came to consult you about, Mr. Herbert," she said. "I am looking for some Bible verses on a particular theme—not on the theme of moderation, but on the theme of being patient and waiting on the Lord's own good time."

He was startled at first that she had cut into his incipient sermon, but then he was appeased by her deference to him. "Ah!" he said. "Now, there is a topic that we may find well represented in the biblical text."

But for a moment more he said nothing; instead he looked at her, as if a new thought had come into his mind. His hesitation was odd and a little unnerving to her.

"Waiting," he said again. "Waiting for the Lord's own good time. Yes, that *is* an important theme—and of course, part of it is recognizing the Lord's own good time when it arrives."

As if to give her more practice in patience, he kept her waiting still for a few moments longer; and then he rose abruptly from his seat and went to a secretary's desk that stood in a corner of the study. It had been part of the furniture of the room for as long as Elissa could remember, but it had never served as anything more than a stand on which the copious overflow from the book presses could be lodged. He now began to remove these books and to deposit them rather hastily on whatever other horizontal surfaces offered. "Do be helpful, Miss Wyatt," he said, "and assist me in clearing this desk."

She stepped forward at once to do as he bade her. Though he had limited his own efforts to moving only a few books at a time, when he had her at his disposal, he shifted an enormous load of volumes into her arms—so many she could barely carry them, though she was by no means a weakling. She turned away, seeking a spot for them, and could find none readily; so she had to cross the room, the books threatening all the while to slip from her straining fingers, to an open area of the floor. Despite her care in laying them down—she actually sank to her knees in an attempt to break their fall—they still thumped roughly on the floor.

"Do have a care, Miss Wyatt!" exclaimed Mr. Herbert. "Those are not French novels!"

I hope not, she thought; for not one of the volumes could have weighed less than five pounds.

She went back to the desk for more. Mr. Herbert now ceased moving books himself, except to load her arms. It really was remarkable how many books the desk had accumulated; but evidently that accumulation had occurred over a great many years, because when she was through distributing the volumes elsewhere in the study, she found her front and skirts were covered with a bitter-smelling, brown dust.

"Now, Miss Wyatt," said Mr. Herbert, indicating the chair belonging to the desk, "sit you down, sit you down, while I bring you some ink."

She made shift as well as she could to dust the seat of the chair, which was truly filthy with neglect, and there she perched herself while he brought an inkwell, a quill, and a sheet of scrap paper. The last turned out to be an old list, apparently from his student days, recording charges paid to a washerwoman in the course of a university term.

Having thus equipped her, he went back to sit at his desk, hauled a volume off a stack near at hand, and looked through it until he found the page he wanted.

"Now, Miss Wyatt," he said again. "Do you write down the passages that I shall cite to you."

He now began to cite Bible passages by book, chapter, and verse, not giving any of the text; though he evidently had some of the text before him, since he chose some passages to give her and rejected others. Elissa had never seen a concordance, but she immediately grasped the nature of the book he was using; and she would have preferred that he had merely shown her the page and let her copy it at leisure; for his instructions to her were garbled and hasty. He sometimes told her to write down a citation, and then changed his mind, insisting that she scratch it out; at other times he misread the citation, and only discovered he had done so after reading several intervening citations, so that she accidently corrected the wrong numbers, only to have him scold her for doing so when he double-checked whether she had done what he requested. He gave her none of his reasons for choosing some verses over others, and she had the distinct impression that he was discarding some that might have been of interest to her. The pen he had given her, too, was ill-trimmed and balky, depositing blotches of ink on the sheet and thus inevitably on her fingers and hands; and though this was one of the hazards of writing in that time, it increased her sense of becoming gradually soiled. She did not mind good, honest dirt when it was part of a task; but the ink stains in this case were bothersome to her because they were so unnecessary.

All in all, the process was very demeaning to her and irritating to them both. And it was very mechanical. She could not help contrasting it with the conversations she used to have with Daniel on biblical subjects. Daniel had all the verses he needed at his fingers' ends, and no need for ink; when he had spoken to her on this particular topic, his words were alive, and she had felt uplifted and strengthened and eager for more knowledge; whereas Mr. Herbert only made her feel (against her own better judgment) that the Bible was a dead letter and that further research in it for this purpose was likely to be dry and unproductive.

This unhappy exercise continued for an incredible length of time. Mr. Herbert searched through the concordance entries for *Wait, Waited, Waiteth, Waiting, Patience, Patient,* and *Patiently;* and just when Elissa was congratulating herself with relief on his coming to the end of these, he hit on the idea of trying other related words, such as *Expectation, Expected, Expecting.* When he finally ground to a halt, he remained sitting at his own desk, again oddly silent, and looking out abstractedly through the rather dirty window at the rectory yard and the empty road beyond it.

"Well, sir," she said, standing up at last to put an end to the visit, "I am very grateful to you."

He held up his hand imperiously. "Please, Miss Wyatt," he said. "Wait." He did not seem to be aware of the peculiar irony of his giving her that directive at that particular time; nor did he soften this command by so much as a glance at her, but continued looking away.

This she found to be very odd behavior indeed, but she sat down again, facing toward him, and waiting, per his orders.

It must have been five more minutes before he began to speak again; and then she immediately wished she had defied him and run out of the house when she had had the chance.

"I am not unaware, Miss Wyatt," he said, "of your purpose in making this request to me. I admit that I was not sure at first what you meant by it; but now I feel confident. It is, of course, a sort of reproach to me, but wonderfully subtle and graceful and feminine; and I feel the exquisite delicacy of your reproof even as I smart under it. For we are, of course, advised to accept reproof. *He that heareth reproof getteth understanding;* and I have got understanding through this your mild and courteous reproof of me this day."

"Mr. Herbert," she said hastily, "I truly intended no—"

He held up his hand imperiously again, and he laughed in a dry, hollow way that reminded her of the ruffling of the pages of an ancient and dusty book.

"Do you know, Miss Wyatt," he went on, "I have oftentimes looked into that corner at that disused desk and thought of you sitting at it."

She looked at the battered desk in dubious wonder at this surprising declaration.

"I have often thought of you sitting there," he said, "taking dictation as I compose my treatise, or assisting me in my researches—organizing my notes alphabetically or topically, for example. There are so many ways in which you could assist me."

"It is very kind of you to think of me in that way, sir—"

Again the imperious gesture for silence.

"Miss Wyatt, you know that I was once married."

"Yes, sir."

"I tell you, if there is any verse of the Bible that burns in my mind and torments me, it is Proverbs 5:18: *Rejoice with the wife of thy youth.* The wife of my . . . *early* youth is gone; I shall not be vouchsafed her presence on this earth again. What I believe Solomon was there saying was that it is by marrying young and growing old with a spouse that we experience the fullness of marriage that God intended for us. A man who loses his wife at a young age can never again experience all of life with the same spouse, so his life is bound to be impoverished in comparison with the life of a man who has met life's difficulties and challenges, tasted its joys and pleasure, all with the same wife.—Do you see what I mean?"

"I believe I do, sir," she said. "Please accept my condolences for the grief I can see that you still do intensely feel."

He did not appear to have heard her reply, or to care about it. "But," he went on, "we make do with what we are given, and bless the providence of the Lord. It is written in Philippians: *This one thing I do, forgetting those things which are behind, and reaching forth unto those things which are before.* We must constantly look before us and give up those things that are in the past."

"This is good advice, sir," she said. "Indeed, very holy advice." Again he gave no sign of having heard her.

She had seen at once where all this talk was tending, though exactly how it was going to get to its destination, she was not sure; and its progress caused an increasing sense of horror and panic within her. She had to fight the impulse to blurt out something about needing to be elsewhere, and to bolt from the room. Only the fact that she lived in this small village with this particular clergyman—that his company really could not be avoided—made her seek instead for some more courteous resolution of this crisis.

"However," he said, "be all that as it may—I am still young, I dare say. If I marry again, I may be assured that my wife, no matter her own age, will look upon me as eminently young and marriageable."

She was quite surprised at this reversal of direction. She looked at him now with the critical eyes of a woman contemplating a man as a potential husband; and, though she was a little ashamed of her lack of charity, she felt a strong revulsion from him. He was far, far too old to ever elicit her interest. The very verse he had quoted about rejoicing in a spouse of one's youth militated strongly against her ever accepting him. He had, furthermore, many qualities that she disliked, and these were borne in upon her notice in particular by the way he had treated her on this very afternoon. And she had now learned that if she married him, she would be a slave of his study as well as of his bed and his household.

No, the picture of herself as this man's wife was impossible to frame in her mind even for a second. But Mr.

Herbert, not mindful of her frame of mind, pressed on in contradiction of that good Scholastic maxim, *Cum negante principia nequit disputari*—or, approximately: "Never dispute with someone who does not accept your premises."

At that moment he turned to her, or at least twisted his torso about in his chair to face her. "And now you come to me," he said, "and rightly question my intentions. How long must you wait for the query that you have known to be on my lips for years? Why do I wait, you would ask?"

And thus the old scholar proved another old principle of logic: *Parvus error in principiis, magnus in conclusionibus:* "A small error in the premises leads to a huge error in the conclusions."

"Sir," she said, "I had no such thing in my mind. I have been very troubled of late and sought some consolation from the Bible; and as you were the best qualified to point to passages where I might find it, I turned to you. If I have given you an impression that I never intended, please accept my deepest and most humble apologies."

"Miss Wyatt, there is no need to be coy," said Mr. Herbert in a dark tone. "If there is anything I despise, it is coyness and double-dealing."

"And so do I, sir, so do I.—Now, I ought to be going back to Aeons' End; my father and sister will be looking for me. I thank you for the list of passages; I shall look them up at the earliest opportunity.—Oh, the notion of an opportunity reminds me, sir: perhaps after the Sunday service we may speak on the matter of Mr. and Mrs. Linnett; it does seem that they will need some assistance during Mrs. Linnett's lying in."

He was scowling at her; and as she made her way through the towers of scholarly detritus toward the door, he suddenly said, "It is that Newsome fellow!"

This gave her pause; it seemed an accusation she should meet.

Before she could decide what to say, however, he went on: "Still! That Newsome fellow! Do you seriously think he will want to marry you after what has happened?"

She gave him a sharp look. "He? *He* not want to marry *me?*" she said. "Why, I should not have the man if he came crawling to me on his knees!" And she instantly regretted the intensity of feeling she had revealed in her protestation.

"I am glad to hear you say it," said Mr. Herbert, "but I see it is all bravado. I know your past feelings for him; he deceived you with a glorious seeming; and you, young and inexperienced as you are in the ways of men, were taken in. It is all perfectly clear to *me*. But *Nihil violentum perpetuum:* 'Nothing violent lasts forever.' It is as I said, Miss Wyatt: We must *forget those things which are behind, and reach forth unto those things which are before.* He is behind you, and I am before you: a life with me is before you."

She could not stifle a shudder of revulsion, which included a kind of proud tossing of her head. It was a purely natural and corporeal response. And as such, it highly offended Mr. Herbert.

"What, girl?" he said. "Do you truly think that *anyone* will want you or your sister after what has happened? It is at great risk—nay, I say, at great *cost* to my own reputation, that I make you an offer of marriage. It is only because my own reputation is stainless that I know it can wash the blot out of yours. You may take shelter with me from the opprobrium of the world. I have in fact confided my intentions to the bishop in a private conversation—laid out all the facts of the case before him—and received his reassurance that my marriage to you would be a most charitable and Christian act. And would you reject this free offer of my house and home?"

"I am sorry, Mr. Herbert—"

"Why, is that *natural?* Do you not wish to have children, Miss Wyatt? I am told that women crave children above all other things. Would you go through life as a spinster, and never bear the fruit of your womb?"

"Mr. Herbert!" she said in an offended tone, hoping to obtain his silence by shaming him for this inappropriate topic, since she could not gain it by open appeal.

"What?" he countered. "Surely you do not think that your personal attractiveness is so great as to guarantee you a husband?"

This unexpected turn in the conversation caught her quite off guard, and she stared at him with an amazement that seemed to suggest to him that he had hit on a profitable line of attack.

"Surely you are not so vain, Miss Wyatt," he said. "Your *figure* is certainly excellent—you are a fine, healthy woman. But your *face*—only a man who loves you could think it anything but plain."

She looked at him, truly looked at him; and if he had not been infatuated with his own superiority, he would have been very chastened by that staring appraisal of him; for it would have told him, as no words could, how she believed that if the personal attractiveness attaching to him and the personal attractiveness attaching to her were put into the balance and compared, his would sink mighty low.

But as if that insult were not enough, he began another objection. "And your personal fortune, Miss Wyatt—the state of your family's inheritance and affairs—"

"Mr. Herbert," she said firmly, "good day!"

And she walked out of the room, out of the house, and into the sunlight again at last; giving illustration, through the fact of her removal from the scene, of another fine axiom: *Contra factum non fit argumentum*—or, in English: "Against a fact there is no arguing."

How many times did she shudder with disgust as she walked home?

Well, she thought finally, *this means I positively must go away, I must go to Bath. He has left me no choice. He and I must have a month or even a few months of time to forget this conversation, or we shall not be able to face each other.*

As she approached her house, it seemed a sweet refuge against the kind of future Mr. Herbert proposed; but even as she felt its security, she remembered that her safety there could not last forever. If she did not make other provisions, the day might come when she would look back on Mr. Herbert's rejected offer with regret.

And the idea of arriving at a condition so degraded as to make being the wife of Mr. Alfred Herbert seem a desirable state—*that* was a terrifying thought indeed.

✳ 13 ✳

Heaven and Earth Exchanged

Her passions are but cold,
She stands and doth beholde,
She retaines her looks estrangde,
As if heaven and earth were changde.

—Old Song

That very afternoon Elissa posted a letter to Louisa advising her of her intention of traveling to Bath at once. Given the necessity of making a few preparations, she could not leave as instantly as she would have preferred.

She would travel on the same plan she had used on the trip to London: Dick Broad would accompany her. This time it happened that Dick Broad rode on the outside of the coach, as there was no room inside for him. This was not optimal, since she might well be made the victim of another passenger's rudeness, inside the coach out of Dick's observation and indeed beyond his ability to intervene; but before setting out, she and Dick had surveyed the passengers inside, and they had all seemed innocuous. They consisted of a large lady in late middle-age; an elderly lady, who, as it turned out, was completely deaf and heard not a single word during the entire journey; and a funereal-looking elderly man, who never uttered one.

Elissa was not five minutes from Deepclough, however, before she realized that the company of the middle-aged lady was going to be a trial. She was the sort of person who absolutely must talk at all times, and of course must have someone to talk to, and would seize on anybody available to fill that office, without any consideration for whether her victim wished to listen to her or not. She immediately gave Elissa to know that she was Mrs. Amelia Sebastian from Oxford-town, widowed, on her way to Bath to take care of her ailing sister, who was afflicted with chronic ague, headaches, cataracts, arthritis, rheumatism, toothache, and fainting fits; that she herself was liable to all these ailments and more, including lumbago, double vision, numbness in the hands and feet, pain and gas in her innards, and sometimes jaundice, though thank goodness she had been free of that for almost a year. She had been left an annuity of £100 by her late spouse, the most sainted man who ever lived (a label Elissa could well credit, as martyrs die young, practically by definition); and this income, to Mrs. Sebastian, was a severe reduction in circumstances, for during her marriage she had lived in one of the finest houses in the town, with fourteen servants to keep it up—and yet here she was now, traveling alone on a public conveyance.

And there was more—so much more. She happened to notice Elissa's rather smart traveling dress, and at once felt the texture of the cloth, gauged its quality, asked how much it cost, advised her to choose something pink next time (her own clothing suggested that she favored that color), and in the process pawed Elissa over in a manner that would have had her shouting for Dick Broad if the perpetrator had been a man (the somber gentleman opened his eyes wide at this rifling of the young lady's person, and the deaf lady gawked in wonder). Then she went on to described her own clothing in detail: what fashion plates it was based on, who the seamstress was who had made it, how much she had paid for it, how many times she had worn it . . . and on through all the gowns in the trunk in the boot of the coach, nay, even the very shoes, stockings, and stays. Other topics of her discourse included the latest novels she had read, as she was certain that Elissa, being a fashionable gentlewoman like herself, must want to read them, and she was convinced that a recitation of the plots in detail would persuade her to do so. She spoke disparagingly of the countryside through which they were passing, characterizing the handsomest fields as bleak and frightening and lonely, and wondering whether highwaymen lay in wait behind every tree. She fretted about the length of time the journey was taking, questioning whether she could withstand the call of nature for long enough to reach the first change of horses; she moved about restlessly, complaining of aches and itching, and sometimes quite crushing Elissa with her ample person, which, though well doused with perfume, still smelled like a pair of wet kid gloves that has been inadvertently left in a drawer and grown moldy and goatish.

Nor was all this enough. She relentlessly required notice from Elissa that she had been heard in everything she said. She wanted to know the particulars of Elissa's family and station in life; whether she was married, in prospect of marriage, had sisters or friends who were married, what her settlement was to be, where she was going, why she was going there, her age and general health, her favorite novels (she let Elissa know that she found her choices too dull and severe), what she had had at breakfast before leaving, who was escorting her, who would meet her in Bath, with whom she would be staying there, how much income her hosts had, what ailments they suffered from, and on and on with the endless but feeble inventiveness of the torturer. She inquired into details so personal that Elissa was scandalized, and only evaded having to give answers by maintaining a stunned silence until Mrs. Sebastian had rattled on to something else: for example, whether her bladder was full, what time of the month it was for her, at what age her monthlies had begun, whether her stays cut her so unmercifully as Mrs. Sebastian's own, what she thought of the French style of undergarment, whether she would ever wear so sheer a cloth as the French ladies were said to favor. She squeezed Elissa's waist with both hands, both admiring it and scolding her for starving herself; she put up her hands unconsciously to rearrange Elissa's hair (Elissa was able to shy out of the way of this unwanted ministration long enough for Mrs. Sebastian to distract herself); and she leaned over, with a great deal of puffing and groaning, and plucked one of Elissa's shoes off her foot to examine it and exclaim over it.

All this provocation Elissa conceived as a test of her Christian patience and humility. She responded calmly and evenly, never evincing her disgust and dislike; she was cheerful and kind and solicitous, helping Mrs. Sebastian to make herself as comfortable as she could and consoling her for her worries and her aches. And though this warmth on her part did have a good effect, it could not overcome the seemingly infinite extent of her companion's gaucherie.

At last they arrived at the inn where Elissa was to change to the commercial coach bound to Bath. The vehicle was already in the yard, but it was not scheduled to leave for an hour. Mrs. Sebastian preferred to sit at a table in the inn, and so Elissa was able to escape her by the simple expedient of not accompanying her. She walked around the edge of the yard, in conversation with Dick, but eventually she realized that he was already eager for another meal, and she gave him leave and means to obtain one. She herself continued her circuit.

After about a half-hour, another coach from the east rattled into the yard. Among the men on the top of the coach was a figure she knew at once: Mr. Blaickie, Daniel's servant.

She had happened to be passing the open door of the stable when she saw the man, and she abruptly shrank back under the protection of its lintel and posts, though she still remained partly in view of the coach.

She had a fleeting, desperate hope that the servant might be traveling without the master; but this proved vain after the coach came to a halt and Daniel descended from within.

He could and would have seen her had he looked in her direction, but he seemed deeply preoccupied with his own thoughts. He even seemed to be grieving.

And as she perceived this, she felt a pang that was a mixture of sorrow for him and perverse satisfaction.

Nor did Mr. Blaickie see her; he looked more travel-worn than Daniel, and even a little disoriented after his journey on the swaying, bouncing roof of the coach in the bright, fresh air.

Master and servant met together and conversed for a moment, and then immediately went into the inn together.

She leaned against the doorpost, feeling suddenly disoriented herself—actually dizzy with the strength of her emotions. She felt anger against him, not only for the familiar causes—because of what he had done, and because he had evidently expected to make explanations to her—but because now, seeing him, she had the dreadful thought that if, in crossing the inn yard, he had seen her and turned toward her and come to her and held out his arms, she would have stepped within them without an instant's hesitation. She found herself even wishing he *had* done so, that he *would* do so still; wishing that he could make some explanation that would take away her pain.

But that was impossible. Nothing could make his past actions go away. And no matter how weak she might feel now, she would never forget, never forgive him; and though she might forget her pride for a moment, she would never be able to live with him as a wife—not knowing, as she did now, that he was capable of such a despicable act.

The fit of weakness passed off. She now assessed the situation: The coach on which he had arrived had evidently reached its terminus; it was being drawn away into the livery barn. There were only four inside seats in the coach to Bath, which she and her three former companions had already booked through to Bath. That meant that if Daniel was to continue on the Bath coach, he must ride on the outside with Mr. Blaickie and Dick Broad.

The sudden thought of Dick reminded her that he was in the inn at this moment. Surely either Daniel or Mr. Blaickie would recognize him. Daniel had seen him at Aeons' End many times last summer; and he would then guess that Elissa, or at least one of the Wyatts, might be with him.

Her best plan would be to board the coach at once and wait out of sight there. This she did immediately, congratulating herself on not having been seen when Daniel first arrived. With a little luck, she might get all the way to Bath without meeting him face to face.

She sat for some time alone and unnoticed in the coach. No one even approached the vehicle except for a porter who periodically brought luggage and loaded it.

But after a lengthy interval she heard Mr. Blaickie's voice: she at once recognized his distinctive accent, with its half-suppressed Scottish burr. He was evidently accompanying the porter to supervise the transfer of his master's trunk.

She froze and listened as the trunk was stowed. Then the two men paused, apparently for lack of any other pressing task, and traded commentary on their occupations in a desultory manner. At one point the porter said, "I have no objection to my master, but my mistress—! *He* is as easygoing as anybody could want, but *she* always has an eye open for me, and I can never slack a moment."

"I have got as good a master as a man could ever wish for," said Mr. Blaickie, "and he has no wife, so there is no one to turn him against me. I often think he is better to me than I would be to myself if I were my own man."

"Is that so?"

"Aye. He makes me eat and drink and rest when I would otherwise drive myself."

"He maketh thee to lie down in green pastures, eh?" leered the fellow.

"You laugh, but those words have come to my mind many a time. If he has any fault, it is that he is too good for me. He would never endure me except that he has mercy on my failings."

"And why is so kind and good—and so rich—a gentleman still a bachelor, eh?"

"There is no lady good enough for him, that is the plain and simple reason."

"And has he never wooed one?"

Mr. Blaickie was silent a moment. Then he said, "One, yes. Just one. One I thought might be good enough for him after all."

"But she turned out not, eh?" leered the porter.

"We have a saying where I come from," said Mr. Blaickie: "*Lang and lazy, little and loud, red and foolish, dark and proud.* And she were dark and proud, that one. Hair as black as . . . as black as the inside of night, and prouder than . . . an angel of God's own vengeance. She thought herself too good and too fine for my master, she did."

Then, after a thoughtful pause, he added, "The fool!"

Inside the coach, Elissa's cheeks were burning so brightly that she could feel the heat smarting her eyes. *Proud!* she thought. *By God, Mr. Blaickie, you have never seen* proud *yet! Not such* proud *as you shall see if I ever encounter your master again! Then, I do swear, you shall see* proud *and know what* proud *is! And as for you, Mr. Blaickie . . .*

But then she thought of an apt Bible verse: *Take no heed unto all words that are spoken; lest thou hear thy servant curse thee.* And so she was, with respect to Mr. Blaickie's part in this at least, reproved and chagrined; and it struck her, in this moment of humility, how extraordinary it was that this servant, for all the time he had spent with his master, had no ill word to say of him.

Mr. Blaickie, too, is deceived, she told herself. *May God grant he never be undeceived!*

At that moment the men outside became conspicuously silent; and then she heard Mr. Blaickie say Dick Broad's name in some surpise, and heard Dick Broad reply, "Mr. Blaickie."

"You are far from Deepclough this morning," said Mr. Blaickie.

"Not as far as you are from Madeira," said Dick.

She could only conclude that Dick must be seeking her. There was no way to avoid it: she must reveal her presence to Mr. Blaickie.

"Are you looking for me, Dick?" she asked, without leaning forward to look out the open window of the coach.

In a moment, his face appeared at the window, kindly as ever, but now darkened with concern. "Ah, there you are, Miss," he said.

"Are we leaving soon, Dick?" she asked.

"If I might talk to you a moment, Miss—in private, like."

At this point it seemed that Mr. Blaickie and the porter took the hint and left them, because Dick turned to watch, and only after he had seen them at a safe distance did he turn back and say, "Miss—did you know that Mr. Daniel Newsome has taken a seat on this coach?"

"I had guessed as much, Dick," she said. "It is bad luck. And now Mr. Blaickie knows we are here, and he will certainly tell Mr. Newsome if he does not know already.—Is there any chance we might hire a postchaise, do you think?"

"I have already asked about it, Miss; the fellow says he hasn't one at present."

"Well, perhaps that is for the best. I should not like to let Mr. Newsome think that I am the least put out. He cannot get a ticket for an inside seat, in any case; we know that. And if you can endure his company and that of Mr. Blaickie until we reach Bath, then there will be no harm done."

"But he *has* an inside seat, Miss. One of the seats came free, and he has taken it. To do him justice, he cannot have known you would be riding on the same coach. I was careful to keep out of his sight, and Mr. Blaickie did not see me either until just this moment. I would have avoided him still, but I thought you should know, and there was no help for it."

The news that she would be riding in such close quarters with Daniel was very dismaying. In a kind of claustrophobic panic, she immediately rose from her seat and climbed down out of the coach.

"What would you like to do, Miss?" asked Dick.

"I do not know," she said, in confusion she could not hide. "Let us ask if there is a later coach to Bath."

"I have asked already, Miss. None today. We could stay over here, though, if you like."

"No, then Miss Bright will be worried for us. We must go on today. Is there nothing we could hire to take us?"

"They were quite definite about it, Miss."

"And no other livery or coach or carriage for hire in the town?"

"We shall surely miss this coach if we go looking for another now; and there may not be another."

"Ah, Dick! You are so sensible—I am grateful to you. No, I told you a moment ago that I would not let Mr. Newsome see that I am discomfited, and I shall stick to that resolution. Do you ride outside and be civil to Mr. Blaickie as necessary, and I shall ride inside and endure the presence of Mr. Newsome."

A fire came into her now at the thought, and she added, "Nay, indeed, Dick, I shall welcome the opportunity to show him that I care nothing for him."

He smiled wryly. "That's the spirit, Miss," he said. "And if you cannot bear it, rap on the roof or give a shout out the window, and I shall stop the coach, and we shall hire a farmer's cart to go on in, if need be."

"Very good," she said. She smiled at him with gratitude for his support. Then she turned the conversation by saying, "Is my trunk aboard, Dick?"

"Not yet, Miss. I shall make certain of it." And away he went.

She remained standing by the coach, feeling defiant, and now refusing to hide.

She expected that Daniel would come to her the moment Mr. Blaickie told him of her presence; and indeed now both Daniel and Mr. Blaickie came forth from the inn and looked straight toward her. Daniel paused; Mr. Blaickie turned discreetly away.

Then Daniel started toward her, striding with unconscious urgency, taking off his hat as he came.

She drew herself up; she fixed her features in a mask of absolute disdain.

He stopped before her, looking at her almost wildly.

"Miss Wyatt! Miss Wyatt!" he exclaimed in a strained voice.

She did not answer or even look at him for a long moment; instead she looked away over the inn yard as if at some intriguing object. She was counting in her head: *One . . . two . . . three . . .* until full ten seconds had passed. Then, after glancing at him for a moment as she might have at someone unknown to her, and again looking away over the inn yard, she said, in an utterly cold tone: "Good morning, Mr. Newsome."

She did not even curtsy to him; only nodded, in a stiff and cursory manner.

She could feel his astonishment and hurt as though it were a wind buffeting over her.

What did you expect? she thought. *That you could shatter my sister's hopes and then take up with me again as if nothing had ever happened?*

"Miss Wyatt," he said now, "I beg you will do me the honor of listening to me for five minutes."

Elissa now saw Mrs. Sebastian exit the inn and catch sight of her in her turn; and it was a simple matter to look away from Daniel and remain silent until her fellow passenger had bustled up to them.

"The rolls! And the tea! Dreadful!" said Mrs. Sebastian. "And what is this delay? I never heard of such a delay. If this were the King's Mail, someone's head should roll for this. But these private companies! They are a power unto themselves, you know—they care nothing for the ordinary passenger."

On she went, through all of Daniel's precious five minutes. Throughout this time, Daniel stood by, staring at Elissa as if he did not even notice that Mrs. Sebastian existed; and Elissa, for her part, paid no more attention to him than if he himself had not.

Then there was a stirring of folk in the yard. The last of the luggage was brought along and loaded; the coachman climbed to his seat, the guard gave a blast on his horn, and the passengers crowded around the coach to board.

The other inside passenger besides Daniel and Mrs. Sebastian and Elissa was the elderly deaf woman. When Daniel saw this lady was to have a seat inside, he assisted her, though he moved as if in a dream, as if so preoccupied with his thoughts that he barely knew what he was doing.

"Do you go up next, Miss Wyatt," said Mrs. Sebastian, yielding precedence for reasons unknown. Elissa would have protested, but she realized this was a stroke of luck, as it meant she could choose a better seat; and she took the lady up on her offer.

Daniel would have given her his hand in assistance, but Dick Broad, who had been standing by waiting for this moment, was too quick for him and did the honors himself. Once inside, Elissa took the seat next to the elderly lady.

When Mrs. Sebastian boarded, she at first said, "Nay, Miss Wyatt, you must sit next to me!" But Daniel—the coachman now being urgent that they should depart—entered too promptly and took the only remaining seat, which was beside Mrs. Sebastian and diagonally across from Elissa. It was, Elissa thought, the best possible seating plan that could have been contrived in such a confined space.

In a minute more the coach was underway. Elissa looked out the window, refusing to acknowledge Daniel's presence in any manner; but she felt his emotions as if she were within the close of his arms. He was shocked, distressed, confused, uncertain what he ought to do. For the first mile, Mrs. Sebastian, rejoicing in her fresh victim, talked at him, but he seemed not to hear; yet gradually he seemed to get a grip on his feelings and his thoughts, to master himself; and he began to respond to Mrs. Sebastian's impertinences with measured answers, calmly, almost as if the distraction she provided from his anguish was salutary and appreciated. More and more he entered upon the lady's conversation.

And Elissa, despite her initial *schadenfreude* that it should be Daniel rather than herself who had to cope with this difficult companion, was now stung by her own pettiness. For he dealt with the lady even as had Elissa herself: with patience and kindness. It was extraordinary to see—or rather, to hear, since Elissa still would not look at him. There was not another gentleman in all England who would have been as kind as he was with such a troublesome fellow-passenger. Sooner or later, out of self-defense if nothing else, any other man would have cut her off, or looked out the window in brooding silence, or pretended to read, or focused his attention on the younger woman seated on the other bench; but not Daniel. *You would think she was his own mother,* thought Elissa at one point.

Indeed, as the journey wore on, she began to feel that Daniel had surpassed her own patience with Mrs. Sebastian. Whereas Elissa's kindness had been the product of self-discipline, Daniel's had every hallmark of genuine feeling. When Mrs. Sebastian wanted to chat, he chatted; when she pried into his life, trying to find private details she had no right to know, he dexterously turned her questions until she was again talking about the subject most dear to her heart—herself. He soothed her even as Elissa had not been able to; he reassured her about her future, which must have been a frightening prospect to her in her change of circumstances; he even made her laugh; he even made her laugh at herself, which is the most salutary form of laughter in the world.

It was extraordinary. It was Daniel as he ever had been. It was unbearable.

Why, she thought, *oh why could you not be a pure villain? Why could your character not be one consistent evil, of a piece with what you did to Merry? Then I could hate you with ease and be proud in it! I can only understand your goodness as deceit; and yet even in that conception of it, my belief is all at odds with my understanding.*

Meanwhile the coach bore them steadily on their way. The weather was fine; the roads were in good condition; when they stopped to change horses, the shift required no more than the legendary four hundred seconds, and none of the inside passengers even descended from the coach. Elissa began to have hopes that they would arrive in Bath with no worse embarrassment than she had suffered already. There in Bath Daniel might stay overnight, or he might continue at once; but she had no doubt that he was headed for Falmouth, and perhaps ultimately to Madeira. When she thought of this, her heart was wrenched inside her; in her mind's eye she saw him, as if utterly alone, sailing over hundreds of miles of black and fathomless sea; she thought of the months he might be away; and she yearned to stop him, even at the same time she wanted to send him on his way in cold silence.

But she was summoned out of these consuming and contradictory thoughts by Mrs. Sebastian's speaking her name.

"Ma'am?" she said, for the first time turning about to face the lady fully.

"I said you must meet my new acquaintance," said Mrs. Sebastian. "This is Mr. Newsome; Mr. Newsome, this is a most delightful young lady, Miss Elissa Wyatt."

It was utterly ridiculous. She looked at Daniel, and he looked at her. Exquisite pain was etched on his face; on her own she felt only an expression of disdain, like a cold, clay mask that she longed to peel away.

"Sir," she said in an absolutely glacial tone.

"Madam," he said. His voice was so grim and tormented that she could hardly hear it. It was like the gasp of a man on the rack.

"Miss Wyatt will be staying some time in Bath, Mr. Newsome," said the officious Mrs. Sebastian. "I am sure your paths will cross; I am sure you are very much in the same set. Not my set, I am sorry to say! Not now, not ever again.—Do you stay long in Bath, Mr. Newsome?"

"My plans are not certain," said Daniel.

"Well, then, perhaps an acquaintance with this young lady will inspire you to make your plans more sure," said Mrs. Sebastian, in the sickening and coy tone of the matchmaker.

"An acquaintance with me," said Elissa, "could not possibly afford Mr. Newsome any reason to prolong his stay in Bath. If I were his only reason for being there—a supposition that is not remotely in the realm of the possible—he would do much better to travel straight through to whatever far corner of the world may happen to be his destination."

If she had kicked Daniel, she could not have shocked and hurt him more. He almost physically recoiled at her words; and for her part, she almost writhed with abhorrence of her own cruelty. But she told herself that it was better for both of them—for all of them, for Merry and her father and even Charles as well—that she should be utterly honest and direct.

"Oh, but your feelings are not engaged," said Mrs. Sebastian, with a smug little smile. "You have as much as told me so yourself."

"Indeed, that is true," said Elissa brutally. "They are not in the least engaged."

"Then there can be no harm in having a friend such as Mr. Newsome while you are in Bath," said Mrs. Sebastian.

Elissa only turned away in silent disdain and resumed looking out the window.

"Well," said Mrs. Sebastian to Daniel, "I can see you have your work cut out for you if you mean to make a dent in Miss Wyatt's heart. And I now see why such a handsome young woman is still single!" To Elissa she said, "Be more sparing with your haughtiness, my dear Miss Wyatt! You may find yourself alone forever if you do not relent. Every man loves a challenge, but no man will pursue you for long if you keep up that frosty front!"

For some reason this impertinence cut Elissa to the quick. It seemed to take her own cruelty to Daniel and twist it back upon her. The tears started in her eyes, and there was no way to hide them except to turn her face completely away from Daniel.

That motion, however, was so sudden and desperate that she knew he saw it for what it was: anguish. And what did he do? He immediately drew Mrs. Sebastian's attention away from Elissa—talking to that lady emptily and prettily on the empty and petty topics that Mrs. Sebastian preferred. And Elissa felt his kindness thrown over her like a covering and protecting cloak.

Bath is not a city but a symbol. One feels it on arriving there: its setting cannot be called an amphitheater, but still the town rises up from the banks of the Avon, the little river that bisects it, in broad increments to a high coomb in the north, or to equally high hills in the south; and though it rises thus, it turns as it goes, to look downward, as if to see into its own heart. And though it is a little place, as cities go, from the very beginning dramas have played out on its stage that have been every bit as romantic and absurdist as those to be found anywhere we human players strut and fret. Even John Wood, the architect of its famous crescent, seems to have sensed that his houses ought to be ranged like the curved tiers of seats in a theater. Or perhaps it is more to be compared to the theater of anatomy, and the hot and murky waters of its famous springs are the ichor that pulses in the exposed yet still-living organs of its passions. What you will; but there is something remarkable about that little place that forces conclusions. Perhaps Sulis, the ancient goddess of the place, dethroned and ridiculed, lurks still and takes her vengeance; for she was ever known to carry out with zeal the curses called down in her name.

Down into the center of this playhouse the coach ran, announcing its entrance with the clash of iron tires on cobbled streets; and Elissa leaned back in her seat, still determinedly facing away out the window, counting in her head, counting to nothing, just to fill the dreadful vacuum there so that nothing else would rush in. Mrs. Sebastian had fallen into a drowse; and Daniel, as Elissa sensed more than saw, was sitting in a state of shock, looking before himself, but seeing nothing.

They pulled up at the White Hart. Then all was a bustle: passengers descending from the roof, some servants tending to horse and luggage, another opening the door of the coach, Mrs. Sebastian reviving and beginning to talk again—indeed, covering everything with talk as thickly as a plasterer parges a wall.

Daniel was by the door, and in the obvious order of decoaching, he descended first. He made no move, however, to displace the servant who was there to "hand" the ladies down, as the saying went; and besides, Dick Broad was standing by as a second. But Daniel did stop there too, immediately beside the coach, and watch, perhaps as if waiting to see if he was needed, or perhaps too stunned to move on.

The elderly woman descended next after him, in the order determined by her prestige and her proximity to the door; and then Mrs. Sebastian.

"Where are you staying, Mr. Newsome?" asked Mrs. Sebastian when she had safely set both feet on the ground.

"With friends," he said.

Mrs. Sebastian would have felt no compunction in pursuing the information she wanted by means of further questions, but at that moment she sighted an acquaintance who had come to meet her, and she was gone away with a great cry of greeting and protests of the discomforts of the journey. Elissa never saw her again, even in that little town; a circumstance that either reflected the great difference between the circles in which they lived, or sprang from some minor mercy of God.

But when she herself had descended, she inevitably came face to face with Daniel again at close quarters. He made as if to speak to her, but she turned abruptly away and said to Dick, "Let us hire a porter for the trunk." She detested the obviousness of her suggestion, and of her desire to snub Daniel by it, but she persevered in both.

"Very good, Miss," said Dick. He understood exactly what she was up to, and helped her by stepping between her and Daniel.

She and Dick went away together across the inn yard. It took only a few seconds to find two men willing to carry the trunk.

"Where to, Miss?" asked one of them.

Elissa looked about and saw Mr. Blaickie not far away, busying himself with Daniel's luggage. She strongly suspected that he was all ears to discover her destination.

"Just follow along," she said. "I know the house."

"Very good, Miss."

And that was all it took. She went out of the yard and walked away, and she did not once look back. If Daniel meant to stay over in Bath, it would not be because she had encouraged any hope that by doing so he would see her again. But she could not help brooding on the fact that her plan to escape the thought of him by leaving Deepclough had produced exactly the opposite effect.

❋ 14 ❋

Scorn

Know, falsest man, as my love was
  Greater than thine or thy desert,
My scorn shall likewise thine surpass:
  And thus I tear thee from my heart.

—Hammond

No. — Queen's Square was a pleasant, well-kept-up townhouse in one of Bath's sunnier and more open districts. Perhaps its only defect was in being so narrow; but for a household in straitened circumstances in those times, a small house was understood to be a big excuse for not partaking in expensive indulgences like large parties and superfluous staff. Between the modest size of the house and its location within Bath, one from which all points of interest were readily accessible, many economies could be effected with little loss of prestige or comfort.

The manager of this thrifty haven was so absorbed in toting figures for the household accounts of Mr. and Mrs. Boulder, her uncle and aunt, that she did not even hear Elissa enter, or Dick and the man-of-all-work carry away her trunk upstairs; and since Elissa told the housemaid, who doubled as the cook, that she would announce herself, Louisa did not have even that warning of her friend's arrival.

Elissa found her at a desk in a sunny sitting room at the back of the house, with her long, brown hair wrapped up in a practical version of the then-fashionable turban, studying the conclusions of her accounting with evident satisfaction. She did not look up until Elissa had actually reached her side and touched her on the arm; and when she realized her friend had arrived, she leapt up, catching Elissa in her arms, hugging her almost off her feet, and bussing her on both cheeks with a laugh.

"Once again you come stealing upon me unsuspected!" she said to Elissa.

"Hardly, my dear," said Elissa. "You knew I was to come this afternoon."

"No, it is your old trick!" insisted Louisa.

"I did not want to give your maid the trouble of escorting me to see you. Between you and me there is no need for formalities."

"Indeed not! Indeed never! My darling Elissa, let me just look at you and delight in you!"

And she stood back and looked at Elissa from head to toe, her pleasure manifest on her face. Then she came close again and unconsciously smoothed Elissa's hair and dress, more like a mother than a friend. Not that there was anything awry with either hair or gown; this gentle touching was just Louisa's way of enjoying things that were tidy and pretty and in perfect order.

Indeed, before the further scenes play out in Bath's little theater, something more extensive must be said about this new persona.

Louisa was a shaken mix of contradictions, of sweet basil oil and rose water. Elissa had always loved her for being serious, and Merry had liked her for being somewhat mischievous. Elissa sometimes thought that she herself would be more like Louisa if no counterweight to Merry's lightness had been required. Louisa's portion of seriousness, in any case, gave her a strong practical bent; and having discovered in school that she excelled at mathematics, or at least the lower form of it that was then taught to women, she cast about for some use for her skill and found it in the household of Mr. Josiah Boulder and Mrs. Catherine Boulder—her Uncle Joe and Aunt Kitty. For that couple was financially inept to a degree that jeopardized their own continuing security; and when Louisa had swept in, during a harrowing domestic financial crisis some years ago, to declare that retrenchments must be made and to draw up a budget and to keep strict accounts, they greeted her like a saving angel. Instead of being reduced to ruin, they had moved to Bath and rented a comfortable if somewhat small house in the town, where they thrived, being released from the worries of maintaining their finances by the simple expedient of spending exactly what their wise young niece allowed them to spend, and only that.

Louisa's family had encouraged this unusual arrangement: it brought Louisa "out," into the company of a higher class than she would readily have encountered in the neighborhood of Ryderly Hall, her own rural home. And it was not long before the gratitude of the Boulders, and Louisa's zest in managing them, had grown and transcended their practical origins and become a marked affection on both sides. The Boulders were very innocent, amiable, and sociable; they loved nothing more than being with others in society, and next to that they loved talking about others in society, though in a kindly and concerned rather than a malicious fashion. To them the world was a marvel of human varieties, and they could never get enough of it. As a result, they were widely viewed as a pleasant, if somewhat bland, addition to any dinner party or other gathering, and were invited everywhere, as an afterthought, and their hosts and hostesses took the same satisfaction in their utility that a mechanic feels for the dollop of grease that makes his gears and wheels run smoothly.

Louisa made an appropriate third to them; she had a bit of wittiness about her, but not too much. She was chatty; that is, she was not as effusive as Merry, but not as inclined as Elissa merely to speak only when her speech was needed, and until then to merely observe. She was rather plain than pretty, but always neat in her person; she had a young if unexceptionable figure, so that even the most superficially minded hostess could invite her without feeling either threatened or disgusted by her. In her appearance as well as her character, then, she was a kind of a blend of Elissa and Merry: in her proportions of height and bust and hips, she was exactly in the middle between the sisters; and her plain features were a kind of aesthetical averaging of Elissa's traditional good looks and Merry's more idiosyncratic winsomeness. Indeed, Louisa's appearance stood on that precarious middle ground that women call attractive, but men call ordinary: when her face was lit by high spirits or exertion, she won second glances, but otherwise she was not likely to be much noticed or remembered.

Her great flaw arose not so much from a defect in her character as from the general defects of the society of that era: she was a husband-hunter. ¶ Like Elissa, she craved a field in which her competence might prove itself; and in that time and place, marriage was the only good option. But unlike Elissa's interest in marriage, Louisa's was not spiritual, not founded in the metaphysics of joy and sorrow; she only wanted a way to show that the 2 + 2 of her abilities could produce the 4 of success in some undertaking. If Elissa soared, in her understanding of marriage, to a cosmic viewpoint, in hers Louisa kept both feet on the ground of domesticity. ¶ Accordingly, her requirements for a spouse were, in Elissa's view, rather low. She wanted only a man who was respectful of her and willing to indulge her inclination to household management. On him, when she found him, she was ready to bestow a warm affection, one that might begin in the headiness of anticipation and resolve soon after marriage into the steadiness of a relationship reinforced by a good regulation of respective roles. Of course, what neither young woman understood is that men who can meet even these modest qualifications are few and far between. ¶ Besides the aforesaid unexceptionable physical qualities, Louisa brought into the marriage mart a potential settlement of some three thousand pounds, a fact that her uncle and aunt freely related to any and all of their acquaintance; and one would have thought this respectable amount would have made her more the hunted than the hunter. She was cheerful, thoughtful of others, pleasant to be with; she had no oddities of voice or manners or interest that would have deterred a potential suitor; her smiles and her laughter were not irritating, but piquant and contagious; she knew how to dress to draw the eye without offending it with immodesty; she was religious, but only insofar as was the average Briton of the period—that is to say, she kept God strictly confined to His nearby house, to be visited only on Sundays, and never let Him intrude on her conversation or activities at other times. And yet here she was, at nearly the same age as Elissa, as perfectly husbandless as if she had nothing to offer. ¶ All this had made her a little desperate, Elissa thought; and there is nothing like desperation in a woman to frighten off a possible husband. A man who would readily face a cavalry charge in Spain, a cyclone in the Indian Ocean, or even a tiger in the Kashmir, will call a skirmishing retreat when he encounters a husband-hungry woman. That is simply the way of it; and though Elissa had given her friend advice on this point, some of it quite direct and candid, Louisa could not correct her behavior. When an eligible man entered the room, her eyes lit up; she grew about as giddy as her sensible character ever allowed; she moved toward him and made fast to him as a ship of the line comes about and maneuvers and finally grapples an enemy—and with about as much obviousness of intention; and she became blind to the effect this particularity of notice had on the object of her interest. Some men, it is true, did seem to find this interest in them to be intriguing; but those were the ones who were later found to be married or engaged. ¶ Despite Louisa's eagerness to find a mate, she had never fallen in love. In this she was unlike Merry, who had been in love any number of times. Louisa was, when all was said, too sensible to lose her head over any man with whom marriage seemed impossible or even impractical. Or so it seemed.

All these augends and addends of Louisa's personality totted up to a certain sum that had remained constant over the years; and Elissa, try though she might and did upon occasion, could never increase that total by even a unit. There are such people, dear to us, but falling far short of what they could easily be. Their potential for growth promises much, but they can never achieve it, because they can never be brought to want to grow inwardly; and they remain utterly intractable, if only because they cannot imagine themselves in a bettered state. When the two girls were very young, Louisa's immutability had frustrated Elissa; but when they were at school together, the young teacher who had become Mrs. Harmony had counseled Elissa against trying to improve her friend's character. "Louisa is not up to your level, dear," she had said. "You must simply accept that fact. She is a lovely young lady, in her way, and she will always be a good friend to you. Be content with that." When Elissa had protested that in every respect Louisa's learning was the same as her own, her teacher had said, "No, my dear, I am not referring to what is in her head, but to what is in her heart. She may learn as much as she likes—learn infinitely much if she likes—but she will never be your equal in spirit." And there was so much truth in this advice that Elissa had finally taken it and desisted.

The difference between them made for a little gap that showed itself in otherwise unaccountable lapses. It was, to choose an example most germane to this little drama, one of the reasons Elissa had neglected to communicate to Louisa the news of Merry's wedding in the time before that event. The Wyatts would not likely have invited Louisa in any case, since in those days family weddings were generally smaller affairs. But Elissa would in the normal course of things have shared such exciting news, as well as given a full review and analysis of the prospective groom. But now she was grateful that their correspondence had fallen away during that period, and she was determined to say nothing on that painful topic. Later she wondered how very differently the course of her own life and that of Louisa might have run if she had.

Such was Louisa's character. Now she has been brought on the stage properly; and so let her scenes play out.

For those with the leisure to be culturally busy, life in Bath was full of all kinds of activities that were at least nominally improving. And for the purposes of most of those who attended them, it was enough that the mere reputation of improvement clung to these gatherings. Indeed, they were more pleased if a given event achieved somewhat less than actual improvement and simply provided entertainment; for as many a sage has observed, most people treat life as something to be got through as pleasantly as possible, and avoid anything that might improve them or, even worse, lead insidiously to some change in their opinions. If only life and the universe had a purpose—then there might be some reason to pursue perfection; but since in a circular calculation it does not, well, let us make merry. And of course, the opportunity *to be seen* at such events was all that some required. Most likely that subgroup of attendees thought their *being seen* contributed more to the improvement of the audience than did the actual performers.

Mr. and Mrs. Boulder had no such pretensions of conferring benefit to others in this way, and they had no appreciation of literature or music; but they attended every concert, every reading, every salon that was open to them or to which they received an invitation, without even pausing to consider their reasons. When asked about the singer last night, they would smile happily and praise and bless the performance with hearty good will, though Mrs. Boulder had really spent her time admiring the singer's gown and wondering if that bust really measured forty inches, as everyone said, and Mr. Boulder had unknowingly used the interval to catch forty winks.

At first Elissa embarked on this round of activities with some dread that she would encounter Daniel everywhere she went. She did see him from time to time, usually on the other side of a hall, even though she restrained her scanning of the crowd and steeled herself to act as naturally and unconcernedly as possible. But curiously enough, his attendance at these events proved quite erratic. Or perhaps not so curiously; for she soon detected a correlation between the quality of the event and his presence. Those concerts she thought frivolous or poor, those lectures or readings that seemed shallow or boring, he never even entered upon. Evidently his greater experience of such things led him to a more judicious assessment of their likely value.

He did not approach her on these evenings. She did once catch him looking in her direction; and he wore again that haunted, oppressed expression she had seen on his face during the coach ride; but she soon ceased to fear his accosting her at public events.

There was another type of gathering, however, where his presence was more difficult to minimize; these took place in private homes. Again, she did not always find him in such places; indeed, the same rule seemed to apply: if a host and hostess were trivial, shallow, insipid, Daniel was never found in their house. Over her first few weeks in Bath, she realized that this scruple on his part ruled out all but just two particular families there. In these households, the master and mistress were decidedly literary and artistic, and discussions and readings of poetry and philosophy might feature in the leisurely conversations that took place after the gentlemen had rejoined the ladies, along with an occasional performance of music by one of the participants. Here no one played cards, or even thought of playing cards—perhaps not even Mr. and Mrs. Boulder, who with their usual amenability went along with the company's preference for intellectual discussion, even though they could not have joined in it and scarcely understood a word that was said.

These two intellectual gatherings were quite frequent—the hosts in each case had an insatiable appetite for good conversation—and since the schedule of the two salons overlapped, she soon found herself seeing Daniel several times each week. These encounters with him were far more trying than a distant sighting of him at some concert. If dinner was served, he would be present somewhere nearby at table; in the hours after dinner, he would be somewhere in the drawing room. Such encounters were full of anguish and embarrassment, which had to be stifled and concealed with artifices she had never practiced before.

At the very first of these, Louisa detected that something was wrong with Elissa; she approached her at once when the ladies had withdrawn and said, "What is it, dear? Are you not feeling well?"

Elissa understood immediately that there was no point in denying her distress, even if she had been inclined to tell an untruth about it. "The situation is awkward for me," she said, "for reasons I shall explain later. I know one of the other guests, that is all I shall say now."

"Do you wish to go home? I shall be glad to make excuses for you and accompany you."

"No," said Elissa. "I do not wish to give the gentleman the satisfaction of knowing how discomfited I am."

"Ah! Then let me assist you by staying by you and conversing with you."

"That would be much appreciated, my dear friend. Let us talk of something light and easy—the old school days or something that comes readily to mind."

And so Louisa plunged into a pleasant rattle on their time together at school; which was sufficiently distracting until the gentlemen came, and of course Daniel among them. But even then, Louisa, seeing Elissa falter, only redoubled her efforts to keep the talk between them bobbing along, until a more general conversation arose; which was, or would have been, very interesting to Elissa; but as it was, she waited in dread of hearing Daniel join it.

He did not—determinedly, she thought. Finally their host turned to him and said, "But our friend Mr. Newsome is very quiet tonight. Have you no opinion on the relative merits of the Greek tragedians versus our Shakespeare, sir?"

Then, along with the rest of the room, Elissa looked at Daniel. Any failure to do so would have been conspicuous.

He reacted to their host's question as if awakening from a dream, even shaking his head slightly as if to clear his thoughts.

"But your mind has been elsewhere," said their host with a smile.

"Indeed," said Daniel, "taken away elsewhere by the subject itself. I have been thinking of one difference between Sophocles and Shakespeare—that the former is austere and otherworldly, as if our thoughts and affections here were merely trivial designs imprinted in fading colors on the insubstantial weave of our existence; whereas the latter is earthly, even earthy, and present to us, as if our thoughts and affections were themselves the very warp and woof that make up our lives."

"And which view do you favor?"

"Oh, Shakespeare's. I suppose at one time I believed that I could dwell on the austere heights from which the Greek playwrights look down on the struggles of mortals; but now I know better. We are of the here and now; we are dust animated for the duration of our lives, and I believe God wishes us to think and feel intensely. πᾶν κτίσμα θεοῦ καλόν: 'All things created by God are good.' And one of those created things is passion. Without it, we are nothing; and those who would live without it are like those who would dwell in their bedchambers and never venture forth."

Their host laughed. "A properly romantic sentiment, Mr. Newsome. I would never have suspected you of harboring such a thought!"

"As I say, I did not always."

"And what changed your outlook?"

Daniel was silent for a moment. In other gatherings, certainly some of the women would have tittered at the question, but here everyone remained respectfully silent with him. Then he said, "Life. The joys and difficulties of life in themselves. I never lived until I felt them—joy and sorrow. For a long time I thought I knew them, though I did not. Now I see them for what they are: not illusions, as the Stoics and the Eastern sages would have us believe, but the stuff of which our true and best reality is made."

"A pointedly vague reply to a too-blunt question," said the host, again with a smile. "But it is clear that much experience lies behind it, and we must respect that.—So we have you decidedly in favor of Shakespeare, I take it?"

"Much as I love the Greeks, yes, Shakespeare is to my heart."

The conversation moved on, but it did not matter: Elissa was undone. The mere word *passion* had been enough: she thought of the way Daniel had looked at her, during that wonderful summer, of how he had saved her, how he had kissed her. And added to them the words *joy* and *sorrow,* which they had much discussed, and which had meant so much to them.

What shall I do? she asked herself. *How can I live without him? If I cannot have him, why should I live at all, why* pretend *to be living? For life without him is not life at all. Daniel, Daniel, why did you do that terrible thing?*

"Dear," Louisa whispered to her, "you are absolutely white. Let us go home."

Elissa only took Louisa's arm at the wrist—their hands lay close to one another on the sofa—and squeezed it, so as to say: *Not now—bear with me: an interval must elapse before I rise to leave.*

Louisa understood; but she also looked wonderingly at Daniel, guessing now that he was the cause of her friend's distress.

Somehow Elissa endured another hour. Then she gave the nod to Louisa, who cleverly staged their retreat on the good grounds that Mr. and Mrs. Boulder were tired.

She did not trouble Elissa with further questions that night, though her parting kiss and embrace were particularly heartfelt and kind.

The two of them were accustomed to walk mornings alongside the river, on a towpath that ran downstream; and Louisa waited until the bustle of breakfast and planning for the day was past, and they were alone together on their walk, accompanied only by a servant at a discreet distance.

She waited, in fact, until they had reached a bench that was the farthest extent of their accustomed walk. It was set back a yard or two off the path, and here they could talk without being heard, though they could still be seen by their accompanying servant.

There was no need for preamble. Both of them knew what they would be discussing.

"It is Mr. Newsome, then?" said Louisa.

"Yes," admitted Elissa. "I knew him in Deepclough last summer."

"Deepclough! Do you mean that dour Mr. Newsome has spent even a day in your cheerful little valley?"

"Dour he is not, my dear, any more than I am. And why should he not spend time where he chooses?"

"Why, he is a man of the world, a traveler. Everyone knows that he divides his time between Oxfordshire, London, and Madeira. And recently he has come into a great fortune, though I believe there is some scandal attaching to it."

"You have met him before?"

"Well, hardly *met* him. I have known him from previous years and previous such gatherings as we attended last night. He is a *very* prepossessing man, in my experience of him. I do not believe I have ever spoken to him, or he to me. I should be frightened to! He is all brain and coolness; though I have to admit that he is always scrupulously polite. I was quite surprised to hear him speak so of *passion* last night, and I think all the rest of the company was as well."

She now looked sidelong at Elissa. "Perhaps you had something to do with teaching him his new view of such things?" she asked mischievously.

Elissa ignored this probing jest; instead she said: "Our neighbors, the Rowcliffes, are his uncle and aunt; that is all."

"That *was* all, perhaps, when he arrived; I am sure it was sufficient reason for him to disembark in your little valley. But he must have had some other reason to stay there, and I mean, to stay there long enough to break your heart."

"My heart is *not* broken," insisted Elissa.

"Ah, my dear, I fear it is, much though you would like to make it whole by saying it is not. I have thought there was some wound or trouble in you since the moment you arrived, and Merry's letter to me certainly implied there was; but I could never pin it down, and I did not wish to ask about it, as it was clear you were trying to put it behind you."

"I do not deny that his behavior *has* hurt me in the past," said Elissa. "But of this you must never speak to anyone."

"Of course not," put in Louisa. "You may depend on that."

"And you are right, I am trying to put it behind me. I am determined not to let his conduct, past or present, determine my actions or my feelings any longer."

"Very good!" said Louisa. "That is the spirit, my dear. Only tell me how I may support you in that resolve, and I shall do it."

This promise, however, was immediately abrogated when Louisa went on: "But are you sure he is not in love with you?"

"Louisa!"

"I am not teasing you, dearest. He is wealthy enough for anyone, or so I hear; he is serious enough even for my favorite dark muse; and though his looks are not particularly attractive—"

"He is among the most handsome men I have ever known!" said Elissa, before she knew what was coming out of her mouth.

Louisa gave her a startled glance. "Do you really think so?" she asked.

"No!" said Elissa confusedly. "Of course he is . . . plain and . . . savage looking. You are right. I used to think him . . . *rather nice looking,* when I liked him. But now that I know what kind of a person he is, I think him . . . ugly, positively ugly."

Louisa seemed puzzled. "Do you really, dear?" she asked.

"I do," insisted Elissa. And yet that word, "ugly," seemed almost blasphemy to her.

"Because you do not really seem to believe your own words," Louisa went on.

"Ah, Louisa!" said Elissa, now beginning to fight off tears, "Do not tease me about him! I am wretched, and he makes me so! I never thought he would be here in Bath or I never would have come. I came to escape the thought of him, and yet here he is, lurking about so that I shall never know when I shall encounter him."

"I shall *not* tease you," promised Louisa. "I only ask you if you have really thought matters through. More than once after Mr. Newsome spoke last night, I saw his eyes turning to you, as if he could not help himself. Talk about wretched! I think he outdoes you in that, or at least if I judge by the way he looked. Do you really wish not to love him? I think if you showed him a little favor, he could easily be induced to love you, if he does not already. And he is *so* wealthy! I have heard that his seat at Landshome—"

"Landseye," said Elissa in correction.

"What, dear?"

"Landseye; the manor you mean is Landseye, the one he has just inherited. His own seat is at Lakeholm Hall; it too is in Oxfordshire."

"*Two* estates!" enthused Louisa.

"Had he a thousand, I would not marry him!" exclaimed Elissa, hoping to cut Louisa short. "I detest him! I scorn him! I shall have nothing to do with him! And I wish that, as you are my friend, you shall not speak to me of him, or of my having anything to do with him. You must be in league with me in this, dear, not against me."

"Of course I shall," said Louisa stoutly. "But—"

"No 'buts'!" said Elissa.

"Yes—very well. No buts. But if you ever wish to tell me more—"

"No 'buts'!" said Elissa again.

"Yes," said Louisa, a little chastened at last.

She took Elissa's arm then, to comfort her; and after Elissa had had time to compose herself, they rose and walked back along the river without saying any more of Mr. Daniel Newsome.

Though Louisa broached several different topics, and Elissa tried to engage with her on them, their conversation was artificial and dull. But fortunately, still it was on other topics; for when they were returning, and were just stepping forth into the street again after winding their way up to it via a side path, they immediately encountered Daniel.

Elissa and Louisa both forgot what they were talking of and came to a dead halt. They were directly in Daniel's way, and perforce he, too, stopped.

It was a long moment of agonized consciousness for all parties.

He broke the spell by doffing his hat and bowing to them and saying, in a strained voice: "Miss Wyatt; Miss Bright. How do you do?"

Elissa responded with the same curt nod she had given him in the inn yard, looking away. Louisa was more polite, and curtsied, and—though it was Elissa's place to respond, as the elder, and the better acquainted with Daniel—said to him, "We are well, thank you, Mr. Newsome. And yourself?"

"I am well, thank you."

The conversation came to a stop they all felt to be brutal.

"It was an interesting discussion last night, do you not think?" he said.

Elissa was not able to keep her eyes from him, and saw that he was speaking to her in particular; but she refused to answer, and so Louisa spoke for them both: "It was, sir; but so it always is at Mr. and Mrs. Foran's."

"I wished you had spoken more," Daniel said to Elissa. In fact, she had not joined in the general discussion at all.

"Good day, sir," she said to him. She moved out of his path and started up the street in a direction opposite to that in which he had been going, and Louisa had to hurry to rejoin her; and unlike Elissa, she could not resist the temptation to look back when they had gone some distance farther.

"He is still standing there, staring after you!" she whispered to Elissa.

"Let him!" said Elissa.

"My dear, where are we going?"

"Back to the Boulders', by the shortest route!"

"But this is entirely the wrong direction for that."

"God forbid we should fall in with him and continue the conversation any further! I do not care if we have to walk round by Timbuktoo; I shall not speak to him again as long as I live!"

"Have you never encountered him before in walking about Bath?"

"No, never. It has been most strange, but I have been most grateful for it."

"I believe he stays with a friend, just outside the town, and only comes in for particular reasons."

"But what does he *do* here?" asked Elissa. "He cannot be furthering his business, which is so precious to him. Why does he stay? Why does he not go away?"

"I would say you must ask yourself those questions, not me," said Louisa. "But he has been known to linger here in this way before; it is not utterly out of character. I believe he has a few particular friends he likes, and they mean a great deal to him.—Elissa, what *has* he done to you?"

"He has made me very unhappy, that is all I shall say. He has done something unforgiveable—I shall add that. That is all you need to know.—I am sorry, dear, I do not mean to be savage. But let us not talk of him! Dear God, let me not think of him! Grant me one minute of the day when I may not think of him!"

They walked on for a time in silence, but Elissa could sense Louisa's continuing astonishment at the intensity of her feelings.

Then Louisa said, in a wondering tone: "I cannot help saying it, darling, but . . . there must be some terrible misunderstanding between you."

"Oh, believe me," said Elissa bitterly, "it is no misunderstanding! It is that I understand him too well! It is that I was brought to an understanding of his character before I made the fatal mistake of marrying him!"

"Did it go so far?" said Louisa in amazement. "Elissa, why did you never write me any of this?"

The tears rose in Elissa's eyes now. "Because when it was happening," she said, "he was my whole world. He filled my whole world. He and I were—we were one person . . . though still *deliciously* two. I cannot explain it!—No, I *shall not* think of it anymore. It is over. Please do not tease me about it, Louisa. I know you love to do so—it is a fault of yours, dear, and usually I love you all the more for it; but in this case, you must overcome it."

Louisa again took the rebuke and said no more.

Gradually a change came about in Daniel's habits. Elissa began to see him much more often as she went about Bath—not only in the common street, but at events where he previously could not be found. He did not go out of his way to accost her, but inevitably meetings occurred as she turned a corner or entered or exited a shop or some public gathering place. These went off with the same sort of strained salutation and quickly terminated conversation as had their meeting near the river. But he never attempted to converse with her either in these chance meetings or when they were in company at Mr. Foran's or elsewhere.

When she saw him abroad during the day, he was never accompanied by anyone, and she thought this strange, too. None of those gentlemen who knew him, whom she knew to be well acquainted with him by the way they behaved toward him at evening parties, was ever by his side. She herself made a point of never going out without Louisa, who soon became zealous to protect her and prompt at responding for them both when Daniel made the queries that the courtesy of the day demanded.

These little *faux* meetings—why was he subjecting them both to this distress? For they clearly gave him extreme pain; that much was obvious from his expression and his air of continued bewilderment and grief. She fought bitterly with self-reproach for hurting him, and with her longing to love him despite the hurt he had done her. She vacillated between a blaze of anger and disdain when in his company, and a flood of pain, grief, regret, remorse, rue, sorrow, and weeping at night when she recalled the moments when she had cut him.

She managed to avoid meeting Daniel alone, without Louisa present to intervene, for full five weeks. But toward the end of August, her luck ran out when she had to go out on an errand by herself. They caught sight of one another simultaneously when they were a great distance apart on the street. Though she had thought through in advance what she must do in the case of such an eventuality, her plan vanished from her mind at the sight of him, and she knew not whether to continue onwards and ignore him, to turn into a shop or another street, or to reverse direction. In this state of fluster, she could think only to cross the road; but to her dismay, he crossed as well, very deliberately, when he saw her do so. He could only be intending to meet her and speak to her.

Well, if that was the case, she would show him how little she cared for him. She drew herself up, she looked straight ahead, and she walked on with what she thought must be a very persuasive affectation of carelessness, first glancing in a shop window, then nodding to a passing acquaintance.

Barely a minute passed before they came face to face. He halted directly before her, and drawing a letter from within his coat, he proffered it to her urgently.

"Elissa!" he pleaded. "I beg you will have mercy on me and *read this letter!*"

And she swept by him without a look or a word.

How he reacted, she did not know, since she did not look back. But she herself felt as if her heart, her very lungs, all her vitals, were being torn from her as she walked on, as if they were left behind with him, and she must live on, hollow and aching, without them. It was agony; and she went onwards up the street without seeing anything, without knowing any longer where she was bound; and only came to herself some minutes later, still walking at a brisk pace, and quite out of the way she had intended to go.

Dear God, she prayed, *have mercy on me! I cannot do that again. I have not the strength for it. I shall break, and then he shall see how false my* hauteur *really is. But what choice have I? Nay, this is true torment! I shall go home—when I come to the Boulders again, I shall tell Louisa that I shall go home as soon as Dickon can be dispatched to fetch me.*

So much for the beauties and comforts of Bath, she told herself. *It only goes to show how our thoughts can make a prison of any paradise.*

Louisa tried to dissuade her from her plan to go back to Aeons' End, and succeeded so far as to make Elissa promise to return when Mr. Newsome had left the vicinity of Bath; which Louisa was sure would happen the moment he realized that Elissa was no longer present there. Then Elissa wrote home, asking for Dick Broad to come at the earliest opportunity. She had good reason to think that he could be in Bath in another two days; and with that relief in sight, she grew calmer. She must only endure another forty-eight hours of waiting.

She resolved to stay within the house until she departed; but it happened that the Boulders had already received and accepted an invitation to dine at the home of Colonel Andrews on that same evening. This man was the other friend at whose dinner parties Elissa had previously encountered Daniel. The Colonel and his maiden sister ran a kind of literary salon, though one without pretension. On this occasion two authors from London were to attend, and Mr. and Mrs. Boulder, who found celebrities fascinating, were especially looking forward to an evening in their company. Now, in her state of upset, Elissa declined to accompany them; but once she saw how they accepted her decision with their usual childlike resignation, and heard them say they would stay home with her, she could not thus deny them the pleasure of the evening. They were all appreciation and joy when she changed her mind. Only Louisa guessed what this simple gift to them might cost her friend.

When she arrived at Colonel Andrews's, Elissa thought she might have escaped the encounter she dreaded. Daniel did not attend dinner. But when the gentlemen joined the ladies in the drawing room after the meal, Daniel was among them. She heard him apologize to the hostess; there had been some trivial but intractable cause for his coming late. It seemed deliberate that he took a seat as far from Elissa as possible; but perhaps also deliberate that he found a seat that faced her across the room. Meanwhile, one of the London visitors sought her out—she was incontestably the prettiest woman in the house—and she forced herself to speak with him with more animation than she truly felt.

It was not as if Daniel stared at her or watched her surreptitiously. He, too, seemed to be doing his best to behave as naturally as possible. He carried on a conversation with several of his neighbors, often making them laugh at something witty he said. After almost an hour, he shifted his attention to another group of guests, and moved his chair closer to them, turning it ninety degrees in the process. Elissa could not help thinking that it was evidence, if she had needed it, that he found their mutual presence as difficult to bear as did she.

The evening wore on. Her usual sense of amusement now had vanished; the talk seemed merely that of idle wags, foolish with their own importance. She thought how far inferior the conversation was to the talks she used to have with Daniel. Ultimately, she began to feel almost ill with the tension of the situation. Tea was served, and a cup only exacerbated the stimulation of her nerves; she was sorry she had taken it. Louisa began darting her those significant looks, and Elissa guessed she must be looking poorly—perhaps pale and anxious. But she told herself that she had only to bear up for this one evening, and she would likely never see Daniel again.

Or perhaps that last thought was what kept her sitting there, unwilling to leave.

Colonel Andrews called for their attention. On some whim arising out of a conversation he had been having, he asked each person to recite something he or she had learned in school or childhood; those who were musical might sing or play something at the pianoforte. In those days, most ladies and some gentlemen of that class had studied music, and memorizing verse was such a common accomplishment that everyone was able to participate. The Colonel himself began the exercise by reciting an ode of Pindar in Greek. It was very beautiful: dark and strange and evocative of an ancient world that was, after all, not so very far in the past.

Others recited passages from Shakespeare, sonnets by Milton, or odd and beautiful poems Elissa had never heard before, by poets whose very names were unknown to her. One young woman recited something from Chaucer, another something in German.

The turn was being passed along clockwise through the room, and Elissa could see that she would be one of the last called upon, and that Daniel was well ahead of her in the order.

She did not dare attempt to sing; she felt too ill with tension, and she feared she might botch the playing or the words and only embarrass herself. She thought instead of a short prose passage she had memorized at school.

But even as she fortified herself with this decision about what she would recite, her mind went back—as it always did, as it did time after time; as it seemed to do minute by minute every day of her life—to that summer. She had to restrain herself from looking toward Daniel before it was his turn; she yearned to hear what he would say, and yet she dreaded the effect it would have on her.

Finally the moment came. "Mr. Newsome," said the Colonel. "What do you have for us?"

"A song," said Daniel.

"You will sing for us?"

"If you can bear it."

"Why, of course, sir; we shall be delighted. I have rarely heard you sing, but it is always a pleasure. What is it?"

"Something that has been much on my mind of late—a song I learned once when I was shooting in Scotland. I happened to take shelter in a shepherd's hut during a thunderstorm, and we traded songs while we waited out the rain."

"Capital," said the Colonel. "So many of those Scots songs are beautiful; and of course we all admire the Bard of Ayrshire."

Despite this encouragement, Daniel seemed to hesitate a moment longer. The Colonel looked at him in mild puzzlement as he paused, and his expression seemed to decide Daniel once and for all; he rose and went to the piano. There he sat on the bench, tested the keys with a few notes as if taking the measure of them; and then, playing an accompaniment sometimes soft and sometimes bold, but always stirring, he sang this old Scottish air:

> Black is the color of my true love's hair,
> Her voice is like the sweetest air;
> She's the wisest maid in all the lands:
> I love the ground whereon she stands.
>
> I love my love, and well she knows,
> I love the ground whereon she goes.
> Though she no more on earth I see,
> I shan't serve her as she has me.
>
> The summer's passed, the world has changed,
> Our ease has passed and we're estranged;
> But still I hope the time will come
> When she and I shall be as one.
>
> So fare you well, my own true love,
> Our summer's passed, but I wish you well.
> And still I hope the time will come
> When you and I shall be as one.
>
> I love my love, and well she knows,
> I love the ground whereon she goes.
> She's the wisest maid in all the lands:
> I love the ground whereon she stands.

The song would have been simple and even trite if robbed of its tune and exposed in print—like the heap of torn feathers a hawk leaves behind to mark what was once a songbird;

but when sung by living breath, it was moving to all in the company, and there were murmurs of appreciation when it concluded. To Elissa, however, it was far more than a passing, sentimental song, it was a pitcher that poured all the lost sweetness of Daniel's love into her mind again; and as if displacing all the anguish she had been living with for months on end, the anguish she had felt most acutely in these past few days and weeks, it forced that bitterness to rise and overflow in a long, choking sob.

Even if she had been able to restrain that first outburst, there would have been no hiding her continued emotion. She put her hands over her eyes, but the tears ran through her fingers; she tried to hold her breath, but a second sob of grief welled from her, and then another, as painful as if the air were being pulled from her lungs with a hook.

Everyone at the gathering, even the good-hearted Colonel and his sister, turned to stare at her in surprise—who could not have done so?

Louisa took her urgently by the arm and said, "Come, dear—you are overtired! Come home with me!"

Elissa rose to her feet, keeping her hands over her face in mortification, and Louisa led her out of the room—she could not have moved without her friend's help, for she was blind with her weeping, and still concealed her eyes; but once they gained the passageway, she took her hands from her face and stumbled onwards to the door of the house by herself. She realized vaguely that Louisa had stopped for some reason, while she herself fled as though from a conflagration and did not look back.

"Sir!" she heard Louisa say in a reproachful tone.

Then came Daniel's voice—broken and low: "Of course—you are right. Forgive me."

Only then did Elissa realize that he had risen from the piano and pursued her as far as the passageway.

It seemed to her that it took an age for the servants to find and bring to her and Louisa and Mr. and Mrs. Boulder (for the latter pair insisted on leaving now, too) the wraps they had worn. At last they were all out in the street and walking home.

"Excuse us," said Louisa to the Boulders. "We shall go a little ahead of you, if you do not mind."

"Of course, dear," said Mrs. Boulder sympathetically. "Go right ahead."

"Indeed," said Mr. Boulder, helping as best he could by pretending he was not aware of the real reason for Louisa's request, "We have not your nimble feet, girls; do you go on as you will."

So Louisa led Elissa on ahead, and Elissa herself was nothing loath to leave the Boulders and their servant well behind.

"I am sorry!" Louisa said to Elissa then. "I could not have dreamed he would do such a thing to you! I would never have let you go to the Andrews' if I had thought it."

"No, it is I that am sorry," said Elissa. She found her voice was hoarse and barely within her control; but she spoke on, trying her best to speak rationally. "I have exposed myself to gossip and embarrassed you all. A young lady with a broken heart—there is no choicer bit of gossip in all of human affairs! I was the only woman there tonight with black hair, and that will compound my exposure—my shame will be all over Bath by daybreak. I am only glad I am going home. May God speed good Dickon in coming to me, so I may go away and try to forget all this! Oh, I am sorry, Louisa, very sorry! I thought I was stronger than this! Yet these events have shown me how very weak I am."

"And you loved him so much! It is terrible! But Elissa, if you could only have seen his face when I stopped him from following you—and that song! That song!"

"Yes, that song! It made me remember how I used to feel when he sang for me. When he sings, there is something about him—he is like an innocent little boy again, like some boy in a choir, a choir of angels; and one feels, listening to him, 'Here is a being without sin, a being who *cannot* sin.' But of course that is impossible."

"And it was for *you* he sang so. Oh, Elissa, I am sure he loves you still!"

"Who can doubt it!" cried Elissa then. "But what is the love of such a man worth? Nothing! Nothing at all! Who could love such a man? A two-faced, lying . . . who cares about him?"

And then she burst into sobs and tears afresh, giving the lie to her own malediction.

❊ 15 ❊

Debacle

Goe, goe, and if that word have not quite kild thee,
Ease me with death by bidding me goe too.
O, if it have, let my word worke on me,
And a just office on a murderer doe;
    Except it be too late to kill me so,
    Being double-dead, going and bidding goe.

—Donne

Elissa thought she would pass an ill night; but the power of her emotions had drained her of energy, and she slept soundly and woke feeling physically refreshed, if still emotionally devastated. She could at least reassure herself that an end to the particular torment of seeing Daniel was now near: she expected that Dick would arrive sometime later in the day and that they would begin the return to Deepclough by the earliest coach tomorrow.

It was perhaps this assurance that made her foolhardy. Or was it regret, regret at leaving the place where he was?

After breakfast, Louisa had some errands to attend to in the town. Elissa was suddenly too restless to remain in the house; it was a fine day, likely her last in Bath for some time; and between the pathetic pity of Mr. and Mrs. Boulder and her refusal to let the thought of Daniel confine her, she found herself willing to brave the streets of Bath one more time. Furthermore, she told herself that her friend could cut short any attempt Daniel might make to approach her.

Their walk about the city was entirely uneventful; they saw Daniel nowhere. At length Louisa came to the last of her errands. "I must return a book to Colonel Andrews's sister," she said. "I ought to have taken it back last night, but I forgot, and I promised her particularly that I would have it in her hands today."

This house was at the moment nearly the last place Elissa wanted to go. "Could you send it, dear?" she asked, thinking that the servant who accompanied them might be dispatched for this purpose.

"Under the circumstances, I should like to see it personally delivered and make my own apologies," said Louisa. "But you need not come. Take a turn on the path by the river, while I go on to the Colonel's; Beckman will go with you."

"Ah, that would suit," said Elissa. "I shall say goodbye to our pleasant walking grounds, at least for now, and promise them an early return—when the coast is clear, as the smugglers say."

This agreed, they parted ways at the entrance to the path, and Elissa descended on it to the river. She had time to kill or spend at will, so she dawdled along the bank, the servant Beckman following behind at his usual distance.

As she came to the end of her customary walk, she was surprised to see a man rise from the bench there and step forward to meet her. For a second she had the sort of apprehension that, in this broken, subcelestial world, women walking by themselves in a lonely place often feel when a male figure looms forth from the shadow; but then she saw that it was Daniel Newsome. Of him at least she feared no physical danger.

But to signify her displeasure, she turned abruptly away from him. Beckman, reading her gesture as one of alarm, and concerned by the sudden appearance of the gentleman, doubled his pace and came up to her.

"Is everything all right, Miss Wyatt?" he asked.

There was something about the urgency of his question, and what it suggested about his knowledge of her feelings, that persuaded Elissa to play down this unfortunate meeting. "It is very kind of you to ask, Beckman," she said. "I am quite all right."

Then she turned back to face Daniel.

She had only to curtsy, he had only to bow; then she could withdraw, and that would be the last time they would see one another.

Of this ritual she commenced her part with a frozen shadow of a curtsy; but he, after returning her civilty with the requisite bow, did not complete the role set out for him; in fact, he did not allow her to complete the role set out for her, for he strode nearer to her even as she was turning away and said, "Miss Wyatt—if you would be so kind as to permit me a brief conversation with you."

She wanted to refuse his request, just as she had refused him in all their other encounters, just as she had deliberately disregarded his offer of the letter. But now—perhaps it was the effect of that song he had sung last night; perhaps it was the earnestness of his gaze; perhaps it was the thought that if she let him have his say, she might convince him to leave her alone once and for all.

"If you wish, sir," she said in a cold tone.

She nodded to Beckman, who had been standing uncertainly nearby, awaiting further assurance from her. Her gesture was as good as a command for him, and he retreated along the towpath until he was out of hearing.

"Would you sit with me?" Daniel asked then, indicating the bench with a motion of his hand.

She stared at the bench and then at him, and it dawned on her that this was not an accidental meeting. He had known that she sometimes took this path. Now she did not feel surprised at encountering him again; instead she felt trapped. But there was nothing to do but play the game out.

"Very well," she said.

He offered her his arm to escort her to the bench, an action which in the custom of the time was only proper; but she pretended not to observe it and went to the bench independently. He could not but feel the slight she intended, but he bore it stoically.

He followed her, and after she had seated herself, he sat as well, at a distance that she was relieved to find was appropriate to the strained relations between them.

She thought to make some trifling comment about the warmth or the fairness of the day, but a glance at him gave her pause: he was looking at her very intently, obviously about to plunge into whatever topic he meant to discuss, and it would have been rude to pretend otherwise.

Instead, then, by way of indicating her wish to have the business begun and thus over with the sooner, she said: "Sir?"

But he seemed, now he had come to it, not to know quite how to begin. He turned away from her and looked over the river; he took off his hat and laid it on the bench. He gave the impression of a man mentally stripping off his coat preparatory to undertaking a great labor or even a fight.

After an awkward interval of thus priming himself, during which she gave him no quarter and no assistance, he said: "Miss Wyatt, you must have thought it very strange when I did not return to you as I had promised."

His reversion to this topic almost robbed her of breath. She thought it unseemly that he should mention it at all— not just unseemly, but morally wrong, as if some stranger had killed a member of her family, had never paid for the crime, and yet had dared to seek her out and bring up the subject with her as a matter of idle conversation. For a full minute they sat in further silence. He grew more and more nervous as the interval lengthened, but he said nothing more; he only watched her and waited in an agitated manner. At last she decided that conveying her irritation in anything but the most cursory fashion was liable to prolong the conversation rather than bring it to the swift end she preferred.

"'Strange'!" she said then, quoting him. "I thought it . . . more than *strange,* sir. I thought it very *wrong.*—But that is in the past; there is no point in discussing it."

He seemed very surprised at her words. "'Wrong!'" he repeated, now quoting her. "And yet you say there is no point in airing this matter?"

"What good would it do? What change would it accomplish? I now know why you did not come back—indeed, when you *did* come back to Deepclough on my sister's wedding day, I wished you had not."

"Wished I had not?" he said.

"You repeat me most accurately, sir."

He seemed bewildered.

"But I *had* to come back," he said. "I was compelled to come back. And what a journey it was—by God, it almost broke me, and I dare say I am a strong man; it almost broke my body, and it certainly broke my heart."

"Oh, I am sure," she said coolly.

He stared at her in what seemed to be amazement; and she felt a pang, almost of foreboding—she could not comprehend what she felt; but she knew that the Daniel Newsome she had loved that summer would never have boasted. This near approach to such a thing bespoke an earnestness that was all at odds with his behavior toward Merry.

But she did not withdraw her remark, or speak again to soften its insulting tone; and her refusal to moderate what she had said seemed to finally break down the last of his reserve; and what tumbled out of him then was stranger and more unexpected than anything else he could possibly have uttered.

"Dearest Elissa," he said, "I do not know under what further mistake or hurt you labor, but you *know* what my feelings were for you then, and *they have not altered.*"

So great was her astonishment at this, so great her sense of offense, that she rose to her feet and looked down at him, even stared at him. And yet for all her outrage, she felt as well another feeling too, one that frightened her: a sense of joy that could not be chased down and crushed, but dodged about among her other, hostile feelings like a lamb skipping about among tigers.

As a gentleman, he could not remain seated when she stood; so he rose too, but he immediately implored her to be seated again. Of this suggestion she would have no part, and her contemptuous question brushed it aside: "What is *this*, sir?" she said. "What do you say to me?"

Forced to the point—forced, as she thought, to give up any attempt to guide or control the interview—he drew himself up and said, "It is simply this: I love you; I have always loved you; I always shall love you."

"You! You can say *that?*"

It was clear that he could scarcely believe what he was hearing; that his surprise at her disbelief was as great as her surprise at the claim he was now making. But he shook off this perplexity and, with every evidence of deep perturbation and confusion, protested: "For the love of God, *be my wife*, Elissa. If I cannot make you happy, I shall die in the attempt, die with some gratitude for the opportunity to make the attempt. I *shall* make you happy, Elissa! You *know* I am devoted to you."

"Devoted to *me!*" she repeated. It must have struck him, too, that they were continuing to quote one another in disbelief, but he made no remark on it; and he would have had no time to do so in any case, since she immediately went on: "You have indeed a *strange* manner of showing your devotion, if I may borrow the word with which you began this astonishing conversation, inadequate though that term may be. I would sooner say that you have a manner of showing your devotion that is inherently incredible—inherently paradoxical!"

He shook his head in what seemed continued bewilderment. "What can you mean?" he asked; and then asked again, but now in a tone that wrenched something inside her: "Dearest Elissa, what can you mean?"

"Mean!" she cried. She was almost choking on her own speech now; she was becoming incensed at his obtuseness. "Why, sir, I only mean that you broke the heart of my sister! Was *that* not a most strange manner of indicating your devotion to my happiness? Do you think that I—that I, the Elissa Wyatt whom you know me to be, not only the sister and the friend but veritably the *mother* of Miss Merry Wyatt—that I could ever be happy with a man who had dealt that dear girl such a careless and wanton blow? Happy? With a man who first threw every obstacle he could in the path of her imminent happiness, and when that did not avail—when he found his schemes in that regard crossed by the very lady to whom he was supposedly so 'devoted'—that is, sir, *by me*—he rode in from Falmouth caked in mud to the thighs, crying, '*Let the marriage not proceed!*' Was not the very drama of that event an insult to us all? And yet you say you are devoted to me! Indeed, I believe it—devoted to my misery, to my hurt, verily, sir, *to my degradation.* If *this* be devotion, do please, I beg of you, spare me it—I consider with terror what your enmity would be, if *this* is your devotion!"

He was absolutely blank with astonishment. He could not speak. But she was not speechless; instead, all the hurt of the year past came raging forth like an avalanche in the icy agony of her disdain. On she went: "You say you were *compelled* to stop that wedding. I have heard, sir, *why* you were compelled to stop it. Your cousin told me: My sister was *not wise enough to keep him on a straight course.* My sister was *too much like him.* My sister was *not wealthy enough.* You went to Madeira, to find a lady there of whom you knew, one who had good sense and good gold, who would make your cousin a good wife. Do you deny this?"

"No," he said, shaking his head. "I . . . deny *saying* none of this. It *had* to be said—it had to be done. I *had* to find a way to draw his attention away from your sister. Do not the facts show that what I did was right? The minute I was not by his side, he went against his own promises to me and returned to your sister—and he determined to finalize the union before I could return to England to give him my blessing."

"Which you had no intention of ever giving him!"

"Indeed," he said forcefully, "which I would never have given him! I would have laid down my life to stop him marrying her! And as I have told you, I very nearly did—I veritably bribed the packet to run when she ought not, in order to make Falmouth in good time. What we went through on that voyage was in itself a tale of horror, but it was nothing to the horror I felt when I first opened his letter to me in Madeira and learned what he was planning to do!" He seemed to shake with revulsion as he said this, and his patent disgust at the idea of his cousin marrying Merry only further incensed her.

"Well, then," she said, "let me put you and your supposed love for me to this test: It was *I* that brought that horror down upon you, for it was *I* who brought them together again."

"You!"

"Yes—it was *I* who found him in London, *I* who persuaded him to return to us and to the girl who loved him. What does your supposed love for me say to that?"

And then his reaction was indeed most strange, for he seemed almost to smile; and he looked on her in that old loving way; and, easily overpowering her own will in the matter, his love worked to quench her anger for him.

"I did not know this," he said. "I had no way to know it. Charles never told me—but his silence on the point was only natural. Any discussion of it would have brought up all his anguish again. And I myself urged him to forget your sister if he could, so I did not inquire into the particulars. But I must say, it makes complete sense to me—it explains much to me that I did not understand at the time." And here he exclaimed, with something very like a laugh: "That it should be you! Of course it *must* be you. Who else would have the strength of intellect, the tact, the good graces to make it happen without offense to the parties involved? That it should be you who toppled all my plans! There is an irony in it, but it is an irony of virtue, not of vice."

"Is *this* meant to be flattery?" she cried. "And if it is, do you think I shall be swayed by it? You heap one astonishment on another! I cannot follow your thinking, sir! It is not thinking at all, but raw impulse. One moment you loathe my sister, and the next you protest your affection for me—if you can bring yourself to believe that those two feelings are at all compatible, Mr. Newsome, you do most seriously mistake the lady with whom you have to deal, for to me they are utterly at odds! Do you think I could lay aside my love of Merry for—for what? For your wealth, for your land, or to be the mistress of Landseye? To be fêted as Mrs. Daniel Newsome? What kind of a woman, what kind of a human being, what kind of a *Christian* would I be if I could do such a thing? Perhaps, yes, I could do it if I were the kind of woman whom such as a man as *you* could love—one matched to your double-dealing nature!"

At this blow of the dagger, he again could not speak; he was staring at her helplessly. Now he seemed to her like a man hearing a relentless judge declaring his crimes—like a man hearing the tale of his sins on Judgment Day; and she, his judging angel, did not spare him, she did not have mercy on him.

"Is this, then, why you lay in wait for me here," she said, "at the end of my accustomed walk—skulking in these shadows here, perhaps to bully me and frighten me, or, as you thought would be so simple, to *tempt* me with the reward of your favor, into betraying my sister, my own dear flesh and blood?

Was it your plan all along to pay your addresses to me here? For it certainly seems so. And why? Did you believe that after what had passed between us, you owed me the specific declaration you have now made? Well, if so, sir, consider the obligation discharged! You are now free to seek any other wife you like. Fly to your heiress in Madeira, or choose one more conveniently in Bath or London—whatever you will. Between you and me, all obligation is over, all relations are severed; I shall never reproach you for not keeping the vow you had implied to me—not when there is so much more— so very, very much more—that keeps us apart!"

She came to an abrupt halt in her vituperation, though she felt she could have gone on all the day, could have chased him up the walk to the town itself, heaping curses and insults on him. But as she looked at him, now, he seemed . . . not like a criminal, but like a man being wrongfully beaten, even like an innocent child or animal being whipped, one that could not possibly understand the nature of the wrong it had supposedly done. The anguish in his eyes was so extreme that she could not bear it; her love for him flooded back into her consciousness, and she again did that very thing she least wished to do—she burst into a storm of tears and sobs; she sagged onto the bench again, and held her head between the palms of her hands, and felt as if she could not breathe—gasped between her sobs, fetched forth her handkerchief and pressed it over her eyes to hide them, and prayed that he would simply go away.

And even as she loved him again for what she had once thought he was, she hated him again for what she now knew him to be; and at this moment, when she was furious with him because he was witnessing her succumb to emotion, she felt pained almost most of all that he should see her exterior appearance disarranged by tears and emotion; and for this she felt doubly the fool.

He, for his part, did not spare her; though it was not vituperation that he cast on her, but something even more painful: his own self-reproaches. He sat down on the bench beside her, but this time not so distant from her; and he leaned forward, with a kind of stiffness, as though it was all he could do to keep from putting his arms around her, and as if he was holding himself back.

"My God, Elissa!" he said. "What you must think of me! I . . . I have thought since that day, since that day that I returned from Madeira . . . that I did not do right. I should have sought out a better way. I have seen your distaste for me, your wish to be as far from me as you could; and I have understood that dislike, even while I mourned it. It is only natural. My presence must bring to you recollections of the most awful kind; it cannot help but turn your thoughts toward that dreadful day. But Elissa! Before that day—before that day, we had all that glorious summer! I loved you—all that summer—it would not be true to say that I loved you to distraction—I loved you to *attraction*, I loved you until every atom within me was turned to you! *And so it still is.* To me there is nothing else in all the world but you. Since I first loved you, I have not said, or done, or thought anything without consulting my memory of you, my love for you. You are ever present with me. It is as the poet says: I shall never cease to think of you, of my Elissa, so long as this soul rules these limbs. I—"

But she interrupted him, spitting out a protest that was almost unintelligible: "And *you* say this! You, whose maxim is that one ought to choose a wife in the most cold-hearted manner possible? Nay, sir, I beg you shall not torment yourself any further with any thought of me! For I assure you, I school myself constantly *never* to entertain any thought of you!"

"Elissa," he said urgently, "this devotion to you is no torment to me—far from it. This is my joy! It is the air I breathe, the earth upon which I walk, the sky to which I raise my eyes! This love is the greatest gift that God has given me, and I love you second only to God Himself!" He seemed to be casting about for some further way to express himself, and now he eagerly added: "Do you remember how, at the beginning of that summer, we spoke of the zest one must take in life in order to endure it? Well, for me you *are* that zest, you are fully and completely all I need to live."

"I do not ask to be!" she said bitterly.

"Did either of us ask for this? No, *this was given to us without our asking.* This is a grace, Elissa! How a man, who in the abstract seems so eminently capable of living without anyone else at all, should find that he cannot live without a woman, without one particular woman, who in my case is you, Elissa—this is all strange, and I rightfully use that word—it is all a mystery, all something God has ordained, and I do not know the reason for it, except that it is *right,* that I feel its *rightness* every second that I love you. *So* God has ordained, and *so* do I love—so do I love *you.*"

She could not speak, but she groaned as her love and her pain twisted upon one another.

He leaned still closer to her, and she was wrenched both by the thrill she felt at his closeness and by the disgust she felt at herself for feeling that thrill.

He whispered: *"Dearest!"*

A sob broke from her.

"Dearest!" he said again. "Dearest Elissa! Can you not love me as you did then? For I know you loved me—I know it! You confessed as much on that day . . . you know when, you know how. The last day I saw you, when we stood in the wood together alone . . ."

Another bitter sob broke from her; and for a minute it silenced him.

"There is some mistake," he said then. "There is something misunderstood between us. I know that often, merely by acting by the best values and by the highest morals, we can yet find ourselves in an intractable and untenable circumstance in life; and perhaps that has happened here. I am sorry that Merry was hurt—as sorry as I am that Charles was hurt, that you were hurt, that your father was hurt—indeed, I swear to you, I was hurt myself, I labored under that pain until I thought it would break me. But I *did what I had to do*. Not well, I admit—oh, clumsily, and you may fault me for that forever. But something had to be done, and I was the one who must do it. Give me credit for having faced it like a man and for having made it happen—that terrible break between them."

She groaned and shook her head in contradiction of what he said, but she did not trust herself to speak.

"But now," he went on, "all that ill has passed behind us. You said so yourself. Can we not go on with our lives—with our life together?"

At this outrage she found her voice again. "Forget, do you mean?" she cried. "Are we to forget what you did?"

"We can never forget," he said. "But we can forgive those whose fault this is."

"Fault!" she cried, repeating him one more time. "And how were Merry and Charles ever at fault?"

"Never," he said emphatically. "They never committed any wrong—they suffered wrong. But why should that stop *us* now?"

She felt again as if she could not breathe; she actually wondered if she might die of the extremity of her emotion. All she could think to do was to terminate this conversation as quickly as possible. "Go away!" she said. "Go! Just—go! I shall not listen to one word more of this! I do not understand you, and I thank God I do not understand you! To understand you, I would have to think as you do, and of that—praise God!—I am incapable!"

She ceased speaking and struggled to get her sobs and her breath under control, and at length she did so. During this long interval he sat beside her without speaking, seeming to be in a kind of panic, as if uncertain what to do, actually unable to go, and thinking there was something still to be said that would convince her.

Finally, however, he rose to his feet. She refused to look at him; she was afraid she would burst into sobs all over again.

"I understand your disgust for me," he said. "As I have owned, it is only natural. I had hoped it would not be so; but I see that it is."

He paused as if he hoped still for some denial of this statement from her; but she gave him none.

Then he said, in a bizarre, dull, toneless voice: "I shall not importune you again. I am for Madeira, or some other far place; I shall take ship as soon as I am able."

He took up his hat; and she could not help raising her eyes to look at him once more, for an instant. He was gazing away along the river, as if he did not recognize where he was, or as if he did not know where to go. He took one step away from the bench and then he paused again.

"Forgive me for hoping," he said, in his former, loving voice. "On the strength of the feelings that we had for one another that summer, forgive me for my hope, at least. It was my hope that we, you and I, would build in our love for one another a house for all our hopes, for all our future."

He turned, and without another word, without a bow or any other gesture of farewell, he went along the riverside in the direction away from the town.

She did not look at him as he departed. Only when she thought he must have walked past the nearest bend in the river did she raise her head to make sure he was quite gone.

He is mad! she thought. *I cannot think what he intends by all this! To so coolly acknowledge that he did wrong in separating them, then to maintain that it* had *to be done, to boast of his having been the one to do it—to own how much he hurt them both, and then to brush it aside as a thing of the past, as if I, too, might as lightly forget it! It is all madness, that is the only explanation for it. I cannot fathom him! Where is the man I loved, the man whom I loved even as he says he loves me now: so that I think of him every minute . . .*

And the knowledge and the truth she had so often tried to deny came to her again in all its certainty: that just as she truly did think of him every minute still, she would think of him every minute for the rest of her life, though God chained her to this existence for eternity.

Oh, God, she prayed, *may* death, *at least, take this doomed love away from me, if sooner time cannot!*

The memories of that sweet summer surged over her like a tide, and with a groan she lay sideways on the bench, drawing her feet up off the ground, holding her head, curling into the pose of a sick child, and weeping, blindly and hopelessly, remembering, remembering, remembering.

And thus she still lay on the bench when the servant brought Louisa hurrying to find her, though then she was no longer weeping, but rather in the final stupor that excess of emotion leaves behind it.

✻ 16 ✻

The Tigress Repents

O tigress heart, who hath so cloakèd thee,
That art so cruel, covered with beauty?

—Wyatt

Elissa did not find Dick Broad at the Boulders' house when she returned. This was a disappointment, but there was still the chance that he might arrive on a later coach. Now she was quite determined not to set foot outside the door until she could make a beeline to the conveyance that would take her back to Deepclough. Indeed, she would confine herself to her bedroom, beg off dinner, and see no one but Louisa.

But for the moment, Mr. and Mrs. Boulder were not at home, so it was safe to sit in the parlor with her friend; and though she had no wish to speak of what had happened on her walk by the river and remained silent on that score, the silence between them was a restorative one. Louisa rang for tea, and the two of them took it together. Eventually Louisa began a gentle conversation on other topics, practical matters, and it was useful to Elissa to join in from time to time as she was able.

Thus they had sat for several hours when the maid brought in the post. There were three letters; and Louisa discovered immediately upon examining them that they had all been sent from Deepclough. One was for Elissa from Merry, so there was little wonder in its origin; but the other two—one addressed to Louisa, and one to her aunt and uncle—were from Louisa's cousin, Mr. David Boulder, who until that moment had not been known even to be in England, or anything less than five thousand miles away in India. It was such a portentous development that Louisa immediately sent a servant after Mr. and Mrs. Boulder and then opened her own letter. Elissa, to keep her company, did the same with her own; though she had little taste at that moment to indulge Merry's latest whimsies.

But Elissa found that Merry had outdone herself in seriousness. The letter covered the better part of two sheets in very small writing; which, though hasty, was unusually neat, as if the writer were determined not to let her customary slovenliness of hand mar or impede one instant of her communication. At first Elissa thought it might consist of commissions for her to perform in Bath before she came home; but she saw at once that it was dated before her own letter could possibly have reached Deepclough.

This is what she read:

Dearest Elissa, My Sister,

You must, or at least, may know from Louisa or her aunt and uncle that Mr. David Boulder is come back from India. I do not know what she has told you of his adventures there, or how much she yet knows of them, since he has not gone to Bath or seen his parents or cousin since he returned. Indeed, he came direct to—but I get ahead of my story, which is what you always tell me not to do.

How shall I explain it to you so that you shall not be quite overcome by it? We all always liked him, you and Papa and I and of course George; and he liked me especially, and used to tease me until I blushed, and always made a great show of kissing me like a cousin, though he was not! And he danced with me four times at the Houghtons' ball before he went to India, though I was but sixteen, and he seemed especially sorrowful to take his leave of me—do you remember, dearest? And I was quite mad upon him in those days, and thought my heart had broke forever when he was gone. How you teased me for it, but I have got the laugh on you now.

You see, dearest, *he has paid his addresses to me, and I have accepted him.*

So you see, darling, I shall be not *Merry,* not your plain old *Merry* any more, ever again, but *Merry'd!* I am utterly mad upon him, just as in the old days, and he is quite mad upon me, but you will think him perfect for me, because though he is mad upon me, he is quite sensible in all other respects, and has Papa in a state of awe with his decisions about this or that matter of business, even though when it comes to gardens dear David would not know a poppy from a carnation.

We are determined to be wed as soon as possible, though David says it shall probably be October before all is quite ready. We shall take our bridal tour in Scotland, where there are both beautiful sights to see and birds to shoot. And we hope you and Louisa will come with us! I hope, indeed, that you yourself will *always* be with us—David is to take back his family's estate, which is not so *very* far from Aeons' End, and you may either live with Papa and come visit us, or live with us and go visit Papa, until Aeons' End passes out of our hands, when you may come to live with us *forever!*

My hand is exhausted with this great letter, so I shall write no more. Do come home as soon as you can and help me prepare for the happiest of days!

Your only and most loving, doting, adoring, silly, but now happiest sister,

MERRY

P.S. You can have no objection, darling, as David is quite approved by Papa and was loved by our own dear George, and he is quite wealthy. He returns from India a made man, with an *independent* fortune of I do not know how many tens of thousands of pounds—I believe it is from the diamond trade or some mine or other, but you must ask the man himself for all the details and amounts; for as you know, neither Papa nor I have any head for such things. With love, M.

This truly was an enormous epistolary effort from Merry, who seldom wrote more than a paragraph, and that paragraph never more than trifling news and gossip, jumbled together almost unintelligibly; but to top it there was a note from John Wyatt, written on a slip of paper and loosely enclosed. Elissa could not remember ever having received a written communication from him, so it was with some wonder that she unfolded it and read:

> What Merry writes is true, my dear. If you are quite well and quite willing, do come home as quickly as you can, and let us rejoice together in this change in outlook!
>
> Your loving
> PAPA

Even her father's note had a postscript, which was, in fact, longer than the main part of the note:

> P.S. Mr. Boulder is his own master and quite scorns toilsome negotiations over the settlement, so all that nonsense shall be kept to a minimum. They are both eager to marry at once, and I see no reason why they should not. So you must come home at once and help your sister be wed.

When Elissa looked up from this double dose of astonishment, she found Louisa sitting back in her chair opposite, beaming upon her, and waiting until Elissa had finished her letter, which must have been considerably longer than the one Louisa's cousin had written to her.

They rose simultaneously from their seats, and Louisa rushed to her and embraced her, laughing delightedly, though Elissa was still speechless with wonder. Then, since Elissa persisted in a condition of some shock, Louisa drew her to a sofa, where they sat down again, this time side by side.

"Can it be so!" said Elissa then. This surprise, coming so soon on her emotion of the morning, took on the tinge of that sorrow, and she could not quite make up her mind to be glad about it.

"Can it be so? That my cousin marries your sister?" asked Louisa. "It would seem we each have testimony to it, my dear. Shall I read you his letter to me?"

"Oh, if you would, I should be very keen to hear it. This is all so strange—and yet, now that I have a chance to think on it even this little moment, it is not so strange at all. Merry *did* have quite an affection for Mr. Boulder before he went away."

"And he for her," said Louisa, "as you shall see." And she read the letter aloud:

Dear Cousin,

Sorry to dash past you from Southampton, old girl, but I was quite mad to get home to Gloucestershire. Why, you will say? Well, the cause of my disrespect to you and Father and Mother is Miss Merry Wyatt. I never told you this, though perhaps you noticed it, but I always thought she was the one for me—the mere thought of her has made me smile in the darkest times, and there have been plenty of those where I have been. She has just this day agreed to marry me, and I dare say she will lift my heart every minute for the rest of my life. She is to write to her sister and I to you and Father and Mother to give you the news, and we hope you and Miss Wyatt both will come to Scotland with us on our wedding tour.

How adorable she is! She makes me positively shiver with gladness, she is such a merry thing! As for her looks, I thought her pretty enough when she was sixteen, but she is quite the little beauty now. But I could go on in this vein all day. I will soon come home, and you will see how happy she makes me, and then I know you will love her too, for you have always looked out for my happiness. If the elder Miss Wyatt has any objections, I pray you may soothe them away and assure her that your cousin will cherish Miss Merry until his dying day.

DAVID

P.S. She has told me of her engagement and her near miss at matrimony. How sweet and earnest her confession was! As if I could fault that gentle soul! How magnanimous she seemed to think me, when I brushed it all aside as of no importance! And all the time I was only thanking God that He had preserved her for my arms, and preserved me in my labors so that I might be the one to have the honor of taking care of her.

P.P.S. I have written you of my business successes before, so I shall not weary you with them again, but I am home a wealthy man, Louisa, and you must prepare your uncle and aunt for a return to their former circumstances.

"An excellent letter, is it not?" said Louisa when she had finished reading it. "I mean, for a man who is obviously head over heels."

"It is a most excellent letter," said Elissa. "I could not possibly want a better. It seems he appreciates her most especially for her greatest virtue, her cheerfulness and lightness of spirit; and his longing to cherish her and keep her well is exactly what I would want to hear from a suitor."

"Oh, I do assure you, David is the steadiest young man you will find in all England," enthused Louisa.

A pang went through Elissa at this; the old pang, as she thought upon Daniel, whom she had once thought just that, the steadiest young man in all England. But pushing this pain aside, she said, "Well, I am glad to hear as much from you. Indeed, I always thought that of David—that he was steady. We were all so glad that he went out to India with George. I have sometimes thought that if George had stayed with him there, instead of coming home alone, he might still be alive today. Your cousin just had that . . . that *aura* of good common sense, you know; when he made a suggestion, it seemed good simply because it came from him."

"Precisely!" said Louisa. "You have described him *precisely.*"

"He is the perfect match," Elissa, went on, "for my mad Merry, my dear Merry; he will steady her, and if he is in need of someone to lift his spirits, she will do that for him. She will sit in his lap like a fairy, and kiss and tease him till he smiles! And I would guess that for all her small stature, she will be a good *breeder,* as they say, and give him as many sons and daughters as he could want."

"Is it not a blessing," said Louisa, "that there is someone for everyone? If I were a man, I would not notice Merry for looking at you; and yet here is David, in every way a sober and serious fellow, who sees that he needs a bit of lightness in his life, and very sensibly falls in love with it where he finds it!"

"Yes," said Elissa, but speaking more pensively than Louisa, "it is a blessing that there is someone for everyone. Perhaps it even might be said that in the abundant good that God sheds on us, there are many possible partners from whom we could choose just one to happily make our own. But we do not always find one of those matches, or if we do, something occurs that tears us from them."

"But what is this near approach to matrimony he speaks of?" said Louisa. "I declare, you came to me full of secrets, dear. I would be quite hurt did I not know there must be some good reason for your keeping it all to yourself."

"Ah, yes—I am guilty of concealing it from you. But I hope you will forgive me. It is all too painful. Mr. Daniel Newsome's cousin was to marry my sister. It got as far as the altar, I am afraid to say."

"What? Do you mean that literally? To the altar?"

"Yes, to the altar, to the very ceremony; but then it was called off."

"Called off! But by whom? How?"

"By Mr. Daniel Newsome."

Louisa rolled her eyes as she understood. "No wonder!" she said.

"Yes—no wonder I loathe and detest him."

"But on what grounds did he call it off?"

"On the sole grounds that in Mr. Daniel Newsome's opinion, the bride he had in mind for his cousin was better than Merry."

"What!"

"Yes; it is unbelievable, but so it was."

"But that is in no way even lawful! And how did he ever prevail upon his cousin?"

"I am afraid his cousin is too much guided by Mr. Daniel Newsome."

"So it would seem!"

"Now you see why I have not spoken of it. I am surprised that the news has not gone from one end of Britain to another; but I suppose that fortunately the Wyatts of Aeons' End are too humble to be of much interest to gossips elsewhere. Imagine the shame of proceeding *to the very altar* and then being jilted. It was devastating to Merry, and indeed devastating to us all. The fewer people know of it, the better. And may I say that it is very generous of dear Mr. David Boulder to overlook the shame of it."

"But it is no shame at all on Merry," protested Louisa.

"Indeed, that is what any good and sensible person must say; but there are many who are not so good and sensible as you, Louisa."

"Well, the person who matters most is David; and as you see, he is quite content with the match he has made."

"Yes, thank goodness. He will appreciate her."

"And this new wealth of his," Louisa went on. "Do you realize what he means by this about my uncle and aunt? He will pay off the mortgages on his family's estate, he will take back the home where he grew up; and I have no doubt that he will call his parents back to live there. They will have no more need of me, I dare say. I shall likely return to Ryderly. Or perhaps David and Merry will invite me to their home. I should like that."

"Or perhaps you will come to live with us at Aeons' End," said Elissa.

"I should like that, too," said Louisa.

They spoke more of the match, both then and later in the day when the Boulders came home; and Elissa was able to both learn and recall things she knew about David that made her increasingly satisfied with this turn of events.

Though the older by a few years, David had been a great friend of her brother, George, both in childhood and at school and university, which the two had attended together. They had, or so Elissa always believed, formed a common front against the debaucheries into which young men in their situation might stray: gambling in particular, though there were others even worse. At times she had suspected that David had the firmer anchor down in virtue, and that he kept George's mooring there from dragging with the tides. For David, the temptations were fewer because he had been doomed, as it had seemed in those days, to inherit a distressed estate; it was clear to him from an early age that he must shift for himself. He went out to India with George, and from what Elissa had heard, he had become deeply immersed in business by the time George left to come home. Winning the good will of the local ruler, he had begun a placer operation near the Kollur diamond mine on the River Krishna. His initial finds gave him the wherewithal to purchase a larger mine that had been believed to be played out. Of his further luck, he had sent some preliminary information home in a few letters to his parents; but now it appeared he had discovered an untapped seam.

His passion for Merry had been a source more of amusement in the two families than of anticipation. From the time she was old enough to awaken a romantic interest, he had teased her and flirted with her whenever they were together; and for quite an entire year before he went off to India, she had been convinced that she would marry him. He did not, however, pay his addresses to her: she was, after all, still very young at the time, and he was a man of very uncertain prospects.

But now all that uncertainty was over. Merry had escaped marriage to another—if very narrowly; and he had escaped the dangers of a foreign land and returned to find her a willing bride.

For all Elissa's pleasure at this match, the prospect yet evoked a more difficult emotion that she felt, if fleeting, still recurringly. And that was puzzlement about Merry's ability to forget the enormous betrayal wrought by the Newsomes. That Merry could so forget was of course a blessing; but for some time Elissa could not help feeling that it was somehow wrong and against nature. After much thought on this, not only later that day as she packed her things to return, but the next day as well as she journeyed home, in the end she came to understand that such forgiveness, or at least such forgetting, was not against *Merry's* nature. It was only against her own.

And she saw that now her pain must come not so much from what Charles had done to Merry, for that seemed to have providentially turned out well—no, Merry's future seemed to be turning out even better than it would have, had that doomed marriage proceeded.

Rather, the origin of her pain must now lie, solely and finally, in what Daniel had done to her, to Elissa Wyatt herself.

Upon her return to Aeons' End, Elissa was subjected to a frenzied welcome from Merry, and a quieter but deeply pleased greeting from father. She took tea with them both, and the talk was all of the coming wedding, as if they had not already been through this before, and not so very long ago. Finally John went away to his garden, and Elissa looked at Merry, and Merry at her, and they moved to the sofa to talk more privately together. Merry put both her arms around Elissa's neck, and Elissa her arms around Merry's shoulders, and they leaned their heads together, and they were silent for a time. Finally Merry spoke.

"Do you see how happy I am?" she said.

"Yes, yes, I do, dear," said Elissa. "And you are not a bit happier than you deserve to be. You shall make him happy, and I do believe he will keep you so as well."

"You like him, I think?" said Merry brightly, smiling at Elissa.

"You know I like him; I have always liked him."

"I know you do and always did so; but I like so much to hear you say you like him that I had to ask you. It will be so . . . comfortable with him. Not because he has made his fortune, I mean, but because I do believe we will make such good and useful company for one another."

"Yes, I know what you mean. He was a good boy, a kind boy. When George brought him home on holidays, David always defended us against George's quizzing and his little tricks. And David will be especially good and kind now that he is grown into a man."

"In some ways, it will be like having George back," said Merry.

Elissa smiled at this, though she hoped Merry had never said anything like it to their father; for in legal respects, David Boulder could never be even remotely like their lost brother: he could never inherit Aeons' End. But after a moment her smile faded and she said, "And I gather that you have told him all about . . . Charles Newsome?"

"Yes," said Merry. "I told him everything."

"Absolutely everything? About how you loved him, and how he stood up at the altar with you, and then ran away at the urging of his cousin—and how he broke your heart?"

Merry smiled a little. "Oh, he did not quite break it, I think. That is what I have discovered since David came home."

"But you did tell him all this? I do not mean to bully you, dear; but just think how important it is that he know everything. We do not want something that you forgot to tell coming out later, as if you had been hiding it from him. It would cast a shadow on your happiness, and maybe even prevent the marriage."

Merry looked more serious at this thought, but she insisted again that she had told David everything about her previous engagement and how it had ended. "I did not hold a single thing back," she concluded. "I even told him about Papa and Mrs. Newsome, which I did not like to do. I would have stopped at telling him about Charles, but once I began, there was no halfway measure. You cannot tell one part of that story without telling all of it."

"Indeed, you cannot.—But what do you mean when you say you told him about Papa and Mrs. Newsome? Do you mean that you would have become Mrs. Newsome?"

"No, I mean Charles's mother."

Elissa was extremely puzzled. "But what has she to do with Papa? Do you mean *Charles's* papa, who would disinherit him?"

"No," said Merry. She seemed to be reluctant to be specific, but she added, "I mean how our papa and Mrs. Newsome met again at Rowantree after Mama died."

"After Mama died, you say? I never heard such a thing. He mentioned knowing Mrs. Newsome a little when he was growing up; but they were both sent away to school at a young age, and he seldom saw her, even at holidays. He told Charles so last summer—do you not remember? If he had met her when she was grown up, I should think he would have said so then."

"Of course Papa never said anything about it," said Merry. Her tone was that of one who felt hunted, and she looked sad and a little frightened.

"Merry, dear, in any event you are talking nonsense. What does some odd, forgotten detail about Papa and Mrs. Newsome meeting once or twice at Rowantree when they were grown up have to do with what you needed to tell David?"

Merry looked at her solemnly. "*You* know," she said. "You know what I mean."

"If I knew what you meant, dear, I would not be so puzzled! Whatever are you talking about?"

"That was how it happened," said Merry. "It was at Rowantree. The summer after I was born, after Mama died. If they had not met there, and fallen in love, and . . . done what they ought not, then Charles and I could have been married."

Elissa stared at her sister in fear for her senses. "My love," she said, "what*ever* are you saying? I have never heard such madness in all my life! Papa and . . . Mrs. Newsome? You are saying they had . . . relations? Merry! This is the maddest thing in the world!"

"It is what Daniel told us," said Merry.

"Daniel? When? What are you talking about?"

"In the church that day—on my wedding day. When we went into the vestry, Daniel and Charles and Papa and I, and Mr. Herbert."

Since Elissa was in a state of confusion and said nothing, Merry went on. "I supposed you knew—later I mean. Did you not know? Did not Papa tell you, or Daniel?"

Elissa was silent, for her brain was silent; her faculty of cogitation had come to a dead halt. The whole matter would have seemed a flight of bizarre fantasy, had Merry not looked so guilty.

"Are you all right, dear?" asked Merry worriedly. "You look so pale!"

Elissa, struggling to say anything at all, came out with the word "What?"

"I said, 'You look—'"

"No, I mean: What did Daniel tell you?"

"So you do not know?"

"I thought I knew! But of these things I have heard nothing—and what does it matter even if Papa and Mrs. Newsome had relations? How could that affect you and Charles?"

Merry herself now looked pale. "Because, dear," she said in a faint voice, "it means that Charles is . . . my *brother,* my half-brother. Your brother, too; your half-brother. You truly did not know this?—No, I see from your face that you did not. It is wretched, I know, wretched; but I have got past it, and you can too."

The room seemed to have grown dark. The sky, the world outside the house as seen through the broad parlor windows, seemed to have grown dark, though the sun still shone; it was as if some dark body were eclipsing the solar disk. Elissa had that pain in her chest that told her she had stopped breathing, but she did not know how to make it go away.

"I shall show you, dear," said Merry, as if fearing that Elissa would not believe her. She rose and went to the family Bible, opened the front cover, and took up a sheet of folded paper that lay there. This she brought back to Elissa, and sitting beside her again, spread it open to show her what it contained: a table of names and parentage.

"I made this up for myself after the wedding, just to be sure about everything. I did not show it to anyone, or at least not on purpose; but Papa found it after you went up to Bath, and though it hurt him to look at it, he told me it was quite correct. Maybe it will help you understand, too, dearest."

Elissa stared at the sheet with wide eyes. This is what she saw:

Mr. Charles Newsome's papa is	Mr. John Wyatt
& his mama is	Mrs. Agnes Newsome
Elissa and Merry Wyatt's papa is	Mr. John Wyatt
& their mama is	Mrs. Jane Wyatt

"Do you see?" said Merry. She pointed to the end of the first line and said, "Our papa, Mr. John Wyatt, is Charles's papa as well as yours and mine; and he ought not to be. Mr. James Newsome ought to be his papa."

This table, written out as it was in Merry's girlish hand, was so pitiable, and yet so horrific, that Elissa could not bear to look at it. She put forth one hand, seized upon the sheet of paper, and crumpled it into a ball.

"*This?*" she cried, staring at the shaking fist in which she had crushed the paper, "*This* is what Daniel told you? That Charles was your brother?"

"Yes, dear."

"It is *a lie!* It is all a lie, a capital lie—it is a foul lie he made up to keep you apart! What will that man not stoop to! As God is my witness—"

"No, dear, it is the truth," said Merry simply; and something in her tone made Elissa pause in the imprecation she was about to utter.

"How do you *know* it is the truth?" she asked.

"Because Daniel had an affidavit from his mother. It was all signed and sealed and quite official. And in the affidavit she told how she had had relations with Papa at Rowantree that summer after Mama died. And when she realized she was carrying a child, she became frightened and went home to Landseye. And Mr. Newsome knew that it was not his child, because they had not had relations for quite some time; but he did not want the scandal, so he said nothing to anyone, and he took her away to Portugal, and she gave birth to Charles there. And they stayed there quite some time, and they lied about Charles's age when they returned—they changed his age by just a few months—so no one could do the figures and tell that he could not be Mr. Newsome's son. And Mr. Newsome came to love Charles in spite of it all, but he would not leave Charles the estate. He told Mrs. Newsome that it was a wrong thing to deprive the line of the Newsomes of even a penny in preference to someone not of the Newsome blood. That is why he was determined to leave the estate to Daniel.—Oh, and I am forgetting: There was an affidavit from Mrs. Newsome's maid, who had been

with her since she was a girl. She knew it all, and she said
it was all true."

Merry was very pale throughout this account, and she
hung her head as she spoke; and she concluded by repeating,
in a voice hardly louder than a whisper, "No, it is all quite
true, dear."

Elissa bolted up from the sofa; but she had not gone more
than a few paces when she turned on Merry and said: "But
Papa! What about Papa! Did he not deny it?"

"How could he deny it?" said Merry simply. "It is all true.
Mr. Herbert asked Papa if it was true, what the affidavits
said, so far as he knew; and Papa went white, absolutely
white, and he would not look at us, and he said that so far as
he knew, it was; though he had never known anything about
how Mrs. Newsome was with child and had had a son. You
see, they fooled even Papa. And . . . I think Papa really loved
her, Elissa. Deeply, deeply loved her; and it broke his heart
all over again when she went away. That is why he never
married again. That is the real reason, not all the reasons
he gives when he talks about it. You yourself guessed at this
once, and told me about it; only you thought it was someone
Papa loved *before* Mama, not afterward. You could not have
believed that Papa would do such a thing, so you told yourself he loved this other woman *before* he met Mama.

"So you see," continued Merry, when Elissa would not
speak, but stood where she was, staring at Merry, "Daniel
had to stop us. Thank God he stopped us!" And for a
moment she looked awed and frightened and she shuddered
with revulsion. "Thank God for Daniel Newsome! You see,
he did not know anything about it until he and Charles
went to Landseye after that summer, *our* summer, the summer that you and I spent with the Newsome cousins. You
remember: He gave no reason for going at the time, but it
was because Charles wanted to marry me and Daniel wanted
to marry you. They wanted to tell Mr. James Newsome and
Mrs. Agnes Newsome about it. Daniel had an idea that if

they approached Mr. James Newsome in just the right way, he might somehow prevail upon the man to leave at least some of his money to Charles.

"Then everything turned out much differently than everyone thought. Mr. James Newsome grew even more ill and died soon after they arrived there. And Charles told his mother about me, and she realized that the woman Charles had chosen for his wife was, of all the women in the world, one of the very few that he absolutely must not marry.

"But she did not want Charles to know, if she could prevent it. She called Daniel to her alone, without Charles, and she told him the whole story, and told him he must stop the match; but, if he could, he must do so without revealing the reason. That is what she made him promise. And Daniel made her give the affidavit, and the maid, too, because it was such a serious matter, and he called as witnesses some trusty men known to his aunt, and swore them to secrecy.

"First of all, he tried to distract Charles. After Mr. Newsome died, Daniel took Charles away to London; he filled his head with all that talk about how Charles and I were not right for one another and would come to ruin if we married—about how Charles had no money and how I could not bring enough to the marriage. I imagine he even let Charles think that he, Daniel, could not give Charles much, just to discourage him. He knew Charles did not want me to suffer any ill, including poverty; and I suspect that he played on that idea a great deal and frightened him. But I am sure that whatever he said, there was truth in it, because of all the people on earth, Daniel Newsome cannot tell a lie.

"And you know Charles," she said. "Daniel could make him do almost anything, I do believe. At last Charles promised that he would not see me again, for my own sake.

"That is where the other part of the story starts, you see. There was a girl Charles had once liked when he was very young, the daughter of the steward at Landseye; and she had liked him. She liked him first, and a great deal more than he liked her, I believe; I think, indeed, that he was drawn to her more by her attention to him than because he found her truly appealing. But it was not a match Charles's father—I mean, Mr. James Newsome—would ever have approved; so when her own father saw their liking for one another, he married her off quickly to a man who was a factor in Madeira, and that fellow took her away to his home there. She did not love the man at all; but for his part, he was old and soon he came to dote on her. A short while ago, she became a widow, a very young widow; and she is a pretty thing, and there was every sign that she still liked Charles, and now she is very wealthy. So Daniel went away to Madeira to try to persuade her to come home.—Charles, of course, would not go to her in Madeira, as you know. I have heard that some people in the village say that he had been to Madeira or was going to Madeira or that he had a wife who had left him and gone there, but that is all nonsense. He has never been out of England in his life, not even to Scotland or Wales. I dare say that the nearest he has been even to Falmouth is Deepclough.

"In any case, dear, that is where Daniel went—to Madeira, to secure this wife for his cousin. And then Charles broke his promise, and came back to us; and you know what happened then. He wrote to Daniel that he was marrying me, and you may imagine what a terror Daniel fell into when he received that letter. He hired a ship at once to take him home, but it was not a very big ship, and they ran into terrible storms. Then they were pursued by the French for four days. And fever broke out on board, and the men were dying of it, and Daniel himself became ill, but he shook it off, as he must get to Charles and stop us from marrying."

"How do you know all this?" asked Elissa. Her voice sounded strangled and muffled to her, as if she were speaking in such a way that the words never left her mouth; it was all sharpness and shock. But Merry tried to evade the question by continuing with the story.

"You saw how Daniel came here," she said. "I do believe he was half-dead when he arrived. He told us about Papa and Mrs. Newsome; he showed us the affidavit, and he read it to us."

"Merry!" cried Elissa. "How do you know all this—what you call the second part of the story? You could not possibly know it!"

Merry's account now came to a halt.

"How? Merry?" insisted Elissa.

Merry shook her head and her shoulders and her whole upper body, as if shrugging off some last clinging reticence.

"He came back," she said.

This would logically seem to refer to Daniel, but somehow Elissa sensed that it did not. "Who?" she demanded. "Who came back?"

"Charles," said Merry.

"He *came back!*" cried Elissa.

"Yes," said Merry, "he came back. We had loved each other so much, you know; he had to come back and tell me how sorry he was.—Oh, do not be so afraid, Elissa. It was about two months after the wedding should have been; he stayed somewhere nearby just overnight—not at Rowantree—and sent me a message in the evening; he walked up, and I met him, out beyond the garden, and we talked together. Neither you nor Papa ever knew anything about it. No one did; and you are the only one who knows now. Charles was very calm, and so was I. It was very strange, dear. I cannot tell you how we felt; but I know he felt as I did. It was like a fire that has gone out, that one has let go out, because it is dangerous; and one is only grateful that it did not catch fire to the world and destroy everything. He told me all about what Daniel had gone through to reach us in time; he told me all the little details I would never have known, and it meant a great deal to me to know them. Then we shook hands, and he went away. And it was then that I began to get better, truly better and happier. Before that, I had been trying to be happy, for you and for Papa, and I think I fooled you and him and even myself a little. But then I truly did begin to be happier again. And then, when David came, I was ready again. I had put all that mistake behind me."

"And you told David all this!"

Merry looked at her curiously. "Of course."

"But . . . these *details?*"

"But you yourself said just now that I had been right to do so."

Elissa felt as if her head would burst; she gave a groan and held her temples. "Yes!" she said. "Yes, you had to tell him! Indeed, you did, but—I never knew *what it was* you had to tell him!"

"So you truly did not know?"

"Oh, Merry, *dear* silly Merry! However was I ever to know? No one told me! Papa did not tell me, *you* did not tell me—Daniel did not tell me! Oh, dear God, *why* did *he* not tell me?"

But Merry was ready with an answer to this as well. "Because," she said, "he did not believe that it was his secret to tell to anyone, except those whom it most directly concerned. His aunt made him promise that; and of all the people on earth, Daniel Newsome would never break a promise.—He must have thought that I would tell you, or Papa would. It would be a natural thing to assume. But I did not; and I see Papa did not. Neither of us could bear to talk of it or even to think of it. Papa and I are alike in that. So I expect Daniel assumes that you know, even if you do not."

At this point, the memory of the conversation by the river tore like shrapnel through Elissa's brain. She uttered an inarticulate cry and turned away and went out of the room.

Merry, thoroughly frightened as she perceived the intensity of Elissa's response, ran after her. But there were no sobs coming from Elissa's lips, and no tears from her eyes; she was caught in a shock and grief so deep that it could not yet find expression.

"Elissa, where are you going?" said Merry.

"Out," said Elissa in a wooden voice.

"Let me come with you," said Merry.

Elissa struggled to form words. "No," she said, "I must go out alone. I must walk—I must have some time to think. I promise I shall come back to you the same as I ever was—or as near to that as I ever shall be again; but I need some time to think."

"Of course," said Merry. "If you wish; but might it not be better *not* to think about it at all? That is what I have tried to do. But I know that *thinking* about things is the kind of thing you do; so if you must do it, you must."

Elissa only turned away painfully and went out of the house.

She went along the ridge. The day was fine enough and dry enough that she might have walked twenty miles; and when she reached the end of the ridge she turned about and walked back; and when she was approaching the house again, she turned about and went back along the ridge. Perhaps she did walk twenty miles, or ten at least, without ever going more than a mile or two from the house.

It was the worst, the most agonized and dreadful walk of her entire life. She hardly saw where she was at any moment; it was like a driven march, such as a broken soldier makes, trying to find his way home alone, wounded and hungry and thirsty, after he has escaped from encirclement by the enemy.

What have I done? was her chief thought, which sounded in her brain and rose in a hoarse half-murmur over and over to her lips. And also: *What must he think?*

And, if it could be represented in a more connected thought, this was what ran through her mind: *What did I say to him? Oh, what did I say? And how shall I ever recall those words now they have flown? How shall I ever undo the hurt I caused him? Which is on top of the hurt he suffered for us all, trying to carry and conceal that sin of long ago, trying not to let it hurt anyone else. If it had not been for my meddling, Charles would have married someone else and never thought of Merry again, and she would have married David and never thought of Charles; but no, I had to take matters into my own hands, like some kind of devil working to everyone's hurt! And thanks to me Papa must have his face thrust into his old sin again—poor Papa! How pale he was there in the church, how sick to death of himself! I do believe if it were not for his garden, he would have done away with himself for very shame. Oh, no, it is all my fault, for foiling Daniel's good purposes and dragging everyone through the mire of this forgotten error!*

Lines from an old poem came back time and again to make a kind of carillon ringing in the background of these thoughts:

> Only the actions of the just
> Smell sweet, and blossom in their dust.

Oh, Daniel, she thought, *how sweet is the fragrance of your actions now! I trampled them into the dust—and yet now they blossom again, blossom again, and fill my mind with the scent of their goodness, their justice!*

Over and over again these thoughts went round; and each time she thought them she would end up asking herself: *Just exactly what* did *I say to Daniel, and he to me, the other day in Bath?* And she would review it in her mind, blenching and shaking as it came back, almost word for word, and she saw how they had misunderstood one another and spoken past one another over and over.

He had begun by speaking of how strange she must have thought it, when he did not return as he had promised. Of course she had thought it strange; but she saw now, as she had not seen then, that he expected her to have subsequently understood why he had not returned. He expected her to have learned at last, from Merry and her father, that he had gone away in a desperate though roundabout attempt to prevent that forbidden marriage.

But she, knowing nothing of these circumstances, had told him *she wished he had not come back at all;* because he had done so only to stop the marriage.

Then he had told her that his feelings for her had not altered from what they were in that summer they had spent together.

But she, knowing nothing, *had been outraged at his claim to love her still.*

Then he had proposed marriage to her, so desperately and abjectly that it would have melted the heart of any woman less fierce than a tigress.

But she, knowing nothing, *had scorned him,* giving as her reason his having broken her sister's heart.

What must he have thought of that, knowing what he knew, and not knowing that she knew nothing?

She *had reproached him* with the counterfeit reasons Charles had given for his cousin's intervention in the marriage: that Merry was not wise enough, nor wealthy enough, nor different enough from Charles himself.

He had refused to deny that he had said those things to Charles; he had quite rightly and sensibly insisted that something had to be done.

In her ignorance *she had boasted* of having been the one to bring Charles and Merry together again.

In his love for her, he had seen this only as another evidence of the qualities in her that he loved.

In reply, she *had scorned his love again, released him from any obligation to her, declared all connection between them now severed.*

And she remembered how he had looked—like a child being beaten for something it has not done. That look had broken her; it had made her remember her love for him, even while in that moment she had virtually shouted out what she had thought was her hatred for him.

And she remembered how he had met her vituperation with only more protestation and confession of his love.

Finally she *had sent him away;* but not until he was as broken as her cold hatred could make him.

My hatred, she thought. *I met his love with nothing but hatred.*

Yet there was one thing she now knew with crystalline and icy certainty: she did not hate Daniel Newsome. She had never hated him. The confusion and ambiguity of her dreadful agony on the bench by the river at Bath was gone forever. She did not loathe him; he did not disgust her. She had loved him all along, all through the time she thought she was hating him. The hate, she realized now, was just a story she had told herself, founded on a pastiche of doubts she had never really believed. She had only paved over her love for him with desperate, stony lies; and the lash of this truth, this great stinging truth that she had at last learned, had broken open that flimsy paving and shown what lay beneath it: a well of love deep beyond fathoming, clear to the eye of the soul and cool to the brow of the spirit and sweet to the tongue of the mind. And she was thirsty, thirsty to drink from it; she had not known how thirsty she was. The throat of her soul was parched and cracked; the fibers of her spirit were drawn and desiccated; the spirals of her brain were shrunken and dry. And so now it was as if she lay down on the very parapet of that well and drank and drank and could not have her fill.

And yet . . . what good would it do her to drink her fill now? She was like the rich man in the parable who deserved not a drop to cool his burning tongue. She had flung away all her opportunities to have Daniel's love, as if they were cheap and meaningless. Another poem taunted her, and she heard it as if from his lips, and spoken to himself:

> Quit, quit, for shame! this will not move,
>   This cannot take her;
> If of herself she will not love,
>   Nothing can make her:
>   The devil take her!

She would never have them back now, those chances. What man could endure that raving and love on? She must have seemed utterly senseless to him, insane, in her ignorance of the true facts. She had stood ranting triumphantly while the bridge between them, set afire by her own hand—her own words—burned to ashes and fell in on itself; she had burned it, only to discover too late that that bridge had led to a bright future, and that she was on the wrong side of the river of decision. An ancient sin had parted the bride and the groom—not just Merry and Charles, but she and Daniel.

It came back to her with powerful force, too, that he had said he would go away—to Madeira or some place else. Perhaps he would go marry the young widow he had once hoped to unite to Charles. Certainly he would find someone else; after all, he had a responsibility to his lineage, which he must feel very strongly. And why should he not find a wife? Did he not eminently deserve one? And as for her, she would be left here in the vale of Deepclough, looking back endlessly on the summer when she had loved, when she had been loved, when she had been respected and honored, even adored, by a man of perfect good sense, of mild and sweet temper, of intelligence, of resourcefulness and physical strength and courage—and of good looks as well; for she now found that all the times she had told herself that Daniel was ugly—they all turned to vapor in her memory. In her memory, she saw him quite clearly; and how handsome he looked to her, in her memory! How fine, in every respect, in every particle of his person, in every attribute of his being. That image, the handsome Daniel, was what she would ever look back upon as the loving husband she had lost.

Somewhere in her endless marching back and forth on the ridge, in the endless rememberings and self-scourgings and self-reproaches and self-recriminations, she broke. She sat down in the long grasses; ultimately she lay down and hid among them; and the storm of pain that she had felt by the river in Bath was nothing to what she felt now.

She wept as only a woman can weep, for only a woman is strong enough to weep so; she wept as only a woman can weep who has lost the light of her life; she wept like a widow.

Act III

A Durable Fire

But true love is a durable fire,
In the mind ever burning;
Never sick, never old, never dead,
From itself never turning.

—Raleigh

✣ **17** ✣

Shall Love Starve?

I hate a fool that starves her love
Only to feed her pride.

—Suckling

She was not sure how she survived to the end of that day. When she returned to the house, all the menservants were out looking for her, and Merry and her father were waiting anxiously in the parlor for some word of her. She apologized to John and Merry, but she could not quite soothe their concern away, for what she had done was utterly unlike her. They ate a late supper, quite silently; the servants returned one by one, and she apologized to each and slipped each one a coin of her own money for their trouble and their own late supper; but they were so glad to see her safely returned that they scarcely heeded the gift. After supper she sat for a time with Merry and John, but she would not play or sing for them, though they asked it of her, perhaps as proof that she was really all right; but it was a proof she could not give to them. After a decent interval, she excused herself and went to bed.She wept herself to sleep. Her mirror the next morning showed her pale and ill, her eyes dark and worn.

Somewhere in the process of washing and dressing, inevitably catching glimpses of that ghost in the mirror, her spirit began to rise in her again. She sat on the edge of the bed then and looked directly at herself in the glass, as if reveling in her defeated air, in order to disgust herself and rouse a fresh courage in herself, a fresh will to live.

I shall never have him back, she said to herself. *But I owe him an explanation. As I hope to be a good Christian, I owe him an explanation, an apology, and whatever amends I can make to him. I wish there were some good deed I could do him, some way to make him stop and realize that I do not hate him, no matter what I said. And if he could go beyond that and realize that I love him still, have always loved him . . . but that is impossible. He could never be brought to believe that, after what I have said.*

The first possibility that came to mind was to write him a letter.

There were, however, several serious obstacles to this in her mind. The first was that in her time there was a powerful taboo against an unmarried woman writing an unmarried man. Of course, women did so all the same; but only women of a certain sort, or desperate women; and at the idea that he would think her such a woman, her now fragile self-esteem shrank in dismay.

Still, to this objection she thought: *Well, am I not desperate? What do I have to lose? Can I descend any more than I already have done in his good opinion? Impossible!*

Another obstacle that presented itself was that the letter might disgust him because of its proximity to his offer of marriage. Might he not look at her explanation as the contrivance of her craven second thoughts about having rejected him? Or of greed as she realized she had let Landseye slip through her fingers? Would it not seem a declaration of her willingness to be false, to say anything, as long as she could have back the offer of material comfort she had so forcefully rejected?

And then she felt a still more powerful qualm: might it not even hurt him? After all, when a woman has stabbed her dagger into the heart of a man, does it help him, as he lies there bleeding, if she then tells him it was all a mistake? Would not an apology, an explanation, only pry apart the wound and let it bleed the more? Or to state it without metaphor, would it not be better to let him go on and marry happily elsewhere, without any intimation of the reason for her mistaken fury against him?

There were more doubts as well, crowding into her mind and urging her to give up the writing of any letter; but she resolved to at least try to compose the thing, if only to see if it was possible to articulate her thoughts and feelings. Whether she would send it or not was something she could decide when she had it in hand.

It occurred to her further that she must speak with her father about what had happened. It would be a topic painful in the extreme for both of them, but she must have some confirmation of the facts Merry had presented. Her sister did have a way of misunderstanding things she was told at times, and also of inadvertently misrepresenting matters; John Wyatt's acknowledgment of the situation would be definitive. She would follow him to the garden after the morning meal and speak to him in private there.

In the meantime, she took further care with her dress and hair and person in general before descending to breakfast; and this was to be her rule for some time to come, because she could never stop hoping that she might somehow meet Daniel without expecting to do so. And if she did, and if he chanced to see her . . . he must not be able to scorn her in his own turn for any frowziness in her dress, her hair, her complexion, her bearing. She had never been less than perfectly neat in all these things, but there is always a further level of care to which a woman can take them, or at least she imagines so. Even if there was not in Elissa's case, her concern would have found expression in her actually fretting over these matters and never being quite satisfied with them.

Ironically, it takes a woman to notice, or at least consciously to notice, this extra care; and Merry saw it immediately when Elissa joined her sister and father in the breakfast room.

Elissa took a somewhat perfunctory meal, waiting for John to rise from the table and go out into the garden. When he at length did so, in accordance with the informality of the English morning meal, she decided to sit on for a few minutes more to avoid arousing the curiosity, if not the suspicions, of her sister.

It was, however, too late to avoid that. As soon as John was gone, Merry immediately asked Elissa if she was well.

"I am, dear," said Elissa, determined to brazen out this challenge.

Merry regarded her in silence for a few seconds, and then said, "Will you tell me what it is?"

"What *what* is, darling?" The endearment came from her lips sounding very stiff and cool and did not help her pretense.

"You cannot fool me, you know," said Merry. "Something has gone wrong."

"Is not what I found out yesterday enough to account for any uneasiness you see in me?"

Merry considered this for a minute, and Elissa thought she had successfully put her off the pursuit. But then Merry said, "No, it is not."

"Then what else would it be?" countered Elissa.

Merry thought for a rather lengthy time. It was unusual for her to cogitate on any one subject so long and so continuously, and her brow was furrowed with the effort. She kept studying Elissa for clues; and perhaps it was in the crisp perfection of the way she had done her hair that she found the answer.

"It is Daniel, is it not?" she asked finally.

Elissa looked at the open door of the room before she could stop herself; and this signaled to Merry that she was on the right track. She rose and closed the door, and then she came and sat down beside Elissa.

Who made a fair show of insouciance for another half minute or so, taking a tiny morsel of very dry toast and a sip of lukewarm tea.

But then her head began to droop, and the tears began to run again.

"Oh!" she said in disgust at herself, irritated that she was already ruining what little repair she had been able to make of her looks. She dried her eyes with her napkin and sat up straight in her chair, summoning her will to repress her emotions, and staring directly ahead, though her view was nothing more than the wall over the sideboard.

Merry touched her wrist tentatively, as if she wanted to take her hand, but did not dare.

"It *is* Daniel," said Merry. "You are afraid there is no chance of him now."

"I *know* there is no chance of him," said Elissa. "And yes, that *is* why I am . . . so upset. If I had *only* known what he told you!"

"But I could not bring myself to tell you," said Merry, uneasily, a little fearfully.

"Ah, dearest, dearest Merry, you have no idea how fatal your reticence was! But I do not blame you. It is I who am at fault. I should have trusted him! I *knew* he could not be an evil man, and yet I told myself he was, I . . . I believed *myself,* when I should have believed *him,* I should have *believed* him to be what I *knew* him to be."

She turned her palm upward so that Merry could take her hand, a gesture that her sister accepted gratefully.

"But why should . . . all that stop him," said Merry then, "from . . . from loving you and . . . marrying you?"

"It should not," said Elissa. "Except that I did something terrible, because I did not know. On Friday last, in Bath, he paid his addresses to me, and I refused him."

"You refused him!" exclaimed Merry. "But you love him! Why did you refuse him?"

"Because I thought he had contrived to separate you and Charles. I thought he had deliberately ruined your happiness forever."

Elissa could see that the enormity and finality of this act did not immediately penetrate to Merry's understanding; and indeed her sister at once said, "But now you know! Now you know he was not to blame!"

"Indeed I do," said Elissa. "But it is too late."

"But . . . he will come to you again. He will ask you again! He loves you. If ever a man loved a woman, *he* loves *you.* Anyone could see it in his eyes, in his entire bearing toward you. They say that when true lovers quarrel, they shake the very earth, and the world turns to winter; but then they come together again, the universe is mended, and spring leaps up from the ground. You would be the first to tell *me,* if I were in your place, that it is all a mere lovers' quarrel."

"It is not a mere lovers' quarrel, darling. It is the quarrel of two very serious people; and so the damage it has done is irreparable."

"Elissa, you do not know your own value as I do, and as others do who love you. To him, as to all of us, you are an angel; he will not let you go because you have made one mistaken refusal!"

Elissa laughed curtly and bitterly. "But such a refusal it was, dear Merry, that no man, not even Daniel, could ever conceive of making any repetition of the offer to which it was given. Such a refusal! I poured out on him all my hatred and all my hurt—not only the hurt I felt for myself, but the hurt I felt for you."

"Oh, Elissa!" said Merry, in a groaning voice, as she began to understand. "If you reproached him on my behalf, then you must have been fierce to him indeed!"

"Fierce is hardly the word for it. If I had been a tiger, I would have laid his breast open and eaten his beating heart. Nay, that would have been kinder than what I did!"

"Oh, Elissa!" said Merry again. Elissa did not know what seemed worse to her sister, the metaphor or the reality, but the seriousness of the facts were now definitely penetrating to her apprehension.

After a moment, Merry began, "But can you not . . ." But her voice trailed off.

"Can I not what?" said Elissa. "Go to him? Tell him I am sorry, that it was all a mistake?"

"Yes; yes, that is what you should do."

"Impossible! Impossible! I would not blame him if he struck me down for the sheer impertinence of it!—Though of course, he never would do such a thing. Still, Merry, I said such things to him as to make him never care for me again. I cannot unsay them; I cannot return to his good opinion now."

"But he *loves* you! And he must have known somehow that you *did not know*. He must have seen that the conversation was mistaken in some way!"

"Why should he think I do not know? Could he imagine for an instant that you or Papa would not have told me what happened that day? He must think I am simply insane or vicious. He cannot *want* me anymore. That is what I must live with."

"But you *love* him!" said Merry.

"Yes, dear, I do love him. That I now know, again, as I knew it before all this misunderstanding began. But it is too late. My knowledge is too late. It will never be undone, all this misunderstanding."

"But you must try!"

"I have no hope of any such attempt. But if it reassures you in any way, I can tell you that I am determined to apologize to him. That much I am convinced I must do."

"How will you do that? Will you go to him? Because I am sure that if you go to him and tell him to his face how you did not know how things stood, he will renew his offer at once."

"I shall *not* go to him. If we happened to meet, and I could contrive a time in private with him, I would tell him then; but I seriously doubt he shall ever come to Deepclough after the thrashing I gave him, and if we ever did chance to be in the same place at the same time, I am sure he would turn away and avoid me.—No; I have thought of writing him. But I am not sure I shall carry it through. Of course it is not proper, but at this point I hardly know if I care about that."

Merry, having been raised in the customs of her times, seemed taken aback at the thought of such a letter; but after considering it in silence for a moment, she said, "You *must* write him, though it is a terrible thing."

"I shall write the letter and then decide whether to send it or burn it."

"Oh, if you can bring yourself to write it, give it to me, and I shall send it, I shall make sure it is sent!"

"No. If I write it, I shall be the one who sends it." She looked at Merry with bitter humor. "You may look to the chimney above my bedchamber, and if you see smoke coming from it, you will know my decision.—Now, darling, I must talk to Papa for a few minutes before I make the attempt."

"You will talk to Papa about all this?"

"Yes, I think I must."

"He does not like to speak of it, you know. It was terrible for him."

"I am sure it was. But I cannot write Daniel until I have heard what Papa has to say."

"I suppose that is right," said Merry, though she did not sound convinced.

Elissa rose to go, but Merry tugged her hand and made her pause.

"Elissa . . ." she said.

"Yes, dear?"

Merry looked up at her in a frightened way, as if she was considering saying something that she thought would draw pure wrath from her sister. She said: "But it was not so *very* wrong, was it? I mean, Papa and . . . Mrs. Newsome. They must have loved each other very much, and needed each other very much. And we are to forgive those who sin, are we not? And if no one had ever found out, what harm would there have been in it?"

"Of course we are to forgive them, dear; there is no question of that. I think you and I have both forgiven them. I daresay we never even reproached them. But do you not see, Merry, what harm it did? To you and Charles, and to me and Daniel Newsome, as well as to Papa and Mrs. Newsome? That is the problem with doing wrong, dear: it spreads like blood in water. That is why there are all those rules and vows and promises, because they keep one walking straightly down the long cord that belongs to one, out of all the cords in the great web that binds us all together. If we thrash about and tear something from this cord and something from that and try to put them together by our own rules, the whole web falls apart. That is the greatest *natural* reason to do right—do you not see, Merry? Because by doing right we do the least harm to others in the long run. The rules were not made to oppress us; they were made to keep us safe and whole, keep us living as freely as we can within the human web. Even if God had not given those rules to us, they would have been discovered bit by bit by those who did wrong and suffered by doing so. The benefit of morals is not always so clear, I admit; but I do believe that there is one."

Merry lowered her eyes as if she could not bear to look into Elissa's at that moment; but she also held her hand tightly, as if she would not for the world have let her go.

"You are so much wiser than I am," she said then. "You see these things more clearly than ever I could. To me it is all murky and dim. But I do hear you, Elissa, I do understand what you are saying. It is just so . . . hard, so unfair."

"We only make it hard on ourselves by wanting what we cannot have, dear, and by disobeying what is right—by doing what is wrong, in order to get it."

"Yes," said Merry. And she kissed the back of Elissa's hand, following her old habit.

Elissa said, "I will go see Papa now."

Elissa had heard that Mr. McBean was to go to Gloucester on an errand that day, and that it was Jim Riggins's day off; so she had some assurance of speaking with her father in private. She found him about to begin the digging up of a new flowerbed.

"Papa," she said, "I must talk to you."

"Ah," he said. "What is it that my dear *serious* daughter wishes to say? That will be something worth listening to."

"Yes, it is not a trifling matter.—Will you sit down with me for a few minutes?"

"Of course, dear. I ought not to begin work so suddenly after breakfast, in any case; I know that, but I was tempted when I saw that McBean had not yet dug up this bed, and I was thinking how I might have it all finished when he returns with those new peonies."

He struck his spade into the ground and went to the nearest bench, which was under the shade of a thickly grown grape arbor; she followed him and sat beside him.

"Now, what do you have on your mind?" he asked with a fond smile.

It hurt her to hurt him, but she must. Still, she was unsure how to begin; and while she hesitated, he continued in the same fond vein.

"If I had known how my daughters would turn out," he said, "I would have given you Latin names. I would have called you *Gravissima* or *Severa,* and Merry *Hilary* or *Letitia.*" He chuckled happily, though it was an old joke; she had heard it many times, and knew that the Latin had been supplied by Mr. Herbert upon her father's request.

"Then today call me *Gravissima,* Papa," she said. "For I have something very serious and sad indeed that I must ask you about."

Elissa had never noticed that he had the same way of looking frightened as Merry.

"Oh," he said, at once uncomfortable and mystified. "What would that be?"

"Papa," she said, "I never knew until yesterday what it was that Mr. Daniel Newsome told you in the vestry at Merry's wedding."

In the space of a breath he went from appearing merely uncomfortable to looking fully miserable.

"I must ask you," she went on. "Is it true, what Merry told me? She does not always apprehend quite correctly, and I need you to corroborate what she said. Is Mr. Charles Newsome our half-brother?"

John, apparently unable or unwilling to speak, nodded curtly.

"And of course you knew nothing of it until that hour?"

This provoked him to speech. "Of course I did not!" he said. "Would that I had! I would have put a stop to their . . . friendship long before that. But indeed, I knew nothing. I did not even know that she . . . that Agnes had borne a child."

"A child," repeated Elissa. "Yes, that is what he is, what he still is. He is a sweet, good, harmless person."

"He *is*," agreed John emphatically. "I daresay I . . . loved the boy. He is not George—I daresay he is not half the man George was; but I loved him. He reminded me of his mother, and I loved that in him, though I could never say that to him or to anyone."

She found that even though the morning was warm, she was shaking with something like cold; and even though she did not in her heart reproach her father, she was so sickened by her own pain that she blurted out: "But Papa . . . oh, how did it happen, Papa?"

And to soften the hurt of her question, she took one of his hands in hers and held it.

He gripped it tightly, but he could not look her in the face; he looked away over the garden; and she had the impression that he was seeing back into time. For a long space he did not answer, and then he said: "It was after your mother died, you know. I did not know if you knew that, if Merry told you that.

"I loved your mother," he went on. "I dare say I . . . loved her too much. I worshiped her; and every time Mr. Herbert says we must not make idols of others, I think of her. She was so . . . beautiful; she was simply and exquisitely perfect . . . in many respects. Such a woman! A woman like no other I ever knew; though I must say that you, Elissa, have her good qualities, and I often see them in you. In that way, I often see *her* in you. In many respects, you are the woman I loved in her, the woman she was meant to be, but could not be.

"For she had other qualities as well, which you do not have. She was hard, somehow. She wanted things a certain way. She would not let things bide as they were; she had to change things—and people—to suit her way of thinking. Your mother . . . liked me, perhaps even loved me in the beginning of our marriage. But gradually she came to dislike me, because she could not change my love for this garden. She hated that love in me. Not that she was jealous of that love, but she thought it was unmanly—or perhaps she only said that because she could not understand why she did not like it."

"Papa," said Elissa, "if that is true—if she hated your love for your garden—then she cannot have truly loved you."

She had assumed this declaration might support and comfort him; and he did shake his head in affirmation of what she said, but only miserably.

"As you know," he said then, "I have never been much of a one for remembering anything I ever heard out of the Bible, unless I hear it a thousand times. But there is one story I always recall. It haunted me like a curse in those days especially, when I was married to your mother. It is about King David, and how one time he danced for God. And his wife saw him, dancing like a fool, and she despised him for his dancing."

"Yes," she said. "Michal, it was."

"Michal, yes. I could never forget that story, because that was the way your mother felt about my gardening. I suppose my gardening, petty and meaningless though it may seem to everyone else—*that* is my dancing for God. And yet she hated it and held me in contempt for it."

"Oh, Papa!" she groaned. And the tears began to steal forth from her eyes yet again.

"And Agnes—I mean, as I suppose I should call her, Mrs. Newsome—was much put upon by her husband. He was not a bad man in most respects, but he had this fault, this one, terrible fault: he was a philanderer. At the sight of a pretty face, a fine figure—he lost his head.

"Agnes came to Rowantree at the same time your mother died. She fled here to Deepclough. She was sick to death of Newsome and his ways. She was determined to sue him for criminal conversation, and it would have been a trifling matter to prove it on him a dozen times over. As for me, I was sick of life. I had lost the wife I loved; and I hardly knew which hurt more, that I had lost her, or that I had never had her love, only her contempt. I suppose I had been hanging on, year by year, expecting that I would win her over in the end, but after she died there was of course no chance of that. I know this is shocking to hear, but I was very close to the edge of life—very close to death, very close to finding a way out by myself. I even forgot the garden; that is how close I was to death. Even my garden seemed futile to me! That dancing before God . . . all useless. Only the thought that I could not leave George and you and my new little child—that is all that kept me alive. I was not so far gone and so depraved by grief that I forgot *you*, the three of you. But even that link to life was fragile.

"I used to ride all day, ride and ride, going nowhere, to no purpose. One day I started out as usual by riding along the ridge, and I came to the Rowcliffes' orchard—where you like to walk, Elissa—and I met Agnes there. She was praying—I suppose for some enlightenment about what she ought to do—under the great rowantree. Perhaps she ought to have been praying somewhere else; it might have all come out differently if she had.

"I had been acquainted with her only slightly in child-hood, but we knew each other enough to speak to one another. And one word led on to another; and that meeting to another; that day to a week, that week to a month, that month to a summer."

Here he lapsed into silence. Elissa could see that though he was not telling the next part of the story aloud, he was telling it in his head, in his heart.

"So kind!" he murmured after a time. "So good! You may see in the Newsome cousins that same kindness and good-ness. So sympathetic! It was as if she knew all my thoughts and feelings before I spoke them. Days we spent together . . . day after day. In that season, no one came into the orchard; and in any event, it had a door we could and did lock. There no one could find us or see us, and we met there, alone. It was a kind of Eden in ruins. To us it became a sacred place, our hiding place from the world, where we could be together.

"She was to be divorced, and I was a widower. We spoke of marrying, and we had experience of marital matters; I suppose that made it easier for us to stumble. And we loved one another. All that summer! It was the most beautiful summer of my life, even though it was filled with the fresh pain of losing your mother, because it was *our* summer."

Elissa flinched. *Your summer!* she thought. *So you, too, had your summer, Papa.* The parallel between her father's love for Agnes Newsome and her own love for Daniel was overpow-eringly oppressive. It seemed that her love was as doomed as her father's had been: it would consist solely of a glorious summer, followed by a lifetime of regret.

He was silent for a minute, but again, not silent inside; Elissa could see that. Finally he said, "I cannot describe it to you; it is sacred in my memory."

She wanted to say, "Yes, Papa, I understand"; but she gave him more reverence by saying nothing.

Then he continued. "But we quarreled," he said. "I do not remember over what—and it could not possibly matter, whatever it was; but we *did* quarrel, and I think she was frightened by that, more frightened than I could understand at the time.

"We did not meet for several days. Then one day I woke up and realized what a fool I had been. I went to apologize to her—I went direct to Rowantree. But there I learned that she had returned to her husband.

"It made no sense to me at the time, but now I know how it was. She had discovered that she was with child, and not by her husband. They had not had relations for some time—he would not stay true to her long enough! As a result of our quarrel she had some doubt about whether I would stand by her and marry her, or so I believe. Her case for divorce was now lost before it was begun, as Newsome could easily prove criminal conversation against her, even more easily than she against him. She must have wanted at all costs to avoid scandal and secure a home for the child that was to come.

"She told me nothing of this. I was left to be mystified, to invent reasons. I would guess now that she feared that I would try to lay claim to that child of mine in some way if I knew of it, so she never told me.

"I was deeply hurt. I dare say I have never recovered from those two swift losses—first your mother, who did not love me, and then Agnes, who loved me too much."

Elissa, remembering what Merry had said on this point, now asked: "And is that why you never married again?"

He thought about this for a minute, and then he replied, "No. The real reason I could never marry again, after I lost Agnes, is that I thought of what had happened between your mother and me. I could never bear to watch another woman slowly but surely come to dislike me for what I am. I could not *inflict myself* on another woman. That is what I felt it would be. It is a wretched thing to watch—the good will of your spouse gradually dwindling away because she does not understand you and has her heart fixed on some other object, which like as not seems trivial or uninteresting to you."

"But how awful, Papa! That Mama disliked you for the very thing you loved best!"

"Yes," he said. "But I think that so it is in many marriages. But it would not have been so with Agnes and me."

Elissa thought this was more than the simple insistence of his ancient affection; and so she asked, "What do you mean, Papa?"

He looked into the distance again and his face grew haggard at the recollection of his loss, at his own pointless regret for what had never come to be, which now never could come to be.

Then he said, in explanation: "She loved gardens."

Elissa saw it all in an instant, with an insight rarely granted to one her age and on her side of marriage: How Mrs. Newsome had come over her father like a blessing and a blessed blow as they had spoken of this mutual passion, this mutual desire to dance before God. It must have been a blinding dream for both of them—for her in what seemed at that time to be the dissolution of her wedded union, for him in his grief at the loss of his own marriage, difficult though it was.

Then her father said something strange—strange words that she never forgot. He seemed to be speaking in a dream or a daze; he seemed to be both unaware of her and deeply aware of her, trying to teach her something that in her youth she could not know but should know; something that, if she could grasp it, might make all the difference to her in times to come.

"But it is not just that she loved gardens," he said. "She *was* a garden. A woman, you see . . . when she has her youth upon her and she is fertile . . . the earth . . . soil, she is like soil. God made us to be . . . fertile, like the soil, and everything about it is . . . blessed by God, the whole way we go about getting a child. The joy of it . . . there is nothing like it. I would say it is magic, but that would demean it. It is not magic, it is reality. God gives us this blessing; we are so fertile that we . . . run over with it. Even the smell of it, of a man and a woman together, is like the earth, overpowering, sweet, damp, rich, so rich that in the moment, in the time of it, you feel as if it is all the wealth you could ever desire. And so it should be! In that moment God lends you His creative power, His blessed power. And to squander that gift is . . . I will not say it is the most dreadful thing we do against God, but it is one of the most dreadful. As she and I learned to our cost! If we had been within our rights as husband and wife, it would all have been different. But instead it was wrong, and our son was hurt, and dear, innocent Merry. It is a dangerous, a tricky and difficult thing, possessing the power of fertility. We must use it rightly. If we do not, it is like sowing just anything, for the sake of sowing; and when it comes up it may be some noxious thing, or even some beautiful thing, but all out of place, and it must be cut down after all—as Charles was cut down."

And then his voice dropped to a murmur, as if he had forgotten that she was there and thought he was talking to himself. He murmured: "Yes, I say, she was a garden unto herself; and a man would gladly lie down on the black soil there and stay, stay there, in the rain and the sun and the storm and the wind, melt into her, until there came forth from her . . . God's child. Our children are not *our* children, they are God's. We think they are ours, but they are no more ours than the hollyhocks or the corn or the hops we plant."

How long he would have gone on if she had not stopped him, who knows; but she felt he was saying things she should not hear, and evoking images in her mind that no child of a parent wants to see; and besides, she had a sense that whatever it was he was saying was something he could not communicate. It was something each person had to learn when the time came, or fail to learn. It was like any moment when the beauty of creation shot into one's heart: it could not be told, it could only be lived. And yet she thought she guessed at some of what he said, because she had dreamed of her body in the childmaking act and the childbearing act, and her fertility lay on her like a weight, a comforting and welcome weight, but still a pressure, as of gravity. And her fear that her fertility would all be in vain—that weighed upon her as well, but in a different way.

She put her free hand on her father's arm to shush him, and he instantly ceased speaking. He looked at her as if he had awoken from a dream and was not sure where he was or what he had just said.

"It is all right, Papa," she said.

He nodded, accepting her reassurance.

She had one more question for him then.

"The Rowcliffes," she said. "Did they ever know anything?"

"About Agnes and me? No, they never knew. All they knew was that she wanted a divorce, and they . . . I think they hated her for that. They never cared much for her, you know that; they disliked her for the very reason for which she deserved to be loved—because she was a *daughter;* but at the idea that she might bring scandal on the family, they were done with her, they gave her up. They wanted her to go back to her husband; and only when she finally did, at the end of that summer, then they were willing to visit her from time to time, on very rare occasions, and only to see Charles. From things Charles said to me about her—and you can imagine how thirsty I was for any word of her, even as late as last summer—I believe they barely spoke to her even when they did visit."

She had an image of that poor woman, trapped between her unloving parents and her unfaithful husband, bearing an illicit child in her womb—how lonely she must have been. She had had Charles to love, but it was a love that would offend her husband the more she showed it. And Charles had grown up strangely useless in his kindness and sweetness, so useless that even his own mother had turned to Daniel when, at the very end, the difficult things had to be done and the difficult secrets told—and kept.

She sat there with him for some time, and neither spoke. They could find nothing more to say.

At last she thought of the letter she must write. She rose and kissed her father on the forehead, and she turned to walk away, but then another thought came to her and she paused.

But it was not just a thought, it was an inspiration, in the more literal sense of the term: a breathing into her of a spirit that seemed not her own. It was an idea so tremendous and awful that she both simultaneously knew it was right and had to be accomplished, and yet could not imagine how it could ever be brought to pass; it was so terrible that it would hurt them all, and yet it was the only thing that could save them all. Her voice, her breath, ordinary words themselves seemed choked in her; but she spoke up somehow anyway, thinking that this must have been how the prophets of old spoke, knowing that they would be hated for what they said, but driven to say it anyway.

She did not even look at him; she was still facing away, as she had halted in departing from him.

She said: "You know, do you not, Papa, that you must acknowledge him?"

She could sense, more than see, how he raised his head and stared at her and gaped at her.

"No!" he said.

"It is true, Papa. You must."

"But . . . Merry! Think what would be said about her! That she stood at the altar with her own brother!"

"It is terrible, Papa; it is a terrible, terrible thing; but you must do it—for the sake of what is true and what is right."

"Never!" he said.

She stood there for quite some time without moving; then she said: "Someday you shall know that I am right."

He seemed to be bewildered, even frightened. So great was her moral power that he was shaken by her pronouncement, even as he rejected it.

She did not want to push him any further, not now. It was not the time for that.

So she went onwards; she left him.

She left him to the consolation of the only spouse that had ever remained true to him, his garden; and her own thoughts turned back to the only true spouse she herself could ever have had.

In those days, writing was not a simple act of seizing one among a superfluity of writing implements and scrawling on a sheet made of dried wood pulp. ¶ The pen was a feather plucked from a goose; its tip must be sharpened with a knife into a particular shape, so that the ink would flow neatly from the hollow of the quill, which formed a small reservoir, though not one so capacious as to obviate frequent returns to the ink bottle. Elissa had the knack for this deft whittling, and in fact everyone in the household brought their pens to her to be sharpened; and now the thought that this letter would be read by Daniel compelled her to use especial care. ¶ The ink of those days, too, was wretched stuff, and ran everywhere. It always made one's fingertips black, and then seemed impossible to wash off; and naturally it was liable, unless one exercised extreme caution, to splash on the clean and rather expensive sheets of paper. ¶ Which was rag fiber, thick, laid in texture, but creamy, so that any blot or correction or inky fingerprint made upon it stood out as a telltale of haste or indecision or carelessness. And Elissa was determined that not a single drop should mar this letter; it would be as pure and without flaw as a sacrificial lamb. ¶ Her handwriting was, in the eyes of Merry and John and everyone else in Deepclough, nothing less than a marvel. She herself took no pride in it; she simply considered the necessity for the perfection of one's hand a fact of life. She would not appear in person before anyone in undress, and handwriting was the clothing of thought; it must be as neat and appealing as her garments, and as well fitted, both to her self and to the style of her day.

Her preparations were soothing; but when the time came to set pen to paper and begin to speak in that medium, her mind went blank with wordless agitation.

Slowly she beat aside the mute spell that her shame had cast upon her and drew the words up from within her one by one. She did not, as one might today, scratch out words or change her mind about how the wording ought to proceed in mid-sentence, for writers in those times had not the luxury of doing so; she composed in her mind, she set down what her mind told her to, and it was complete.

And despite this certainty about what she had written, on this occasion she copied it all out in a still fairer hand and tucked away the flawless first copy in a drawer of her writing desk.

And all her toil, which lasted nearly an hour, had this meager result:

Wednesday, 3 September, 1812

Aeons' End
Deepclough, Glouc.

Dear Sir:

I write to you to make an explanation and an apology.

Only yesterday I learned the true nature of the revelation you made to my father and sister on the day of the latter's abortive wedding in May. I need not tell you that this knowledge puts your motives and actions in a completely new light. If you will—if you can—look on the statements I made in our most recent interview as the words of one conjecturing your motives in ignorance of them, I have hopes you will judge me less harshly than you must most justifiably at present.

It grieves me deeply that in my misapprehensions concerning this matter, I charged you with sins against my family of which you are wholly innocent. You were then and

have always been a friend to us, and my recompense for that
fair dealing was abominable, though I beg you to understand
that it was so only because of my ignorance of the true facts.

Your most humble servant,
Elissa Wyatt

When the letter was thus complete, she at first took courage from the words she had written in it. Was it not, when
seen in one light, just a very simple matter? A misunderstanding, as Merry had said, such as lovers have all the time.
If she had not done such terrible injury to his feelings in
repulsing him, she would have had no doubt about the two
of them overcoming this misunderstanding.

But other words sounded in her thoughts more loudly now
than did the words of her letter; they were the reproaches
she had uttered in Bath.

Yet those bitter words only made her the more keen now
to get the contrite words of this letter into his hands, and
before his eyes, and into his heart.

And so she decided she would send it.

And yet now a new difficulty arose: Send it where? Was
Daniel in residence at Landseye now? Or should she send
it to Lakeholm Hall, his own family's house? Furthermore,
in those final moments in Bath he had made a vow—or
a promise, or a threat, or was it just an expression of his
despair and sense of futility—to go away, to Madeira or
some other far place. To send it to him in Madeira seemed
impossible; that would be launching it into the void; and
furthermore, the letter would too likely then be seen by eyes
that had no business with it. In fact, now that she thought of
it, who would see it if she sent it to Landseye or Lakeholm
in his absence? Perhaps his manager there would open it, or
not open it, but might in either case think it a minor social
matter, something to put on a pile of odd letters for his
master's attention when he returned; which might not be for
a year or more.

These thoughts led on to others. What if he was still in Bath? What if she could find him there and hand him the letter herself? Perhaps now he would scorn to read it, as she had scorned to read the letter he had tried to hand to her. But then she could speak to him, at least, in person—track him down and surprise him, as he had surprised her, and tell him what the letter said.

Countering this: Maybe it was simply too late for any apology. This likelihood tormented her, or rather, she tormented herself with this likelihood.

But the thought of returning to Bath grew on her moment by moment.

She determined not to send the letter to Daniel at present, not until she knew his whereabouts and could make the sending to him count. The letter she must write and send instead would be to Louisa, begging for an invitation to return. Or was that even necessary? Louisa and the Boulders would welcome her back at any time. If they needed some excuse to give their acquaintances, they could say that she had come to Bath to make purchases for her sister's wedding.

Still . . . what a fool she would look! Having burst into tears in a public gathering, embarrassing both herself and Daniel; running away precipitately from Bath, and obviously from Daniel as well; and then, just as wildly and suddenly, running back. Even if she did not care how the business appeared to others, would not Daniel find her urgency, after she had repulsed him so determinedly and consistently, repulsive in itself?

She could not decide if her reluctance to run back to Bath was only foolish pride in her, or something deeper, an instinct that told her she must make her apology to her lover thoughtfully and calmly. He had loved her passion once, she knew that; but it was a strong passion, a serious passion, all the more powerful for running deep beneath a calm surface; it was not the flighty impulse of a Merry or even a Louisa. In her collectedness, she must reassure Daniel that she was *not* a fool who flew off in the wrong direction and leapt instantly to the wrong judgment. In her mind's eye, she saw the moment of her apology to him: her contrition for her mistake and her love for him should be legible in her features and her very posture. She would not cringe, she would not fawn; she would stand as upright before him as she always had when she was sure of his love. But he would know, looking on her face, that she was deeply sorry and grieved for having hurt him in her mistake.

Though these conflicting feelings battered her for quite some time, she did eventually conclude that one thing she could safely do was to write to Louisa and ask to return. She did not want to lie about her reasons, though the temptation to give the upcoming wedding as an excuse was very strong. So the note read as follows:

Dear Louisa,

Upon my arrival here, I found that my circumstances were quite otherwise than I had supposed. Would you and Mr. and Mrs. Boulder find it too strange if I were to return to you in Bath at once? I have business there of great consequence.

I am sorry that I cannot now say more concerning the reasons that call me back. Nor will I ever be able to do so; but I hope you will trust me to be acting with the best will and judgment of which I am capable.

Your most affectionate friend,
Elissa

To this letter, Elissa had every expectation of a quick response. But in this she was disappointed.

A week went by, a dreary, wretched week; and then a new week began beyond that. Every day she looked for the letter, was inwardly wild for it; and it did not come. Having sent the letter and made her request, she could hardly take it upon herself to appear in Bath uninvited; so she could only wait.

At last, a fortnight after she had sent her letter to Louisa, she received the following reply:

Miss Elissa Wyatt
Aeons' End
Deepclough, Glouc.

Monday, 14 September, 1812

Dearest Elissa,

Please accept my apologies for the delay in my response. I have been in a turmoil here; and if that alone were not enough to occasion the delay, then there is the further difficulty that my turmoil impinges on your affairs and has left me all uncertain as to how to write you. I hope you will forgive me! And I mean: not just forgive me for the delay, but for this other thing I have done. I did not mean to hurt you, dear; but you must know of it before you return to Bath, in the event that it affects your wish to do so.

Immediately after you left, I was overcome—quite overcome—in a most unexpected way, and with a suddenness I would not have thought possible; and that distracted me to the point that I let your letter lie unattended until the difficulties of answering it have now become almost insurmountable.

There is a certain gentleman out of Oxfordshire whom you know—know too well, in fact. I do not think it is necessary to specify him any further. Letters, as you know, often fall into the hands of servants or others, and the matter is so delicate that I would avoid any stranger apprehending this business as long as I may. Think of the man whose connection with me would make my relations with you and your dear family very awkward, and you will have all you need to identify him.

He first visited here with some others on the day after you left; and though his spirits seemed low at first, they have improved daily; and I cannot but hope that the cause of this is my own company, since he has come to us every morning since that first visit, and we have met by agreement at several concerts and dinner parties. My uncle and aunt concur that his interest in me has grown most particular; and—how it pains me to say it to you, of all people!—I myself am so head over heels for him that sometimes I think I do not know myself in the mirror.

He is, as you must know, quite extraordinary, and perfectly suited to my own temperament. My affection, or I might say my passion for him, cannot be simply a deceit born of the wild flutter that begins in me the moment I hear his voice in the passage. There is depth in it, reality in it, such as was never in any of my hopes of marriage before.

He has told me his side of the history of the breach with your family. I cannot fault you for severing relations with him—I see how painful it must have been for you all. But on the other hand, I do not think he himself is at fault in any way, and I rely on your sense of fairness to concede that.

Can you forgive your friend for this? That is what I must ask you. And though I have dreaded telling you what has happened, I have also craved your company, and longed to hear from your own lips that you can and do forgive me.

The full truth is that he has not proposed marriage as yet, though given the extraordinary interest he has taken in me, I anticipate his doing so any day; and it would not be too much, dear friend, to say that I daily pray and hope he shall. I grieve to add this complication to the friendship between you and me when we are so close to being united as sisters (or cousins, at least!) through David's marriage to Merry; but to me it is clear that Providence has appointed this, and I am swept along willy-nilly.

My dear, you know that if you have any need to return to Bath, whether for a purpose great or a purpose small, or even simply to purchase something for the bride, or for no purpose at all, I should be very glad to have your visit at any time or in any season, as would my aunt and uncle. Do not even think of needing to ask us.

Indeed, let me make it quite explicit: Come at once! Come now, and do not pause to write me in return.

The fact is, my love, that it is I who must do the asking—indeed, the begging—for I need you urgently, and greatly wish to see you again and to hear your opinion of the situation. Do at least write to me and tell me what you think of me! Tell me that you still love me, and that in spite of this prospect, we shall still be friends! For if in gaining a husband I lose a friend such as I have in you, it will be a sore loss on top of my happiness.

With all my love,
Louisa

After Elissa had read this letter, and read it again, in a state in which horrified comprehension and utter disbelief vied with one another to rule her thoughts, she remained sitting in the drawing room for quite some time in shock. This was indeed the most shattering news she could possibly have received, short of Daniel's having perished from the earth.

Louisa! she thought, when she could finally think again. *Louisa and Daniel! Is it possible?*

Much though she loved Louisa, a consciousness of her friend's shortcomings and, indeed, of Louisa's shallowness overwhelmed her. These were failings Elissa had always tried to deny, as one does in the case of a dear companion from childhood; but in the present circumstance, there was no submerging them in the current of her affection any longer; they bobbed to the surface and could not be forced down. Louisa . . . well, Louisa simply *would not do,* not for Daniel. That was her first objection: Louisa was not good enough for him.

And later, looking back on this moment and considering how she had reacted, she hoped it was some sign of a nobility in her that she thought of Louisa's future marriage in those terms—not as a loss to her, but as a disappointment to Daniel. Louisa simply could not offer him what she herself could.

That theoretical consideration was all well and good. But as a practical fact, such a marriage was all too superficially plausible. In those times, given the limitation of social circles, it often happened that a man who was refused by a woman then went on to marry her best friend or sister or cousin. Elissa knew of several examples within her own acquaintance. It appeared that having lost Elissa, Daniel had—with that resoluteness in him that was admirable—looked about for another wife, and found a candidate in Elissa's best friend.

And as the second wave of her pain and remorse surged over her, Elissa began to see how Louisa might well seem eminently suited to be any man's wife. She was not flighty as Merry was; she had a good head on her shoulders. She was no great beauty, true, but a man like Daniel would care little for that; she was attractive enough, she was healthy, she carried herself well. And most importantly, she was no raging tigress, as his last choice had proven to be. This irony cut deep: that Louisa should seem by contrast with Elissa to be more calm and serious.

But indeed, this marriage held out the prospect of endless misery for them all. Elissa might someday, remaining unmarried, go to live with her sister in the house of Mr. David Bright, whose cousin would then be married to Daniel. It was inevitable that Elissa and Daniel would be brought together, and inevitable that he would someday realize what sort of misunderstanding had taken place between them. Then too, though his morality would continue sterling and he would never waver or misstep in his marriage to Louisa, how could Louisa fail to realize that Daniel had preferred Elissa to everyone, that they had only been separated by a misunderstanding, and that it was a preference that could never change? And Elissa—how could she fail to remember that summer every time she looked at him?

But on the other hand, how could she protest this marriage? What right had she to fault either Louisa or Daniel? Should she not simply bow out and leave them to find their way to whatever happiness they could?

Her remorse and shame counseled this course; but then her passion and her pride rose up in defiance; and for those hours of anguish the struggle went on inside her until she literally thought she would go mad, or perhaps already had gone mad.

Finally she remembered to pray; and the answer that came to her was that she ought to go to Bath. If she should find there that Louisa's marriage to Daniel had advanced as her friend hoped it might, Elissa should bless her and Daniel, retire to Deepclough, and face the drear march through the future as best she could.

Accordingly she rose from the sofa and went to set in motion the return to Bath, dreading what she would find there, but also hoping that somehow it would turn out for the best.

❊ 18 ❊

In Greatest Pain

Of all pain, the greatest pain
Is to love, and love in vain.

—Prior

The journey to Bath was difficult; there were delays caused by exhausted horses and by a breakdown of one of the coaches. This gave Elissa plenty of time to rethink her decision to journey there; and it was only natural that long second thoughts should force her mind in the direction of regret. But so much had been entrained in her going, from the packing of her trunk and her goodbyes to her father and sister, to yet another imposition on the time and good temper of Dick Broad, that she would have been ashamed to call a halt and turn about.

Bath greeted her again, and fairly; for it was all sunshine on this day. It seemed impossible that the world could be so bright when her present day stood mired in misery, and future pain seemed to be hurtling down on her. This very day might be the end of her hope; and yet as she walked up to Queen's Square once more, occasionally nodding to her previous acquaintances as if she had not a care in the world, the city breathed its pleasantries into her ears as if nothing could possibly go wrong on earth.

There was a little bustle at the door; the maid answered the knock; Louisa came hurrying out of the parlor at

462

the sound of Elissa's voice, both beaming with joy at her arrival and yet abashed. She made much of her and bid the Boulders' manservant help the porter from the inn carry the trunk upstairs, and directed Dick back into the kitchen to take some tea.

Then Louisa and Elissa were left alone in the passage; and Louisa, embracing Elissa and putting her lips close to Elissa's ear, whispered: "He proposed marriage this morning! And I have accepted him! And I hope that it shall all come right with time, and that you and your family will not be hurt by it."

Elissa froze.

"Come," whispered Louisa. "He is here, in the parlor. You will say hello to him, will you not? For my sake? Greet him, at least?"

And Elissa, though she could make no answer aloud, let herself be drawn along the hallway to the parlor door.

Her thoughts were in an uproar in her head; if she had not been in shock, she would have refused to enter the place until she had had a chance to think and to calm herself, to ready and steady herself. But no opportunity was given her; she was brought straightway into the parlor and face to face with the man.

"Mr. Newsome," said Louisa. "Miss Wyatt. There is no need to introduce you; but I dearly hope that you will find a way to be friends still, for the sake of us all."

It was Mr. Newsome, indeed; only it was not *that* Mr. Newsome who came forward at Louisa's bidding and held out his hand; it was Charles.

Elissa looked at Louisa. "This is your Mr. Newsome?" she asked.

"Indeed it is, my dear."

"This is . . . your fiancé?"

Louisa, growing a little troubled at this odd interrogation, said, "Yes, dear; this is he."

For a lengthy moment, Elissa felt as if the world were churning around her; and perhaps it was, as her reality shifted to accord with this new understanding.

But then her spirit moved within her again, and turning to Charles, she said: "Ah, Charles! Do you offer me your hand to shake? Is this to be our greeting, after all we have been through together?"

And she stepped to meet him, and setting her hands on his shoulders, she kissed him on the cheek.

He blushed with delight; and then he seized her in his arms and gave her a buss on her own cheek.

"Dear Elissa!" he said. "You do not hold it against me? All of it? Any of it?—I give you my word, I had no idea when I met Louisa that she was *your* especial friend."

"I am glad you did not, if it would have made a difference to you," said Elissa. "But you know now, and I am glad of it." Now speech fairly burbled up out of her in her excess of relief and delight: "As for what has gone before," she said, "I shall never hold any of it against you. We have all suffered cruelly in this trick the fates have played on us.—But please, for the love of God, tell me where Daniel is."

"He has gone back to Madeira," said Charles, a little sorrowful at the thought.

"Already? He is gone already? We cannot summon him back from Falmouth?"

"No, I am afraid not. He took ship two days ago."

"Two days! We missed him by two days! Oh, how dreadful!"

"Yes. I knew he was in Falmouth waiting for a ship Madeira-bound, but I only heard this morning that he had gone. He has written me that he may be gone for as long as a year. But I could not let that news stop me from paying my addresses to Miss Bright."

"No," said Elissa. "That would not be right. Certainly Daniel would not want his own affairs to prevent you from speaking to her on such a subject."

"But Elissa," he said, reverting to his former anxiety, "you *do* forgive me? For everything? I would not fault you if you could not bear to see me again."

"Bearing a grudge against *you* is the last thing in the world I could ever do," she said. "Indeed, I am now duty-bound to do that which I would have gladly done all along, if the secret of your birth had been known to me—I mean, to love you like a brother.—But my head is whirling with all this. Let me sit down and have a moment to think."

"Of course," said Louisa. "Do you just sit down and rest for a minute, and I shall call for some tea. And you have just made your journey from Deepclough, too. It is too upsetting, I am sure, even though it is good news."

"Yes," said Elissa, even as she sat down. "It is very good news. You can be sure, Louisa, that I think your choice is good enough for my best friend, because I thought him good enough for my very own sister. You have got a sweet-tempered and good man for yourself; God bless you both. Now give me a minute—"

And she pressed her palms against her temples, as if to caution her friends with that gesture not to intervene in her thoughts.

"I shall just call for some tea," Louisa whispered to Charles. "She could use some, poor dear." And she slipped out of the room.

For several minutes Charles restrained his natural enthusiasm; but eventually the silence was too much for him. He had that same trait as his half-sister: he abhorred a lull in the conversation as nature abhors a vacuum.

"Is Louisa not wonderful?" he asked. "You have known her and loved her for ever so long—tell me, is Louisa not wonderful?"

Elissa smiled at him. "Yes, Charles, she is wonderful. And you are well matched, well matched indeed."

"I know a union between us will be awkward for others, and in many ways," he said.

"Well, so be it. That should not be an obstacle to your happiness. I shall certainly not let it be an obstacle to my being happy for you."

"I am glad you think so, Elissa!"

"Still, it is striking to think that you will be married to the cousin of the man whom Merry is to marry—that a brother and sister will be married to cousins. Louisa has told you about Mr. David Bright and Merry?"

"Yes, she has," said Charles. "I was very pleased to hear it. I believe this Mr. Bright is an exceptional gentleman and loves Merry very much. I could not have wished anything better for her; and you know I wish her the best."

He was so earnest and enthusiastic and sweet that she could have forgiven him far more than he had asked her to; and she smiled on him again and said, "Then do not be concerned any further about any difficulties, Charles. Let me ask you about Daniel again, for I must know how I may write to him. I have something I *must* tell him, and yet I have no way to say it."

Charles's high spirits were a little dampened by this reference to his cousin's affairs. "Yes," he said. "He said something about your being displeased with him. He did not say more—he never does, you know; he is the soul of discretion. But he was very unhappy when he went away."

"We had a misunderstanding," said Elissa, though as she said the words she wondered if the understatement amounted to an actual falsehood. "I should like to set it right—I have hopes I could set it right if I could write to him. How do you write him, when he is in Madeira?"

"I send a letter under separate cover in care of the manager, Mr. Curtis, at Lakeholm. He assembles a packet of business and personal letters for Daniel periodically. If you like, I shall write to him and enclose a letter from you."

"That would be very kind of you," she said. "But it sounds as if this is lengthy process, this assembling a packet. And how often does he actually post it?"

"Oh," said Charles, "I am not sure, really."

"And especially considering that Daniel has just left for the island—it would seem that Mr. Curtis would not see a need to send him correspondence for quite some time, perhaps even months. Would it not be better to write him directly, via the ordinary mails?"

"It could be done," admitted Charles. "But Daniel always told me that to be sure of reaching him with a letter, I must send it via Mr. Curtis.—I say, Elissa, send it in both ways. Write him by regular post, addressed to the firm in Madeira, and give me a copy; I shall make sure that Mr. Curtis has it."

"You would do that? I should be very grateful to you."

He was obviously deeply pleased to be of possible service to her. "Think nothing of it," he said.

"And the name of his firm in Madeira is . . . ?

"Newsome and Son."

"That is straightforward."

"But really, Elissa, it is the worst sort of luck that he has gone to Madeira just now. It makes me think of . . . before, you know—how it all happened, and he went off to Madeira after my . . . after Mr. James Newsome and my mother died. But this time he did not go for my sake, I can tell you that."

"Do you mean, to find you a bride?"

"Yes," he said, laughing in embarrassment for the past. "He told me that after having encouraged me so vigorously to marry the one woman in the world whom I *must* not marry, he is chastened, and shall never again promote my marriage to any particular lady.—No, I think he must be going to Madeira for himself." Then he seemed to catch himself; he blushed again with regret and embarrassment.

Yes, Elissa thought. *He can only have gone to Madeira for himself this time. And he will be gone for as long as a year! What other reason can he have for staying away from England so long, but to woo a woman—that particular woman whom he once had marked out for Charles?*

"Does he like her?" she asked Charles bluntly.

Charles was further embarrassed, but he could not quite pretend he did not know whom she was talking about. "Susan, do you mean?" he said. "Miss Bruit that was?"

"The widowed lady in Madeira, yes."

Charles shifted about in his chair in pure embarrassment. "To tell you the truth," he said, "there did seem to be some—how did Daniel put it?—some transferring of affection to him when he went there to propose to her on my behalf."

"I am sure," said Elissa painfully. "And she is . . . lively, and pretty, and wealthy, in addition to being now well disposed toward him."

"Yes," admitted Charles reluctantly.

To herself Elissa thought: *He will come back married, if he ever comes back at all. My only hope is to get that letter to him.*

The conversation suddenly lapsed; but in a moment they were saved from the embarrassment of this new silence by Louisa's return to the room. Elissa now learned that Louisa and the Boulders were to meet Charles at a concert later that evening; and he, needing time to dress for it, said goodbye to Elissa. His plan was in fact to depart first thing in the morning and to be absent for several days, as he was to journey to Ryderly Hall and seek the permission of Louisa's father, Mr. Samuel Bright, to marry his daughter.

The endearments and farewells between the lovers, though there was nothing exceptional or improper about them, now struck Elissa as painfully familiar. Once, and not so very long ago, Charles had addressed those looks and those words to Merry; but his love for her had now withered to a fraternal form. A different woman was the center of his little universe. This was as it should be, as it must best be; but Elissa could not help finding it strange and even shocking that what had once seemed a thriving love had been so readily redirected to another. She could only trust that with time she could grow accustomed to the change—and hope that his cousin's affections were not so readily shifted.

For her part, Louisa could not have done more to accustom Elissa to the new state of things; for after Charles had left, and the tea had been brought in and served, Louisa wanted to talk about nothing but her fiancé. She rattled on about his good qualities, while at the same time showing a fairly clear understanding of his faults; and gradually Elissa came to see that she loved Charles in quite a different way than she herself loved Daniel. To Louisa, Charles was not just a husband, he was a project. If Elissa had wondered briefly whether Charles's silliness would someday wear on Louisa's level-headedness, or if her good sense would soon become an object of ridicule to him—for that is often the ironical fate of the more practical spouse—she had to conclude that it would most likely not be so. It seemed probable that Charles's need for Louisa would feed their love for one another impartially.

The taking away of the tea things occasioned a break in Louisa's soliloquy, and with it she seemed to realize she had been doing virtually all of the talking. She now took up her needlework, as a signal that she was changing the mode of the conversation, and said: "Well, my dear friend, what do you think of all this? And I do hope you will speak freely. You of course have known Charles far longer than I. Was it a mistake for us to fall in love so swiftly?"

"It *is* very sudden," said Elissa. "How long have you known one another? You said you met him immediately after I went away."

"Yes, it is just a fortnight since," said Louisa, with a little laugh. "But I made up my mind very quickly that he would suit me. And for once I kept your saying in mind, and I think you may take a fair share in the credit of this match."

"What saying is that? I cannot think what you mean."

Louisa laughed and said, *"The hunter chases the hart until he catches it; but the man chases the maid until* she *catches* him."

"Oh, that old thing! Yes, you did well to follow that bit of ancient wisdom. And I think the outcome proves you did. As for the suddenness of it all, I am sure many a good marriage has been made on shorter acquaintance. And if my longer acquaintance with you both is of any consequence, I should say that you will do rather well with one another. Charles is so . . . open, and kind, and candid, and affectionate; and you yourself are affectionate and good-natured as well. I think he will be very pleased to be helped and directed by you, and goodness knows, he needs that. It was something that Merry could not have done for him, and we were all concerned that they were too much alike."

"Merry will not hate me?" asked Louisa with sudden anxiety. "She *ought* not, since David will love her so well."

"No, I can promise you that. Merry shall be quite happy with David and never look back. Besides, there is the reality of her relationship to Charles that will always make her stop and think. No, you are quite safe from that difficulty. Still, as I told Charles when you were out of the room, it is strange that my sister and brother will marry two cousins."

"Matters have become tangled, have they not?—Well, it could be worse. What if you did not have such a decided dislike for his cousin? If you had married *him*, we would make quite a merry chain of cousins indeed."

As she said this, she darted Elissa a mischievous look; but she must have regretted her teasing upon seeing Elissa cringe with pain. Her attitude changed instantly, and she asked, "Is there no hope, dear?"

"None," said Elissa. "Or very little. You know perfectly well that I love him—love him to distraction. But he and I have had a great misunderstanding, and I do not think that I can now put it to rights."

Louisa put the needlework down in her lap decidedly and gave all her attention to Elissa. "I last saw him the same day I met Charles," she said, "at Mr. and Mrs. Foran's house in the evening. It was the day after you left. I shall never forget it; it was the second time I had seen Charles that very day. Daniel brought Charles with him to dine there. And I must tell you—how miserable *your* Mr. Newsome was!"

"Was he so?" said Elissa in a faint voice. "And is that good news for my hopes, or bad? Should I rejoice that he was miserable? I do not think I ever could.—Did he say anything?"

"Hardly a word the entire time, and when someone inquired into his low spirits—he could not conceal them—he muttered something strange about being 'murthered,' and about going away soon."

"'Murthered'? Was that the word he used?" asked Elissa, with a quick horror.

"Yes. I recall it distinctly. It made no sense."

Unfortunately, it made all too much sense to Elissa. For a moment she could not see the room around her; she was away from there, in time and place, back in the garden, standing beside him, singing one of Campion's old airs. And the words of it went like this:

> When you must home to shades of under ground,
> And, there arriv'd, a new admired guest,
> The beauteous spirits do engirt thee round,
> White Iope, blithe Helen, and the rest,
> To hear the stories of thy finisht love
> From that smooth tongue whose music hell can move;
>
> Then wilt thou speak of banqueting delights,
> Of masks and revels which sweet youth did make,
> Of tourneys and great challenges of knights,
> And all these triumphs for thy beauty's sake:
>   When thou has told these honors done to thee,
>   Then tell, O tell, how thou didst murther me.

And she felt she *had* murdered him, or rather, murdered their love. And what if her rejection of him did, through breaking his health—or worse—prove the end of him?

In this thought that harsher fear came back to her from her previous broodings: What if he loved her still? If he did not hate her, then he must love her still; and if he still loved her, how he must be suffering! She knew the depths of her own suffering; but she had the consolation that she now knew she had made a mistake. He had no such solace. He must think her doubly mistaken: as he must see it, not only had she been wrong about him, she had been wrong in not coming to realize she had been wrong about him.

If he loved her still, that is. And the more she contemplated the pain she had caused him, the more impossible she thought it that he could ever care for her after that. And that reckoning was both a relief to her, because it meant he could not be suffering as greatly as she did; and an augmentation of her pain, because it meant he would never allow her into his heart again.

"You are very silent, dear," said Louisa gently.

"Yes; I am sorry.—Now, do you tell me: What are your prospects? Did Daniel ever arrange an income for Charles?"

Louisa looked a little grim. "He has given Charles an annuity of several hundred pounds."

"Several hundred? Do you mean three or four or . . . ?"

"Can you believe that Charles has actually forgotten the exact amount?"

"I am afraid I can. But it is a virtue in him to care nothing for money. Still, only a few hundred; I am surprised at that. I would have thought Daniel would have given him more."

"Oh, but I am convinced that it was a wise thing Mr. Daniel Newsome did, to restrict the amount for now; for surely Charles would spend it all on this thing or that. I think it would make him the victim of unscrupulous men, and his cousin cannot watch over him night and day. He did say something to Charles about increasing it should he ever marry; and Charles thinks that he named a figure, but he cannot recall *that* either. What he has now is all very well for him as a single man; but if we are to set up housekeeping together, we shall need somewhat more."

"You seem to do marvels with very little, as far as the Boulders' housekeeping is concerned," said Elissa.

"Oh, yes, I should take Charles with what he has, there is no question of that, and I am sure we would do very well. But my father will not let me marry anyone unless the man's income is ample and secure. He has always told me so."

"So you are telling me that as of yet you *have* no prospects?" said Elissa. "That you *cannot* marry Charles?"

"I am afraid that is the way of it. We must write to his cousin and ask for a clarification of the future annuity. And of course it must be stipulated in the marriage settlement; it cannot be a mere idea drifting in the wind. My father has always expressed a dislike of private annuities, and I am afraid that he does so somewhat justifiably, because one cannot depend upon them. So Mr. Daniel Newsome's departure at this juncture is most inconvenient! We must write to him, and then wait to hear from him, and then wait until we have settled all these matters properly and legally, and then, and only then, plan the wedding."

"It would seem very convenient then, to recall Daniel from Madeira, so that he can provide ironclad reassurances."

Louisa darted her a laughing glance. "Yes," she said. "It would be most convenient to have Mr. Daniel Newsome back. Convenient *for the sake of all concerned.*—But he might not come, you know. I am sure that he can conduct all the business at a distance."

"But much more quickly and effectively here. Once your father has met Daniel, he will have no doubts over the soundness of any annuity he might be offering."

"If my father can be brought to share your high opinion of Mr. Daniel Newsome—yes, I am sure any resistance from him would vanish! And I make no doubt that your own business would go much more . . . *quickly and effectively* as well. But in any case, surely the fact of his cousin's forthcoming wedding will bring Mr. Daniel Newsome back."

"Perhaps. Or perhaps not. Perhaps the very fact that you and I are friends might deter him. He well knows we are, as he saw us always together."

"But in any case, even if he came back for the wedding, that will only happen after we have all the articles of agreement in hand. So our engagement is likely to draw out to an unpleasant length."

This likelihood now frightened Elissa. The more time Daniel was in Madeira, the more time he had to make a marriage there.

The only thing she could do to speed his return was to find some way to speed the marriage between Charles and Louisa. And this she could only do by securing a living for Charles somehow. And she, Elissa, must be the one to do it: Charles himself was not constitutionally able to bring this about, and Louisa, for all her competencies, had little opportunity to do so.

And with her recognition that the best hope for effecting their marriage lay with herself, Elissa instantly saw the plan in her mind. In outline it was rather simple, but there were complexities within it that would involve a good deal of time to arrange; it would not bring Daniel back to England tomorrow, but there was a chance it would do so sooner than he would return on his own. There was no guarantee that it would have its effect before he married another, but it was the only plan she could conceive that lay within her power, and she must try it or forever regret that she had not.

And it had the great additional advantage of being the right thing to do for moral reasons—a characteristic which those expedients to our personal goals do not always possess.

Louisa had taken up her needlework again and now peered curiously at Elissa over it. "What is it, dear?" she asked. "You look thoughtful, and yet relieved, as if you have just thought of something very good."

"Perhaps I have," said Elissa. "Time will tell."

"And does it have to do with you and Mr. Daniel Newsome, or with Charles and me? Or with all of us?"

Elissa smiled—not too much, as she did not mean to encourage Louisa to hopes that might fall through; but enough to give her friend something to dream on.

"I shall not tell you any more about it," she said. "You have guessed that I have something in mind; and that is as much as you shall know for the present. I only want one promise from you."

"You have only to ask, my dear, since I know you cannot ask any wrong thing."

"You must invite me to your wedding."

"Why," exclaimed Louisa, "of course I shall do that! I hope you shall be my bridesmaid."

"Yes, bridesmaid would do very nicely," said Elissa.

And having made that mysterious remark to tantalize her friend, she turned the conversation to a new topic.

❈ 19 ❈

A Doctor of Law

Were you the doctor and I knew you not?

—Shakespeare

Elissa did not go to the concert with her friends; instead she stayed at home; and weary though she was, she copied her letter to Daniel over carefully, addressing it to him care of his firm in Madeira.

The next morning she walked out early and mailed that letter. When she heard that the postage to Madeira was two shillings and eightpence, she could have groaned; not for the expense, but because the amount only reinforced in her mind how far away Daniel was, or would soon be.

Then she entrusted the original fair copy to Louisa, well sealed, to give to Charles when he returned to Bath, so that he could mail it to the manager at Lakeholm, with instructions to send it on to Madeira as soon as possible.

Though this seemed a long chain of communication, after she had set it in motion she felt somewhat lightened in mind. After all, even if one of the copies of the letter went astray, they both could not. Surely they both could not. Not *both* of them.

That morning she also paid a hasty farewell to Louisa and the Boulders, for she had determined to return to Aeons' End at once with Dick Broad.

The surprise of her father and Merry when she returned late on the very day after she had departed was equaled only by their pleasure in the fact. She promised them an explanation, but did not hurry it; she waited until the following morning.

And because she wanted to tell her news to each of them separately, she waited further until John went out into the garden, as she knew he would immediately after breakfast; and then she took Merry aside into the parlor and shut the door.

"This is very mysterious, dear," said Merry. "You do not have bad news, do you?"

"No, not bad news. But surprising news all the same.—Sit down for it."

They took their usual places side by side on the sofa.

Elissa had said nothing to Merry of the letter from Louisa she had received before she left. At that time, of course, she had thought that it was about Daniel; and in any case, she had been too uncertain of the outcome to lay out the possibilities to her sister. So at least she did not now have to unsay anything she had said before.

"It is news about Charles, dear," she began.

"Ah!" said Merry, with a genuinely fond smile. "Tell me, what of him?"

"He is to be married."

Merry beamed with delight at this development. "Is he?" she exclaimed. "That is wonderful! I would not want him to be alone, especially now that David and I are so happy. If he is to put *all that* behind him, he must have someone to help him take his mind off it."

"Indeed, dear, it is a godsend."

"And who is it to be? Whom will he marry?"

"Well, that is where matters become complicated. Of all the people in the world, he has fallen in love with—Louisa Bright."

This robbed Merry of speech; she stared and made no reply.

"I know it is odd, and striking," said Elissa, rushing into the silence. "They met in Bath in the normal course of things—it was all quite natural. He had no idea of our friendship with her.—Now, I know what you are thinking, dear: it is very strange. But you know he needs looking after, and you know she is just the one to do it. And I do believe she loves him very much."

"Of course," said Merry, in a faltering voice, but with an attempt at a smile. "Now that you say it—I had never thought of any such connection between them, of course . . . but it is . . . rather a good match, I think."

"Indeed it is."

Merry was looking about somewhat distractedly, but her smile was increasing in its certainty. "I never thought of it before!" she said. "But what a lovely idea—Charles and Louisa. Yes, I like it: *our brother* and Louisa. We have always loved Louisa, and we love Charles as well. What could be more perfect?"

And Elissa, seeing her rise to this occasion with such strength and clarity of mind, could not help suddenly weeping for her.

"There, there," said Merry, caressing her sister. "Do not worry about me. I know that is why you are crying—because you are worried about me."

"No, dear," said Elissa, "I am crying because I am so proud of you for doing what is right, and for putting *all that* so resolutely behind you."

"But what else could I do?" said Merry. "And besides, with you for a sister to model myself after, how can I help doing what is right, or at least trying to?"

This made Elissa weep the more. "You are sweet to say so," she said. "I dare say you have been far more saintly through all this than I have! I was such a Jezebel to Daniel, such a Fury! I sinned terribly in that, and I shall pay the price for it. If I had been as kind as you, and as Christian, and spoken softly to him—as I ought to have! As he deserved of me!—I would not now be in this terrible situation."

"It will all come right, dearest," said Merry, repeating her assertion of a few days ago in well-meaning but futile ignorance. Then, with a more practical impulse, she said, "Have you sent the letter to Daniel?"

"I have done so, both directly and under cover through Charles. He will receive it as soon as is possible; in a couple of months, I suppose.—But dear Merry, I do not mean to talk about Daniel and me; I mean to talk about you and what all this will mean for you. It will be awkward at times, you know, because you are marrying Louisa's cousin. You will see Charles from time to time, surely."

"And so it should be," said Merry. "Why, I am his sister, am I not? I should not like to cut off all knowledge of him. He is a good man, and as innocent as a lamb—why, he is as innocent as ever I was."

She smiled reassuringly at Elissa. "Do not worry, dear," she said. "I think it is as you have always told me: there is a Providence working in our affairs, though we do not always see it. And you would also say that God has given us the gift of the passage of time to be a balm for our little hurts here on earth, until He can heal them finally in His house at the end of time."

"Did I ever say that? Though I admit it does sound like something I would have said."

Merry laughed. "It is only that you cannot believe I ever listen to you, that is all," she said. "And I do not blame you. But I find now that I *have* been listening to you, even though I did not always know I was."

"Yes, so it seems. But if only I had listened to myself!"

Merry laughed and wiped away her sister's tears; and then Elissa took Merry's hands in her own and held them.

They sat then for some time in silence, holding hands; joined in that sweet manner, but each thinking her separate thoughts.

Elissa found her father alone, by good chance. He had laid open a bed where roses were to be planted, and Mr. McBean and Joe Wiley were elsewhere in the garden, digging up the stock that was to be set here. John was resting after his part of the task, which was unusual for him. As it seemed to her, he was simply living in the morning. Or perhaps he was thinking of events of long ago; events that were leaving their deep traces in the lives of his daughters even now.

He acknowledged her coming with a smile; and when she tried to sit down beside him on the stone bench, he insisted on putting his coat down first so that she would be more comfortable. He had guessed that she would be sitting there for more than just a few minutes.

"Now, what is all this about, dear?" he said. "My sensible girl does not dash off to Bath and then return the next day without some good reason, some important reason, which she is likely to need to tell me."

"I hope I do not dart about like a distracted bird, Papa; though these days I feel that perhaps it is so.—I will be as brief with you as I can: Charles Newsome is to be married."

She saw him wince at the name of his son.

"Is he?" he said then. "I suppose that is . . . that is a good thing. Yes, it is a good thing. After all, Merry is to marry now; he should too. All the better."

"There is one difficulty, Papa. By the Providence of God, the woman he has met and fallen in love with and paid his addresses to is none other than Louisa Bright."

He trembled as an oak does, when the storm strikes it, and one hears from deep in its heart the complaint of an old wind-shake.

"Louisa!" he said, looking at Elissa, but sightlessly.

"Yes, Papa. So it must be."

"But *must* it be?"

"So they have chosen."

"But did *God* have to so choose? Will he not let my poor child be? Must Merry suffer on for my sin without end?"

"It is all right, Papa. I have told her, and she is glad for him. It is a good thing. Louisa is perfect for Charles. We have always loved her, and she will take good care of him; and he of her, so far as he can."

"But Merry will meet him again—she cannot help it. Why, Louisa Bright and David Boulder are cousins! And then she will suffer again. And everyone will know her shame."

"And exactly what is her shame, Papa? That she came close to marrying her own brother? Well, we would all admit that it is not exactly what anyone would like to go through; but it was stopped in good time, thanks to Daniel Newsome."

"No, *not* in good time. It should never have gone so far. After myself, I blame Agnes. She should have told me."

"It is too late to blame anyone, Papa. We have to go on; we have to continue our lives and make the best of them. And I do believe that the marriage of Charles and Louisa *will be* the best thing. I think that through this, God is teaching us to accept what has happened, to come to terms with it."

He flinched again.

"Papa," she said gently. "He is *your son*. He is *our brother.* We love him. What is there to be afraid of?"

"Scandal," he said. "In a word, scandal. No one knows the truth—but imagine if anyone did! How they would look at Merry! The girl who almost married her brother—the girl who loved her own brother *in that way*. The world will see what it wants to see—scandal—and say that they had an unnatural love for one another."

"Papa, which is more important, our having the company of a son and brother we love, or the gossip of fools?"

"I would not mind," he said, in evident mental pain, "if only Merry and you had not been hurt by all this. I would gladly carry the weight of my sin alone; but that it should be visited on you, on my beloved daughters—that is beyond my enduring."

"But it has *not* been visited on us, Papa. Merry will be happy with David, and I think you will agree with me that she will be happier with him than she would have been with Charles had Charles never been her brother. David will care for her better, certainly! There is no denying that. And I think that what happened—I think it made her a little more serious, a little less flighty, so that when David came back, she could appreciate him more than ever."

"Yes," he said, "I have thought the same. But what about you? Were not your own dreams shattered when that secret came out at last?"

She was silent for a minute, trying to think how to deal with this shadow on the rosy picture she was painting.

"Daniel and I," she said at last, "have had a misunderstanding. I have taken steps to set it right. I have written to him, Papa. I am sorry; I know it was not proper, and I should have communicated with him through you. But I hope you will forgive me for that."

"Of course I shall forgive you! But will a mere letter set it right? He was . . . so *perfect* for you, and then that terrible barrier was thrown up between you. I am afraid that it can never be set right."

"It can and it will, Papa," she said firmly. "If it is God's will, it shall be set right, and Daniel and I will be reunited. If God wills otherwise, I will accept it." And then, looking away into nothing, she repeated, in a voice so faint it could hardly be heard: "Somehow I will accept it."

He took her hand for a moment and gave it a mute squeeze. But then he withdrew his grip and sat with his head bowed forward, signaling the oppression of his spirit with every bone and fiber of his body.

She gave him a minute to rest, as it were, and then she took a deep breath and moved on toward her goal.

"Papa," she said, "there is something you must do."

He raised his eyes to hers. "What would that be?" he asked. "If it is anything to help you and Merry, you have only to let me know what it is. But otherwise I am useless. I have only my garden; and when I die, that will be lost and ruined."

"What do you mean, Papa, you have *only* your garden? Working in a garden—why, that is as important as anything we do in this world, short of loving one another. It is as great—nay, even greater, I think—than literature and art, than poetry and painting, than natural philosophy or mathematics, than theology."

"Ah, but all those things live on after us to help future generations. A garden can be overgrown in a year. It is a temporal and temporary thing."

"Papa, everything we do on earth, all our little accomplishments, are temporary. They shall all be swept away on the Last Day, in the end of the age. It does not matter if it is the greatest poetry or the most useful of sciences: it will all be so much dust in the wind then. Yes, a garden is . . . time-bound. But so is everything. What difference does it make if those other things last a bit longer? They have no higher status in the eyes of God for doing so. God looks upon you, laboring in His Garden, which is this world He has made for us, and He loves you for loving Him so, through your work. Tomorrow *is* the end of the world, if you see things through God's eyes. We are no more than a blink there; the universe is no more than a blink. But we must go on planting roses and writing poems. That is what He wants us to do. As you have said yourself, that is your way of loving Him."

He took her hand again in gratitude for her words; and this time she responded by joining her other hand to their mutual grip and holding fast to it.

"And that is why, Papa," she said, "I must urge you to this other most difficult thing. We have only a few moments before we die, that is the truth of it, even if we live on for decades; we have only a blink of life and a little sleep, and then the end of the age. So we must *do* now, we must *act* now, we must do what is right and live by God's will *now*, while we can. And the right thing to do, Papa, is for you to acknowledge Charles Newsome as your son and heir."

He stared at her; he gripped her hand so fiercely in his surprise that he hurt her; and then he roughly pulled his hand away.

"No!" he said. He shook his head. For once, for perhaps the first time in her life, he was angry with her; or perhaps he was only still angry with himself.

She did not say anything for perhaps a minute. Then, very gently and quietly, but still very firmly, she said: "*Yes.*"

He stared at her again in something like outrage. "No!" he said again. "By God, Elissa, you have always been a good and obedient daughter to me—where does this rebellion come from? I will *not* hear of this! This is madness! It would only drag you and Merry through the mire! Through scandal! It is best to leave everything as it is and pray that the secret remains undiscovered until we are all dead and buried!"

"Papa," she said, "it is not your daughter who tells you to do this. I am nothing. Your conscience tells you to do it, because *it is right.*"

She could not leave this statement standing bare of any confession of the benefit to her; and turning her eyes away again, she went on, "I admit to you freely that I have hopes still—somehow, in spite of the terrible things I have done to Daniel, I still hope and pray that he loves me. And if Charles and Louisa marry, Daniel will certainly return from Madeira, where he is headed at this time. And if I meet Daniel at their wedding, at Charles and Louisa's wedding, perhaps I may reconcile with him—I pray I may do so. These are all my petty mortal wishes, my petty machinations. But even if Daniel and I . . . even if we are *over,* if our love is finished, still this thing that you must do will stand as an injustice forever if you do not do it. You must not let an injustice flow from that old sin, Papa. You must set the old sin right by acting rightly now."

He was furious. He did not trust himself to speak. He glared out over the garden, refusing even to look at her.

She took another breath and went on; and as happened when she felt deep emotion, even if it was not strictly grief or joy, she began to weep, to weep without sobbing; the tears simply dropped from her eyes, though her voice was steady.

"If you do not do what is right, Papa," she said, "then a further great wrong shall be done. And you know what it is: Mr. Crustall shall inherit this house."

"Crustall!" he exclaimed, so suddenly and vehemently that he startled her. "Do not fling Crustall at me! You know as well as anyone how I have striven to exclude him since George died! I have told you it is impossible, and you yourself know it is!"

"Is it, Papa? Has not God now put the means in your hands at last?"

He guessed something of what she meant. "Charles is my natural son," he said. "As such he is not a legal heir. That is a basic principle of the law of England, as sure as ever there was one."

Her argument now hung by a thread, but she went ahead with a show of boldness.

"Papa," she said, "remember how you used to read us that old document that goes back to the founding of Aeons' End, that lists all our ancestors?"

"The abstract of title, yes," he said. "That is what it is called."

"And somewhere, back on that list, a natural son was adopted and made the heir of the line. Do you not recall?"

She could tell from his surprise that he did now recall what she meant. It was not something the Wyatts liked to remember: "the taint of bastardy."

"Well, yes," he said. "But that was . . . the way I understand it, that son was made possessor, but was never considered legitimate. But his son was, and all the sons from him. It was as if the Wyatt line leaped over the illegitimate heir. That was the way my father explained it to me."

"Then could not something similar be done about Charles?"

"But that must have been five generations ago. That was centuries ago. And in any case, that does not matter; all that matters is what my father and I set down when we resettled, upon my majority."

She must have looked blank at this legalese, and some of his anger ebbed away.

"Dear girl," he said, "you know nothing of what you are asking. This is the way of it: When I came of age, my father offered me an annuity that would last until I became life tenant, on condition that I would join with him and break the entail by the suffering of a common recovery. It is all customary, my dear; everyone does it. I would have been without a penny until he died if I had not agreed—though I would have done what he asked in any case, as I loved my father and was an obedient son."

He could see that his explanation had not really helped.

"What it amounts to," he said, "is that my father and I were able to establish new conditions for the possession of Aeons' End going forward. We did not change much. But one thing your grandfather did insist on adding to the new settlement was that if I should not have a male heir, Aeons' End should pass to his sister's son, if she had one, on condition that he take the Wyatt name when he acceded. That is where Mr. Crustall came into all this. Your grandfather was fond of his sister and did not like the man she had married. And indeed, he turned out to be a drunkard and a gambler who beat her and drove her to an early death. But not before she gave birth to this son, this younger Crustall."

"Can we not—what did you call it—break the entail again?"

"No. It can only be broken by a private act of Parliament. Which, as you can imagine, would be virtually impossible to obtain. Not that the House of Lords is not always meddling in these things, and passing this act or that to adjust these settlements one way or another; but the settlement in this case is so clear about the line of succession that the Lords would never wish to break it for a . . . for a bastard son. No, the settlement is carved in stone."

"But how did our ancestor make his natural son a legal heir? And why cannot you do the same?"

At this acute question, John looked puzzled. "It must have been part of the entail then," he said, "or part of the deed of conveyance, or whatever instrument it was they used to pass on the estate."

"But might it not be preserved there, in some way, to this day? You might not have noticed it when you read the papers so many years ago, because you meant to have a legal heir."

"Indeed," said John wryly, "I never read 'the papers,' as you call them. The deed of settlement goes on for I do not know how many dozens of pages. I would not have the faintest idea what most of it meant."

"Then it might be buried in there."

This brought John to silence, in which he remained until she pressed him: "Might it not, Papa? If the deed goes on for ever so long, and you have never even read it, might not some clause in it allow for a natural heir?"

"It is not impossible," he admitted. "But neither is it very likely. The law does not like natural children. They complicate matters; they have a way of coming out of the woodwork at awkward times and spoiling things for the legal heirs, and they make claims that cannot be supported. For one thing, they seldom have the right . . . written pedigree, do you see, acknowledged and witnessed by all."

"But you have an affidavit from Agnes Newsome," she said. "That will help establish that Charles is your son."

"True," he said.

"Then we ought to go to Mr. Vaughn and ask him to reread the deed in that light, looking for some way that Charles may be declared your heir, and so—I am sure there is some legal term for it, but I mean so that Charles may supplant Mr. Crustall."

"No," said John, resuming his stubborn tone. "I will not go back to Vaughn again."

"But you admit there is a chance. Why will you not seize at that chance?"

And now John grew adamant. When it came to going to a third party outside the family and revealing the taint that lay on his house, he could not find it in him to say yes; and the more she urged him, the angrier he became.

Finally the workmen returned with the peonies to be transplanted. He stood up from the bench to indicate that the topic was closed; but she persevered a moment longer, and in desperation said to him: "Very well, Papa. If you will not go to Vaughn, at the very least let me look at the deed."

"You!" he said. "You would not comprehend a word of it, any more than I could. I doubt if even Mr. Vaughn understands the half of it."

"Let me try," she said.

And with an ill grace that was most unusual in him, he assented to this, if only to silence her for the time.

John made his continuing displeasure in Elissa's proposal known to her by refusing to bring out the papers for a week. Nor was he the only father in the world impeding Charles and his chances in life; in the meantime, Elissa received this note from Louisa:

22 September, 1812

Dearest Elissa,

> Bad news! The worst news!
>
> My father will not allow us to marry.
>
> Charles freely stated his circumstances; my father, who Charles said had seemed delighted, even eager, at the appearance at last of a suitor for his spinster daughter, listened with kindness enough, but then said that he could not allow his daughter to marry a natural son, a man without standing in

society, rejected by his own adoptive father and left penni-less, relying only on the mercy of the cousin he would have displaced from his rightful inheritance. And when he put it like that, what did Charles do but *respectfully agree with him!*

It is all perfectly awful.

Charles of course told him *everything*—after all, he had to explain why his wedding with Merry was broken off at the very altar, an event that would otherwise have prejudiced my father against him forever. But Charles, as you know, is never more winning than doing what he does best, which is to innocently tell the truth. And my father was perfectly decent about it all, and actually thanked him for explaining the circumstances, and said that of course it must have been very difficult and awkward, and he did not hold *that* against him.

Indeed, I almost wish he *disliked* Charles, and I could hate him for it! But who could dislike Charles? No, this is all a very *practical* calculation that my father has made, that Charles's birth shall harm my prospects and the prospects of my future children. And being founded on what my father sees as good sense, it is unassailable!

What *are* we to do? What *are* we to do?

The last thing on this earth I should like to do is to marry without my parents' blessing. Then poor Charles truly would be an outcast! And it would be all my fault, or the fault of my family, which would be the same thing. If I must *leave my father and mother and cleave to my husband*, I shall do it; but I should be very sorry about it, and we are decided that it shall be our last recourse. Poor Charles truly is miserable about it all, or as miserable as ever a man of his sweet and buoyant spirits could be; he seems to think it is all his fault that he was born out of wedlock.

Some might have counseled us (and I know you would not have been one of them) to have withheld this information from my father until it was too late for him to make it the foundation of an objection to the match. But neither Charles's open character nor my love and respect for my father would allow it. And the irony that his natural father should be *your* father, whom my father has known and respected since they were both boys—and that Charles should be *your* brother, you whom my father has doted on as a friend of mine since we were both girls.

And sadly, my dear, there is some bad news for you as well. When Charles returned to Bath with his ill report, we were so distraught that neither of us remembered the letter you wished us to send, not even when we determined on writing Mr. Daniel Newsome for counsel, and not even when Charles did so and posted the letter to Mr. Curtis at Lakeholm. Only then and at last did I remember you, my dear friend, and your own pressing difficulties, and Charles and I were then all chagrin. He made good by sitting down at once and composing a cover note to the same Mr. Curtis to whom he sent his first letter, and we went out together and posted it at once. So you see, we have patched up the error as best we may, but it was not done as thoughtfully as we should like.

I must say, the whole notion of this Mr. Curtis only further alarms me. From what Charles says, he is the keeper of all Mr. Daniel Newsome's correspondence, and if he should judge a letter from a lady to his master to be of slight import, he will not send it on to Madeira at all. Apparently he would see himself as acting in Mr. Daniel Newsome's best interest in doing so. Thank goodness you have sent the letter to Mr. Daniel Newsome directly! I quite approve of that, for all its boldness. *Both* letters cannot possibly go astray; *one* of them must convey your message to him.

In the meantime, we are at our wits' ends about what to do.

With all my love,

Louisa

In Elissa's day, such a development was dire indeed; it meant that Louisa would, if she carried through with the marriage, be shut out of her family and even a large part of her circle of friends. Young people then had not the same freedom of action and independence as they do now, and there was a censure attaching to illegitimacy that is almost inconceivable today; without being recognized, accepted, and supported, an illegitimate child had at best blighted prospects.

But Louisa's news only reinforced Elissa in her determination that her father should recognize Charles, not only legally but socially. When she first received it, she rose at once, letter in hand, to go to her father and relate it to him; but then, in a flash of awareness that seemed to come from outside herself, she paused, deciding that this news must be held back until it could be utilized most effectively to shake her father in his obstinacy.

As for the effect of these developments on her own situation, Charles's oversight meant that her own letter under his separate cover might be retained by that fearsome censor, Mr. Curtis, and never be sent on to Madeira. Then too, Charles's own letter requesting Daniel's help might bring his cousin back from Madeira before either of her letters reached him; and though his early return would be a blessing, he would in that case come home unaware of her repentance.

Distance and time! she thought. *There is no way on earth to overleap them. I can only send Daniel my love, and hope that his own love for me steadies him and brings him home before it is too late.*

At length Elissa prevailed upon her father to surrender the papers she required. It was only by annoying him severely by repeated requests that she was able to shame him into keeping his word to her. His discourtesy was utterly out of her experience of his character; she hardly knew what to make of it.

When he did finally take her into the office and fetch forth the papers, she found that—as she had suspected—they had been immediately accessible all along. Out of an enormous, brass-studded chest that had always been a part of the furniture of the room, and was never even locked, he took a thick packet of parchment and handed it to her with an air almost of disdain.

"When you are quite finished," he said, "you may put it back in the chest yourself. I need not tell you that you must guard the thing; it is not the only copy, by any means, but the expense of making another would not be trivial. Read it here, or in the drawing room, or in your own room; but do not leave it lying about in the meantime."

"Yes, Papa, I understand."

He went away; and she, to avoid the distractions of servants and sister, took the document to her own bedroom, where she had a desk at which to work.

But it was only a small lady's desk, and the top was barely sufficient, as it turned out: the document, when unfolded and then fully opened, consisted of parchment sheets of enormous width that had been sewn together along one edge. She did not attempt to count the pages, but the entire thing was as thick as her thumb. She had quailed from the first at the mere heft of it, but the array of verbiage that now met her eye was even more daunting: the lines crawled across the page for a foot and a half, so closely written that one could easily lose one's way while returning from the end of one line to the beginning of another. Furthermore, the document was written in an odd script. It was not what is commonly called old English or blackletter, or in the court hand that succeeded that style, since it had been written in the late 1700s after those affectations had become obsolete; but it was not a form of handwriting she had ever seen before. As she stared at it, turning over the pages with a sense of hopelessness, incomprehensible terms seem to swim up at her out of the sea of ink: *incorporeal hereditaments, enuring to, messuage, peppercorn, recital, remainders, seizin, personalty, jointure, defeasance, tenant to the praecipe, disentailment, assurance, dock, general power of appointment, hotchpotch*; to say nothing of fragments of Latin that the lawyers had apparently sprinkled in for effect: *ex parte una, ex parte altera, de me et heredibus meis, in perpetuum, sciant presentes et futuri, cum pertinentiis.* And hopeless it all certainly made her; for she sank down on the chair before this morass of legal jargon as though it were an impassable Slough of Despond.

This will never do, she thought to herself. *I have not the education to understand this. And yet I must read it—I must find something on which to hang my hopes—and to get for Charles that which should be his.*

She went to the door and called to Lucy Brown, asking her to bring up some tea. Then she returned to her desk.

And so began her strange journey into the law; veritably an alien world where nothing was called by its familiar name and the intention of all seemed to be to cloak simple facts in mystery, to encrust them so thickly with words and words and words, that under this carapace the true sinew and bone of the meaning could only seldom be glimpsed.

For days her journey lasted. It was often interrupted by the claims of the household upon her time and energy, and not only was there the usual business to be conducted, but Merry's wedding was now approaching, and preparations for it consumed a good part of each day. When she did study, she often had to stop and rest because she had ceased to be able to think straight, or because her eyes ached. Whenever she and her father met at mealtimes, he would give her a long, hard look across the table to see if she was finally willing to concede defeat; but she, affecting cheerfulness as best she could, greeted him lovingly and said nothing of her difficulties or her fears.

And this was what the deed contained—if indeed it was a deed, if that was the proper term for it.

It began with the date and the particulars of the parties involved: her father and grandfather and others identified as trustees, including several of the Vaughns, who had been attorneys to the Wyatts since time out of mind.

Then there began many pages of paragraphs beginning WHEREAS, which described the property of Aeons' End and its history through the centuries. Here the legal terms were particularly dense and tangled as they tracked various lawyerly stratagems and fictions, conditions for the inheritance of putative heirs who had never come to be, conveyances, breakings of entails, new settlements of the property, the dowers barred from and the dowries bestowed upon wives long dead, encumbrances anciently incurred and discharged and lifted, fines levied to end entails, heirs intestate, legitimate issue, life tenancy, bequests to persons now mere names, codicils of revocation, alterations by estate act, and the like.

Then came another great patch, marked off by the word WITNESSETH, which, after many preliminaries, commenced a minute description of Aeons' End and the personal properties that descended with it. There were odd exceptions to this property, consisting of parcels of land once attaching to the estate, but disposed of or traded for other properties, some of them under different forms of ownership—fee simple and fee tail and fee general, copyhold and freehold—in transactions all scrupulously recorded though for all the difference they now made, those lands might well have fallen off the edge of the earth. It seemed that not only had her ancestors once owned most of the eastern half of Deepclough Valley, but properties in Wiltshire, Devonshire, London, and even the Isle of Wight, all here detailed so minutely that one might have walked their ancient lines by the instructions laid out.

The fourth flood of verbiage was indicated by the words TO HAVE AND TO HOLD in looming capitals. She did not reach that point for some days, and it took still longer to plow through it. It seemed to describe trusts of various kinds. She could see that one trust had been created to give her father an annuity until he became life tenant of the property himself, taking over from his father. Two others had to do with her mother; one was about pin-money, and another, called a jointure, was for a purpose she could not puzzle out. Here too were the monies to be given as settlements for her father's female children; these she readily recognized. Old servants were mentioned, and various annuities and life tenancies granted to them.

From this she plowed along into a new continent of verbiage that had to do with the entail—that is, with the person who actually was to inherit. It was then that she came upon this paragraph:

> . . . Obed Wyatt his lands, tenements and hereditaments whatsoever, with the appurtenances in the county of Gloucestershire aforesaid, and *to and for the uses,* intents and purposes hereafter limited, and to and for no other use, intent or purpose whatsoever, that is to say, *to and for the use* and behoof of the said Obed Wyatt, for and during the term of his natural life, without impeachment of and for any manner of waste, and after his decease, *to and for the use* and behoof of the said John Wyatt, for and during the term of his natural life, and after his decease, to and for the use and behoof of the first son of the said John Wyatt lawfully to be begotten, and *to the use* and behoof of the heirs males of the body of the first son lawfully to be begotten; and for default of such issue, *to the use* and behoof of the second son of the said John Wyatt lawfully to be begotten, and the heirs males of the body of the said second son, lawfully to be begotten; and for default of such issue, *to the use* and behoof of the third son of the body of the said John Wyatt lawfully to be begotten, and the heirs males of the body of the said third son lawfully to be begotten; and for default of such issue, *to the use* and behoof of the fourth son of the body of the said John Wyatt lawfully to be begotten, and the heirs males of the body of the said fourth son lawfully to be begotten; and so severally and respectively to every of

the heirs male of the body of the said John Wyatt lawfully to be begotten, and the heirs males of the body of such heirs males lawfully to be begotten, according to their ages and seniorities; and for default of such issue, or any such legal issue dying intestate, *to the use* and behoof of the male, begotten whether lawfully or naturally, nearest to the direct male line of the Wyatts of Aeons' End, hereinafter the *Wyatt Heir,* for and during the term of his natural life, and after his decease, *to the use* and behoof of the first son of the body of the said Wyatt Heir lawfully to be begotten, and the heirs male of the body of the said first son lawfully to be begotten; and for default of such issue, *to the use* and behoof of the second son of the body of the said Wyatt Heir lawfully to be begotten, and the heirs male of the body of the said second son lawfully to be begotten; and for default of such issue, *to the use* and behoof of the third son of the said Wyatt Heir lawfully to be begotten, and the heirs male of the body of the said third son lawfully to be begotten; and for default of such issue, *to the use* and behoof of the fourth son of the body of the said Wyatt Heir lawfully to be begotten, and the heirs male of the body of the said fourth son lawfully to be begotten; and so severally and respectively to every of the heirs male of the body of the said Wyatt Heir lawfully to be begotten, and the heirs males of the bodies of such heirs males lawfully to be begotten, according to their ages and seniorities . . .

She was extremely tired when she read this passage, and her eyes were aching and stinging; and at first it seemed just more dreary lawyer's language. But when she reached the middle reaches of this Amazon of verbiage, with its constant reiteration of *son* and *heirs males* "lawfully to be begotten," and as she was foundering, so to speak, in the act of fording it—she was struck by the sudden lonely variation "the male, begotten whether lawfully or naturally, nearest to the direct male line of the Wyatts of Aeons' End." And on this male, who came into possession only in default of her father's legal heir, it seemed that all the future ownership of Aeons' End came to rest.

And in time, after much puzzling over the matter, she realized that this was where Mr. Crustall came into the picture. It was the only place that any other heir beside the son of John Wyatt was mentioned.

But there was no question—in *her* mind, at least—that Charles Newsome was more directly in the male line of the Wyatts than Mr. Crustall. Charles was the son of John Wyatt; Mr. Crustall was the son of John's aunt, one Julia Wyatt, who had married a Mr. Xenophon Crustall. She had a sinking feeling, though, that Chancery would prefer the legal cousin to the illicit son, if its judges were ever asked their opinion.

But why was that language allowing a natural son to inherit in the deed of settlement at all? This puzzled her still more; and she went to bed that night wondering over it.

And as sometimes happens, after she had slept for about half the night, and had partially awakened, and was drifting between wakefulness and dreams, she seemed to hear her own voice telling her the reason.

She sat bolt upright. And so that she would not forget the thought she had suddenly had, she rose from bed and wrote the reason, the possible reason, on a scrap of paper, by the light of the moon that came in the window.

Though she would have preferred to approach her father immediately with her discoveries, by the time she had made them Merry's wedding was nearly upon her. Her father seemed to have assumed that she had given up her attempt to decipher the deed, since she had failed to this point to report any headway on it; and rather than awaken his irritation at this juncture, she stifled her impatience and put off any further discussion of Charles and his prospects until after the wedding had taken place. Enforcing this delay on her will was not easy, and she could not have done it without many a prayer for strength. She was all too conscious that every day she waited was another day for Daniel to be drawn into a marriage overseas. But she would not spoil Merry's wedding by putting her father out of sorts in her pursuit of Charles's hopes and her own.

So the day of the wedding arrived without further incident to relate. What shall be told of it? It was a wedding; that should suffice; its details, so poignant and striking at the moment, were, when looked at *sub specie aeternitis*, mere generalities. The bride was young, and her excitement and affection—bubbling over—as well as the awe she felt at the solemnity of the event, elevated her common prettiness to an actual beauty; and for a day, the red-headed women of the world might be said to have overcome the common prejudice against them, and to have outshone even those who are fair-haired. The groom went through his role in a kind of shock of joy, unable to believe his own great good fortune and the blessing of God. You would have thought he was a man in a dream who had stumbled into a cave of wonders so extraordinary they could not be remembered, much less retold, by the awakened mind. The father of the bride was shaken by the enforced view of successive generations that comes with weddings; he sensed, beyond the powers of his articulation, that legion of fathers at his back, the fathers who before his time had brought a daughter to the altar and bestowed her out of their own care into the love of another man—full he was, of hope and dread at the same time, stricken by his own sense of awe at the unstoppable movement of time and growth and change in human affairs, proud of his child and at the same moment humbled by the littleness of the two of them, first father and daughter, and now new husband and wife, mere grains of salt in the dissolving oceans of humanity and eternity.

As for Elissa, in her heart too all was as it should have been, as it had been for countless sisters of the bride before her. Her joy and sorrow were so blended on that day that she neither knew nor cared whether the tears she shed and the smile she beamed forth upon Merry were tears and smiles of pain or delight; for there is a smile of sorrow that can be seen on the faces of those who feel seriously and thus suffer deeply. She keenly felt the loss of the constant friend and companion of her youth, the girl who had indeed been nearly a daughter to her; and yet her spirits were exalted by Merry's joy and hope. And she longed, she dared, to hope that Merry's wedding and its joy were a forerunner to her own; even as she feared and dreaded that they were not, but were instead a fleeting, meteoric vision of what she might have had, once might have had, but now never would attain.

That this was the second time preparation had been made for this woman's wedding heightened rather than dulled its effects. Though Elissa and (as Elissa suspected) John Wyatt would have confessed to considerable anxiety lest something unexpected should intervene to spoil this wedding as well, they repressed that concern, of which they saw no visible trace in the bride. And the village too, which thronged to the church in even greater numbers than before, seemed determined to see the event through this time, and in conspiracy to let no recollection of the former abortive wedding mar the splendor of this. Even Mr. Herbert, for all the dryness of his delivery, seemed touched by the radiance of the bride and her final success in embarking upon matrimony. Indeed, he was apparently inspired by the wedding; for in a remark aside to Elissa later in the day, he mumbled something about how he prayed that certain hopes that had seemed to be dashed forever might yet be fulfilled through the Providence of the Lord. She immediately seconded that prayer—but with different parties substituted. As for Louisa, who as a friend and cousin of those marrying might otherwise have figured as bridesmaid in the event, she prudently stayed away, so as to awaken no recollection of Charles by her mere attendance.

The wedding breakfast went off with the perfect blend of sobriety and hilarity, and the bride and groom boarded a touring barouche to travel to the lake country and Scotland. Though Elissa would have much liked to fare with them, her own affairs were too urgent to permit her to do so; and as she saw the married couple depart in a mutual glow of excitement and contentment, she thought it was really all for the best that they should be alone together. Merry, in particular, must learn to depend upon David in those ways in which she had previously depended on Elissa; and that transference would not have come about as readily if Elissa had followed them on this first journey, symbol as it was of their larger journey together.

She went to bed expecting to weep herself to sleep. But now her own project forced its way into her thoughts—her plan to advance Charles and to recall Daniel from his self-exile over the sea. And so it was rather hope for a future husband than regret for a lost sister that kept her eyes open and her thoughts alive long after her body itself had given up all need for wakefulness.

The next day, the very day after Merry's wedding, she rose up at the usual hour; but instead of turning toward the breakfast room immediately upon descending the stairs, she went into the drawing room to the table where the great Bible lay always open. There she took a few minutes to copy out some verses from a psalm she had thought of. Then she went to breakfast with her father, saying nothing as yet about the purpose she had set for this day.

At noon her father was in the garden; she brought him his midday meal. Again the circumstances were perfect: no one was with him, and it was natural for her to remain with him while he ate.

It had been over a month since he had handed the deed over to her for her perusal, and he was no longer angry and perturbed; the wedding had worked to soften his irritation and make him forget the whole matter, and as always, the garden itself soothed such emotions, drew them and carried them away. Still, she knew that he expected her to capitulate; he would know that she was by nature too forthright to let the subject drop without an admission that she had been wrong and he right; and though there was no overt reason that she should raise the topic now, she thought she could detect some such anticipation in his air throughout the time he ate his meal.

During this interval, they talked abut the wedding, and both laughed together fondly over Merry's joy in it, and commiserated with one another over the loss of her bright presence in the house. But at length, when he had finished eating, and she had folded his napkin and placed it with cup and plate in the basket she had brought, she said, "Papa, I must talk to you again about Charles."

"Yes," he said. "I expected as much. I expected you would wait until Merry's great day was past.—It is no shame, you know, to say you are baffled. You are no doctor of law."

"No, indeed I am not. I am no Portia. But I am John Wyatt's daughter; and as such I have a head on my shoulders."

"Indeed you do, dear! And I shall take such credit for your brains as I can get, believe me. I have many a time had your good sense imputed to me, out of your hearing, when among friends, and I have never refused the honor of it, though I truly think your fine intellect was something that came down to you from your mother or from someone else and skipped over me. I am glad you have had the sense to see that what you proposed can never come to be."

And he smiled fondly as he said this, thinking their quarrel now over.

"I am sorry that I must not let you be deceived in that, Papa."

He looked at her, surprised and hurt.

"I have a question for you," she said. "A difficult question, an ugly question. But an important one."

He was stonily silent.

"And that is, sir: Was your cousin, Mr. Crustall, born out of wedlock?"

It seemed that she could see him turn pale beneath the tan of his face. For a long moment he could not speak to her; he glared at her, as one does at another who has deliberately caused one pain.

"Is *that* in the deed?" he said harshly.

He could not have more directly admitted what she had needed to know.

"So it is true," she said softly, looking away from him.

He grew very agitated now; he shifted about; he rose up, he sat down, he stretched forth his workstained hands as if against fate and then cast them down as if they were useless.

"Maybe it is true, and maybe it is not," he said then. "My father never knew. He could never be sure. It was covered up too well—he was left in the dark about it. His sister was taken advantage of, we knew that much; but whether the scoundrel married her first, or married her in time, or married her at all, we never knew. It was done in France. The records were demanded when the settlement was drawn up, but they were not produced, and it seemed better to go ahead without them than to let my sister be tainted by our doubts. I myself wanted to go there and ascertain the truth; but the years slipped by me, and by the time I might have been able to set out, France had descended into such chaos that it would have been madness to undertake the search. We knew that if he did marry her, it was without articles of agreement or anything of that kind, and that fact alone made my father suspicious. But my father loved his sister, and he wanted her son to come into the property if his own line failed."

"That explains the language of the deed, then," said Elissa.

"What language?" he asked curtly.

"It says that in default of a proper heir, Aeons' End shall pass to the male nearest in line, whether begotten legally or naturally."

"Yes," he said. "Your grandfather must have made the lawyer word it that way so that no one could ever question Crustall's right to inherit. What if someone knew that Crustall was a . . . was illegitimate? They might throw it in his face and try to deprive him of the estate; they might threaten him and blackmail him. No, it must be solid, a solid bequest and inheritance. And so it was; and so it is. Our line has failed, Elissa; failed in the male side, at least; and in our case, the female side, for all its excellence, does us no good."

She drew a deep breath; she turned to him and put her hand on his; and she said, "But do you not see, Papa, that it is that very wording that gives Charles his hope? He is the nearest male to you in a direct line—your own son, naturally if not lawfully. And a son is closer than a cousin can ever be, especially a cousin tainted with the same stain of . . . of bastardy."

For a time he did not comprehend what she was saying. He looked at her blankly, as if his mind was revolting from consideration of her words; but then she saw understanding begin in his features, as a kind of flicker, which suddenly became a flash of full comprehension.

He gripped his head with his hands.

She saw that somehow this sudden realization that Charles *could* inherit only made his pain the worse.

"No," he said.

"Papa," she said, "it can be done. It *must* be done. It is only right for you; it is only right for Charles."

"No," he said again.

"Papa—"

He cut her off. "No!" he said. "It cannot be done!"

"But it *can*, Papa. No one ever paid any attention to that clause because it never mattered before. Until George died, the clause never mattered at all; and after he did so, it seemed it could point only to Mr. Crustall, because you did not even know you had a natural son."

"Never!" he said. "Even if it *is* so, I shall *never* acknowledge him."

"Why not, Papa?" she asked urgently. She saw that his mind was set and determined, and suddenly she was frightened that she could not set it free, no matter how determined her own mind was.

"I have told you already!" he said. "I shall never do it because it would bring scandal on the both of my daughters."

"I do not think so, Papa. Merry has told David Boulder all about it. He does not care. He loves her."

He was surprised at this news. "Well," he said, "he no doubt assumes we shall continue to hush it up. If it were to come out in public, he would be humiliated and angry."

"I do not think so, Papa," she said again, very calmly.

Now he went on the offensive. "Your Daniel has left you," he said. "And why? Because of the scandal, *that* is why; because he is afraid of the scandal that his attaching himself to you would bring down on him. And every gentleman would fear the same—there is not a one of them good enough for you, good enough to overlook something that is not your fault—that your sister almost married her brother, because of the sin I committed over twenty years ago!"

She mustered her strength to combat this line of argument. "If I had not driven Daniel away," she said, "because I misunderstood his motives, we would now be married, no matter what the scandal. I have heard him say as much, Papa. Of his willingness in that respect I have no doubt whatsoever, though I fear it cannot have survived my abuse of it. And besides, even if it *were* so—if Daniel were such a coward as to be frightened off by mere talk—we Wyatts must do what is right."

"No!" he said again.

She waited for a few moments, and then she said: "Then Mr. Crustall shall have Aeons' End."

But this did not give him pause.

"Yes, Crustall shall have it!" he said. "There is no preventing him! Do you not see the bind I am in? If I do what you propose, I sacrifice my daughters to save my son; if I refuse, I save my daughters and let my son fend for himself. And I tell you, given that choice, I shall save my daughters! Not only because I love you both more, not only because you are finer people than my son—God forgive me saying it, and God help Charles in his weakness—not only for those reasons, but because you are my *daughters,* and I would protect you and favor you over ten thousand sons. *That, that* is what *my heart* tells me is right!"

She thought of two revelations that might make him reconsider. But she waited and let him sit in silence for a minute.

Then she said, "Papa, you never knew that I have met Mr. Crustall—that Merry and I have met him."

He stared at her.

"Of course," she went on, "the word 'met' is far too polite for our encounter with him. It was early in the summer before last, shortly after we became acquainted with the Newsome cousins. You were not at home; the servants were all at the back of the house. I was in my room, and I heard a man come in at the front door and speak to Merry."

John sat up on the bench, staring at her still, but even more intently, and his jaw, though clenched shut, moved grimly, as if he were working his teeth against gravel.

"I went downstairs at once. It was Mr. Crustall; he had frightened Merry, and I am sure he would have done worse, but I came into the room and told him to leave. When he would not, I sent Merry to find Dick Broad. After she had gone out, Mr. Crustall began boasting about how the estate would be his—and how he would have one of your daughters as his wife into the bargain."

John was white with his fury. It was a strong medicine she was ladling out, but she kept dosing it.

"But it is worst than that, Papa. When he realized that he and I were alone in the house, he came after me. I seized up the paper knife to defend myself, but he took it away in a trice, and he forced me down on the table."

John stood now, and the loathing and hatred in his eyes was such as she had never seen in him before; he was clenching his fists, and if Crustall had been within his reach, he would certainly have killed him.

"And he lay on top of me," she said.

Her father's eyes were slits no wider than the edge of that paper knife she had wielded at the time.

Then she said: "But before he could do anything more than paw at my skirts, Dickon came in, and dragged him off of me, and hauled him out of doors. I did not see all of what Dickon did, but I believe he broke Mr. Crustall's arm. I know he drove him across the yard, beating him every step of the way, kicking him and knocking him down again every time he stood up, until I caught up to him and stopped him."

She paused a moment to let the lesson sink in, though John's agony was patent already.

Then she said: "That is Mr. Crustall, Papa. This is the man who will inherit your estate, the home of the Wyatts. That is the perverted blood that has tainted the blood of the Wyatts. You say you have done everything to stop him. Not yet, not yet, Papa! There remains this to do: to acknowledge your sin and your son in the eyes of the world."

He was silent, almost writhing in the perplexity of his inner pain. She was frightened again, thinking that the lesson was too much for him, too weighty for his moral fiber to bear; and she went on hurriedly and earnestly.

"Papa," she cried, "this is Providence! You *have* a son, a good man, a man whom you love and who loves us, who may inherit Aeons' End. Our prayers have been answered! What stands in your way? Pride? Papa, when we sin we give up our right to pride. With Adam we gave it up! And with Eve as well, with Eve as well, and to my utter anguish do I know that!"

He sat down on the bench again, leaning back, holding his head, and staring before him, sightless with rage.

For her it was one of those moments that in the natural course of things must come to us all, whether in the extreme age of our parents, or in our own extreme youth, when we see that we are stronger than our parents are. And in Elissa's case, she saw that she truly was morally superior to her father, superior in her willingness to act and to do what was right. He was weak. He wanted only to hide from the world in his garden; and though she did not blame him for that, she would not allow him that resort and refuge now.

"There is more," she said. "More, and perhaps the worst of it. Mr. Samuel Bright—your friend from of old, Papa—has told Louisa that he will not permit her to marry Charles."

"There!" he said. "I told you—the scandal!"

"You do not see what it means, Papa. It means that in your hands lies the power to change Mr. Bright's mind. If you accept Charles as your son—if you make him the heir to Aeons' End—Mr. Bright will surely take a new view of the matter. He will give his blessing, and then Charles and Louisa will be happy, instead of struggling through life as best they can with blighted hopes, outcasts of their own families. Think of what has happened to Charles! He has been rejected by Mr. James Newsome; by you, his own father; and now by the man who would be his father-in-law, Mr. Bright. And all because of the circumstances of his birth, for which he is not to blame!"

He hid his face in agony once again.

"Papa," she went on, "I shall do it all. I shall go to Mr. Vaughn, I shall give him orders as to what must be done, and I shall see that he does it properly. You need not stir a finger. Rely upon me; rely upon my love for you; rely upon my will, for I shall see it all done. Only reconcile yourself to welcoming Charles here again when we have made our move. For of this I am convinced: he must be here, living in this house as your acknowledged son, as soon as possible. We must not cede to Mr. Crustall a single inch, for he will fight us all the way. Possession is nine points in the law, as they say; and we shall put Charles in possession as soon as may be. Mr. Crustall shall doubtless make his arguments, his protests, and carry out his suits, but they shall not avail—not if Charles has lived here for years as your acknowledged son. And we have the affidavit that proves he is so, by nature if not by law; and the settlement allows for him to stand in after George."

And even in this hour when he was overwhelmed on all sides and his pride was being beaten down, John Wyatt felt his love for his daughters again, and his love for injured Merry in particular, and he said: "But what of Merry? How can she come to us here, if Charles is here?"

"That is still to be seen," she admitted. "I think in time even that will be easy for them to bear. But the point is that she need not come. She may bide at David Boulder's home. It is not far from here, Papa; we may easily visit as often as we like. I know you do not like to leave your garden, but it will be a short journey, and even shorter if we make it for Merry's sake."

He was silent for some minutes; she could see that he was in an agony of indecision. Then she unfolded the scrap of paper she had brought with her, the one on which were written the lines she had copied that morning; and she read it aloud, in a soft voice, very gently; and he looked at her as a child looks at a teacher and listened in a kind of awe. She read:

> Rest in the Lord, and wait patiently for him: fret not thyself because of him who prospereth in his way, because of the man who bringeth wicked devices to pass.

> Cease from anger, and forsake wrath: fret not thyself in
> any wise to do evil.
> Evildoers shall be cut off: but those that wait upon the
> Lord, they shall inherit the earth.
> For yet a little while, and the wicked shall not be: yea,
> thou shalt diligently consider his place, and it shall
> not be.
> But the meek shall inherit the earth; and shall delight
> themselves in the abundance of peace.
> The wicked plotteth against the just, and gnasheth upon
> him with his teeth.
> The Lord shall laugh at him: for he seeth that his day is
> coming.
> The wicked have drawn out the sword, and have bent
> their bow, to cast down the poor and needy, and to slay
> such as be of upright conversation.
> Their sword shall enter into their own heart, and their
> bows shall be broken.

"So you see, Papa," she said in conclusion, quietly and certainly, "the meek *shall* inherit. Charles *shall* inherit Aeons' End; and Mr. Crustall shall be cut off."

Then, with nearly the same violence that had inflated it, his resistance collapsed. He knew that what she urged was right and that she would not let him retreat from that certainty.

He looked up at her now haggardly, painfully, and said: "I thank God that He blessed me with you, Elissa! I thank God! He took my wife, He took my son, but He left me a daughter who is as good as a son to me—nay, better, as she is as strong in mind and heart as a man, but still a woman."

These words, which were overpoweringly sweet for her to hear, brought the sting of salt to her eyes; and she kissed him for his praise, though at the same time she thought of her great mistake, and she was humbled.

Then she said: "So you are agreed, Papa?"

"I am agreed. I am agreed.—But Elissa, *why did you not tell me* of this violence of Mr. Crustall? Why did you conceal it? I would have brought charges against him at once!"

She was ready for this question. "Because I was afraid, Papa, that a false story would go about that he had violated me, and perhaps Merry too. You know how rumor twists everything. If the world caught even the faintest reek of any story that we had been assaulted, others, even good men and women, might have shrunken from us as dirtied creatures. And we were also afraid for Dick Broad, for I believe he gave Mr. Crustall quite a severe beating; and when a coachman beats a gentleman, even a fraudulent gentleman, he may well be hung for it. It was all too much to risk. I do believe Mr. Crustall has learned that in coming here he thrusts himself into a hornet's nest. He will not be back anytime soon. And if you take heart and acknowledge Charles Newsome as your heir, Mr. Crustall shall never return, not before aeons' end, and not even then. By then he will be in the hell he deserves."

Having accepted Elissa's plan, John Wyatt would hear nothing of letting her consult Mr. Vaughn by herself. For this she was grateful; for the law was one of the many fields of activity in the world at that time that were considered the exclusive domain of men, and she would have met with great resistance from the attorney for that reason alone. As it was, she thought it likely that once Mr. Vaughn understood the reason for John Wyatt's visit, he would be scandalized that Miss Wyatt was in his office at all.

Under her father's direction, she wrote at once to Gloucester, where Mr. Vaughn conducted his practice. Mr. Vaughn's clerk soon wrote back; and on the appointed day, John and Elissa set out for town. The journey was uneventful, marred only by her silent and fruitless regrets: it seemed that any time she rode in a public conveyance for the rest of her life she would be put in mind of that difficult journey to Bath with Daniel; and now she wished she could have back that accidental meeting with him; for surely now she knew how to make better use of it.

The attorney's office was in Eastgate Street; a fine, modern building—not at all the cramped garret up crooked stairs that she fancied to be the habitation of all lawyers. An underclerk greeted them and ushered them into the clerk's office; and that man in turn called for tea and refreshments, begging their indulgence for a slight delay in their meeting with Mr. Vaughn; but she might even have thought the postponement contrived, so pleasantly did their little tea proceed. The clerk was a man of middle age, who seemed delighted to have a female visitor to the office; he was all gallantry and compliments; the tea was fresh and hot, and the cake first-rate.

Well primed with this, they were at length brought onward into the inner sanctum where Mr. Vaughn presided. He too was gallant toward Elissa, though more condescending in his manner than his clerk had been; but after he had finished with his compliments, and had seen his visitors settled in their chairs, his attitude toward her markedly changed, and he seemed determined to overlook her existence.

"Well, John," he said to Mr. Wyatt, "your letter was not forthcoming about the reason for your visit here. Will you be needing articles of agreement for Miss Elissa Wyatt as well as Miss Merry?"

"No," said John. "That is not it at all."

"Ah. Then . . . ?"

Now he had come to it, John did not know where to start. And after sitting in silence for quite some time, and evincing discomfort that transcended common embarrassment and attained even to anguish, by both turning in his chair and looking everywhere but at Mr. Vaughn, he said to Elissa, "Do you see? I do not know where to begin telling this sad tale."

"Begin with the most difficult part, Papa," she said to him, in a calm, gentle tone. "Put that behind you, and the rest will be easy."

John did not take the advice, but he was ashamed enough to begin somewhere, at least.

"You know," he said to Mr. Vaughn, "how we have looked for anything that might save Aeons' End from the hands of my father's nephew, Mr. Crustall."

"Yes," said Mr. Vaughn, looking disappointed to hear this topic raised again. "We have examined every possible avenue. There is no hope for it, I am afraid."

"Well, there *is* hope for it, after all," said John.

"Oh, really, John," said Mr. Vaughn. "I cannot believe you have come all this way again to moot some proposal about the inheritance. I have virtually memorized the document; there is not a crevice anywhere in it where any handhold could be found to forestall this Mr. Crustall."

"I know that you have studied it thoroughly," said John; "but you did not know all the facts."

Mr. Vaughn leaned back in his chair, not sure whether to be surprised or suspicious.

"Well, I think I did and I think I do," he said. "What fact could you adduce that would essentially alter our understanding of the purport of the entail?"

Again John was reduced to silence; and silenced he sat, in an anguish of shame that he could not find his way out of.

"The fact is," said Elissa quietly, "that my father has a son who may inherit."

Mr. Vaughn did not condescend to speak to her; instead he said, "What, John? But we know your son perished on the passage from India."

Still John could not utter a word.

"My brother George did so perish," said Elissa. "But that is not the son of whom I speak."

Mr. Vaughn was more befuddled than thunderstruck by this announcement. But whether confused or astonished, he was still not compelled to recognize Elissa's importance to the discussion; he persisted in looking to John for an explanation.

And finally John said, "It is my *natural* son. I did not know I had one until recently."

Mr. Vaughn was immediately irritated; but curiously enough, he was not the least morally offended, which had seemed to Elissa to have been the difficulty John anticipated. "Ah, a *natural* son!" Mr. Vaughn said. "Well, such a son is what the law calls a *filius nullius*—a son of no man. He cannot inherit, whoever he is; your deed will be quite clear about that. Yes, the law is always quite clear about that— *legal heir of his body*, that kind of language. I am afraid you have traveled all this way for nothing, if that is the peg on which your new hopes are hung."

John was miserable; but not, Elissa guessed, because of what the lawyer was saying. Rather, the whole matter of Charles's illicit status had plunged him back into the realm of memory, and he was reliving in his mind that summer with Agnes Newsome, and wondering how something so sublime had had an outcome so difficult to master. She saw that he would not be able to speak in explanation of their discoveries; so again she spoke for him.

"I beg your pardon, sir," she said. "The deed of settlement does in fact allow a natural son to inherit."

Mr. Vaughn now looked at her at last. "Miss Wyatt," he said, "with all due respect, the law is not a lady's province. A lady knows nothing of the law. You must take my word for it; and what is more, I most respectfully request that you do not break in on my discussion with your father any more. Do go see Mr. Welch again, and he will give you another cup of tea—and of course some cake, if you wish it. Your father and I will be finished here shortly, and then he may take you shopping for something you like—a new hat, or some gloves, or some of those accoutrements that so please a lady's heart."

Instead of replying, she took from a portfolio a copy of the relevant passage of the deed; and this she brought and laid before the attorney as he sat at his desk, staring at her.

"I have copied out the germane portion for your convenience, sir," she said.

He picked up the paper as if in disbelief about its mere existence, as if he expected it to turn to vapor in his hand; and after fixing her with a long, displeased stare, he began to read it, mumbling as he did so: "'Obed Wyatt' . . . 'behoof of the first son *lawfully* to be begotten,' you see, it is as I say . . . 'use and behoof of the heirs males of the body of the first son *lawfully* to be begotten' . . . and second, and third, as usual— really, there is nothing out of the ordinary about this; you would *know that* if you knew the least thing about the law— but you are a woman, Miss Wyatt—really there is nothing . . . 'and for default of such issue . . . to the use and behoof of the male, begotten . . . whether lawfully or . . . *naturally.*"

And here he came to a hard stop.

She went back to her seat to await further developments.

"Odd!" he said finally. "I have read this deed I know not how many times, but I have never noticed anything of this sort."

"That is likely because you were not looking for it, sir," said Elissa, "and it was lost in the *uses and behoofs of the heirs males* and so forth."

"But this is not a true copy," said the lawyer, flicking the paper away from himself dismissively. "If it was you who copied it, Miss Wyatt, you must have made a mistake."

For answer she drew the full copy of the deed from the portfolio and brought it to him. She had the page marked; she opened the document to that passage and pointed it out to him. Then again she returned to her chair.

He read in silence this time.

When he was finished, he passed his hands over his head, smoothing down what little remained of his hair; then he rubbed his hands together in an indication of perplexity. It was clear that he did not know what to think.

"But why would the language have been changed in this way?" he asked John suddenly. "It is out of all precedent."

John, looking haggard, made a motion to Elissa to reply in his behalf. And thus the conversation was to continue, Mr. Vaughn putting his questions to John, and Elissa replying, without any notice from the lawyer, as though she were some kind of interpreter.

"We believe," she said, "that it was because my grandfather, Mr. Obed Wyatt, feared that his nephew, Mr. Crustall, might be proven illegitimate, and so be denied the inheritance."

Mr. Vaughn's mind jumped to another puzzle. "But John," he said, "why did you never tell me of this other son?"

"We did not know of the existence of my half-brother until this past year, sir," said Elissa.

"But why did you never tell me that Mr. Crustall might be illegitimate? We might have pursued that course in our earlier attempts to block him."

This Elissa could not answer from sure knowledge; but she said, "I believe my father was reluctant to bring that discredit on a relative, sir."

"But if Mr. Crustall *is* illegitimate, then he would be equal in status to this *filius nullius,*" said Mr. Vaughn.

"But see, sir, where it says, 'the male nearest to the direct male line of the Wyatts of Aeons' End.' That is my father's son, sir, not my father's nephew."

This stopped Mr. Vaughn for a minute; but then he said, "Well, who *is* this natural son, sir?"

"He is Mr. Charles Newsome," said Elissa.

Mr. Vaughn was utterly taken aback. "What?" he cried. "The fellow who was to . . . the fellow for whom I wrote the settlement for Miss Merry Wyatt?"

"The same, sir," said Elissa.

Mr. Vaughn looked pale and almost queasy. "And so that was why the marriage . . . ?" he began.

"Never came off, yes," said Elissa when he did not finish.

He smoothed his thin hair down again and for a moment looked as if he might whistle with astonishment; but he restrained himself with an effort.

Elissa said: "The connection was discovered, very fortunately; but—very unfortunately—only at the last minute."

"I see," said Mr. Vaughn, for lack of anything else to say.

"As you know, Mr. Charles Newsome was disinherited by his putative father, Mr. James Newsome," Elissa went on. "It was a mysterious business when it happened; but it is clear now that the reason behind it is that he was not legitimately an heir to the Newsome estate."

"And now you would make this man *your* heir, sir?" Mr. Vaughn asked John.

"That is my father's wish," said Elissa.

"To forestall this Crustall fellow? Is that it?"

And here John Wyatt showed he had been hanging on every word; for he spoke up at last and said: "No, sir. It is true that I would forestall Crustall; you know I have long wished for that. But even more important is to put Aeons' End into the hands of my son. For Charles *is* my son."

"And will he take the name Wyatt?" asked the lawyer.

"I hope so. I see no reason he should not; though perhaps he himself will see one."

At this point Mr. Vaughn heaved himself to his feet and walked about the room. He seemed at first to be seriously displeased; he repeatedly smoothed his scalp and veritably shook his jowls, and he frequently muttered broken phrases of protest. But Elissa soon saw that it was not any immorality but the legal irregularities of the case that bothered him: for example, at one point he mumbled to himself, "Precedent! How could anyone so defy precedent as to write such a clause!"

After many minutes of this irritation and perplexity, it seemed that the idea began to catch hold of him; for he now muttered, "But to make it work! To keep the estate in its proper line! Now *that* would be *coup*."

And when at last he had fully warmed to this new reality, he stopped his pacing and muttering and turned to John.

"This fellow Crustall will fight it, you know," he said.

"Oh, I am sure he will," said John wearily. "But can we carry our case against him, if it comes to that?"

"Oh, it *will* come to that. The law does not like these bas—I mean, it does not like a *filius nullius*. But even if Crustall maintains that he himself is legitimate, the language seems clear in favoring your natural son, and in the end I think it will be irrefutable. I *think* it will; I *believe* it will. Enough so that it is worth a try, I do believe."

"There is another difficulty, sir," said Elissa, "that makes the settling of this business a matter of urgency."

Mr. Vaughn raised his eyebrows and looked at John expectantly; but John in turn looked at Elissa.

She explained: "Mr. Charles Newsome hopes soon to marry. But the father of his intended bride is unwilling to ally his daughter to an illegitimate son. It is our hope that once he knows Mr. Newsome has been acknowledged and made the heir of Aeons' End, his views on that subject will soften."

"Ah," said Mr. Vaughn. She could see that the idea of this added challenge intrigued him. "Well," he said, "I should think that the news that his daughter is to become mistress of Aeons' End will work on him quickly enough.—Where does Mr. Charles Newsome reside at present?"

John looked at Elissa.

"In Bath, sir," she said.

"Well, that is not far at all," said Mr. Vaughn, speaking again to John. "Summon him and let me know when he arrives. I shall come to you at Aeons' End and we shall work out the details there; and in the meantime I shall consider how best to move forward, and of course I shall study the deed again lest we find anything in it that would thwart our purposes."

He paused for a moment, and then he crossed the room to where John sat and said to him: "Sir! I rejoice that at last our long efforts to thwart this scoundrel Crustall have some hope of fruition!" And he wrung John's hand with considerable pleasure.

That was the end of the meeting. In paying his farewells and ushering them out, Mr. Vaughn bowed to Elissa and simpered at her as if she were no more than a pretty face; as if she had let loose from the powerful bow of her brain not a single fletched word the entire time.

On their return home from Mr. Vaughn's office, Elissa composed the following letter on her father's behalf:

Aeons' End
Deepclough, Gloucs.

Tuesday, 10 November, 1812

Mr. Charles Newsome
in care of Miss Louisa Bright
No. —, Queen's Square, Bath

My dear Charles,

My father, as you know, is not much for taking up pen and setting hand to paper; he does better at taking up a spade and setting it to good loam. Thus he bids me write you with our news, which task I consider a great honor as well as a joy.

Great good news should be shortly delivered, so here you have it: My father wishes you to take your place at Aeons' End as his son and heir.

You will at once hope, as do we, that this development may help sway the opinions of Mr. Samuel Bright and win his blessing for your marriage.

Let me further enlarge the joy we all feel in this news by requesting that your fiancée herself testify to my father's longstanding respect and affection for her. He will welcome her to Aeons' End, when the time comes, with the joy of one greeting a daughter returned. As for myself, my delight in your bride can only be increased by my living with her here as a sister.

To hasten that day, my father bids you repair to us at once so that you and he may consult with our attorney and begin to determine how you shall overcome Mr. Samuel Bright's objections.

I must add one final remark, lest the circumstances weigh upon you and cause you any anxiety. My dear sister wishes you and Louisa all blessings. As you know well from Louisa, she was married two weeks ago to Mr. David Boulder, so you may now call her a cousin as well as a sister. She and David are on their wedding tour at this time, so you will not meet her at Aeons' End in this interval; though we all hope that you may do so at a future date, with all the amicability of friends holding each other's best interests at heart.

With joy and affection,
Your own true sister,

Elissa

A few days later, Elissa heard the sound she had been listening for almost since the letter had left her hand: the hoofbeats and the creaking of a postchaise ascending the drive to Aeons' End. She ran to the door—turned briefly to send Mr. Jens to find her father in the garden—and then went on into the drive, reaching it just as the carriage drew up.

It was indeed Charles. As she saw the expression on his face, she hoped he had not been suffering this extremity of emotion all the way from Bath, for he seemed quite overcome as he looked up at the front of Aeons' End, and as he climbed down to set foot again on the property that was now to become his, and as his gaze shifted to behold his sister.

She went to greet him immediately, taking his hands and standing on tiptoe to kiss him on the cheek.

"Welcome home," she said.

A pang went through him, evidenced not only by the tears that sprang into his eyes but by a kind of joyful tremor. For a moment he looked at her, and then it was not enough merely to hold her hands; he caught her in his embrace and held her so tightly she nearly felt crushed.

He released her.

"There, there," she said. "Change, change—who could have known what we would all come to be to one another— brother and sisters, you a brother to Merry and me, and sisters the three of us, Louisa, Merry, and I again. And you Papa's own son all that time!"

"Yes," he said in a voice hoarse with emotion. "I dare say I loved him as such from the first! Such a good man, and so after my own heart; or should I say, so much was I after his."

She heard footsteps on the gravel and turned to see her father approaching from the garden. "Here he is," she said to Charles. She stood back a few steps and let son and father meet.

For a moment they seemed hardly to know what to do. First Charles bowed to him; then he held out his hand, and they shook hands heartily; then John Wyatt abandoned the handshake as insufficient and embraced him.

"Welcome home, my son," said John in a broken voice.

"Thank you, Father," said Charles.

"Father! Father!" repeated John, as he was struck by the newness of that name, spoken by Charles's voice. "Yes, your father welcomes his son home. And yet this is not the story of the Prodigal Son; it is the story of the Prodigal Father!— But you have had another father all these years. That cannot be changed now. Call me Father if you will, but I shall not mind if you call me by my own name instead."

"My other father is gone," said Charles. "So I *shall* call you Father."

John seemed very pleased.

"Well," he said, "we cannot stand here all the day, though it would certainly take that long to count our blessings. You need refreshment after your journey.—Jim, fetch Mr. Newsome's luggage into the house.—Come away, my boy. We have much work to do! These settlements! Between the lawyers and the father of the bride, there will doubtless be endless fuss and delay over the details. But we must have you married promptly, so you may bring your wife to live here alongside you. Miss Louisa Bright always was one of my favorites."

As John said this, he took Charles by the arm and began drawing him toward the door; but Charles stopped him, and right there in the dooryard, with the postilion still in the act of pocketing his tip, and Jim Riggins and Mr. Jens gathering up the luggage, he said: "One thing, sir, I wish to make very clear from the start."

"And what is that, my boy?"

"If you will permit it, sir, I should like to take the name Wyatt. That is only proper for someone who is to carry forward the line of Aeons' End. And more importantly, I feel as if I have always been a Wyatt—as if I never knew my name until you . . . until you called me home."

"I, permit it?" said John. "I will rejoice in it, my boy!"

"My *other* father—Mr. James Newsome—he never really saw me as a son. So it is no loss to him, or I should say, no slight on his memory."

"Indeed not, sir. And I think . . . I think your mother would have approved as well."

"I should like to talk to you about my mother, if I may, sir."

"Yes, my boy, we shall talk about all that, all that. We shall have many a golden hour in the garden, to talk as we work."

"Yes," agreed Charles happily. "I have been looking forward to that since I received Elissa's letter. And even before, I dreamed of the garden."

They went off into the house together, arm in arm.

Elissa stayed behind a moment as she heard Jim Riggins ask Mr. Jens to which room he should take the luggage.

"The great bedchamber," said Mr. Jens. Elissa was surprised: no one had slept there since her mother had passed away. Mr. Jens, seeing her expression, added: "The master says it is to belong to the new young master and his new wife."

"So he *is* to be master of Aeons' End," said Jim.

"As well you know a hundred times over," said Mr. Jens. "You and all the village too."

So should it be, thought Elissa. *Let rumor work on our side for once. The future master has come home to his rightful place.*

❋ 20 ❋

A Messenger

Behold, I will send my messenger, and he shall prepare the way before me.

—Malachi 3:1

Charles brought good news—of a sort.

He had heard from Daniel at last. Of course, he had left the letter in Bath in his haste to reach Deepclough, and the account he gave of it was far from satisfactory to Elissa. This is what he said, somewhere in the middle of their celebratory dinner on the day he returned: "Oh, by the way, dear Sister, you will be interested to know that I have heard from my cousin."

She froze in the act of cutting her meat and stared at him.

"A few days ago," he said, "shortly before I received your letter. You will be pleased to hear that he is in good health."

She was brought up short by the realization that this fact was, indeed, of the utmost importance to her. "I am very glad to hear it," she said.

"He expressed himself delighted to hear of my forthcoming marriage."

"Well, that is very good; but we did not expect otherwise, I think."

"Yes," said Charles. He turned then to John and said, "And what have you done, Father, with that allee—you know the one, where the arbor was blown over?"

"If I may," said Elissa urgently, "before you enter into this other topic, Father, and Charles—was there no more in your cousin's letter?"

Charles looked blank and said, "Well, I suppose—yes, there was more; it was about a page in length."

"Did he . . . did he answer your queries about the annuity, and whether it shall be increased on your marriage?"

"That is the first thing Louisa wanted to know too," said Charles, as if congratulating himself on detecting this similarity.

"Indeed, my Brother, it is the material point. Did he say anything?

"Yes; he said he would take the matter in hand and let me know soon what amount his estate and business could promise with certainty."

"Well, thank goodness for that! Did he give any indication that he had received . . . your second letter to him?"

"Well, no, he did not mention it. Louisa pointed that out particularly when we read the letter. But as she said, why should he refer to the communication from you? It is not properly our business."

"Yes, that is so," agreed Elissa reluctantly. "Why should he mention it? You are right."

"And Louisa also says that the annuity is now a moot point—or not moot, really, since we shall be glad of any augmentation of income my cousin sees fit to make to us; but I do not think it will be a material point with respect to obtaining Mr. Samuel Bright's blessing. Surely that must be forthcoming soon, now that . . . now that I have my family, a true family." And he turned back to Mr. Wyatt and smiled and opened his mouth to speak of that allee again.

But she would not let him.

"Nay, Charles," she begged, "can you not tell me more? What did your cousin . . . how did he sound, in his letter?"

"Oh, as I said, he assured me of his perfect health."

"Indeed—a blessing, a blessing. But did he tell you of his doings in Madeira?"

"Oh, he never does," said Charles. "I think he feels it would be taunting me with the beauties of a place I shall never see. Not that I care, you know; but it is most thoughtful of him just the same."

"But . . . not a word of society there?"

"Oh, there is not a great deal of society in Madeira, I expect. No."

"Well, what did Louisa think of the letter?"

"She thought that my cousin did not quite sound cheerful. That was what she said. But she has seen him mournful many a time, she said, and this letter was of a piece with that. I myself thought it just Daniel in his usual style. I was very pleased to have his blessing on my marriage, I can tell you that."

"Well, of course you were. That is most excellent, though we all know that he *must* approve Louisa. But did he say anything about whether he is returning to attend the event?"

"No; but he hardly could, since we have not set a date."

This was maddening, but she now let him go on with his query to John, consoling herself with the plan of writing at once to Louisa to obtain better information.

But when it came a few days later, Louisa's letter only corroborated what Charles had said. Daniel had written cordially but very briefly; he had expressed affection for his cousin, said he remembered Miss Bright and believed her to be a lady "of excellent good sense and warm disposition"; made a promise about the annuity that was vague but clearly sincere; reported his own good health; gave Charles and his fiancée his best wishes; and—signed his name. That was all. Louisa did think the letter seemed a trifle depressed; but she thought the man had a depressive tendency, so she was not surprised by that.

As for whether Daniel had received the separate letter with Elissa's enclosure, she said there was no way to be sure.

Well, thought Elissa, *if that letter via Lakeholm has gone astray, at least the letter I sent to him directly must have reached him. I wish he would reply to it; but if he does not, I can scarcely blame him.*

Elissa was sure that Mr. Vaughn could conclude their business in a month's time and Charles and Louisa would wed in January. But no more could the Law have done *that* than the will and the work of God could be revealed in a day.

To spare the lawyers some blame in the delay that then took place, however, it must be said that Mr. Samuel Bright proved a Gibraltar against which the glacier of legal opinion and familial persuasion ground with apparent futility for what seemed to Elissa and the two lovers to be an aeon of time.

Not an aeon in fact; but a full seven months.

Of course, Mr. Bright could not even be approached afresh until some formal recognition of Charles's new status had taken place. It was not enough that Mr. Wyatt publicly declared him his heir and acknowledged him as his son, or that Charles now lived at Aeons' End, or that he changed his name to Charles Wyatt. He must be recognized as heir in a strict settlement of the estate; and though Charles was compliant in every possible point required of him, Mr. Vaughn (and the many counselors he brought in to assist him) wished to make the new arrangement "ironclad and impregnable"—those were the very words Mr. Vaughn used; and Elissa, for one, thought the welding of new iron plates to the document, and the layering of legal ruses within it to prevent its impregnation by any contrary force, would never come to an end.

At length, however, this tower of legal babble was erected, and a new appeal was made to Mr. Samuel Bright. Louisa began it, though Elissa thought this to be an error in strategy. Her pleas were roundly rejected by Mr. Bright. Next Charles himself went again to Ryderly; and though

Mr. Bright treated him openly and considerately, he was sent away without any encouragement. Next John Wyatt made the journey. He too was greeted with friendliness, but he too failed to make any progress against Mr. Bright's prejudices, which seemed to be becoming more firm rather than less.

Finally the lawyers, led by Mr. Vaughn, met with Mr. Bright's lawyers, and they in turn communicated with Mr. Bright. The pecuniary soundness of the estate of Aeons' End was laid out in full for the opposing side to consider. The months during which the outcome hung fire convinced Elissa and Louisa and Charles to hope at last; but then Mr. Bright's lawyers delivered, and the answer was still no.

Charles wrote again to Daniel, explaining these difficulties, and asking for some indication of what the annuity might be, in the hope that with this source of income added to his daughter's prospects, Mr. Bright might weaken in his resistance; but in return Charles received only a short note saying that arrangements were being made, and that though they were drawing out to far greater length than Daniel wished, he hoped to conclude them soon. To Elissa, this letter was even more frustrating than the last, but the two lovers took hope from it.

During this time Elissa had feared that Mr. Crustall would reappear and damage Charles's prospects in the eyes of Louisa's father. Yet during this long interval, nothing was heard from the man. He was either unaware that his heirship was threatened, or was unable to employ lawyers to oppose it. One rumor that reached Aeons' End through Mr. Vaughn put him out of the country, in the West Indies; another that came through Elissa's London correspondent, Mrs. Harmony, made him an invalid in the north of Ireland. Furthermore, Mr. Vaughn received an anonymous scribbled note, threatening violence if he did not cease assisting the Wyatt family in their legal business, and some thought it the work of Mr. Crustall, though others ascribed it to some cowardly busybody and troublemaker.

And there were busybodies aplenty when it came to the Wyatts' affairs. Elissa had thought rumor might work to their benefit for once; but . . . it was such a delicious scandal: How the daughter had nearly married her own brother! How the bastard son was now the acknowledged heir! How Mr. Bright of Ryderly Hall could not be brought to bless the man's marriage to his daughter! How the would-be groom pined in Deepclough, and his would-be bride in Bath, with never a sign that their wedding day would come! From such tattle, Mr. Wyatt and Charles hid in the garden; but Elissa went forth and met it, when it dared to voice itself in her presence; and her calm and matter-of-fact response to it had a great deal to do with the reason it finally began to die down. Though of course, the sheer weariness that sets in after a topic has grown old was also persuasive; and in six months and more, any topic of gossip grows annoyingly old.

The Rowcliffes needed nearly that long themselves before they could even bring themselves to speak to the Wyatts. After all, their daughter was involved; and though they cared not so much for that, they were concerned that any imputation against her would affect her brother, and with him, the new young Rowcliffe, his son. But as the novelty of the idea wore off, they gradually began to see the advantages of the rehabilitation of their grandson. Yes, he had lost Landseye; but was that not only right? And he had come into a very fine old place instead; and was that, too, not perfectly right?

And yet all who busied themselves in the matter seemed to feel that it could not finally be resolved for good and all until Mr. Bright gave his blessing to the marriage. And on this head, the situation seemed quite hopeless until Daniel finally sent word of his assistance—through a very unexpected messenger.

One morning at about eleven o'clock on a day in late June, Lucy Brown came to Elissa in the office, where she was doing the household accounts, and said, "Please, Miss, there is a man here to see your father and Mr. Charles. I have sent Jim into the garden for them, but I thought you might want to know that he is here. It is that Scotsman as is servant to Mr. Daniel Newsome."

Elissa rose to her feet in a panic of joy.

"Mr. Blaickie!" she said, in a voice hoarse with its own urgency. "Here! In England! At Aeons' End! Certainly his master cannot be far!"

"He said nothing of his master, Miss," said Lucy, as if seeking to restrain premature hopes.

"No, of course he did not. Not after the way I welcomed him the last time he came on his master's behalf!—Oh, please God that nothing is amiss!—But no, he has surely brought news about some contribution to the marriage settlement— and about whether his master is to attend the wedding."

"That is what I think, Miss. He came to the front door like a man on business, not to the back door like a valet. And he is carrying a little case that might have important papers and such. I put him in the parlor—I hope I did not do wrong."

"Of course not," said Elissa. She abruptly abandoned her accounts and went past Lucy and out of the office; and she fairly ran to the parlor and burst into it.

Mr. Blaickie was standing by the window. He was dressed in a dark traveling coat, and his boots still bore the dirt of the long walk up from the village, where it was likely the morning coach had set him down. The case of which Lucy had spoken—it looked as if it had once served the military as a dispatch case—was firmly trapped under one arm. As she entered the room, he turned to her; and as he saw who it was, his face became grim and affected a blankness of thought and emotion.

But by this she was undeterred. She went to him joyfully, saying, "Mr. Blaickie! How good to see you again!"

He bowed stiffly, but said nothing more than, "Ma'am."

In the excess of her happiness, she now put her hand on his forearm and stood looking on him in a blissful silence, smiling. At this impulsive display of her feelings, his surprise overwhelmed his resolution to show no emotion; but the emotions he now showed were dislike and distrust.

Yet still Elissa was so glad of the sight of him that she thought nothing of this. "Here you are!" she said. "In England, in England!"

"Indeed, ma'am," he said, continuing to be puzzled at this reception, so very different from his last at Aeons' End.

"And where is your master, sir? Tell me, oh, tell me, where is your master?"

"Why, he is in Madeira," said Mr. Blaickie.

This was a blow, and she flinched with it; but in another moment she said, "But he is well? Tell me he is well."

"I left him in *exquisite* health, ma'am," said Mr. Blaickie.

"And he is . . . has he . . . ?"

But she could not bring herself to utter the question. *Was he married?* She would have to rely on Charles to find that out.

"Ma'am?" asked Mr. Blaickie.

"Has he made any plans to return, I mean."

"Ah, no, ma'am. He is to stay in Madeira, I believe. I have brought papers to advance the marriage settlement of his cousin, Mr. Charles Newsome."

Another blow. She felt physically weak and went away from Mr. Blaickie, to sit down and try to think.

When she had done so, she looked at him again and saw that he was still regarding her warily and, she thought, somewhat cynically.

"Oh, Mr. Blaickie," she said, "do forgive me for that other time—for all those other times. I did not treat your master well. I did not understand him—I did not understand wyhat he had been through, what he had done on our behalf. I was mistaken—I was in error."

He eyed her with a coolness that indicated continuing suspicion; he said nothing.

To this point she had acted and spoken without reflection; but now it occurred to her that she could send a message by Mr. Blaickie. It would not be a direct one, certainly; but when Mr. Blaickie saw Daniel again, the servant would be sure to report to the master that the previously rude and cold Miss Elissa Wyatt now seemed strikingly altered.

She rose again and indicated a chair near to her. "Please, sir," she said. "I beg you will sit down. You have traveled far; do permit me to offer you the relief of resting, now that you have arrived.—Nay, you must be needing some refreshment: I shall have some tea brought for you—"

"If you please, ma'am," said Mr. Blaickie, "I broke my fast at the inn before I climbed the hill."

"Oh, but you must have been traveling since quite early, is it not so? Would you do me the honor of sitting with me?"

He looked baffled. "And how should I, a servant, honor you, who is my better, ma'am, by sitting with you? I am not accustomed to standing about in gentlefolk's parlors, let alone sitting in them. Indeed, I would not be here except that I am the servant on the business of a good and honorable man, a man good enough for *anyone.*"

"Then that is exactly why you would do me honor if you sat with me. Because you are the servant of Mr. Daniel Newsome. And I, too, am his servant, though he does not know it—does not know it yet, and may never know it."

It would not have been too much to say Mr. Blaickie was flabbergasted. When he could speak, he said: "You, ma'am? His servant?"

"Yes, his servant. And since you and I are equals in serving him, let us be equals in sitting together—just this once, this precious once, if at no other time."

He hesitated. She could see the process of decision reflected in his features—whether he should reject her request or accede to it.

"My dear sir," she said, "we are taught to forgive others; indeed, we are commanded to do so by the Lord Christ. I beg leave to appeal to that law on my own behalf. Will you forgive me for the way I have treated your master? I promise you that if you do, you will see I bear a reformed and regenerate heart."

This seemed to be language he understood, and an appeal he could not deny. He came to the chair she had indicated, and though he insisted on waiting until she had seated herself again, he then sat as well, or at least on the edge of the chair. He rested the dispatch case in his lap, holding the handle of the thing with his left hand, and looked to her for further illumination.

She said: "I will not rehearse all the pain and suffering that Mr. Daniel Newsome and my family went through. Suffice it to say that when I rejected your master, I had no idea why he had put a stop to my sister's marriage. I thought the worst of him, because I had nothing else to think, no other information to know him by. I thought his act arbitrary, or even worse—deliberately destructive to my sister's hopes. I hope you can see how I would have thought that, since I possessed no other knowledge."

This narrative of events was so opposed to that which Mr. Blaickie had assumed for so long that it took him a long moment to even begin to understand. He seemed still to need a definite push in the direction of comprehension. So she said, "I knew nothing of the connection between my father and Mrs. Newsome so long ago. So I knew nothing of the connection between Mr. Charles and my sister."

"You knew . . . nothing?"

"Nothing. Not until the time your master left England for Madeira. And by then it was too late to go to him and tell him that I knew at last how mistaken I was."

Finally she thought she saw something new in his expression. It was not a softening, but a new alertness, an active exploration of a new opinion of her.

"And now, you see," she went on, "it has all turned out well. Mr. Charles is to marry my dear friend, Miss Louisa Bright. And my sister has found great happiness, through the grace of God, with another gentleman. Both Mr. Charles and my sister are quite content in their new affections."

He still remained silent.

"For me," she said, "the most important thing is that I have learned at last the true role your master played in the entire business—not the role of a rogue and a reprobate, but of a rescuer, a saint. I would say that I have forgiven him, but of course I never had anything to forgive; I can only say that I have learned I had no need to forgive him. It is I who seek to be forgiven for the way I . . . for the way I misunderstood and . . . and scorned him."

His eyes were locked on hers piercingly, as if he were, in that close gaze, testing the sterling of her heart for any base metal of insincerity.

"Do you think he *can* forgive me?" she asked.

Scot that he was, and loyal to his master, he seemed reluctant to speak at all; but having been directly questioned, he would not be so rude as to remain silent. "That is for the master to say," he said. "We none of us know if we deserve to be forgiven, not truly. But I know this: he *can* forgive. He can forgive anyone who is honestly contrite. I have seen him do it."

"Then there is hope for me?"

He made a gesture with his free hand. It was noncommittal; a way of responding without truly answering. It was not the means of communication that servants ordinarily used with their social betters; but she knew that though the two of them might play those social roles, they were indeed spiritual equals.

"No, of course you cannot say," she said. "And of course I should not ask you to. But let me ask this: I have sent him a letter explaining all this. Do you know if he has received it?"

He thought for a moment, and then he seemed to decide he would not be betraying his master's confidence by answering her question. "I do not know all his correspondence by any means, ma'am," he said. "But I do not believe he received anything of a personal nature while I was with him in Madeira, except for a communication or two from Mr. Charles Newsome. But I would not know—not certainly."

"Well, does he have any plan to return for the wedding, for Mr. Charles's wedding?"

"I do not know, ma'am. He did not give me information on that point."

"But surely he must have told you his further plans. Are you to return to him in Madeira?"

"No; I am to go to Lakeholm and await further orders."

"Ah, then . . . he might have you return to Madeira, or he might have you wait there against his own return to England."

"That would be right, ma'am."

"So he did not want to risk your making the voyage back to Madeira unnecessarily. Then it would seem he *is* undecided; we may at least guess that there is a possibility he may return."

"You know all I know on that point, ma'am."

"Well, I should like to . . . to explain to him in person. That is all. I am sure you understand."

This appeal to his understanding brought a further, unexpected warming in his response to her.

"Oh, I do, I do," he said. "When the need comes upon one to beg forgiveness, it is a powerful need. One might even call it a kind of craving, ma'am. A good craving."

"Indeed it is, Mr. Blaickie. And . . . will *you* forgive me, if I say I am sorry for all I did, and if I promise never to act in such a way again?"

"It is not for me to forgive anyone, ma'am."

"Oh, but it is, Mr. Blaickie—because you and I are his fellow servants, as I have said; and because I have done something that might well be unforgivable. I became . . . *disloyal,* I *doubted* him; and a fellow servant can and indeed ought to take offense at that on behalf of his master. I judged Mr. Newsome without giving him the opportunity to explain himself. And if I did not give him the opportunity to explain, why should he owe the same to me?"

Mr. Blaickie had a ready answer: "Because that is not the manner of it, ma'am—forgiveness, I mean. If we were all treated as we deserve, every last man Jack among us would be broken and cast aside; aye, ma'am, and every Jill too."

"Indeed that is so, Mr. Blaickie—and every Jill too; and I the first of them."

"And Mr. Newsome is someone who models himself on the Great Forgiver, the one who forgives any sinner who is truly repentant."

"I know he does," said Elissa. She was not surprised to discover that Mr. Blaickie had a religious bent; it must have been much of the reason Daniel had taken him into his service.

"So you will not find him slow to forgive where it is deserved," Mr. Blaickie said, completing his syllogism.

"Then I shall cling to that hope," she said.

They sat in silence a minute, she leaning forward and smiling on him, and he on the edge of his seat, regarding her with a curious expression that made her think of the parable of the shepherd who has found the lost sheep. It was as if he had found her, found a good opinion of her after all, among all the bad opinions he had of the world at large.

"May I read you something, ma'am?" he asked then.

The request was odd, but she at once said, "Of course, Mr. Blaickie."

He drew from the pocket of his traveling coat a much-battered book. When he saw her looking at it curiously, he said, by way of explanation, "Rutherford."

This meant nothing to her. "Ah, Mr. Blaickie," she said, "you must forgive me something else—my ignorance in this as well. I have no notion who Rutherford is."

"'Tis all right, ma'am. I had no such notion myself until the master gave me this book. He thought I should like it, and he was right; he is always right about such things. Perhaps someday he shall give you such a book, ma'am. Perhaps he shall; I have no idea."

"I shall hope that, too," she said, "though I am not worthy of it—I feel all unworthy of it."

"Well, that is the very reason I wanted to read you this passage, ma'am. A lovely passage. It has given me much comfort." He thumbed through the book until he found what he wanted. "Here, ma'am," he said. And then he read, his voice again picking up the accent of the land of his birth:

> You owe charity to all men, but most of all to lovely and loving Jesus, and some also to yourself, especially to your renewed self; because your new self is not yours, but another Lord's, even the work of his own Spirit: therefore to slander his work is to wrong himself. Love thinketh no evil; if you love grace, think not ill of grace in yourself. And you think ill of grace in yourself when you make it but a bastard and a work of nature. For a holy fear that you be not Christ's, and withal a care and a desire to be his, and not your own, is not, nay, cannot be bastard nature. The great Advocate pleadeth hard for you; be upon the Advocate's side, O poor fearful client of Christ.

He read with such fervor, and put such depth of feeling in every word, that she wept, though in that first acquaintance with the passage she caught perhaps only half of the full meaning.

"Now," he said, looking with approval on her shining face, "is that not beautiful, ma'am?"

"Indeed it is, Mr. Blaickie. Oh, Mr. Blaickie, I should like to copy those words out, if I may. I should like to study them, to get them by heart."

"Well, then," said Mr. Blaickie, "I know what I must do, for I have got most of this book to heart. I must give the book to you." And he held it out to her.

"Oh, no, Mr. Blaickie! Not a book you love so well!"

"Nay, Miss Wyatt, ma'am, 'tis not the only good book in the world. There is one even better; and I shall content myself with that."

"But I *could* not! Not a book that *he* gave to you."

"Well, then, bethink yourself how sometime you may give it back to me. But in the meantime, take it as an earnest that there is in *that man's* heart a power of forgiveness that other men do not have."

On those terms the gift could not be refused; and so she took it from him. And indeed the implicit promise that she would have an opportunity to return it to him made a thrill run through her.

Then she heard her father and Charles in the hall, and both she and Mr. Blaickie stood to greet them.

Mr. Blaickie did not figure much in the subsequent discussion. He merely opened the dispatch case and produced a letter from Daniel and a sheaf of legal documents under separate cover. Charles read the letter aloud at once. It conveyed the news that his cousin was promising him an annuity of four thousand pounds per year, to be secured inalienably by the Lakeholm property, for the duration of his life and that of his wife. At the time of his writing the letter, Daniel had heard from Charles about the articles of agreement drawn up on the basis of Charles's accession to the heirship of Aeons' End; but this only meant his offer was the more generous. His London attorneys were to draw up any papers necessary for any further articles of agreement between Charles and his in-laws; these were to be based upon the authenticated documents Daniel had sent with Mr. Blaickie. It seemed that the long delay in

arranging matters had come about through the difficulties
of repeated communication between Madeira and London.
But the result was all that Elissa would have expected of
Daniel: he had set to rights once and for all his inadvertent
misappropriation of the estate Charles would have received
from his adoptive father. It was all done with both crisp
executive certainty and loving forethought.

But in all the letter there was no mention of his returning,
indeed ever returning, to England. Obviously, he could have
arranged matters far more readily if he had come home; but
he had not done so, and from this circumstance Elissa had
to conclude that he was determined not to attend the wedding. There was in fact no mention of the wedding per se,
except insofar as the hope was set out that it could take place
without meeting further obstacle.

Charles was as much struck by this omission as Elissa.
"His *not saying* he is coming home is almost like his saying
he is *not coming* home," complained Charles. And he questioned Mr. Blaickie about Daniel's plans, just as Elissa had,
and received similar answers. "I shall be very sorry if he does
not come!" said Charles finally.

Silence met this lament. Elissa did not dare second it
aloud; she was afraid she could not keep her composure.

"I say," said Charles to Mr. Blaickie then, "is my cousin
courting anyone there in Madeira? Is that the reason he is
reluctant to come home?"

"I would hardly know, Mr. Charles," said Mr. Blaickie,
with true Scots stubbornness.

"Oh, come, man, you would certainly know. Is he courting anyone?"

But Mr. Blaickie held fast to his claim of ignorance, and
though Charles badgered him for several minutes, he could
not budge him. Finally Elissa interfered.

"You cannot expect the man to give any such news of his
master, even if he has it," she pointed out. "You would not
like your servants gossiping in that way about you, Charles."

Charles conceded the point.

Then the little gathering broke up—Charles to write letters to Louisa and to his cousin, and Elissa to take Mr. Blaickie to the kitchen to have some kind of meal before he departed for Lakeholm; for she was as insistent that he fortify himself as he was determined on proceeding to Lakeholm at once.

She meant to see him again before he left, but he slipped away while she was busy elsewhere. In a servant, such a silent departure was not rude, but rather expected. Still, she was a little hurt by it, since she hoped she had made a friend of him, and she had hoped to coax from him some further shred of information about Daniel's plans.

But she told herself: *Even if he has no news to report of Daniel, at least I have given him something remarkable to report of me. And that is nothing less than that I have put on the new woman.*

❖ 21 ❖

The Work of Patience

Let patience have its perfect work.

—James 1:4

Charles's letters were sent; and by return of post, so to speak, Louisa came to Aeons' End.

Elissa would have taken her to seek Charles in the garden, but Louisa asked her to wait; and seeing that her friend had something to say, Elissa instead called for tea to be brought.

But it was a hot day; neither of them found she wanted the tea when it came. When Lucy Brown had left them alone with it, Louisa left off her cheerful broadcast of the news in Bath and lapsed into an uncharacteristic silence. A worried silence.

"What is it, dear?" asked Elissa. "This latest news is tremendous; you can hardly be grieved to find yourself wealthier by far than even Aeons' End could make you."

"No, of course I am not sorry for that," said Louisa. "It is that I have come to a decision—a very difficult one, a very painful one."

"Ah," said Elissa.

"Yes—I daresay you know what it is. I shall go ahead with my marriage despite my father's refusal to bless it."

Elissa only nodded to show her understanding.

"Of course you know how difficult this is for me," said Louisa. "I can count on you for that. Everyone else in the

540

world is likely to be looking at me and saying, 'You fool! Of course you shall marry the man without your father's blessing—he has an estate and four thousand pounds *per annum* into the bargain.' But you know it is not that simple."

"Indeed, I know it is not. I perfectly understand. The mere thought of ever disappointing my own father in such a matter makes me sorrowful."

"Yes," said Louisa, seizing eagerly on this. "'Disappointing' is the very word that describes it. Of course I may flout his wishes—I am of age and, as I have said, the world at large will be on my side. I am quite sure our acquaintance in Bath will not care a wit what my father does or doesn't do; they have as much as said they think he is a silly country squire. But the pain it gives me to cross him, and in such an important matter—I am sorry for that, and shall always be sorry for it. I only hope we can be reconciled in future years. When I think of never seeing my parents again, and perhaps my own brother, because I have disobeyed my father—that makes me feel unutterably sad."

"Of course it does," said Elissa soothingly. "You would not be a good daughter if it did not. But I do believe they will come around. I have known your parents as long as I have known you—since we were girls of five—and I know them to be kind. Your father is only trying to protect you; and once he has seen that his fears have not been realized, he will receive you again. He is not a proud, intractable man. And until then, you shall live in the heart of your new family—with Charles and my father and me—right here in your new house; and be loved as you could wish."

Louisa did not reply; but the look she gave Elissa spoke her gratitude. After a minute or two of silence between them, her expression changed into one of dread mingled with a grim conviction, and she said: "I have determined to go home and make one last attempt to persuade my father. If I cannot do so, I shall tell him I shall marry without his blessing. I dread it; but Charles and I have waited long enough. It is time to act."

Instead of answering aloud, Elissa took her hand in sympathy and held it; but rather than strengthening Louisa's resolve, this expression of affection and concern broke her friend's reserve, and she began to weep."

"There, there," said Elissa. "It shall all come right. Only pray that their hearts will open to him and all shall come right. I suspect your mother has been at least secretly on your side all along; and Charles has said that your father does not dislike him and treats him with kindness and respect."

"That's the very thing!" said Louisa through her tears.

"What do you mean, dear?"

"I mean they should like each other very much. One of Charles's passions is shooting, you know. I dare say he likes it next best after gardening."

Elissa had been dimly aware that Charles liked the autumn shooting, but so did most men of her acquaintance, with the conspicuous exception of her own father.

She said: "And your father—yes, I recall; he does love shooting inordinately."

"And my brother has no use for it. So I thought it might be something my father and my husband could share—a mutual pursuit that might bring them closer together, as gardening has brought Mr. Wyatt and Charles together."

"I see," said Elissa.

A thought struck her suddenly, and she was silent as Louisa regained control of her feelings and wiped her eyes.

Then she said, "Dear, I have an idea."

"What is that?"

"Let me see what I can do to talk Mr. Bright over."

"You?" said Louisa.

"Yes, I. Everyone else has tried; why should not I? Your father and I have always liked each other."

"Indeed, that is true; I think he wished you to marry my brother at one time—I think he still wishes it, though he has had to acknowledge that the two of you have no leaning in that direction. Papa has always had a place in his heart for you—he has always told me what a fine figure of a woman you have grown up to be."

Elissa laughed a little at this. "And he said 'woman' rather than 'young lady,' did he? Well, then, he will be all the more likely to listen to me, I think.—Will you let me try, dear? If I fail, you have lost nothing but a day or two. You may make a journey to him the very next day after I return."

"Oh, Elissa, if you could persuade him!" said Louisa. "But I scarcely see how you could do it. First of all, you are a woman; and it is so hard to make headway against male presumption of that kind. A father's presumption, I mean."

"What, are women without persuasion, Louisa? I doubt that; I would rather say we have been renowned throughout the ages for our persuasiveness, though not always to the glorifying of our sex."

"Well, if you *would,* if you would attempt it, I shall be grateful to you, even if you fail. I know that in any case you shall be deft as always and make matters no worse."

"Have no fear of that," said Elissa.

So it was decided; and after speaking for a while on other matters more cheerful, they went into the garden at last to find Charles.

Once the plan was announced, Charles was delighted; he seemed to think obtaining his father-in-law's blessing was now a certain thing. John, however, was dubious. "I am not sure what you can do, Elissa," he said. "You will seem the outsider, I think, stepping into the question."

"I am Louisa's old friend, and an old friend to Mr. Bright's family, Papa," said Elissa. "Those will have to be my credentials."

John in any case acquiesced; and arrangements were made for the carriage to take her to Ryderly on the morrow. For the rest of the day the spirits of Charles and Louisa were light.

When all came inside to change for dinner, Elissa took the opportunity to follow Charles to his rooms. He now had two: not only the master bedroom, but an adjacent chamber made over to his use, which had been gradually filling up with possessions retrieved from his various places of residence over the past years—Landseye, Lakeholm, Rowantree, London, and Bath.

She was so quick in pursuit that his servant, a man by the name of Dover, had not yet arrived to dress his master.

"May I speak with you a moment, Charles?" she asked.

"You know you may at any time, my dear sister," he said.

"This may seem an odd request—indeed, I know it is. But you must humor me."

"Whatever you wish, Elissa; simply tell me what it is."

"I wish to see your guns."

Why is a man never properly astonished by such a question? Charles could never have understood why anyone might *not* want to see his guns; so with great enthusiasm he took her into his storeroom and showed her his armory, which consisted of four birding pieces.

Even she, though she scarcely knew what she was looking at, could admire the exquisite workmanship of their steel and wood. Each was delicately engraved and checkered, and they possessed a lean grace that reminded her of a wolfhound.

He would have gone on for some length about the merits of each, but she stopped him by raising a hand. He looked at her inquisitively.

"And which is your favorite, Charles?"

"Why, this one; this one Daniel gave to me. It is a William Young, made in Suffolk. Damascene steel, do you see? That refers to this pattern in the steel, where they worked the layers together with repeated forging. Thirty-inch barrels; nineteen gauge. Shoots as true as your line of sight. You shall not find a better gun in all Britain, I dare say."

"It is indeed both a terrible and a beautiful object, Charles, though I am no judge of such things. But here is the question I would ask you: which do you love more, Charles—this gun, or Louisa?"

A startled laugh burst from him. "Dear Elissa," he said. "What a question!"

"Then you would happily give up this gun for the chance of making her happy?"

"In a heartbeat," he said.

"Then have it put in the carriage tomorrow when I leave for Ryderly."

He was speechless.

She smiled at him. "Will you do it?" she asked.

"Why—I—of course I shall! You know I shall! But you mean to give it to Mr. Bright, do you not? And do you really think it will . . . do you think it will help?"

"I rather think it will, if the matter is properly handled."

"Well, then, God bless you, Elissa. You are welcome to it—Mr. Bright is welcome to it. I know Daniel would wish it so, too. What is a gun? I shall buy another—you know I could buy a hundred such if I wanted, now."

"See to it that you do not," she said, with a smile. "Ten such, if you like, Louisa shall not object to; but a hundred may be too many."

He gave another startled laugh; and after she had given him a peck on the cheek, she left him and went away to dress for dinner.

Ryderly Hall had not the antiquity of Aeons' End. It possessed the advantage of having been laid out by Charles Bridgeman, but to Elissa's mind, the artificial beauties of its plan only showed how Nature, with the assistance of that latter-day Adam, John Wyatt, had made Aeons' End the more breathtaking.

One approached up a long, straight drive that lay between two ranks of lime trees, hundreds of them. Indeed, all here was regulated and rectilinear; one exited the drive not onto a curving sweep but onto a boxy graveled area before a house whose shape was ruled absolutely by symmetry and line, rectangle and square. It was as if the architect had never proceeded in his studies into the use of the compass, but knew only the straightedge as a tool of his trade. Here was simply *too much* dwelling for any ordinary family, and especially for the Brights, of whom four made up the full number. The manor-house and grounds were splendid, true; but their splendor was a burden unto itself, only kept up by a vast upkeep, no small part of which included the pay, housing, and feeding of a small army of servants. One admired, but one said, "How glad I am that this is not mine!"

And so Elissa thought, as she stepped down from the carriage and paused a moment to look about her. At her left was the main garden of the place, which to her mind had always seemed a student's exercise in right angles and diagonals that would have been a positive embarrassment to Euclid; at her right was an extensive planting of trees that seemed to have borrowed its design from a checkerboard. All she saw—garden, park, and broad and extensive house façade— was in exquisite repair; and though as a housekeeper herself she could not but admire it, its perfection was oppressive. *Perhaps*, she thought, *if a little flaw had been allowed in all this, a little flaw might have been allowed in Charles as well.*

She was shown into the parlor while a footman took Mr. Bright the news of her arrival. At her order, another footman brought the gun in its case and set it on a table behind the sofa where she had taken her seat; and so high was the back of the sofa, and so low the table, that the gift was blocked from view. In a few minutes the first footman returned to say that Mr. Bright would be delayed, but had ordered tea and cake to be brought for her refreshment in the meantime.

She need not have been concerned that Mr. Bright would notice the gun behind her; he had eyes for nothing but her when he entered. He could be a formidable sort of man: he was physically large and portly, and in attitude he seemed determined to get assurances of his importance from everyone he met, even if he must badger both meek and noble to get them. But this was mostly a seeming. He was more sensible than proud, and his chief flaw was he thought the main purpose of good sense was to preserve appearances. He had a further, if minor and very particular, weakness as well: he and Elissa had that certain rapport that a young woman and an older man sometimes achieve, in which she knows she is admired, and he knows she knows, and yet each is perfectly easy and comfortable in the knowledge that nothing will come of it, that both parties may enjoy the admiring without adverse consequences. And now, when she rose and curtsied to him, and he took her hand and bowed in response, each wore a little smile of pleasure in the meeting.

"Well!" he said. "This is most unexpected—Miss Wyatt visiting Ryderly, and not in company with my daughter. And yet being alone I must extend to you all the more welcome on behalf of the Brights.—I imagine the young lovers have sent you to me, have they, as a kind of ambassador, to plead their case?"

"Indeed they have, sir," said Elissa. "Only I should rather say that it was my idea."

"Ah! Well, my dear, I must tell you at once that you shall not succeed in changing my mind. But let us not allow that to mar your visit. Mrs. Bright is out at present, but she will be as delighted as I am. Our Sam, I am sorry to say, is not at home. You know he has always doted on you."

She smiled at this wishful statement. Sam had always been friendly to her, but had been too puzzled by her seriousness to think seriously of marrying her.

Mr. Bright now added: "And you must stay over—you must not go back today."

"I have not come equipped for that, unfortunately," she said, "but I thank you for your kind offer."

"Well, let us have tea. Let us sit together like old friends and gossip a bit. You were always so good as to listen to an old man fill your ears with the doings of his estate."

"Indeed, sir, I always take a genuine interest in such matters. You know what a homebody I am."

So they sat down amicably and drank tea and ate cake—
Mr. Bright ate quite a bit of cake, even while he spoke—and
chatted on ordinary subjects: her father's latest gardening
feat and her sister's marriage, Mr. Bright's various improve-
ments and repairs to Ryderly, and Sam's enlarging prospects
and the possibility of his becoming an MP.

It was only when Mr. Bright was quite talked out that
Elissa reverted to her purpose.

"We have had a delightful talk, Mr. Bright," she began.

"Ah, my dear, we have; and you will not spoil it, will
you?"

She smiled at him. "I shall not say much, I hope. Will you
tolerate it, so that I may return home and say I have done
my best?"

He was by now in such a good mood that he smiled in
acquiescence, though at the same time he shook his head to
show that it was all hopeless.

"You know, sir," she said, "that my father has adopted
Charles Newsome as his heir; and indeed, that as a consequence Charles has taken the name Wyatt."

"Yes, your father himself told me as much."

"And of course that means that he is established as the
future master of Aeons' End, and as a link in the lineage of
the Wyatts from the past into the future."

Mr. Bright raised his eyebrows to indicate he thought this
was an irregular way to get an heir and carry on a lineage,
but he was too sensible of the lady's feelings to point it out.

"And marrying the heir of Aeons' End is no mean security for a lady's future, and the future of her children," she
went on.

"Indeed it is not," said Mr. Bright, willing to be affable
where he could.

"Nor is my brother Charles in any way an unkind man.
His disposition is utterly sweet and gentle, and he will
always treat his wife with the utmost respect."

"I have no doubt that his wife, whoever she may turn out to be, will always be pleased with his temperament," said Mr. Bright. "I shall allow you that."

"I shall cite two other advantages of the match that attach to Charles," said Elissa, "but first let me mention a fact about my dear friend Louisa, your own beloved daughter, about which we may between us be quite open and candid."

"And what is that?" asked Mr. Bright, surprised at this turn of the conversation.

"She is not growing younger," said Elissa. "A tendency that I feel the more keenly because it is also true of myself."

"Why, that is preposterous!" exclaimed Mr. Bright. "You are both young gals if there ever were such!"

"You say so, I think, out of kindness to me. I am sure you, as a father, feel some anxiety that she will not achieve the marriage she has long desired."

He was silent and sad; he did not attempt to counter the point she had made.

She went on: "I said I would mention two other advantages to the match. Here is the first: We have just the other day received news from Charles's cousin, Mr. Daniel Newsome, to the effect that he is settling on Charles an annuity of four thousand pounds. It is to be secured inalienably by Mr. Newsome's estate at Lakeholm, and is to last for the duration of the life of Charles and his wife."

"Hm!" said Mr. Bright, impressed despite himself at the size of this increase in Charles's prospects. "Four thousand pounds, do you say?"

"Yes."

"*Per annum?*"

"Yes."

"Hm!"

He was a little confused; and he now made the mistake of looking at Elissa, as she sat before him, attentive and beautiful; and he only grew a little more confused.

"Well!" he said. "I believe you said that there was another advantage. I doubt you can top the four thousand pounds, though, and I warn you that I am still proof to your persuasion, even with that addition to his property.—Good gracious, the man has a way of coming up in the world, does he not? Born a—I mean, an illegitimate; raised in one of the finest homes in Oxfordshire; sent up to university; has the unflagging support of his cousin, who by all accounts is a gentleman of the first water; meets the daughter of Ryderly Hall and wins her affections in a matter of days; is adopted into an old family, a fine old family—one of the finest in all Gloucestershire, and I shall be the first to say it; and now is to have an additional income from Lakeholm, which is famous for its prosperity in our part of the world.—But I warn you, to all this I am proof!"

"Well, then, I would have you look at something," she said.

"And what is that?"

She rose and went around the sofa to the table behind it; and without being bidden, he followed her. He saw the gun case at once, but so unexpected was it that he did not realize what it obviously held.

"This, sir," she told him, "is not a gift or a bribe; it is an offer of fellowship."

"My dear Miss Wyatt, I beg you will be less mysterious."

"You may ask my father, and he will tell you: gaining a son, even when one has or has had one, a son who will stand by you in your own avid pursuits, is like gaining a further extension of one's lease on life. If Louisa *may* marry Charles—if you, sir, should give her your blessing—you will find your life enriched by his company in one of the pursuits you hold most enjoyable in this our mortal life."

Mr. Bright was staring at her, his thought in suspension.

She undid the clasps of the case and turned back the cover, and for the first time in this interview his attention was drawn away from her.

For a moment he merely looked at the gun, and then he said: "It is a splendid piece! But what is the meaning of it? Do you mean to say that young Charles is . . . keen on shooting?"

"It is one of his greatest passions," said Elissa.

"Really! How did I never know of this? Why, he may come to Ryderly if he likes to shoot—I shall not begrudge him that. You know, our Sam is not much in that line; it is the only way he has failed me."

"That is very kind of you, I am sure, Mr. Bright. But I mean to tell you that Mr. Charles Wyatt would like to offer you this as a token of his esteem, no matter what your decision on his proposal to your daughter."

"But I could hardly accept it! What, take this wonderful gun from him and still say no? And if I did take it, and agree to their marriage, it would be like accepting a bribe, would it not?"

"Mr. Bright—my dear Mr. Bright—I can only say that he intends it as a token of esteem for you *as the father of his future wife.*"

The emphasis was unmistakable. He was once more startled and almost gaped at her. He understood what she was telling him: that he risked losing his daughter entirely if he did not give his assent. His future relationship with Louisa stood in the balance: he might give her up on a point of principle, or he might bend a little, and not break up his family—indeed, he might happily increase it.

For a long moment he was staggered; but he kept looking at Elissa, who did not let her gaze drop from his for an instant; and in this, again, she won him over.

He laughed aloud. He stepped close to her and put one arm around her shoulders, giving her a squeeze that would have crushed a slighter woman. "By God!" he said, "You are a clever one! I do believe you have won me over! Aeons' End and four thousand pounds! Louisa married off and the mother of children—a house of her own, a house such as she has always wanted!"

"And a son to shoot with," added Elissa.

He laughed long and loudly again.

"And a son to shoot with," he repeated. "Why, it is not so bad! This is the modern age, after all. There is a blot on many a scutcheon, many a noble scutcheon—"

"And in any case, it would not be on yours," she put in.

"That is another point!" he said agreeably.

"Mr. Bright, you will never regret it," she promised him.

"No—no, I doubt I ever shall. Think how happy it will make Louisa. And her mother! Why, Mrs. Bright has been at daggers drawn with me since Charles Newsome first came to ask my blessing. We may have a little concord in the house again, I do believe."

"And truly, sir, Charles wishes you to have the gun. You will not deny him the pleasure of being able to give you that, will you?"

Mr. Bright laughed and took up the gun, which he held in his hands, turning it this way and that and admiring it. "No," he said, "I shall not deny him that pleasure.—Besides, eh, he must give me *something* for my daughter, do you not think? Though my wife will tease me no end for taking this in exchange.—Well, let her!"

"Then the marriage shall go forward, and you shall see Charles at Ryderly for the shooting."

"Indeed, I had *better* see him for the shooting. Let them not plan their wedding tour during *that* season." And he laughed to show her he was only half serious.

This was all very well, and for several days after Elissa's return with the news, Aeons' End was the scene of great rejoicing. But Mr. Bright, having acquiesced in theory to the marriage, did not cease presenting further practical obstacles, or at least complications. He decreed that the negotiations for the settlement should take place at Aeons' End, which was midway between Ryderly and the offices of the lawyers in Gloucester. While in Deepclough, Mr. Bright and his attorney were to stay at the village inn, while Mr. Vaughn would stay at the house. (That stipulation lasted for only one night, however, out of the two that were required, the inn providing only rather rough lodgings.) Mr. Bright further insisted that he and Louisa and their attorney should sit in the parlor at Aeons' End, and Mr. Wyatt and Charles and Mr. Vaughn and a clerk in the drawing room, and that messages should be sent back and forth between them as the terms of the settlement were hammered out. This was not an unheard-of procedure, but it was utilized more in the alliance of vast dukedoms than in marriages between ordinary gentlefolk.

The great advantage that Elissa gained by this formal negotiating process arose from her being the messenger between the parties. It never occurred to anyone, except John Wyatt, that she could actually understand what she heard spoken; and the lawyers discussed the pros and cons of the terms as frankly before her as if she had been stock or stone. She found that she could linger in each room after handing over the latest written communication from the other party, and explain it, or add a tempering context to it, and even propose responses to it. In this way she became essential to the negotiations without either party really being aware of her role.

And more than once she saved the marriage when, through some misunderstanding or arrogance on the part of the lawyers, the parley was likely to come to ruin. The basic fact was—a fact that she kept presenting to both sides when they seemed to have forgotten it—that the match was very much to the advantage of both bride and groom, and they would be heartbroken if it could not be brought about. It is certainly helpful to have a woman present to remind men of basic facts such as these, particularly when their own suspicions and insecurities are likely to lead them into open war, as was the case with the lawyers. Not that Elissa could not have done far more than this; just that she did have this stabilizing influence.

It took all day to hash out the details of the agreement, which in the end looked very much like the terms that had been initially proposed. Charles was to become heir of Aeons' End and settle upon his wife a large jointure and ample pin money; stipulations were made about Louisa's future maintenance (Mr. Bright, having long marveled at how few servants the Wyatts had, was insistent that she should have her own maid); and settlements were made on her children, and in particular on her second and later sons and all her daughters.

Very late at night the provisional articles of agreement were drawn up, read out, and signed in the presence of all. A bottle of very fine claret was brought forth from the cellars, and all drank to the success of the marriage. All were jovial—John because the legal lineage of the Wyatts was now secured, Mr. Bright because he felt he had played a bad hand very skillfully and because the union that he had feared would be a stain on him would instead do him credit as well as benefit his daughter. The actual deed of settlement was to be composed and signed at a convenient date after the marriage; what was in hand now was sufficient for the engagement to go forward—for the banns to be read and for the wedding to be planned; which latter must include the finalizing of the most elusive item: the date.

And the setting of the date brought to the fore what had been a continuing source of puzzlement to Louisa and Charles. It was now the end of June. They still had not heard from Daniel as to his intentions; and it would be convenient, before they choose the day of their wedding, to know if he even planned to attend it. Elissa counseled them to select a date three months distant, but to be willing to delay the match if Daniel wrote to say he was returning; and this advice they took in part. A three-month delay seemed infinite to them; so they compromised on two months and a fortnight.

Accordingly the wedding was set for the end of September. Louisa returned to Ryderly Hall to undertake the preparations with her usual zeal for organization and management; and as her father's estate was an easy distance from Aeons' End, Charles frequently rode there, and on occasion she returned the visit. As for Elissa, during the early part of those months of preparation, she went often to visit Merry in her new home.

It was one of those junctures of life in which all the old patterns break open and reveal the unfolding of new structures to come. To the two younger women involved, it seemed that the horizons of their lives were not expanding gradually, but racing outward to the very farthest bounds of earth. Yesterday Merry had been a flighty girl; today she was a wife, the mistress of a large estate, and was soon to be a mother. She was in a state of ongoing bliss, and she went about with the air of one blessed, one whose every hope had been met and more than met. Yesterday Louisa had dwelt almost as a dependent and servant in the home of her uncle and aunt; now she lived in a fever of anticipation of the fulfillment of her dreams: a splendid home of her own, which she herself would one day run; and an amenable husband—also to be guided by her superior abilities, of course. Added to these were the additional benefits of a new father and sisters already known to her and beloved.

The men in this picture were moving into the future with an equal eagerness. Merry's pregnancy sealed David Boulder's affection for her as nothing else could have. And the greater the affection that fell upon her, the merrier and the Merrier Merry became, and the more still he loved her. Yesterday he had been deep in the cares of business in a foreign land; today he had reclaimed the family estate and had cast off its mortgages and the leases that encumbered it, and had brought his parents home to live in it again along with his new bride. Charles went about with an air of having arrived, for the first time in his life and all beyond his deserts, at a standing place that would not slip from under his feet; he could not believe his good fortune. Yesterday he had been drifting through the world, propped up by his cousin, without aim or prospect; today he was the heir of a goodly estate, the fiancé of a woman who would indulge him, but wisely and not beyond prudence. And he had a new name, and at once began calling himself and signing himself *Charles Wyatt;* and he had as well a new companion in his authentic father.

As for John, he put aside his shame and his regret for the past in the delight of again having a son and heir. Yesterday he had felt burdened by sin and failure; but he had been faithful throughout, his pound had gained ten pounds, and today God had given him back authority over his seed and its future. The two of them, John and Charles, now became more like brothers than father and son. Often as you went about on the property, you were likely to hear them, distantly beyond the labyrinthine hedges of the garden, talking about plantings and fountains and walks and trimming and edging and pruning, as if there were no other topic in all the world that could be talked of. Indeed, any other bride might have been hurt to see how gardening filled Charles's fair head; but Louisa, practical as ever, told Elissa quite frankly that she was delighted to see this occupation of his, and welcomed it in preference to the fixation with gambling and drinking and coarser pursuits in which men so often indulged. When father and son came back to the house at the end of the day, they were mellow with happy weariness and the success that only such workers as the gardener and the craftsperson truly know, of having made the world more beautiful, following God in creation, in at least some small way.

Elissa could see these changes and overturnings as if from a perspective beyond and above them all. The changes in her own life seemed more stubborn; but she had the consolation that yesterday she had been sunk in the darkness of her error and her pain, and today she was waiting and hoping.

But her hopes were more complex than her sister's and her future sister's. And the dark side of hope is fear; and so she was fearful as well.

As the wedding neared, Elissa went to visit Louisa and Merry less and less. She could not have said why, but she wanted to be at home, even if her time there was lonely. Perhaps she *wanted* to be lonely; that thought occurred to her, and it seemed there was some truth in it.

She struggled a great deal with her sense of having wronged Daniel. From all sides she seemed to hear herself accused: the lawns where she had sat with him said, *Where is he now, who gazed upon you then with such delight and love? Why did you drive him away?* The river, the mill pond, the dam where she might have died, all these seemed to reproach her for having wounded the man who had been her salvation. The mere sight, let alone the hearing, of Mr. Herbert, seemed to be whispering in undertone: *And is this the fate you would prefer?*

Indeed, her womb reproached her for its emptiness; her arms were wearying of hugging only her own waist, her own knees.

At times she tried to while away the hours till he could be hoped to return by singing and playing the songs they once had sung and played together. But now she found they afforded no pleasure, or only a piercing one. So many spoke of hard-hearted women who disdained and scorned their lovers (and in fact, a vast portion of older English lyric was devoted to that theme). The pain seemed inescapable. Songs he and she had once smiled over because of their excess now took on a sharp and specific personal meaning, and indeed seemed understated in comparison to the depth of her grief and the grief that he, too, must be feeling, or must have felt when she was scorning him from her. When she tried to sing those words in Campian, "O bitter grief, that exile is become Reward for faith," all she could think of was how she had driven him into exile. She read how Campian wrote:

> The cypress curtain of the night is spread,
> And over all a silent dew is cast.
> The weaker cares by sleep are conquerèd;
> But I alone, with hideous grief, aghast,
> In spite of Morpheus' charms, a watch do keep
> Over mine eyes, to banish careless sleep.
>
> Yet oft my trembling eyes through faintness close,
> And then the map of hell before me stands,
> Which ghosts do see, and I am one of those
> Ordain'd to pine in sorrow's endless bands,
> Since from my wretched soul all hopes are reft
> And now no cause of life to me is left.
>
> Grief, seize my soul, for that will still endure
> When my crazed body is consum'd and gone,
> Bear it to thy black den, there keep it sure,
> Where thou ten thousand souls doest feed upon.
> But all do not afford such food to thee
> As this poor one, the worser part of me.

Now these lines became the voice of Daniel's unheard thoughts and produced in her a sickness of heart almost physical in its intensity. This wretchedness of Campian's was no exaggeration; it was what she herself would feel if—when—she knew for certain that she had lost him forever.

At such times she could not stop herself from wallowing in her pain. She let each poem hurt her as much as it possibly could and then turned almost eagerly to another. This next shaft of Campian's in particular was one to which she often returned, imagining that Daniel sang it to himself:

> Harden now thy tired hart, with more than flinty rage;
> Ne'er let her false tears henceforth thy constant grief
>   assuage.
> Once true happy days thou saw'st, when she stood firme
>   and kind,
> Both as one then liv'd and held one ear, one tongue, one
>   mind;
> But now those bright hours be fled, and never may return;
> What then remains but her untruths to mourn?
>
> Silly Traitress, who shall now thy careless tresses place?
> Who thy pretty talk supply, whose ear thy music grace?
> Who shall thy bright eyes admire? what lips triumph
>   with thine?
> Day by day who'll visit thee and say 'Th'art only mine'?
> Such a time there was, God wot, but such shall never be:
> Too oft, I fear, thou wilt remember me.

And that was, indeed, what she most feared: that her life would become one long and fruitless remembering of the man she loved. As another old song had it: "Life is a death where sorrow cannot die."

Perhaps her loneliness in that time was a kind of penance. Or perhaps, paradoxically, it was the only way she had of being with Daniel: that is, by feeling, every minute of every day, how he was absent from her.

By contrast with her dark thoughts, the book Mr. Blaickie had so surprisingly and impulsively given her provided a solid comfort during those days. The Rutherford in question turned out to be one Samuel Rutherford, a Scottish

Presbyterian preacher and writer who had run afoul of King Charles II at the Restoration and was ultimately accused of high treason. Whatever his political history, his letters were extraordinary—poetic, passionate, and deeply Christian. Not only did Elissa memorize the passage Mr. Blaickie had read to her, but she wrote out new versions of it in her own words, varying them as the personal significance of the piece seemed to change day by day. One such version read:

> I owe love to all humanity, and most of all to the Most Human, to Jesus beautiful in His love. And because I owe love to all, I ought to love myself, and especially because I became a new person when I came to love Him. It was His spirit of love that made me new, and so my new self belongs to Him. So to speak or think ill of myself would be to wrong Him. Love thinks evil of no one; and if I love the grace that has come upon me in this love, then I cannot think ill of its working in me, of its transforming and renewing me. And yet that is exactly what I do when I believe that my repentance and renewal came upon me through some personal action alone and so can fail and decay. Surely, if I have a most holy fear of *not belonging* to Christ, and likewise a deep care and passion to be His, and not to belong to my own mere self—that holy fear and longing is not, cannot be, the result of my own weak doings. I must trust in its power. Indeed, the great Advocate pleads hard for me; I owe it to him to believe in my newness and set aside my fears that it shall fail me.

But that was just one of a hundred ways she could have rewritten the passage, just one of the hundred offspring of its pregnancy.

Her meditation on the variations of its meaning constantly gave rise to a further consideration of whether or not Daniel would forgive her. She took heart at what Mr.

Blaickie had said; and yet inevitably even his assurance that forgiveness would be forthcoming led her to think: *Of course, being forgiven is one thing. Being loved again, the way he loved me once before—that is quite another.*

❈ 22 ❈

A Miss Takes a Shot

Therefore a health to all that shot and miss'd.

—Shakespeare

Another comfort to Elissa in this time, besides her reading in Rutherford, was her growing appreciation of Charles. She had previously thought that if, of the characters of the two cousins, Daniel's was the one that must be declared most positively to be good, still Charles's character could be described negatively as lacking in all badness. But during that time of waiting she grew to love him for his own sake. She began to think that she, and perhaps even Daniel, had been too gloomy about him out of their concern that he might go astray. She had always thought of him as weak and unable to cope with the ordinary realities of life; but she came to see that the fault lay not so much with him as it did with the corruption of human life in general. He himself was angelic and innocent; it was not his fault if that goodness put him at a disadvantage in this world. He was like an angel indeed, like a happy spirit who had fallen through some gap in the spheres and tumbled to earth, a stranger sent to test them all in their love and hospitality. He only needed his Daniel, his Louisa, his Elissa, his father, to direct and protect him; and by helping him, they climbed to heaven beside him.

Thus she grew more and more content with the idea that he would be Louisa's lifelong partner. With Louisa to guide him, he would find his way to a great deal more good than he would have, had he been left to his own whims or to the direction of a wicked or a stupid or a lazy or a greedy or a silly wife. And he would also bless Louisa in his turn. The oppression of living with a bad spouse only those can understand who have endured it, and Elissa knew nothing of that; but she sensed that Louisa would blossom all the more in his innocent company, and that their children too would thrive between Louisa's earnest and directive motherhood and his beneficent paternity.

Charles's conversion from hunter to husband and husbandman was not quite complete, however. Summer was coming to its close; the shooting season was soon to be upon them. At times there was a particular sting of coolness in the morning air, or a damp and mist hanging over the hills, and Charles would look about him and begin asking questions about which manor in the vicinity had the best shooting, or perhaps say something about riding up to Ryderly for a day or two when the shooting started.

When the first of September arrived, the hunter in him could not be restrained; but he compromised with it by declaring he would not leave Aeons' End without first trying whether the yew wood on the hill would suffice for him. He pressed his man, Dover, into service as his loader, and prepared to walk the hill for the afternoon. Having made this decision, however, he was still loath to leave John, and he spent some time hanging about and saying hopeful things about how his father might come with him. But John—who had always scorned shooting, to the point of neglecting any upkeep of his own lands directed toward that purpose— would have none of it, and was even a little irritated at Charles's teasing. As an act of mercy to them both, Elissa offered herself as a substitute and was accepted.

How Charles expected to shoot a bird when he would not hush long enough to surprise one, Elissa could not understand. He rattled away on the usual variety of topics as they ascended the hill, and even as they walked through the parklike expanse under the great dark evergreens, weaving about in an erratic manner that he seemed to think would afford them more luck.

Even if Charles had managed to keep silent, the hill really did not have enough understory to provide shelter to ground birds, and he would probably have hit upon no prey there in any case. Eventually, as the day was drawing to its end, they found themselves at the crest of the slope on the far side of the hill. This land was, in its upper portion, rocky and waste wold, with some shrubby growth beneath several fine specimen beeches; and upon seeing the undergrowth, Charles said, "Now, here is some shooting!—I say, is this our land, Elissa?"

"Yes," she answered him. "As far down as those fields you see at the bottom of the slope; there is a wall there that marks the property."

"I should walk the lines with you and Father someday," he said.

She made no answer; for she was looking now at a figure who was rambling across the slope a few hundred yards below them. She did not recognize the man, though at the same time she felt a dread of him.

Charles followed her gaze and saw the figure as well.

"Who is that?" he asked directly.

"I cannot say."

"Is he shooting, do you think?" asked Charles. "Has Father given anyone permission to shoot here? That is something else I suppose I ought to know. Though why someone would come *here* to shoot, I could not say."

She did not answer for a moment; she was too preoccupied with her puzzled uneasiness at the sight of the stranger.

"He's carrying a gun, Master," said Dover rather unhelpfully.

"So he is," said Charles affably. "You are right about that, Dover."

"I do not recognize him at this distance," said Elissa. "Let us go back; it is late."

But the man had noticed them and had now bent his course abruptly in their direction; it would have been rude in them to turn away when it was obvious he wished to speak with them.

"He may only be passing across the hill, not shooting at all, and he wishes to explain himself," conjectured Charles.

"I do not know anyone who has Father's permission to shoot here," said Elissa. "And he was walking about as though he were looking out quail."

"But he has no dog, Master," said Dover.

"Neither have we," Charles pointed out.

The man was drawing near at a rapid pace, though he walked somewhat unsteadily. Elissa was suddenly sure that he was at least slightly drunk, and probably very much so. The unpleasant nature of her reaction to him grew upon her slowly as she watched him approach; it evolved from a vague dislike to a strong though inexplicable loathing; and finally, as she recognized the man, it became active revulsion and fear.

"It is Crustall," she said suddenly.

Charles was startled at this announcement. "Are you sure?" he asked.

"I am sure. Let us go." And she turned back at once, assuming her example would draw Charles away from confrontation with the man.

"You go," said Charles.

"You must come too," she said. "He is up to no good. Do not become entangled with him."

"My dear, I shall not run from a man on our own land."

She had not realized that Charles could be cool when he needed to be. She stopped and turned again to face Crustall. If Charles would not avoid the man, then she would not leave Charles.

Crustall had now closed to within about fifty feet and stood glowering up the slope at them. She had somehow forgotten how ugly he was.

"It is the Wyatt bitch," he said. "I know her. And who does she walk with, on my land?"

Charles, in his goodness, was too astonished to reply. Not so Elissa.

"This is Wyatt land," she said. "And we shall thank you to leave it, Mr. Crustall."

"I am only enjoying a little foretaste of my inheritance," said Mr. Crustall. And then, to Charles, he said: "And you, pup—who are you? The bitch's boy?"

At this Charles got over his astonishment.

"I am Charles Wyatt," he said. "And you owe us two things, Mr. Crustall: An apology to the lady for the foul language you have used, and a prompt departure from this land, to which you have no right either now or in future."

"You are this new so-called heir!" exclaimed Crustall. "Why, I have my luck today! It was you I have been hoping to find!"

And with that prologue and nothing further, he leveled his gun at Charles and fired; and Charles gave a groan of pain and surprise and sagged to the ground.

From that moment on, reality altered; the very air in which Elissa moved seemed to become a sticky, suffocating fluid that bent the light in some ghastly way. She threw herself to her knees beside Charles and pulled open his coat.

Crustall must have been telling the truth about seeking out his rival, for he had not fired buckshot, but a single ball; in other words, he was not carrying a birding gun, but a soldier's musket. The ball had struck Charles somewhere in the rightmost part of the torso; it might even be no more than a glancing blow—she could not at once discern the seriousness of the wound, since Charles was clutching it, and it was bleeding effusively, and his garments concealed it. She drew her handkerchief from the pocket of her pelisse, tugged Charles's hand away from his side, packed the handkerchief hard against the wound, then returned Charles's hand to its original position, and pressed her hand over his.

She looked at his face. At the same time he raised his eyes to hers; she could read continuing astonishment in them.

"It is not so bad," he said, his voice soft and constricted. "I think it broke one of my ribs, but it is . . . not so bad."

"We must keep the pressure on it," she said. "We must not let it bleed out."

She looked about for Dover, thinking to direct him to summon help, but he had thrown his gun down on the ground and was running away; she shouted to him, but he seemed not to hear, or at least he paid no attention.

Then she heard an ominous sound of metal on metal.

She looked toward Crustall. She had forgotten about him, assuming that he, too, would run away as quickly as possible, once he had seen the results of his shot. But he had stood his ground.

And worse than that, he was reloading his gun; the sound she had heard was that of the metal ramrod in the barrel, packing a new bullet home.

"That's right, Missy," he said to her as he saw her start. "First I shall finish him off, and then I shall have you. By the time I am through with you, you shall have no choice but to marry your cousin Crustall. And wouldn't that please your father now, Missy?" His voice was slurred and his movements were jerky and only barely effective; he was clearly quite drunk.

But his intentions were clear; he had stated them, and she knew now that he had every capacity for carrying them out.

The thought of her friend Louisa came suddenly to her mind. The idea that this stupid and spiteful man should deprive her friend of the happiness that was to come with her marriage to Charles—this was insupportable. Later she wondered why she had not thought of Charles himself, or of the grief Daniel would feel at the loss of his cousin, or that which her own father should feel at the loss of his son; and it seemed to her then that it was Louisa who leapt to mind in this instant because of her own loss of Daniel.

But at this moment all she knew was that she could not permit something so stupid and wrong to take place.

She rose to her feet. Charles's shotgun was lying on the ground where he had dropped it; she stepped around him with exacting care, then picked up the gun.

It was very simple, really: you held the stock of the gun against your shoulder, you pointed the barrel, and then you squeezed the trigger.

The crack of the shot made her ears ring. The violence of the recoil surprised her; the stock twitched viciously and bruised not only her shoulder, but her ribcage and the inside of her arm. The muzzle kicked upward, and the smoke of the powder hung for a moment in the air and left her unable to see the results of her shot.

Then the smoke cleared away. She and Crustall were facing each other over the same interval as before. He was staring at her as if he meant to say something, but he seemed unable to speak. As she watched him, she saw drops of blood emerge randomly on his face and throat and hands.

He worked the ramrod in the barrel of his gun again, but fitfully this time, as if he was forgetting what he was about.

She put Charles's gun aside and picked up the gun Dover had been carrying. This one had twin barrels and twin triggers; and this gun, too, she leveled at Crustall and discharged.

This time he did not remain standing; he toppled backward as though the whiff of lead shot had pushed him over.

She did not dare leave Charles there on the hill, in case Crustall somehow contrived to kill him. Their enemy was still writhing about; he was clearly still alive, and Elissa did not put it past the power of the man's hatred to come after Charles even in his wounded state. She managed to get Charles to his feet, and they set off through the darkening woods—she walking on his unwounded side, holding him up with both arms, and he leaning heavily on her, dizzy with pain, and his right hand under hers, both still clutching the sodden handkerchief to his side. Her last glimpse of Crustall over her shoulder showed him up on all fours and crawling away downhill.

She saw no sign of Dover, but apparently the man had run back to the house, for they were soon met by Dick Broad, and not far behind him came John Wyatt, crying out in a panic for them, and Jim Riggins and Mr. McBean and Joe Wiley and Mabel Dean and Lucy Brown, all straggling along behind their master, all frightened as well. Lucy had had the wit to bring several sturdy wool blankets, of which they made a kind of litter, and they carried Charles the rest of the way, each of the eight of them gripping a twisted handful of the cloth.

The weirdness of the flowing of time that had begun with that first shot continued. Later Elissa could not remember large parts of what happened: how they brought Charles into the house and put him in his bed, summoned the surgeon, and sent word as well to the magistrate. But she did recall how the surgeon came, and how she, Elissa, stood by Charles the whole time and helped the surgeon clean the wound and stitch it up. Then the surgeon told her: "It is a dirty and painful wound, but I think I have got the cloth out of it, so it will not rot in there. That one rib beneath the wound may be broken through, I really cannot tell; at the very least it is badly cracked. There was not as much powder behind the shot as there might have been, I think, and thank God the aim was poor. Unless it turns putrid and we have infection and fever, he shall recover."

Then time began to return to its normal pace. She remembered her father taking the doctor downstairs to see him out; and there was Dick Broad, hanging about by the door of the room—not only inside the house but even upstairs, where a coachman did not belong. She went to him and said, "What is it, Dickon?"

"Beggin' your pardon, Miss Wyatt," he said, "but did you know I warned your father and young Mr. Wyatt about Crustall's bein' about?"

"No," she said. "I did not know that, Dickon. When did you do so?"

"No more than three days ago. I heard it when I was over in Limmervale, that he had been hangin' about the Red Hart, drinkin' too much, and boastin' how he was to come into Aeons' End after all. And when folk'd ask him how, he would put his hands up like this—" and here, making a gun barrel of his arm and a hammer of his thumb, Dick mimicked a man shooting—"and then he 'uld just nod and wink and laugh all harsh-like."

"And what did my father say when you told him this?"

"He grew very angry and said he did not want to hear of it."

"Well," said Elissa, "now he has heard of it in a way he cannot ignore. I am sorry they did not listen to you, Dickon. You must never hesitate to come to me if you have information of that kind. My father just does not like to hear it, as you say; and in the meantime, it could make all the difference to us, to all of us.—Did you know that tonight Crustall threatened to finish what he started that day you drove him out?—But I think we shall soon have heard the last of this fellow. After what he did today, the law will make short work of him."

"I hope so, Miss Wyatt," said Dick.

"But you must tell Sir John what you heard. That establishes beyond any doubt that Crustall had forethought in the attempt, and makes it all the more serious."

Sir John Gunne was the local magistrate.

"Indeed I shall tell His Honor that, Miss," said Dick.

"And Dickon—"

"Yes'm?"

"You must find me a steady man who can take a message to Miss Bright at Ryderly. She must be told at once."

"Aye, Miss Wyatt," said Dick. "Gippy Murton's Billy is the one for it. I shall send the bwoy for him straightway."

"I shall write a note for Billy to take," said Elissa. "God forbid we should leave him to his own devices to communicate this news."

Dick agreed to this, and with these necessities taken care of, she returned to nursing her brother.

Sir John Gunne, Justice of the Peace, arrived early the next morning. He was an English squire very much in the old mold. By rights the Wyatts should have held the magistracy, but John Wyatt could not be bothered with it, and John Gunne took to it with zest. It allowed him to build up a legend about himself; but fortunately, the legend really only took place in his own head, and for all his boasting about the severity of his application of the law, there was more than one broken man who had been grateful to receive a warning and a dismissal for a crime of poaching that might, if adjudicated by someone else, have sent him to the Southern Hemisphere.

The worst of Sir John, as Elissa saw it, was that he was a merry old man who doted on pretty girls. He was far worse in this respect than Mr. Bright, who was selective in his appreciation of the opposite sex and restrained and courteous in his expression of that appreciation. Sir John was convinced that his flirting and his somewhat broad remarks were received by all women with great pleasure, and each mark of irritation or disgust with him, whether it was flushed cheeks or flashing eyes, only confirmed him in his belief.

A further flaw compounded this vice. He loved bad puns and rhymes. Indeed, he had written a poem about himself in forty stanzas, of which these are two of most innocuous:

> A girl in a fuss gets a good buss
> From that lover of fun and hater of none,
> Your old John Gunne.

> Quick as a rhyme, he judges the crime;
> And then with a pun, justice is done
> By old John Gunne.

In short, John Gunne was—much like Mr. Vaughn, and as some would say, all representatives of human law—inherently ludicrous, being inevitably a shadow of a higher law and a living failure in respect to enforcing it, and thus somewhat jealous of the honor done him; and yet he was all the law to be had in the district, and so he was indeed honored. And so when Elissa was informed that he was waiting to speak with her in the parlor, she told herself that it was a very important matter, in fact a matter of life and death, and that she must bear with his gaucheries as best she could and persevere in establishing the facts of the case.

He was all happiness at having a truly serious case on his hands; but under the example of her seriousness, he grew more grave than she had ever seen him. The presence of her father in the room also helped him curb those little flirting comments that she found so obnoxious. He listened to her account of the incident with appropriate closeness of attention, interrupting only to ask questions which, if not always useful or even relevant, were at least soberly put. When she had concluded, he walked her through the story again, focusing on particular facts that he found significant, such as that Crustall had approached them, and not they him; that the man had given no warning, and fired at Charles from a distance, while not under attack himself; and that he had threatened Miss Wyatt with rape.

When this second account was given, he said, "Well, Miss Wyatt, the first thing I would have you know is that neither you nor your new brother will ever be in danger from this fellow Crustall again. Yes, we took him up last night. He had not got far. And the case for premeditate murder is about as clear as we could ever ask for. I heard he was calling for gin and lawyers, but we mean to be more generous with another commodity: we shall give him all the rope he likes."

She was a bit taken aback by Sir John's coarse imagery; but she expressed approval of his capture of the culprit and then asked: "And what sort of condition was he in when you arrested him, if I may ask?"

"Condition, Miss? Why, he was drunk, drunk as a lord."

"I did not mean that, Sir John; I meant with respect to his wounds."

"Oh, he was at Mr. Hanby's house having a fair sowing of lead shot pulled from his flesh a bit at a time." Mr. Hanby was the surgeon in nearby Limmervale. "He did not seem to be enjoying it; which is all to the good, in our opinion."

"In other words, my second shot did not do for him completely," she said. "That is good news. Though he greatly deserves the punishment he will no doubt have, I would not have liked to be the one to execute it."

"Indeed, Miss, I doubt you even hit him at all with that second gun."

She was surprised, but said, "I shall not argue it with you."

And here he finally lapsed into his usual form, and out came the rhymes and puns that had been in preparation all this while. "Do not mistake me, Miss," he said. "We could wish you had shot *lead* into his *head* until he was *dead*. That would have been a *capital shot,* do you see, and prevented a *capital offense.* But you only broke the *crust* of the fellow, who has plenty of it—*all* of it, as a matter of fact, if you see what I mean. As a *noisome* fellow, he could not abide that a *newsome* fellow was to come in and take what he thought was his own. But a fool's bolt is soon *shot*. Indeed, he *thought* with a *shot* to alter his *lot*; but he *caught* him some *shot* that *taught* he *ought not*."

"Would I had never had *need* to commit the *deed*," she said, humoring him. Though her effort was lame, he appreciated it.

"It was well you missed with that second shot," he said, "as it keeps you from being dragged any further into this matter than you have been. Do you see? Indeed, Miss Wyatt, it is all a tale of *hit* and *miss*. We may say, *Miss*, that though you had one *palpable hit*, you also had a *capital miss*. And in any case, though you are not a *capital shot*, you are a *capital Miss*, which makes you a *hit* with me! And I would say to any other such fellows who go up against Miss *Wyatt*: 'Don't *try it!*'"

"Your *wit*, Sir John," said Elissa, now rising to the occasion, "is as scattered as birdshot; let us hope your *wits* are not the same. But I think not, for in this case your judgment is as *capital* as the crime."

Mr. Gunne laughed delightedly. "Oh, for a pretty gal like you," he said, "to perch upon my knee and fire off squibs all the day long!"

"Better wish for no such thing, Sir John," said Elissa. "My *gun* could not hit a *squab*, but my *squibs* can hit a *Gunne*."

"They may—they do!" roared Sir John happily.

At this moment, she heard a bustle at the door of the house—it was Louisa arriving—and that gave her a good excuse to escape Sir John's humor, or what passed for such.

❊ 23 ❊

The Day Comes

Disdain me not that am your own,
Refuse me not that am so true,
Mistrust me not till all be known,
Forsake me not now for no new.

—Wyatt

Charles recovered very rapidly. Indeed, Elissa thought that he would not have dared to sicken, much less to die, with Louisa looking after him.

He was determined to stick to the date they had set for the wedding; and though at first Louisa would have none of it, he soon demonstrated that he would be mended enough to wait at the head of the aisle.

The shock he had been through seemed to have settled his mind about one thing. He was now convinced that Daniel would attend the wedding. He did not even write to his cousin about his misadventure with Mr. Crustall, saying that the message could never reach him in time—that he must already be on his way. "He will be here if he must walk on water to do it," said Charles. And he said it in a tone that suggested that he really believed his cousin could do exactly that if he wished.

To Elissa, it seemed the remaining weeks crawled by. She was secretly convinced that she was as eager for the wedding to come as the bride and groom, for she felt the event would be tantamount to her own wedding; and yet at the same time she dreaded the arrival of that date, for she felt it might establish finally and certainly that she would never be wed.

At length there were but two weeks remaining. It was a wet, cold day, and Louisa, who had lingered at Aeons' End to ensure, as she said, that her fiancé lived to marry her, forbade Charles even to walk in the garden. She was to go home on the morrow to resume the preparations for the wedding; and to take advantage of their last day with her, John and Elissa kept the lovers company by the fire in the drawing room.

And at about one in the afternoon, Merry came home.

It seemed to Elissa that the clouds seem to pull apart and roll aside when Merry descended on their gray day. Without any announcement by any of the servants, there she was at the door of the drawing room, smiling; and David behind her, perhaps more tentative, but following the lead Merry's mood gave him.

She looked . . . almost beautiful. No, she *did* look beautiful. She was not just pretty with that sort of pert, hasty prettiness she had always had. She was happy, she was even merry as in the old days; and the blush of her motherhood was on her, that rosy aura that women often have in the first few months of pregnancy, and the contented glow that comes with a happy marriage. The maternal pounds she had gained suited her; she no longer looked like a straw that would tumble in any wind, but like a being of some solidity; it was as if her body had decided to emulate that of her sister and be a woman, be a child no longer. David looked at them all, and then at Merry, and then back at them, as if he were saying, "Here she is! Is she not the most wonderful thing you have ever seen? And she is carrying our child as well—the only thing that could possibly make her more precious to me." His adoration was almost comical.

"We happened to be on our way home from Gloucester," Merry announced, before any of them could move a muscle in their surprise. "And all of a sudden I knew I could not stay away any longer."

Elissa was the first on her feet. "Of course you could not," she said. "Welcome home, dear Merry!" She went at once and embraced her, and they clung to one another tightly and, for a moment, a little weepily.

John was next, and kissed her and greeted her with a fondness almost inarticulate, as if he had been repressing his love for her so that it would not hurt him in her absence.

Then Charles came forward; and for a long moment it seemed all held their breath.

But Merry would not let them wait and fear for long. She met Charles in the middle of the room; she held out her slender hand; and she laughed brightly.

"Greetings, dear brother," she said. "*Dear* Charles! How wonderfully everything has turned out! Do you not think so?"

"Indeed I do," he said. And then the two of them laughed happily together, and the pain and the trouble of their misadventure vaporized under the effect of that laughter.

She looked over her shoulder and said, "David!"

David came to her side.

"This is my brother Charles," she said. "Charles, this is my husband, Mr. David Boulder."

David extended his hand to Charles, Charles took it, and they exchanged greetings without a trace of awkwardness.

"I have heard you are a very fine fellow," said David. Elissa could have kissed him for his generosity.

"And I have heard you are the *perfect* match for my excellent sister," said Charles.

"Well, I do try to be," said David, "and I shall *always* try to be."

"Then let us be friends," said Charles impulsively.

"By all means," said David.

They looked at one another with sincere approval. The only awkwardness was where the conversation ought to go from there; and Elissa put a stop to that by saying to David, "Now, give your cousin Louisa a kiss before she begins to sulk for lack of it."

They all laughed at this; they would have laughed at anything anyone said. Indeed, over the next few hours, until David and Merry resumed their journey, they laughed a great deal, all of them.

Later Elissa thought that only Merry could have done it—make them forget the difficulties of the past so readily. But Merry, better than anyone, understood instinctively, with an emotional certainty unmarred by intellectual doubts, that life is only a moment, and there is no time to brood on old mistakes, to harbor jealousies or ill-will toward others. There is only time for moving forward into more love.

When Merry had gone, the day was no longer dark. She had washed the last stain off the line of the Wyatts and out of the halls of Aeons' End.

Elissa knew that on the day of the wedding she might have little chance to talk to Daniel. She had been to many a marriage service and wedding breakfast; she knew how little serious conversation ever took place among the members of the wedding party. The most she could hope for was to hand him her letter—the letter with which she had pursued him since the day she had learned the facts of her error concerning him. If he allowed her no further communication but that, she would at least know she had done all that lay within her power to explain to him and to apologize.

On the day before she was to go to Ryderly, she took advantage of the relative peace and quiet of her own house to sit down and copy over the letter. First she read it through, looking for any way she might make it more earnest or more abject:

3 September, 1812

Dear Sir:

I write to you to make an explanation and an apology.

Only yesterday I learned the true nature of the revelation you made to my father and sister on the day of the latter's abortive wedding last year. I need not tell you that this knowledge puts your motives and actions in a completely new light. If you will—if you can—look on the statements I made in our most recent interview as the words of one conjecturing your motives in ignorance of them, I have hopes you will judge me less harshly than you must most justifiably at present.

It grieves me deeply that in my misapprehensions concerning this matter, I charged you with sins against my family of which you are wholly innocent. You were then and have always been a friend to us, and my recompense for that fair dealing was abominable, though I beg you to understand that it was so only because of my ignorance of the true facts.

Your most humble servant,
Elissa Wyatt

But she saw nothing in this she would change. The date on the letter, along with her profession of ignorance of the facts previous to that time, was the most powerful persuasion she could muster.

Having set forth the original again, she added this cover note:

Dear Sir:

Enclosed please find a copy of a letter written to you on 3 September, 1812. The original was sent directly to you in Madeira on 18 September of that year, as was a copy under Charles's seal on 22 September. I hope you will forgive these repeated communications of the same information, but I cannot rest until I know that you have received the facts concerning this matter, which the enclosed will make known to you better than anything new I might write. The gist of it is that I was not apprised in a timely manner of certain circumstances having to do with relations between your family and mine.

Your most humble servant,
Elissa Wyatt

This note she folded around the original letter to form an envelope, and sealed the whole new letter with wax.

Thus the letter was prepared; but what if she did not even have time to hand it to him? If she did find a private moment to do so, it would be no more than a moment indeed; to be caught, to be observed by half the gathering, in the shameless and forward act of handing him a note would be a disgrace to be avoided at all costs. So to overcome this difficulty she devised a curious stratagem.

It is the strange custom of our own times that all in a party of bridesmaids should wear dresses not only of the same color but of the same style. This procrustean practice of forcing women both tall and small, wide and thin, into the same sort of dress has the unfortunate result that at most only one of them, and more probably none, wears anything that might be flattering or advantageous to her particular figure or coloring. Perhaps this is just as well, for the cardinal rule of the bridesmaid, the most basic principle on which she prepares for her role, the absolute law that she must never break—is that she must never be more beautiful than the bride. It is not, after all, *her* day.

In the times in which Elissa Wyatt lived, women were less uniformitarian about the bridesmaid's costume. Each friend of the bride wore what suited her, and no attempt was made to create a flanking bevy in solid apricot or lavender or mauve. The result was not as eye-catching, perhaps; but then again, sometimes the viewing of eye-catching sights has more in common with catching one's eyes on something sharp than with resting them on something happily stimulating.

Thus it was a dress of her own choosing that Elissa was to wear to the wedding. And that which she had chosen was of a color that set off her dark hair and eyes to good effect. It was finely sewn of very handsome fabric, opaque but silken, of a foreign weave, in which one could discern, if one had the opportunity to inspect it closely, stylized acanthus leaves worked into the cloth by some marvelous trick of the loom. It was not deeply cut at the neck, it did not plunge away recklessly close to those twin limits of the acceptably seeable, the paps; but somehow that modesty made the neckline even more provocative—it is curious how this counterintuitive fact holds true, through age after age, though fashion seldom appreciates it. Over the breasts the gown was fitted tightly, and beneath the breasts it had a panel composed of embroidery all in a matching thread, which cheated the high-waisted fashion of the times and drew in the flanks of the dress from the bust as far as the hips. Beneath this, on her torso, she would wear stays to the midriff, very finely crafted, and so light in weight as to be imperceptible through the gown. The skirts fell from her hips, exposing not even an inch of her leg or even her ankles, until they reached the tops of her shoes, which were such as we might sooner call pumps or even dancing slippers; the toes of which, peeping out alternately with each step she took, exhibited an inset of silver brocade on the top of the foot.

Into this dress, behind the embroidered panel, she now undertook to sew—for like most women of her time, she was an excellent seamstress in her own right—an invisible pocket just large enough for the letter she had written to Daniel; and when it was in place, she contrived a closing for it by stitching in a loop of thread and reconfiguring one of the decorative buttons on the edges of the embroidered panel. The letter, once inserted in this pocket, would thus be immediately at hand, ready to be produced instantly if opportunity arose, and yet undetectable until then. Until then it would be, as well, heated by the warmth of her heart, caressed by the beating of it; and she could only hope it would carry that heat and the effect of that pulsation to the man she loved when she put it in his hands.

When she had completed this final preparation, she put on the dress and consulted the looking glass. She was not a vain being, by any means, or prone to imagining greater beauty in herself than she possessed; but for all her modesty, as she stood there before the mirror—stood tall there before the mirror, straightening her back so that her breasts rose and her waist narrowed—and as she thought of Daniel, of meeting him again on the day after tomorrow, of communicating to him that critical knowledge he did not yet possess; and as the light of hope woke in her countenance, faint but undeniably present, and lit her natural good looks with a further supernatural, spiritual tinge; then she felt a pang of guilt.

It grieved her to do what she must do, as she loved her friend, and could not have been happier for her; but she hoped that Louisa would never notice.

For she knew, despite all her modesty, that at the wedding she would break that absolute law that must govern the bridesmaid.

The journey to Ryderly Hall was brief and pleasant. Little rain had fallen since that day when Merry had stopped at Aeons' End; the roads were dry, but had not yet been reduced to headache-inducing dust. Despite the superplus of rooms at the Hall, Louisa had reserved rooms in a nearby inn for Charles and John, and one for Daniel as well, should he appear; but when the carriage stopped there briefly, it was quickly learned that Daniel had neither arrived nor sent a message that he was on his way. Even Mr.

Blaickie, who might have been expected to meet his master in Gloucestershire if Daniel was bound for the place, was conspicuously absent. Until these sad facts were established, Elissa's heart pounded mercilessly within her; and when she knew for certain that Daniel was not present, that organ seemed to shrink inside her, or to draw at her blood in vain, like an unprimed pump, as if her very life had become a vacuum. In a fit of gray sickness and unease, she continued on to Ryderly, where she was to stay the night with Louisa.

Her hope and her heart began to rise again, however, when the carriage turned into the long drive toward Ryderly; for against all common sense, she thought there was a good chance that Daniel had gone to the Hall first; after all, he could not know that the bride had prohibited the men of the groom's family from entering her house till the wedding was complete. This hope continued for several minutes of acute suspense, during which she was welcomed by Louisa and bustled into the house and up to the bride's dressing room, all without being able to ask if any other guests had appeared. Finally she found an opening to say to Louisa, with some semblance of nonchalance, amid the chatter of the seamstress and the lady's maid and Louisa's mother, "Has everyone arrived?"

"All my family and my aunt and uncle are here; David, as you know, is not attending, though I hear that there is much new easiness in that quarter." Then she added: "Was there any news of Mr. Daniel Newsome at the inn?"

Elissa's spirits lapsed again. "None, I am afraid," she said.

"Really? I am surprised at that—did you know he sent a quantity of very fine wine?"

Elissa's heart did something indescribable in response to this news.

"No," she said. "I did not know—I had no idea. We ought to send a message to the inn to let Charles know."

Here she could see that Louisa began to struggle between her hopes for her friend and the realities that her own good sense painted for her.

"Yes, you are right," she said. "I shall see that he hears of it." Then: "We may take it as a hopeful sign."

"We may indeed," said Elissa, "or at least, I hope we may. I hope it is not just the sum total of his notice of his cousin's marriage—one might well say that between his generous settlement and this wedding-day gift, he has done more, far more, than most cousins ever would."

"Indeed," said Louisa. And then, straining for a brighter prospect, she said: "But they were so close, Charles and he. I cannot imagine he will not come."

But I can too easily imagine it, Elissa thought.

She asked, "The wine was shipped from Madeira, I suppose?"

"It is Madeira wine, but it was shipped most recently from the Newsomes' London warehouse. Papa says it is Malmsey, the best Madeira produces; it is called *Casa Solitária.*"

"Well," Elissa said, "I suppose it is a good sign that it comes from London. It might mean that he is in England— that he did not bring the wine with him, but had to have it shipped from his warehouse here."

"I am not sure its provenance means anything," said Louisa, as her logical side got the better of her. "He could just as well have sent orders to London from overseas, or requested his manager do so from Lakeholm."

"Yes," admitted Elissa. "I suppose it cannot really reassure us much."

Louisa looked as if she could have said more on the subject, but on thinking that it would not be encouraging, she refrained.

The rest of that day and its night passed without any further communication from the inn. As is common at such events, the different parties progressed pell-mell toward their destined meeting at the church as if neither knew of the other's existence. For Elissa, the suspense continued at a lower pitch, and not even the frenetic preparations and buoyant spirits of the bride's family and servants could distract her from the great question: *Would he be there?* It gave her a curious emotional detachment from the thought that her best friend and her brother would soon be wed: she felt like someone riding in the tumbril to the guillotine who catches a glimpse of a wedding party on the steps of a distant church. *What is their joy to me?* she caught herself thinking at more than one point.

But even as she thought such things, she would catch herself, and say a penitent prayer in remorse for her self-centeredness. *Truly,* she thought, *there will be life beyond that disappointment. It is only that I do not know what shape that life will take, and I will always measure it against what might have been. I will always think how close we came, Daniel and I, to peace on earth. Beyond tomorrow I will only have the waiting for the end of time. I shall try to be useful, and there is indeed much in that, and God will steady me in it. But to have come so close! Truly that will leave a bitter taste in the mouth of my soul forever.*

The bridal day dawned. The house was up with the sun, and much of its inhabitants well before. Thanks to Louisa's marshaling of the domestic forces, the family was seated in the carriages and on the move at precisely the proper time. Not even then did Louisa let slip her need to control events, but she seemed to gain happiness from the very smoothness of their flow, like a gambler who has counted all the cards and knows they can only be played one way.

The church of the parish of Ryderly was a very small and very ancient structure; it might almost better have been called a chapel in the stricter and more British sense of that term, denoting the size of the hall. The entrance was on the south, where the morning sun gilded the faded green ivy on the walls and over the door with lingering tints of fleeting and shimmering auroral metal. To the west lay the churchyard, the near edges of which were bound tightly in a wall of treacle-colored Cotswold stone, but the far borders of which were lost among the very beautiful and ancient yews and oaks that surrounded the church grounds to the north and merged into a wood almost daunting in depth and darkness. On the east was a pretty little rectory, clad in massive, healthy rose bushes, bedight with a few late roses, of which John Wyatt must have murmured fond approval; and between the rectory and the church a little stream ran, bridged by a diminutive arch just wide enough for the rector on those Sundays when he must hurry to vesper services, still wiping the last traces of an excellent repast from his mouth with his handkerchief.

On this day, however, the rector was not the last to arrive. To be sure, he would not be late to the wedding of the daughter of the squire of the parish. When the carriage with Louisa and her mother and Elissa drew up at the church, and that with her father and brother behind it, the rector was already inside, with those neighbors and friends who had been invited; and with *the bridegroom's party.*

But even to *think* "the bridegroom's party" was to commit a *petitio principii,* a begging of the question. Was it proper to assume there was a bridegroom's party at all? For if it existed, it consisted in its entirety of Daniel Newsome.

In the intervals in which she was not thinking of *the bridegroom's party,* Elissa participated in Louisa's delight as far as she could. And Louisa was very much enjoying herself. But if she had given herself over to joy, it was a sensible sort of joy: she giggled and laughed outright at the typical little setbacks that occur on wedding mornings, as if she had foreseen them and already disallowed their power to disturb her—the hem in her mother's dress that caught on the carriage door and pulled out, the one curl that now declared it would defy the previous instructions of the hot iron. After all things were considered, a less nervous bride could not be imagined. Everything was perfect: she was marrying the man she adored, a man who adored her; the morning was clear and splendid; her best friend was beside her, her parents and brother in attendance, and all were in approval of her choice. The future would, perhaps, not be so flawless and blissful (for futures never are, or at least not when they first arrive, though they do tend to improve in retrospect); but at least she and her husband had the prospect of a good living on a fine old estate; and in any case, today was today, and precisely because of her greater prudence and good sense, she would enjoy it far more than many a bride giddy with joy.

But for Elissa, even this practical form of enjoyment produced painful stabs of memory that at unpredictable moments thrust their way between her ribs into her heart, that heart so challenged, so often elevated and so often cast down, by these circumstances. For a moment there, Louisa's smile and her laugh had seemed like that of another bride on another day on her way to marry this same man. On that day, too, Elissa had hoped from minute to minute that Daniel would be present. And what pain it caused when he did appear, what error—an error that had grown as it tumbled onward through her life until it had jeopardized and even perhaps slain her own best hope for love, companionship, happiness. Perhaps if he did come to his cousin's wedding on this day, it would be the completion of the pain that had begun then: he would scorn her, in some subtle but unmistakable way, or she would learn that he was already married to another—that she was too late.

This was her state of mind as they descended from the carriage before the church and lingered for a long moment, waiting for the men of the Bright family to join them. Both the bride and the bridesmaid were looking about them, and again it was as if they had exchanged roles. For the bride was appreciating the beauty of the morning, and the setting of the old church of her childhood, which she loved so well; she was anticipating seeing Charles, handsome and happy, waiting for her before the altar; she was riding on her strength of character as a skiff playing in a wild surf rides safely to land in the curl of a wave.

But the bridesmaid felt almost a panic. She felt as if she were hanging on to the shreds of her character by her fingernails. She was furtively attempting to determine if any of the carriages ranged along the edge of the lane might belong to Daniel; but there were many vehicles there, some private and energetic in their bright, new paint and varnish, and some hired and tired from long use without refreshment; they could tell her nothing. Among the coachmen and footmen who peered curiously back at her she saw not one familiar face—specifically, no Mr. Blaickie, whom she had hoped to find among them.

Mr. Sam Bright, Louisa's brother, went forward and inquired of the ushers at the door whether everything was prepared. He gave Louisa a signal, and the bridal party took its places in order of ritual precedence: Mrs. Bright, on Sam's arm; and then Louisa and her father, Mr. Samuel Bright; then Elissa, feeling suddenly bereft of company, alone behind them as the Maid of Honor.

They proceeded into the church; or perhaps *processed* is the word; but things were simpler then, and there was a far smaller supply of artificial theatrics in the ceremony. The power of the event was deemed sufficient, and no pomp had to be concocted to serve in place of it: marriages were for life, not temporary alliances of convenience or the tentative results of impulse or half-hearted expectation, as they are today; and that looming permanency of commitment was enough to elevate the poignancy of a wedding to that of a living and authentic Greek drama.

The congregation rose from their seats as the bride's party stepped over the threshold, turning to see the bride; and those on the aisle leaned into it and craned their necks, some smiling, and some already weeping; and all this curiosity had the maddening effect of blocking Elissa's view of the front of the church. As did Mr. Sam Bright's broad back; and it was not until that man had conducted his mother to the family pew and had himself stepped aside into it that Elissa could at last glimpse those who stood at the end of the aisle.

At first she saw only Charles and the rector behind him. But then—when she was almost upon them—she saw Daniel standing beside Charles. She had no further chance to prepare herself. She looked directly into his eyes and found him looking directly into hers.

He straightened a bit as he saw her—she must have done the same. He looked grave, and yet there was a kind of benignity in his countenance as well; and this was what broke her heart again upon the instant. It was as if he had been resurrected in her mind. She *remembered* his goodness, all in a flash, as if she in herself had been too petty to retain a knowledge of the height and depth of his spirit and character, and must be taught it always by the constant sight of him. He was too good a man to punish her for her errors by repelling her notice with haughtiness. Indeed, he was too good a man for any sort of falseness or pride. How could she have imagined he would scorn her, even in some unspoken fashion? He was *Daniel.* He could never have done such a thing.

And yet that goodness of his would make this day all the more painful to her—she saw it now. He would be gravely courteous to her; he would scrupulously observe every article of good manners with respect to her. And that would be worse, far worse, than if he had displayed anger toward her; for his kindness would only teach her once again what she had thrown away.

Like the self-inflicted blow of a penitent, too, came the thought that he was beautiful. She could not conceive how she had ever, in those times of their previous estrangement, thought him ugly or even anything less than the finest creature to look upon that God had ever made. Indeed, in the popular phrase, he looked veritably like a god to her. Thus would a god stand before all, a human god, radiating calmness and power, goodness and beauty. In the days when she had a quarrel to keep with him, she had made herself as beautiful as possible to punish him; but now she felt that all that beauty had been hollow, because it had been built on an error and put to the purposes of an error, while his entire being had always been built on truth and put to the purposes of truth. And truth is inherently beautiful, beautiful from the inside out.

This realization was devastating. It was as if she could have no beauty unless it were reflected from him; as if, unless she borrowed his truth, she could have no truth herself and so no true beauty.

She took her place along with the rest of the bridal party; the ceremony proceeded. She, Elissa, neither saw nor heard any of it. Even that awful moment when the congregation was commanded to tell whether there was any reason why Charles and Louisa ought not to be wed passed altogether unnoticed by her. It seemed to her that there were no other people in that little church but her and Daniel. Yes, there were some ghostlike forms here, and a vague resonance in her mind of words they were saying; but what were they, compared to the reality of her own breathing body, and that of that one man who was once again close to her, and perhaps for the last time?

Thus she remained, in a world of her own, for what seemed a dozen hours, full seven hundred and twenty minutes, raised as the last tedious extension upon an age that had endured since the furthest beginning of time.

Then the service was complete. She rose, mechanically, aware that she ought to accompany Louisa as she went to sign the registry; and as she went, Daniel fell in beside her.

If, before then, time had spun itself along with infinite slowness, like the wheel of an overturned cart spinning and spinning slower and slower to no purpose, now it ran like bright water through her fingers—through her bleeding fingers, and now time was stained scarlet with her life, for it seemed to be carrying away her life as it ran. The registry was signed; the wedding party had left the church and were standing before it. It was as if she could not think fast enough to follow the movement of time, as if she only knew what was transpiring after it was past. It occurred to her that this was how the aged must feel as they viewed the actions of the young accelerating into incomprehensibility.

Daniel took Louisa by the hand; he smiled on her with all the power of his generosity and gentleness of character; and he said, "You know you have my very best wishes, Mrs. Wyatt. I shall not be able to join you at breakfast—"

Here both Charles and Louisa protested, but in vain. Daniel bowed to Louisa gravely, and continued: "I regret it must be so. To stay would be—impossible. But I shall be at Lakeholm by the end of this day, and I look forward to seeing you there at your earliest opportunity. Perhaps you can stop there on your bridal tour? Either tomorrow, and for as long as it pleases you, or at the end of your journey?"

"We most certainly shall!" responded Charles. "We shall be with you for dinner tomorrow, Daniel. But can you not stay? Can you not stay for an hour or two? This is too much—to leave now, after I have not seen you for so very long—and on my wedding day!"

"So it must be," said Daniel, in that quiet tone he used, the tone that could not be denied; and indeed in his case, Elissa knew, the more quietly he spoke, the more confirmed he was in any decision. "I must go," he said, "but you have goodly company to entertain you; I do not fear you shall lack for that, nor do I think that if you were without it my company would make up for its absence. No, I must go, and at once.—God bless you both." And he embraced Charles, showing great warmth and affection in that act. One of the two cousins emitted a sound like a stifled sob; and Elissa was not at all sure that it was not Daniel.

Then he broke off. His expression was now reserved and calm, and yet there was a peculiar urgency about his motions. He nodded one final time and turned away. The other well-wishers crowded in upon the bridal pair, who must then pay them attention, whether they wanted to or not.

But Elissa, again, saw nothing of them. She saw only Daniel walking away. He was already a dozen, two dozen, three dozen feet from her, and still she felt as if she were in some evil dream, unable to move.

Then she broke free of the inertia that had bound her and hurried after him.

She saw which carriage was his—it was one of those hired for the occasion—by the sudden attention the coachman and the footman paid to him when he approached it; the footman opened the door smartly, and the coachman, already sitting on his seat, gave a nervous little jerk of the reins. Daniel had reached the door and had even put one hand forth upon the doorframe to climb into it when she caught up with him.

"Mr. Newsome," she said.

His back was turned to her when she spoke. She saw him freeze, as a man does when he hears some dreadful animal behind him that he had hoped to have escaped; and the sight of that consciousness in him hurt her and humbled her yet again.

But this was her great chance; she would not let it pass, no matter how much she must abase herself to make use of it.

He turned slowly about.

"Madam?" he said. Then it seemed that he felt this title was too cold and formidable; or perhaps the sight of her softened him somehow; for he amended his greeting to: "Miss Wyatt?" This too, must have seemed too dry; for he added: "Yes. How may I be honored to serve you?"

She plunged ahead; and now that the moment had come, she was relieved to find that her voice was quite firm and audible: "Did you ever, sir, receive a letter from me when you were in Madeira?" This was the critical question; and if he answered yes, she had only to make her best apologies and withdraw.

But instead he said, with evident surprise: "From you, Miss Wyatt? No, I did not."

"I did send you a letter, in two copies by two separate means, as I considered the matter very important and very urgent. I sent one by the regular mails, and one under cover of a letter from Charles, via your manager at Lakeholm, Mr. Curtis."

He did not speak for a moment; his expression was inscrutable, but if anything he seemed somewhat irritated by this news.

Then he said, in a tone that seemed cool to her ears: "I cannot say what happened to your letters. I regret to report that I did not receive either of them. I do know that within the last year one of the mail ships to Madeira was closely pursued by the French, and the crew sank the mails, as is their duty when capture threatens. Other pieces of important correspondence went missing at that time, I know that. Perhaps your letter was among them. As for Mr. Curtis, he is notorious for holding back personal letters; he thinks them of little account, and though I have reprimanded him for it, I receive so few such things in general when I am away that I do not think the lesson has been brought to stick with him."

He paused again. He was clearly waiting for her to make the next move.

Her hand went to the button on the panel of her dress; and she thanked God that she did not fumble at it, but undid it and removed the letter from its hiding place smoothly. He stared in considerable surprise at this performance—she felt renewed chagrin as she thought how it must be to see a lady undo a button, as if she were undressing, and draw a bit of paper out of a hidden pocket beneath her bosom. She had not thought of that appearance when she came up with this clever idea! But she persisted; she held out the letter to him.

"Here is a third exact copy of that letter, sir," she said. "If you would do me the favor and honor of reading it, I should be forever in your debt."

He stared at the letter and did not move. She could not understand this, and it frightened her.

"I *beg* you, sir," she said, in a softer tone.

Now he raised his eyes to hers. Whether he could read there her regret and humility, she did not know; but now suddenly he moved, and took the letter from her, and he spoke and said, "Of course, Miss Wyatt."

He put the letter inside his coat.

"Is that all you would require of me?" he asked then.

The question almost overturned her intellect. *Require of you!* she thought. *If I could require anything of you, the first would be—take me with you! Or stay, stay until I may explain everything!*

And inspired by this thought, she said, "Will you not stay to the wedding breakfast, sir?"

He looked confused; very confused. Clearly, this was the last thing he had expected her to say. But for the very reason he was unsure, it seemed, he adhered to what he had previously decided. "No," he said. "I may not. It is impossible. I thank you for your urging me to do so, however."

He made a motion to go. She saw that he was leaving indeed, and that she could not stop him. And so she curtsied to him, lowering her eyes as well as her body; and when she looked again into his eyes, she saw that he was surprised and struck by the respect she had shown.

"Madam," he said again. He bowed to her.

Then he mounted into the carriage. He sat back out of her sight, facing forward. She heard his voice calling to the coachman: "Drive on!"

The footman sprang to his post; in a moment the carriage was underway; in less than half a minute it had wound out of sight on the country lane.

❦ 24 ❦

The Wedding Feast

When thou art bidden to the wedding, go and sit down in
the lowest place; that when he that bade thee cometh, he
may say unto thee, Friend, go up higher.

—Luke 14:10

What was she to think?

That was Elissa's question to herself as she
returned with the wedding party to Ryderly Hall
for the wedding breakfast. Daniel was at this moment in
possession of her letter, that was all she really knew. But he
might wait until the carriage was passing through the fields
and then tear it to pieces unopened and strew those scraps
from the window. He might leave it there in his pocket,
unwilling to read it and mar the day, and he might eventually forget it. Perhaps his servant might find it in a week and
draw it to his attention again; and he might throw it in the
fire still unread. *A woman, now,* she told herself, *a woman
could not have restrained herself from reading such a letter; but a
man, and especially a man who has felt himself spurned, might
take relish in doing so.* And then she remembered how she had
once shredded and another time rejected the written appeals
that he had made to her, and she shuddered.

Or he might read it immediately, and understand her
apology, but not be able to overcome the pain she had
inflicted on him. His reading of the letter guaranteed

nothing. She might in a week receive a gracious note from him, thanking her for her communication, and expressing vague good wishes for her health. That might be the end of it—of everything.

Perhaps he would make such an answer because he had married already. There was no telling if he had, and there was no asking Charles if his cousin, in the short time they had been together at the church this morning, had said anything to that effect—her doing so would be too embarrassing, too improper.

No, there was only waiting left to her; waiting and hoping that he would read that letter and find it in his heart to come back to her.

The breakfast proceeded as such meals commonly did. At first it was somewhat somber in the aftermath of the emotions the ceremony had evoked, and—what was probably more telling—because some of the guests were still recovering from a lack of sleep or from the previous night's celebrating. But after this initial sobriety, the party gradually grew more merry. There was in that era no taboo against strong drink at any time of day, and the good wine Daniel had sent began to flow, into glasses and then into throat and belly and blood; and the volume of talk and of laughter began to increase by amounts so slight that the change was not immediately perceptible. But after an hour the great room of Ryderly Hall gave back every voice relentlessly; and Elissa began to feel out of touch with her own thoughts, as if she could not hear them.

She had one cup of tea, and then another. Though Louisa pressed a glass of wine upon her, saying it was from Daniel, and she took it from her friend with a smile, she only put it aside.

Yes, the tea kept her wakeful, but to what purpose? Perhaps she would have done better, she thought, to have sipped the wine and dulled her senses; but she wanted her mind to be as lucid as possible so that she could think clearly about Daniel. And he was all she could think of, even though she knew not what to think about him.

Eventually the tea had its side-effect, and she was compelled by nature to leave her seat; and on her way back to the great room afterwards, she met Louisa in one of the long hallways.

Her friend was flushed pink with happiness—and perhaps with the good wine as well; but only with a little, for she was too sensible to have more than half a glass. When she saw Elissa coming toward her, she bent her course so that they virtually collided; and she seized upon Elissa, embraced her and leaned on her with a happy little laugh. It was one of those moments, rare on that morning, in which Elissa really forgot her own troubles and remembered her friend's joy.

"You are my *sister* now," said Louisa in her ear, still leaning against Elissa, and letting her friend hold her upright.

Elissa gave a short laugh. "I suppose I am," she replied. "How odd that I never *really* thought of that until now!"

"It is not odd at all," said Louisa. "You have had your thoughts fixed on *other* matters—I understand, my dear; truly I do."

"If I have neglected you, my dear friend," said Elissa with a sudden pang of guilt, "I am very sorry."

"There is no need to be," said Louisa. She stood straight again and made as if she would walk on, but she did not release Elissa's arm, and so came to a halt after taking a single step. And Elissa, attempting to move onward in the opposite direction, was restrained from doing so.

"You are behaving rather strangely, dear," said Elissa.

Louisa smiled. "Am I?" she said. "If so, it is only because I have a secret, and I cannot decide whether to tell you or to let you find it out for yourself."

"Well, of course *I* think you would do better to tell me."

"Of course you do," said Louisa, "and so I shall." Then she leaned toward Elissa again, bringing her mouth close to Elissa's ear.

"He has come after all," she said in a whisper. *"He has come; in the end he has come, as we knew he would."*

Before Elissa knew what she was doing, she had seized Louisa by both arms; and her first words were "Who? Who has come?"

But the question needed no answer. It was purely rhetorical, if impetuosity can be said to have a rhetoric.

"Why?" Elissa asked then. "Why has he come? Did he say why he changed his mind?"

"I do not know, my dear," said Louisa, smiling mischievously, and making a show of shaking her head gravely. "All I know is that he said before that it was impossible for him to *stay;* and now it seems that it is *even more* impossible for him to *stay away.*" And she laughed affectionately, and drew her arms free, and gave Elissa a little push down the hall.

And nothing loath, Elissa went, and hastily—and then she thought that perhaps she went too hastily. Before she reached the door, by exercising all her will, she had achieved some control over herself. She paused for a moment before she stepped forth into the line of sight that would show her if he was present; she caught her breath; and then slowly she went into the room.

It was true: he was there. John had yielded his own seat by Charles (most likely in order to go quiz the rector about his late roses), and Daniel was now sitting by Charles, on what would be the far side of the wedding couple from her seat. He and Charles were conversing, affably as always; and yet Daniel still had that air of coolness, of reserve about him.

When she returned to her seat, both the gentlemen rose from their places, and Charles said to her, "Look who has come after all! Is this not splendid?"

She wished she had anticipated this moment and planned the right answer. The right answer would let Daniel know that she was full of joy and yet still contrite. The wrong answer, however, would appear presumptuous and put him off. And caught between these extremes, she could not say a word, and only curtsied to him, and sat down abruptly, so that they might sit as well; and she was so . . . perhaps *frightened* was the word, frightened of misusing this opportunity, that she could not even smile at him, which would have told him more than any words.

"I say, Daniel," enthused Charles, "I believe you have a way of plucking the very power of speech from these ladies! No sooner did Louisa see you than she ran out of the room without saying a thing; and now Elissa comes back, and she is no more capable of answering a simple question than her friend!"

Elissa felt the heat rush into her cheeks, and Charles saw that he had embarrassed her. He laughed and held out his hand to her, as if to ask her forgiveness; and with a smile— the smile she wished she had smiled at Daniel, and which was now altogether too joyful to be explained by his simple gesture—she took his hand in hers for an instant.

"There, do you see?" said Charles. "The lady is as loving and sweet as ever she was, though she does not speak."

At this Elissa positively had to turn away. The gentlemen sat down again and resumed their conversation; which was maintained mostly on Charles's side. In a few minutes, Louisa resumed her seat, and then she joined Charles in speaking to his cousin.

Very well—Daniel had returned after all. But what good could it do Elissa? She could not speak to him, nor he to her, in this noisy and public gathering; and he merely sat there by Charles, listening to his brother and his new sister fairly *prattle* about this thing and that—for however different they might be in other respects, they both loved to talk. He made no attempt to look past them and meet her eye.

Suddenly her understanding took a new swerve, as drastic and consequential as those of the atoms of Lucretius. *This is all,* she thought, *This is all there will be. This is his way of telling me: "I have read your note and I thank you for it. Let us be civil to one another hereafter. The love between us that once was is gone and can no longer be; but when we meet, let us be decently kind, and say the proper things, and not burden others with the irrevocable and painful change that has come upon us."*

Then she thought: *Is that the way he feels? Can it be? Has he so easily rid himself of the last sparks of the fire of affection that were left after I stamped out that blaze so determinedly? Is there nothing to make him hope, to make him desire, as I hope, as I desire?*

Sometimes, as she attempted to swallow this bitter, bitter lozenge of pain, she looked away from the three of them; at other times she looked directly at him, begging him in her thoughts to look at her, even once, to reassure her with just one gaze that all feeling for her was not dead within him.

And on went the feast.

If the wedding service had crawled through time, this meal slept through it. And the feast was worse than the service, because there was noise, endlessly, and only snatches of intelligible conversation, and a constant increase in the false conviviality of drink; there were people to whom at intervals she must be polite, and servants whose offerings she must refuse; and Daniel not eight feet away down the oaken board.

At last the tedium of her torment was broken by Charles, who stood from his seat and called for silence in the hall so that his wife could speak.

"I have a surprise," Louisa said, "a little treat for everyone. My very best friend and Maid of Honor, Miss Elissa Wyatt, has agreed to sing a song this morning."

Elissa looked up in considerable alarm; but on consulting her very distracted memory, she found that she had promised something like this in some reckless moment weeks ago. But she had not thought out how it would put her on display in front of Daniel. She went cold all over; but Louisa took her by the hand and drew her to the side of the great room, where a piano stood ready.

There was a tense, whispered conference when Louisa thrust the sheet music into her hands.

"Oh, dear, why did you not remind me?" said Elissa. "I had forgotten all about this promise!"

"But you know the song," said Louisa. "I know you do. I heard you sing it once at school. You cannot have forgotten it—you sang it so beautifully then. Do not be silly. Everyone is waiting."

And in fact everyone was; so there was nothing to do but summon up the appearance of calm, and sing as well as she could.

The piece was an old bridal song by John Ford:

> Comforts lasting, loves increasing,
> Like soft hours never ceasing;
> Plenty's pleasure, peace complying,
> Without jar, or tongues envying;
> Hearts by holy union wedded,
> More than theirs by custom bedded;
> Fruitful issues; life so graced,
> Not by age to be defaced;
> Budding as the year ensu'th,
> Every spring another youth;
> All what thought can add beside,
> Crown this bridegroom and this bride.

To sing these good wishes for Louisa and Charles should have been a pleasure; but they told her only what she herself might have lost, and without her attempting any such thing, her delivery had a haunting undertone of sorrow, which only made the lyrics richer and more poignant.

The guests, who were merry enough to have applauded the braying of a donkey, were entranced by her singing, and broke into a loud and long applause when she was done, and called for more; but she refused any encore and went resolutely back to her seat.

As she did so, Charles turned suddenly, reaching up his right arm to touch her shoulder in appreciation.

He flinched. Elissa knew it was because of his wound; she had seen him flinch like this many times since he was shot. Louisa, too, who was right beside him, immediately realized what had happened and said, "Have a care for your wound, dearest."

Charles laughed the pain off, but he did as she told him, and faced forward in his seat so as not to twist his torso.

"What wound are you talking about?" asked Daniel with considerable concern.

"Where I was shot, that is all," said Charles. "It hurts like that sometimes when I raise my arm. The surgeon says it will take some time for the pain to go away completely—perhaps a year or two."

"*Shot?* You mean . . . what! Did someone hit you in error when you were out birding?"

Louisa said to Charles, "Daniel does not know about it, dear. You did not write to him about it."

"Ah," said Charles, "of course, that is so. The fact is, I *was* out shooting; but it was not just a few pellets of shot that hit me, old man. That fellow Crustall, who would have come into Aeons' End—he tried to kill me."

Daniel was silent—the horror was plain to read on his face—and Charles blundered on with the story. "I was out shooting on the hill at Aeons' End, you see—not very good shooting there, either, by the way. I shall have to think if anything can be done about it."

Daniel's expression distinctly conveyed his impatience with Charles's digression into the maintenance of good birding grounds, and Charles, seeing it, resumed the story: "We had gone over the top of the hill—it was getting on toward sunset, rather late; it was like that day we shot at Fenestall, do you remember? When that dog got caught in the slough and we had to form a chain to draw him out?"

"Charles," said Daniel, "for once in your life, tell me the pertinent facts without the ornament!"

Charles laughed, and then winced a little. "Yes," he said, "I do wander about in telling a story. But there is not much to tell in this one. This fellow Crustall had been out looking for me with his gun, and we happened across him—"

"Whom do you mean by 'we'? You and Dover?"

"Well, yes, Dover was there, though he was not worth much, as it turned out. Elissa was with me, and it was she who saved me."

"Elissa!" exclaimed Daniel.

Charles made a humorous face and said, "Yes, my dear cousin, the selfsame lady of that name—she whom you see sitting beside me."

Daniel looked at Elissa momentarily as if to confirm that they truly were talking about the same person; but then he turned back to Charles. "And what happened?" he said.

"Well, this fellow Crustall fired a glancing shot that hit me in the side—here. Hurt like the bite of a dog, I can tell you! Like that time I got bitten in Lambing Minor, do you remember?"

"Charles, stay with the story! You were *shot* by this man—did the ball break any of your ribs?"

"We believe it did break the one rib," Louisa put in.

"And?" asked Daniel of his cousin urgently. "What happened then? There you were, standing there on the hill with a piece of lead in your side. Did you simply walk home?"

"Oh, no, I fell down at once. The pain was quite unbearable, I assure you. If it had not been for Elissa, I would be lying there still—only perhaps at a level six feet lower. Dover simply ran away—*he* was quite useless."

And now again Daniel swung his gaze to Elissa. She felt the blood mount into her cheeks, but she stared back at him, still stuck in her anxiety, and thinking to herself, *This may be the last time I ever have the chance to look into his eyes.*

"And what did Miss Wyatt do?" asked Daniel, still looking at her, but obviously speaking to Charles.

"Why, she picked up my gun and shot Crustall—that is all."

Daniel was literally taken aback—he leaned backwards several inches as though he had been pushed—but he did not speak, and he did not take his gaze from Elissa.

"You see, Crustall was reloading," added Charles. "He was planning to come and finish me off. And when her first shot did not stop him, she picked up the gun Dover had thrown down—it was that nice double-barreled shotgun, you know, that I bought off Sam Jones at Oriel—"

"Forget Sam Jones!" snapped Daniel, turning again to his cousin in his frustration. *"What happened then?"*

"Why, she shot him again. That stopped him. Unfortunately, the shot did not kill him, but it put an end to his troubling us any further. He went to gaol and now awaits his interview with the rope. At any rate, Elissa helped me return to the house, and she nursed me till Louisa came."

"And you are all right now? The wound has healed but for this . . . residual pain now and again, when you are careless in how you move?"

"Yes, quite so," said Charles.

There was a rather lengthy silence between the two cousins; and then Charles said, "What is it, Daniel? Have I done something wrong?"

"You? No, no, of course not. Your only sin has been in telling your story in your usual maddening fashion. I am sorry if I seem to act strangely, but you will understand that the idea of someone attempting to murder the cousin who is so dear to me is quite shocking, especially when I learn of it so casually, so . . . accidentally. But now I know that all is well, so the manner of the telling does not matter."

And Charles, instantly reassured, turned the topic to something more pleasant.

If Daniel does not look at me now, Elissa told herself, *I shall know that he means me to forget about him. If he does not give me just one glance to say, "Well done, Elissa," I shall know that he no longer cares for me as I do for him.*

She watched him then for a full five minutes and he made no move to look in her direction again.

However, he did not look anywhere else, either. He seemed to be looking at nothing.

Finally, in a moment when Charles and Louisa had fixed their attention upon one another, Daniel rose and passed behind them. Elissa could not help turning toward him as he approached, and thus she was all attention when he paused for an instant and said, in a voice no one else could have heard, "I shall be in the garden, if you would do me the honor."

Then he walked on without waiting for a reply or even looking at her further.

She felt lightheaded. Her heart was pounding audibly in her ears; she darted a look about to see if anyone had noticed him pause and speak to her; but no one had seen, not even Louisa and Charles.

How long? she thought. *How long ought I to wait? It must not be too long, or he will think I am not coming; and it must not be too soon, or people will guess that we have gone out to be together.* To wait at all seemed an excruciating extension of her torment; but she told herself, *I can wait a little longer. After all, I have waited for him my whole life.*

She compromised on two minutes, and counted the seconds off to herself so slowly and with such power of will that it was probably more like three minutes before she rose and went outside.

The garden at Ryderly, though arguably overregulated, was deep and extensive enough to afford corners where a lady and a gentleman might sit and converse quietly and privately. To do so was of course improper; but that was her last concern at this moment. And in any case, without such little improprieties, private conversation between unmarried men and women in those times would have been impossible.

She discovered Daniel as she had once before, at the end of a path, waiting on a bench. Perhaps he too was struck by the similarity; he looked uncomfortable as he rose and waited for her approach.

She stopped before him. Again, she knew not what to say. It was up to him to speak; she felt so powerfully in the wrong that she thought she must leave it up to him to say whatever he meant to say without her invitation or request.

Now he did not avoid her eyes; instead he looked sharply at her, and yet without ever shedding that grave and quiet strength he had worn like a shield on this day.

"I thank you for so graciously allowing me to speak with you, Miss Wyatt," he said.

This was not a good beginning at all; his manner was too stiff, and her heart sank within her. She had too much to say, and so could say nothing; again she curtsied to him, and again he bowed to her. This frigid little ceremony completed, he made a gesture toward the bench, and she sat down; but he remained standing and commenced to pace about. *What an advantage!* she thought. A man's advantage, according to the custom of the times. She would have liked that—to be able to move and fret off some small part of this intense energy of feeling inside her.

When he began to speak, he quite surprised her with the irrelevancy of his remark; and her heart sank further.

"Of course you know," he said, "that I was slightly acquainted with Miss Bright in Bath."

He looked at her briefly for an affirmation; and having received it, though only in the form of an intensely attentive but otherwise blank look, and through the absence of any denial, he continued: "I formed a good opinion of her then,

I assure you; but still, our acquaintance was so very slight that my estimate of her character could not proceed very far. That is why it meant a great deal to me to read, in my brother's letter, of the larger circumstances surrounding his betrothal."

She could guess at what he meant, but she wanted to hear him say it explicitly. "May I ask of what particular circumstances you speak?" she asked.

He was puzzled by her question. "Why," he said, "I understood in particular from Charles's letter that it was you who discovered the terms of the entail that favored him, and that it was you who persuaded your father to acknowledge him as a son."

"I believe I may claim some credit for that, yes."

She was unsure whether or not he smiled for an instant at this remark, but there was no doubt that he shook his head. "No one could imagine," he said, "that the credit for this deed belongs to anyone other than Miss Elissa Wyatt. No other person but Miss Elissa Wyatt is so clear-sighted as to have seen that solution to my cousin's difficulties, or so bold and certain in her love and action as to attempt it, or so competent as to bring it to a successful conclusion."

This was deeply pleasing to her, but her conscience pricked her; and though she did not make a full confession of her motives, she managed to say: "But throughout, I felt I was doing only what ought by rights to be done. Charles *is* my father's son; he *ought* by right to inherit Aeons' End."

"But you mistake my point."

"Indeed, I believe I do, sir. Please explain it to me."

"Why, I have done so already. The difficulty is that you, in your modesty, have not heard me. I said that *it was you* who assisted him toward his marriage."

"And I have allowed as much. But as I have said, I was only doing what was right."

He paused in his pacing; he definitely smiled; he almost laughed. "That fact—that you were only doing what was right—does not detract from what we owe you; for if you were only doing what was right, then you deserve the more credit. You were not acting out of a selfish motive, but out of a moral one. As a general rule, the world does not acknowledge and repay those who act by the rule of rightness rather than by the dictates of self-interest; but that only means that it is the more incumbent upon me, upon all who love Charles, to express our gratitude."

Here she offered at least a partial confession: "I cannot say, sir, that I acted *only* unselfishly."

He seemed further amused, and made this observation: "But only a moment ago you claimed that you acted *only* out of an abstract sense of what was right. So it seems that now you retract what you previously said."

"I am afraid, sir, that by imputing a purity of goodness to me that I do not deserve, you have forced me to admit that my motives were mixed."

He said nothing further on that point, but went on: "But there was more than that in Charles's letters to me. He seems to think that he succeeded in winning his bride only because he had your recommendation and support."

"That is not so, either; when I first returned to Bath after Louisa had met him, she had fallen deeply, even instantly, in love with him."

"But you could have cast a rope down to her in that well of love into which she had tumbled; you could have created in her a resolve to reject him, and steadied her in that rejection, if you had wished to do so."

"But, sir, I cannot take credit, again, for following my own bent. I saw the advantages of the match for both of them."

"Yes; it is my very definite impression that Louisa is a good person—intelligent, capable, and yet sweet- and even-tempered; a very rare human being."

"Indeed, she is so. I am happy to confirm it from long acquaintance."

"Of course," he added, stealing a glance at her, "my point is—my point all along has been—that she is *a friend of yours,* of Miss Elissa Wyatt's; and that is all the recommendation I need. That is why the larger circumstances of which I spoke confirmed me in my understanding that Louisa Bright was a person worthy of the cousin who has been so dear to me all my life. If you approve her, she must be worthy."

Whether this had indeed been his point all along, or a fresh turn he was making in the conversation, it was in either case very pleasing to hear. She would have said something to keep his remarks tending in that direction, but he went on: "And as her friend, you have worked on her behalf, and on behalf of Charles, to make their marriage not only possible but prudent, and, we can hope, successful for each. He brings his unflagging good humor, his absolute lack of moodiness, which is something a woman does not often find in a man; and he brings his newfound home, his newfound family, father, sisters. She brings a matching good cheer and, as I hear from him, a good head for overseeing the use of their mutual wealth, which is a responsibility he would otherwise entrust to those who might bilk him of all he has. She brings as well a religious seriousness which—though not as admirable as your own—will yet go far to repairing a fault in Charles that I myself have never been able to remedy."

Elissa thought that this was an overly generous estimate of Louisa's religiousness, but she was not about to correct it. To rationalize this omission, she told herself that perhaps Louisa would *become* more serious in this respect as time went by.

During the brief moment when she was struggling with this little mistake of his, he became silent, looking with an abstract gaze across the garden. It now struck her that it was all well and good that his tenor so far had been approbatory, but she expected he would now issue some great adversative; she felt an agony to read his mind, but her mental effort to that purpose was in vain; and he left her in silence to feel the pain of that failure for another long minute.

"No," he went on then, "I say you have managed all this for the best of all, and—I do not speak for anyone else, though I know I could include all our families; I speak only for myself—I am deeply grateful to you for it, humbly grateful to you for it. Not only could I not have carried off such a plan—not have dared to—I could never have conceived of it."

She spoke up at once. "I am pleased, sir," she said, "to have pleased you by it; for—I shall confess it—that was no small part of the selfish intention of which I have spoken."

This remark won her the gift of a glance from him, but she could not read it. He apparently had a mental outline of the remarks he meant to make, and he hewed close to it.

"So much for Charles's letters," he said. "If you will bear with me, I shall ask you further about the one you gave me today."

She could not frame an answer; her mouth seemed suddenly too dry. Fortunately, he did not wait for one.

"In your letter," he said, "you wrote of being a fool for not understanding certain circumstances."

"I did," she managed to say.

"Let me understand you, Miss Wyatt."

In a tense voice, almost too soft to be heard, she said, "Instruct me, sir, in which points I ought to explain, and I shall address them most willingly."

Thus urged, thus invited, thus even begged, what did he do? He seemed puzzled; his eyes roved over the garden unseeingly. She might almost imagine she heard audibly the tumult of thoughts and feelings in him, but she knew not what that agitation meant.

Finally he said, as if forcing himself to a brutal act: "The date on the letter you enclosed—I believe it was only two days after our conversation in Bath. Is that the day on which you became aware of the reason I called a halt to your sister's wedding?"

"I learned the reason late on the day before that date, sir, from my sister. It took me quite some time to assemble my thoughts enough to compose the letter."

She could see his jaw tighten, and she guessed that it was with self-reproach.

"That day—the day you wrote the letter—was the day I made up my mind to return to Madeira," he said.

This coincidence was no great surprise to her, but it seemed to be affecting him deeply.

"If only!" he murmured to himself.

The words made her flinch, but she could not judge from them to what they referred. Was it to a general regret, or to a more specific one—such as an engagement or marriage into which he had entered?

They remained for several minutes without speaking. He seemed to be in some other world, but she was very much in this one, hanging on every moment, waiting for him to say some word more, fearing he would not, that he would simply walk away. She did not watch him throughout, though from time to time she darted a look at him, half hoping he would notice it and so return it; and again she did not dare address him first.

At length he spoke, but it was as though he were speaking to himself, even though he was, in actual fact, addressing her. "So you were in ignorance of my motives from the time of the wedding until after our conversation—until the day after our final conversation in Bath. All that time! Why, it must have been months—it was full four months!"

She leapt at the opening this afforded her to press for her exoneration. "Yes, all that time," she said. "All that time I was blind to the truth, though I felt the pain of it and knew nothing of the cause. All that time, I was blind and a fool— as I said."

"A fool!" he said, in a tone of abject disagreement, dismissing the mere idea.

"What other name do I deserve?"

"You were no fool," he said. "You of all people are the last who shall ever deserve that title."

"But I am," she insisted, feeling stupid for saying so, but unable to stop herself.

"Then I need to tell you that I do not see you as such. If you were not told why I acted as I did, there was no way you could have known, no way you could have guessed the reason I undertook that act. Who could guessed at the connection between my cousin and your sister? It was bizarre, it was wildly improbable; and yet it was so."

Then he said again: "Four months!"

Pain passed over his face as he said this; for that moment he looked almost haggard. And, with agonized emphasis, he added: *"What you must have thought of me!"*

"You *know* what I thought of you," said Elissa in the grimmest contrition. "I did not stint to tell you at the very first opportunity, the first moment I had in private with you."

He closed his eyes in pain at the recollection.

If leaping into oblivion myself, she thought, speaking to him with her thoughts, *could bring your pain into oblivion as well, I would do it!*

It was an extravagant thought; but so the thoughts of lovers are.

"Yes," he said, "you did tell me what you thought of me, what you felt toward me. I understand it now. I could not understand all it at the time; I was sure that you must have known why that wedding with Merry was broken off, why it must be broken off."

She replied: "Merry was too . . . I might almost say *too bewildered* to tell me. She did not know how to think about what she learned that day."

"Yes, yes, Charles was the same way. It was as if I had confronted him with a problem in higher mathematics and told him he must solve it before he went on living. He simply could not understand how to think of it. I did not understand him at first; but gradually I came to see that the only way for him to go on was to forget what had happened—forget, as only he can."

"He and Merry," said Elissa.

"Thank God if so it is for her, too. May she live to have the happiness her innocence deserves."

Then he ceased speaking again; and after a minute, when she could not bear the silence between them, she said: "I think that the last time we spoke on this subject, we made the mistake of indiscriminately mingling various aspects of it together—I spoke of one subject, and you thought I meant another; and we did so over and over, to the utter confounding of all communication."

"Doubtless that was so."

"Well, then, now I urge you to leave aside what I knew or did not know about what *you* did. Let me speak on another head—on the subject of what *I* did, before their attempted wedding. I told you of this in Bath: I was the reason of their coming together after you had worked so hard and successfully to separate them—and to separate them without inflicting on them the anguish of their ever knowing their true connection. That error is one I shall never outlive."

"It was no error at all," he said with a firmness and evenness of tone that sent a thrill through her. "I would have done just as you did had I been in your situation. And what is more, I would have thought it a noble act."

"But you *were* noble throughout, though it cost you bitterly, and I was never noble, only driven by my love for my sister and for my own will. If I had not meddled—if I had left well enough alone—matters would have come to their safe and proper outcome without anyone paying the cost—your cousin, or my sister, or my father—or you."

He seemed stirred by what he saw as something wrong in her words. "When a good act reveals a concealed sin of long ago," he said, "is that the fault of those who do the good, or is it the fault of the sinners? I cannot think that your acting in love as you did can be an ill thing. It was not *reckless;* on the contrary, it was well and even nicely reckoned and reasoned. I sought to cover over the past, and I failed through your good motives—and, I might add, through your superior skill in *managing* our two beloved but rather flighty younger relations. You outflanked me quite easily. I only felt like a fool for thinking I had escaped so readily from the inconvenience to my feelings that did inevitably come about. By that, I mean the pain that came to me from forcing my cousin and your sister to confront the moral error of the parent they shared."

"But I *doubted* you," she said. "I should have trusted that you would always do right, even if I did not understand how what you were doing could possibly be so."

"Nay, *I* should have trusted *you,*" he said. "I should have called you into the vestry on that morning of the wedding, with Charles and Merry and your father, and told you what I knew, told you from the beginning. But as I explained to them all on that day, the secret my aunt had confided to me was not mine to disclose; she had specifically enjoined upon me that I tell no one if I could find a way to avoid doing so. Still, I assumed *they* would tell you, they *must* tell you, and particularly Merry, whose heart was always open to you. It was a further error in me to make that assumption. But as we have said already, we overestimated their ability to grapple with the truth and master it. We thought they were as we are, preferring to know what must be known, and not to shrink from it."

She began to speak, but he interrupted her, something he had never done in all her acquaintance with him; but such now was his determination toward confession that he could not stop himself.

"Nay," he said, "I should have formed a far better plan even than that, and I have thought so, over and over, since the very day of that would-be wedding."

"What better plan could there have been, given the circumstances?"

"Only this: I should have insisted upon an exception to my aunt's stipulations. I should returned at once to Aeons' End the moment I knew the truth. I should have sought you out in private and told you the whole story; and with your assistance—I say, between the two of us, we could have formed a plan for saving my cousin and your sister from the pain and embarrassment that instead resulted from my reticence toward you. If I had acted toward you as if you were then what I felt you to be—*my wife,* or at the very least, my betrothed—then all would have been well. But I did not do so, not only because of my promise to my aunt, but because . . . because I was afraid you would be disgusted with me when you learned the truth, that you would feel a union between us to be impossible. And my fear of your rejection became an established fact when you rejected me. It is as the apostle says: I ought to have 'renounced the hidden things of dishonesty' and not have 'walked in craftiness.'"

"You wrong yourself! You wrong yourself, sir!" she said.

He seemed somewhat surprised by the passion behind this protest; again he seemed confused. "Forgive me, madam," he said, "if I do not seem logical. My thoughts, my understanding, my feelings have undergone such a revolution in the last few hours that I scarcely know what I am saying."

If she had dared form hopes on the basis of this impulsive utterance, they would have instantly been undercut; for now he said, "No, no: my feelings have undergone no such a revolution, no such change. They are as they were when I awoke this morning."

He was very abruptly silent; he turned away in a motion she understood to be remorse at having said too much. It seemed to her the worst possible halting place: she dared not make any assumption about what his feelings were that morning, or at any time since their conversation in Bath.

She herself was now in the greatest agony she had felt in this entire conversation, and she could not so much as look at him. After a minute of this, she forced herself to say something to put an end to the silence: "Nay, you will not turn me aside from my self-reproach by taking the blame on yourself. I knew you were good, and yet somehow I contrived to think you bad."

"I think not," he said. "I think in your heart you went on knowing that I was not as bad as circumstances made me appear. Otherwise you could not forgive me as you have."

"Forgive you! What have you done that needs my forgiveness? My father asked that very question of me on the day of the wedding, but I did not understand him. It is myself I struggle to forgive.—Do you remember what you said in that hour when you saved me on the river in Deepclough?"

He looked blank and uncertain. "What I said?" he asked.

She had no doubt he remembered perfectly well what he had *done*—how he had held her and kissed her—even if the words she alluded to now escaped his memory. She plunged on: "I was holding on to the lash end of the whip as you drew me to shore; and as I came near the bank I was tempted to jump out before it would have been safe to do so. But you told me not to; you said, 'The whip will save you, but the leap will not.' Do you remember?"

He now looked only puzzled. "It seems like something I might have said at that moment," he allowed.

She went on: "Call me a symbolical fool, if you will, but those words have haunted me ever since, until what has happened between us gave them meaning. The whip is the cutting end, do you see, the painful end of truth. If I had held to it throughout, I would never have betrayed you. Instead I jumped—to the wrong conclusion."

He was silent for a moment; then he said, "That is what we all do."

"Yes, we are not willing to catch and hold the lash of truth! We are not willing to cling to what we know in our inmost hearts to be true, though we live by that truth every day, as we *must*, because there is no other way to live, because the truth is the reality of the universe. Instead we jump too soon to what we think is salvation, and we drown between ship and shore."

"Yes," he said. "So it is. Having faith, acting on it, bearing ourselves onwards as we know is right—we *do* fail in that."

He looked around at the garden. As he did so, the tension in his expression melted away for a moment, and he smiled; though he seemed a little sad, too, as if remembering happier times; which apparently was the case, for he said, "This garden—any garden—must now put me in mind of your father's wonderful garden, though any other garden is, and necessarily must be, inferior to his own creation. But the fragrance even of these late roses here puts me in mind of the fragrance of the roses there; and so it puts me in mind of our days in that place. And I daresay, the fragrance of my memories outdoes the fragrance of all earthly roses; it is the fragrance of the very *rosa mundi*, the rose of the universe, with all its bloom and thorn. Its roots are in the heart of God. That is what we forget, time and time again: that both the blossom and the thorn of our lives spring from the heart of God, from God's love for us. Here we are, debating which of us is to blame for what has happened; but ultimately it all comes out of the heart of God, and tends towards God's purposes. Which are love and nothing else."

Then he seemed to shake off his musings. He looked at her now; and now his gaze was not reserved or glancing, but again straight and piercing; and she remembered how he always used to look at her in those days, and the same thrill, the *bliss*, went through her.

He said, "Forgive my directness, but there is one point I must pursue further."

Her heart was thumping, yet over its roar in her ears she managed to frame a response: "Please do, sir."

"Your generous treatment of my cousin," he said, "tells me that you do not find the Newsomes so utterly repugnant as I thought." And then he added, like a man on trial adducing one more argument in favor of his acquittal: "And Charles told me in his letter. . . he told me that you do in fact care for me and do not abhor me for . . . for what I am to you—that is, a relation, through the affinity wrought by a moral error. We are, in the eyes of the law, first cousins, because you are half-sister to my first cousin. That in itself is . . . not dreadful. It is the manner in which you and I *became* cousins—that is what I long believed to be the cause of your evident disgust for me; and it may still operate upon you, still disgust you and make you wish never to see me again."

He had carried off this much of his query coolly, but here his voice broke, and he had to pause a moment to regain his composure. Then he went on, this time evincing considerable emotion.

"So do tell me," he said, "if you feel any such disgust; and if you do, do forgive me for keeping you away from the wedding breakfast. I would never have done so if I had not been urged to it by the appearance of a possible presentiment in my favor on your part."

She was even more stupefied and speechless than she had yet been on this day. How much could she say? What was he prepared to hear? That she considered him a friend—or that she considered him her beloved in this world?

For too long, though probably it was only seconds, she sat without uttering a word; and he looked increasingly uneasy, and as if he was about to bow in apology and flee. Finally, to forestall this, at all costs, she said the first words that tumbled out of her mind.

"How could you *ever* think that?" she said.

He looked more uneasy still. "Think . . . *what* in particular, Miss Wyatt?"

She saw that he might well think she meant *think that I care for you.* She uttered a hasty clarification: "Why, think that I found it unpleasant to be with you—think that you disgusted me!"

He seemed surprised by the question; he cast his gaze here and there, as if seeking the answer in thin air, in the order of the garden.

"Why," he said, "it was the way you so decidedly rejected me on those occasions when I saw you after the wedding—to say nothing of what you said to me when I . . . when I spoke to you by the river in Bath. I believe you yourself said as much at the time—or agreed to as much when I said I understood you to have those feelings; I mean, that you found my presence unwelcome, as a reminder of the relation in which I stood to you, as the cousin of your half-brother."

"And you believed that?"

"I could all too readily believe it. Being related to a man through sin is hardly a commendation to a lady's feelings for him."

"But I said what I did only because I was laboring under such a terrible mistake, sir, as I have told you—told you several times on this very morning. Is there no way I can say it so that you believe me?"

And here a tear mounted up over the lower lid of one of her eyes, and ran down her cheek, not quickly, but lingeringly, as if saying to him, *I dare you not to see the evidence I offer, sir, that you are loved.* And he watched the progress of that tear with a kind of amazement and fascination and regret, as if he wanted nothing in the world more than to brush it away, but could not believe in its existence enough to dare to do so.

Yet still pressing on, he said: "But my fear still is that the very thought of our strange relationship disgusts you—the very sight of me, my presence, is a reminder to you of that ugliness; and though I am grateful that you do not think as ill of me as once you did, I do not presume to imagine that you have set aside all the distaste for me that once you so clearly felt."

Another tear mounted up and ran forth, from Elissa's other eye, and another from the first; and they, too, began their slow course down her cheeks, and he stared at them and at her.

And finally she broke—she spoke without reserve.

"But have I not," she said, "evinced to you with every action I have taken that I have no such distaste? Nay, I shall convict you out of your own mouth: Did I not labor mightily to bring your cousin into his inheritance at Aeons' End—as you say? Have I not argued like a Portia in the scornful face of the law, to win him what could rightfully belong only to him? Have I not welcomed him with open arms into my ancestral home, and blessed his renewed companionship with my father? Did I not bless my closest friend when she came to me and told me she was to marry him? And when his murderer shot him down, was I not the one who took up a deadly weapon to defend him—using these very hands you see before you, far more familiar though they are to instruments of music than to instruments of violence? Were these actions, oh, dear, *dear* man, were these the actions of one who finds you *distasteful?* Every assistance I ever gave Charles, for all he deserved it, I confess was done in some good part as a banner to you, emblazoned with the sign of my love, and signaling to you that my love for you had never been lost or vanquished, no matter how long I fought the invisible demons of error and confusion. Call me conniving if you will, but was there any other way I had to declare to you that I had been mistaken, and now knew it? Was there any other way to conjure you back from Madeira? And if there had been any other way to bind you more securely into my life—if I had discovered it, I would have made use of it! I shamelessly confess it! Any *good* thing that I could have done, I would have done! Oh, Daniel—how, in the face of all this, could you doubt that I love you, love you still, love you as I always did, love you more than ever?"

He was swaying on his feet as if he were about to simply fall over.

"I think," he said, in a hoarse voice, "that you forget the effect your virtue has on others! The idea that you would be disgusted by me as a reminder of . . . of the sin of others—the idea was utterly credible to me!"

"What virtue that is truly virtue would ever despise love, my dearest?" she said. "I reject this as a reason. This cannot be the reason you were uncertain of me! Were you not, rather, uncertain of yourself? Were you not disgusted with me, because of the relationship in which I stand to you?"

"Never!" he cried instantly.

And then, as if casting about for a final explanation, he said, in a hoarse voice, "I think, Elissa, that you underestimate the power of your own eloquence! That I stand before you today and speak these words is a miracle, considering what you said to me in Bath!"

She burst quite openly into tears now, and she tilted her head back, and closed her eyes, and said, in a voice as hoarse as his own: "Yes, yes, *my eloquence!* How great it became, when I struck the one I most love, to hurt him! May God forbid such eloquence in me for the rest of my life! Better I should cut out my own tongue at once than let it cut *your* heart ever again!"

His reserve—or whatever was left of it—now broke as hers had, and he came to her and drew her up and held her to him. He spoke; his voice was choked, but she understood him: "Then you *will* marry me, Elissa?"

Between the tightness of his embrace and her own emotion, she almost could not speak; but she gasped out, "With all my heart."

He gave a sound between a sob and a groan; and she put her head against his shoulder and buried her face against his neck, and they gripped one another tightly.

"But," she said then, in a whisper.

"What? What is it, dearest?" he said.

"You are not married? You did not marry in Madeira?"

"No," he said.

"Are you sure?"

He laughed softly. "My love," he said, "I will prove it to you. I shall demonstrate it with logical precision!—Were you there, in Madeira?"

She was confused by the question, so he repeated it: "Were you?" he said. "My love, was Elissa Wyatt there in Madeira when I was there?"

"No—no, I was not. But someone else was there, I think. Someone else who, if she had any sense in her head or fire in heart, would have been glad to marry you."

"Perhaps there was someone there of that ilk. And perhaps she was forward in letting me know of her willingness. But the point is that *you* were not there. And that means I did not marry when I was in Madeira. Because once I met Elissa Wyatt, I could never have married anyone else. Since I first met her, I have awoken every morning loving her more than the day before. Even when she drove me away from her in despair, I have loved her not one bit the less. Without her, I was doomed to be alone for all time, because I loved her and never ceased to be true to her. No, I have not changed— not in all the time I have known her.—No, dearest: you must never fear about what happened in Madeira. I had descended to hell; I was a man already dead. I was waiting to be resurrected, though I had no hope of it. I never loved anyone there; I thought only of returning to you."

She groaned in anguish or joy, or both together.

He must have thought she was not going to be able to stand anymore; he made her sit on the bench, and then sat down beside her and held her in his arms; and then he kissed her, and she kissed him. That kiss—a sweet, stinging kiss it was, like the touch of the lash of truth again, but a sweet touch, a mild touch, a burden bearable because both material and unworldly, both physical and spiritual.

"We have come back," he said then.

"What do you mean, dearest?"

"Back to where we were that summer, back to those days in the garden."

"Yes!" she said. "We are back here again, and we can go on from here as we could not then. But make me one promise."

"As many as you like."

"Never speak to me, or let me speak, of that day by the river in Bath."

He laughed a little. "It is already dear to me," he said.

"Oh, Daniel! How can you say that? Even in jest!"

"I am not jesting. I am already arrived at that wonderful retrospect I shall have on my deathbed, where I see my life as valuable only for the hours that I spent with you. And that was one of them. What else will our misunderstanding do, but convince us to be certain of one another, and not to leap to conclusions—or to confusions? I think we will be gentler with one another, dearest, because of all that we have been through. We have been allowed a glimpse of how terrible life would be if we lost one another, and so we shall never do or say anything that would put our love at risk."

"I do believe it," she said.

They looked at one another, and it was true: they had never truly lost one another; for there was the Daniel she had loved then, the Daniel who had been there always, throughout, though she could not see him for her own mistakes; and here was the Elissa he had loved, the Elissa who had loved him even when the fog of error was over her and she could not see the Daniel she loved.

"Our love has won through," he said.

She began to weep even more at this; and he held her tightly again, and kissed her and caressed her hair and her cheeks and her shoulders. She wanted to stop crying, but she could not; it felt wonderful to weep now, knowing as she did that all was well, and she wanted to tell him not to mind her. But to soothe her he began to sing in a low voice, and that was so wonderful that she made no attempt to stop him.

How blessed it was, how magical, but better than magical, how real it was, to lean against him, and hold him while he held her, and listen to that beloved voice in her ear, easing away her pain forever. It was as if she were dying to her old life and rising, wakening to a new one.

He sang an old air with words again by Campian, a lover's song indeed; and as long as she lived thereafter, she never forgot the sweetness of its final lines:

> Yet be just and constant still,
> Love may beget a wonder;
> Not unlike a Summer's frost,
> Or Winter's fatall thunder:
> They that hold their Sweet-hart true
> Through ev'ry pain and sighing,
> Live most bless'd with joy and love
> Unto their day of dying.

THE

BEGINNING

www.ingramcontent.com/pod-product-compliance
Lightning Source LLC
Chambersburg PA
CBHW050943210726
48287CB00004B/1117